LOOKING FOR TROUBLE

A Cassidy Adventure Novel

by

Kelly Rysten

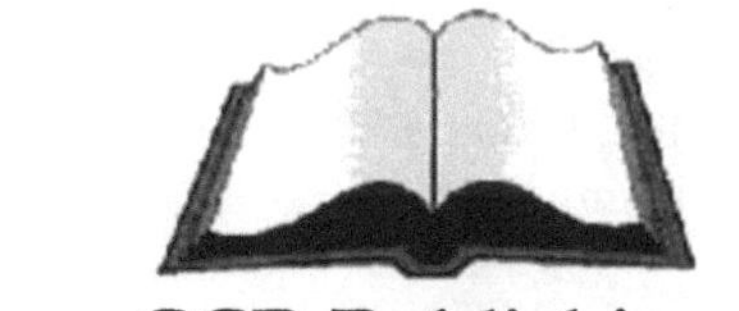

CCB Publishing
British Columbia, Canada

Looking for Trouble: A Cassidy Adventure Novel

ISBN-13 978-1-77143-249-8
First Edition

Library and Archives Canada Cataloguing in Publication
Rysten, Kelly, 1960-, author
Looking for trouble : a Cassidy adventure novel / by Kelly Rysten. -- First edition.
Issued in print and electronic formats.
ISBN 978-1-77143-249-8 (pbk.).--ISBN 978-1-77143-250-4 (pdf)
Additional cataloguing data available from Library and Archives Canada

Cover artwork by Kelly Rysten: www.kellyrysten.com

This is a work of fiction. Names, places, and characters are a product of the author's imagination or are used fictitiously and are not to be considered as real. Resemblance to any events or persons, living or dead, past or present, is purely coincidental.

Extreme care has been taken by the author to ensure that all information presented in this book is accurate and up to date at the time of publishing. Neither the author nor the publisher can be held responsible for any errors or omissions. Additionally, neither is any liability assumed for damages resulting from the use of the information contained herein.

Publisher: CCB Publishing
British Columbia, Canada
www.ccbpublishing.com

To Henry Daniel (Dan) Saastamoinen, my father, the librarian, who asked me to publish Cassidy's stories. It's because of him the books have reached printed form.

And to my husband, Gary, who supports me and encourages me.

Without these two men the books wouldn't have been published. Their influence in my life means more than words can say.

Other books by Kelly Rysten

Kelly Rysten is the author of the Cassidy Callahan Adventure Novels. Cassidy Callahan is a young woman who grew up on a quarter horse ranch. Given free run of the local hills she developed an eye for tracking, and with the help of Detective Rusty Michaels, she joined the local search and rescue team to track lost hikers. Unfortunately she is also a terrible trouble magnet, and her job brings her into contact with more trouble than the police can keep her out of. One adventure follows another as Cassidy tracks her way from one mishap to another.

The books are:

Triple Trouble
Published 2009 – ISBN 978-1-926585-41-3

Car Trouble
Published 2010 – ISBN 978-1-926918-03-7

A Cache of Trouble
Published 2011 – ISBN 978-1-926918-87-7

A Double Dose of Trouble
Published 2012 – ISBN 978-1-77143-025-8

A Shot of Trouble
Published 2013 – ISBN 978-1-77143-107-1

Kelly is also the author of an action adventure romance novel that incorporates the hobby of geocaching. College student Gwendolyn Brody agrees to enter a geocaching contest to help her friend Tony win a trip to the Caribbean. Follow their hilarious cross country trip as they accidentally grow ever closer to each other.

Geogirl
Published 2014 – ISBN 978-1-77143-150-7

PART 1

LOOKING FOR TROUBLE
(in all the wrong places)

Chapter 1

The stillness of the house wrapped around me. It felt oppressive. Old Frank was gone. He was gone and some things you just can't bring back. When a person is gone it's final, which is one reason my job is important to me. I'm a tracker. Personally I don't know enough first aid to keep a person alive but I can bring in the people who do know. In the morning I needed to do just that. It was going to be a rough trail to follow. A man missing two days. The area he disappeared in was notorious for bad tracking: rocky, dusty, hostile, and rugged. It matched my mood.

My husband, Rusty, came home, saw all the camping gear, and his heart sank. I was going away. Rusty is a tall, sandy haired, blue eyed, hunk of a detective and he loves me way too much for his own good.

I stood over the gear trying to decide what I needed. My choices changed a lot depending on who I was going with on the search. My team consisted of four EMTs and me. Of course, the whole search and rescue organization was made up of many more people, with many more talents than I possessed. But I was good at one thing: finding people, following their tracks until we came to the person. This time I was going with Victor, so I had to bring everything. Anything he thought I needed I better have on hand. It was standard procedure to have a trail ready pack at all times. Sometimes I have to grab it and go. However, this call gave me the luxury of time because I couldn't track at night. I would take off first thing in the morning, ready to hit the trail at first light.

"Babe, what's wrong?" Rusty asked.

"I know Marcel Clayborn's situation is more important than a funeral but my heart just isn't in this search. I'll go, and I'll find him, but this pack is going to weigh a ton. My thoughts are going to weigh more. The miles are going to be long."

"You don't have to go."

"Yes, I do. You know I won't turn down a search if they really need me. And they really do need me. This is not a trail that Victor can follow. It's going to be overnight, maybe two nights. I hope not. Marcel has been lost for two days already. I don't know how much time he has left. If I'm not back by Friday afternoon, can you call the ranch and tell them what happened?"

The ranch was where I grew up and where my family still lived. It's a quarter horse ranch about four hours drive north of where I lived in Joshua

Hills.

"You can't miss Old Frank's funeral," Rusty said. "You'll be miserable if you don't go."

Old Frank was the ranch foreman for longer than I could remember.

"I know, but if Marcel has a chance, I'll stay on his trail. Preserving life is more important than honoring death, even if it doesn't feel like it sometimes."

I began picking up things, the heaviest things first. I decided if it was necessary, and then packed it for the search, or put it in the camping box to be stored out in the garage. The camp stove, needed. I placed it in my pack positioning it for good weight distribution. The tent, unfortunately, needed. Sleeping bag, needed. Water purifying system, needed only because I was going with Victor. Clothes, one change of lightweight tracking clothes, the bare minimum. Food, three days worth. Water, arg, water, the curse of backpackers, three days worth. This was going to be a very hot, dry search. I doubted I'd find a spring or a creek but I'd try. Matches, knife… all the little things that get lost in the bottom of a pack and never get used because I forget they are there. And cookies. I opened the freezer and took out a bag of cookies hoping Victor was hungry for them so I wouldn't have to carry them for long. Then I took out another bag of cookies and left them on the counter for Rusty. After I packed my backpack, and tied down the tent and sleeping bag, I packed a suitcase just in case the search ran long and we had to make a run for the ranch.

A hollow, lonely feeling loomed at the edge of everything I did. I sat in the bay window of our bedroom and gazed out to the hills where the deer came from, even though it was too late for the deer to arrive. My dog, Shadow, slept curled in a ball by the bed.

"Think you could leave the sadness behind long enough to enjoy a dinner in town?" Rusty asked.

He was asking for minutes. It would take all evening to go eat dinner in town but it would be time spent together, not him working in the office while I cooked dinner. When Rusty proposed to me he said he wanted every minute I'd give to him. Searches robbed us of minutes. Trouble robbed us of more. Work and daily life encroached on our minutes. With a search just around the corner he just wanted to get a dose of minutes, full minutes, together.

"I'll try," I answered.

"That's my girl," he said, wrapping his arms around me. I soaked up his strength. We stood there for a long time until finally he kissed me on the forehead. "Are you ready?" he asked.

I looked at my clothes: old jeans, old t-shirt, dusty moccasins.

"Is this a date or just dinner?"

"Babe, you're fine. Don't worry about it unless changing will make you feel better."

Rusty had just come from work so he was still dressed in brown slacks, sports coat, and tie. Maybe dressing up *would* make me feel better.

"Give me half an hour," I told him.

I went to the closet and picked out a cheery dress. I hadn't worn a dress in months, not since the Christmas party at the Schroeder's house. The weather was warm so I chose a little white sundress with beachy graphics on it. I curled my hair so it would look perky and fun. I slipped on a pair of pumps and was ready to go. I stepped into his office and he had taken off his coat and tie, untucked his shirt and rolled up his sleeves.

"Rusty! I changed clothes so we'd match and now look at you."

He turned around, looked at me appraisingly, and smiled, "Maybe you changed clothes for the wrong reason."

He pulled on his coat, buttoned one button and looked dressed up again. It was no fair.

"Where can we go where we won't end up working?" he asked.

"I know this little hole in the wall place that only has five tables and one waitress. What's the likelihood of running into felons with only five tables, a waitress and a cook?"

"Sounds like the kind of a place I'd go if I was a crook," he answered.

"I can just close my eyes. If I don't see them, they aren't there, right?"

It's a fact; I'm a magnet for bad guys. When we went shopping for our wedding rings the store was held up. When we went to a restaurant they sat at the next table. I'd had drug dealers walk up to me, strike up a conversation and tell me their profession. What was it about me? It didn't happen consistently enough for me to decide, just often enough that I worried about it whenever I went out. I needed blinders, that's what I needed, so I could only look at Rusty and people would think I was weird and back quietly away.

"Why don't you show me who you're looking for, so I'll at least know them when I see them?" I said.

"No, but I do have one you could identify with," he answered. "She's a lot like you."

"Really?" I asked, interested.

"Yeah, she's a cat burglar. Ever since I met you I thought I sure was lucky you were on the right side of the law. This woman is sixty-five and has hit ten houses in the past four months. She's invisible."

"How do you know who she is then?"

"We're not sure. We've compared notes with other agencies and when a similar string of burglaries stopped in Northridge they started up here. Many communities within a few hundred miles have had similar cases."

"You think they are all related?"

"There are too many similarities to ignore it. This picture is five years old."

He held up a computer printout showing an older woman. Agnes Cooper. She looked like anybody's grandmother. She was slim, petite, and colored her hair a dark brown. Her face was tanned and lined but she looked young for her age.

"She looks like Chase's girlfriend," I observed.

Chase was a friend of the family, a retired cop and part time tracker who lived in the San Diego area. He was sixtyish and would make a good cat burglar, too. I'd tracked him and been tracking with him. He was single and available but too eccentric for most women's tastes. Although he would grudgingly enjoy some companionship, he knew the likelihood of marriage at his age was slim so he tried to enjoy his solitude.

"Look at this. It was taken in Riverside six years ago."

I looked at the picture. It was a slim figure, dressed in black, a black ski mask pulled over their face. The person was sneaking behind a bush in a yard next to a house. I looked at the shoes. This person would be hard to track. They knew what they were doing. The shoes fitted close to the person's feet and were as black as the rest of their clothes. Not moccasins, not water shoes. Rock climbing shoes? As a tracker, shoes interested me and movements intrigued me. I wished I could observe this person for a while.

"Is this Agnes?"

"I'll ask her if I catch her. What do you think?"

I held up the two pictures next to each other.

"It could be, but I don't think so."

That got his attention. "Why?"

"The head is shaped differently."

"How can you tell with all that hair?"

"Imagine her without the hair. What shape is her head?"

"How should I know?"

"Okay, picture Agnes stepping out of the shower, her hair is plastered to her head. Does it look like this picture?" I asked showing him the picture of the person in black. "To me Agnes is slimmer, her jaw is smaller, her neck is thinner, the forehead is shaped differently. If this picture is on your computer try taking away the background, see the profile you get. It'll be different from Agnes's profile."

"Are you sure?"

"No, it's just a feeling I got."

"Just like when you profile while you track?"

"Yeah."

"I'll try it."

"Is Agnes a professional? Or is this some kind of hobby? What does she steal?"

We climbed into the Explorer and Rusty pulled out of the driveway and headed for town.

"She has a record but she hasn't been caught since those pictures were taken. She got off pretty easy since they could really only link her to a fraction of the charges they suspected her of. Then she plea-bargained. She did two years. Nobody really knows how long she has been at it."

"Interesting."

"The burglaries I have been involved in have involved jewelry and credit cards."

"Any extremely recognizable pieces? Have you asked Hazel about Agnes?"

"Hazel? Our neighbor, Hazel?"

"Yeah."

"No, why would a housewife who lives up in the foothills outside town know Agnes Cooper?"

"I've got a feeling about Hazel. She knows more than you think she does."

"That's because Hazel's nosey. Why would she know Agnes Cooper?"

"Something tells me Hazel has connections. She doesn't just sit at home knitting. She is too social for that. I bet she goes down to the senior center and gets involved in their activities. We need a spy in the world of the senior citizens."

Rusty thought I was kidding, but I wasn't. He wouldn't pursue that idea, but I might. First dinner, then Marcel Clayborn, then Old Frank's funeral. Sigh, I had a full week ahead of me but at least the cat burglar case had me thinking of something besides sadness.

"Thanks," I said brightly. "I feel better already. With a puzzle in my head I can think again."

"Don't think about it too much. I don't want you involved in this."

"How dangerous can a sixty-five year old cat burglar be? Is she armed?"

"We don't know. She hasn't shot anybody yet."

"There, you see?"

Our conversation at dinner was limited. Talking about the search would get Rusty down. Talking about the ranch and Old Frank would get me down. Talking about Agnes Cooper made Rusty worry about me pursuing his case. I thought it was safe to bat the subject around a bit. As we sat in Trujillo's wondering what we wanted to eat I asked, "So, what kind of places does she break into?"

"Just like you would expect, upper-class homes. We're convinced she watches a house until she knows the family's schedule and breaks in when they are likely to be gone for a while, although she has been known to break in while a woman was home alone in a large house. I think she is getting overconfident. It is pretty gutsy to break in with people in the house."

"How does she break in?"

"She just finds the easiest way in that she can. Usually it's an unlocked window she can pry open. You'd be amazed how easy it is to break into most people's houses. She has even entered second story windows. Most people consider the second story windows to be safe so they just leave them open in the summer to let the heat escape and allow the air conditioning to circulate. What convinced us that she stakes out a house first is that a family hid a key right before going on vacation. It wasn't a simple hiding place, like over the door or under the mat. The key was hidden between two boards on the inside of the backyard fence. No breaking and entering. She used the key, let herself in, took what she wanted and left. She even locked up behind her and put the key back so no one would suspect a thing. She wears gloves. She never makes a mess, doesn't ransack a house. She leaves a house in such a state that nobody suspects a thing until they discover something missing. The things she steals are so small the theft often goes unnoticed for weeks."

"Interesting. I'd almost hate to arrest her. She sounds like someone I'd like to meet."

"I told you, she's a lot like you."

"Do you have a recent break in?"

"It won't be by the time you get back from your search. Besides, most of the houses she breaks into are very carefully landscaped and gardeners visit weekly wiping out any outside evidence."

Trujillo's was frequented by most of the police force. Someone from the force could be found there most evenings. Kent Jacobsen wandered over and then dragged a chair over to our booth.

"What's up?" he asked.

"Nothing. I'm just getting ready for a search," I answered.

Kent looked at Rusty. "Just a search?"

"Just a camper gone astray."

"That's a relief. Don't think you've run into problems on those searches. It just seems to be felons who give you trouble. It's like you're a magnet for trouble or something."

"Thanks, Jacobsen. I think your food's ready."

"I've already eaten," he said. "I heard that's going to be a killer search."

"That's why they called me," I said confidently.

"You think you can make rocks talk."

"That's silly," I said. "Rocks don't talk. Dirt talks. Rocks whisper very,

very quietly. Sometimes you have to put your ear down to the ground to hear them."

"Very funny. Seriously though, do you think you can find him?"

"Yeah, I'll find him."

"Is she always this confident?" Jacobsen asked Rusty.

"I've haven't seen her misjudge a search yet," Rusty answered, somewhat dodging the question. The fact was I was always positive starting out. I wasn't always happy with the results.

Chapter 2

My alarm went off at four a.m. My goal was to be at base camp at first light. Rusty groaned when the alarm went off.

"It's okay, go back to sleep," I told him.

I showered and dressed in my regular tracking clothes: camouflage pants, and an olive drab t-shirt. I debated whether to wear moccasins or hiking boots. The hiking boots won because of the rocky terrain. I put them on grudgingly. I liked to feel the ground beneath my feet.

After my shower Rusty paced the bedroom nervously. He was always a jumble of emotions when I went on a search. I thought it was funny to see my big, tough detective; eyes full of concern, arms reaching out for reassurance. Every time I was out of his sight for more than a day his loneliness and worry grew. It didn't seem to matter that I was safely hiking the mountains with an EMT, I was armed, and had help at the touch of a button. I think the problem was he trusted me; he trusted me to get into trouble. And he knew his idea of danger was different than mine, so he worried.

Victor picked me up on his way into the mountains. He pulled up about five in a search and rescue car.

"Remember, if I'm not home by Friday afternoon, call the ranch and tell them what's going on."

"You'll be home in time. Take care of my girl out there."

"I will. I always do."

Lou Strickland had everything he could come up with that he knew I needed. Unfortunately, there wasn't much to go on. Like usual, Marcel had not brought extra shoes on his camping trip. A small patch of ground had been taped off where Strict had found a few good tracks. Other than that I was pointed in a general direction. No talking to Marcel's family, no picture, no shoes to gain some knowledge from. Okay, if a few good tracks are what I had to work with, it's what I would study so I sat by the tracks and sketched them and labeled the tracks with the little bit of information I could squeeze out of them: worn heels, a tread. I measured the stride. It wasn't much to go by. I felt my enthusiasm slipping a notch and it was already pretty low to begin with.

"Can you give me a starting place?" I asked Strict.

"Not until you tell me what's wrong."

"Nothing's wrong."

"You're not acting like yourself. Normally you'd be a half-mile down the trail by now. You're dragging. Why are you dragging?"

"Am I? Lou, I'm sorry, nothing's wrong. I'm fine. A friend of mine died. When I'm through here I'm off to a funeral."

"Who was it?" Lou asked, concerned.

"To be honest in the twenty-six years I've known him I don't think I've ever heard his last name. I always just called him Old Frank. Last time I visited the ranch I found out he was sixty-two when I was born. No wonder I always thought he was old. Lou, he was like a grandfather to me and more. He taught me how to think, how to ride horses, how to get along in the woods, how to shoot, how to get along with my dad. He was my grandpa and mentor and teacher and friend. I don't think I'd be here right now if it weren't for him. He had a stroke. And his funeral is Saturday."

Lou finally gave me the hug he usually greeted me with. I wanted to pull back. I didn't want sympathy. Maybe I'd been a little standoffish when I'd arrived.

"Why didn't you tell me when I called?"

"It didn't matter. I'd still have gone out. Now let me get going. It'll be better when I get on the trail."

But it wasn't. The part of the trail that I could follow with my eyes I tracked easily but my mind was such a jumble that I wasn't profiling and when I got to tough spots I had to reorganize my thoughts to make room for the puzzle before me. Lou had called Victor aside, I assume to fill him in on what I'd told him.

I stood over a rocky patch of invisible footprints trying in vain to concentrate. What would Old Frank tell me to try? I thought. He'd say, "People take the easy way. They're lazy bums. So if'n you cain't see the tracks look for the easy way." Or he'd say, "Them rocks sure are slanty. If a man had to walk on those rocks he'd have a hard time walkin' straight." So I looked at the slanty rocks and pictured a man walking across them and I pictured how he'd have trouble walkin' straight and where the easy way would lead him to, and sure enough, the tracks were there. When I saw the tracks there on the ground a big lump formed in my throat. I marked the trail and walked away from it. I sat on the ground, backpack and all, and tried to get my emotions under control.

"Cassidy? Are you okay?" Victor asked.

"I've got a ghost telling me how to track," I said, my voice breaking. "Did Strict tell you?"

"Yeah, he told me."

"My thoughts even sound like him, bad grammar and all. We gotta get going."

He gave me a hand up and I found the tracks again.

"Would it help to talk about him?"

"I don't know. I don't even know if I can."

"How long have you known him?"

"He worked for my dad when I was born. So… my whole life. I know him better than my dad."

"How can that be?"

"You have to know my dad. Rusty wouldn't be surprised."

"What's your earliest memory of him?"

I thought for a minute and smiled, "He used to meet me at the bus stop. I rode a bus to school all my life because we lived so far from town. Old Frank was supposed to meet me at the bus stop and walk me home. This was when I was six. There was a kid at school who had leg braces and one day I was curious what his tracks would look like, so I got off at the same bus stop that he did. I hid in the bushes and then tracked him home. I was standing outside this kid's house with a whole basket full of new information and no idea how I was going to get home. So I walked back to the bus stop and I started following the road the direction I remembered the bus going to get to *my* bus stop. I was doing all right, for a little kid. I wasn't lost. The bus only took five minutes to get from one bus stop to the next so I thought it couldn't be far. Old Frank pulled up in the old ranch truck and he was hoppin' mad. 'Dag nabbit, Trouble!' he said. 'What'd you get off early for? You sceared your mom spitless!' I hadn't even thought about consequences. I was just curious and when I got curious the question in my mind became top priority. 'I just wanted to see what a kid's tracks were like if he wore leg braces. I just followed him home. He didn't even know I was there,' I said. 'An' how was you goin' to get home?' he asked me. 'I'm walking,' I told him. 'An you think walkin' is goin' to get you there?' I told him I thought it would. He told me to get in the truck so I did. Then he says, 'If a kid can walk three miles an hour how long will it take 'em to walk nine miles. Nine is three plus three plus three.' I had to think. 'So, that means they'd be walking one plus one plus one?' He helped me see that if I walked home I wouldn't get there until after dinner time *if* I could walk three miles an hour. He was that kind of a guy. He didn't just yell at a kid. Everything was a reason to think. And he was on my side. When he got the lecture over with he asked me, 'So, what did you learn about tracking a kid in leg braces?' I told him that the tracks were a lot like a normal person's but there were brackets where the braces fit with the shoes and maybe the walk was stiffer. He admonished me, saying, 'you ain't ever to make fun of a kid in braces, or glasses or in a wheel chair. Not ever. It's only by luck you ain't the same way.' I never had made fun of other kids and he wasn't scolding me, just passing on a word of advice."

"You could track people as a kid?"

"Yeah, the ranch hands were the easiest. The whole ranch was dirt and I was Dad's messenger boy so I was always tracking down the hands."

"Don't you mean messenger girl?"

"No, my dad wanted a boy so he raised me as a boy."

"What did Old Frank think of that?"

"Nothing. I took to it and I thrived on it so he didn't worry about it. If I'd have been unhappy or rebelled against it he might have stepped in and stood up to my dad. But that wasn't the case. I thought it was great being raised as a boy. I got to go tracking and hunting and I grew up training horses. It wasn't odd that I wanted to join the military. In my eyes guys got to do what they wanted and girls had to wear dresses and wash dishes and dust and learn to sew. I thought I had it better than my sister because I got to do whatever I wanted. It just happened that I wanted all the chores a boy would do. I split firewood, fed the horses and brushed them when the hands were through for the day. I mucked out stalls, painted fences and learned how to fix the truck. Of course, the subtleties of tracking didn't come until much later."

"How did you learn the subtleties?"

"Years of careful observation and tracking. Every movement people made got catalogued. Every movement they made I imagined a track to match it and it got catalogued in my brain. As a kid it was a crude system. It was more just a matter of satisfying curiosity. As an adult I watch people and I track them even when they don't leave tracks. Every movement is a potential track and every track has a corresponding movement."

"The stories that float around the station say you can spot a person who is going to commit a crime before they do it. Is that true?"

"I'll tell you I have spotted people who I thought were up to no good and I was right. I won't say I can do it all the time and I won't guarantee I am right all the time."

"How do you do that?"

I stopped to figure out the tracks. Victor was used to frequent pauses in my story telling. He waited patiently while I studied the ground. As long as Victor kept me talking I seemed to do better. I could track with one part of my brain and talk with another part so the part that was sad got shoved aside. The track turned and then turned again. Marcel was wondering if he was sure he knew where he was. This was one of many thinking stops he had made. I found the direction he headed and started walking again.

"You can understand that every movement leaves a corresponding track, right?" I asked.

"Yeah, I can see that."

"Would you accept that every *intention* has a corresponding movement?"

"Every intention? No."

"What about frequently? Do intentions *frequently* have a corresponding movement?"

"I don't know, I never thought about it."

"Okay, well, say you are walking down the mall and the guy in front of you glances at every bag and purse he comes near? What would you think?"

"I doubt I'd notice what people are looking at. But if I did happen to notice that, then I might be suspicious."

"Most people don't notice. But I do. Since I watch movements I notice things like that. Did you know that even something like a guy watching for a purse to snatch leaves evidence of it in his tracks? Even eye movements if you follow the movement down to the feet, *might be* reflected in the tracks if one were skilled enough to see it."

"Are you?"

"No, not even close. But I have seen eye movements reflected in the movement of a person's feet because I am watching for it."

"Cassidy, did anyone ever tell you you're weird?"

"Yeah, I tell myself that all the time. But most people think I'm a nice type of weird. I don't tell people that I think like that. Most people don't know I watch every move they make. In academy we watched surveillance tapes of robberies. I could spot the robber way before anybody else in class. Their intentions were exhibited through their actions. Robbers would check their weapons and the class didn't notice. They would fiddle with their keys and shift back and forth nervously, watch video cameras and take stock of their getaway while standing in line and yet nobody seemed to notice they were fixing to rob the place. I didn't understand how they could *not* know. In class we watched the tapes so we could see the process, what we might be walking into if we were called into a situation like that. But I saw all the things that led up to it and wondered why someone didn't do anything to stop it."

I talked and tracked, stopping when I got stuck. I studied the ground while Victor waited patiently.

"Do you really want to know all this or are you just keeping me talking so I won't think about Old Frank?"

"It's interesting to me. It doesn't matter why we're doing it."

"I guess I do remember him from before I was six. He'd always been around. My mom says he used to haul me out of the paddocks when I was just a toddler. He thought the horses might hurt me. I don't remember a horse ever hurting me until I started riding. I started riding when I was three and I was left to ride on my own when I was five, just a very gentle, easy to manage horse that was my friend and wouldn't hurt a fly. Old Frank worked me up through the horses until I was riding like hellfire on the work horses. When the work horses weren't enough of a challenge I started trying to ride the horses in training. So I do remember Old Frank from before I was six."

The tracks were fading more and more as we got closer to the rocky hillsides. Please, don't even try to go up those hills, I thought. Tracking could be fun but it could also be mind numbingly challenging, too. Looking for that one piece of a track that would point the way. A slight indentation with an edge that looked like a person had made it. A tread. A scuff. Anything? The tracks were disappearing and we progressed slower and slower until, finally I was forced to get down to ground level. Crawling on the ground with a thirty pound pack on my back got old real fast. I stood and took it off, propping it against a rock.

"Don't let me forget it," I told Victor.

"How can you forget your pack? It's almost a part of you. It's got all your food and water in it."

"Just don't let me forget it."

"Okay."

I knelt down again looking for clues. There was no plants, no sand, just rock and fine gravel. I looked for scratch marks on the rocks and found a few. Was it enough? I examined the scratch marks and looked the direction they pointed. I wasn't sure enough to just leave the spot behind, even if I was only moving a few feet away, so I marked the last clue. This was feeling hopeless. I looked at all the rock ahead of me. "Don' choo let what mightn't be stop you from what *could* be," Old Frank said in my head. And later when I was truly exasperated, "Oh, no you don't. You ain't run out of options yet. You get back in there and run your options out first." I finished examining the rock. One little scratch mark. It could have been made by anything. I stood and brushed my hands off.

"How far have we come?" I asked Victor.

He took a few moments to plot our location on a map.

"As the crow flies? Two miles."

"Damn. We've spent all morning going two lousy miles?"

"If they were the right two miles they weren't lousy ones."

"We've got to do something to put these rocks behind us. This is ridiculous. And I'm still hearing Old Frank in my head."

"Yeah, what's he saying?"

"That we haven't exhausted all our options yet."

"Smart man."

"Okay, next option."

I looked at the area ahead. Rough rock, sparse vegetation. Was Marcel hiking at this point or did he consider himself lost? He had stopped a few times and his tracks looked like he'd been thinking. But maybe he had just been watching something, or deciding which way to go. If he was just hiking his decisions would be very different than if he thought he was lost. I marked my spot so I would know where to return if my ideas didn't work out. I followed the known trail and kept going, watching the ground. Okay, so my choice of hiking paths didn't pan out. I walked an arc zigzagging across the area I thought Marcel had crossed. An hour of zigzagging and I was ready to throw in the towel. My spirits were at an all-time low. I went back to my marker and looked for the next direction to try.

"Cassidy, eat something," Victor said. "You'll feel better."

I wasn't sure I wanted to feel better. I had settled comfortably into my blue funk and it felt like too much bother to try and climb out of it. I got out the bag of cookies and let Victor take a couple, then I took one for myself. How could you not feel better after a chocolate chip cookie break? After the cookie I thought I ought to have some real food so I dug out my trail mix and picked out the M&Ms. Victor just watched, arms folded over his chest.

"No wonder you never grew up," he said.

"I bet if your wife thought chocolate would keep her young she'd convert," I joked back. "Besides, I didn't see you turning down any chocolate chip cookies. Just think of the green M&Ms as vegetables, the red ones as berries, the brown ones as meat, and the orange ones as cheese and you have a balanced meal right here in a bag."

The search didn't look quite so bleak after that. I still didn't know how I was going to find Marcel's trail but at least I could look at it with a tracker's eye again. I tried another direction, walking until the soil got better, then walking a large half circle around the last sure track. I was looking for a dirt-colored indentation in the dirt. Or a rock colored scrape on a rock. Tracks always wear camouflage. They blend in and they are good at it. I had to change the way I looked at things to see them when they were faint. Any change in the normal pattern of the ground was something to investigate. Most people would say there is no pattern to the dirt on the ground, unless they were looking at dunes that had been scoured by the wind into a washboard effect. Think of randomness as a pattern. If you take a bunch of randomness and add just one pressure point, or one line, that one thing suddenly stands out. The static on a television screen is a good example. All these random dots coming and going, but if there is an interruption or small change in the power a line will appear in the randomness. So it is with tracking except it's not all black and white. It's all dirt colored or rock colored. And the change is very subtle. Walking through the scrubby, rocky, barely forest I was looking for something very faint that said a person had been here. When my half circle didn't reveal anything I continued the circle on around. When that didn't help I widened the circle. Scanning, scanning, with an analytical eye, searching the randomness. When I finally found the tracks again I could see why the circling had finally paid off. Marcel had turned around. Why do people always choose to do unpredictable things on rock? Two hours I had spent on one spot in the trail. I ran back for my pack, exasperated.

"We're back in business," I told Victor. I fished out the cookies again and offered some to Victor. He took two, as did I, then I stuffed the bag gently back in my pack, zipped it up and shrugged into the straps. I pulled the hip belt snug and shifted it around as I walked. Victor got up calmly and followed. There was no use hurrying. Tracking was slow and his even pace would keep up. All he had to do was keep me in sight.

I returned to the track I found, just a corner of a heel print, but the heel is always behind the toe so I had a direction and I was back to moving from track to track. My frustration started to fade as I settled into my comfort zone again.

"Told ya you weren't outa options yet," Old Frank said.

I was back in business but everywhere we turned we ran into rock of some kind. When night fell we were a mile and a half from base camp but we had tracked much farther than that. At dusk we set up camp and went about our activities in relative silence. Normally I kept up a friendly banter with Landon or Victor on a search. If I had to go with Rosco it was a quiet search. If I had to go out with Thez *he* kept up a constant flow of friendly chatter. That evening, with Victor, I was sad, tired, and frustrated. My emotions were wearing on me. My pack weighed a ton. Little setbacks felt like giant obstacles. Little things faded in importance. Eating was a little thing. I didn't want to bother. I just wanted to go to bed so morning would arrive faster. However, I knew it didn't work that way. Going to bed without dinner only caused me to wake up hungry during the night.

"I've never seen you that stuck before," Victor said.

"That's because I've never been that stuck before," I answered as I shook out my tent. If I'd been alone I wouldn't have even bothered with the tent.

"I need to call Strict and give him our coordinates."

"Tell him to just look west and he can see us," I said sarcastically.

I set up the tent, carefully hammering in each tent peg with a rock. Victor was precise. If I didn't peg my tent he would tell me that it might blow away. If I didn't use a rain fly it might rain. If I went without a tent he would offer me his. He was a father and a gentleman and I bore the brunt of that grudgingly and happily. I liked Victor. I enjoyed his company on searches but I sure wish he would ease up in some respects. Landon was nearly as bad but he'd come to accept some of my quirks and eccentricities. When I thought about my camping quirks as eccentricities Chase came to mind and I wondered if I was gradually becoming more like him. I could camp any way I liked with Chase. He often slept in a hammock on searches so when I simply rolled out my sleeping bag and climbed in he didn't question me, didn't offer me a tent. He knew I chose my own conditions and he left me to choose for myself. I wondered if Chase would go to the funeral. Chase didn't know Old Frank well. He had only met the man once, or was it twice? But Chase knew Old Frank was the man who had taught me to track. He respected the old cowboy, and he had a vested interest in the goings on at the ranch, because Patrick was there. Chase watched out for Patrick and me, making sure the art of tracking didn't die. Even though he lived in San Diego he kept tabs on us. He'd been doing long distance mentoring with Patrick, and he appreciated Old Frank's presence and involvement in Patrick's life. And now Old Frank was gone.

I was setting up my stove as these thoughts rattled around and then dragged me along with them into deep sadness. I set the stove aside and walked. I kicked rocks. I brooded. I struggled, trying to control my emotions. Victor went about his camp preparations keeping one eye on me. He wouldn't get emotionally involved but he'd be assessing the situation, ready for an answer when Strict asked.

Old Frank was gone. That meant Patrick's backup was gone. And what exactly did a seven year old need backup for? Well, if he was like me as a seven year old, which so far seemed very likely, he needed Old Frank's brain. The old man encouraged Patrick to think. He had been developing the same inquisitive mind in Patrick that he had in me, more so since he had more time to devote to Patrick.

Chase had hinted that he knew a man who could train horses and teach Patrick to track but I couldn't imagine a person like that. A person with those particular qualities was rare. There was just no replacing Old Frank.

The light was fading fast. I needed to get back.

When I got back to camp Victor was going through our evening check in with Strict.

"Yeah, it was a disappointing day but it was a rough trail. Everything about this search has been hard… Yeah, she's doing okay. Don't worry…It's bound to affect it some but she's not letting it stop her. It's the rock that held us up today, not Cassidy…No, don't call us back…I know we're close enough but Cassidy is the only one who could track this search. We'll check in tomorrow. G'night."

I finished assembling my stove, pumped it up and lit the burner. Pretty soon I had a pot of water heating. I looked around in my backpacker food for something that wasn't very filling, but it all looked alike. I looked for one meal that I liked better than the others and they all tasted alike, too, so I just grabbed one. Spaghetti. Okay, so they might taste different. I put the spaghetti back and pulled out chicken and rice.

"You're not yourself tonight," Victor observed. "You usually have camp set up and dinner half cooked by the time I get my pack off."

"Sorry, I'm being pokey because I don't care. I don't want to bother with the tent. I don't want to eat."

"What will you miss most about Old Frank?"

"From the past, just his ornery old cowboy attitude. For the future, he was the one who helped my nephew follow his tracking genes. The boy is only seven and already shows talents for tracking. I've tracked with him a little, stalked deer with him. He's got the right mindset for it but my sister won't encourage that part of his education. Old Frank would. Old Frank would challenge Patrick's mind. That influence is what will be missed the most."

I poured water into the pouch of backpacker food and folded the top down. I propped up the pouch against my pack and waited for it to cook.

"What do you think of this search?"

"If there wasn't a person counting on us, I'd quit. But I won't. As long as we know Marcel is still out there I'll stick to the trail."

"Do you think we'll find him?"

"Yeah, we'll find him. I just hope we find him in time. Today was mind-numbingly difficult. If I ever get to relive a day in my life, I'd never choose today. I've got a whole list of days I would go back and relive but today's not one of them."

"Really? What would you choose?"

"I'd like to see Old Frank's expression when I was eight years old and I jumped off the barn roof. I'd like to relive the time I went home to the ranch to recuperate from a bout of trouble and Rusty drove up and surprised me with a visit for my birthday. I didn't even know it was my birthday. That's how sick I'd been. He just showed up and I was so happy! I hardly knew him. I only knew I loved him and he showed up anyway. I'd relive that day a hundred times. I'd go back and jump out of the airplane again. My parachute barely opened and I thought I was going to die. Now that I know I lived through it, I'd do it again."

"You're kidding."

"No. Normal bouts of trouble make life exciting. It's man made trouble I can do without."

"Cassidy, allow me to define *normal* for you. Normal is what happens to everybody else. Your trouble is not normal. Normal does not include jumping out of an airplane with a faulty parachute. Normal people don't jump off roofs."

"If I'm not normal it's half genes and half Old Frank's fault. He never encouraged me to be normal."

We stayed up late. Usually we turned in shortly after dark in order to get a good night's rest and be ready to get up with the sun. I tracked during daylight hours so it was important to me to be ready as soon as the sun was up. When we finally went to our tents, I knew it was going to be a very short night. It was a very troubled night, too. I tracked in my dreams. I tracked Marcel through impossible rocks and I tracked Old Frank around the ranch. I had always known Old Frank's tracks. Even when they changed and finally became a weary shuffle I knew it was him. His tracks degraded in my dream and each tiny change brought a stab of pain as I watched him fade from my life, through his tracks. I woke in the night longing to snuggle closer to Rusty, but he wasn't there. Loneliness smothered me. My heart ached. Frustration made me worry about the tracking the next day. The sun came up and I wanted to turn it off again and go back to sleep. I was exhausted. I pretended I was back in the Marines and forced myself up anyway. I prepared and ate a packet of oatmeal just out of habit. I broke camp and packed everything up. It was a new day. I found the trail again while Victor finished up packing.

When Strict checked in with us he asked to talk to me.

"Cassidy?"

"Go ahead, Lou."

"Victor says you've had a hard time of it."

"No kidding, this is the toughest trail I've had yet."

"What's the trouble?"

"Rock. There's nothing I can do to hurry it. There's no way to get rid of the rock. It's just plain old, tough tracking."

"Do you need help?"

"No, Chase is the only one who could possibly help and he's too far away."

"You sure?"

"Yeah."

"Rusty called. He's worried about you."

"I know. You know what to tell him."

Strict had been fielding Rusty's calls ever since I'd started tracking for him. He'd known Rusty long before I came along so I left the guys to their own battles regarding me.

Marcel's trail started out faint and it got worse. It was slow, track to track tracking. There was no walking along, just watching for the next track. I knelt by the tracks, tracing the hints I could see, following the hint a few feet farther, looking for the next track. At the rate we were going we'd find Marcel dead. I despaired when the trail led straight into the rocks again.

"Victor, this is impossible!"

"I agree. I don't know how you've come this far."

"Maybe it's time to split up. One of us can circle the rocky area and find where Marcel left it."

"I don't know if I'd see it, but I sure won't see anything here."

"Well, give it a try."

I stayed on the rocks trying to spot any signs at all of Marcell's trail and Victor took off to find the end of the rocks and search for signs of tracks. He wouldn't venture far.

Okay, Cass, the rocks, focus on the rocks. I was so tired of focusing on the rocks. I took off my pack and got down on hands and knees. I picked up tiny rocks, looking for pressure points, scrapes, anything in the spot where the next step should have been. I measured from the last track and moved over hoping Marcel had turned. I worked my way, slowly in a circle around the last track. I was sitting there cross legged moving small rocks, hoping for hints beneath them when a quick, dark blur shot out from under the rock and ran up my pants leg. Pain shot up my leg from the back of my calf!

"Oh shit!" I exclaimed, jumping to my feet. Oh, man, it hurt! Imagining squished bug all over my clothes and leg, I slapped at my pants leg trying to kill whatever it was that ran up there. Big mistake! It stung my hand, too! Right through my pants leg! I frantically began pulling at shoe laces, trying to get my boots off as squirming feelings brushed against my leg between the skin and the fabric of my pants. What was it? I pulled off my hiking boots and pants, hoping Victor was still circling the rocky area. "Damn it, where are you, you stupid critter? *What* are you?" I shook out my pants and a large brown scorpion ran away and hid under another rock. Oh it hurt! The sting sites burned and I didn't know what to do. I didn't know if this was the worst of it or what else I could expect. I pulled on my pants again with difficulty. My hand barely worked. My fingers were getting stiff. Pain shot up my arm and my leg. I paced around cradling my right hand and trying not to put much weight on my left leg. Where was Victor? How far away was he? I was sure he would know what to do.

"Victor!" I called out as loud as I could. I cupped my hands and called again, "Viiiictor!" I sat and examined my hand. The site of the sting was red and my hand felt like the inside was on fire. The pain radiated farther as the poison spread.

Victor came jogging up. "What is it? Did you find something?"

"Yeah, I found a scorpion! The stupid thing ran up my pants leg and stung me on the leg and when I tried to kill it and it stung my hand."

How he managed to laugh with a worried look I don't know. The guys were mastering that look. I noticed it a lot when trouble hit. When he'd finished with the mental picture of what had happened he got back to work.

"Did you see what kind it was?"

"No. It was just a scorpion."

"It wasn't yellow and ugly?"

"No, it was brown and scorpionish."

"That's good. Yellow is bad news."

"Hell, *this* is bad news."

"I can tell you it's not going to kill you. This *could be* the worst of it. Let's hope you don't have an adverse reaction to it. Can you walk?"

"If I can dance around and get out of my pants, shake them out, and get back into them again, I think I can walk. Did you find anything?"

"No, not yet."

"Damn."

I could walk but my left leg hurt like hell and within an hour we could tell this was going to throw the search way off. First the pain radiated farther from the sting sites. Then, I didn't tell Victor for a while, but my hands and feet began going numb. I started salivating like crazy. I felt antsy. I had to keep going. I had to. I became fixated on finding the tracks. It didn't matter if it was the logical method. I felt pushed to go on. When my feet were well and truly numb I began having trouble walking. Finally, Victor put a stop to the search.

"Cassidy stop. You're reacting to the poison. Your extremities are numb, aren't they?"

"We can't stop! We're only three miles from base camp. We've been on the trail for two days. We can't stop!"

"Hush, listen, you're displaying all the symptoms. There's nothing we can do except wait it out. How far has the numbness spread?"

I sat down, defeated, "Even my face is numb," I admitted. "But I have to do something. I can't just sit here!"

"Then I'm *telling* you. You *are* going to just sit here. Until you can feel again and your vital signs return to normal, you're going to sit here. I'll set up camp. It could be hours; at worst we'll be here overnight."

"Overnight? No! We can't waste a whole day!"

He seemed amused by my attitude, a calm that I'd frequently seen in EMTs when they are faced with emergencies. He just remembered this was the effect of the poison and gently prodded me in the direction I should go. "I'm setting up your tent and you're going to get out of the sun and wait this out. I'm telling you, that's what you're going to do."

I tried to help Victor with the tent but I couldn't tell how hard I was grasping things and my right hand hurt like crazy making any coordinated effort impossible. The numbness was scary. It felt like it would take over everything and leave me drifting. I was scared to lie down in the tent. I was afraid I'd pass out from sheer numbness.

"All the odd things you are thinking are part of the reaction. Just don't listen to them. An agitated feeling is normal for a bad reaction. Just ignore it."

When he had the tent set up he spread my sleeping bag out.

"I want you to lay down in there and wait until I come back. I'm going to circle the rocks like we were planning on doing and I'm going to call Strict. He might want to try another method."

I lay in the tent as low as low can be, numb, sad, lonely, and extremely agitated. Fighting the urge to track was difficult. I was trapped in a mental war with myself. How could the stings hurt so badly if I was numb all over?

Victor took my pulse and blood pressure. The pulse was fast. The blood pressure low, normal for a scorpion sting, he said. He looked at my eyes.

"If you notice your vision changing in any way, call me," he instructed.

He left the tent and I heard him call Strict.

"Strict, it's Victor."

"Go ahead," Strict answered.

"We've got another setback..." He walked out of my hearing, I presume to circle the rocky area. I curled up on the sleeping bag, miserable. I couldn't lie still because I felt antsy but I was so numb I couldn't do anything. I faded in and out, dozing nervously, losing track of time. I thought I heard a helicopter in the distance. The search had expanded. I hoped they were not coming for me. I'd feel like a total failure if I didn't finish this search. I would blame myself for the outcome if I didn't do everything I could. I was already kicking myself for letting a dumb bug get the best of me. Just a stupid scorpion. And why did I have to swat it with my hand? That was one of the *stupidest* things I'd ever done. My thoughts wandered from my stupidity to what Victor was doing, to Rusty, to Old Frank. I'd never catch up to Marcel before Friday afternoon. I wondered if we could make it to the ranch in time on Saturday if we left early. My feelings spiraled down further and further until I couldn't do anything. Every corner of my mind was either antsy from the poison, sad from grief, or frustrated with my situation. Physically I was okay, just incapacitated. I lay there for hours until, finally, Victor came back.

He crawled into the tent. "You okay?" He quietly asked my still form.

"Yeah, still numb, though."

"How do you feel?"

"Like I'm trapped. I can't move without feeling pins and needles. I can't think without getting sad. Did you have any luck?"

"Maybe, you'll have to take a look. I've got the place marked and I'll go back and try to get farther but I wanted to check on you first. Your pulse is still fast. Look at me. Okay. Isn't this fun? Just normal type trouble. It makes life exciting, right?"

"Very funny. I heard the helicopter."

"Yeah, we're kind of in a time crunch. We're going on four days. Marcel needs to be found."

"It would help if his buddies had called earlier too."

"Well, there's not much we can do about our position so we might as well make the most of it. If you'll be okay, I'm going to check out that possibility I spotted. If it's Marcel we'll be back on track in the morning."

"In the morning? I can't stand this idleness. I'm not waiting here until morning!"

"You'll stay there until I say," he told me.

After he left I crawled out of the tent, cursing a mile a minute because the stings hurt like crazy whenever I put any weight on the that limb. When I got out of the tent I was dismayed because I couldn't track Victor. He was as untrackable as Marcel. I cursed the hard ground, the pain, and the situation. Since I was out of the tent I went to my pack, unzipped it left handed, and pulled out the cookies. I took a bite but I was so numb I couldn't chew well or swallow right. After a terrible coughing fit I gave up on eating anything.

Victor came back and saw the bag of cookies.

"Cassidy, I swear, you're as stubborn as they come."

"Didn't do me any good. I can't eat them. What did you find?"

I handed over the cookies, left-handed.

"I can't tell. I think it was a person, but I can't tell if it was Marcel. We'll go back in the morning."

As evening wore on Victor set up his tent and began dinner preparations. I crawled out of the tent thinking perhaps it wasn't quite as painful this time. Perhaps the numbness was wearing off a little too.

"Don't bother heating water for me," I told Victor. "I can't swallow. My throat's numb."

"You should try," he said.

"Not if I have the same reaction I did to the cookie. I'd rather skip that."

I went to my pack and got out a bottle of water. I sipped that for my dinner. I went to bed hungry, numb, sore and very discouraged. Victor called Strict for our nightly check in. I went through my nightly ritual of wondering where Rusty was and what he was doing but I pictured him worrying about me and it made me sadder.

I woke up in the night and the numbness was mostly gone. In the morning the only things to remind me of the scorpion sting were two very sensitive sting sites. I cooked dinner for breakfast and Victor felt better about our situation.

"Show me where you found the tracks," I said.

I limped after him. When he showed me the tracks he found, I was impressed. I wouldn't have thought him capable of spotting tracks that faint.

"We'll have to follow them to know for sure," I said. "Should we take that chance?"

"I say, there's very little chance of it being anybody else. If you think it was a person it's a good chance it was Marcel."

"Let's follow it then."

The day was brighter. We had tracks again, a day of rest, and breakfast. The only thing that hung over us was time. We had to find Marcel as quickly as possible and even with a good trail the pace was slow. The helicopter showed up later in the morning. They buzzed overhead and we waved. They reported our position to Strict. We now had a day and a half to find a man missing four days. The fact that the helicopter hadn't found Marcel was worrisome. I thought if he had heard a helicopter overhead he would have done something to attract their attention.

I hit the trail ready to put in a full day. I tracked as quickly as I could, moving from track to track, pausing only long enough to verify I was on the right trail.

Victor had saved us hours of frustrating work. He just seemed to think it was part of being a team. If one person runs into trouble you just do what you can to achieve the goal. He had done well.

I couldn't move very quickly. Each step still brought a jab of pain from my leg. My right hand was useless. I couldn't put any pressure near the sting, which, unfortunately, had gotten me square in the palm of my hand. When I swat something I swat it good and hard. I needed to remember to not swat scorpions.

The tracks led us on. Time was weighing on both of us. We didn't know how much water Marcel had started out with but it was bound to be gone. We searched the map for springs and creeks but we couldn't find any that seemed likely places for Marcel to go, so time was precious. I grumbled to myself about spending a whole day laid up, especially due to stupidity. Okay, Cassidy, I told myself, so you flubbed up, you're still the one who can track this trail the fastest so get after it. Your sergeant is standing behind you giving you an order and you better track this trail or you'll be doing KP for a week. Nope guard duty. It was guard duty that I had hated. Anything with activity I hadn't minded. Guard duty was boring.

When I asked Victor for our position I was encouraged. We were making good time. The tracks were staying visible. Marcel was doing logical, predictable things. The rocks had given way to more open ground. We had spent two and a half days on the trail and, unless some accident befell Marcel, he had at least a two day head start on us. It looked bleak, even with this breakthrough. We could only hope that something had stopped Marcel from continuing and even that thought held little promise. What would have stopped him? An accident? Injury? Lack of water? Usually a lack of water drove people to look for it and that could prove fatal. There was very little water in these mountains and to go looking for it used up precious physical resources.

Marcel's tracks looked old. They were eroded from the wind but, fortunately, not from the rain. One thing I could count on in these mountains was dry tracking. It was very rare for a rainstorm to interfere. The tops of the tracks were rounded from the wind but the tread was still visible. I was glad to see the footprints led farther into the mountains. There was more shelter from the wind in amongst the trees and more protection from the sun. Sources of water were more prevalent, although still rare. Another thing that gave me some hope was that Marcel watched for trees he could climb to get an idea of his whereabouts. Tree climbing would use up time, time we could use to our advantage catching up.

Morning faded to afternoon and we ate lunch on the trail. Afternoon faded to evening and I kept on until I couldn't see the tracks anymore. Another night. We would be starting day four. Friday. The day we were supposed to drive to the ranch. The day we were running on empty. We had a little food in our packs. I had an extra backpacker dinner because I couldn't eat it the night of the scorpion sting. Victor and I could split it. I had a couple of oatmeal packets, a stick of jerky, some trail mix and four chocolate chip cookies. Victor dug through his pack. He cooked his last backpacker dinner. What was left was a packet of powdered eggs, a granola bar and a cinnamon roll wrapped in plastic.

"I'm good for another day," I said.

"Me too," he said hesitantly. It wasn't much to go on but we could do it.

"If you can stand oatmeal for breakfast you can save your eggs for later. We can pool our resources."

He nodded. "I need to get back to work one of these days, too. I told them this was likely to be a long one but I've never been gone this long. They're going to think I got lost and send out a search party."

"I hope they call Strict for the search party."

"How are you doing?" he asked.

"Okay, the stings are going away. I was able to concentrate on tracking today. I just wish I could make it to the funeral but that's not looking likely anymore. My dad won't be happy with me. He says women shouldn't be traipsing around in the mountains looking for people. Of course, when he said that I was looking for a violent criminal. Maybe he'd feel different about this search."

"What would Old Frank say about it?"

"Old Frank was proud of me. He said if he ever had kids he hoped they lived life like I do, jumping in with both feet."

"Did he have kids?"

"Not that he knows of," I laughed. "He was never married as long as I knew him either. Maybe he was married before I was born. He never said and I never asked. He was just Old Frank. He never seemed lonely for any one person. The ranch was his family. He could have had a whole other life before my dad hired him on. I don't know. It's weird to think that we only know about his life from the ranch on. I wonder what he did before."

Sixty-two unknown years. That really seemed odd. More than twice my lifetime, lost to time, forgotten, only known to Frank himself. Anything could have happened. My cranky, old, adopted grandpa could have been a soldier in the war, a cattle rustler in the old west. Something told me he had always worked with horses. Even when he could hardly walk he could ride with ease. His mannerisms revealed a lifetime of horse sense. Even when he walked around the end of a fence he placed his hand on the post as he walked around it, just like he'd place a hand on a horse's rump to let them know he was there. Imagining all the old mannerisms made me feel lonely again. It was things that most people didn't even notice about him that brought back the memories. I doubted anybody else noticed his habit of placing a hand on things as he went around them. Nobody else knew that to go over a paddock fence he placed his foot just like he would into a stirrup and swung his other leg over, just like he was mounting a horse. When he handed me a quarter for the gum machine at the grocery store it was always palm out, fingers back, like he was giving a sugar cube to a horse.

"Cassidy?" Victor said waving a hand to get my attention.

"Sorry, my thoughts kind of wandered away."

"It's okay."

Our discussion turned to the search.

"Any chance of finding Marcel tomorrow?"

"I doubt it. The tracks are still old. We're not catching up to him. Tomorrow it'll be five days, so it's not looking good."

We got out the map, found ourselves on it, and speculated about the terrain ahead. It looked more pleasant than what we'd done so far. At least that was encouraging. The direction we were heading was into deep forest. It didn't make sense to me. If I was lost I would follow a creek or wash downhill. Around here, downhill led to a campground or highway. If one could walk far enough, downhill led to Joshua Hills to the north or the L.A. area to the south. But people seldom thought that way. They left trails for wilderness; they left roadways and cut cross-country. It didn't make sense to me.

“What would you do if you were lost up here?” I asked Victor.

“I doubt I could get lost up here. I’ve walked so much of it with a map and GPS. Maybe Marcel was a boy scout. They say to find a high vantage point and try to get your bearings. He has tried that a couple of times.”

“I wish he had read the part of the book that says to find a safe spot and wait to be found.”

He nodded.

As I snuggled into my warm sleeping bag I thought about Marcel out in open. I’d slept out in the open in weather like this. It was cold, although not dangerously so. The water problem was what bothered me the most. A cold night was minor trouble, but being lost without water was major trouble. I searched my heart for Rusty and wondered what he was doing. It was unusual for me to be gone three nights. I was sure he had found out about the scorpion by now. He called Strict for a nightly report. He always called after dark and he knew how to read Strict’s answers. I wanted to reach out and ease his worries. The pain from the stings was easing and only ached when I put pressure on them. In the morning I expected to be nearly back to normal.

The next morning the challenge was not rocks. It was the opposite: pine needles. The forest was covered with them. It goes against the nature of a tracker to disturb the trail, but four days worth of pine needles had fallen over Marcel’s tracks. At times I could see where the pine needles had slid under Marcel’s feet. Those areas I could cross quickly. Where walking was level though Marcel’s footprints were only a slight indentation in the blanket. It had sprung back up and more needles had fallen, hiding his tracks. I tried looking at it from ground level and sometimes I could make out very subtle indentations. I lifted the needles like pickup sticks, one sprig at a time to reveal the larger indentations below. It didn’t often work. I came to celebrate steep uphill climbs because it forced Marcel to leave a good trail.

Victor could see the trail was wearing on me again. My brain was fried, just thinking of all the impossibilities and trying to pull out the visible from the invisible.

“Taint invisible, Trouble, it’s just subtle. You gotta get down to subtleties. Think like a blanket of pine needles. What are you hiding? Where is it? It’s there somewhere’s. You just gotta think subtle like.”

My brain feels like Jell-O from thinkin’ subtle like, I thought.

There was a fallen tree. Marcel had stood next to it. The indentations in the pine needles were obvious here. He’d broken off pieces of bark and thrown them into the woods. The fresh wood beneath the chunks stood out like a beacon. I looked over the tree; very few pines needles rested on top.

Pieces of bark were scuffed on top. Fairly recently. I climbed up on top of the tree and walked the trunk until I came to a freshly broken off branch and when I looked to see where the branch had fallen I saw Marcel.

"Victor! I found him!"

I jumped off the tree and knelt down beside him, afraid to reach out. Victor jogged around the end of the tree. I felt for a pulse. I couldn't find one, but I didn't trust myself to be able to find one right away. His skin was cold but not like dead cold. As Victor took over I got back to tracker mode. Marcel had been here for some time, but he'd been able to move around a little. He'd been here at least one night, maybe two. He'd pulled pine needles around him. He'd had water for a while after he fell. The empty bottle was tossed aside.

Victor slipped into automatic and the staccato transmissions fired back and forth over the mountains.

"Ten sixty-five found." Missing person found.

"Ten forty-five?" What is the condition of the patient?

"Ten twenty-three." Stand by.

"Ten four." Okay.

"Cassidy, we're going to need a pick up. Look around for an open area."

"Okay."

"No wait, help me get him where I can see better."

Something didn't feel right about that. It was a tracker thing, not an EMT thing. He knew not to move a person unless it was absolutely necessary. He was thinking a fall from a tree, no big deal. He was thinking maybe Marcel had sheltered there. I saw something different.

"Victor, I don't think we should."

"I can't see a thing in here."

"I know, but…" gee I hated disagreeing with the authority. "Victor, call an ambulance."

"I can't even tell what shape he's in."

"Call an ambulance and the guys will help you. Something's wrong that we don't know about. Marcel pulled pine needles over him for warmth, but he did it while he was lying down. He only moved his legs as much as they shifted while he used his arms. I think it would be dangerous to move him without help."

He stepped back and examined the situation from my point of view. It only took a few seconds. He didn't see it in as much detail as I did but he acknowledged the observation. He sighed and looked at what he had to work with.

"Okay, find a pick up area."

I set out to find a clearing where a drop could be made.

"Ten forty-five B," Victor fired back to Strict as I jogged off to begin my search. Patient serious. I knew it was just a starting point to get things moving. The condition could change at any time but better to play it safe and call it serious.

I chose a direction and took off in search of a flat area where a helicopter could land, or at least drop a cable. The first area didn't pan out. It was too thickly forested. I began hiking in the gentler direction, and found one farther away than I liked. Still, it was a good pick up spot, highly visible from the air, close enough that our GPS coordinates would lead the pilot to the right area. I jogged back to Victor. He'd removed the pine needles.

"What can I do?"

"Did you find a spot?"

"Yeah."

"I hope the helicopter can find us before dark."

He had a point. It was late afternoon. It could take hours for a helicopter to take off from LA and find us, just one tiny speck in the mountains. I always felt tiny when I knew a helicopter was looking for us. The mountains grew and the little clearings and canyons shrunk. When the light began fading I took two flashlights to the pickup spot and waited for the clatter of helicopter blades. I might not be a good EMT but I was willing to do anything else that was needed. Flag down a helicopter? No problem. I stood in the middle of the open area and waved my arms, flashlights shining. When the helicopter had found us three men were lowered on cables. They brought a basket to transport Marcel in. I led them back to Victor and Marcel, then got out of the way. It took them a while to stabilize Marcel for the ride to the hospital. He was young and fit but he had been injured, out in the open and without water too long. The three had taken a toll on him. I stayed out of the way while the men worked. Victor saw me sitting there and sat with me.

"He'll be okay," he told me.

I just nodded, hoping it was true, wondering if my stupidity had cost him in some way. I never found out. We landed in L.A. and Marcel was rushed off to ER and I found the hospital lobby. The lobby was usually a relatively quiet place so, rather than fighting the crowds in ER or the waiting rooms, we usually met in the hospital lobby. I found a quiet corner and called Rusty.

"Cassidy?" he said on the first ring.

"Hi."

I had so many things battling it out in my head. I just hoped he didn't hit the wrong buttons.

"You okay?"

"Yeah, I'm fine. I'm in L.A."

There was a long pause. He knew a flight to L.A. meant a close call, and a close call usually involved a major guilt trip on my part. On the bright side he knew I'd found my man.

"Strict said it was a tough search."

"The toughest one yet."

A long pause.

"I'll be there as soon as I can."

An hour and a half I waited while thoughts of the search battled it out with the memories of Old Frank. The last four days had taken a toll. I was physically, mentally and emotionally exhausted. Victor found me when he had finished his EMT duties and Rusty arrived to give him a ride to the compound where he picked up his own car.

Shadow went nuts when I walked in the door. I had to sit while he jumped all over me, getting caught up on four days worth of petting. When he finally settled down it was Rusty's turn. I needed the hug on the big brown couch as much as he did. I slid into his arms and found that certain spot where we fit together just right. As I finally let my guard down the tears came. I felt his concern change a little until it felt like comfort. Tears he could deal with. Tears were normal. There were lots of other things he worried about, but he could comfort me, so he felt better.

"Oh, babe, it's okay. If you're worried about the funeral, we'll make it," he said softly into my hair.

It wasn't just the funeral. It was the mental strain. It was four physically demanding days. It was feeling trapped in a numb body with nothing but negative thoughts. It was being far away from home when I needed familiarity. I needed a meal and a good night's sleep, time to sort out my feelings and give my brain a rest from invisible details. I wasn't ready to deal with life yet, much less death.

"Are you okay?" he asked.

"I think so, sort of."

"Do you want to try and get there tonight?"

"If we leave now we'll get there at two a.m., but we can sleep in. If we leave in the morning, we have to be on the road at six and not stop. Both of them sound like too much."

"This doesn't sound like you. Are you sure you're okay?"

"Yes, it's been a hell of a week. What did Strict tell you?"

"He just said it was really tough, almost impossible tracking conditions. He said you were having a rough time of it. We talked about Old Frank."

So he didn't know. He thought I was blaming myself for the slowness of the search.

"I had a rough time up there for other reasons besides emotions and a tough trail. I did something really stupid and it laid me up for a whole day."

He waited while I stewed.

"I got stung by a scorpion," I almost laughed. "You should have seen me, and I'm glad Victor didn't. It ran up my pants leg and stung my leg and when I tried to squash it I got stung again. I was dancing around in the woods trying to get rid of the stupid scorpion, cussing a mile a minute. It hurt like crazy. Then I reacted badly to it. I spent a whole day stuck in the tent while my whole body went numb. I wanted you so bad. I just wanted to be held. I wanted you to take away all the sadness and frustration even if it was for just a few minutes. I was so miserable."

"Where was Victor when all this was going on?"

"The trail went cold. I was searching the rocks for tracks so I sent him to find an exit point. It was a logical course for us to take. He came running when I called, and he made me stop when he knew I was having a reaction to the sting. I'd have kept going but he made me stop. It was a bad reaction, too. It was awful. If Victor hadn't been there to tell me it was normal I would have been terrified."

"My girl, when will you learn? You don't have to go through all this. You're allowed to turn Strict down."

"No, I can't. I couldn't live with myself if I just left people out there when they can be found. While I was laid up Strict sent out a helicopter but they didn't spot Marcel. He'd fallen off a dead tree and hurt his back. He was half buried in leaves and half hidden under the trunk of the tree. They couldn't have spotted him from the air if they'd looked for years and searchers would never have thought to go where we finally found him. He was almost impossible to track. I almost gave up but Old Frank wouldn't let me."

"You might as well admit it. You can't kill Old Frank. He's just a part of you."

I snuggled closer trying to fight off the tears again.

"Why didn't Strict tell me about the scorpion?" Rusty asked.

"Because it was just part of the search. Things happen. We deal with them. We dealt with that. It didn't leave any lasting effects. It was a long delay but just part of the search. I just hope it didn't cost Marcel."

"What about the ranch. Do you want to leave now?"

"I don't want to think about the ranch. I just need time, just a little time."

"Babe, it's after ten. If we're going to the ranch tonight we need to call."

"If we leave in the morning we'll be pushing it," I sighed. "We better go tonight."

"I had to go shopping and repack a little. Your mom called and said not to wear black. She said to bring something cheerful to wear. So I found a bright western shirt in your closet and I went shopping for something western for me."

“You’re kidding! You didn’t need to do that. What did you buy for you?” I’d never seen Rusty dressed western before.

“You’ll see.”

Chapter 3

I took a five minute shower while Rusty loaded the Explorer and we took off on a long, dark drive to the ranch. Mom and Dad left the front door unlocked and we got to the ranch at nearly three a.m. We slipped in, locked the door behind us and went quietly to my old bedroom. I set the alarm for nine and we fell into bed.

I heard the door open a crack and gently close early in the morning. My mom checking on me. Rusty stirred, too, pulled me close and we went back to sleep.

Long before the alarm went off I woke up. It was funeral day. The day I had to say good-bye forever. I'd have to keep my emotions in check, so it was going to be a tough day. I tried to figure out how cops did it. How did they set their feelings aside and just deal with the task at hand? I'd never know.

I let Rusty sleep and wake up with the alarm. I showered and dressed and went to meet my somber family. My mother and Martha were in the kitchen.

"When did you get in?" my mom asked with a sympathetic hug.

"About three. It was a rough search. I had to catch a ride with the ambulance and ended up in L.A. I didn't get home until ten."

"I'm glad you could make it."

"What have you got to eat? I just did a four day search on three days of rehydrated backpacker food. I'm ready for some real food."

"Now that's what I like to hear," said Martha. "Usually it's a job just to get you to eat."

My dad came down stairs and stood in the doorway. Things were a little strained between my dad and me, but it was unnecessary.

"Welcome home, Cassidy," he said.

"Thanks dad," I answered.

"How long can you stay?" he asked, surprisingly. Usually it was my mom who asked.

"I don't know, Dad. I got home from the search and we just jumped in the truck and took off. We haven't even talked about it. I could use a few days off. I would love a walk on the beach and a ride in the hills."

"Did you know your tracker friend is here?"

"My tracker friend? Chase?"

"Is that his name? He just asked where he could find you. When we said you weren't here he asked if you were coming. We said we expected you before the service. Then he asked where he could find Patrick. I informed him that Patrick was only seven years old and I'd have to get Jesse's permission before I sent him down there. Last I saw him Patrick rode up to the house and led him back down to their house. Patrick was real excited. What is it about that guy to get a young 'un so worked up?"

"He thinks like Patrick does. They understand each other."

"It's a rare thing to see a kid respect an old man like that. Patrick was the same way with Old Frank. They played chess and dominoes. Patrick would drill Frank with questions and Frank answered them with the patience of a saint."

"Did you notice that both men have a respect for Patrick, too? They see something in him worth encouraging. Whatever it is, they nurture it. It was important to Old Frank. It's important enough to Chase to bring him all the way from San Diego. Chase came to pay his respects, but he also came here to see how Patrick is doing. They met when I had to take Patrick with me to San Diego at Christmas."

I found Chase exactly where I expected to, in the tree house beside Jesse's house. Chase wouldn't stay in a hotel and he'd feel like he was imposing on the family to be put up for the night. He had been awake a while and he slid down the rope when he saw me walking down the road. He stood there, hands in the pockets of ragged cargo shorts. His t-shirt was from Tacky T-shirts where Rusty's brother, Cody, worked. It showed a guy carrying a surfboard and said "Life's a beach." His hair was tied back in a ponytail. He wore sandals. I winced inwardly wondering what my dad had thought when Chase came to the door.

"You ready for some breakfast?" I asked.

"It was a short night for you," he pointed out. "I saw you pull in this morning."

"Yeah, it was. I had to finish a search before we took off. I didn't know if I was even going to make it. Come on up to the house."

"Can't. I promised Jesse I'd stay with Patrick."

"No problem," I told him. I climbed the rope to the tree house and there was Patrick, sound asleep. "Real trackers get up with the sun," I told Pat.

"Aunt Cassidy!" He yelled, instantly awake. "Oh boy! Oh boy! Mom said you might not come and you came! I knew you'd come. I asked you to, just like I ask the deer and you came!"

"You knew I'd try. Chase and I are going to the ranch house for breakfast. Go ask your mom if you can come, too."

He slid down the rope and ran into the house on silent moccasined feet.

"I can't decide if he's an adult trapped in a kid's body or seven going on twenty," Chase said.

"I know how you feel."

Patrick rushed outside and grabbed my hand. "I have to show you something first," he said. He dragged me into the house and into his bedroom. There he pulled a shoebox from under his bed. "I'm collecting tracks!" he said excitedly. In the shoe box was a plastic tub of plaster of Paris. He pulled out a few solid plaster lumps. On the back, in sloppy first grade printing they were labeled: Jimbo, Bandit, jackrabbit. "The cotton tailed rabbits like to stay on the grass so it's hard to get their tracks. So I only have a jackrabbit. It took me a while to figure out how to mix the powder. If it's too stiff the plaster squashes the track and if it's too thin it falls apart when I pick it up."

"This is really cool, Pat! What made you think to do this?"

"Mom was making sand candles and when I saw her making the mold for her candles I thought about tracks in the ground. So I asked her if I could use some of her wax to try and get paw prints from the ground. She said I should use this stuff instead so I wouldn't have to heat it."

"Bring it up to the house and show Uncle Rusty. Maybe we can find more tracks for your collection."

He brought the box along and we headed to the ranch house knowing Jesse and Wyatt would catch up soon and James would show up with the rest of the ranch hands. Patrick reminded me of Shadow, running twice the distance in his excitement as we walked back to the ranch house.

"You should really take a room in the ranch house," I told Chase. "It's no problem for them. They don't mind you staying there. All the rooms have their own bathroom, so you don't even have to wait for a shower. It's handy, if confining."

At breakfast Patrick was running off at the mouth.

"Chase said we could try and find a deer track. I told him where the deer are and we're going to go see if we can stalk them. And I want to get a horse's hoof print but they are so big. And I want to get a hoof print of a horse without shoes on."

"Try the colts. They don't wear shoes until they are a couple of years old. While they are out in the paddocks growing, they go without shoes. How's Snoopy?"

"He's great. Chase, can you ride? I can only ride in the hills with an adult but I bet my mom would let me go with you."

"Yeah, I can ride. I grew up riding Indian ponies."

"Oh cool! The Indian ponies on TV look like my horse. Were they pintos too? Snoopy is a pinto."

"Patrick! I swear, you're monopolizing the whole table," my mother said. "Let other people talk too!"

"What's monopolizing mean? That's a cool word. Monopolize. It sounds like it takes talent. What's it mean?"

"I swear, one of these days you're going to talk so much your jaw is going to seize up and you'll get lockjaw," Mom said.

Just then Rusty walked into the room and that started Patrick on a whole new victim. He was just excited to see everybody but his excitement came out his mouth. He showed Rusty his small track collection and told him about his plans to add to it. At least with Patrick around nobody had a chance to be really sad. His enthusiasm was contagious.

The ranch hands were not nearly as enthusiastic about the day. They dragged in from their early morning chores, ate a joyless breakfast, and left to get ready for the funeral.

"Come on, Pat," Jesse said. "No playing until after the service."

Thus, with all of us now thinking of the hours ahead we all went somberly to our rooms to get ready.

"Chase, do you want a room? There's plenty. Go get your things."

He went outside and returned with a small duffle bag. I led him to a room a couple of doors down from my room, a smaller room with a view of the hills.

"You're fine the way you are as far as I'm concerned, but if you want to freshen up there's a bathroom in here. You're welcome to stay as long as you want."

"That's a nice little tree house Patrick has," Chase said.

"Thanks," I replied. "I built it. Did you notice the bullet holes in it? Just a souvenir from a bout of trouble."

"Patrick wasn't in it was he?"

"No, just me."

"Figures."

I changed into the western outfit Rusty had packed. It was a turquoise and red plaid western shirt. I tucked it into jeans and pulled on my cowboy boots that lived in the closet at the ranch. I curled my hair and put on makeup. I looked in the mirror and a fifteen year old high school kid looked back. In fact, I thought, didn't I get this shirt in my junior year of high school?

Rusty put on a blue and red striped western shirt. It was still new, not a wrinkle on it. He'd bought new jeans too. If he brought out boots and a hat I was going to laugh. He rolled up a kerchief and fastened it with a western slide. Okay, I was laughing now, boots or no boots.

"What's wrong?" he asked.

"Nothing, it's just strange to see you dressed like that. You don't need to change in any way. My family likes you just fine in your regular clothes."

"But your mom said…"

"And she wouldn't have said a thing if she thought you would go out and buy new clothes just for this. She just knew Old Frank wouldn't want his funeral to be black and dreary."

"Should I change back?"

"Wear what you want. Just be prepared for some strange looks from Steve and Randy."

Steve gave Rusty a lopsided grin, "After the service I'm going to teach you how to rope and tie a calf."

"Steve, leave him alone."

"Cassidy can do it," Steve told him.

"What?"

"Rope and tie a calf."

"You can?" Rusty asked me. "Is there anything you don't do?"

"I don't make fun of people just because they dressed nicely for a friend."

Randy poked Steve in the ribs and said, "Rusty, are you applying for Old Frank's job? You need a bigger belt buckle and where's your hat?"

"You don't wear a hat." Rusty pointed out.

Steve handed over his black, beaver felt Stetson. Rusty put it on his head just as Jesse walked in the front door.

"Whoa, you look like you just stepped out of a Sheplers catalog!"

The cemetery was spring green. Birds flitted from one oak tree to another. A large crowd was gathered to see Old Frank off to his final resting place. He hadn't wanted a fancy memorial service. In fact, we were told, he wanted a backhoe to dig a hole and he wanted to be buried with the horses in the field. Since it was illegal to do that he had to opt for the little backhoe at the cemetery. His casket was placed in the ranch buckboard and Old Frank's horse pulled it to the gravesite. Steve, Randy, Zack, and James were pallbearers along with Old Frank's two close friends from the barbershop, Hector and Bert. Hector and Bert weren't much help with the lifting, being nearly as old as Old Frank, but they were honored and touched to carry their old friend's casket.

A minister addressed the crowd and I wondered if Old Frank approved. He wasn't a religious man but neither did he scorn religion. He thought there must be a god and he thought that god must be nuts to create someone like me. He'd told me when I was a kid it would take a whole host of guardian angels to keep track of me. He pondered whether there would be horse racing in heaven but he doubted it, at least until God created a new earth and people got greedy and started betting again. He seemed to think people in general messed things up, but he conceded he rather enjoyed messing things up more than working hard at perfecting them.

When the minister asked us if we'd like to share a few words about Old Frank we all rolled our eyes when Patrick jumped up. The minister looked at Patrick with surprise. The whole ranch family knew Patrick would say anything, any time, but to have a seven year old take the platform for an eighty-eight year old man took the minister by surprise.

"You want to say a few words?" the minister asked.

Always taking things literally Patrick confessed, "I doubt it ends up being just a few." Then he stepped up to the microphone and stood on tiptoes. He looked at the arrangement and lowered the microphone before an adult could stop him and surprised everybody again when he did it right. "I think you all need to look around you," Pat said, his voice breaking a little. "You see lots of old folks, because Old Frank was around long enough to know people a long time. When you see old folks, think of what they have to give. They have special gifts that they can only give to young folks but young folks don't want to receive those kinds of gifts. They should. Old Frank gave me time. An' he gave me stories. He didn't see a no good mischievous kid. He figured out which way my mischievousness ran and he ran with it. He showed me how to do things the right way so's I wouldn't get in trouble trying to figure out the wrong way. He played games with me, partly because he was bored, but partly because, he said, it kept our minds sharp. He liked games with numbers. Easy games like dominoes. We played a lot of dominoes because he said it was good for my math. I got an A in math every time. Maybe it was Old Frank that got an A. Old Frank didn't get to finish school. That's why he made me work hard at it. He said you're stuck with your brain as long as you live. The more information you stick in there the more useful it is as time goes by. So he spent hours stuffin' my brain. Old Frank was smart, even if he didn't finish school. All you young people… let some old folks help stuff your brain. An' all you old folks find a young person who appreciates you an' do like Old Frank."

He stepped down and the minister wiped a tear from his eye.

"Well spoken, young man, well spoken. You should have my job."

Jesse was crying now, whether for Old Frank or because of Patrick I wasn't sure. Mom was on the verge of tears, too. Several people got up and said that Old Frank was a great guy and he sure would be missed. I felt an invisible nudge. Rusty wasn't going to prod me but he knew I had things to say. I stepped up, reluctantly. I was used to getting up in front of people. I spoke to school classes regularly. But I wasn't used to getting emotional in front of a large audience and I didn't trust myself to stay on guard.

"Most people saw Old Frank as a grumpy old cowboy out of place in sunny California. Maybe he was, but there was more to Old Frank than meets the eye. My generation at the ranch called him Old Frank because I'm the oldest and Old Frank was sixty-two when I was born. So I always thought he was old. He was younger than many middle-aged people I meet, in his heart. He was devoted to finding the good in a person and nurturing that thing. In my case he taught me to think. I wouldn't be able to do my job today if it weren't for Old Frank. Those of you who went to school around here know I'm a tracker. None of you know it was Old Frank who encouraged that in me. Twenty four hours ago I was on a mountain outside L.A. finding a man who would have died had I not gotten there in time. His chances are still iffy. He led me on the toughest search of my life and I would have given up if it wasn't for Old Frank. His wisdom echoed in my brain. His stubbornness pushed me when I couldn't see the way. And now a man lives who might have died. Old Frank saw something to nurture in me. If you knew him for any length of time he saw something in you, too. Think. What was it that Old Frank encouraged in you? When you find it, continue to nurture that in yourself. You'll be a better person because Frank chose wisely what he helped along. He did it with horses. He did it with people and he had an open mind. Who would have thought to encourage a young girl to be a tracker? Nobody. Nobody but Old Frank. When you see something good in a person, encourage it. Nurture it. Help it along. Continue what Old Frank started. And don't try to nurture people into society's molds. Sure the world needs doctors and lawyers, corporate CEOs. But Old Frank didn't let money get in the way of what a person was truly meant to be. The world needs people to follow their own set of tracks out of the mold society places on them. Old Frank saw what people really wanted to be and he helped them be that. Artist? Ditch digger? Tracker? It didn't matter to Old Frank. The world needs ditch diggers, too. Take up Old Frank's mission in life and find some good to encourage. The results will surprise you."

Dad got up and gave a big long speech about Old Frank's talents with the horses, how many horses Old Frank had trained to be winners. If there was someone from the society page to write about Old Frank's passing, they would quote Dad and I thought that was sad. Sure Old Frank loved the races. He'd won and lost his share betting and he'd spent a lot of time in the barns, getting horses ready for the races. People all over the west would miss him in the barns and winners circles. But when all the hoopla was over Old Frank didn't go for a champagne dinner and celebrate. He'd be found in the barns with a patty melt in one hand, a horse trying to take it from him. He'd push the horse away and switch the sandwich to the hand with horsehair all over it and keep eating, talking to the grooms like he was one of them.

Several other people got up and spoke. Hector joked about their barbershop days. Randy spoke about being raised by Old Frank. Dad would have taken the credit for that but Randy didn't give it to him. Sure, Mr.

Gordon had done his share but he hadn't been down there with the boy showing him how to muck out a stall. He didn't sit in the bunkhouse and help him with algebra. Old Frank did that.

When everybody was either talked out or tired of listening, the group moved to the next phase of the day, which was food. There was a reception in town, which Frank would have loved to go to. Anywhere with people and food was a place for Old Frank. I wasn't hungry. As everybody filed away I found an out of the way place and I sat. Watching. Watching a wooden box with a blanket of flowers on it. A winner's blanket. The service wasn't where I wanted to say goodbye to Old Frank. This was it. One on one. I wanted to be left alone. I wanted my tears to be between Old Frank and me. I wanted him to see that it was just him that mattered to me, not all the speeches and the food and the society page. Rusty came and sat with me. Chase stood at a respectful distance.

"Babe, they won't bury Old Frank while people are watching."

"I don't care. I'm not here to watch him get buried."

"Then what are you here for?" he asked kindly.

"Minutes," I answered, "just sharing minutes."

"Hon, Old Frank's been gone for a week. He doesn't have any minutes."

"But I do," I cried. "I haven't used them all up yet."

He sighed and stuffed down his emotions.

"Come with me, you'll feel better once you get back in the swing of things. Let's go to the reception, get some lunch, go riding out in the hills."

"Rusty, I don't want to feel better. It feels wrong to feel better. Please, just let me be sad for a little while. Go on to the reception. Tell them I'll be there soon."

"I can't stand to see you like this. It tears me up. I can't go to a reception and smile and talk to a bunch of people I don't know, when I know you're out here miserable."

Chase walked up and laid a hand on Rusty's shoulder. Rusty looked up and followed Chase a few steps away.

"Come on," Chase said quietly. "She just needs some time to mourn her own way. You can't make her mourn like everybody else. She'll never be like everyone else and you know it. Take a walk and talk to me about Patrick. Tell me what Mr. Gordon's plans are."

Rusty looked to me. He didn't know what Dad's plans were but he could talk to Chase.

It was just the two cemetery workers and me now. I sat there for a few minutes, then got up and spoke to them.

"I have a silly request," I told them. "This old man taught me to follow people's tracks. He practically raised me. All I want to do is leave my tracks for him. Just two boot prints in the bottom of the grave. Can I do that?"

"How are you going to get out?"

"I thought maybe you could give me a lift with your backhoe."

"No. We'd be fired."

"If I accidentally fell in you'd *have* to help me out, right?"

"I guess so."

"So I'll accidentally fall in. If you'll help me out I'll let you get back to work."

They took the fake grass cloth away from the grave and I jumped in. I walked to where I figured Old Frank's heart would rest and I put two plain boot prints in the dirt. His tracks would forever be in my heart. It was the closest thing I could come to it being the other way around. I don't know why it mattered for me to do that. But I felt a little better for it. The younger guy gave me a hand up out of the grave and I looked down at my boot prints, plain as day even from up on top. I kept my promise and got out of their way. I heard the machine lower Old Frank's casket into the grave and as I walked away one of them called out to me, "Ma'am?" He held out a shovel. I walked back and took it. I was only going to throw in a shovel full and leave, but one shovel full led to another, and before I knew it the men were sitting under a tree and I stood there shoveling dirt. In my mind I was mucking out stalls in the barn and Old Frank was standing there shaking his head saying, "Trouble, what'd you do this time and how long are you in for?"

And I answered, "Two weeks. I back talked a teacher. She said Matthew Rogers started a fight but I could tell by the tracks that Matthew was barely involved. It was Barton Fartston who hit Randy. She won't believe me but I know Barton's tracks. And Matthew was just part of the group. Barton pinned it on Matthew but they won't believe me. Now me and Matthew are both in trouble and Barton's off scot-free."

"Some things just ain't fair," Old Frank told me. "Why didn't you tell your dad? He put you to this, right?"

"It was the talking back that did it. I doesn't matter if I was right. I still back talked the teacher."

"Well, I guess you're right there."

And so we were all right except Barton Fartson and I was mad at Barton so I kept shoveling. And I was sad about Old Frank so I shoveled harder. The two men sat there shaking their heads watching me work, not realizing it was therapy, just thinking I was nuts. They got out their lunch and settled in with their sandwiches. Rusty came back and looked over the situation. Chase stood there hands folded over his chest, smiling, glad I found a way to work off my sorrow. Rusty came up behind me and gently grabbed the end of the shovel when I brought it back. I stopped. He released the handle when he saw that I was focused on the present again and I dropped the shovel full of dirt in the grave, then jabbed the shovel into the dirt pile. I looked over the pile and saw that I'd put a good-sized dent in it.

We drove to the reception arriving half an hour late. Fortunately, it was a buffet. We chose our lunches and looked for a place to sit down.

"Cassidy! Where have you been? And just look at you!" My mother said.

"It's okay, mom. Old Frank would approve."

"Old Frank would approve of a lot of things I wouldn't."

I looked around. There were a few open chairs here and there except for the head table. Only my dad sat at the head table. Everybody else was seated with the town folks talking and swapping stories about Old Frank. Dad looked lonely but I wasn't going to put myself at the head table either. Old Frank wouldn't have sat there. Head tables were for people of status and Dad was the only one who counted status in that way. A woman walked up and talked to Dad. Mom shook her head.

"That woman has to be *everywhere*!" she said with disdain. "I swear; she's on the hunt."

The woman leaned low over the table. Dad pretended not to notice as he spoke to her. He pointed out Mom, Jesse, and me to her. When she turned to find us I saw who it was, Misty Montague! She turned back to dad, he said something, and she looked back our way. Oh man, I was going to have my work cut out for me now. I quickly found a spot in amongst the people making sure there were only three chairs. I led Rusty and Chase that direction and we sat down, moving used plates and a few wrinkled napkins out of the way.

Chase saved the day, distracting Rusty by asking me about this really tough search I just returned from. I was glad to have the distraction and went into all the detail I knew Chase was interested in. Rusty rarely heard about my searches in detail. I thought it would bore him, but he listened intently. Chase interrupted me a few times asking pointed questions. I think he was trying to assess the scope of my tracking skills. Only hearing about the intricacies told him how my brain worked as I tracked.

"Well, well, if it isn't our little woods elf," said a voice behind me. I looked up and there stood Misty Montague in all her sequined, spaghetti strapped glory. "Welcome back, Cassidy."

"Thank you," I said and then I had to be polite so I made introductions. "Misty, this is my husband Rusty Michaels and a friend of the family, Charles Downing. Guys, this is Misty Montague. We went to school together."

"Pleased to meet you," said Chase as he gave me a strange look.

Rusty just looked at Chase and said, "Your name is Charles?"

"You knew that," Chase said.

"No I didn't. I've never called you Charles. Cassidy, how did you know his real name was Charles?"

"That's how they introduced him to the class at police academy," I answered; glad they weren't paying much attention to Misty.

"Ooo, police academy. Our little woods elf is getting more citified." Chase just laughed. Then to Rusty she said, "I can tell by your outfit that you are a cowboy," and Chase laughed even louder.

Misty didn't like being laughed at, especially by a sixty year old beach bum. Even in jeans and a collared shirt you couldn't take the beach bum out of Chase.

"What?" she asked.

"Ma'am, I'm afraid you've got it all wrong," Chase told her.

I smiled as Misty became indignant. I didn't really want her to know what we did. It would only encourage her. If there was one thing Misty liked it was a challenge, particularly a handsome challenge. Chase would be too old for her. Rusty was definitely in the danger zone here but he knew Misty's reputation. She might be beautiful and rich but she was basically not a nice person. At least Rusty didn't have enough money to be a successful investment, but at this point Misty didn't need money. Misty collected husbands. She was one year older than me and had married and divorced three men. And that was *after* high school. In high school she was worse.

"It was nice of your dad to do this for Frank," Misty said. "He must have thought a lot of Frank."

"He was like family," I answered. "I never heard if Old Frank had any real family. In all the years I'd known him he never talked about ever having a family."

"I heard he was worth millions," Misty said.

"That's silly. If he was rich he wouldn't live in a bunkhouse with two other guys and nothing but a pool table and some poker cards," I answered. But in the back of my mind I was thinking it would be just like Old Frank to sock away his money and live the life he liked, in a bunkhouse on a ranch, just an old cowboy.

"You never know. I had one husband who was rich and the only way you'd know it was he had a penchant for Mercedes," Misty said.

"But Old Frank never even bought himself a car! He borrowed the ranch pickup to go to town."

"Why fork out twenty thousand when you can keep it plus interest?"

"Misty, don't you have something better to do?" I asked, tired of her greedy thinking.

"Oh, yes!" she exclaimed looking at her watch. "I'm late for a pedicure!"

Only Misty would put her toenails over a funeral. Of course I was sure she wasn't really there to mourn Old Frank. She was scoping things out. Funerals, weddings, store openings, beach volleyball tournaments… anything that drew the community drew Misty.

When she was out of earshot Chase leaned forward, "Okay, I'm curious. Why'd you use my real name?"

"I didn't want to give her any ideas," I answered.

"What kind of ideas?"

"Misty collects husbands. If I introduced you as Chase it would pique her interest. Believe me, you don't want to be chased by her."

"Why? She looks like fun. I'm single. Can't a guy have any fun?"

"Sure," I answered. "Just ask any of the local guys how fun Misty can be. Then come back and thank me."

He changed the subject. "When do you figure it's safe to talk to your dad about a horse trainer?"

"It's never safe to talk to my dad about anything he didn't think up first."

"What are you saying?"

"Can you think of a way to put the idea to him so he thinks he came up with it? You know he needs another hand. The trick is to make him think he came up with the idea of also finding a tracking teacher for his grandson. I'm not sure he wants Patrick to be a tracker. Since I've become a tracker he's only seen one dangerous thing after another happen to me and so far Patrick seems to have gotten the trouble gene, too."

Chase looked at Rusty who nodded.

"You both probably got it from *him*," Chase said.

"Trouble never happens to Dad. He's led a charmed life."

"He's a carrier."

"That's not a bad idea, let him think we got his inquisitive mind. Who knows where it really came from, but if you build up his ego he's more likely to see that wonderful brain he handed down needs fine tuning."

"When?"

"How long are you going to be around?"

"I hadn't set any time limit. I know I'm likely to overstay my welcome shortly after the funeral. They don't see any reason for me to stay and visit."

"Tomorrow then?"

"Should I talk to Patrick first?"

"Talk to Patrick about what?" Patrick said behind us.

"No, you shouldn't."

"Shouldn't what?" Patrick asked.

"Talk to Patrick first."

"Why?" Patrick said. "I'm always the last one to hear about everything."

"And you tend to get overexcited about things before we even know for sure if anything is going to happen," I told him. "Now let us talk."

Patrick ran off, looking like he was going to find Wyatt so we resumed our conversation.

"Is he willing to hire someone who is a little different from what he's used to?"

"If they show promise, he is willing to hire anybody who will accept the conditions and do their best to fit in with the guys. The ranch hands have to work closely together so it's important that they get along. If they live in the bunkhouse the fit is even more important."

"Okay, then, will the guys accept someone who is a little different?"

"Sure, as long as they try to get along, the hands will do their best to keep things running smoothly. Why?"

"Because this guy is a little different. The ranch hands aren't really that different to him. He's used to the dress and the talk. But they aren't used to people like him. His name is Elan. He calls me Demothi. It means *talks while walking*. He calls me that because when we first tracked together I would tell him what the tracks said to me. He was amazed that the ground told me stories but eventually he showed some talent in tracking. I taught him. His grandfather taught him. He isn't as good as you but he has a feel for the earth and for the way animals think. When he tracks people, he generally finds them but he doesn't think like most people, therefore, he takes the tracks very literally. In some cases it helps because he doesn't assume anything, but sometimes some speculation is a good thing. He has a lot to teach Patrick, but Patrick has a lot to teach him, too."

"What!" we heard from under the table along with a big *thump* as Patrick hit his head on the underside.

"If you're going to learn stealth. It's got to start with your mouth," Chase admonished him.

"But you didn't know I was down here," Patrick said defensively, "Or you would have stopped talking about me."

"He's got a point," said Rusty.

"Do you know Elan wants to train horses?" I asked.

"He knows horses, grew up with them. He knows how they think and how to get them to learn. His home for the past 25 years has been a three room house twenty miles from town. He's ready to try anything new. The thought of living just like his family has for the last five generations grates on him. He wants to see the world. Here he can stretch his wings, see a different side of life, try a different environment and do some good at the same time. He's never drawn a paycheck, never had to. His family is pretty self-sufficient."

"When can he come?"

"He's there now. He came with me but he didn't want to intrude on a time of grieving."

"Where? Why didn't you invite him into the house?"

"That's your father's job. Your father is the head of the house. It's his job to protect the people under his roof. If your father invites him in friendship he will gladly come in. But, in respect for your family, he's stayed away to give you space to grieve. He was fine last night. He slept in the Bug. He's probably spent the day wandering the hills. While he knows we are gone maybe he's ventured onto the ranch to see if the horses are well cared for. He wouldn't work there if the horses were neglected. It's just common sense things. He comes from a different culture so he comes to you a little differently."

I was beginning to see why Chase was a little different, too. My mood had brightened considerably with new possibilities. Patrick had sat quietly trying to figure out what we were talking about and who he could possibly teach anything to. I didn't want to get his hopes up. There was still the possibility that my father would not hire Elan and Patrick would be devastated. If Patrick knew what we were talking about, he could accidentally spill the beans to my dad and that could make the whole thing backfire.

"This can't wait until morning," I decided aloud. "Elan cannot spend another night in the Bug. Dad would be angry to think we left a guest to sleep in the car. We, at least, need to invite Elan in to spend the night in the house."

Our discussion seemed to have come to an end but my mind was going a mile a minute. A teacher for Patrick! We had to make this work.

Chapter 4

People began leaving the reception hall, going off to their own lives. I dreaded going back to a ranch to face years of memories, but now with a plan in place I wanted to get back to meet Elan. To me it was awful for Chase to bring someone along and then just leave them to their own devices at a stranger's house. I knew Chase was different from most people and that this was in part due to his being raised in Elan's environment. The two men didn't see this like I did, but I still felt a need to get back to the ranch and check things out.

When we arrived at the ranch Zack and Randy had already started their evening chores. I bet they were glad to have a day with minimal chores. There would be no rigorous horse training, just feeding and tending, and lots of talking.

I jumped out of the Explorer, scanning the ranch for signs of a stranger. I scanned the ground for unfamiliar footprints. Rusty smiled, glad to see me almost back to my old self.

I went to the old Bug and picked up Elan's tracks. I knew they weren't Chase's. They were very different. They were slightly smaller and more graceful than Chase's tracks. They led to the back of the ranch where they wandered a bit. Elan had observed the ranch from the shelter of the trees. He took his time and moved from tree to tree. This place probably looked odd after what he was used to. White fences, close cropped green grass. The bright red barn. The huge ranch house. The house was like a hotel. There was a whole wing of private rooms, each with its own bathroom.

Elan spent the morning observing the movements and people around the ranch. After we left for the funeral he slipped back down and walked amongst the horses. He watched the horses in the pastures and quietly walked from horse to horse in the barn. He had jumped away, startled, when Satan charged the gate to his stall. It was a reinforced gate, because the devil horse had broken the first two, but it made a racket when the 1200 pounds of cantankerous stallion charged it. Elan stepped close to most of the horses, probably petting them. It was hard for a horse person to get near a horse and not touch them. A horse person naturally reaches out to meet a friendly horse. He had kept a respectful distance from the house. I caught up with him in the oak woods in back of the property. He was lying in the grass just waiting and when he noticed movement he sat up. He stood in one fluid movement and walked down the hill to us, smiling. He was short and slim. His black hair, bound in a ponytail, hung down his back. He was a young, handsome Indian man. He stood erect, yet relaxed.

"You bring strangers," he said to Chase.

"They are only strangers to you," Chase replied. "This is Rusty. I've known him longer than I've known you. This is his wife, Cassidy."

"It's good to meet you," he said extending his hand. We shook hands and he stood, quietly for a moment, then said, "Which of you is the tracker?"

"That would be Cassidy," Chase said.

Elan raised his eyebrows, "Tell me, where did I go today?"

"You walked the fence, watching the horses, you visited the horses in the barn. The big, black horse charged the gate and made you jump. You walked down the row of stalls petting the horses. You particularly liked the big gray horse and the buckskin. You looked at a racehorse and leaned forward. I don't know what you were doing. After you left the barn you walked around the outside of the ranch house. Early in the morning you wandered in the hills and after you checked out the ranch you came back here to wait."

"The race horse has odd looking knees. At first I thought there was something wrong with them but I think, if I looked more closely, they are fine."

"The man who died? His name was Frank. The horse you were looking at is named Frank's Choice. Frank could spot the talent in a horse. He knew that horse could run. It's in his blood. I have ridden him and he *is* fast. There's nothing wrong with his knees. I'm willing to bet Frank put his money on that horse because people would see his knees and not bet on him, making him a long shot in the betting booths. That would be just like Old Frank. The horse isn't ready for the track yet. He's finishing up his training. The gray horse is mine, although I don't get to ride him often. The ranch hands work him like they do the rest of the horses while I am gone. The buckskin is just a workhorse around the ranch. I think Steve favors him, too."

"One horse puzzled me. A little paint. He is like a puppy, following people. Yet he lives away from the ranch in a large pasture. He's no work horse. He's no quarter horse. You won't breed him, yet he is socialized and well trained."

"That's my nephews' horse. Patrick has worked with him. He's ridden by a kid."

"I'd like to meet that kid."

"You will, but first you have to meet my father."

When Dad got home we gave him some time to get settled. I thought it would be better to get a feel for the situation first, so Rusty, Chase and Elan waited inconspicuously outside. I went to Dad's office and knocked quietly.

He glanced up wearily. It had been a long week for him. I hated to drop ranch work on him.

"Cassidy. You doing okay, kid?"

"Yeah, how are you?" I answered quietly.

"I've been better. What did you want?"

"I have a surprise for you. I didn't know about it until I got to the reception. And I don't know if you're going to be happy about it or not. I'd like you to keep an open mind."

Oops, that made him wary.

"I'm about as open minded as they come."

Yeah, right.

"What do you think of Chase?"

"I don't know. I don't know the man. He looks like a bum."

"What if I told you he was a retired police officer from San Diego? Would that change your opinion of him?"

"Why does my opinion of your friend matter that much to you?" he asked, not beating around the bush.

"Because Chase has a friend. He brought him along. He'd like to train horses for you. But, Dad, it's more than that. This man wants to work with Patrick, too. He's an Indian. He's related to the man who taught Chase how to track. Chase is the best tracker I've ever met."

"How many trackers have you met?"

"Well, one, but that's the point. Tracking is a rare talent. Patrick has it. If he had a person to go tracking with he could easily get better at it than I am. To find a person who is good with horses and knows how to track is a rare find. I'm asking you to give this man a chance."

"You talk about Patrick like he's the only one who exists over there. What about Wyatt? I won't favor one kid over the other like you do."

"I don't favor Patrick. Wyatt just hasn't taken an interest in things around him yet. He barely speaks to me. He stays in the house with Jesse."

"The door lets people in as well as out."

"Dad, we're not talking about me here. I'll try to pay more attention to Wyatt if you think he needs it, but we're talking about a horse trainer. I talked to Elan a little bit. Just from the few minutes we talked I know he's experienced, maybe not with horse racing but with horses. He knows more than Zack. He'd get to know the boys just like the other hands do."

"And you think I should take Chase's word on this guy?"

"Yes and no. I admit Chase has a vested interest in Patrick. Chase sees tracking as an art and he worries that it's fast becoming a lost art. When he sees true tracking talent he nurtures it, much like Old Frank did in me. But Chase lives in San Diego. He can't teach Patrick like he wants to. So when he heard you might be looking for a new hand he asked Elan if he'd apply for the job. Patrick almost worships Chase because Chase is a walking encyclopedia of animal lore and tracking knowledge. If Chase was around, Patrick would soak up all the knowledge he could. Patrick is a walking information sponge right now and Elan can teach him what he wants to know."

"But you want me to hire him as a horse trainer."

"I'd appreciate it if you would give him a chance."

"And you say he's here?"

"Yes, but he won't come in without an invitation from you."

"This is a hell of a time."

"I know Daddy, but you've wanted to hire someone even before Old Frank passed away. Chase came to pay his respects, all the way from San Diego. I think Elan is from Arizona. The least you can do is talk to them. If you don't want to do it now I'll take them riding in the hills."

"Send Patrick to me," he said.

Gulp. "Okay, so you'll think about it?"

"I'll think about it. Stick around."

"Yes, sir!" I said happily.

I jogged out the front door and down the lane to Jesse's house. She answered the door and invited me in.

"Dad wants to talk to Patrick," I told her.

"Dad does? What did Pat do this time?"

"Nothing. He's thinking about hiring a new horse trainer and he just wants Patrick's opinion."

"Since when is Patrick advising Dad on how to run this ranch?"

"Since about ten minutes ago. He'll be fine. Dad just wants to talk to him."

"Well, I guess he better get up there. I know how Dad hates to be kept waiting."

Jesse found Patrick outside snooping around in the bushes.

"Patrick," she said. "Your grandpa wants to talk to you. Go on up to the ranch house and be respectful."

"What'd I do this time?" Pat said.

"Nothing," I answered. "I'll explain a little on the way."

Pat jumped on his bike and I stopped him. "Slow down. I need to talk to you on the way. Grandpa's going to ask you some questions and I want you to think before you answer him."

"What kind of questions?"

"You know I can't second guess your grandpa. Maybe tracking questions. Maybe about what you want to be when you grow up. It might be serious questions and it might be fun questions."

"Why is he asking me?"

"Because it's your opinion that matters."

I sure was right when I said I couldn't second guess my dad. When we arrived back at the ranch house Dad wasn't in his office sitting behind his big, scary desk. He was out on the porch talking to Rusty, Chase, and Elan.

"Thank you, Cassidy," Dad said, then to Patrick, "I need some help and seeing as how you're affected by this decision I was hoping you could help me make it. This is Elan. He wants a job as a horse trainer. I want to know if you'd hire him."

"Sir?" Patrick asked totally taken by surprise.

"Show me how to conduct an interview to hire a horse trainer."

Patrick was embarrassed, but disobeying his grandfather was unthinkable. He tried to keep his expressions levelheaded as he frantically tried to figure out how to follow through on the request. His Grandpa never wanted help with anything. There had to be a catch, but the only way to find out what was really going on was to obey orders.

"It's good to meet you Elan," Patrick said nervously. "My name's Patrick Marshall." Then to his grandfather, "Grandpa, we can't do a training interview at the house. We gotta do it at the barn."

"Why's that?"

"Because it's not what I think, it's what the horses think. If the horses will listen to him that's what matters most."

The men nodded in agreement and so we headed for the barn. On the way Patrick walked with Elan.

"We train quarter horses here," Pat said. "The trick is to know which ones are born to work and which ones are born to race. We don't breed a lot of horses but we train the few into the best horses around. Unless a horse is obviously born to race we train them to work. That means trail riding, rodeo, herding, you name it these horses can do it. We don't work the racers the same, 'cause they don't think the same. Their brains are just different. They got lots of go and hardly any stop. A work horse needs more stop in 'em and a thinkin' brain. Do you agree?"

Elan tried not to snicker. He was half amused and half impressed to see a seven year old take on the mantle of one of the grown up ranch hands.

"Of course, I agree," Elan said. "To force a work horse into the stress of the track would be cruel. Likewise, to limit the racehorse to the stop and go chores of the ranch would frustrate them. A horse has a mind of its own, just like people, except horses are at the mercy of the people around them."

We had arrived at the barn.

"I want you to choose a work horse. This is Chet, Mack, Buck and Shasta.

Pick the horse you want to work with and saddle him up. Then saddle up Frank's Choice and take him down to the track."

Dad pointed the way to the tack room. Elan quickly looked over the horses and chose Buck. He led Buck out to the open area of the barn and carefully saddled and bridled the buckskin. Then he clipped a lead rope to Frank's Choice's halter and led the skittish colt into the main part of the barn. The young race horse was antsy. He didn't know this man. He was a little hard to handle even under normal circumstances. Elan talked to the horse quietly in a mixture of Navajo and English. He ran his hands over him, calming him. He checked his knees, feeling for tenderness or hot spots. He grinned remembering what I'd said about Old Frank's choice of racehorses. When Frank's Choice had settled, Elan saddled him and bridled him, stopping when the colt got agitated, patiently working with the motions of the horse. All the while Patrick just watched. Watching how Elan handled the horses. When both horses were saddled he clipped the lead rope to the bridle of Frank's Choice and mounted Buck. He led the prancing racehorse all the way to the track. Frank's Choice tried to shy away but a quick jerk and a cluck or two of horse speak and he followed along. Buck, steady as ever, just glared at the spunky colt.

"Now, take him round the track three times."

"Three times? But this is a quarter horse. He's not meant to run three laps."

"I didn't say run 'im three laps. I just meant ride him three laps."

Dad stood there arms folded, taking notes. Elan dismounted and tied Buck to the fence surrounding the track. I watched Patrick. What was he looking for in a horse trainer? He seemed to even note how Elan tied the reins to the fence. Elan led Frank's choice away from the group to introduce himself to the horse. He seemed to admire the colt's sleek coat and man and horse appraised each other for just a few seconds before Elan swung easily into the saddle. A slight grin spread across Elan's face. Every horseman knows the feel of a quality horse when he is in the saddle. There is just a spark there that isn't in a downtrodden, ill kept horse.

Elan put his heels to the horse and was pleased with a quick response. He let the horse get warmed up and when it was obvious Frank's Choice was itching to run he pulled him back just a bit. He settled himself firmly in the saddle, crouched down, but not low, a spring ready for action. He gave the racehorse a kick and Frank's Choice reached out. He accelerated, looking for that perfect speed that ate up the ground and warmed his muscles. Elan pushed him for a little more but didn't hold him there. This wasn't a race and he wasn't going to use up a good horse for a demonstration. He talked to the horse with his hands, legs, feet, and body position, aware that the rider gave the horse a clear message through touch. Elan took Frank's Choice around three laps but he didn't run a complete lap. He watched the horse as he rode and responded to its signals. He brought him up to a slow pace to see how the racehorse responded to a restraining hand. Frank's Choice fought it but in a way this seemed to please Elan. He came back grinning.

"Frank was right. This horse will drive the bettors crazy when he runs his first race."

Patrick simply turned to his grandfather and said, "Go for it!"

"What?" Dad said. "You'd hire him after watching him saddle two horses and ride around for fifteen minutes?"

"Yes, sir."

"You didn't ask him if he's had any experience. You haven't asked him if he's been to the races. You didn't ask him if he's worked at other ranches."

"Sir, I can tell you, he's been around horses all his life. He's never been to an official race, but he's seen a few on TV. He's worked with his horses and he's been around other horses but he's doesn't have a fancy… what's it called? A paper that tells what jobs you had before."

"A resume?"

"Yeah, if you looked at his resume you wouldn't hire him. But if you ask the horses, they'd hire him right off the bat."

"Well, I'll be a monkey's uncle," Dad said.

"He knows more'n Zack. He's got more experience than Randy, though Randy has a feel for horses you can't match. I say if he's as good as what you got and what you got's good, go for it!"

"So you'd hire him?"

"Yes, sir."

"What if I told you Elan isn't just a horse trainer? What if I told you he was a tracker?"

Patrick's eyes got real big. He almost jumped up and down but he restrained himself, gave his grandpa the biggest hound doggie eyes you ever saw and said earnestly, "Grandpa, you can't let him get away."

"Thank you, Patrick, you answered my questions. You can go home now."

"What?! But I got a zillion questions now! I can't just go home! I'll drive my mom nuts!"

"Very well, you can stay but let us talk adult talk for a while. Cassidy, would you put the horses away?"

"Sure."

I rode Buck and led Frank's Choice back to the barn. I unsaddled both horses and put Buck in his stall. I brushed down Frank's Choice as he danced around. I talked to him as I tried to follow his nervous movements. I looked over his funny-looking knees. Yup, Frank had chosen this horse just to play a joke on bettors at the races. He was fit as a fiddle with odd shadowy spots on his knees that would fool almost anybody. I could imagine the race announcers asking how we could think to race a horse like that. I never listened to the horse races but I became determined to catch Frank's Choice's first race.

Patrick hung on every word as Dad took Elan around and introduced him to each of the ranch hands and told him a little about them. Then he showed Elan the bunkhouse. It was one large room with four beds, a table and a separate bathroom. It was like a modern version of the old west bunkhouse. It was heated and air-conditioned. It had hot and cold water, closets and dressers. The hands ate their meals at the ranch house with the family.

The ranch hands seemed very accepting of Elan, but I thought Elan was due for some culture shock. The ranch was very different from where he'd come from. It was even different from most California ranches. Something just set it apart. I couldn't really put my finger on it but I thought anybody would experience a bit of culture shock moving there.

Dad asked for some time to think and went to his office. I doubted that he was really going to think. He was going to talk to Mom or Steve but we wisely gave him the space he asked for, and found something to do.

Patrick was nervous. "I didn't know what to do!" he said. "Grandpa pulled a fast one on me!"

"It's okay, Pat. You did good. You didn't do what he expected, but you did better. You assessed the situation in your own way and you came to the right conclusion."

"You could'a let me know how much was hangin' on it! What if he says no?"

"Then we'll just have to accept it."

"I gotta find something to do," Pat said. "This waiting is driving me nuts. Can we go find those deer tracks?"

"We don't have time before dinner," I told him. "We'll go out there tomorrow."

He thought for a moment then said, "Aunt Cassidy, do that trick where you cross the whole ranch without leaving a track. See if Chase or Elan can figure out what you did."

"No, I don't want you to know how I do it."

"Aw, come on."

"No, if you knew how I did it you would try it and it's not something a seven year old should be doing."

"When'll we know something?" Patrick asked.

"I expect him to make a decision before dinner time. He knows we are all waiting and he'll have to say something at dinner."

"I know!" Patrick said. "If he's going to make a big announcement he'll call mom and make sure everybody's gathered for dinner. So if he's going to say yes he'll call Mom and make sure we're all going to be there! All we gotta do is go to my house and see if we got invited to dinner. If he's going to say no he'll do it in private an' he won't want a bunch of people there hounding him about an answer. All we gotta do is see if Mom got a phone call and then we'll know! He'll have to call Mom before she starts cookin' dinner so he should call soon."

"Are you sure you don't want to be a detective when you grow up?" Rusty asked Patrick.

We walked down to Patrick's house and sat under the big oak tree while Patrick went and did his undercover work. He left the front door open and ran into the house.

"Hi, Mom! What's for dinner, I'm starving!" he said innocently.

"I don't know. If you're hungry grab a cookie."

I could imagine the frustration and the expression on Patrick's face.

"Can I take one for Aunt Cassidy and Uncle Rusty? And Chase and Elan?"

"Sure," she said absentmindedly.

Patrick came outside with a sack of cookies and no information.

"I've never been disappointed about getting a cookie snack before," he informed us.

We fell silent, waiting until Patrick couldn't stand it anymore.

"At least tell a story," Patrick said.

"I was just here a few weeks ago. I've only had one search since then and Chase already heard all about it."

"Did you see any animals on your search?"

"Only one, but I didn't tell Chase about that."

"What kind was it?"

"It was ugly! And it was very small. It ran up my leg and its sting hurt like crazy! Believe me, you never want to get stung by a scorpion!"

"A scorpion! What did you do?"

"I did the worst thing I could have done!" I exclaimed, building up the story.

"You hit it," said Elan smiling. "It's the first thing everybody does and it's always a mistake."

"Yup, I swatted it good and hard and you know what happened?"

"It stung your hand," Elan said. "If there's one thing everybody knows in Arizona, it's that scorpions are no fun and they can sting you even when they're dead."

"Did you kill it?" Patrick asked.

"No, Elan is right, it stung my hand too. Then my leg *and* my hand hurt like crazy but that wasn't the worst of it. The poison from the scorpion made me get numb all over. I couldn't feel anything with my hands or feet. Even my ears and nose were numb and I couldn't swallow except just a little water."

"But it didn't kill you," Patrick said.

"Obviously. Victor said my reaction was bad but it felt worse than it was. I was glad because what I felt was pretty scary!"

"Now I've got the creeps," Patrick said scratching his arm. "I'm gonna feel creepie crawlies on me for the rest of the day."

The phone rang inside the house and Patrick leaped to attention and ran into the house.

"Patrick, close the door!" scolded Jesse.

"I'm just getting my tracks book," Patrick said.

He went to his room and quietly eves dropped on the way.

"No, I haven't started anything… Sure, I'd be glad to not cook for a day!… All right, we'll be there… Pat? Can you run out and tell your dad we're eating at the ranch tonight?"

"Sure, Mom!" his voice cracked with the excitement.

"Patrick, are you okay? You're acting really weird today."

"Me? I'm fine! I'm even finer than fine. I'm great!"

"Okay, listen for the bell."

"I will. I wouldn't miss this dinner for anything!"

"Are you sure you're okay? I feel like I'm missing something here, like the whole ranch knows something I don't."

"It's okay, Mom, you'll find out at dinner."

"I hope so."

Patrick leaped off the porch and clasped me in a hug then he jumped up and down. He grabbed his bicycle and rushed off to tell his dad about dinner. If there was one thing he wanted it was a dinner befitting a big announcement from his grandfather.

Dinner was a study in contrasts. Half the table was still in funeral mode. The ranch hands were subdued. Dad seemed tired. Mom and Martha were not ready for things to return to normal. They missed Old Frank. Wyatt was his normal, happy, little boy self. The rest of us sat on the edge of our seats, waiting. Rusty was more laid back than the rest of us. He knew life would go on no matter what Dad said but he also knew how much I wanted this to happen. Patrick barely stayed in his seat.

As Martha placed the last bowl on the table, Dad stood. I expected him to wait until the end of the meal to make his announcement, but there were strangers at the table.

"If I could have everybody's attention, please," he said. "We have dinner guests and I'd like to make introductions. I'd like you all to meet, and make welcome at our table, Elan and Chase. Elan would like to hire on as a horse trainer. We'll talk about that further after dinner but it looks like, if he's willing we'll see about a three-month trial period. Some folks couldn't stand us for three months so we'll see if we pass muster. He may put in his three months and high tail it for Arizona, but we'll see. Most of you know Chase as Cassidy's tracking teacher from San Diego. He's a good friend of Rusty's family an' I reckon they know what they're about. Chase, you are always welcome at our table."

"Thank you," Chase said with a controlled grin.

There were handshakes with the people that Chase and Elan could reach and friendly chatter from the rest of the family.

"I want to know why Patrick is so excited about this," Jesse said. "I've never seen him like this before except maybe when he knows Cassidy is coming to visit. So, Pat, tell us, why are you bouncing off the walls?"

Patrick waited, letting the tension grow. This was important to him and he wanted everybody to know. When all eyes were on him he said simply, "Elan can track!"

All eyes swiveled to Elan. "Well," he said, embarrassed, "tracking kind of runs in my family. My great grandfather taught Demothi to track. In my family the skills are passed down from generation to generation and so, even though the skills for tracking are not needed as they once were, the connection with the land is still there. Demothi thought that if Patrick and I work together we would both improve our tracking skills."

"Patrick, Elan is not being hired on as your babysitter," Dad warned.

"I know, Grandpa. But we can be friends, too, can't we?"

"I would hope so."

"Who's Demothi?"

"It is my family's name for Chase," Elan said. "It is a Native American word for *talks while walking*. He was given it by my grandfather because Chase would tell what the tracks said to him as he tracked."

"Cool! Will you give me an Indian name too?" Patrick asked.

"We will have to wait and see what name you fit. Right now I would have to name you *talks always*, but I know there is more to you than that. You must earn your Indian name."

"Oh man, if I gotta earn it, I gotta decide what I want to be known for. That means I need to work on my tracking and my stalking. What else am I good at?"

I could see the wheels turning. Patrick had a goal, to earn the ideal Indian name.

"What does your name mean?" Patrick asked Elan.

"I was named when I was a baby, so I didn't have the option of earning my name. Elan means *friendly*."

"Aunt Cassidy, what does your name mean?"

"I've never bothered to find out. I know Grandpa liked it because it was an old west name."

"You've never looked it up?" Jesse asked.

"No."

"I did. I think the meaning of your name is very appropriate. It means *clever*."

"So what does your name mean?" I asked knowing if she looked up my name she surely looked up her own.

"Well, the book didn't have a meaning for Jesse but it said it was derived from Jessica and Jessica means *rich woman*."

Rusty laughed out loud when he heard that. Jesse glared at him.

"What?" she asked.

"Mr. Gordon you sure know how to pick 'em. Cassidy lives by her wits and Jesse lives at the mall."

The deer were alert and we really had no chance to close in on them with a party of four riders. Patrick was determined to try and I knew to have four of us out there would be useless. Two, at most, could stalk together, if they shared a common goal and had experience. So I waited with the horses as Elan and Patrick went out together. Patrick knelt before the herd and went through his ritual. At least that's the way I thought of it.

"What is he doing?" Elan asked.

"He says he is talking to the deer. It's something he came up with on his own. It's harmless and it puts him in the right frame of mind so I haven't stopped him."

"You doubt him?"

"I don't believe the deer can hear him. I don't try to talk to them. But it can't hurt for him to try."

"And what do you think the deer think?"

"They think the grass is good here or they wouldn't keep coming back."

"Maybe you need to listen to the deer."

"I enjoy the deer. I like being with them but I have never heard a deer speak."

"Maybe you listen with the wrong ears."

Patrick stood, still focused on the deer. We stood watching and he stepped forward not waiting for an adult to guide him. He needed supervision because of his age but he trusted the deer. As Patrick walked we all looked at each other.

"Have you done this before?" I asked Elan.

"Not with this kind of deer, only animals in general."

"Go ahead, Patrick will surprise you."

And so Elan followed Patrick out into the clearing. They had to walk a ways before they came within stalking range. As they grew closer their posture gradually changed until they were in a stalking crouch. I wanted to try it, too, but I knew Elan and Patrick needed to learn to work together.

It was a lazy day. It felt good to sit back and listen to the hills. I was content knowing Patrick was in good hands, able to get out and investigate the world around him, ask questions, and find answers. I was glad Patrick had possibilities before him instead of sorrow over Old Frank. I knew by the time Patrick was my age Old Frank would be a distant memory but Old Frank's influence on Patrick's life would last a lifetime.

Elan let Patrick lead, observing the youngster's movements and the way he read the deer. When they got within a hundred feet the deer didn't let them get closer but they didn't run away either. They simply kept out of reach, like they knew these slow humans were no match for them. The two were able to observe the deer from close quarters but they were never able to close to the gap. Patrick returned jubilant. He'd spent time with the deer. Quality time when the deer could get to know him. He felt it was important that the deer know him so they would get used to him and let him get closer next time. Before he left he mixed up the plaster and filled a clear deer track with plaster of Paris. He marked the spot so he could come retrieve the dry track later.

We rode back, Patrick cheerfully talking all the way. His little horse looked happy and perky listening to his chatter. When Patrick's voice rose Snoopy's ears swiveled.

"Do you like stalking the deer?" he asked Elan. "I can only come out here with an adult so I have only done it two times. My mom and dad don't care about the deer and Steve and Randy are always too busy. And Zack can't stalk 'em worth beans. He doesn't have enough patience. Grandpa is too busy being the big boss. Even if he isn't doing anything he's being the boss of the ranch."

"What does your grandfather do with you?" Elan asked.

"He'll talk to me, if I go talk to him. He will tell me stories, mostly about Aunt Cassidy and my mom and ranchin' in the old days. He likes maps. If he's got a map out he'll ask me to do things he thinks are hard, like find a town in this and so county, or which way is north, or name three towns on highway five. If I do something he disagrees with he'll call me into his office and give me heck for it. That's why I was scared to come when he wanted me to interview you. I thought he caught me on the barn roof."

"I told Steve to cover those meters so you couldn't do that. I told him you'd figure it out, since you knew it could be done," I said.

"Yeah? Well, he didn't do it fast enough. Did you know you can spy on half the ranch from up there?"

"Yeah, I know."

Chase just smiled as everyone quietly lived up to his expectations.

"You're not mad at me for goin' up there?"

"Do you know how to walk on the roof without being heard? Do you know how to walk without falling off?"

"Yeah, I wear my moccasins and I walk like I'm stalkin', feeling my way like you taught me and then my steps are nice and quiet."

"Then I'm not mad at you, but you're taking a chance doing it. Sooner or later you're going to get caught."

"Yeah, I can't wait. I bet Steve says, 'There you go again. You're just like Cassidy.' He says that a lot. I got a lot to live up to. What can I try next?"

"Come up with your own adventures."

"Aw, but if I try your adventures and come up with my own then I get twice the fun!"

"A kid can only take so much fun without killing himself," I said. "I'm lucky I grew up."

We all rode to the barn and I automatically went through the motions of unsaddling and brushing down Shasta.

"It's a rule at this ranch, you ride a horse, you groom him. Unless it's just a walk to the track and back like you did with Buck, the horse gets unsaddled, brushed out, anything it needs you take care of before you put him back in the stall. After a while it'll be second nature. I've come off the trail barely able to walk but I still groom my horse. I think the only one that'll give you any trouble is Chet. He doesn't like his hooves messed with. He's still manageable but he's fussy. And don't do anything with Satan. He's earned his name. He isn't rideable. He'll turn on you, charge you, kick you, and bite you. Don't even try to pet him."

"This seems a very pleasant place to live," Elan said. His English was too precise, too refined. It seemed odd to me.

"Yeah, that's one reason I don't live here. I can only stand so much pleasantness before it grates on me. Don't be surprised if it grates on you too. When Rusty, Chase and I go home things are going to get mighty quiet. I can't wait to get my hands on some unpleasantness. Rusty's got an interesting case. I'm going to pick his brain and I've got some ideas to try."

"What kind of a case?" Chase asked.

We walked to the house ready to see if Rusty was bored to tears. He wasn't. I stopped. I knew I shouldn't have turned my back on him for more than an hour or two. He sat on the porch swing and next to him acting her voluptuous self was Misty Montague. Rusty was pleasant to her. He wasn't uncomfortable with her advances, but hardly anything made Rusty uncomfortable. He was at ease in any situation. I had to check my actions. One of Misty's biggest assets was the jealousy of others. She would undermine the wife. Make her look bad. I had to be pleasant and assertive and I couldn't let her beat me down. I needed to be self-assured. My family and the hands were nowhere to be found. They knew they would have a hard time being pleasant. Rusty stood and walked down the steps. He smiled and wrapped me in a hug.

"Did you get to stalk the deer?" he asked.

"I let Elan go out with Patrick. I just had to show them where the deer are found."

"Wow, that took self-restraint. I thought you'd be the first one out there."

"Elan wanted to go and he needed to see what Patrick was capable of. They did pretty good, and had a lot of fun doing it. I can stalk deer at home."

"I can't believe it," Misty said. "You look the same as you did in high school."

"Thanks," I said, although she didn't mean it as a compliment.

I was dusty and windblown and smelly and there was Misty in a fancy pants suit, fresh from the cleaners, diamonds sparkling. Her pedicured toes poked delicately out of high heeled sandals. Her fingernails matched her outfit.

"Do you ever change?" She asked.

"Yes," I said. "I've changed a lot."

"Oh really? Tell me."

And I realized she wasn't interested in the ways I had changed inside. She wanted to know if I drove a fancy car, if I could go to the department stores and buy whatever I wanted. It made me mad.

"I'm a survivor. You drop me anywhere and I'll find my way home. I've been beaten and lost and I've lost loved ones and no matter what happens to me I bounce back."

"You were like that in high school, too."

"Thanks."

She didn't like that either.

"Well, I must be going. Will I see you before you leave?"

"I don't know. I don't know how long we're staying."

"Toodle-oo," she said and did her runway walk down to her white Mercedes. She got in gracefully and waved to Rusty on her way out.

That woman made me so mad. We were opposites in every way imaginable. In a man's eyes, she was everything I wasn't, and it made me mad, but I couldn't let it show. I wasn't jealous of her. I felt sorry for her, but sometimes the difference was hard to distinguish.

I took a quick shower and changed clothes for lunch.

After lunch Dad called a meeting in his office. He wanted the rundown. Chase, Elan, Rusty, Patrick and I sat in front of his big desk.

"Elan, you want to train horses here? You know it's going to be a lot of manual labor. There's a lot of dirty work involved in running a ranch. Are you up to it?"

Elan had been taking notes. "Yes, sir," he said.

"You'll do as you're told? Steve is your supervisor. He's a fair and reasonable man. Do you anticipate any problems?"

"Do you?"

Dad raised an eyebrow.

"Mr. Gordon, I won't make trouble for them if they won't make trouble for me."

"You're used to a little opposition."

"Yes, sir."

"You'll not get it here. If you do, let me know."

"Sir, these things are not solved by an iron hand. I'm used to proving myself. All I have to do is show them I am a man, the same as them, and they will learn. We may hit it off just fine. It may take all three months. It may take longer, but as long as the ranch is running smoothly I have no need of help."

Dad nodded. "Patrick?"

"Yes, sir?"

"I'm telling you again, Elan may know how to track but he is not here to baby sit you. He has a life of his own. If he goes tracking with you, that is his gift to you. You don't ask for a gift, do you?"

"No sir."

"You will not ask Elan to take you tracking. You may ask him questions, just like you do all the ranch hands. I do expect you to ask reasonable questions. You are growing up into their job so I expect you to learn it gradually and take on responsibilities just like Cassidy and your mom did growing up here. When you get old enough I'll hire you on. Right now you're still learning. Do you understand your position here?"

Patrick got right to the heart of the matter that was on his mind.

"Sir? I know I got a job to do. An' I know Elan's got a job to do. An' I know Mom and Cassidy pulled their weight. An' I plan to do that, too, but can I be a grandkid, too?"

Dad's eyes softened a bit. "You most certainly can."

Patrick relaxed a little.

"So," Chase said to Elan, "you really want to stay?"

"I do," he answered.

"I'll keep in touch," Chase told him. "I call up here every few weeks anyway."

Dad raised an eyebrow again.

"Patrick has tracking questions," Chase explained to him.

"He keeps tabs on lots of people, in his own quiet way. He calls Lou Strickland and Schroeder," I told Dad. "I'm used to it."

"How did you know?" Chase asked.

"I just know. You leave tracks," I said.

Chase loaded up his things after the meeting, shook hands all around and headed back to San Diego. Elan watched Demothi drive away and turned to survey his new home. He was on his own in this strange, new place. He took his things to the bunkhouse and settled in.

Monday the ranch was pretty much back to normal, except for the obvious absence of Old Frank. The ranch felt settled and peaceful. I decided it was time I became acquainted with my other nephew. I walked down to Jesse's house and knocked. She came to the door and invited me in. Patrick was at school but Wyatt ran out and peered at me from around the wall of the hallway. He was as quiet as his brother was talkative. Jesse was on a scrap booking spree and Wyatt was using the little bits and pieces of paper that were left over to glue together a collage. If the shape wasn't quite right he snipped at it to his liking, but he talked very little. I decided to get down to his level while I visited with Jesse. So we talked and I glued.

Wyatt was thoughtful and kind. If he thought I needed something he'd find it in amongst the scrapbooking supplies and I put it to use whether I had that thing in mind or not.

When Rusty came looking for me I felt like I hadn't made much progress but Wyatt ran up when we went to the door.

"When will you come back?" he asked.

I knelt down and looked into his sparkly hazel eyes.

"I'll see you before I leave."

He just said "okay," and went off to find a toy. Accepting of anything, easy going as his dad, he was his own little person. Someday I'd know him better.

We walked back to the ranch house lazily strolling up the long drive from the highway to the house, hand in hand. The road bordered a large paddock where three horses grazed. It was a quiet ranch day, each person off doing their job in harmony. I thought it was too peaceful for my liking. I was itching to get home, on the trail, anything. I lacked purpose at the ranch. I felt like a visitor. I needed to do something. My job here was finished. I'd come to say good-bye to Old Frank. I'd done that. I was glad the quiet, empty place Old Frank left was filled. It wouldn't be the same, but it would be different in a good way. Chase had pulled a fast one on me bringing Elan along. I hadn't planned on talking my dad into hiring a new hand. Thankfully, Patrick came through with flying colors.

I heard tires crunch on gravel and Rusty and I moved to the side of the road. A sleek, white Mercedes sports car slid up the road, stopping next to us.

"Need a ride?" Misty asked innocently.

"No thanks, we like the walk," I replied. She looked like she worked in a jewelry store. She was wearing a crisp, black and white pants suit. Her hair was carefully styled. There wasn't a spot of dirt on her car. Everything about her looked like it just walked out of a showroom.

She drove on up to the house and dusted off the porch swing before sitting down to wait for us. I was tempted to go back to Jesse's house but it was too late for that. Misty would know we were avoiding her and take it as a challenge. She looked at my dusty jeans with distain. The only way she would be caught in jeans was if…hmmm, I didn't think Misty would wear jeans. I wondered what she wore when she was in her cowgirl phase and couldn't remember. I remembered her in a white hat with a silver hatband, white boots; she had to have worn jeans to ride in. I bet they were specially made for her to accentuate all the right places. Then I remembered the cowgirl phase had happened while I was in the Marines, working in a sea of sand, sleeping in tents, getting up at the crack of dawn, working all day and falling into my cot at night wanting to sleep dead to the world but needing to stay alert. What a contrast.

"What have you been doing today?" she asked as we walked up.

"I was visiting with Jesse and making a collage with my nephew."

"How quaint. I bought a custom-made collage once to hang over my mantel in my bedroom. It came out beautifully. I like to stand there and find all the pieces of my life in it. It's made up of photographs and things from my past."

I bet there wasn't one unflattering picture in the whole display. No picture of her eating spaghetti as a toddler. No pictures as a nine year old with a big pink grin on her face from eating a wedge of watermelon with her hands. No pictures showing skinned knees.

Misty stayed for dinner and the table was remarkably quiet. Polite conversation floated around but the only real conversation took place between Patrick and Elan. Misty asked Elan irritating and insulting questions and he attempted to answer them without losing his temper. I couldn't figure out if she was just ignorant or trying to put him down. She asked him if he spoke English and what "how" means. When that backfired she turned to Rusty. She didn't get the answers she was hoping for from him either. When she asked what he had done that day, he said he and Randy had done target practice.

"I can't stand the thought of awful guns. They are so loud and violent."

"Uncle Rusty needs to stay in practice for work!" Patrick said. "He's a detective and he catches bad guys! And they don't get away, do they Uncle Rusty?"

Rusty smiled, although he didn't usually tell people what he did. "Hopefully not," he told Patrick.

Misty was taking notes. She was plotting something. She just needed time to put pieces together. I didn't like it.

"Sometimes Aunt Cassidy tracks down bad guys too!" Patrick went on. "If they leave tracks she can follow them!" Patrick rambled on and everybody ate in peace glad for Patrick's chatter. Everybody, that is, except for Rusty and I. We didn't appreciate Misty knowing our life story from a seven-year-old's perspective.

I went back to Jesse's house the next day, like I promised, and spent some time sitting on the floor again, talking to Jesse and watching Wyatt practice ABCs. He was precise. He didn't like sloppy letters so it took him ten minutes to do a row of As. If one came out sloppy he erased and rewrote it. Sometimes he had to move to a new spot because he wore a hole in the paper erasing. If Patrick were doing the same thing he'd get it done as quickly as possible figuring if you can tell it's an A that's good enough. Then he'd be out the door with his eyes to the ground. Wyatt seemed more accepting of my presence rather than eager for my attention while Patrick saw me as a tracking companion and endless question answerer. I wondered if Elan would last the three months with Patrick tagging along through his afternoon chores.

Chapter 5

I had been home a few days when Strict called.

"Cassidy? How soon can you be at Creekside campground?"

Creekside? I knew that trail inside out.

"An hour, maybe two. I just need to call Rusty and grab my pack."

"I'll have everything you need when you get there."

"You seem unusually rushed. What's up?"

"I'll explain when you get here."

"I need details as you go," Strict said. "Not the nitty gritty details from track to track. When Stella stops I need to know why. I need to know what happened."

Stella was an eleven year old girl with epilepsy. She could control her seizures if she took her medication but she had to take the medication on a strict schedule. The seizures themselves were not dangerous to her at first but the longer she had been without her medication the worse they became. Stella's mother sat still as she listened to Strict tell me about what I was looking for.

"The seizures won't harm her but falls will."

"How long do the seizures last when she has them?" I asked.

"They start out small, maybe five minutes but as they get worse they can go on for an hour or more. We're worried about falls. We're worried about her having a seizure near the creek. We want this kid found before she can hurt herself."

"How long has been gone?"

"Overnight."

"And how long since her medication quit helping."

"We don't know for sure, maybe twelve hours. Epilepsy is not a predictable disease. She medicates on a worst case basis. We can't predict how her body is going to react without the medication under these circumstances. The doctor's worst case scenario didn't include being lost in the woods overnight."

I could see why we were in a hurry now.

Stella's mom added, "When she comes out of a seizure she will be confused. Once she stops and thinks she will know what happened but while she remains confused she may do irrational things. She will walk quickly and nervously. She might run in a direction that makes no sense. I think this is how she became lost. She had a seizure and acted before she thought about what she was doing."

"When Stella stops I want you to tell me what you think happened. We will be able to predict a little bit what you can expect."

Landon and I both nodded. "Got it."

Strict showed me a picture of Stella and handed to me a pair of her shoes. There were very distinct wear marks on the soles and even on the sides of her shoes. The shoes she wore when she got lost were very different so I couldn't count on the wear marks being exactly the same, but seeing the shoes she left behind helped me form a picture of her hiking style in my brain that would follow me for the entire search.

"Why did you wait overnight to call if Stella needed medication?" I asked.

"We were out looking. We thought she couldn't have gotten far. She isn't athletic. She hadn't been up in the mountains before so she just wanted to look around."

"What does she have with her? Any food? Any water?"

"No, nothing. She was just going for a walk. We thought she would turn around when she got hungry or thirsty."

"What was she wearing? Is she prepared for the heat or the cold?"

"Jeans, a t-shirt and tennis shoes. She didn't need a jacket."

Thez joined the group as a precaution. Landon brought him up to speed as we walked.

There were tracks all over the forest near the campground. At first it was difficult to distinguish Stella's tracks from the others. Tracks crisscrossed Stella's trail. If her family had known anything at all about tracking they would have stopped when they found her tracks and followed them but they didn't. They just wandered the woods calling out to her. I could tell which tracks were Stella's because they were the only ones that fit the profile. And they were on the bottom. It was tedious following partially buried tracks, but this was the kind of challenge that made this *my* job. Following tracks is simple, but the intricacies of the art required a trained eye.

I slowly pieced together Stella's trail while Landon and Thez patiently followed. She had explored the campground thoroughly and it took me a while to work my way out of view of base camp. Eventually though, Stella followed the creek out of the campground. When she climbed up to the trail the hiking was easier. Other hikers had obscured her tracks here too but I could watch for places where people had left the trail and decide if it was Stella's trail. Most of the tracks I found off the trail were left by kids wanting to hike faster than their parents. The kids would rush ahead and then step to the side of the trail to wait for their parents or they would leave the trail for a moment to investigate something while their parents caught up. The small footprints always rejoined the big ones. All except Stella's. I was grateful for her time on the trail. It allowed me to walk at an almost normal speed.

When she did leave the trail it was at a spot where many people detoured. There was a small swimming hole in the creek below and the laughter of swimming tourists echoed off the canyon walls. Stella followed a short trail down, visited with the people at the swimming hole, then followed the creek, crossing back and forth a few times by hopping rock to rock over the narrow stream.

There is just something about a creek that draws people. It isn't the source of drinking water. It is just the pleasantness of a creek. They are bordered by green, something usually lacking in these desert mountains. They are frequented by animals. The trees have water so they grow tall and shady. The last time Stella crossed the little stream she forgot which side of the creek the trail was on. She walked through the woods as if looking for the trail. She seemed to remember that she could see the creek from the trail so she returned to the creek, but at this point the creek and the trail had turned and were no longer close enough to be seen. Round and around she looked, but she looked on the wrong side of the creek. At one point she stopped and soaked her feet in the cold water. Before she left, she drank from the creek, the toes of her shoes pressing good solid tracks into the creek bank. At this point in her exploring she was just a normal eleven-year-old girl, a bit lost in the woods, unafraid, still thinking. I was glad to see that. If she had remembered that the creek flowed right through the campground she could have just followed it back but she seemed focused on finding the trail. When she was rested she walked directly away from the creek and into the woods beyond.

After Landon got the story of my last search and laughed at my little escapade with the scorpion, Thez took over and the two men talked as they followed me.

It was late in her day of hiking when hunger and thirst had taken their toll that Stella began having problems. Her tracks suddenly changed mood and direction. Her steps became irregular and roamed. The picture in my mind was of listlessness and confusion. When the tracks suddenly stopped I felt a sudden stab of helplessness as I read the ground before me. I held out my arm to stop Landon and Thez from going around me and walking through the scene I was trying to decipher. I walked the perimeter of the area. I examined a nearby tree for signs of a fall against it. I looked at the small plants that had been crushed during the seizure.

I radioed Strict, like he asked me to.

"Go ahead, Cassidy."

"Stella was lost well before she had her first seizure. I'm standing there now. Right before she fell her footsteps got sluggish and confused looking. There's no sign of her hitting herself on rocks or trees. There's plenty of crushed vegetation."

"Can you give me an idea how long the seizures lasted?"

"Hold on, Landon can help with that. He's dealt with seizures before."

"Ten four."

Landon joined me and I pointed out what I saw.

"It's a fairly large area. Do you think all this was done during one seizure?"

"It's hard to tell," he answered. "Show me where she fell."

I showed him the spot.

"And there's no footprints until she leaves the scene. Can you tell what kind of motion produced what we're seeing? Was it side to side motion or top down motion."

I examined the plants. None of them looked like they had been crushed from above. They had all been pushed over from the side. Some of them had been ground into the soil from repeated quick movements. In several spots I could see where the seams of Stella's jeans had pressed into the ground. I explained to Landon what I saw. I could read the motions to him but I didn't know anything about seizures. He listened carefully before reaching for the radio.

"Strict, I think this was a fairly minor episode," Landon told him. "I don't know how long it lasted. I doubt it was more than half an hour. It's possible that it was two short seizures. Does she follow some kind of pattern when this happens?"

There was a short silence while Strict conferred with Stella's mom.

"Yeah, it's more likely to be two short episodes. Her mom says if she tries to do too much right after a seizure it can send her into another one."

"Then I think that's what we're seeing here."

As Landon talked I found the tracks leading away and began tracking once more. Stella's tracks revealed an almost random, almost drunken pattern at first but she stopped and waited for her mind to clear. When she went on she was steadier on her feet, though her direction didn't make sense. At this point in the search I was taking in facts. The ground was an information board and I was reading the posts. At first it was just memos. Steps steady. Direction south. Tread readable. But as I tracked the posts began getting wordier. I need to get home. I'm thirsty. Where am I? How do I find my way back? What will happen without my medication? And after the seizures came upon her they continuously increased, becoming more prolonged and violent. Her seizures were always preceded by irregular footprints. I examined the ground closely noting there was blood on the ground. I looked for where it had come from and found small, sharp rocks just under the soil. As a tracker I disliked rock. It hid and disguised footprints but these rocks were different. They bit and tore and I felt every scratch and scrape as I imagined Stella convulsing here, helpless. I had to sit down and gather my wits. Surely I could track as fast as she was traveling. With her frequent and prolonged stops I should be able to catch up.

As night fell we were disillusioned. Stella had a day's head start on us, but after seeing the scope of her situation we fell into the mindset that we would come across her soon. I imagined a very tired and physically stressed young girl. Beaten by her situation. Scared. Hurt. I couldn't just set up my tent and eat a warm meal and sleep the night through knowing she was out there scared and hungry.

"You have to stop," Landon told me. "You know when you have to stop. You have to stop when you can't read any more and there's nothing you can do about it."

He was beginning to know me too well.

I handed over the chocolate chip and walnut cookies. Landon was very specific about his cookie preferences. I didn't even bother trying to divide them up and hand them out slowly. He knew, when they had thawed they were his. And he would share. I knew he would because he and Thez were both bachelors. Both ready for a cookie handout whenever one came along. I imagined all the woman cops out there cringing at the fact that I baked cookies for my search partners. But, hey, they liked me for it. I certainly had backup if I ever needed it. It was a small price to pay for a little life insurance and Landon had been there for me more than once. He'd tell me it wasn't because of the cookies. And he'd wink at me while he said it. I figured I would owe him cookies for the rest of my life.

I cast around for a tent spot. This was a decent place to camp. I just wasn't ready to stop. I stood in the little clearing willing the sun to reverse its course. I longed to track just a little farther. But I knew Landon was right. If I continued, I'd miss something and we might not run across another good camping spot. I had to stop while the conditions were right.

We were all a little bummed out, Landon and Thez because they knew what Stella was going through, and I because, well, I knew what she was going through from a different perspective. I had experienced what it was like to be alone in these mountains, wondering if I'd get home again. Stella needed protection, to be home, comfortable, safe and secure.

I set up my tent reluctantly, reluctantly because I thought it was unfair that I got a tent when Stella was out in the open. I didn't need a tent. She did. I wished I could send it to her, make it appear all set up before her, sleeping bag and all. But I couldn't do that. So I set it up so the guys would know I was camping in the comfort of a nice, safe tent. I cooked my dinner so they would know I was getting a nice, hot meal. While it was rehydrating in the bag I pulled out a flashlight and circled the camp, a flashlight shining a welcoming beacon that I hoped Stella could see. I walked around the camp twice and on the second pass I thought I heard a noise. I stopped and shined my flashlight towards the sound. I couldn't see what it was but I could definitely hear it. My heart leaped. It was the sound of a young person running through the woods, cursing the darkness, stumbling, crying softly.

"Hey guys? Come here. Bring your lights."

When they had found their flashlights we advanced in the direction the noise was coming from.

Stella stumbled into our flashlight beams, emotional, disheveled, hungry and hurt. She saw the guys' uniforms and fell to the ground crying in relief. I swallowed a lump in my throat. This was why I hiked miles of rough terrain. This was why I followed track by track through sand and rock and over creeks. So I could give people hope where none existed. Landon and Thez went forward. It was going to be a long night for me, and a cold night because I'd give Stella my sleeping bag. But I was glad I could. I guided the party back to camp and started cooking a backpacker meal for Stella, too. Landon and Thez did a physical examination, gave Stella the medication she needed, and treated the numerous scrapes and cuts. Even with the medication she had seizures until her system evened out. Landon spent hours with her gently helping her through the convulsions. She woke embarrassed and confused.

"Do you see what you need to do when she convulses?" he asked me.

"Yeah, I hope I can do it in the dark, one handed."

"If you have trouble just wake me."

Stella's seizures grew less intense as the night wore on. By morning I was mostly just dozing, sitting up. I was stiff, sore and cold. I sure didn't want to get up and hike back to base camp.

We took our time in the morning. We cooked a big breakfast by backpacker standards and Stella ate more than all three of us combined.

It felt a little weird when Stella began talking. To me someone who faced health crises on a daily basis would be hardened and overly grown up. I was mistaken. Stella's main concerns were the same as any eleven-year-old girl.

"My mom is going to kill me."

"I doubt it. If she was going to kill you she wouldn't have called the police to come find you."

"She's going to ground me for life."

"She'll be careful. You have to expect that out of a mom."

"She'll keep me at home and I'll never have a boyfriend and I'll never go to the prom."

"You're only eleven. There's plenty of time to be a kid before you have to worry about a prom. And you'll be surprised how understanding guys can be. Don't let a simple thing like having seizures keep you from doing what you enjoy. If anything it should make you want to obey the doctor's orders so you won't have them. If you are careful to control your condition you should be able to do almost anything."

"Nobody wants to go out on a date with a girl who would embarrass them."

"Stella, you're too young to date. You could outgrow the epilepsy. And I wouldn't go out with a guy who based his whole relationship on whether or not you were going to have a seizure. If a guy is that conceited you don't want to go out with him anyway."

"How far is it back to the campground?"

"It's just a few miles. Landon, can you find the way back?"

"Yeah. Why?" he answered.

"Because if you will lead I'd rather follow. I can read as I walk and I'll see a seizure coming on."

"I know the way back, but it's going to feel really weird having you behind me. It's like a married couple trying to switch sides of the bed. It just feels wrong."

"He's used to following me because I'm a tracker," I explained to Stella. "I usually have to go first so I can see the tracks."

With me behind Stella we were able to avoid any major convulsions. When her steps faltered I called a halt and we waited for clarity to return.

"Thez, you're doing a lot better in the woods. Have you been out camping a lot?"

"No, this was just an unusually quiet search. I was so glad Strict called me. The short notice prevented Victor from coming, so I was next on the list. I had to get out of that office."

"You used to do rescue work all the time. Why don't you go back to it?"

"Technology. All the things I trained to do they don't do any more."

"How'd you get a name like Thez?" Stella asked.

"That's another reason I don't go back to rescue work. If I did that full time I couldn't make the performances."

"Thez is an actor," I told her. "Thez is short for thespian. They've called him that since before I knew him."

"Have you been on TV?" Stella asked Thez.

"I prefer the stage. I feel more connected to the audience."

We talked as we walked and Landon led us down the mountain and to the trail. Due to frequent updates, Stella's mom knew exactly what to expect so she didn't smother the kid when we finally appeared down the trail. Her eyes reflected care and concern. She wrapped Stella in a hug and cried quietly. Strict gave me a shoulder hug. "Nice work," he said.

There was a surprise waiting for me when I got home. There was a sleek white sports car parked in my driveway. I got out of my Jeep Wrangler and eyed it suspiciously. Rusty was still at work. I was dead tired. I'd been hiking and tracking and camping in the dry, dusty mountains. I was filthy and looking forward to getting cleaned up before Rusty came home. I couldn't track my visitor on cement but maybe I could see hints of their passing on the grass. They obviously were not in the front yard so I walked around back. The grass of the yards was overgrown and needed cutting so it was easy to see that a person had walked through it recently. I followed the bent grasses to the side yard and to the gazebo and there sat Misty, in the gazebo, smug as can be, until she saw that it was me.

"What are you doing here?" she asked.

"I live here," I answered. "What are you doing here?"

"Visiting," she replied with a hint of over confidence. "Rusty said he didn't know when you'd be home."

"That's because he never knows when I'll be home. I was on a search. Searches can take days."

"You should stick closer to home. You never know what's going to happen while you are gone."

"Obviously."

"Aren't you going to invite me in?"

"No."

"How rude."

"I never was very good in the tact department. I went to school, graduated, went to school in the Marines, too. The only place they ever taught me about tact was in police academy and then we were holding loaded guns while we tactfully arrested people. So I'm kind of lacking in tact right now. Besides, I believe in giving people the respect they deserve and so far you haven't done anything to deserve mine. I'm going to go unpack, shower and rest up before I make dinner. Have a good day."

The house was quiet for just a few seconds and then Shadow tackled me and went through his welcome home routine. Somehow he thought he could be petted while he attempted to engage me in a game of tag. I wasn't up to a game of tag. I unpacked my pack throwing away the trash and putting my filthy clothes in the dirty clothes bin. I took a long, hot shower wishing Rusty was there. After I was done I slipped on shorts and a tank top and looked out the front window. Misty's car was still there. I dried my hair, brushed it out and looked again. The car was still there. What was she up to? I went outside and she was still sitting in the gazebo. Shadow rushed up to greet her but she nearly climbed up onto the rail to get away from him.

"Get down you filthy animal! I told you, back! Get back! Cassidy call off this brute."

"He's not a brute. He's a friend. He's been my friend a long time. At least *he* can take a hint."

"Well, hint at him to get back!"

"Shadow, come," I said simply. Shadow came and stood in front of me. "Sit. Stay."

Misty climbed down off the gazebo rail.

"How can you live with that dirty thing in your house?"

"He's part of the family. I've had him longer than I've known Rusty. He's trained. He's obedient. He's smarter than some people I know. I've only met one person more loyal to me than Shadow and that's Rusty."

"Really? Rusty? How do you know?"

"I just do. Rusty has stuck with me through thick and thin. He's had women after him from the time he started working at the Joshua Hills station and he only let one of them work their way into his heart. She was killed in a car chase and he didn't look at another woman until I came along. I haven't done anything to attract him. He just chose me for some reason. And he's stuck with me ever since. I don't know why. I'm just glad he did."

"How very interesting. And you are certain he's that loyal to you?"

"Misty, I know what you're up to and I'd appreciate it if you would leave."

"I bet you would. I might leave, but you can't get rid of me that easily. I know where to go."

"Good, then go there," I said and then realized what I'd told her to do.

"Thank you," she said and did her runway walk, crisply tailored skirt swishing all the way to her car. When she got in she let a lot of leg show. She smiled as she closed the door and started up the engine. It purred. She waved as she drove away and I ran into the house to call Rusty. I felt like an idiot. An insecure idiot. But I couldn't let Misty in on that little fact. It was one of her handiest tools. And when I talked to Rusty I felt like I sounded like an insecure wife.

"Hey!" I said brightly when he answered his cell phone, "I'm home."

"That's great. I missed you. Did you find your man?"

"The first day. We just found her late in the evening and there was no need for a pick up so we hiked out this morning."

"You're sounding good. I guess it went well?"

"Yeah, it went as well as it could."

“That’s my girl.”

“We had company when I got home.” The line went eerily quiet. “I’m afraid I wasn’t very nice to her.”

“I think it’s the only way you’re going to get through.”

“Misty has selective hearing… And she might be on her way down there. She also has selective interpretations.”

“I think I’ll go stake out a house or question a witness or how about if I just come home?”

“It’s still early.”

“Long as I get the job done, right?”

“I’ve got a job you can do if you come home in time. It might take a while.”

I got two things out of that conversation: Rusty knew who my visitor had been and he was avoiding her. It was half bad news and half good news. It made me wonder why he was avoiding her but at least he was making the attempt. Many guys would love to be pursued by Misty Montague.

It was heartening to see Rusty pull up into the driveway beaming at me even before he got out of the Explorer. I had thought about changing clothes, dressing up a bit but I decided it would look like I was trying to compete with Misty. Nope, if I was going to win this little battle I had to be myself and myself was wearing shorts and a tank top. Since I’d just showered and expected to rest up and do a few chores around the house I hadn’t bothered with a bra. He bounded out of the truck and I met him halfway down the sidewalk. His eyes were smiling and his embrace was happy and warm. His brown sports coat wrapped around me in the hurry and the smell of him was inside. I basked in the warmth.

“Come here,” he said. I couldn’t get much closer but he lifted me and I wrapped my legs around his waist and he carried me into the house and sat down in our spot on the couch. “I didn’t get my minutes in before you left. I have some catching up to do.”

“Strict was in a hurry and I’m glad he was. The girl I was looking for was pretty beat up by the time we found her. Strict was right to hurry. I hate taking off on you like that, but I like the way you catch up on your minutes.”

His hands strayed underneath my tank top.

“How do you do it? You drive me crazy just by coming home. When I heard your voice my whole day turned around.”

Fingers glided up my leg. Although he could have, he never assumed I would make love to him. He might lure me into it, but he always stopped at inconvenient times to allow me to back out if I wanted to. Heck, I never wanted to. One look, a few touches and I was ready to drag him into the sack.

So it was that I woke up in a dimly lit bedroom with a trail of clothes leading down the hall, the sheets and comforter a tangled mess and a wonderful contentment as I pulled all the warm closeness that I could out of him. I felt the comfort dragging me back down and let it take me, sleeping next to him.

An hour or so later he woke up and pulled me close. "Now look what you did, it's too late to go to town and it's too late to cook. I worked up an appetite and all we have is cold pizza, half a sub sandwich and a cheesecake."

"I betcha if you give me a minute I can make the cold pizza into warm pizza," I said.

"I betcha if I give you a minute you could make me forget about food."

"That's only a short term solution. Every time I make you forget about food you get hungrier."

"We could smear the cheesecake all over each other and take care of both needs at once."

We joked back and forth in wonderful familiarity and laughed at the trail of clothes leading from the den to the bedroom. We heated up pizza in the nude, then both sat and jumped back up because of the cold seats on the dining room chairs. We moved to the couch and ate pressed together. Conversation began as thoughts returned to matters at hand.

"Agnes is teasing us. She is getting way too confident. She moves from one area of the city to the other. She has to be staking these houses out and studying the flow of activity. She always seems to know just when to break in to be undetected. She has patience. I'll give her that. She is subtle too. People don't even realize they are missing things for weeks after she breaks in."

"Is there any pattern to it? Is there any way to second guess what she might try next?"

"Only the fact that expensive jewelry is involved. But she doesn't pawn the items. She either does it to keep the jewelry or she sells it far away from here where people don't know her."

"Well, that's one way Agnes and I differ. I can't imagine wearing expensive jewelry just to show it off."

"You don't need jewels. You are a jewel. I see you and all I can think is how beautiful you are and why did you choose to spend your forever with me?"

"I must be like those geodes that are all rough on the outside and you have to break them to see what they really hold."

He didn't like the comparison. He was too used to people trying to break me.

"Any idea what kind of car she drives?" I asked curious about this cat burglar he was looking for.

"No, we've been watching for someone casing out houses but anybody can sit in a car in a neighborhood. They might be waiting for a friend, a carpool. People wait in cars for any number of reasons and we don't have a description of her car so it's a rather vague thing to go on."

The wheels in my head were turning. I still thought Hazel was the best bet, even if she didn't know anybody like Agnes she would talk endlessly about the workings and gossip at the senior center. I'd at least have some ideas to go on. I made a mental note to go over to Hazel's house the next day.

Chapter 6

"Cassidy! It's so good to see you. You never visit."

"Sorry, I've had searches come up and had to go up north for a funeral and then more searches. I haven't been home much."

"What are you working on now? I know you don't just come over here to chat with an old lady. Some reason always brings you over and I'm always fascinated to see what it's going to be next!"

"Well, now that you mention it, I'm looking for someone. She is sixtyish, small, in great shape for sixty. She has a penchant for expensive jewelry and manages to get expensive pieces with startling regularity. I thought someone like that might show up in your groups occasionally."

"You just described half the women in the elite group."

"The elite group?"

"You know, the rich, the uppity ups. I'm not one of them. They have teas and bridge nights and garden parties. They don't care about me. I'm the Boggle champion and the Scrabble champion in our circle of friends."

Her husband, Wally called out from the other room. "That's because you use your whole vocabulary in a single day!" He never interfered or eves dropped on Hazel's conversations unless he could compliment her. At least that's the way she seemed to take it. I thought he was just being sarcastic.

"This woman would probably hang out with normal people because she wouldn't want the uppity ups to out class her."

"Hmm, small, sixtyish, you know sixty year old people in great shape don't usually hang out at the senior center. They think that place is for old people. People only go to the senior center once they really feel old. Why, I know a few people in their sixties and seventies, even their eighties who have groupie friends at the gym! If she's in great shape maybe she goes to a gym."

"You can't show off expensive jewelry at the gym. It just gets in the way."

"I'll ask Melba Troast and Winnie Dixie. I've got a few connections between the Boggle group and the uppity ups. I bet we can come up with some names if we just try."

"She can't know we're looking for her. If gossip makes its way to the wrong ears she'll take off for another city."

"So she's new around here?"

"Within a year or two."

"Well that narrows it down a lot! Most of the people I know have been in Joshua Hills for decades."

That got the ball rolling. Then I got to thinking that it couldn't hurt to check out the gym. I hadn't thought to watch for Agnes there but it made sense that a sixty-year-old cat burglar had to stay in shape. And it made sense for her to go during the middle of the day when there was no use staking out houses. So I drove down to the gym and staked out a spot on an elliptical machine because the elliptical machines were stationed higher than the treadmills and gave a better view of the room.

I quickly found out that there must be hundreds of women in town fitting Agnes's description, so I began wandering. I feigned ignorance about how the machines worked while an older person was near and then talked to them while we fixed the problem.

"These seats never budge!" I said struggling with the handle and lifting the seat to adjust the machine. "I get a better workout adjusting the machines than I do using them!"

"Here," a woman said. "You pull and I'll lift. How far do you want it?"

"Just a notch or two." Actually, I didn't really want to move it at all I just wanted to break the ice and talk. The seat moved and I got on even though it was now set all wrong for me. "I don't know how you do it. Here I am only twenty-six and I see people all the time here your age that can out do me!"

"Thanks," she said. "I'll be seventy-two in August."

"Seventy-two? I'd have never guessed. I try to guess how old people are and I always guess young here."

"That's because exercising helps keep a body fit and a fit body looks younger. It really does help. I feel so much better after coming here. Look at that man. How old do you think he is?"

"Sixty?"

"He's seventy-one and came in second in the state in weight lifting for his age division. What about that woman?"

"Fifty?"

"I think she's sixty-four but she claims she is sixty. Her husband is sixty-eight and he says she lies about her age."

"If she looks fifty why does she say she is sixty? Why not just go for fifty while she's at it?"

"Too many people know her husband. She wouldn't want people to think a fifty-year-old woman would marry a sixty-eight year old man. Better to be a young looking sixty than an old looking fifty."

And so I went from machine to machine working out with all the wrong settings and talking to a most interesting set of people. By the time I went home I could hardly move.

"What's wrong with you tonight?" Rusty asked. "You act like you just ran the L.A. Marathon."

"I did! I went to the gym and talked to all the old people there. I must have used every machine in the place! Those old people almost killed me!"

"Wait a minute. You went to the gym to talk to old people?"

"It was Hazel's idea. She said old people in good shape don't hang out at the senior center. They go to the gym. I figured a cat burglar might have to stay in shape but the old people at the gym can all out do me."

"You went to the gym looking for Agnes Cooper?"

"I'm lucky I didn't find her! I was in no shape to do anything about it if I did. I'm going back tomorrow. If a seventy-five year old woman can out stair step me I'm in trouble."

He smiled. "I don't want you looking for Agnes Cooper. She'll slip up one of these days. I'm worried about Hazel scaring her off."

"I didn't give Hazel a name, just a set of characteristics to watch for. If she finds anybody matching the description she'll be over here on the double. I just hope she doesn't try to walk here again."

"Forget about Agnes Cooper."

"I can't. You got me curious. She isn't dangerous. She isn't going to come after me with a loaded gun. She won't even know I'm looking for her. I can slip into circles that you don't have access to. The police don't go to Boggle matches at the senior center, but I could, if I just talked to Hazel and expressed an interest."

"Boggle matches?"

"Yeah, Hazel's the area Boggle champ. You didn't know that?"

"No, but it doesn't surprise me in the least. Hazel probably runs through the entire dictionary in a day. What makes you think Agnes goes to *our* gym. There's four others in town."

"Our gym is the most popular. If a woman wants to develop a group of friends she's going to go where people are."

"Well, I'm not going to tell you to stay away from the gym. And I won't stop you from talking to the neighbors. But I really wish you would just drop the hunt for Agnes Cooper. There are bigger fish to catch out there than a sixty-five year old woman who likes expensive jewelry."

"But Agnes is doable. I can find Agnes. It just takes patience and connections. I can make connections. Plus, if I can find Agnes under the right circumstances she can be brought in easily instead of running her down in some midnight chase through a neighborhood."

He sighed knowing he couldn't stop me from thinking about it and I bet he kicked himself for even mentioning Agnes to me in the first place.

The good news was I was going to be in good shape by the time I found Agnes Cooper. I had been a regular at the gym for a long time. I trained there before academy and easily ran five miles. Then we had moved out of town and the gym seemed a long ways away and the hills nearby invited hiking and exploring. Hiking and exploring were okay exercise but I'd let a lot of things slip without knowing it. I could hike. I could carry my pack. I could shoot dead on. But I was getting out of shape as far as the gym went.

I knew if Agnes went to the gym she could go any time of the day or night but I thought she would go during the day because she would be on stake out when families were coming and going and she would be breaking and entering under cover of darkness. I tried all the weight machines. I attended aerobics classes. I even did yoga. But I didn't see Agnes.

"Have you tried the water aerobics class?" Hazel asked me when I came to her aching and discouraged.

"Water aerobics? I had enough trouble keeping up in regular aerobics."

"Older people go for water aerobics because it provides a workout without stressing the joints. You ought to try looking there."

"Did you talk to Winnie and Melba?"

"How could I not? Wally thinks I talk a lot but that's because he never goes near them!"

"Did you figure out anybody that matched my description?"

"No, everybody we could think of had been in town much longer than two years. But I'm not giving up! I've got eagle eyes for this woman. What did she do?"

"If I told you that, word would get out and she'd make a run for it."

"Are you saying I'm a gossip?" she said in mock offense.

"I was counting on it. I need a gossip right now."

"Wally!" she called out. "Wally, get in here."

Wally peeked around the wall.

"Have you noticed any attractive sixtyish women with expensive jewelry? Has anyone come on to you lately at the matches or games?"

"You'd actually ask him that?"

"When you've been married as long as we have nothing surprises you anymore. Everybody knows the widows are notorious flirts. As long as they get flirted back to they are happy. So, my husband flirts with younger women? I think it's funny. Just as long as he doesn't score!" I laughed to myself thinking of Wally scoring with some widow lady. "You just wait, Cassidy, some day you're going to be my age, and when you are every widow in the county is going to be after Rusty. You better be on your toes."

I better be on my toes right now! I thought. Divorcées can be just as bad, even worse.

I went to the gym when a water aerobics class was scheduled. I walked through the locker rooms to the pool to see what was involved. I saw women three times my size squeeze into colorful spandex and I thought, no thanks. Cat burglars hate water.

Next, the city offered classes to senior citizens. I looked over the offerings. How to Make a Quilt in a Weekend. Cooking for One or Two. Creative Courtship. I wondered about that one, then decided that's where all the widows got their tips from. Self Defense. It showed a picture of a person using their cane as a weapon. Hmm, maybe Agnes would take a self-defense class, if she was worried about getting caught. Yeah, and maybe she's a retired karate teacher, too. The more I thought about Agnes Cooper the more I wanted to meet this woman and it didn't really make sense. All she had done was break into a few houses, okay, well, many houses, and take some jewelry. There was only one piece of jewelry I cared enough about to be upset about its loss and I wore it all the time so I couldn't really identify with the victims, but I could identify with Agnes. I could see why she did what she did. I thought it would be fun to break into a house and see if I could navigate inside without detection. I didn't want to take anything and I didn't want to scare a hapless family half to death, but the idea held appeal to me, nonetheless. If I could choose a victim I decided it would be Chase. He'd broken into my house undetected. I thought it would be fun to surprise him for a change. I was almost sure he'd identify me *before* he shot me. Okay, enough day dreaming, Cass, what's your next step? I didn't have a car, or an address, or a pattern. I only had a list of characteristics and a picture. I was sure there was a pattern somewhere. The police just had not discovered what it was yet.

Rusty accidentally gave me the break I needed to make another stab at Agnes. He went off to work and left Agnes's file on his desk. It seemed wrong to open it. It was none of my business. But I was good at seeing things other people missed. What if I could see something in it that the police passed over? I didn't pour over every page leaching out all Agnes's secrets. I wasn't interested in her past arrests or where she went to school or her last known address. I was sure the police had paid Agnes's address a visit. What I found of interest was a list of places she had broken into and a few pictures of jewelry she had stolen. Wow, she did have an eye for the spectacular. I couldn't imagine a woman showing off a ring like the one pictured without everyone in the room remembering. I made a quick copy of the list of houses and pocketed it. I got out a map of the city and looked up each address in the order they were hit. Then I drove to the houses and studied them to find similarities. Very quickly, I wished I had paid closer attention while I had the file handy. I'd like to know how she broke in and what made her decide to. Sitting outside a house thinking about how I would break in didn't help a whole lot. I watched the house in the afternoon when I thought moms would be picking up kids from school and taking them home. I really wanted to be there in the evening when the people were getting home from work but I needed to be home cooking dinner during that time.

The house I staked out first revealed very little to me. Agnes could have broken in easily in broad daylight here. The neighborhood was quiet. The upstairs windows were open. It was a large brick affair, a mansion compared to normal houses. It was custom built, to be sure. None of the houses in this neighborhood looked alike. My Jeep seemed out of place. This neighborhood was the home of rich people's cars, not dirty off road Jeeps.

When a car finally pulled up, a uniformed person got out. It was an older car, and they parked on the street. The woman came back and pulled cleaning supplies from the trunk and entered the house using a key she already had. I looked over the car. No advertising. Later, a BMW pulled up to the house, the garage door opened automatically and closed before the driver exited the car. I had to leave before the woman in the uniform left. I hadn't learned much at all but I wasn't discouraged. I had a whole list of houses. Something would turn up.

Chapter 7

"You and Rusty are as elusive as an escaped convict," Misty said as I stepped out of my Jeep.

"That's good."

Her eyes narrowed.

"Misty," I said. "Go home. You're wasting your time here. You're not welcome. You're getting nowhere."

"It just so happens I am home and I have business here. And you don't know that I'm getting nowhere. These things take patient persistence."

"I bet they do. Joshua Hills is not your idea of the ideal place to live. You'd be miserable here."

"I *do* have business here. I have investments to check on."

"Good, go check on them."

She left in a huff and I realized I'd done it again.

The next house was small, in a poorer section of town. Typical middle class. A family lived here. A family with small kids. A plastic kid sized picnic table and slide were in the front yard. This time it paid off to be there as school got out. A woman walked from the front door carrying a baby and went down to the street. I was tempted to follow but before I could an older woman exited the house with a toddler. They played in the front yard until the woman came back, an older child in tow. I realized there was a school close by. I made notes next to the house on the list- mom, three kids, grandma? The two older kids played in the front yard for a few minutes while the women talked and then they herded the children inside. A short time later the older woman came out with a list shaped piece of paper and her purse. She got into an older tan sedan and left. I argued with myself for a second and then instinct told me to follow her. I pulled out and caught up at the light at the end of the street. I could just about have followed her on foot. She went to a grocery store less than a half mile away. Okay, I thought, I can go grocery shopping. There were a few things I could pick up, too.

I parked my Jeep and went into the store, only halfway following the woman. I really only wanted to run into her a few times to get a closer look. I looked for dinner ingredients and found steak on sale. Then I thought about what I needed to go with steak. In and out of the aisles I went running into the woman a few times. I noted a leather purse, crisp dry-cleaned clothes and…and lots of jewelry. Expensive jewelry. As we were checking out she noticed me looking at her rings. Oops.

"They're my last link to a past long gone," she said. "My husband had a booming business here for forty years and he lost it all five years ago. He gave these to me, God rest his soul. I refuse to give them up even when things get rough."

"Don't you worry about someone stealing them?" I asked, hint, hint.

"I didn't used to, but after a burglary a few months ago, I do. I wear these all the time now. I can't bear to lose them. It broke my heart to lose the few that were stolen from me."

"Whoa, you should insure them babies!" the woman behind me exclaimed.

"I did, but I still miss the original pieces. I could never replace them. They were gifts, gifts I'd never part with."

"I'm sorry you lost them," I said. "Maybe you'll see them again someday. You did report the theft, didn't you?"

"Yes, I did, but I really have no hope."

Uh oh, she'd said *the words*, those words that drive me into a set course. I would find this woman's jewelry. As soon as the word hope entered the picture I wanted to restore it. I lived on hope. I hoped trouble wouldn't strike. I hoped for another day with Rusty. I couldn't count on another day but I could hope and so hope drove me. It drove me to look for people lost in the mountains. It drove me to look for a woman's jewelry. I thought as long as hope held out for me I'd see a lot of adventures, and I hoped this one wouldn't be too adventuresome. Mild adventure was fine right now. Grocery store interrogations. That's the way I preferred to work.

I went back the next day and parked at a different angle. It was an older house. Single story. Agnes probably had no problem finding a loose window. Large shrubs provided lots of dark corners to hide in. Even though it wasn't the house of an uppity up, Agnes had known to strike this particular house. She knew that woman had jewelry. How did she know?

The next day I drove around to the other houses on the list but they were big, lonely houses. I could sit there all day and only see a cleaning lady or a gardener. The owners had two incomes, the kids were in school or daycare or had lives of their own. Agnes could have broken into those houses any time of the day. It was the little, old house that drew me back. It had a life. It was interesting. And the grandma there had a story. It was the best clue I'd had yet so I went back as early in the morning as I could and I watched the house. When the grandma left it was always in the tan sedan. She went out frequently but never stayed out long. I followed her to the bookstore where she bought two romance novels. Later in the day she went to Wal-Mart and bought flowers. She went home and put her things away and spent an hour or so planting flowers in the flowerbeds. The toddler helped. She had to guard her patience. Maybe that's why she went out frequently. She always made sure she was home when school got out so the mom could walk down to the school and pick up the older boy. It felt like I was eves dropping, watching this family go about their daily lives. I felt like an intruder, a well-intentioned intruder, but unwelcome all the same. I wished I could see the dad come home from work. A piece was missing to the puzzle, but he must have come home in the evening like Rusty because I never saw him. I hoped he existed.

"You sure have been out a lot," Rusty commented one day. "What have you been up to?"

"Following a hunch."

"Uh oh."

"I promise, it's harmless. I've been following a grandmother around town. So far she's showed me where to get a good romance novel, where to buy bedding plants for the yard, where to go to donate used books if I want to get rid of them, where to buy Chinese chili paste and where to take my clothes for dry cleaning half off, if I have at least ten items on Tuesday afternoons."

"So, where does your hunch come from if all she does is typical little old lady errands?"

"Eventually she is going to lead me to the place she met Agnes."

"Agnes has met her?"

"She didn't say that, but I'm willing to bet."

"What makes you think that?"

"She doesn't fit the pattern. All the houses that were broken into were big fancy affairs. Agnes could have broken into those places any time. I watched a few of them. I could have been in and out of those houses ten times and nobody would know."

"How do *you* know?"

Ooops! Skirt the question, Cass.

"I watched them. They are empty all day. Nobody comes or goes except a cleaning lady or gardener and Agnes is not a cleaning lady. I know you checked out the housekeeping companies these people hire. Then I ran across this little house in an old neighborhood. No one would think to break into that house for anything and yet Agnes stole several valuable pieces of jewelry from this grandmother. Agnes knew to hit that particular house even though it didn't appear to have anything valuable in it. I think she talked to this grandmother. So I have been following her to see if she goes anywhere she would run into Agnes. See? It's harmless."

"Cassidy," he said, and he meant business. "How do you know about these houses? How did you find out about this grandmother?"

Time to fess up.

"Would you be mad if I told you a careless person left the information in plain view and I just happened to read it?"

He put his hands on his hips and looked at me sternly. I was glad he loved me. I could imagine some punk kid seeing that look and slowly melting into the sidewalk.

"Did I do that?" he asked.

"You did."

"And you narrowed it down to this one house and this one person?"

"I did, but only on instinct and because the people in the other houses are never around. This family does things. They are home when I can be out watching them. I have to leave to cook dinner so I never see what happens there in the evening."

"And I suppose you'd like to."

What? Was he offering to go on stake out with me?

"I'm curious, your file is backwards. Usually you have a crime with several people's backgrounds in it. This time you have Agnes at the front with all these crimes in the back. Are you really convinced Agnes pulled off all these burglaries?"

"Show me the house. And tell me about this grandmother."

We ate a quick dinner and then got in the Explorer and headed for town. I led him to the house I'd been watching. As he drove, I talked.

"And the one time I spoke to her she was wearing rings on every finger because she was afraid they would get stolen if she didn't keep them on. I'm convinced Agnes knows this woman, maybe not well, but they have a connection. I'm betting it's a social one, which is why she hasn't led me there in the daytime. That's when this woman would be dressed in such a way to draw attention to her rings."

When we pulled up to the little stucco home Rusty looked at me weird.

"This house? This is the house you've been watching all this time?"

"This is the home of the grandmother I've been following," I corrected him. "She comes and goes a lot. She doesn't have a lot of patience with the kids so I bet she goes out in the evenings if she has someplace to go."

"This house doesn't match the pattern at all."

"That's why it might be the one link. Something had to make Agnes choose this house. It wasn't a chance drive by that made her choose it. The big, fancy houses, yes, those were hit by chance, but not this one. This one has secrets."

He smiled and we settled in for a long, quiet evening and quiet it turned out to be. I was glad to note there was, indeed a father in the house, but the dad came home and almost immediately the parents left and grandma stayed home babysitting.

"Do you want to follow the parents?"

"No, it's Grandma we're interested in."

"I doubt there's much reason to stay."

"I don't know, I think we should stay."

"Why?"

"Did you bring the file?"

"It's at the office where it should have been when you read it."

"Rats."

"Why?"

"What day of the week did the break in occur? Today is Friday. What if every Friday Mom and Dad have a date night? What if Grandma agrees to babysit every Friday?"

"So?"

"So, I think we should stay."

"Sometimes your logic eludes me."

"Sometimes it pays to listen to it, too."

Hours went by. It was boring in the car. Too bad we couldn't make things a little more interesting. About eight o'clock the house got still, lights went out. Shortly thereafter the front door opened and Grandma came outside and sat in a patio chair under the front yard tree. She brought out a skein of yarn and a crochet hook and added to a project she had started. I guess she didn't need to see it because she only rarely even looked at it. Her fingers flew automatically.

"You want to sit here and watch an old lady crochet?" Rusty asked.

"I want to see if she can finish it tonight," I joked.

After a short time a man walked down the street and into the front yard. He sat down in the other patio chair and he and Grandma talked for hours.

"Bet I could slip in that house and be out before she realized it." I said.

"I bet you could. You really think Agnes broke in while they were in the front yard and the kids were sleeping in the house? She'd have to be pretty gutsy to pull that off."

"You said she was a gutsy lady."

About ten thirty the man got up and kissed Grandma gently on the cheek and walked home. About eleven o'clock Mom and Dad came home and the house went completely dark.

Rusty and I had enough for one night except for one quick stop. I'd gotten Rusty curious. He drove to the station and got out Agnes's file. He read through it a little bit and set it down.

"Well?" I asked. It was my stake out. I wanted to know if I was right.

"It happened at 9 o'clock. On a Friday. It was one of the few thefts that was discovered soon after it happened. The grandma's name is Dottie and she doesn't mention the man at all, unsurprisingly. She just reported that she was outside getting some fresh air."

"I wonder how fresh," I joked.

"Got any other hunches you'd like to follow up on?"

"I still think one of these evenings Dottie will go out for her own night out and when it turns out to be a social occasion Agnes is likely to be there."

"Did you get any more hunches out of this file?"

"I didn't pry. I only got enough general information to give me a starting place."

He took the file home. In the morning, when he left for work, he put the file on the dining room table and said, "Maybe you should pry. Just don't act before calling me."

"Do you want to stake out the house tonight?" I asked.

"You're still set on this?"

"I still think it'll pay off, eventually."

"Pack a picnic dinner and I'll pick you up at four. Maybe eating will help pass the time. Stakeouts were never my favorite thing to do."

"Maybe we can do your favorite thing afterwards," I said playfully.

His eyes got all soft but he checked his thoughts and glared at me instead.

"I'll pick you up at four."

I smiled, "okay."

I decided I'd get more information out of the file than I would watching Dottie pick up her prescriptions and go to the library so I settled in with the file.

Agnes was born Agnes Luella Peruggia, in New York City. I wondered what part of New York City. That might explain why she learned to rely on stealth. She married Isaac Cooper and had three kids. The thefts dated back into the nineteen seventies. Several were confirmed. Many were not. Just as Rusty had said, she was caught and served two years in prison after a plea-bargain. Apparently, two years didn't teach her a lesson. She was suspected in burglaries all over southern California. I wondered what kind of a name Peruggia was so I did a search on the Internet and laughed when I found out the Mona Lisa was once stolen by a man named Peruggia. Maybe it ran in the blood. I compared the picture in the file with the picture on the Internet. I couldn't see a resemblance.

I was sure if I came up with any hunches it was not going to come from Agnes's past. It was going to come from closer to the present. I looked at the cat burglar picture again and I was almost sure it wasn't Agnes. I looked at the mug shots and memorized the features. I was almost sure I could spot Agnes from across a room without seeing her face just because of the way she moved but it couldn't hurt to have a face to go with the actions.

I studied the recent burglaries. There was nothing to indicate they were broken into at night. The few that were confirmed were daytime break-ins; she was discovered by a person like the cleaning lady I had watched earlier. Still, her access points were interesting. She could fit through a very small opening. Sometimes she didn't even open the window farther to get in. She just popped off the screen and slithered through. She even replaced the screens if it was physically possible. Sometimes the victims blamed friends and servants because there was no evidence of a break in, yet the police had the cases lumped in with Agnes's file. Did they really give her that much credit?

The burglaries she was convicted of were similar to the confirmed cases in her recent history. She had been seen by witnesses. Hmm. I wondered if she could be baited. What if Hazel had a neighbor, just down the road who had the most exquisite ring she had ever seen? Could I get her to break into *my* house? Some research was necessary first. Before I invited her over for a break in I wanted to know if she was armed and I needed to make the right connections. At least reading through the file I was familiarizing myself with the way Agnes worked. Usually if I did that a profile would build in my head and when I finally met the person something would click.

Dottie seemed to have big plans that night. We were lucky we got there early because ten minutes after we got there Dottie came out of the house with a flourish. She was wearing a bright purple dress, with bright purple hosiery, with little rhinestones sewn in so her legs sparkled when she walked. Her high-heeled shoes clicked rhythmically as she walked to her car. On her head was a bright red hat with red and purple feathers and silver accents. Dottie was all dolled up!

Rusty and I looked at each other. Would he follow her? He better! This was what we were waiting for.

Dottie opened her car door and reached in. She brought out an outrageous antenna ball with purple and red ribbons streaming down from it. She'd be hard to lose with that thing flying as she drove! Dottie started up her car and backed out of the driveway. Rusty let her get a head start and then pulled out. It was hard to follow Dottie inconspicuously because she drove so slowly. Rusty tried to keep a car or two between us but drivers got tired of following Dottie and passed her. We followed her through town to a park and ride near the freeway. She parked and got out of her car. I looked around thinking the Martians had landed. Everybody was dressed in bright purple and topped with a red hat. The women greeted each other warmly. There must have been fifty of them! What were all these outrageous women doing at the freeway park and ride?

"Do you have binoculars?" I asked.

"Yeah, but now isn't the time. We're too visible. If someone saw you they'd call the cops."

"So? What if one of them is Agnes and I can't see her behind all the feathers?"

"Just wait."

When all were accounted for they boarded a charter bus and it slowly pulled out of the parking lot. Rusty let the bus get onto the freeway before taking off from the park and ride. The women were not going to get away and the bus was visible from a mile away. As we merged onto the freeway Rusty checked his gas gauge. Three quarters of a tank. We hoped it was enough.

At one point when we knew it was several miles until the next exit Rusty pulled up alongside the bus and I watched the women inside laughing and joking together. When some of them saw me watching they waved enthusiastically. I couldn't distinguish individual faces through the tinted glass but they were all smiling, glad to be out doing something together.

Rusty dropped back again and we settled in for a long evening.

"If there was ever a group of ladies who would appreciate Agnes's jewelry collection it would be these ladies," I commented to Rusty.

"Unless they are all former owners," Rusty said glumly, eyes on the road. "What have we got to eat?"

I pulled out a sandwich and unwrapped it halfway so Rusty could hold it easily and drive.

We followed the bus all the way down Highway 14 to I-5 and then followed them south for an hour. I was glad Rusty was used to following people in big city traffic. He stayed on their tail and they never suspected a thing. I brightened considerably when I saw where they were going. Maybe this stakeout business could be fun after all. The Red Hat Ladies were going to Downtown Disney.

The atmosphere at the park and ride was festive, but once the women disembarked at the shopping area of Downtown Disney they opened up even more. They split up and shopped. Many of them bought small gifts for grandkids. Rusty and I wandered from group to group acting like tourists, trying to see if any of the Red Hat Ladies looked or acted like Agnes or wore particularly dazzling jewelry. The festive mood was contagious and I had to remind myself that I had a job to do. I bought a big Lego set for Patrick and Wyatt. Rusty shook his head. He was all work. I figured there were Red Hat Ladies everywhere so we had to go in all the shops and buying something would make me fit in. About seven thirty all the Red Hat Ladies gathered at a meeting spot and went to a jazz restaurant. The constant music all over the shopping area lent to the festive mood. I was wishing we hadn't eaten on the way. The Red Hat Ladies had reservations. They had a head start on us and we couldn't afford to lose them afterwards so we sat outside with the hope that we would get a good look at each and every one of them as they exited the restaurant.

"We need to come here with Patrick and Wyatt," I said as a cartoon character walked by.

"We need to come here with our own kid," said Rusty and we both fell silent. We'd brought up the forbidden topic.

It wasn't that I didn't want kids. I loved kids, but I loved my freedom, too. I thought my time was better spent doing other things besides procreating. I was worried what would happen with a little Cassidy running loose. I wasn't sure two trouble magnets in one household would survive long enough to see the kid grow up. It sounds silly, but it was a legitimate worry, especially after spending a couple of weeks with Patrick. In those two weeks Patrick had called 911 and sent the police to arrest Hazel and Wally's son, become stuck in the top branches of a tree, and been dragged down the mall by a purse snatcher. If I had kids I thought we'd need our own personal search and rescue team. We'd need a tracker, an EMT, and a swat team. Then I reminded myself of the good times we'd had playing in the snow, teaching Patrick how to ride a bike and roller blade, tracking and stalking together.

Rusty was watching me but he was wise not to intrude on my thoughts. He could read me like a book and he knew to talk about it would be harmful to his cause. He did want kids. I knew that. He didn't push. But I knew. He left me alone to work my way through the difficult topic.

Another reason I had trouble with the idea of bringing kids into the world was that I'd seen how life could end. I'd seen an Alzheimer's patient wander the woods looking for a spouse who had died ten years ago. I'd felt what it was like to be beaten and shot at and carried away from a car crash. I saw what I put Rusty through and I wasn't willing to double that. Okay, so most people don't know what it's like to be beaten and shot at, but this was my kid we were talking about. If they took after me at all who knows what would happen. I'd grown up in a peaceful setting, sheltered from the world, yet just my basic personality prevented me from staying in a nice safe place. I was just programmed differently. I wanted to be out there, like Frank said, jumping into life with both feet.

And how would you have your kid live, Cass? Would you have them sit at home and be a house wife? What about a boy? Would you have him sit in an office and, and do what? Accounting? No, admit it, you'd want your kids to be out there getting as much as they could out of life, too. Damn, it was a catch 22. And that's why the subject of kids was the forbidden topic.

"Here we go. You watch the ones on the left, I'll watch the ones on the right," Rusty said.

I'd seen them coming. "Okay," I replied although my methods of observation were different from his and I tended to look at people in general and then focus on details if someone stood out. It was like bird identification. The first thing to notice is the general shape and motions of a bird, this narrows your choices down to a certain type of bird, then look for particular markings to make a final identification. In this case I was looking for a smaller, lither woman, who moved gracefully, smoothly, who kept track of her surroundings, who wore lots of jewelry. It only took a couple of seconds to run through the list. Most of the women were instantly ruled out. By the time all the women had left the restaurant I was convinced Agnes was not one of them. Many of them were small. Many of them wore expensive jewelry. But none of them moved like a cat burglar. Rusty would say, "And how exactly does a cat burglar move when she's not cat burglaring?" But I knew, she would move slightly differently, just as I couldn't help but move differently. It was programmed into the brain. I wished I could get a man nearby to yell, "Freeze! Police!" so I could see the reactions. If Agnes were here we'd see forty-nine Red Hat Ladies go "huh? What?" and stand there looking puzzled. And we would see one who shrunk from sight, becoming nearly invisible within seconds. Then she would put anything she could between the voice and herself and she'd shrink back into the shadows and vanish.

"I think we struck out," Rusty said.

"At least it was an entertaining stake out," I said.

"I'm not going to bother following the bus back. We'll beat it back and find a dark corner where we can use the binoculars."

"You're being very thorough with this group of ladies. What's up?" I asked.

"If I knew, I'd look into it further, but I don't. It can't hurt to give it one more try and call it a night."

I doubted we'd learn anything new by hiding out and watching with binoculars. I'd gotten a good look at the whole group and none of them was Agnes. I was sure of it. Still, I wasn't going to do anything to stop Rusty from reaching the same conclusion.

We drove back to the park and ride and located a dark corner where we had a good view of the bus stop. We finished off the sandwiches and started in on the macaroni salad when the bus pulled up. Rusty watched as all the women disembarked. I sat, watching Rusty, as the binoculars shifted slightly one way and then another. All the women disembarked and he was still watching. Suddenly he brought the glasses down and looked around. I sat up, looking over the situation. Something was up. The ladies were all in a commotion but we were too far away to see what it was about. I slipped out the passenger's door and made my way through the few parked cars that remained late at night. I slipped into the desert bordering the park and ride and stalked my way closer to the group. The ground sloped down and it was easy for me to stay below their field of view. When I'd stalked as close as I could without being seen I still couldn't hear well but I could make out motions and attitudes. The actions said, "It was right here! I parked between Mildred and Sarah and their cars are right here and mine's gone!"

This was interesting. I speculated about who would want to steal that particular car. It could be anybody, or it could be Agnes, knowing a car was available, one that wouldn't draw attention herself. I lay in wait while the women fidgeted and stewed and comforted the woman whose car was stolen. I tried to notice if the woman was wearing an excessive amount of jewelry. I quickly made my way back to Rusty.

"Her car was stolen!" I said. "Is there any way you can get some information out of her, like whether or not she had a spare house key in it and what her address is?"

Rusty looked at me like I was nuts.

"Okay, it's a hunch. But one that could be worthwhile checking out."

It took half an hour for a black and white to show up and when they did Rusty stepped forward.

"What're you doing here?" Jayce Thompson asked.

"It has nothing to do with stolen cars but it could tie into something I'm working on. I have a few questions and then I'll get out of your way."

I left Rusty to his detective work, partly because he was better at it and partly because I didn't want Jayce to know I was there. As soon as the guys saw me at a crime scene they tried to figure out how it could go wrong or who was after me this time.

Nothing interesting happened while Jayce and Rusty questioned the woman. Rusty returned to the Explorer.

"What did you find out?"

"She locks her keys in her car so she doesn't lose them. She has a combination lock so she didn't worry about someone breaking in. The keys were out of sight in the console. And I got an address. Let's go."

"Did you ask her about Agnes?"

"Yeah, but I doubt Agnes goes by her real name. I think she's smarter than that."

Rusty hurried to the woman's house. He had to get out his big, city map and locate it first because it was on one of those residential streets that we had to wind our way in to. The neighborhood was quiet as we drove down one street after another. It was a two story house and Rusty paused half a block away.

"That's the car," he said.

"What? You mean the car was stolen just so the thief could take it home for her? That doesn't make sense."

"Unless they just wanted access to the house."

He pulled out his phone and called Jayce.

"I found the car. Now I need the owner." A pause while Jayce spoke. "It's at her house." Another pause. "Just let her go as soon as you can. I may know who took it shortly after she gets here."

"You think Anges stole this lady's car to break into her house?"

"Agnes is a good locksmith. I'm sure she can unlock a car."

When the woman arrived she looked over her red Mazda MX5. It matched her hat. And her attitude. She unlocked the car with a combination and dove inside. The keys were still there. Rusty instructed her to look around to see if anything was missing, especially jewelry.

I waited in the Explorer. Jayce pulled up and noticed me there.

"Oh, no, don't tell me you're in on this, too?"

"Just barely, I wish I had worn my uniform so I could go in there and know what was going on."

"I think you just got your chance," Jayce said nodding towards the house.

"Cassidy, come here," Rusty called from the front door.

Hmm, this was odd. I knew there were no tracks to follow; everything outside was cement. When I jogged up Rusty said, "I need your input."

"On what?" I said and then realized the whole house had very new carpet and footprints showed up easily. I slipped over to where Rusty was standing.

"Cassidy, this is Verna. Verna, this is my wife, Cassidy. Her area of expertise is tracking. I'd like her to follow the trail through the house and tell me what the person did in here. I'd do it but she seems to get more out of a trail than anyone else."

"Do you have your cell phone?" I asked.

He pulled it out of his pocket.

"Set it to speaker phone so I can talk to both of you." I looked around a little before moving. Even from where I stood I had a few questions. "Before you left the house were the curtains open or closed?"

"Open, I leave them open so I can see in when I get home. I leave the lights on so people think someone's home, too."

"The first thing the person did was stop at the front door, probably to listen for other people in the house. Then they closed the front curtains so the neighbors wouldn't see her poking around."

"Her?" Verna said. "What makes you think it was a woman?"

I looked to Rusty.

"She doesn't yet," Rust said, though I did know it was woman. A woman who wore size six. She wore flat soled shoes with very little tread. They fit her feet closely. The wear was even. All those facts pointed toward Agnes.

"After she closed the curtains she felt more free to look around." I followed the tracks to the dining room and then to the kitchen. "She only glanced in the dining room and the kitchen," I informed them. If she went in the kitchen she came out exactly where she went in and that would be unusual. Can you think of anything you left out that might draw her attention?"

"No, nothing!" Said Verna. "I'm a neat freak. I hate a cluttered house."

I looked in the kitchen again. She was right. She was a neat freak. No dirty dishes, nothing was on the counters except a few canisters, a toaster, and a coffee maker.

"Do you keep any valuables hidden in the canisters?" I asked.

"No, just sugar, flour, corn starch, that sort of thing."

I followed the tracks upstairs. They became muddled with Verna's tracks a little but the thief's tracks were on top. I was surprised when the tracks bypassed the first two doors and went straight to the master bedroom. It was fairly obvious which bedroom the master bedroom was because it had big double doors.

"Whoever it was didn't bother with the smaller bedrooms," I informed those downstairs. "They went straight to the master bedroom and closed the curtains in there too. They glanced in the bathroom. Was there anything in the bathroom they would want? Any rings in the dish? Any necklaces hanging from the peg?"

"No, all my jewelry would be in the jewelry box…"

"On your nightstand," I said finishing her sentence for her. "Why didn't they bother with the bigger one on your dresser?"

"It's just costume jewelry," she said with a worried tone. The jewelry box on my nightstand has the good stuff in it."

"But how did the thief know that? Almost any thief would have gone for the big one first, the small one second, yet they skipped over the big one completely."

Verna gasped, "It's like they knew me!"

"Anything else, Cassidy?" Rusty asked.

"Just one little quirky thing that doesn't involve the theft. As she was leaving the master bedroom she jumped to the side. As I look to see what made her jump, I realize you can see directly from Verna's bedroom door, through two windows, directly into the neighbor's house. From what I see here maybe we should warn them to be on their guard."

"Oh, that woman only has junk. The gaudiest costume jewelry you can imagine." This coming from a woman dressed in a bright purple and red pantsuit and a red hat with purple hatpins all over it.

"How did the burglar get out?" Rusty asked.

"She just went back down stairs and out the front door." I answered.

"Thanks, Cassidy, you can come downstairs now." When I got downstairs he asked. "Do you want to take the truck home? It's going to be a long night."

Sigh, I didn't want to, but there was also no use in me staying. I knew the basics. Verna knew this woman. The woman had been in her house before, had been in her bedroom before. Knew which jewelry box held the best jewelry. Had known Verna would be gone several hours today and knew she tended to leave her keys inside her car. She knew where to find the car and how to get in. A slim jim might have done the trick, or she might have known the combination.

"There was an accomplice involved here or the car wouldn't be in the driveway," I mused aloud. "Now it makes sense why we could never find out what car she drove. It's possible that she is never in her car."

"Now that you mention it," Verna said. "I've heard of people's cars being stolen and then turning up, unharmed in odd places before."

"It's going to be a long night," Rusty said again. He handed me the keys to the Explorer. He called the station to arrange for a forensics crew to come in and collect evidence. I didn't see that they would find much but they had to look anyway. If it was Agnes, she was known to wear gloves during her break-ins. We would at least know if the theft matched Agnes's MO. So far I was willing to put good money on Agnes. It was observant enough and sneaky enough and neat enough to fit her profile.

I took the Explorer home knowing there was no use waiting up. I slipped into bed at two a.m. and woke up, like usual, around dawn. Oh man, I needed more sleep! But it was no use. I was awake for the day. Shadow woke up, too, and once he was awake I knew there was no use trying to sleep. I fed him and ran him through the agility course a few times. That got him wound up enough that he wanted to play. I'd have taken him out in the hills for a hike except I wanted to be home when Rusty got there.

Rusty dragged in around eight a.m. and slouched into the old brown couch. I sat down next to him feeling nearly as tired as he was.

"What haven't you already guessed?" he asked.

"Did Verna identify Agnes from the picture?"

"No, nor from any of the mug shots on record."

"Do you think I should show the picture to Hazel? Did you show it to Dottie?"

"Dottie didn't recognize Agnes's picture either. By the sounds of it, it can't hurt to ask Hazel."

"Agnes hasn't been known for her disguises, has she?"

"Who knows anything about Agnes anymore," he said tiredly. "It didn't work out quite the way we hoped but it paid off to follow Dottie last night. Are you ready to try again?"

"Not unless we both have a nap."

"It's a deal."

About three in the afternoon the doorbell rang and I pulled myself out of the depths of sleep enough to answer it. I took a look at myself in the hallway mirror and didn't like what I saw and didn't care a whole lot. I smoothed down the worst of it and opened the door to a perfectly primped Misty Montague. I groaned inwardly.

"What happened to you?" she asked.

"I've been on a stakeout all night." I told her without thinking.

"Ooo, anything exciting happen?"

"I can't talk about ongoing cases. You know that."

"I bet I could get Rusty to talk," she said.

"I bet you can't because you're going to let him sleep. Good night, Misty."

"It's the middle of the afternoon," she whined.

"Yes, and morning will be here sooner than you think."

She turned with a huff and laid rubber on Lost Hills Road as she headed for town.

Dottie led us to a dominoes game at a friend's house, a pot luck at the senior center and a eightieth birthday party at the Holiday Inn conference center.

I thought another trip to Hazel's house was in order. She opened the door but quickly admitted, "We've been wracking our brains all week and we can't think of who this woman is."

"That's okay; I have another question for you. Have there been an unusual number of stolen cars amongst the seniors?"

"How many is an unusual number? I can't say I've heard of more than four."

"I'd say four is an unusual number for a small group of people." I observed. "Do you know any details?"

I was alert right away when she started her explanation with, "Well, it's the oddest thing, cars are stolen but police find them really quickly. The police must think they are doing a wonderful job recovering cars so fast but I think the thief is just borrowing them. But why would someone borrow a car without asking only to return it?"

"To commit a crime?"

"But the police haven't mentioned to any of the owners that their car was involved in a crime."

"Maybe the police don't know. Can you tell me what was going on at the time the cars got stolen?"

"Well, one was a Boggle match. I was there for that one."

"How long does a Boggle match go on?"

"It depends on how quick people think and how many people enter. It can be a few hours."

"And what happened?"

"I went to the senior center for the match and won handily but when we came out one of the cars was gone. It was found again back at the senior center the next day. Lily says that Carol said that her car was stolen when she went on a bus trip to the State Line. When she came back her car was not where she left it but it was found near her house. We were all wondering how the car thief knew where she lived."

"Have any of these people also had their houses broken into?"

"What? Like a robbery?"

"If it's a house that's broken into it's a burglary but, yeah."

She thought for a minute. "Come to think of it there have been a lot of burglaries lately. There didn't used to be but for the past year it's gotten worse and worse."

"The past year?"

"No, I guess it's been more recent than that. It's awful, isn't it, the way crime is getting?"

"Can you tell me what has been stolen?"

"Well, cars. And credit cards. Cash and credit cards are always high on the list of stolen goods. And jewelry, but that's understandable. Some of those women have jewelry you wouldn't believe!"

Okay, it was time to take the plunge. I'd copied Agnes's picture and removed all the personal information from the page.

"Hazel, does this woman look familiar to you?"

She took the picture from me and looked it over carefully, then hollered into the other room, "Wally! Get in here! Cassidy has a suspect!"

Wally waddled in from the other room and took the picture from Hazel.

"Does she look familiar to you?" she asked. "You see a lot more women of an evening than I do." Then to me, "He's such a flirt."

"Maybe, just maybe. I can't think of her name but she looks a little like what's her name."

"I don't know," Hazel said. "What's her name?"

"If I knew I'd tell you. It's right at the tip of my brain."

"Your brain is as round as your head, maybe it slipped off the side. If we wait long enough maybe it'll slip out your mouth."

I didn't appreciate the mental picture that went with that but I didn't say anything.

"Will you be quiet?" Wally scolded her. "I can't think with you going on about it."

They went back and forth a bit, "Well, what group is she in?"

"None."

"What do you mean none? How do you not be part of a group?"

"By not forming cliques!" Wally said pointedly.

"She's gotta be in some group. Who does she hang out with?"

"No one. She just kind of watches things. She's a wallflower, that's what she is. She's quiet and she watches things from a distance. The only time I've seen her get involved is at the big dances. She dances! Boy can she dance! Makes me wish I could dance too!"

"Okay," said Hazel, losing patience. "So what's her name?"

"I don't know but, if I could dance, I'd be sure to find out!"

"What does she wear?" Hazel was helping me out by leaps and bounds without even knowing it.

"She wears…oh hell, how should I know what she wears? I never examined her outfits before, except those dresses she wears to dance in and her sparkly jewelry. She does go for the sparkly ones, that gal does. Wow!"

"I see," said Hazel with a glare.

"So, let me see if I've got this straight," I interrupted. "Cars disappear when there's a long activity going on. There have been burglaries involving cash, credit cards and jewelry. Not TVs? No big electronics or antiques?"

"Louis had his TV stolen, but that was while he was moving. Someone just walked off with it out of the truck," Wally said.

"And this woman looks like a woman that goes to the dances and usually sits quietly alone observing things," I said in conclusion.

"Yeah, that sounds about right to me."

"Do you have a schedule of the upcoming events?" I asked Hazel.

"Of course! I keep it tacked to my refrigerator."

She went and got the paper and handed it to me. It was water spotted and had food stains on it but it showed the activities for the month.

"Can I copy this? I'll bring it back in a few hours. Do you happen to have one of these for the Red Hat Ladies, too?"

"Is what's her name a Red Hat Lady?"

"I don't know, just a possibility," I said, not wanting to go in that direction at that point in time.

"I don't have one but Melba does. I'll have her give me a copy. She's always trying to get me to go to the meetings with her."

I left Hazel's house ready to take on Agnes. All I had to do was find her.

I was convinced that the next big senior citizen's event or Red Hat Ladies event would bring her out. This time I wouldn't go to the event itself. I would watch the parking lot. I copied the calendar as promised and took the original back to Hazel, then drove quickly to town. I was excited about what I had learned and didn't want to wait until Rusty came home from work to tell him about it.

Chapter 8

The weather was so nice I took the top off my Jeep before I drove into town. I searched under the seats to make sure I had a hairbrush and took off with the senior center calendar of events safely tucked into my pack. I pulled into the police station parking lot and parked, ran the brush quickly through my hair, then bounded up the steps two at a time.

"Cassidy wait!" the desk clerk called out to me before I hit the door to the hallway leading to Rusty's office. I pulled up short.

"Is he busy?" I asked. "I can come back later."

"Uh, you could say that," she said noncommittally.

"Don't tell me…there's a beautiful blond who comes to 'talk business' every day. She drives up in a white Mercedes and she asks for Rusty and makes up some story about a case he is working on and she has more information for him."

"You know?"

"I can guess."

"Wow, you guess pretty good."

"She's pretty predicatable."

"And you're not worried?"

"Should I be? What's Rusty's reaction?"

"Well, he can't exactly kick her out. He's had me make up excuses for him. He's quietly slipped out the back a few times. But they have met in his office a few times."

"It doesn't surprise me in the least."

I went through to Rusty's office and peeked in the little window. I knocked and opened the door a crack, just like I always did. Misty jumped out of her chair with a little screech. She stood there, hands on hips, giving me the evil eye.

"I think it's about time for you to leave," Rusty said.

Misty stomped over to me, turned a spectacular shade of red, out of anger, not embarrassment, and said, "You…you…you…infuriate me! That's what you do!" Then she stomped out.

It was Rusty who was embarrassed. "Cassidy, it's not what you think."

"Yes, it is," I answered. "It's Misty, just being Misty. I watched it for three years in high school."

"Let's get out of here. My office is like a trap these days."

We went out the back to staff parking and took the Explorer to a quiet restaurant for lunch. I kept my news to myself until we were settled in a booth.

"I told you Hazel knew more than we thought!" I said excitedly. "After I asked the right questions we started talking about cars being stolen and the odd way they are found and about some burglaries she had heard of. Look, this is a calendar of events for the senior center. If we stake out the parking lot or meeting area during one of the longer events we might catch Agnes going after a car. If none of those pan out there's a dance the last day of the month and Wally says a woman that looks like Agnes attends the dances. He wasn't sure it was Agnes but he said enough to make me think she was worth talking to. Hazel's getting me a calendar for the Red Hat Ladies, too."

"You got all this out of Hazel and Wally in one morning?"

"I went over there twice. I didn't have much luck the first time, but I had more to go by the second time. I told you, Hazel has connections."

"I guess so. Is this ours?" he said waving the calendar.

"Yeah, I made a copy of Hazel's."

He read through the schedule of activities and chose two likely days.

"I'm going to stake out these two nights, unless the other calendar has more likely prospects on it."

I looked over the calendar and agreed with his choices. One of the dates was in eight days, the other two weeks.

"I think the second one is more likely to work. The group will be at a huge museum an hour away and I bet the more classy seniors will be interested in the Getty Center."

"That's my thinking."

"I just wonder if Agnes will have time to find a new victim by then."

"We'll see."

The subject of Misty never came up. I didn't say I trusted him and he didn't make any excuses. The truth was, I never demanded Rusty's faithfulness. Although I thought he had been trustworthy I had no way of knowing that. My heart said I could trust him and my brain asked why. But they weren't at odds with each other, either. Misty, however was a different story. I could feel a touch of jealousy as she pursued Rusty, but I wasn't going to tell Rusty what to do. I always got a catch in my throat at the prospect of losing him. What would I do, if that happened? I could only blame myself. But…I hoped I could trust him. I just wished I *knew* I could. So, I guess I *was* at odds with myself. I just tried to keep the two sides of myself away from each other. If I could do that everything would be fine.

Chapter 9

"Cassidy?" It was Strict.

"I have a request. You can turn it down. It's not really a search and we don't think the man is lost. I've got a mom asking that someone go down a trail and look for her son. He's been out there four days, with camping gear, trying to get from a campground to a trailhead."

"So, are we dealing with an over protective mom? A medical condition? What's the problem?"

"Hopefully nothing. The guy's blind."

"But he may be fine."

"Yeah."

"So it's just a look see."

"Yeah."

"How old's the kid?"

"Twenty."

"Fit?"

"Yeah."

"Leave him alone."

"What?"

"Lou, the guy just wants to go camping. So he's blind, he wouldn't go out there if he didn't feel capable. There's no reason a blind person can't backpack. I've backpacked blindfolded just to see what it's like. I didn't last long with the blindfold but it *is* possible. He's got a cane or a dog, right?"

"A cane. So you're going to let this guy feel his way through the mountains?"

"Yeah. How many days did he pack for?"

"A week but it wasn't far, unless he got off the trail somehow."

"He'd know if he was off the trail. It's hard to walk without sight off trail. The cane would get hung up on everything. He's on a trail except to find camping spots."

"You want to give him more time?"

"I'll talk to Rusty, but I'm for letting the guy backpack by himself. He may be trying to prove something to himself. Sending out a rescue party isn't exactly going to boost the guy's confidence."

"There's such a thing as overconfidence. If anybody should know that it's you."

"Rusty? I've got a call from Strict. He'd like me to go check on a blind hiker. I told him to let the guy hike in peace."

"But?"

"But he didn't seem too keen on the idea. This isn't the best time."

"There is no good time."

"He's probably fine. If he wants to go camping alone I think he should be able to."

"So, why tell him you're there? You could check on him and pretend to be another hiker and just keep going."

"You think I should go?"

"What's wrong, Cassidy? There's something going on here besides a blind hiker. I thought you'd jump at the chance to track a blind person. You've never tracked a blind person before."

There sure was, but I didn't want to admit I was more worried about a blind wife than a blind hiker. He was right, though, I would like to track a blind person. But it sounded a little like he was trying to get rid of me. I was imagining things. I had to be. He wasn't really trying to get rid of me.

"Okay, I'll go in the morning. I should be able to catch up pretty fast."

I sure would, too, I'd have Misty Montague on my mind the whole time. That would push me. A blind person with a cane should be easy to track.

"Hey Strict, I'll go out at first light, just give me a starting point and an ending point and I'll do my best."

"Atta girl, I'll call Landon."

"No! I want to go alone. And if this hiker is doing fine I'd rather he not even know I'm there. I still think he has a right to camp by himself if he wants to."

"What if he's not okay?"

"Do I have to take Landon?"

"Has Landon been giving you problems?"

"No, Landon's been fine. I'd just like to get in and out with as little gear as possible and if Landon goes I have to pack a tent and…and I'd rather just rough it quickly than pack everything but the kitchen sink. There's going to be no base camp, right? It's just a look see. So why take Landon?"

"Because if Grey took a fall off the trail you're going to need help."

I met Landon at the trailhead at first light. He seemed a bit skeptical.

"I told Strict this was just a quick checkup. I'm hiking in and finding the guy and hiking out. I told Strict I was packing minimally. Get used to it. And don't make a fuss over the lack of a tent. I have what I need."

He still looked at me oddly so I forked over the cookies. That didn't help.

"What?" I asked him.

"Something's bothering you."

"Let's go."

It wasn't hard finding Grey's tracks. Even when I couldn't see his tracks the swish of his cane was plain. It brushed the trail in front of him and went ever so slightly over the side, telling him where his boundaries lay. I hiked as fast as I could and still read. When the reading was good I took note of how his feet came down. Each stride was exactly the same length. He walked confidently as long as he had a clear trail. I read the rhythm of his footsteps and cane strokes and it was like watching a metronome. Step swish, step swish. When he got puzzled about the trail it was easy to tell. His feet spoke volumes.

"Cassidy, you're running from something but it won't work."

"I am not. I'm running to something. I'm getting this over with."

"Why? Usually you like being on the trail. Usually you'd jump at the chance to follow a different type of trail. Something is eating at you."

If there was one person I didn't want to talk about Rusty to it was Landon, so I hiked faster. Landon gave up but then he started dropping farther and farther behind. He knew as long as I was in sight we were okay but he didn't like the separation. It gave him time to regroup and think about the goings on at the station. Just like Hazel had connections through the seniors, Landon had connections at the station. He knew what went on there. He jogged up and confronted me. "You're letting that air headed bimbo worry you," he declared finally.

"I know how she works. She's from back home. She moved down here specifically to target Rusty. I doubt she's here to stay but she's here until he proves to her that she's wasting her time."

"You find more ways to get into trouble than anybody I've ever met," he said laughing.

"This isn't trouble," I said.

"Then what is it?"

"It's annoying. It's frustrating…it's…okay it's trouble. The trouble with this trouble is there is nothing I can do about it."

"Send her packing."

"That's just like challenging her to a duel. She would just get more determined."

"Then have Rusty send her packing."

"I'm not going to tell Rusty anything. If he wants her gone he'll choose to do it but I won't tell him to."

"You're either very brave or very stupid. You think a guy is going to tell a girl like that to get lost?"

"He knows the score. He knows she will drop him like a lead balloon as soon as the novelty wears off. I think he's smart enough to distance himself from her. The problem is Misty loves a challenge. The more he puts her off gently the more she likes it."

"Well, hiking my feet off isn't going to solve it. We should have no problem catching up with a blind hiker, so calm down. Do you know how Rusty handled pushy women before he met you?"

"No, and I was not a pushy woman. I didn't even encourage him."

"Much to the chagrin of those watching. He was charming and polite and always declined their advances. He just wasn't interested. He's not interested in this Misty character. He'll do the same with her as he's always done."

"Then she'll be around for a long time. As long as she thinks there is hope and she can annoy me she's only going to get worse."

"Then don't let her annoy you. Pretend she doesn't exist."

It was easy for Grey to feel his way over this part of the trail. It sloped up to the left and down to the right. All he had to do was stay in the middle. When he came to rocky places his cane felt its way through, followed by his feet. He was used to feeling his way with his feet. He did stumble a few times but he felt his way over the obstacle and continued on his way. On days with a clear trail he made a few miles a day. On days that he had obstacles or confusing places in the trail it slowed him down a lot. Switchbacks took time to navigate. Wide-open spots in the trail were almost as confusing as the obstacles but in a different way. He needed boundaries. As long as there were boundaries he walked around just fine. When he needed to camp he seemed to watch for one of those confusing wide open places. If he could find one he found the perimeter of the area, located the openings that indicated the trail and marked the trail by scoring a deep line down it, then he triangulated to find a tent spot. He seemed to pitch his tent haphazardly and then sleep with his head pointed uphill. It worked. One thing I worried about was him starting up a stove to cook. It was too easy to have flare ups and many times he was camping in close proximity to dry weeds and grasses. What was he eating on the trail? A guy could take only so much granola bars, trail mix and beef jerky.

At one point in the trail deer tracks crossed the trail and Grey's footprints went right over the top of them. I wished he could have seen them. He probably didn't even know they were there.

We caught up to Grey late in the afternoon. I saw him off in the distance and called a halt. We used the GPS to find ourselves on the map and saw we were only three miles from where the trail hit the pickup spot. If Grey had made it this far he'd have no trouble finishing the hike in the morning.

"I say, just let him finish," I insisted. "We're only friendly hikers. You can ask questions that curious hikers would ask but we are not searchers. Got it?"

Sigh, "Got it."

"We can report to Strict when we get to the pickup spot."

I purposely scuffed my feet as we came up behind him.

"Hikers behind," I announced.

Grey stepped aside.

"Hi! How are you?" I asked.

"Tired, but well. I didn't know how hot and dusty this trail was when I started out," he answered.

"How far are you going?" Landon asked.

"Only to where the trail meets the highway."

"How long have you been on the trail?"

"Five days. It's a little slower going when you only have a cane to tell you the way."

"I bet. You have everything you need? Plenty of water?"

He shook the water bottle in his hand and said, "Hmm," then he removed his pack and unzipped a compartment and felt around. He took out two more bottles, shook them to make sure they were full and answered, "I'll make it, no problem. It's nice how folks have been watching out for me. One person marked camping spots for me. They asked what kind of a mark I'd recognize and when they saw a good place to camp they drew a line down the middle of the trail so my cane would hit it."

So that's where the lines came from, I thought.

"Okay, well, we'll be moving on. Have a good afternoon," Landon said.

"Will do," Grey answered.

"Three more miles to go," I said to Landon, though it was more for Grey's benefit. "You ready to hike it?"

"Yeah, though we don't have to hurry. We'll have a ride whenever we get there and we don't have to stop as soon as the sun sets. I think if I were blind I'd prefer hiking at night when it's cool. We only hike in the day so we can see."

We put some distance between ourselves and Grey before we resumed our conversation.

"So," I said. "Mission accomplished?"

"Mission accomplished."

"That was a good day's work."

"I only ate three cookies."

"Keep the rest."

"Cassidy, don't worry about Rusty. He's so stuck on you. I've spent the past year wishing he wasn't. He took a lot of flack from me. He put me in my place more than once. He can handle himself. For a while I thought I'd ruined our chances to work together, but he's patient, too."

"Yeah, he is." I remembered a time not so long ago when Landon and I were not friends. We kind of got off to a rocky start. "Landon, I'm sorry I slugged you."

He felt his jaw and smiled, "It's okay. It's the closest I've come to getting a kiss."

I was tempted to slug him again, but I couldn't. We were fast friends now.

"Besides," he continued. "I deserved it. I was a jerk."

"It's been a long time," I observed. "I'm glad we got things straightened out. I couldn't have asked for a better search partner. You know, we're not tracking any more. You're allowed to go in front."

"Nah, if I go in front then all I have to look at is the trail. If I follow I get to watch you."

"You're worse than Misty Montague," I told him.

"So why are you worried about her?"

"Because she takes her little hobby very seriously. She graduated one year before me and she's looking for husband number four. Specifically she is trying to break up me and Rusty. So far she has just done it by coming on to Rusty but she's been known to fight dirty."

When we had put some distance between Grey and us and we were about a mile away from our goal Landon called Strict for a pick up.

"Ten sixty-five found. He's doing fine. We left him three miles from the trailhead. He'll be arriving tomorrow morning at the latest."

"That's good news. I'll be there in a half hour."

"Ten four."

Landon turned to me. "Why didn't you want Grey to know we were searching for him?"

"Would you like it if you were out for a nice camping trip in the woods and searchers converged on you and told you your mother sent them out?"

"No, I can say I definitely wouldn't like that."

"Well, neither would he. Just because someone is missing one of their senses doesn't mean they are incapable. Grey was just as capable as any other hiker. Maybe more so. He had to take precautions, but who doesn't? Let people show you what they can do and they will surprise you."

"I know, you surprise me all the time."

Strict picked us up at the trailhead and took us back to our cars.

"I need to tell Grey's mom something. Tell me what you saw," Lou said.

Landon answered, "He was in good spirits. We didn't tell him we'd been searching for him. We just talked a little bit and made sure he had the supplies he needed to complete his hike. He told us how helpful people had been. So we left him to finish his hike. Let him tell his mom about the hike himself. Just tell her the guy we found was doing fine, appeared very capable and in good spirits. He should be at the trailhead in the morning."

"Okay, will do. Thanks for going out."

"It's okay. We did some talking. I'm glad we went," said Landon.

When I got home Rusty appeared to still be at work but when I entered the house I quickly realized he was working in his office and the Explorer was in the garage.

"Are you hiding out?" I asked.

"You don't want to know." He answered shortly. He reached into his shirt pocket and tossed a keycard onto the desk. "Here, if you ever want to visit Misty any time of the day or night…" Then he thought better of it and shredded it. He knew I just might pay her a visit if I got mad enough.

"You might want that back if she ignores her restraining order," I said sarcastically.

Chapter 10

A few days later Hazel brought me a copy of the Red Hat Lady schedule of events. The number of different activities astounded me. There were lunches at local cafes. There were shopping trips to the local mall, Santa Monica Pier, State Street Santa Barbara, and the outlet mall in Barstow. There were historical trips to Calico Ghost Town, Bodie and Hollywood. There were picnics in the park and nature walks at the Poppy Reserve. There was an ice cream social at Ida Mae's house and a weenie roast at Flora Bristol's house. There were quilting bees and craft meetings and scrap booking parties. I wanted to see the Red Hat Ladies bowl and shoot pool. I showed the calendar to Rusty.

"We'd have to live in the car to cover all these activities," he said.

"I wonder if Hazel could speculate on who Agnes's next victim might be. Then we might be able to figure out which activity she'd likely go to."

I was hesitant to ring Hazel's doorbell. Hazel was really getting into what she considered a mystery. She was going to know too much too soon. She peeked out the living room window before she answered the door. When she opened it she stared at me eagerly.

"What's the scoop? Have we captured the perpetrator yet?"

"No, but we're getting closer. I was wondering… if you were going to steal some one's jewelry who would *you* target?"

"Me? Well, I'd go after this cute little Christmas pin that Silvia Flores wears all during the holiday season. She bought it in Maui and it's a reindeer wearing Hawaiian print swim trunks and playing a ukulele. It is so cute and I'll never get to go to Maui."

I believed her. That was just the kind of jewelry Hazel would wear.

"What if you were going for dramatic effect and big bucks?"

"Women's jewelry?"

"Why?"

"Because if I were going for big bucks I'd go for Franklin Grossman's collection of gold chains. He thinks he's so hot wearing them to the dances and playing disco fever. If you're talking about women's jewelry I'd pick Simone Randal's or Denise Langhaufer."

"Can you think of what activities they would be most likely to join in on?"

"Simone stays close to home. She is at the center every weekday from nine through lunch. Denise will likely go for the craft functions but she loves the beach so she planned on going on the bus tour up the coast."

"Okay, that helps a lot."

"What are you going to do?"

"I'm going to tell Rusty and you're not going to say a word or else you'll scare off the thief!"

She gave me a *who me?* look and I gave her *a yes, you* look.

"Here we go," I said handing the paper to Rusty. "Hazel said she would target Denise Langhaufer and that Denise would take the bus tour up the coast. We can stake out the Senior Center parking lot that day and see if Agnes shows up."

"Cassidy, you're pinning all your hopes on one trip and one person. You know these things seldom go the way they are predicted. Agnes goes by her own rules. The likelihood of her actually showing up is slim."

"Okay, you go to work. I'll stake out the parking lot. It can't hurt to try."

"Oh, yes, it can. You're not going alone. Letting you go alone is an invitation for trouble."

We checked out the senior center parking lot. It was L shaped. It was impossible to watch the whole lot from any one place and people parked on both sides of the building to gain access to different doors. Knowing this, we took two cars to stake out the parking lot and we arrived early. We drove around waiting for a few cars to show up so we could blend in and then we found an out of the way spot and settled in for a long wait. The bus arrived at seven thirty and fifteen minutes later senior citizens began arriving. The parking lot filled up. Most of the seniors were cheerful, ready to start the day. A few were normally late risers and went inside for coffee. They wore Bermuda shorts and wide brimmed hats to keep the sun off. They carried big tote bags with medications, cameras, and neck pillows. Most of them knew each other and they greeted each other amicably. A few were outsiders and they looked younger. Perhaps they were still trying to decide whether the senior center was the place for them. At eight o'clock they took a head count and waited for three other people to show up. I watched with interest. I liked to see people interact. I watched their feet and translated their movements into tracking patterns. Maybe I was watching a little too close because a large car pulled up beside me. I was just thinking up a good line in case they spoke to me, something about waiting for my Great Aunt Matilda, when I saw a gun appear inches from my face. I froze. I reached for my cell phone on the seat and the man cocked the gun. Rusty was on the other side of the bus. I had to make a fuss, draw some attention but I didn't have a chance. When I shoved open the door to try and run he brought the gun down hard on my head and I fell roughly to my knees.

My head throbbed. I was still inside the Jeep but it wasn't moving. The man with the gun sat next to me. He was big, lean and hard looking. His head was nearly shaved and his scalp under his hair had a tattoo of a skull. Tattoos of thorn branches encircled both biceps. He was tanned, toned and his black muscle shirt didn't hide anything.

"Misty didn't tell me you were armed," said the man. "You could 'a blown me away."

"I hadn't gotten desperate yet," I said. "Who are you?"

"Just a hired man, you can call me Gonzo because that's what I'm supposed to make you. It's also short for Gonzolani, so people call me Gonzo anyway."

"If you're supposed to get rid of me, why are you telling me this?"

"Can't hurt. First on our to-do list is to make your boyfriend think you're gone for good. As soon as our ride gets here we'll send your Jeep for a nice swim and then we'll be going."

"Why not just send me for a nice swim, too?"

"Because, I was told you might be needed later. And I was told you're very hard to kill. So if we do it we want to do it right."

He said *if.* That was a good sign. And he said *later*. That was a good sign, too. I took in my surroundings. We were parked near the aqueduct. Dumping my Jeep in the aqueduct wouldn't fool Rusty for a minute. They might drag the aqueduct looking for me but it wouldn't surprise them to not find me. It was split into sections and small parts of it were dragged a couple of times a year because cars were known to disappear in there. Fisherman accidentally fell in. They wouldn't find me, but it would only verify what Rusty already knew. Something else had happened.

The area around the aqueduct was sparse desert. Not many hiding places. Maybe that's why I wasn't tied up, there was nowhere to run. If I thought I could run I might have tried but I knew I had to wait for my head to clear. I'd never make it the way I felt now. I felt the lump on my head. It was tender. I wouldn't be able to sleep on my left side for a while. I wondered how many times a person could be knocked out before permanent brain damage set in.

Gonzo paced around the Jeep, not really paying much attention to me but keeping tabs on me, too. The ride we were expecting was taking a long time. I began formulating a plan. The best hiding place available was also the riskiest; it was the aqueduct. People drowned in it every year. However, the water was murky and would give me cover. One problem with the aqueduct was the barbed wire and chain link fence that surrounded it. I could easily scale a six foot chain link fence. I had to climb over that and much more to make it through boot camp and police academy. The barbed wire at the top was the only problem.

The desert offered very little in the way of cover. Skimpy mesquite, Joshua trees and little bunches of yellow wildflowers was all the cover the desert offered. There was a shallow fold in the ground about fifty yards away. I was in uniform, which didn't help my chances of going unseen.

Further inventory revealed that Gonzo had taken my 9mm but he didn't know about the survival knife I kept in the Jeep. I looked around the floorboards for other useful things. I found a water bottle and a pen. I couldn't find my cell phone. On the side of my seat I wrote, "Rusty, it's a trick. Quit looking here." Then after considering the matter some more I added, "Ask Misty."

As time wore on Gonzo got tired of waiting and my head settled down to a nice, mellow throb. I decided it was time to take my chances. Barbed wire or not the aqueduct seemed like my best bet for camouflage. I was willing to risk the cuts to get away. I began shifting this way and that, picking at the roof of the Jeep, acting bored, making noise so that, when I opened the door, maybe the noise would blend in with the other noises Gonzo had been hearing. I waited until Gonzo was on the far side of the Jeep and then opened the door quietly. I sprinted to the fence and launched myself half way up it. I scrambled the last few feet and threw a leg over the barbed wire. I bullet zinged past my right ear and then a wild war cry filled the air as Gonzo closed in on me. I pulled myself over and dropped to the other side doing my best to ignore the bite of the barbed wire on my leg and then my forearm. My only goal was to get out of range of my captor. After I had the fence between me and him I sprinted down the aqueduct. Gonzo ran back to the Jeep and started it up. He threw it into gear and it charged through the fence. He pointed the Jeep down the aqueduct and hit the gas closing in on me quickly. I sprinted toward the water and tried a shallow dive. I wasn't sure how deep it was but I knew it was deep enough to swallow up whole cars. Oh, the water was cold! I had to force myself not to gasp when I hit it. The cold closed in on me and I drifted with the current staying under water as long as I could. The currents scared me. I knew the water gradually flowed down hill and the flow looked slow from up top but it had little whirlpools that pulled me down. My lungs were near bursting when I finally made my way up. I was trapped now. With Gonzo in the Jeep he'd be able to keep up with me easily. I couldn't swim upstream. I was going to hit a gate pretty soon and then I wouldn't be able to go farther. I also expected the currents at the gate to be strong. I didn't know what to do! When I surfaced it didn't take Gonzo long to find me and send a bullet into the water beside my head. One wrong move and I could be in trouble. I swam to the far side of the waterway but when I tried to get out the sides were slick with algae and weeds. Gonzo was yelling unintelligible curses and the water was sucking me farther and farther downstream. I knew I was trapped but I didn't have it in me to give up. I made another lunge at the far bank. Getting up what momentum I could I pushed for the most height I could reach. My hands gripped the dry cement and I pushed my arms down on it trying to get some kind of a purchase on the rough concrete bank. I slowly pulled myself up and out of the channel and onto dry ground. Bullets continued to fly around me. I wondered why Gonzo had a gun if he couldn't shoot. Give it to me, I thought, I'd have you on the ground in one shot!

Knowing it would be hard to turn the Jeep around I sprinted upstream until I found the place where the road cut across the channel. The Jeep *kathumped* its way up the other side on two flat tires. At least the barbed wire had accomplished something. When the Jeep hit the pavement there was no use running. I couldn't outrun the Jeep. Gonzo stomped up to me and grabbed me by the shirt front, then he dragged me over to the Jeep. He pulled my climbing rope out of the back and tied my hands. Then he tied the other end to the Jeep and took off. He drove as fast as the flat tires would let him. I ran after him until I couldn't keep up and finally the rope jerked me off my feet and I was dragged up and down the dirt road next to the aqueduct. He was furious. On one of his turnarounds I thought he was going to run me over. Finally, he drove back to our starting place and stopped. I just lay there, beaten, worn and bruised.

When Gonzo stood defiantly over me all I could manage to say was, "You're a lousy shot."

Red faced he said, "Don't you fucking move or I'm heading for Mexico, you in tow. I hear it's a hot, dry desert between here and Mexico. Tires or no, I'll take you for the ride of your life."

"You'd get caught, there's not enough back roads to get there, and the whole police department is looking for this Jeep."

I was wet and then dragged through the desert. It's no wonder Misty chose that time to drive up in her sparkling white Mercedes. She wasn't happy for several reasons.

"Damn it Gonzo, can't you follow directions just once! I told you she wasn't to be hurt."

"It's her own fault. She made a run for it."

"She's just a young woman. I would think a big, strong guy like you could handle a little thing like her."

He just glared at Misty. So she turned her attention to me.

"Well, it looks like our woods elf has changed into a desert rat. You expect me to let you in the car like that?"

"No, I wouldn't. I might bleed on your upholstery. I might smudge dirt on your door handles. Damn it, Misty, this isn't going to work."

"Oh, but it might. You should have seen the look on Rusty's face when the bus pulled away and you were gone."

"I hope you're ready for a real battle because I can be a royal pain in the ass," I warned her. "You aren't the first one to kidnap me but I think you might be the first to survive it. No, I take that back, I do remember one other guy that survived it. He's in jail right now. He'll be there for a while. So you see, I'm not new to this. You're going to lose this little game."

"I'd planned on giving you a lift to my penthouse and loaning you a room for a few days, under lock and key, of course. But I don't want you riding in my car like this. What am I going to do? Gonzo? Get rid of the Jeep. Let's go."

Gonzo pointed the Jeep through the downed fence and drove the Jeep to a precarious position over the water. He got out on the bank of the aqueduct, then he put the Jeep in neutral and gave it a hard push. Down into the murky waters it went, the current pulling it slightly downstream before it finally sank from view.

"Boy, when you make a break for it you don't do it halfway do you?" Misty said. "What did you do?"

"She vaulted the fricking fence and swam the aqueduct," Gonzo said.

"And your response was?" she asked Gonzo accusingly.

"Damn it, Misty, she's impossible to catch. If I didn't have the Jeep I couldn't have done it. If you're planning on keeping her in that penthouse you're going to have to tie her up or drug her or something. You don't have a chance if you leave her loose."

She looked at me crossly. "Did you give Gonzo a hard time?"

"Not as hard as I'm going to give you if you don't let me go."

"I may not let you go at all. Not if I get anywhere with your poor, anxious husband. Don't worry, I'll comfort him in his time of sorrow. But if I can convince him you're dead I'm afraid I might just have to make it true."

"He's going to be hard to convince. He's seen me go through things that would kill most people. You don't know what you've gotten yourself into when you abducted me. You're going to want to let me go just to get rid of me."

"Oh, but I didn't. Gonzo did. I'm just giving you a nice place to stay."

"It's called kidnapping no matter how you look at it. You pay for it, you're as guilty as Gonzo. Even if you know it's going on and you don't try to stop it, you're guilty. You're going to end up behind bars over this. Then you'll see what kind of a place the state provides for people like you."

"Big words for a person in your position. Gonzo, put her in the trunk."

Even the trunk was spotless. Gonzo left my hands tied and used more of the rope to tie my feet, but not before I cracked him in the jaw with a good swift kick. He almost slugged me because of that but Misty stopped him. Hands and feet bound, they closed the trunk and in the dark I could feel the car move. We didn't go far. I could tell we went back to town because of all the twists, turns, and stops. As I rode I worked at the knots. Gonzo wasn't too smart to use a climbing rope to tie me. They are made for good knot tying but they are also made to be untied when needed. Climbers don't want to have to fight their ropes while hanging off a cliff, so the rope is made to untie easily. I worked at the ropes with my fingers and teeth.

It was easy to tell when we arrived at our destination because they shut off the engine and I heard two car doors open and close, then footsteps leaving the car.

I yelled and nobody heard me. Where was I? I didn't really expect them to let me out in a busy place in broad daylight, but I did expect them to be careless and leave me in the trunk without thinking about what I might try. First I tried fiddling with the trunk latch. No good. I was really surprised to find out that Misty wanted me confined bad enough to cut her emergency trunk release. Gonzo must have reminded her that I could escape if they left it intact, but just the fact that she did cut it showed her determination level. I couldn't get my fingers up into the latch mechanism.

Next I tried the exit through the back seats method. I knew many cars had fold down seats that allowed for an expanded trunk area. So, I examined the back of the trunk as much as I could in the dark and located the spot where I would put a latch if I were making a fold down seat. Misty is going to kill me, I thought as I gave the spot a good hard kick. In academy we were taught how to kick a door in. I have to admit, I never got enough weight behind my kick to actually do it. But I had the theory down. I did some serious damage to some doorjambs but in a police situation I'd have to turn the door kicking over to a partner. Back seats of cars, I thought, should be easier. Should be. I quickly found out Misty could use a bigger trunk. I could only move my foot about a foot away from the back seat and I couldn't get much momentum up in the little space I had to work with.

The heat of the day began to dissipate and the cool of the evening was a relief. I hadn't had water all day and my throat was parched. When I heard footsteps on gravel I tensed, waiting. I was planning to kick the trunk open and surprise them but my mind was changed instantly when I saw a tiny spray can pointed into the trunk. I immediately turned my back to the can and held my breath. It was just an instinctive reaction. I knew what that stuff felt like. I didn't want it in my face.

"Aw, Cassidy, you're no fun," Misty said.

"You don't want that stuff all over your car. It's oily and hard to clean off."

"It is?" she asked and started reading the label. I jumped up and grabbed the can still in her hand and pushed the button. I didn't give her much but her reaction was instantaneous and natural. She screamed, then fell to her knees and started rubbing her eyes, exactly the wrong thing to do.

"Ahhhh," she screeched, "Gonzo!" I looked around for Gonzo and the pepper spray. It was on the ground in front of Misty. No time for a second try. I clambered out of the trunk and dashed toward a nearby vacant lot, but Gonzo was on top of me in an instant. I elbowed him in the side and he twisted my arm behind my back. I kicked him in the shin and he eased up but he was more powerful than me.

"I told you I was a royal pain in the ass!" I said as he restrained me.

Misty was on the ground.

"Calm down," I told her. "You're only making it worse. Just wait it out. It'll ease up in about half an hour."

"Easy for you to say. You've never been pepper sprayed!"

"Yes, I have. You're lucky I only gave you a little. I know what a lot feels like. They don't go easy on you in the Marines."

"You're mean!" Misty screamed.

"Wait a minute," I said. "You're the kidnapper, but I'm mean?"

"Yes!"

"I don't think I have a whole lot to worry about if you'll let me pepper spray you."

I think Gonzo was beginning to see the entertainment value in his job.

"My outfit is ruined! And my manicure! Look! Oh, ouch! I can't even look. I can't even open my eyes. You've blinded me! You bitch! You're going to pay for this."

Whatever it was it was worth it. I didn't think she was that determined to have Rusty. A few outfits and a few manicures and she'd run for the hills. Too bad I couldn't do more damage to her car.

"We were just trying to get you upstairs as inconspicuously as possible," Misty said.

"Pepper spray? Inconspicuous? You've got to be kidding."

"I thought it would paralyze you. I'm going to get my money back!"

"You do that," I said.

"Gonzo, I guess we're going to have to get rough again."

He raised the gun butt and I ducked. I tried to grab his arm but he brought it down again and I fell back, stunned.

"If we meet anybody, she's a passed out drunken friend," Misty said to Gonzo.

"A dusty, bleeding cop friend?" Gonzo asked.

"Let's hurry."

Gonzo tossed me over his shoulder and headed for a building.

"At least *look* like you care," Misty admonished him, so he set me down and picked me up again. I could barely think. My brain was scrambled. Oh man, but I was going to be miserable. Every movement brought weird light patterns to my closed eyes and explosions of pain in my head. Even the movement of the elevator hurt and when Gonzo tossed me on the bed in the penthouse I nearly screamed. I lay where he'd tossed me and let myself drift into semi consciousness. It was all I could do. Anything else required movement or thinking.

"Cassidy?" A gentle shaking. Pain exploding behind my eyes. "Cassidy, you're scaring me. You've been like this for almost a day." A day? "Cassidy?" Then to Gonzo, "Bring her food and water. And stay at the door."

Time went by and after a while Gonzo came in with a tray of food but didn't speak to me. The thought of eating made me feel sick. The smells wafting over the bed from the tray made my stomach churn uncomfortably. I knew I should try to eat. I cracked my eyes open and when the dim light slipped in fireworks went off in my brain again. I forced my eyes to stay open. Maybe things would calm down. I looked around the room. No windows, one door leading to a bathroom, one door leading out, Gonzo was on the other side. I rolled over testing the effects of my movements. My head pounded but not as bad as it had yesterday. Okay, first things first, the bathroom, for two reasons; one was obvious. I also wanted to check out any escape options. I kept a hand on the wall as I walked. It was the only way to stay upright. The bathroom was an impossible escape route. No windows, no vents large enough. I was surprised Misty had actually thought this far ahead. The bathroom inspection took a lot out of me. I lay on the bed again and sleep took me. I woke to voices and the clamor of someone entering the room in a hurry. Misty sat on the bed. Gonzo walked in.

"She got up for just a minute today." He looked at the tray. "She didn't touch the food."

"Cassidy?" Misty said. Did I hear a touch of concern? "It's cruel. This thing I've done. I can't watch it."

"I've had worse."

"I didn't mean you. It's Rusty. He's inconsolable. What can I do?"

"You're asking me what you should do? You're kidding."

That made her mad. I'd barely moved since she came in the room. I had to stay very still in order to talk to her at all. But then I thought I might be able to use Misty to give Rusty subtle clues. What would Rusty associate with me?

"What does he like?" she asked.

"He's a guy. He likes anything."

I had to make her think she was manipulating me.

"A car, you think he'd like a car?"

"You're kidding. You want to buy him a car?" What kind of a car would Rusty associate with me that wasn't a Jeep or an Explorer? "He's a guy, you know what guys like."

"But there must be something. Something he's driven before. Something a friend has. Something he's had his eye on."

"He likes his Explorer."

"Something sporty and powerful."

"An electric blue BMW Roadster convertible."

Her eyes brightened as the idea hit home. When Rusty and I first met I'd had the old, tan Jeep Wrangler and my deceased husband's blue BMW Roadster. One look, one drive and he'd be transported back in time.

"Does a friend of his have a roadster?"

"Yeah, Jack."

"Well," she said. "That was easier than I thought it would be. I thought Gonzo would have to persuade you to cooperate. Eat something. Now, we need to get you out of this uniform. What size do you wear?"

"Five. Or seven."

"I wish you could see the news. Your Jeep made quite a splash and when they tied the Jeep to the missing deputy things got real tense. You're famous!"

"Again? Shit."

"Well, I'm off. I think I'll go shopping. I love car shopping. They run a check to see if I qualify and then they let me test drive everything on the lot. Electric blue. To match his eyes? He seems more like a brown guy. What do you think? Doesn't brown just suit him?"

"His Explorer's blue."

"Right," she said pursing her lips. "Now eat something or Gonzo might have to make you."

She paraded out, happy with her plan.

I looked at the plate of food. It was cold but I considered that my fault. I sat quietly for a while until my head settled down and then reached gingerly for some fruit, since it was supposed to be cold anyway. I could only manage a few bites. My stomach recoiled when I tried to eat too much.

Later in the day Gonzo appeared with a bag and inside was a couple of outfits. They weren't what I would have chosen but I couldn't complain either. This was the first time I'd had a kidnapper buy me new clothes. Gonzo stood there with a smirk on his face, especially when I took out the fresh underwear.

"Misty wants the uniform disposed of," he said and crossed his arms over his chest. He leaned against the wall, waiting.

Okay, I could take a hint. I took the bag of clothes and headed for the bathroom.

"Nah uh, here," he said, pointing to the floor.

We had a short stare down. He shrank back but didn't give in.

"You want to fight?" I said.

"Hah! You've got to be kidding."

"No, look, I'll make you a deal. We'll put the clothes in the bathroom. And we'll start over there," I said pointing to an open area of the bedroom. "If you block me successfully from the bathroom, I'll change out here. If I make it to the bathroom, I get to dress in privacy."

He was enjoying this little game so he motioned for me to put the clothes in the bathroom. I went in, set the bag down on the counter and quickly slammed and locked the door. He rammed it from the other side.

"I wouldn't break the door in if I were you. You'll have the wrath of Misty down on you!" I yelled out to him. He backed off so I took a long shower. I was dusty and grimy and I had to pick gravel out of my elbows and knees because of the dragging. My head still hurt and if I turned quickly I had to grab a wall for support but I was enjoying letting Gonzo stew out there. I felt better when I was clean again so I took my time drying my hair, fluffing as much as I could with my fingers. There wasn't much I could do without a hairbrush but at least I felt better. As I dried my hair I looked around. No escape was possible from the bathroom. There was not even a skylight.

I put on the clothes Misty had sent. We had different taste but she had at least kept that in mind. She'd sent jeans and blouses. Not dressy, fitted blouses like she would wear but comfortable, easygoing blouses. The underwear was conservative but attractive. The bra didn't fit right but I wore it and hand washed my old one.

When I came out Gonzo was still standing there. He held his hand out for the uniform.

"Clever," he said.

When I handed him the uniform he grabbed my wrist instead. "Now, how about that fight you promised me?"

"Let me go," I demanded.

I would have fought him if it had come right down to it. I imagined it to be like my boxing matches with Tom, only more painful. Gonzo didn't let go so I pulled back enough so he was concentrating on my left arm full of clothes, then I kicked him in the shin with my steel toed police shoes and hit him with a right hook, snapping his head back.

"Why you little..." he said smirking. He released my wrist and the uniform fell to the floor.

I backed off and assumed a fighting stance just out of his reach. We circled each other watching for an opening. I wasn't going to attack unless he did. I had fought Tom enough to learn I didn't have the power to hurt a guy but if he was coming towards me I was quick enough to get out of the way and I could use his momentum to add power to my hits. And so Gonzo and I danced around the room, me ducking, getting in a strike here and a kick there, him basically tearing the place up in his haste to get at me. He charged me and left a fist sized hole in the wall. I dodged and came around behind him and shoved him further in. His arm disappeared up into the wall and he yelled. Who knew what was inside that wall? Nails, splinters, wall studs? He pulled his arm out and charged me, blood flowing from the backs of two fingers. Since he had all this momentum built up I let him have it in the side with a roundhouse kick. He doubled over gripping his side with his arms, his fingers swelling as I watched. I ran to the bedroom door and he was after me in an instant. I flung it opened and dashed into the apartment beyond. I was three feet from launching myself through a window when he tackled me and I hit my head on the windowsill. Damn it, here I go again, I thought, as I saw the wood coming up to meet my face.

I woke up with two black eyes.

"I'm impressed. Two for two. I didn't think you could do that," Misty said.

"Two for two?"

"Your two black eyes for Gonzo's two broken fingers. Try to stay in one piece for me, please?"

"Tell him next time he wants me to change clothes in front of him I'll break something else. And why should you care if I stay in one piece? You kidnap me and then put Gonzo in charge of me, what do you expect? I hate to break it to you but you didn't kidnap a wimp. I nearly got away. Just a few more feet and I'd have been out that window."

"And seven stories off the ground. You don't want to jump out that window. The elevator is the only way down."

"I don't believe you," I said. "You're just saying that to discourage me from trying that again."

"Go look for yourself," she said.

I followed her into the living area of the apartment. I looked out the window. It really was seven stories up but it wasn't seven stories to the next level. It was only two. It still would have been an awfully long fall.

I took note of the layout of the part of the apartment I could see. It was a large room furnished with expensive furniture. A wet bar stood in one corner and a long dining table filled the bar side of the room. A living room set filled another corner. A fancy chandelier dominated the room. All the wood was a rich dark color. Floral arrangements were displayed on the dining table and the coffee table. It didn't feel like a home though. It felt like a hotel. None of the furniture looked sat on. The tables and shelves looked like a maid dusted them daily. It was too stiff and formal, too rich and fancy. No normal person would live in a place like this. Large, heavy doors separated the living area from…from what? What was beyond those doors? Misty's room? A hallway or elevator?

I ran to the double doors and flung one open. I dashed through into a small room. An elevator stood at one end, no call button, only a place to slide a card.

"Cassidy, come here. There's no way out."

"Then why have Gonzo guard me?" I asked.

"So the rest of the apartment doesn't get damaged like your room did. So you won't jump out of seven story windows. So if my plan works he can dispose of you. Besides, Gonzo is rather useful."

"Where do you find a guy who will beat up women? Most guys could do anything *except* be mean to a woman."

"Gonzo was an escort I hired to make my husband jealous. We got to talking. He changed professions. But he really is a very good escort when one is needed. He looks awesome in a tux. Makes a believable limo driver."

"Is anything in your life real?" I asked. "What do you have that you can be proud of?"

She started to answer, then realized how shallow she'd sound, and perhaps things weren't as real as she wished them to be.

There was a knock on the heavy wood doors.

"Come in, Gonzo," Misty said. "I have some errands to run. I'll be out most of the evening. Order some dinner and keep Cassidy in her room. Cassidy, is there anything you need?"

"A hairbrush," I said, since I knew she wouldn't bring Rusty. "Did you find a car?"

"Yeah, it'll be delivered tomorrow."

"If he asks why you bought it just tell him Rule 642."

"Six hundred and forty two? Is that some police code?"

"No, it's Rusty code. Rule 642 says that if something is just made for you, you have to buy it. It usually applies to outfits but I guess it could apply to cars, too."

"Sounds like my kind of a rule," she said. "Where should I take him for dinner?"

"You're taking *my* husband out for dinner and you want advice on where to go? Now that's tacky! Okay, take him to Zeke's. You *do* eat pizza, don't you?"

"Of course I eat pizza!" she said, offended that I thought pizza was beneath her.

That night I was so lonely, so bored and despondent. I picked at my dinner and went to bed early. There was no use staying up if I was just going to think about Misty and Rusty. Instead I thought about the layout of the apartment. I considered the elevator from every imaginable angle. How could I get access to the elevator? The only way was with a key card. How could I finagle a keycard out of someone without them knowing it? I fell asleep with a plan half formed in my mind.

It was a troubled night, loneliness tempered with hopelessness left me tossing and turning. I was searching for Rusty. His tracks went on and on. I knew where to find him but when I got there he was gone. I missed him. I ached for him. His familiar hug. My arms ached for it. My feet were tired from walking, my legs were leaden and I just wanted to curl up under a tree and sleep but my desperation drove me on. I knew I could find him. I needed to. I was close to tears, stumbling from place to place in my dreams when Misty burst into the room in a rage. The dream dissolved and I bolted upright. She was standing there unsteadily, my 9mm handgun pointed at me. Gonzo ran in from the other room.

"Misty, put that thing down. You don't know how to use it," he said.

"Get out of here!" she shrieked, pointing the gun at Gonzo. Gonzo backed off, hands over his head, his two fingers in a brace, his hand in a splint. That's about the time I realized Gonzo couldn't shoot right handed anymore! In spite of my immediate danger it was a realization that brought hope. "Cassidy! I swear I'm going to kill you with my own two hands! He'll never have me. He almost hit me! When I suggested dinner he got angry and…"

"And it looked like a terrible storm brewing and his voice was like thunder."

She stopped, dumbstruck.

"Yes! That's it exactly. How can you stand it?"

"He won't hit you. He's the kindest man I know. I've only seen him angry when people hurt me."

"But all I did was suggest dinner! A man has to eat! The only way he's going to put you behind him is if they find a body. That's it. And I can't do it! You're too nice to me."

She frantically paced back and forth, knowing what had to be done, unable to do it. I had to buy time. And I had to offer Misty some hope so I threw in my wad. It would make Rusty angry again but it would eventually tip him off.

"You haven't tried the gentle approach. Tell him you aren't asking for much, that you know he's preoccupied. Tell him you only need a *few minutes*. Try cheesecake." Was I a mean cruel person or what? I wasn't sure who I was being mean to, Misty or Rusty. Sooner or later he'd get the impression that Misty was telling him something and then he'd pay attention to her and when that happened she would brighten up considerably. "If he gets stressed out and needs a break suggest a trip to the hideout. If he asks where that is tell him to hike out of Creekside Campground two miles and turn up a canyon where the stream crosses the trail. The hideout is two miles up the canyon at the big pine tree. He'd love camping there. There's no people, fresh water, a nice camping place, rocks to climb. He likes rock climbing."

"Why are you doing this? Why are you letting me makes moves on your husband?"

"Honestly? I'm buying time. Nobody wants to be blown away. As long as I have information you can use you'll pry it out of me. So it pays for me to dish it out."

"Why don't you just kill me? I'm sure you could manage it."

"No, I won't kill you unless my life depends on it or the lives of others depend on it. I have killed before. I hate it. Ask Rusty. It sends me into everlasting guilt trips. I couldn't kill you unless I absolutely had to."

"What about Gonzo? He beat you. He could have killed you."

"He wasn't going to kill me and risk the wrath of Misty. Our fight was because I tricked him. He brought the clothes you sent and was going to make me change clothes in front of him so I challenged him to a fight. When I tricked him out of the fight, and out of watching me dress, he got mad and pressed the fight issue. But he wouldn't have killed me without orders from you."

"Look at you. You're scratched and bruised and have two lumps on your head and two black eyes and you still have a good attitude. How can you do that?"

"It doesn't pay to have a bad attitude. It muddles the thinking. The only way to think clearly is to have a good firm grasp on the situation, so I try to do that. I think my way out."

"Well, it worked tonight. Maybe I'll have better luck tomorrow. Maybe I can pick up the car tomorrow. They had to bring one up from L.A."

"It's too early for the car. Go for the few minutes first and work your way up to the car. If you cook you could try mayojar steak and chocolate chip cookies with no nuts. But start small and work your way up."

When I thought about it I was amazed how many little things Rusty and I shared between just the two of us. I treasured those things. Little things. Minutes and cookies and hugs on the big brown couch.

The next day I got into it again with Gonzo. I was in my room bored to tears and I could hear him watching TV in the next room. The news. The news about me.

"Gonzo!" I called. "Can I watch, too? I just want to know what the outside world thinks of all this. I can't get away. I already tried."

He opened the door, looked me up and down wondering if he could trust me, then pointed to the couch.

"If you hear the elevator, scoot!" he warned.

I sat and waited for the news team to get back to the story about my disappearance.

"Three days after Reserve Deputy Cassidy Michaels vanished while on stake out, she is still missing. An anonymous tip led the police to her Jeep Wrangler, which had crashed through a fence and landed in the California Aqueduct, but her husband, Detective Rusty Michaels, has doubts about the crash's validity. When pushed for a conclusive answer he refuses to comment or declares the information detrimental to solving the case. Her friends all have faith the young woman will be found."

"She's out there somewhere," Landon said resolutely.

"What are her chances? A young woman abducted by violent criminals?"

"I feel sorry for the criminals," Landon said. "They don't know what they've got. Cassidy will pull through. She'll find a way. She's a survivor."

And Kelly, "I have every bit of faith in that kid that a guy can possibly have. Cassidy will persevere. She'll win. I'm counting on it." He paused, like he heard something and needed to identify it. His expression softened. Then he looked directly at the camera and said, "Cass, Kiddo, we're counting on you. If you can see this, just know we won't stop. We'll find you. We *will* find you, if you don't find us first."

I swallowed a big lump in my throat. But that was nothing. They put my mom on and asked her about me. I had to listen to the Reader's Digest version of my life. "Cassidy is a unique individual. If those people think they know what they are doing they better think again. Cassidy sees chances where none exist. She *will* find a way out of this."

I almost couldn't stand it when Patrick pushed his way through the throng of reporters. The presence of a little kid made everybody stop and stare. Patrick had a commanding presence even at seven.

"My Aunt Cassidy is the wiliest, sneakiest person ever born. She finds people who are lost. She would even find the bad guys if they were lost.

She… she can't be gone. She's one of the good guys. She's going to come back. She has to. Too many people need her."

They put Mom back on. "If anyone… anyone has seen Cassidy, call, *please* call. We can use all the information we can get."

"You sure have an odd lot of friends. They have a lot of faith in you. Should I call?" asked Gonzo.

"You know," I said. "The ironic thing about all this is that Rusty had a card to get into this place. Misty gave it to him but he was afraid I'd get mad at Misty and pay her a visit so he shredded it."

"It was a different card. She had to switch hotels when we abducted you. We had to find one with an escape proof room."

"There is no escape proof room. I'll get away eventually. Like they said, all I need is to spot my break."

"You better hope that comes before Misty throws another of her little temper tantrums. I thought she was going to shoot you last time."

"It's going to get worse before it gets better."

"Go back to your room. You don't want Misty to catch you out here. I'll be back in a second."

I went to my room and pulled the door closed, but I held the door knob so it wouldn't lock, and waited. When Gonzo heard my door close he stepped into another room and I silently exited the room again closing the door behind me and slid under the sofa. I was glad the fancy furniture had a little dust ruffle around the bottom edge. Gonzo came back and sat in the stiff-backed chair next to my bedroom door. He was bored. I didn't blame him. If I wasn't worried about getting caught I'd have been bored too. As it was I tensely waited for a break to present itself. Light from the windows helped my mood immensely. I could feel the passage of time. I wasn't trapped in limbo, like I was in the windowless bedroom.

Gonzo sat, he paced, he sent text messages on his cell phone. Finally, he got up and walked to a telephone and called room service. Without looking at a menu he rattled off an order for two and went back to his chair. Half an hour later I heard the ding of the elevator, then there was a knock on the door, and a young man called out, "Room service!"

Gonzo walked to the door and opened it. He didn't let the person in but took the two plates and set them on the coffee table, then signed the receipt. I was tempted to come out of hiding and plea for help but I worried about what the delivery boy might do. I didn't want to endanger him. I knew I was in for a beating if I was caught outside the room, so I watched from under the dust ruffle. As the man turned to leave, a plastic card fell to the floor behind him. It landed in the doorway and Gonzo closed the door behind the man concealing the card from view. My chance. If I could get to it. It called to me from under the door but I had to wait.

Gonzo went to the coffee table and picked up my plate and took it into my room. He'd know I was gone as soon as he opened the bedroom door. I slid out of hiding and shoved Gonzo into the room. I quickly pulled the bedroom door closed behind him and locked it, then I dove for the keycard. There was banging and yelling from the bedroom as I ran out the front door and into the little hallway in front of the elevator. I pushed the card into the reader and pulled it out, then held the front door of the apartment closed while I waited for the elevator to return to the top floor. Seconds stretched until I thought they'd snap and my world would fall apart. The elevator dinged and the doors opened. I watched and counted and let go of the apartment door a half second before I thought the elevator doors would close. I sprinted for the elevator with Gonzo on my heels. He grabbed me by the back of my shirt as the elevator doors were closing and yanked me back. I turned on him and sent a fist up into his nose. While he was bent over, holding his nose I kicked the back of his knees in. I was afraid to call the elevator again. So far he didn't know I had a keycard. I stuffed it deep into a pocket and took my chances with Gonzo. He was furious. When his nose had settled down to just a nice steady stream of blood he grabbed me by the arm and dragged me back into the apartment. He took me to the bedroom and shoved me against the wall, then he pinned me down.

"I told you this room wasn't escape proof," I told him.

"It is if I make you incapable to escaping," he growled. "You have been nothing but trouble for me. You're going to stay in this room until hell freezes over." He punched me in the stomach. "You're going to stay here until pigs fly!" I took a one-two to the head. "You'll stay until I say so." The punches went on and on until I collapsed and quit moving. All the rest of that day I lay on the floor. When Misty came home there was no need to rant at me. She demanded to know what happened. She gave Gonzo an order and he lifted me and put me on the bed, then turned and walked out locking the door behind him. For two days I crawled to the bathroom and back and rested. I was in no shape to escape now. Gonzo was right. I'd stay.

In the late evening Misty would come in and visit with me. She was torn. She hated what Gonzo had done but at the same time she talked about how she thought the only way to get Rusty to turn around was if they found my body, proving to him that I was gone. Rusty's devotion to me was touching to her, too. She wanted that for herself. She had never known a person who was loyal and kind hearted and what she saw of it she craved.

I continued to watch for my chance.

Finally, a day came when Misty decided it was time for me to go. Either it was because she thought she'd won and I needed to be out of the way before she could close in, or she knew Rusty would never give up his search. Whatever the cause, Gonzo came in and ordered me to stand before him. My clothes were spotted with his blood and mine. They were wrinkled from being slept in night after night. He ordered me to change clothes. When he didn't move, I glared at him, "You want to fight?" I asked.

He threatened me with his fist but then turned on his heel and stalked out.

When he came back in we stood toe-to-toe taking stock of each other.

"We're going downstairs. You let out one peep, even one and I'll kill you."

"Then what's to lose? You're going to kill me anyway."

"Okay, you let out a peep and I'll kill you and anybody you talk to. We're going for a little ride, and you aren't coming back. Got it?"

"Got it."

Misty wasn't there when we left. Gonzo guided me to the elevator and we rode it down to a little lobby. A guard waved at us in the lobby.

"Hi! Gonzo, have a good day!" he called out.

"You too," Gonzo called back. When we got to the parking lot he said, "Black Hummer."

He took out handcuffs and cuffed my hands together.

"I saved these from your uniform. I thought they might come in handy, especially after I had to fend you off. I don't want any trouble. I've got your gun and I know how to use it."

Gonzo drove for a long time. At first he drove around town. He carefully avoided getting near police cars.

"Your cop friends have been on the hunt," he said. "What is it about you that all your friends won't accept your death without proof?"

"They know me too well. They've seen me overcome obstacles that they thought were impossible. But I'm used to trouble by now. It's just part of my life, so I deal with it."

"How many guys do you figure are out there?"

"Looking for me?"

"Yeah."

"Besides the police? I have no idea. They all have lives, too, you know. But if Rusty had a clue they'd all be quick to jump to his aid."

He thought about that as he drove around. Then he said, "Aw hell," and headed north on Highway 14. In Mojave he took a turnoff east and drove until the desert got as barren as possible. He found a dirt road and drove until it ran out and then he drove some more, bouncing over the rough desert cross country. I was surprised how far he got off road. It must have been twenty miles of dirt road and at least ten miles off road, through the desert.

"I thought the purpose of killing me was for the police to find a body," I pointed out.

"Sorry, I thought I'd give you a chance. I can't shoot you. No matter what Misty wants. I'm dropping you off and I'm out of here."

"Do you have any water? Any water at all?"

"Nope, sorry. I'll be watching the news."

"If you're out of here, anyway, can I have my gun? I've had it since I was a kid. I can shoot a rabbit from fifty paces."

He threw the pistol as far out into the desert as he could.

"Good luck," he said removing the cuffs. "If I'm to believe half the stories, you'll be on tonight's news, safe and sound and Misty will be behind bars."

It didn't quite work out like that. I still had a long, rough walk ahead of me. I thanked my lucky stars it wasn't summer. First, I found my gun. I checked the magazine and found I had six shots left. I shook all the sand out of it hoping none was lurking in some critical part of the mechanism. It was a chance I would have to take. I put myself in survival mode. A firm determination set in. I bet Landon would have said I turned into Dangerous Tracker Woman. In my mind it was just a mindset, watch for anything to eat, anything with moisture in it, conserve energy, go the maximum distance with the minimum amount of exertion. And above all else, keep on keeping on.

In my line of work I see a lot of people make one critical mistake in the situation I was in. They say, "Oh no, I'm lost in a barren desert. Let's see, I know Mojave is to the southwest so I'll hike toward Mojave." Then they turn out to be five degrees off and walk right by Mojave, without seeing it.

I want to take these people and tell them, "Stick to the known road! It's a long slow death to miss a town by five degrees!"

So I stuck to the known road. I tracked myself back to the Hummer's tread and followed it back. I knew I had to follow the off road portion of the walk in the heat of the day but once I reached the dirt road I could rest and hike at night. I wished I'd kept better track of the mileage on the Hummer so I'd know how far it was to the road. It was far, I knew that. And the dirt road was longer than that. I walked slowly and evenly, conserving energy. When I found shade I stopped. If I felt myself get tired I rested. I lay on top of bushes so air could circulate around me. The heat of the ground could suck all the energy out of me if I let it. I saw a cactus and longed for my survival knife. I thought about using an article of clothing to wrap around the cactus and pull part of it off but I knew my clothes would be full of cactus needles. I needed my clothes as much as I needed water. They insulated me from both heat and cold. I continued until I saw a barrel cactus. There was water in there, but how could I get it? I refused to part with any of the meager belongings I had. Then

I happened to think that my shoelaces could be fashioned into a saw. I unstrung them and tied the two ends together. I wrapped the laces around the base of the cactus and sawed back and forth, back and forth, pulling all the while. At first I made very little progress but when the skin on the far side gave way it went quicker. When the top of the cactus peeled away I reached in and pulled out the pithy inside of the plant and chewed on it. Then, I pulled out as much as I could fit in the tails of my shirt and tied the ends up around it. I grumbled at the time it took to lace my shoes again and cursed the sun beating down on my head.

I continued on, watching for more cactus, sharp rocks that might be useful for cutting into the cactus and places where water might be found. I had little hope of finding water. If there was water, there would be green plants, and there wasn't a spot of green between me and the horizon.

Suddenly a rabbit bolted! I reached for my pistol and remembered I didn't have the holster. Rats. I pulled out the pistol and kept my eyes on the rabbit until it slowed and froze beneath a thin mesquite. I stalked it slowly until I had a good line on it. I didn't want to waste my shots and I wanted to preserve as much of the meat as I could. I took careful aim and squeezed off a shot. The rabbit jerked in the air and fell, dead. I only half celebrated. It increased my chances for survival, but I felt sorry for the animal and I didn't look forward to raw meat. I didn't have a knife to skin the rabbit with and I didn't have anything to build a fire with so raw meat was my only option. Raw meat and cactus. I hated what I had to do. I felt like an animal myself as I held the rabbit down with one foot and pulled up on its leg until it tore open. I tried to think of it like rare steak. I could stand rare steak so I psyched myself up and ate as much of the meat as I could. It was messy, bloody, but the blood had nourishment in it, too. When I'd eaten what I could I stuffed the rabbit's hind legs through the belt loop of my jeans and hiked along with the soft body bumping against my leg.

I marched, just like I had in the Marines, but more subdued. I kept up the cadence and the miles gradually passed by beneath my feet.

As the heat set in I became thankful for my uniform shoes. If I didn't have those on I'd have been wearing moccasins and the heat would have been harder to deal with. I also wouldn't have had shoelaces to work with if I'd been wearing my moccasins. Little things can have big consequences in survival mode.

Toward evening my steps began faltering. I tried adjusting my attitude, finding that next level of determination. It worked for a while but I finally had to stop and rest. I looked at the tire tracks through the desert wondering how much farther it was to the road. I really needed to see the road. The road was hope.

After a rest and a cactus snack, I felt better so I started walking again. When the sun set I kept on, enjoying the coolness. As long as I could see the tire tracks I kept walking. All night I walked through the desert and I finally hit the road in the wee hours of the morning. If I had the energy I would have done a happy dance but I was just quietly relieved. I walked until the sun rose and then I looked for another cactus. I was lucky and located one next to a shadowy place so I bedded down in the shadows, my face towards the ground to avoid getting blistered by the sun. I slept as much of the day as I could and then sawed open the cactus and replenished my supply. The cactus didn't offer much moisture but it was all I had. I was starving, but I didn't swallow the cactus. It was too rough. I chewed the pith and spit it out knowing the moisture I got out of it contained some nourishment. I ate more rabbit, but I didn't like it. I had to force myself to eat it to keep my energy up.

If I hadn't been starving and thirsty and weak I would have enjoyed hiking in the desert at night. As I was, all I could do was keep marching. I knew when exhaustion was near because I lost the beat and when that happened I had to rest.

I held a small, quiet celebration when I realized I'd been out in the desert for two days and still had energy to walk. My steps were weaker, to be sure, but they were still steady. My dad would have been proud of me, out in the old west, making do like the pioneers. I imagined my conversation with Chase when this was all over. Chase grew up in the desert. He knew how hostile it was. He'd want the whole story.

I kept my mind busy. If I only looked at the situation, I grew despondent. I wanted to survive this so I could teach Patrick how to cope in a similar situation. I wanted to see Rusty. Oh, how I wanted to see Rusty. I wanted him to know I was okay. I wanted to feel his arms around me. That's when I knew everything would be all right, when I felt those arms. I saw myself slipping back to a melancholy state and forced my brain into a different process. Thinking could improve a situation or it could drag you down. I changed the subject. Elan. I wondered what Elan would do in my shoes. He was used to land more barren than this.

Again, I hiked through the night. I'd begun stumbling more, even in the cool of the night. A couple of times I hit the dirt hard and I woke up wondering how long I'd been there. Minutes? Hours? I needed help but I knew help wasn't coming. I chewed on more cactus. Pieces of it were crushed in my falls and the precious moisture had been squeezed into my shirt.

My thinking became fuzzier. My concentration was dimming. I kept thinking I could see lights off in the distance. Lights. I kept walking to the lights and after a few hours I was certain they were lights. How far? How far away? I had to force myself not to run. Running would use precious resources and my energy was flagging. I had to conserve. Just keep calm. Just keep walking. Just keep chewing. Keep walking… keep walking… the sun rose but the lure of the highway was too much. I couldn't stop now. I'd seen the lights. The source of the lights was out there somewhere. The land shimmered ahead of me and still I kept on. I should have stopped. I should have slept but I didn't. I reached for another chunk of cactus and realized it was gone. Shoot. I watched for another cactus but it was miles between cacti and I didn't want to leave the road. Off and on through the last three days I had thought about the dirt road and where it might lead and why cars were never on it. I decided it led to a ranch out in the boonies. But why didn't the residents ever go anywhere? I had put my hopes on someone picking me up on their way into town but nobody went past.

At last I noticed I could *hear* the highway. It had to be close if I could hear it! And then I could see it. Cars and trucks zipping by. My thoughts were so muddled I almost stumbled out onto the pavement. I stood watching the busyness. It was overwhelming after the stillness of the desert. The noise, the speed, the sheer number of cars. I needed one of those cars. I needed help. I waved my hands over my head trying to flag someone down, lost my balance and fell over backwards. I got up and waved more frantically. Many cars passed before a big rig pulled over. It took him a quarter mile to stop so I staggered after the truck. A burly driver with a two day old beard hopped out and made his way down the shoulder of the road. He stared at me in disbelief.

"Lady, where's your car?" he asked.

"Don't have one," I replied. "Need water. I haven't had water in days. Please tell me you have water."

"Where'd you come from?"

"Three days walk. That way," I said pointing.

He led me to his cab. It looked a long way up. He handed me a half full water bottle. I forced myself not to gulp it down.

"Where are you trying to get to?"

"Joshua Hills police."

"Joshua Hills is fifty miles away."

"I know. I'll get there. The first thirty miles is always the toughest."

"Climb in," he said. "I can at least take you to Joshua Hills. Do you know where the station is?"

"Yeah."

I barely had the strength to climb into his truck cab. It was smoky and littered with wrappers of various sorts but he cleared a place for me to sit.

"You are either nuts or you have some story!" the trucker said.

"Yeah, maybe both," I answered.

He looked at me wondering if he should trust me. I thought that was ironic. A big guy like him worried about picking up a half dead woman.

"Have you seen the news lately? Say, three days ago? Maybe a week?" I asked.

He was driving but he took time to get a good look at me. It wasn't a very good look, anyway. I was curled into a ball in his seat, my head cradled by the seatbelt, half dozing, weak.

"Damn, lady, you aren't that missing cop are you?"

"I'm a tracker. I'm only half a cop. But, yeah, I'm Cassidy Michaels."

"Woohoo!" he said. "Boy have I got a story to tell now! You know, when you're on the road day after day a little story goes a long way to breaking the monotony of it all. All the truck drivers I met wouldn't bet a wooden nickel you'd be found and now here you are, in my truck. You'll have to tell me what happened to you. I need the rest of the story."

I started telling him about it leaving out the back story and starting with the abduction but as I went along I realized I was mumbling and I didn't know what I'd said. Things got fuzzy and I drifted off. I vaguely felt the twists and turns as the truck came into town.

"Where's this police station?" the trucker asked, then followed my slurred directions until he pulled up beside the building. I pulled the handle on the door and nearly toppled out. I made a grab for the seatbelt, still buckled around me. When I had my balance, I unbuckled and slid from the cab, landing on shaky legs. The driver ran around the front of the truck and walked with me toward the front doors. Activity in the lobby froze as I forced my feet to carry me towards the station. Through the big plate glass windows I could see into the lobby. The front desk clerk quickly picked up the phone and seconds later I saw Schroeder stride quickly into the lobby and hurry out the front doors. I stumbled and caught myself with my hand and continued on. Several cops hurried out right behind him.

"It's okay," I rasped. "He just gave me a lift into town."

"Come, tell me what happened," Schroeder said to both of us.

I shook my head, "Food… and water. And Rusty."

"Rusty's being called right now. Come in. We'll find you something."

I managed to get my feet working again and followed Schroeder into a meeting room. I sat in one of the little plastic desks and put my head down on my folded arms. Schroeder set a paper cup of water on the desk and knelt down beside me. From my level he asked, "Who did this to you?"

"Misty paid for it. Gonzo did it."

"Gonzo?"

"Works for Misty. Short for Gonzolani."

"Where are they? Do you know?"

"Hotel. Somewhere with a penthouse on the seventh floor."

"In town?"

"Yeah."

"You don't know where?"

"No, I was locked in a trunk."

"You didn't get like this sitting in a penthouse. What happened?"

"Misty told Gonzo to kill me… but he couldn't do it. He dropped me in the desert and took off. Black Hummer, headed east."

Officers started lining up around the edges of the room, just curious, not wanting to intrude, ready for orders. Kent Jacobsen stood there with barely contained rage. Schroeder went to the truck driver.

"Can you stick around for a few hours?"

"I got a load to deliver."

"It might be worth your while to stick around. Where'd you find her?"

"Half way between Mojave and Barstow. No car, no food, no water. I thought she must be nuts."

"Yeah, but she's a good kind of nut. Can I get some information from you?"

Schroeder led the truck driver away. He came back with a sandwich and more water. I ate slowly. I wasn't sure what my stomach would handle. The door banged open and Chase walked in. He stood there a second like he didn't expect to really find me there, then he came over.

"I learned a few tricks for desert survival," I told him weakly.

He smiled, "Yeah, what's that?"

"Cop shoe laces will saw open a barrel cactus, if you get a good grip and saw long enough. If you walk at night, it takes two cactuses to make it three days. If you walk during the day you'll feed the buzzards."

"I want you to show me where you came from."

I nodded and took another bite. "We'll need the Bug."

As word got around, the room started filling up with people. It was getting to be too much for me. I was feeling claustrophobic. The chatter grated on my thinking and the activity made me feel nervous. I stood and tried pacing but I was still too weak. I sat and tried to eat another bite and then suddenly the room fell silent. I looked at the door and there stood Rusty, tentatively looking in the window. Like Chase, he wasn't sure he believed his ears. I stood shakily and made my way through the desks to the door. We met in the middle somewhere and he wrapped me in that hug I'd waited so long for. That hug I thought I might never feel again. It was worth all the pain, all the walking, all the striving and forced march, just for that one hug. I melted into it wrapping my arms about him, breathing in the smell of his brown sports coat. He looked around the room and pulled me out where we could be alone. He couldn't talk for the longest time.

"How could she?" he finally said. "My girl. What would I have done? I couldn't stand it. The only thing that kept me going was knowing you. I knew if there was a way, you'd find it. Misty said Gonzo had killed you. She couldn't say where or how. She was panicked. She knew she was responsible. She'd grown to like you and she panicked. When Gonzo didn't come back we thought he'd made a break for it. We thought we'd never know. I couldn't stand not knowing. I had to know something so I searched. I had to. I couldn't stop. I only had vague clues to go by but I couldn't stop. I searched the penthouse. I searched the aqueduct. I called Chase. When he found your tracks on both sides…what made you take on the aqueduct?"

"It was the only cover in sight. It felt safer than Gonzo."

"Chase told me what had happened there. He pieced together how the Jeep tires got flat and that Gonzo had driven the Jeep up and down the aqueduct. He told me shots were fired. It didn't make sense that the Jeep was driven up and down the bank and then into the channel. They were trying to make it look like an accident but it didn't fool Chase for a minute."

"He caught me and beat me. I fought him three times and he beat me three times, but he broke two fingers trying. You saw the hole in the wall? That was from Gonzo's fist."

"You took that guy on three times? Babe, you didn't have a chance."

"I did. Or I wouldn't have tried."

His breathing quickened as he thought about what I'd taken on.

"Rusty, if nothing else I earned his respect. When he was ordered to kill me he couldn't do it. He said he couldn't kill me outright, so he gave me a long shot. He dropped me off in the middle of the desert and took off, said he'd see me on the evening news. It took a few days but maybe he'll be watching when they say I made it."

He released me and stood back. When he saw the black eyes he suppressed a shudder. He lifted my arms, covered with blood.

"It's okay, it's from a rabbit."

"My little survivor. How far was it?"

"I don't know. Chase wants me to show him where it was. We can figure it out."

"You're not really going to take him all the way back out there, are you?"

"Sure, it'll be fun in the Bug. You can come, too."

"Cassidy, you're beaten…"

"I might be beaten but I am *not beat.*"

There was a knock on the door. Rusty answered it.

"Cassidy? I have a bunch of reporters out here who need to see you for themselves," Schroeder said.

"Schroeder, you know how I feel about being on TV!"

"I know, but you owe it to the country. They've been left hanging for nearly a week."

"Look at me!"

"Yeah, you look like you've been through hell and back. It'll back up your story."

"Did you give them the basic story?"

"I don't even know the basic story."

"Great."

I went to the front of the station. The press was generally not allowed inside so I made my way outside. I had to push my way through a sea of microphones.

"Please, I need to sit. I've been on my feet for three days." I worked my way to a planter in front of the station and sat on the edge. Rusty followed.

Fortunately, they were more concerned about my escape than my abduction.

"How did you get away?" a news woman asked.

"I didn't. I was dropped off in the middle of the desert and I walked out. As a tracker and search and rescue officer I don't recommend others try it. You need all your survival skills intact before you try something like that."

"Have the police caught the people who kidnapped you?"

"One yes, the other no. He was last seen in a black Hummer heading east down highway fifty-eight."

"What are you going to do now that you are back?"

"I'm going to sleep for a day straight, then I'm going to get the police caught up on the case. I'll be back to normal in a day or two."

"You've got two black eyes, were you assaulted in your captivity?"

"Yes, I was assaulted."

"How did you cope, knowing you might not be released?"

"Coping is easy, I just don't let them break my spirit. I stay alert. I watch for breaks. As long as I am trying, I am coping."

"Your family and friends described you as a survivor. What do you think of that?"

"They know me well. They've seen me survive under extreme conditions. But even a survivor needs friends. I don't know what I'd do without them. It used to be I thought a survivor was someone who didn't need friends. Then I found out there's more than one kind of survivor. One kind survives out of stubbornness and the other survives out of love. I'm glad I have seen both sides of that coin. Now, if you'll excuse me, I've only eaten cactus and raw rabbit for the past three days. I'm going to go finish my turkey sandwich."

Questions continued to be fired at me but I waded through the crowd back to the station and went to the meeting room where my half sandwich was dry.

I ate it anyway. Rusty, Schroeder, Chase and a detective named Lawrence Parker had a meeting. Tom had a full caseload and Rusty was too close to the situation to be assigned the case, so Parker got chosen. I was uncomfortable. I could talk to Rusty, Schroeder, or Chase. They knew me and knew what to expect. Lawrence Parker was different. He questioned every piddly, little thing until I was ready to scream. I started at the beginning and started again and again. He wanted to know how Gonzo could sneak up on me if I was watching the parking lot. It was so quick and simple.

"I wasn't expecting a kidnapper! I thought the car was another senior citizen or a family member. I was making up some excuse about waiting for my aunt and this guy just sticks a gun in my face! That's all I know. I came to at the aqueduct."

"So you didn't suspect this guy until you saw a gun?"

"It was a bunch of old people. Who would expect a kidnapper to show up at a bus loading?"

The whole stinking week got picked apart. The more he pushed the fuzzier my thinking got. I was ready to drop. I just wanted to go home and get attacked by my bored sheltie and sleep.

"Why did you ask the truck driver to stick around?" I asked Schroeder.

"I had to get a statement from him," he answered.

"That's not why. You told him it might be worthwhile to stick around."

"I'm not supposed to tell you," he said. "Did you see the news at all while you were gone?"

"Only once," I said with a catch in my voice. "It was the one where they showed Landon and Kelly, my mom and my nephew. It was right about then the room service guy dropped the keycard."

"Cass," Rusty said. "Your dad offered a reward for information leading to your return. He didn't want you to know. Let him do his part in his own way."

"So they know I'm okay?"

"You should still call them. They need to hear your voice." Rusty said.

Then Chase added, "Patrick calls every day. He's going to be in big trouble when James gets his phone bill."

"I almost cried when I saw Pat on the news," I admitted. "Do Kelly and Landon know?"

"I don't know. We'll call them soon."

After a long pause I asked, "Can I go home? I need to collapse. I'm not all here. I need to rest. I really need to sleep. I can't go on like this. I…" I realized I was rambling so I stopped.

"Come on," Rusty said. "We're already out of here. We'll see you guys in the morning."

I followed Rusty out barely making my feet work enough to walk. When we got to the parking lot I automatically looked for my Jeep. It was gone. Dunked in the aqueduct. He led me to the Explorer and opened the door for me. I looked in. It looked too hard. Just thinking about climbing in and sitting in the truck. It looked too hard. I turned to Rusty and weakness overcame me. He caught me and I cried quietly. I didn't have the energy for a good cry. He held me there in the station parking lot, his breath coming in quick short bursts. My crying gradually faded but it wasn't replaced by anything.

"Cassidy? Cass... Babe, please… I just got you back… Cass?"

I was limp as a wet dishrag. I tried to move but nothing worked.

"Rusty?"

"Shh, it'll pass."

Flashing lights.

"Rusty, no! Take me home! Please! Take me home," I cried.

He stayed with me while the world got all topsy turvey. He demanded to stay with me at the hospital. He explained what I had been through. Fluids were administered. Everything was a jumble to my mind. People came and went and I couldn't make sense of any of it.

"Rus?"

"Shh, just let the IV work."

"I feel weird."

"Shh it's okay, just wait. I'll be here. I promise, no matter what. Just lie still."

Tears were so close to the surface. Some tough cop I was. Damn, I didn't want to be here. I wanted to go home. I wanted to sleep in my own bed. Please, just let me go home.

Finally, sleep came. I woke up for checkups and tests. While I was awake Rusty talked to me.

"I'm sorry for all the poking," a nurse said as she drew more blood "The results are getting better so it's worth it, right?"

Rusty began telling his side of the story. "I thought Misty was going to drive me mad. I thought she was bad before she had you abducted but she got worse. In retrospect I see what the plan was, to eliminate the competition and use the situation for her benefit, but she started doing things that didn't make sense, even for her. Every time I turned around she was reminding me of you. It seemed kind of counterproductive. At first it drove me nuts. But as the inconsistencies got more and more specific I knew there had to be a reason. I had to step back and think. I made a list of all the semi coincidences and was amazed: Zeke's, cheesecake, chocolate chip cookies. Then she shows up with this car! And what is it? A roadster. A new version of your old car. And when she asked me if it was like Jack's I almost lost it but I'd noticed a pattern so I backed off and talked to her, tried to tease out more information. She'd only say it looked like it was made for me. The thing that clinched it was she referred to Rule 642. I knew then that all these coincidences were coming directly from you. First, I grew frantic. The reminders on top of the search hit a raw nerve. A couple of times I blew up at her. One time she ran away in fear."

"You're scary when you're mad. She came after me with a gun after that but Gonzo stopped her and I fed her more information to calm her down. As long as she thought she had something to work with she was fine."

"After I saw the information coming through I felt more in control of the search but it was right about then that Misty came to me telling me I had to find you. That Gonzo had taken you out. He was supposed to kill you and leave you someplace findable. Gonzo disappeared and then she was frantic. She was so upset I felt bad arresting her. Every day I visited her and grilled her on where Gonzo might have taken you and every day she had no clue, just said he could have taken you anywhere you might be stumbled upon. A dumpster, a back alley, our house… I ran home and searched the house, yards and barn. We went back and dragged the aqueduct again. The only thing that kept me going was that you were supposed to be findable, yet no one had found you."

When he finished telling me about it we realized Kelly was standing just inside the room.

"Kelly, I saw you on TV," I said. "I heard the news and I asked Gonzo to let me watch. He let me out for about fifteen minutes."

He paused thoughtfully as he came into the room. "That's weird, because I didn't plan on talking to you at all. Then I just had this feeling you were out there. It felt like you were hiding behind a tree nearby but you couldn't come out. I thought I better reach out to you while I could."

"It was right about then I was determined I wasn't going to be found. I'd get myself back. I'd find you guys before you found me. After watching the news, Gonzo was impressed with how much faith my friends had in me."

"How long are you in for this time?" Kelly asked.

"Nobody has said, but I assume just until I get rehydrated. If I were tracking myself I wouldn't have given me a chance."

Rusty gave Kelly a knowing look and no more needed to be said.

"You're one tough cookie," Kelly told me.

"What shape is the Jeep in?" I asked.

"It's a mess, full of mud and not worth fixing," Rusty answered.

"Where is it?"

"In the police impound yard."

"Can we go look at it?"

"Sure, why?"

"I want my survival knife back. And I want to show you something," I said.

"What is it?"

"I want to look at it with you. I want to see how visible it is and if it's visible and you missed it you'll learn something from it. I'll show you as soon as they let me out of here. I still need to show Chase where I walked out of. I hope he doesn't try and track me. It's too far, too hot, and too dry. I wouldn't advise a person to do that even *with* water."

I spent a lot of time in the hospital sleeping. When I woke up I felt fine, but when I slept, I slept deeply. I knew when my body was getting back to normal again when the nightmares started.

I was released with admonitions from the doctor to avoid fistfights. He said I wasn't going to survive the next one. Hmm, maybe I wasn't in there because of dehydration.

"Stop by the impound yard on the way home," I asked Rusty.

We found my Jeep. Rusty was right, it was useless now. We pulled on rubber gloves and I opened the passenger door.

"Since this happens occasionally you might want to know to look for clues in odd places. While I was sitting in the Jeep waiting for Misty I found a pen."

I looked at the side of the seat and scraped away the mud. The ink was smeared but legible. He bent down and read: "Rusty, it's a trick. Quit looking here. Ask Misty."

He stood, quietly thinking. "I'll remember," he said. "Tracks come in all forms. I'm sorry. Babe, I'm so sorry. You tried."

"There's nothing to be sorry for. I couldn't do anything obvious and I didn't have much to work with. But I do use what comes to me."

"There were signs all around me. Until it was too late."

"Come on," I said. "Let's go home."

I had a peaceful day with a hyper sheltie trying to play games every time I got up to do anything. I still had to take it easy. Rusty stayed home with me treasuring minutes. We tried walking to the clearing to check for deer but I tired too easily.

Early the next morning the doorbell rang and Chase stood there.

"You ready for a ride?"

"Come in," I said. "You can convince me but good luck with Rusty. Would you like breakfast? I was going to scramble a pan of eggs. I can just add a few more."

Rusty took one look at Chase and said, "No. You're not going back out there. You need more time."

"Rusty, the tracks out there are five days old," Chase said. "We have to pinpoint the site to get an attempted murder charge. You know just saying she was dropped off in the desert won't count. We have to do our homework. I wanted to go, anyway, so they let me do it."

"You can do it, anyway," Rusty said. "It's a Hummer. I know you can follow a Hummer."

"Rusty, I'd like to go," I said. "We can bring a picnic, lots of water. It won't be the same as when I walked it. I can find it if I have the mile marker where I was picked up. I'm sure they got that information from the truck driver. The report will have more validity if I go verify the location. Then it can't be questioned in court."

We skipped breakfast to get an early start and drove through for breakfast burritos on the way.

"Why is this thing so quiet?" I asked. "I thought cool dune buggies made a lot of noise."

"Not if they need to sneak up on illegals trying to cross the desert. I did a lot of modifications to get it to run like this. One thing about Bugs is you can work on them forever. Tinker here, add a roll cage there, add KC lights. There's nothing to them so there's very little to go wrong. One of these days I'll find time to paint it."

It took hours to reach the place where I was picked up. When we stopped he got out and looked around. Nothing. Wide open desert stretched in every direction as far as the eye could see. He wrote down the miles from the odometer and we headed up the dirt road nearby. It was amazing how quickly the miles skimmed by under the wheels of the Baja Bug.

"You know you're wiping out all my tracks on the road. I walked this whole road from the highway to the end."

When we got to the end of the road he wrote down the odometer reading again. He got out and looked at my tracks next to the Hummer tracks. He slipped back into the driver's seat with a grin on his face.

"You're funny," he said.

"What?"

"You track a Hummer through sand. You can't possibly mess up its trail enough to make it unreadable, yet you carefully walk just to the left of it just like any right handed tracker would do."

Chase's eyes lit up as we headed off road but he couldn't speed off and have fun. He had to keep to the trail. I was amused that he very carefully drove just to the left of the tracks just like any right handed tracker would do.

He only ventured over the Hummer's tracks when it was obvious he had to.

The farther we went the more alarmed Rusty looked and the more amused Chase looked. He had to work his way down into washes and back up.

"What was this guy thinking?" Rusty asked.

When we got to the end of the Hummer's tracks Chase carefully wrote down the miles one more time, then he took a GPS reading and wrote down the coordinates. He walked the area. The tracks were worn but readable. Chase followed my tracks out to where my gun had landed.

It was a long slow drive back. It was hard on both men, Rusty because of the sheer distance and improbability of it all, Chase because he could read the toil through my tracks. He frowned as he inspected the barrel cactus.

"Very ingenious to think of using your shoe laces for a saw. You're the only person I know who would think of doing that."

"How would you do it?"

"I'd have a knife on me."

"Normally I do, but all I had was the clothes on my back and a 9mm pistol."

"Most people in your situation would not have thought of getting water out of a cactus. Of those that would most of those would give up trying to get at it. One or two would brave the needles and get at the water. I doubt anybody would think to use their shoelaces."

"It's one of the things I tell people when they want to know about survival. I tell them they have to see other uses for everyday things. I believe in that implicitly."

It took all day to track my trail because Chase wanted to learn as much about me as he could and to do that he had to study each movement. We stopped where I had stopped and I explained things to him after he had tracked the area. Mostly he just nodded, having received confirmation of what he had read. He examined with interest the place where I had shot the rabbit.

"Good shot," he said. "I can't wait to see what you did with it."

The farther we went the tougher it was for both men. When my steps faltered Chase faltered in his profiling. I could see it in him. He was letting the tracks reach into his brain.

"Chase, stop. Look at me."

He sighed and looked at me.

"Take five steps back, forget who you're tracking and start again. You're putting too much into it."

"Can't do that, kid. You don't know what you did. If I was tracking anybody else I'd have found a body by now."

"I know. Don't think about it. I think you've seen enough. We need to go home."

He shook his head. “I want to see it. There’s a lesson in this trail.”

I had to watch as the trail pulled at him. At one point he simply sat cross-legged in the desert sand with his head in his hands. I wanted to stop him, but he wanted to feel it, so I had to watch. At the highway both men sat in silence. There was no victory celebration, just a stunned disbelief.

The silence stretched all the way back to town. Chase typed up a report on his findings recommending a charge of attempted murder for Gonzo. He described the conditions in detail. While the guys were appalled at the cruelty of Gonzo’s actions, I was simply relieved I’d been given a chance, and I’d made it pay off.

Trying to get the guy’s minds off the past four days I pulled out the calendar of events for the senior center.

“No,” said Rusty. “Absolutely not! That’s what got all this started in the first place.”

“But Agnes is still out there, and I still think I’m onto something. While you were out searching for me I bet she broke into Denise’s house. Am I right? Did it follow the pattern I saw in the past burglaries?”

Chase was glad to see my old self coming through again. I’d been rather quiet out in the desert, only venturing out of the Bug to answer questions and clarify Chase’s findings.

“Forget Agnes,” Rusty said.

“Was I right? Did Agnes hit Denise’s house while she was on the bus trip?”

“No.”

I didn’t know whether to be glad or disappointed. Rusty pulled me down onto the couch and wrapped his arms around me. Chase was fixing to make himself scarce when Rusty said, “she hit Mabel Turner’s house instead.”

I perked up. “Did she show at the parking lot?”

“She used the commotion of your disappearance to make off with an unlocked car. She lifted the keys inside the senior center and drove to Mabel’s house. Everything was by the book. But I didn’t investigate it. I only heard about it later. Tom cornered me and we compared notes.”

I got the calendar back out.

“How long has it been since she’s hit a house?”

“That’s it. That’s the last one we know of.”

“So she’s due to strike again,” I said excitedly.

“You’re in no shape to be tracking cat burglars, even sixty-five year old woman cat burglars. You showed me today, you need a few days to rest.”

“Okay, I’ll go along with that if…”

“No ifs. You’re not pursuing this.”

"Grrr, look, the next chance I would have is four days away. If Strict called, I'd go out in four days. So why not stake out a parking lot in four days?"

"For me. Stay away from this for a while, just for me. I know the danger is slight and you wouldn't go unless you felt fit. I admit you figured out the pattern and gave us something more to go on. I just need to know you'll be home when I get here. Give me some time, knowing you're safe and sound. When this is all over I want to go somewhere. The ranch or San Diego or Timbuktu. I want to catch up on minutes. They're too fleeting. Every time I think we're fine trouble attacks and throws a monkey wrench into everything. If trouble was a person, I'd hunt him down and I wouldn't stop. They'd have to lock me up."

I could see the storm brewing way off on the horizon. The storm of Rusty's anger. I ached to make that anger ease. Anything that was strong enough to anger Rusty was pretty powerful stuff. So I decided I better back off for a while.

"A week? I promise to be a regular old housewife, unless Strict calls, for a week. After that I'll be going nuts."

"I'll call Strict and make sure you get a search. I'll get lost myself if I have to," he said.

Chapter 11

A regular old housewife visits the neighbors, right? I rang Hazel's doorbell and stood back, ready for the onslaught.

"Aaieeee! Cassidy! I heard on the news you'd been found. I thought I'd sent you to your doom looking for this jewel thief. Ask Wally, I was fraught with worry and guilt!"

"Yeah," Wally said. "She went to the Boggle match and said, 'that missing policewoman is my neighbor. Isn't it awful! Boohooo.' And all the old biddies gathered around her and patted her on the back and said, 'there, there it'll be all right. You'll see.' And then in her worry and guilt she whomped them at Boggle."

"*Whomped* isn't even a word," Hazel countered.

"It is, too, I just made it up."

"So, Cassidy," Hazel said. "Now that you are safe and sound and home again, tell me all the nitty-gritty details. What did the jewel thief do to you?"

"It had nothing to do with the jewel thief. It was another, completely different case. Don't worry about it. I survived and I'm back. I just have to take it easy for a few days and I promised Rusty I'd stay completely away from the jewel thief case for a week."

"Oh," she said, disappointed. "Well, I guess I can postpone it."

Oh, no, I thought, what has she done now?

"Hazel? What have you been up to? You've been scheming! What did you do?"

"I'm sorry, Cassidy! I thought if you were looking for a jewel thief and she was involved in the seniors groups I could lure her *here* so I added a night to the calendar called A Decked out Dinner. It's formal, well, as formal as folks can get. And they're all going to be wearing their best. I had my white polyester pantsuit dry cleaned and everything!"

"Hazel, do you know how dangerous this could be? What if you lured your guests into a crime scene?"

"I thought you said this jewel thief is harmless."

"Well, she has been so far."

"So, maybe she'll show up to check out the goods!"

Sigh, "When is this Decked out Dinner you have planned?"

"Friday."

"Okay, I'll talk to Rusty, but you better keep your fingers crossed!"

Rusty came home for dinner at his usual time. One of his favorite dinners was almost done. He looked around, looked at me, folded his arms over his chest and, I don't know how he did it but, he glared and grinned at the same time.

"You're cute when you're trying to butter me up for something. What is it?"

"I am not!" I said. "We have this dinner about once a month. What makes you think I'm buttering you up?"

"The fact that you are defensive about it, for one. Babe, you can just talk to me. I'm not that scary, am I?"

"It depends on the topic," I said cringing. "And I'm not doing it for my sake, but for Hazel's. She's been scheming."

"I think I better sit down for this," he said. "Come talk to me."

"First of all, I had nothing to do with this idea except that Hazel knew I was looking for a jewel thief. She thought that if she threw a big, formal dinner everyone would come out in all their best clothes and wear their jewelry and maybe the jewel thief would come to check out the goods. She called it a Decked out Dinner and it's scheduled for Friday. She started planning this as soon as she heard on the news that I was okay, so I didn't know anything about it until today."

"Hazel? Is throwing a formal dinner party? What's the main casserole?"

"Rusty! I don't know. The food is her department. It's her party."

"But…"

"You know we can't let her do this without at least keeping an eye on the place."

"You want to go to the party and watch for Agnes?"

"Do you have any better ideas?"

"How do you get yourself into these things? Why don't you just borrow Misty's engagement ring from her second husband twice removed. It's a rock the size of Manhattan."

"He married her twice?"

"Cass…"

"Actually that's not a bad idea. Maybe Agnes would try and break into *our* house! Maybe Misty would loan it to me to make up for nearly killing me."

"Cassidy, I wish you could hear yourself. No! You are not talking to Misty or going to Hazel's Decked out Dinner. She got herself into this and it'll go fine."

"And Agnes will come and go and not be caught. My real plan only involved mingling and watching for Agnes, or maybe watching the guests come and go. I feel like Hazel did this for us. We should at least make an attempt to catch Agnes if she shows."

"We? What's this 'we' business? You promised."

"I didn't do anything except go visit the neighbors. Hazel brought up all this other stuff. It's going to happen whether we like it or not. When I said that I was grounded from jewel thieves for a week she acted very disappointed and said she could postpone it. But postponing it only makes Agnes less likely to show. Hazel *will* have this dinner now that her friends are expecting it."

"And I suppose, now that you're famous, you're supposed to be her guest of honor."

"Oh, man, I hadn't even thought about that aspect! But then Agnes will think I'm a cop. You think she'll show if she knows there's a bumbling cop present?"

"There's no telling what Agnes is going to do."

He sat there, very irritated. Wacky senior citizen dinner parties involving jewel thieves didn't seem to appeal to him for some reason. Duh, I wonder why. I put dinner on the table and still he sat there thinking glumly about this party.

"Rusty, I don't blame you one bit. That's the same way I felt when Hazel told me. Would you like to go talk to her? Maybe you can talk her into canceling it. I just didn't have the heart."

He picked at his food, thinking. I didn't know how he could think so hard about one little dinner party. It seemed like it would be a simple decision on his part. Just lay down the law and tell me I couldn't go. It's what I expected.

After dinner he went to his office and he was on the phone for a long time. When he was through he still wasn't happy. I didn't push for an answer. He knew I needed one for Hazel. He sat on the old brown couch, his usual office work forgotten. I took Shadow outside and ran him through the agility course a few times. He still balked at the dog walk and I didn't have a lot of concentration to put into training so we stopped and went inside. Rusty was looking glummer. Something had to be done.

"Take a walk with me," I said.

We walked in silence for a while but the cool desert air finally relaxed him enough so he talked.

"Schroeder wasn't too pleased when I told him what happened."

"I don't blame him. I wasn't too pleased myself."

"But we decided, if it was going to happen, we might as well take advantage of it. Clifford and Fraser were not pleased with their assignment either."

"I don't know that I've met them."

"That's because they work undercover. They don't expect to see much action at a senior citizen dinner party."

"Is that why they didn't want to do it?"

He shook his head no. "They didn't like being chosen because they look old."

"So Friday's a go?"

"Friday's a go."

Half of me wanted to jump up and hug him and half of me thought I needed to really think this through.

Rusty continued, "Communication is going to be the big problem. We will stand out enough. Add radios and Agnes won't come near the place. At least you and I can pretty much dress up and be ourselves, since we're kind of honorary guests, anyway. Clifford and Fraser will come scruffy formal, act old, develop a few annoying habits, complain about their arthritis, keep an eye out for Agnes and be on call. If you see Agnes or anything suspicious you'll have to talk to them inconspicuously. And you are not to leave the house. I know, if Agnes makes a break for it you're going to want to take off after her. Don't."

"Well," I said, "I ought to be well enough to party by Friday. I hope my eyes are back to normal. I don't want my eyes to match my little black dress."

"You're going to wear your little black dress?"

"It's the closest to formal I've got. I can dress it up with the necklace and earrings my mom gave me."

"I'm beginning to like this party idea a little more."

Chapter 12

Wednesday the telephone rang and I picked it up. A nervous woman was on the other end.

"I'm looking for Cassidy Michaels," she said.

"You've found her," I replied.

"Her?"

"Yeah, her."

"I'm looking for a tracker."

"You've found her, too. What can I do for you?"

"I'd like to hire you to find something for me."

"I don't look for things. Things don't leave tracks and things that do leave tracks usually have a conflict behind them somehow."

She paused, unsure how to proceed.

"This thing leaves tracks and there's no conflict attached to him."

"I don't find people for money. I find people who need finding. I don't track down philandering husbands. Or disobedient children. I find people who might be in physical danger from their circumstances."

"This isn't a person, it's a dog. A very valuable and rare dog. It shouldn't even be outside for long periods of time."

"Why? A dog is an animal. It should be acclimated to the outside world."

"My daughter was just playing with him outside for a few minutes and a noisy trash truck scared him. He panicked and ran away. I need this dog back as soon as possible."

"What kind of an environment was it in when it got away?"

"Just out in the yard."

"A residential yard? Grass? Dirt? Cement? There's no sense in looking for tracks unless the environment is conductive to tracking."

"Please, please, just come take a look. I'll make it worth your time."

"Okay. I have a dog, too. I guess I can see how you feel. Give me your address and I'll be out there as soon as I can."

At least the lady knew good tracking conditions when she called me. The house was on the outskirts of town. Four small dogs answered the door followed by a very rotund woman in a pink housecoat.

"Good morning," I greeted her. "I'm Cassidy Michaels. I'm here to see about tracking your dog."

"Oh thank you! Thank you for coming! I'm Vivian."

"It's good to meet you. I'm curious. How in the world did know to call me?"

"My daughter. She said a tracker had spoken at her school about safety in the woods. She remembered your name. I couldn't find you in the phone book but she said you had on a police uniform when you spoke at the school so I tried calling the police station. When they heard the name Michaels they put me through to a man. He questioned me thoroughly before giving me your number. He mumbled something about, maybe this'll keep her out of trouble for a day before he gave me your number."

It didn't sound like Rusty but I couldn't imagine whom they would put the call through to except Rusty.

"Okay, first of all I need a description of the dog. How big it is, what color, long hair, short hair."

She began looking around on the floor.

"Lulu! Lulu, come!" she called.

The four little dogs came running back. She picked up one of them, the ugliest little dog I ever saw. It was nearly hairless, gray, about the size of a Chihuahua. I guess I couldn't judge, though, there was a dog for everybody.

"He looks like this," she said. "Except he's red."

"Will I be able to catch him?"

"Oh, I don't know, it depends on how frightened he is."

"How long has he been missing?"

"Oh, for hours! You just have to find him! He shouldn't be out. He'll burn to a crisp!"

"He's only been gone for hours and you're already calling out a tracker?"

Sorry, but I just couldn't see the need for haste.

"He could be miles away! He could be coyote food!"

"Okay, okay, what have you done to try and get him back?"

"I've been calling and calling."

"Did you try a treat? Food usually brings dogs running."

"Look at my dogs, do they look like they get treats?"

I had to admit her dogs were in great shape. Okay, so her missing dog wasn't used to treats.

"I think an exception to the rule might help in this case. I need a way to catch him if I find him. I think I should make a quick trip to the station for a tool and then I'll see what I can do."

"A tool? What kind of a tool will help you catch a dog?"

"It's a loop on the end of a pole. Dogcatchers use them. It won't hurt him. I think I can get close enough to use the pole but if he doesn't want to be caught I can't catch him without it. I'll be back in half an hour."

I rushed off to the station, borrowed the pole from Carla and, took off for my new assignment.

I really needed a new Jeep. I was in a rental car at the moment and I didn't like it. I wasn't used to cars. They felt so low. I wanted another Jeep Wrangler but Rusty had threatened over and over to get me a sports car, something I couldn't get in as much trouble with. I was afraid if he bought a sports car I'd end up getting *that* stuck in the boondocks instead of a Jeep that was meant to be used that way. Nope, a sports car just wouldn't do. I needed wheels that would take me places, remote places.

I pulled into Vivian's dirt lot and got out. I took out the pole and my pack. I only needed the pack to carry water but it had other tracking tools in it as well.

"Hold out your hand." I instructed.

I put the noose over Vivian's hand and pulled it snuggly around her wrist, then gave it a couple of tugs.

"See? That's as much as it will hurt the dog. I'll only use it until I can get a leash on him. Now, what's his name and where did you lose him?"

"His name is Zulu. Zulu the Xolo. It's short for Xoloitzcuintli. And he was just right here," she said as she led the way to the back yard.

The tracking was good but the tracks of the dog were light and small. It would be like tracking a rabbit. I turned to Vivian.

"No promises, I'll put two days into this and then I have something else I have to do on Friday. If my search commander calls, people take precedence over dogs. Did you find a treat that will tempt him?"

She handed me a sandwich bag twisted around a gray lump.

"What is it?"

"Liver. I use it at dog shows to get the dogs to look perky."

"These are Zulu's tracks?"

"Yes."

"Okay, I'll see what I can do."

The first thing I noticed was that the dog had been very frightened and could run very fast. He scattered sand as he laid tracks to get away from the loud noise. I heard a squeaky toy behind me and Vivian was running after me.

"Here, try this too," she huffed and puffed. "He loves a game of fetch with a squeaky toy."

"Thanks."

I took the toy and stuck it in my pocket. Dogs. I never expected to be out searching for a dog. Chase would think I was nuts looking for a dog that had only been gone for a few hours, but I guess I didn't have anything better to do. At least I wasn't thinking about Agnes. That would just tempt me to try something and I had promised Rusty I'd stay away from that situation, except for Friday.

When the tracking got tough I brought out the squeaky toy and squeaked it as I searched. After the dog had bolted, and had some distance between him and the noisy truck, he'd calmed down and did what any curious dog would do. He started investigating things. He sniffed bushes. He chased rabbits. He wandered. A small dog can wander quite a distance in a few hours.

What am I doing out here? I thought. By the time I catch up to this dog he's going to be home watching Tom and Jerry on TV and ready for a game of fetch. Still, it was good tracking practice. If I wasn't looking for a tame dog I might have been tracking coyotes, anyway.

I followed the light tracks as they wandered through the desert. The sun beat down on me. The heat felt more intense than it should have. I walked, water bottle in one hand, dog catching pole in the other. I saw some interesting things out there in the desert. I saw centipede, rabbit and coyote tracks. Piles of bleached bones told me that perhaps Vivian was right to worry about coyotes.

I followed Zulu until he investigated an old homestead out in the desert. The only things left of it were a rough wooden floor and a stone chimney protruding up into the bright, Cobalt blue, desert sky, a sundial in the middle of nowhere. I looked at the shadow. Gosh it must be four in the afternoon, I thought, surprised.

Zulu's tracks went right up to the wooden floor and then jumped back. There was a jumble of tracks that looked like he'd stood there and barked at something. He had dug at a dark hole beneath the floor and jumped back several times. I looked for more tracks but this was all there was to see. Had a hawk got him? I didn't see the usual pattern of a hawk attack. There is usually a sharp scrambling motion and the prints of feathers sweeping the sand before the hawk flies away with its prey. No, a hawk hadn't gotten Zulu.

There was a whimpering under the floor. Oh hell. I wasn't going in there. It was a rattlesnake den if ever I saw one.

"Zulu! Zulu, come!" I called.

A sharp bark, but no dog. I walked around on the old planks trying to make a racket and scare him out. I jumped. I pounded. He wouldn't come out. I tried prying up some of the boards but they had stood the test of time and wouldn't budge. I went back to the hole and stuck the noose in. I felt around. When the noose seemed to catch on something I wiggled it to see if there was any fight on the end of it. When I felt resistance I pulled the noose out. First I snagged a chunk of wood. Why I thought a hunk of wood had moved I don't know. I stuck the noose back in. The floor area was longer than the pole so I might not be able to reach the dog. The next thing I pulled out fought me but I could tell it wasn't a small dog. I eased back to the end of the pole and kept a firm grip as I backed away. By the time I dragged it free of the hole I was pretty sure it was a snake but I didn't know what part of it I had grabbed. If it was large and I had the tail end I could be in trouble. It was mad and it could be longer than the pole. I thought of just leaving it down there but I'd just be in the same predicament if I tried again so I pulled out the thrashing mad rattlesnake and dragged it a long way from the hole. It lunged at my feet and my moccasins felt mighty thin with those beady eyes focused on them.

Right about then my cell phone rang. I wasn't going to answer it but something told me it might be important.

"Cassidy?"

"Chase, you have got the worse timing of anybody I know!"

"What are you doing?"

"I'm wrestling a rattlesnake. Hold on, I need to let it go."

I dragged hard on the pole, released the noose and ran in the opposite direction.

"Will it come after me?" I asked.

"What kind is it?"

"Looks like a diamondback."

"Maybe."

"Will it go back where I got it from?"

"Where'd you get it from?"

"Under a floor out in the middle of the desert. I'm looking for a little dog and I can hear him under the floor so I fished around under there for him and pulled out a rattlesnake instead."

"Damn it, Cassidy, you know better than that. A dog is not worth it."

"I have a pole. It's not like last time when I grabbed the snake with my hand." I looked in the hole but it was dark. "Look, I'd love to chat but I need to get this dog out and head for home. It's going to take some work."

"The dog doesn't stand a chance if it was snake bit."

"You have a cat that was snake bit. He's ornery, but he lived."

"You got it backwards. He lived because he's ornery. How ornery is the dog?"

"Not very."

"Then go home."

"No can do. I promised the owner I'd try. I told her I'd put two days into this search if I had to, so I'm stuck out here. I wish I had a flashlight."

"Use the screen from the phone. It ought to shed a little light in there."

"Okay, hold on. Tell me if you see anything."

"Very funny."

I shined the phone around in the hole. I was met with a rattle. I scrambled back so fast I nearly lost the phone in the hole.

"Cassidy?"

"There's another one in there," I said.

"So I heard."

"Look, I've got to go. I'll never get the dog out if I can't use both my hands. Are you still in town?"

"Yeah."

"Then distract Rusty until I get there."

"Do you need some help?"

"Not unless you can magic in a backhoe. I've always wanted to try one and this would be a good chance. Seriously, it would take you hours to get out here. I'll be fine. I'll call when I'm through."

I fished around in the hole until I found the other rattler. This time I had grabbed the head so it wasn't nearly as dangerous. I took it out to the desert and released it, running away like I had the first time, hoping I didn't run into the first snake out there.

Surely there weren't three in there, I thought, peering in.

"Zulu! Zulu come!" I squeaked the toy and acted excited to play. "Come boy, get the toy!" *Squeak, squeak*. "Get the toy, Zulu!" *Squeak, squeak, squeak!*

I tried waving the chunk of liver around in front of the hole and blowing the smell inside.

"You want a treat? A cookie? You want a cookie?"

A little whimpering answered me but no small dog emerged.

"A car ride? You want to go for a car ride? Let's go!" I talked and cajoled but he wouldn't come out. I began to think he *was* snake bit.

I tried the pole again but didn't find anything. That didn't mean there were no snakes in there. It meant there were no snakes with a body part raised enough to get the loop around it. I knew snakes could be very flat indeed. I listened around under the floor and pinpointed where Zulu was hiding. I thought he was near the back wall of the building so I used the end of the pole to break up the ground and dug down under the floor at the back. I was glad I had plenty of digging experience compliments of the Marines. I had the motion down pat for breaking up soil. I cleared away enough dirt so I could see down under the floor. I saw…boxes, several boxes, some empty and some closed. An empty box moved. Hmm. The box whimpered. No wonder he hadn't come out! He was stuck in an overturned box! I nudged the box over and out shot a panic stricken, little wrinkled dog. I dove for him as he shot out of the hole, but he was too fast.

"Zulu! Come!" I commanded in a friendly voice. I offered the liver again. He sniffed the air. "Come on," I said. "I'm not going to hurt you. Come here. Good boy! Come to Cassidy."

I talked to him and crept closer until I was able to sneak the noose down around his head. I pulled the loop snug and he wriggled and squirmed. I pulled him in, picked him up, and clipped a leash around his neck. He seemed dehydrated and scared but I couldn't see any signs of him being bitten. He probably ended up in the box jumping away from the rattlesnake. The box had protected him from snake and sun and had probably saved his life.

"We need to rename you Lucky!" I told him.

I held him as I looked around in the hole. I still wasn't willing to venture in there, but I was curious what was in the boxes. How did they get down there? There had to be a way to get to the boxes from above so I examined the floor carefully. I tried pulling up boards over the spot where I knew the boxes lay. The sun was near the horizon when, at last I got a board to move. When it moved it moved easily and I knew I was onto something. I pulled two boards out excitedly and put Zulu down so I could use my hands better. I looped his leash around my wrist so he couldn't get away and reached into the hole in the floor. The boxes were old. They were made of wood or metal. I opened one and inside I found coins. I pulled a few out and read the dates: 1923, 1925. I pocketed a few of them and closed the box. I opened another that contained personal belongings, a pocket watch, a journal. I opened the journal and read the dates. Again, the dates were in the 1920's. I put the journal in my pack, closed up the box and replaced the floorboards. I needed to get this pup home.

I carried Zulu because it was easier than trying to walk him. He would walk on the leash but he was interested in everything and I had to coax him along. I wanted to get home before the guys ate dinner without me, so I picked up the dog and set out at a fast walk. I arrived at Vivian's house as they were cleaning up after dinner. I rang the doorbell and waited, dog in one hand, pole in the other.

"Oh!" she squealed excitedly. "You found him! I can't believe you found him! Ashley look! Zulu's home!"

A little girl ran in and gathered Zulu into her arms.

"Well," I said. "I need to get going. I still have a husband to cook for. I'm glad I was able to find your dog. He was trapped and he couldn't have come home on his own so you're lucky you called me."

"Wait! I promised to pay you. It's well worth my while to pay you. This little guy is a champion stud dog. He's worth a lot to me. How much will you accept?"

"Vivian, really, you don't need to. If you pay me I'll just donate it to the search and rescue program, anyway."

"Okay, then you do that," she said as she handed me a check. I didn't look at the amount, just pocketed it and extended my thanks, then practically ran for the car.

I called Chase back like I promised.

"Hi. Mission accomplished?" he asked.

"And then some," I answered. "Are you still in town? Can you stay until tomorrow?"

"Yeah, I suppose. Why?"

"I'll show you when I catch up with you. Are you with Rusty?"

"Yeah, we're at Trujillo's."

"Have you ordered yet?"

"No, we just got here."

"Get a drink and then go someplace where we won't be met by people from the station."

"Cassidy, what are you up to now?"

"I'll show you when I get there. I'm on my way back to town now."

He talked to Rusty for a bit and then said, "Okay, meet us at Si Señor. We felt like Mexican food tonight."

"Okay."

The guys looked at me curiously when I slid into their booth excitedly.

"Cassidy, you're scary when you look like that. What have you been up to?" Rusty asked.

"You didn't tell him?" I asked Chase.

"I thought he knew and I thought you didn't want him to know about the snakes."

"I've been tracking down a little dog. He ran off into the desert and I found him under the foundation of a ruined house. After I pulled two rattlesnakes out from under the floor I kind of decided I had to find another way in. When I found the dog he was in a box. I think he had bolted to get away from the snakes and the box fell on top of him. Anyway, I dug a new spot and got the dog out but then I looked around for how the boxes got down there. There were loose floorboards…and look what was in the two I opened."

I dropped the coins into Chase's hand and handed the journal to Rusty. Chase squinted and turned the coins this way and that trying to make out the dates.

"I couldn't bring it all out. The box with the journal had other things in it, too. A pocket watch. A hairbrush and mirror, just personal things. The box with the coins had lots of coins so I just brought a sampling. Judging by the dates, these things have been down there a long time. I couldn't carry it out so I thought you'd like to go back tomorrow and dig for buried treasure. Even if it isn't ours, it ought to be interesting."

"Can't you do anything halfway?" Chase asked. "You track a dog, something I wouldn't have even bothered doing in the first place, and you end up wrestling rattlesnakes and finding a stash of money and personal affects."

"If someone asks you to track their dog you might consider it," I advised. "It might pay off. I told Vivian I didn't want to be paid, that I'd just give the money to the search and rescue organization, but she paid me anyway." I tossed the still-folded check onto the table. Chase opened it up.

"What kind of a dog *was* it?" he asked. "Made out of gold?"

"It was the ugliest dog I've ever seen. I'm glad he didn't get left under that house, though. It would have been a long, slow death. I suppose, after our curiosity is satisfied, we'll have to track down the land owner and inform him of his good fortune."

"I suppose so," Rusty admitted.

"I suppose we really should inform him *before* we go poking around in it," I said.

"Can't," Chase said, justifying our actions. "We have to go out there and get a GPS reading so we know exactly where it is and who owns it."

"I *knew* you'd be curious. There's lots more boxes down there than the two I looked in. Just remember the snakes when we go back out. They were big ones."

"Cassidy," Rusty said closing the journal. "This is information you don't want to have your hands on."

"Why? I mean, I don't really want to read someone's personal journal to be nosey. It just seems interesting historically. Like finding the *Diary of Anne Frank* or something."

"Exactly why you don't want to know what's in this book. It could be right, historically. Of all the things to grab out of that box, why did you have to pick this?" he said holding up the tattered book.

"It just seemed more interesting than a hairbrush or a pocket watch."

He picked at his food and seemed deep in thought for the whole meal. Chase knew not to press for information in the restaurant. When we got home we both converged on Rusty.

"You've been awfully quiet since you opened that journal. It can't be that bad. What did it say?" I asked.

"I wish I knew where the loyalties lay in this town. I don't even know where to go with it. This could turn the whole city government inside out."

Chase and I looked at each other.

"Look, Rusty, it happened in the 1920's. Today is what it is no matter what happened back then."

"Just forget you saw this book," he said. "What else is at that site?"

"I don't know. I had a squirmy dog to deal with. I only opened two boxes and then figured we'd come back later."

He ran his fingers through his hair.

"Okay, we'll go back tomorrow. Can we get there without being seen?"

"No. It's wide open desert. I bet if we park at the road we'll still be able to see the truck a mile away."

"Damn."

"We could drive the Bug out there," Chase said. "It blends in pretty good in the desert and would hide us from view."

Dawn was still creeping up on us as we headed across the desert. It wasn't far. We had hoped to be out there about the same time that we had light to see by. It was cold. The desert is always cold in the morning. I showed Rusty and Chase the hole the dog had gone through. There was another rattlesnake in the hole. I fished it out with the noose and dragged it away. The guys just shook their heads at me. This was getting to be old hat for me. Unsnake the area, then go in cautiously.

"There could be others but at least we got the obvious one," I said swinging the pole around in the hole.

"Yeah, it's the sneaky ones you really have to watch for," Chase said.

I shined a light down into the hole, then shined it into the hole the dog had come out of. So far so good. I went to the loose floorboards and lifted the two out that I knew about. The guys peered in. I reached for the box that I had found the journal in and Rusty handed me rubber gloves. I don't like gloves but I could see his point.

"My finger prints are already on it," I told him.

Without moving the boxes we carefully removed the contents. Rusty flipped the pocket watch open. It was long dead but started right up when we wound it a little. We brought out the brush and mirror, a wallet, some papers, an old pistol. An envelope containing photographs. A couple of the pictures were printed on tin. There were boxes of record books and one with handmade maps. With each piece of information Rusty got more and more tense. He sat reading while Chase and I were more interested in the old household items, the odd coins and bills. The box of coins didn't have just coins. It was more like someone hid their life savings down there. It was coins and bills, IOUs, and a few checks. Many of the boxes that were made of wood had water damage to the contents. Pages of books were glued together and brittle but important papers had been stored in metal boxes. When we looked further we found dishes and silverware, candleholders. It almost appeared that the residents had packed all their small valuables and hid them, anticipating having to run, only hoping they would be able to come back for them.

"I say we put it all back and pretend we never saw it," Rusty said.

"Can we?" I asked.

"Just watch."

"What about the real owners?"

"It's very debatable who the real owners are. The landowners didn't get this land by legal means. We don't know who the real owners should be. Too many people would like to be the real owners. I don't want to open up this can of worms."

"The real owners…"

"Are dealing with the present just fine," he interrupted.

I looked to Chase. He just shrugged. I wasn't determined to bring all this out in the open so I relented. I stood, a yellowed map in my hand.

Off in the distance a man straddled a dirt bike, binoculars in hand, watching us.

"Rusty? There's a bullet in a box," I said.

Chase looked into the hole at the boxes. He knew there were probably a lot of bullets somewhere down there since we'd found an old pistol but the phrase was a code phrase of sorts between Rusty and I. Literally a bullet in a box meant small things can have big consequences. In this case it was me saying, there's something small you might want to pay attention to because it might be bigger than we think. Rusty didn't bother with the boxes. He followed my gaze, then he made sure his service revolver was handy. The motion wasn't lost on Chase. We all knelt down, making a smaller target, hiding our movements.

When the person knew they'd been discovered they put down the binoculars and quickly rode away.

I stuffed the paper in my back pocket and started moving dirt, filling in the hole I'd first seen the boxes through. The guys repacked the boxes and replaced the floorboards. I used the pole to smooth the tracks off the loose dirt. I was wishing I had a rattlesnake or two to put down there. By the looks of it, though, they'd show up soon enough.

Rusty was nervous all the rest of the day. He went off to work after he got cleaned up but the findings under the house had disturbed him for some reason. He knew something and he was keeping quiet. When he came home from work he didn't come in and calmly put away his things like he usually did. He hurried in the door and found me first. When that was settled in his mind he was able to relax a bit.

When we went to bed I discovered the papers I'd hastily stuffed in my back pocket and so I hastily stuffed them in my dresser drawer.

I climbed into bed and Rusty put his arms around me. "No funny stuff at Hazel's party tomorrow. You keep your eyes open and you tell us if you see anything, that's it. We've got all the bases covered. We've got two cops in house. We've got roadblocks on both ends of Lost Hills Road. There's no need for you to do anything except point Agnes out if you find her. Got it?"

"Got it."

"You're a guest at Hazel's party. A neighbor. Right?"

"Right. How will I know Clifford and Fraser?"

"You'll know."

"No, really, if they are undercover they'll be blending in. How will I know?"

"Cassidy, I'll introduce you, if you want, but you'll know. You can add a beard and some scruffy formal wear to a cop but you can't take the cop out of him. You'll know Clifford and Fraser the same way you'll know Agnes."

I suspected he was right. It might even be fun trying to figure it out.

Chapter 13

Friday afternoon I started getting antsy. Rusty came home to get ready as I nervously paced the house, cleaning things that were already clean. When he headed for the bedroom to change I did, too. I curled my hair so it flipped out slightly. That gave it more volume. Then I applied makeup and slipped on the little black dress. I found the necklace and earrings my mom had given me. I only wore them for special occasions. They made me feel dressed up. I turned in front of the mirror wondering who this other person was. She wasn't as foreign to me as she used to be but I still didn't know her very well yet.

I looked outside and it was breezy so I gave my hair a good coating of hairspray.

"Where are you going to put your gun in that outfit?" Rusty asked.

"I'm supposed to be armed? At a formal dinner party? I thought you said I wasn't supposed to try anything funny."

"There's a difference between trying something funny and being prepared."

"I am not going to open fire at Hazel's party. We're just watching for Agnes."

"And what if she shows?"

"Then I'll quietly point her out and we'll watch her with eagle eyes until she leaves, the guys will close in and that'll be the end of it."

"How can you be so simplistic and complex at the same time? It's one of the things I've never understood about you. Put it in your purse or strap it to your leg."

I kind of had to strap it to my leg. Since Agnes was known for making off with people's car keys I couldn't leave anything in my purse that she'd be suspicious of.

Rusty wore a black suit, vest and tie. I thought he looked too formal but I couldn't think of what he should change to fit in better. Hazel's idea of formal was a white polyester pants suit so I was sure Rusty would really stand out.

"So," I said. "Can you find the gun?"

He ran his hand up my leg. "I hope you don't need it or we may have some men come down with sudden heart problems."

"Are you ready? Should we walk or drive?"

"We might need a car handy. We better drive."

"Just don't leave the keys where Agnes can get to them."

Hazel and Wally's house was a quarter mile from ours. We got there early so we wouldn't stand out coming into a large group of seniors.

"Oh Cassidy! Look at you! I hardly recognized you! And Rusty! I'm glad you could come."

Hazel was wearing her freshly dry cleaned white polyester pants suit. It almost buttoned in front so she wore a frilly blouse under the jacket. It made her look like a crowing rooster. Her double chin didn't help the impression. She had gone to a lot of trouble for this party. Her house was freshly cleaned. All the clutter was cleared away and the furniture was dusted.

Her kitchen was decorated with chickens and I found a big white rooster that matched Hazel perfectly. She had platters of mini pizzas and tacos, stuffed mushrooms, cheese and crackers on the dining room table. I could smell something cooking.

"Wally! Come out! Rusty and Cassidy are here!"

"Dang, suits, why did you have to make this shindig formal? You know we don't do formal. We barely do informal! I haven't worn this suit since Lester Havalind's funeral five years ago."

I thought it was pretty good that people Hazel and Wally's age hadn't been to a funeral in five years.

"What tie should I wear?" Wally asked Hazel. One was bright red. One had pink flamingoes on it. And the other was blue and green plaid. His suit was blue but it didn't match the blue plaid. The red made his face look flushed. The flamingoes just wouldn't do. The only place I'd let him wear that would be on a senior citizen cruise to Flamingoland.

"You don't have anything else?" I asked.

"Only a stiff black one."

"Black is good. It makes anything look formal. If you don't like the suit anyway, you might as well not like it one hundred percent."

He couldn't argue with my logic so, thankfully, he put on the black tie.

The doorbell rang and Hazel was busy so she asked me to get it. I kind of liked being the official door answerer. I got a good look at all the guests and I was able to explain my presence at the party easily. I opened the door.

"Wowie kazowie!" a man said and his wife nudged him in the ribs. "Hazel and Wally got some hot servants! I didn't know they were that well off!"

"Good evening," I said. "I'm Cassidy. I'm Hazel and Wally's next door neighbor. It's good to meet you."

"I'm Phil and this is JoAnn. JoAnn is Hazel's Boggle partner when they play in teams."

"You play Boggle in teams?"

"Sure, you can play anything in teams."

As each couple came in I greeted them and introduced myself. As I shook hands I noted the jewelry or lack thereof. People came with canes and walkers. A few had oxygen tanks on little carts.

Marsha Haskins had better watch out for Agnes, I thought as I shook her diamond-studded hand. I looked her over. Too tall to be Agnes.

Roberta Fisk had beautiful jewelry but she was too old to be Agnes.

In all about thirty people showed up. Most of them knew each other. They visited amicably. I started watching for the two undercover cops. No one had introduced themselves as Clifford or Fraser. I began watching for the odd man out. I didn't think Agnes was here. People were milling around eating the stuffed mushrooms, ignoring the mini pizzas. All the women who were not dressed up in evening gowns were in the kitchen helping. All the women in evening gowns were socializing. I wondered if this was the difference between the Boggle group and the uppity ups.

"What brings you to Hazel's Decked out Dinner?" Roberta asked me.

"She invited me and it seemed impolite to refuse. Plus, Hazel is a wonderful person. She's always so cheerful and upbeat. Nothing ever gets her down."

"Huh! You haven't seen her lose a Boggle game. Why would you want to hang out with a bunch of old people?"

"I don't pay attention to how old people are. They are all interesting to me. In my job I deal with people of all ages."

"Oh really? What do you do?"

Ooops, oh well. "I look for people."

"You mean like a private investigator?"

"No like a rescue worker. I do the finding and the EMTs do the rescuing."

She looked me up and down. Black spaghetti strapped dress, diamond earrings. "You?"

"Yeah, me. I grew up doing it. It's the only thing I'm really good at."

Wally came puffing up talking excitedly, "Cassidy! Cassidy, it's what's her name! She's here being a wallflower."

"Now Wally, that's not nice. There's nothing wrong with being a wallflower. Some people are just more outgoing than others," Roberta said.

"I thought I met everybody when they came in," I said.

"Once things get going people know to just come and go. Many people can't stay out late anymore. They turn in early. So these things never have a rigid schedule," Roberta explained.

Wally remembered he was supposed to be inconspicuous so he whispered loudly, "She's in the den sitting on the fireplace hearth quiet as can be."

I mingled that direction. When I got to the kitchen Hazel nabbed me.

"Would you take this to Melba Troast?" she asked handing me a glass.

"Um, sure, which way did she go?" I asked.

"Look on the patio."

I took the glass and headed for the back door. Hazel had even strung party lights around her patio and put candles on the table out there. I glanced at the fireplace hearth on the way by. There was a woman sitting there just as Wally had said. I tried to get a good look at her without staring. Could that be Agnes? I went out to the patio and looked around.

"Is anybody out here Melba Troast?" I asked.

"That's me," a woman said cheerfully from behind the patio table.

"Hazel asked me to bring this out to you," I said.

"That's because you were the most able bodied person in there," Melba joked. "You must be Hazel's neighbor, the one who rescued her son. I can't tell you how much Hazel went on about that. While you were out there she was certain she'd never see either one of you again. She can be a terrible worrier, Hazel can. The whole group celebrated when Mark was found. We had a party for him at my house, just a little one."

"That's great," I said wanting to get inside and talk to the wallflower.

"Looking back, we should have invited you too, but I was just wanting to share in Hazel and Wally's joy at having their son back. I know what it's like to lose a son but I don't know what it's like to get one back."

"I'm sorry about your son," I said, thinking how many stories these old people held dear to them. How many joys and sorrows they had experienced. One reason I liked older people was because they were time capsules. They held a bit of history and a lot of wisdom and it was interesting to get glimpses of a time gone by. And sometimes it was heartbreaking. "That's why I do what I do. Each person I find is important to somebody. Each life is precious."

"Mark is a dear," Melba said.

"You should see the pictures Mark gave to me from the rescue. I didn't expect him to do anything except maybe stop in and visit when he was in town and then he brought me these one of a kind Mark Mireau prints. I was honored he thought of me that highly. He's a nice guy."

I saw an old man slide lithely between two groups of people talking on the patio and resume a stooped position. Clifford or Fraser for sure. He was looking for somebody. Somebody specific.

"I should go see if Hazel needs any more help," I said and quickly slipped away.

Another man walked quickly, if stiffly in through the backdoor.

Hazel greeted him warmly. "My, my," she said. "Are you new at the center? Come here, let me introduce you to my friend Winnie. I'm Hazel."

"Mike Fraser," he said with an urgent appeal for help.

"Ooo, so macho sounding too," Hazel squealed.

I slipped in the backdoor.

"Cassidy!" Hazel said. "This is Mike Fraser, he's new! I only just met him. I'm so glad to see some new people showing up at my house! Isn't this a lovely surprise! Did you get something to eat yet? I have mini pizzas." She looked over the table. She had a lot of mini pizzas. "Ooo," she said, "I need to get out more stuffed mushrooms and cheese."

Fraser quickly slipped away and I helped Hazel in the kitchen hoping she'd forget about introducing Fraser to her friend Winnie. Hazel gave me a job to do, so I was stuck in the kitchen, I had a wallflower needing observation in the den, and two cops on their way inconspicuously somewhere. Where was Rusty? I glanced around the kitchen door into the den. Okay, my wallflower was still there. Was it Agnes? A woman came over to her and spoke to her. She talked amicably enough but she didn't make a move to join in the other groups. None of her actions made me think she was after somebody's jewelry. She just seemed quiet. So far I'd only observed her sitting down. Hopefully, she would stand up and walk around. I had to find a way to politely leave the kitchen.

"Hazel," I said looking for an easy out. "I don't see many people with glasses. Do you want me to walk around and offer them something to drink?"

"No, that's the wife's job."

"What?"

"If you walk around and offer people something to drink all the men will take whatever you offer whether it's good for them or not. So the wives get the drinks. Believe me they know what their husbands can have."

"I'd never tell Rusty what he can and can't have to drink," I said.

"You just wait. Don't say you'd never until you get there. I bet there was a time you said you'd never wear a spaghetti strapped dress before, too."

I laughed, "You've got that right. There was a time getting me in any kind of a dress was a struggle."

"And what changed that?"

"Mostly, it was Rusty," I said with a hint of admiration in my voice.

"So there, you see, don't be deciding ahead of time what you will or won't do for Rusty. You never know."

An exotic voice beside me said, "She speaks wisely and with experience."

I turned and it was the wallflower. I checked my reactions.

"Hazel has been right about a lot of things. I'm Cassidy. I'm Hazel's neighbor," I said extending my hand.

"Yes, I know," she said shaking hands gently. She wore jewelry but not extravagantly so. The pieces she chose suited her, matched her outfit and were meticulously cleaned. They sparkled like new. "I recognized you from the news. Hazel shouldn't have expected you to come after the ordeal you went through."

"Trouble is my middle name," I said. "If I let it get me down I'd never go anywhere. But I don't. I just keep going. I have to be doing something, bruises or not. I've learned to ignore them. My mother told me as long as I wear a smile people will overlook the bruises."

"It amazes me what people can do if they have to. You have been through much."

"It's Rusty that has been through much," I said. "It's him who has the tough part. I just deal with circumstances. He is left to deal with the consequences. He shouldn't have to do that."

"We all deal with circumstances. Your husband deals with his own. He doesn't think of it as consequences. He thinks of it as his own circumstances. Tell me, when you are driving down the road and someone does something stupid. They cut you off dangerously or they stop suddenly causing you to react. What do you do?"

"I just react to the situation."

"Do you get angry with the person?"

"Of course, we all do."

"Now, if your husband were that person and you knew it, what would your reaction be?"

"I would think he was on his way someplace in a hurry or he was reacting to something ahead of him."

"Yet you don't give the stranger the same courtesy? Perhaps we are each reacting to our own circumstances."

I wasn't sure what she was driving at but she was an interesting person. She walked into the kitchen with an easy grace and got a glass if wine for herself. She went into the living room and disappeared into the mass of people. She didn't just walk in there. She purposely vanished putting an end to our conversation.

"Hazel, who was that woman?"

"I don't know. I don't know a lot of the people here. They just saw the event on the calendar and thought it sounded like fun. I better get the turkey and ham out of the oven."

I went into the living room. I didn't see the woman there. I went down the hall and glanced in the rooms. I felt like I was snooping through the house so I didn't go in any of the rooms but the woman wasn't to be seen. I went out the front door and walked around in the front yard. It was crowded with parked cars. A shadowy figure slipped between two parked cars. I followed. I knew I should go get Rusty, Clifford, or Fraser but there didn't appear to be time. If I turned around she'd be gone or, at best, invisible. I had my sights set on her, so I couldn't let go. Keeping one eye on the dark shadow ahead and one eye on my surroundings, I slipped between the parked cars and followed her. I was one car length behind her and barely keeping her in sight when she slipped into a car and started the engine. I wondered if it was her car or somebody else's. I couldn't follow a car! And I couldn't go get one of the cops without losing her. I wasn't willing to open fire on the car. I couldn't see well enough to hit a tire and I didn't want to cause a panic inside. I watched as the car pulled away and headed down Lost Hills Road. I walked after it trying to keep it in sight. Suddenly the car turned off the road. The only place to turn that direction was… my driveway! I watched as the car parked and the lights flicked off. I hurried down the street by feel. There are no streetlights on Lost Hills Road and, unless there is a full moon, the hills are pitch black. It was dark and I was walking quickly, hoping I was following the pavement, when headlights suddenly appeared and I jumped out of the way. The car stopped and an officer jumped out.

"Police! Freeze! Put your hands over your head."

I complied and stepped into the headlights, hands over my head.

"It's just me," I said.

"Rusty's going to kill you," Ben Tomlin said.

"No kidding. I think Agnes went that way," I said pointing down the street.

"Does Rusty know?"

"No, there was no time. I'm not even sure it's her but she was following the pattern."

"How so?"

"She came to the dinner, scoped it out, chose a target and quietly disappeared when things got going. She headed this direction but I think she pulled off to avoid the roadblock."

He looked me up and down. Okay, I know I don't usually look like this but it was a formal dinner party. Give me a break.

"Nice dress," he said.

"Not exactly my favorite for chasing down criminals in the dark. Look, I want to see where this car ended up. I can't stay on her trail without a visual."

"I don't think you should."

"Why? If she follows the plan she hits a roadblock. She gets caught. Everybody goes home happy."

"I'm not going to count on it."

I started down the street.

"Hold it. What are you doing?"

"I'm going to stay on her trail. If I'm seeing things right she pulled off at my house."

"You're not even armed!"

"Turn around."

He turned his back to me. I reached up under my skirt and pulled out the 9mm.

"Dang!" said Ben, then turned around.

"I told you to turn around for a reason!" I told him.

"The mirror was really dark," he answered.

I started down the street again and Ben was torn. Go get Rusty? Call in backup? I wasn't going to tell him what to do. He was the real cop. He could decide. I only knew what *I* would do and that was to check out the car, run the plates, and see if it was Agnes's or if she filched a car from someone else. Once we had a name we'd be in better shape to make a decision.

The farther I got from Hazel's house the darker the street became. By the time I reached my house I couldn't see a thing but I couldn't turn on any lights without causing huge distractions and drawing attention to myself. I crouched at the end of my driveway behind a bush and listened to the darkness. All I heard was silence. No footsteps. No one moving about in a car. I crept forward inch by inch until I felt a car in the driveway. I identified it as the rental car then looked for another car. There wasn't one. Where was the other car? This was the only driveway visible from Hazel and Wally's house yet I knew the car had turned this direction. I made my way to the side of the house and slipped into stealth mode. I was glad I didn't need to worry about the owners of the house getting worried and calling the cops. It was my house. I inched along the wall using the shrubs and bushes for camouflage. I spotted Agnes making her way around the backside of the house. She wasn't worried about the roadblocks. She was trying to find a way inside my house.

I was fascinated. I didn't want to catch her. I wanted to see her work. I wanted to see how she moved and how she got in. I wondered why she picked my house aside from the fact that the police had blocked off any other victim's houses. I was glad to have this opportunity to see her in action. She moved like quicksilver, her movements flowing. She looked like a shadow, not a real person. She had a tool that she deftly slipped into a window crack and gently pried. If the window didn't move she quickly made her way to the next window. I knew Chase had managed to break into the house but he had shown Rusty the way he got in so I assumed Rusty had fixed that. He was very careful to have the house secure from break-ins.

Window to window she skimmed effortlessly around the house. I followed, careful to stay out of sight. It was easy to do in the dark. I just wished I was in swat team black, not a dress and pumps. When she had checked all the windows she made her way to the back door and used another tool to slip the latch on the sliding glass door. She was in in an instant. Shoot, now she could get out any way she wanted to and I wouldn't be able to see her. Where was Ben? Where was Rusty? Where was Shadow? A loud bark and a startled gasp confirmed where Shadow was. Maybe he would follow Agnes so I could tell where she was. She turned on a light, presumably so she could see what kind of a dog she was up against. Shadow barked and wagged his tail enthusiastically. With the lights on inside it was easy to see who I had been following. It was the foreign sounding woman. She never had told me her name.

I knew that I was supposed to arrest Agnes but I kind of felt like I should leave that to a real cop. I wasn't sure how far the technicalities stretched. Technically, I needed a senior officer to do anything official and all my possible senior officers were elsewhere. I thought that if push came to shove Rusty could be named my senior officer but if so I definitely was disobeying orders by being anywhere near my house. I had strict orders to stay in Hazel's house. But I didn't have time when Agnes left to go looking for help. One second she was there and the next she was gone. When Agnes slipped into the master bedroom I silently slipped into the den and grabbed the cordless phone. I slipped back out and then into the barn hoping the phone worked from there. I had to punch the number in by feel. Rusty answered on the first ring.

"Cassidy! Where are you?"

"At home! Where are you?"

"At Hazel's just like you should be."

"Agnes is in our house. She's going to figure out real quick that there's nothing to steal."

"I told you to stay in the house."

"I didn't have much choice. It was follow or lose her. Get some guys down here. Last I saw she was headed for our bedroom."

"Where are you?"

"I'm in the barn but only so Agnes won't hear me. I need to go check on her. It doesn't take her long to vanish."

"No! Stay put."

"But Rusty! She'll be gone in an instant. I need to keep an eye on her."

"No you don't. The roadblock will get her now that they know she's here. They'll catch her."

"She'll disappear into the hills before she'll drive through that roadblock."

I didn't stay in the barn. I figured if I stayed in the barn it would only give Agnes a chance to escape and sneak around the roadblock. If she found the guns in the house and there was any shooting going on a few bullets could easily end up in the barn. So I mentally weaseled my way out of staying there. I crept back to the house and peeked in the bay window. No Agnes.

I slid around to the office. No sign of her. The office window faced the front of the house so I saw the police cars converge on the house in the reflection on the window. They cruised in quietly.

"I don't get it," I told Schroeder. "I watched her get in. I talked to Rusty for thirty seconds and now I don't see her in there anymore."

"Is she armed?"

"She didn't look armed but then neither did I when I went to the dinner."

He looked me up and down. "Nice dress."

"Thanks."

"You know the house, you know the yards. Make one more circuit and try and pinpoint her before we go in."

"Really? You'd let me do that?"

"Don't tell Rusty."

"Send someone around to the back sliding glass door. That's how she got in. It's the quickest way to disappear into the hills so she'll probably come out that way."

"Right. Be careful."

I slinked into the darkness and approached the guestroom window. There was only a bed and a dresser in the room. No place to hide. If Agnes had gone in there she had searched the drawers and found nothing. The office was similarly devoid of hiding places or places to stash valuables. A computer desk and chair. An easy chair in the corner. The master bedroom looked empty. From the bay window I had a clear view down the length of the room. The closet door stood ajar. The bathroom door was open. The light was off. The dresser seemed untouched. Nothing looked odd about the things on top of the dresser. If I was a jewel thief the master bedroom dresser would be the first place I'd look.

I knew how invisible I was because there were no sounds when I approached the den door. Somebody was supposed to be watching. I crouched low. This part of the house had the most hiding places. The big brown couch curved around the fireplace. The kitchen was nearly out of sight between the den and the living room. No shadows or movements appeared in the dining room adjacent to the kitchen. Everywhere I looked the house looked normal, just like all the other houses she had broken into. I sat underneath the living room window. Something was niggling at my mind. Something felt wrong about the house, but not enough to catch my attention, only my subconscious. What was it?

I joined the group of cops again, appearing silently beside them. Jayce Thompson jumped.

"Cassidy! Don't do that!" he said quietly.

I addressed Schroeder but it was for all to hear. "She's in there somewhere but I couldn't see her."

"What makes you think she's in there, then?"

"I don't know. Something is just off about it. There's only two ways to find out if she's in there and I doubt you want to wait until morning and have me track the area. So that leaves going in."

"And she's not armed?"

"I didn't say that. I said she didn't *appear* to be armed."

Rusty had joined the group. They all nodded. They didn't need me to tell them people can be armed even if they don't look like it.

"If she found my backpacking gear, she probably found my rifle. We can only hope she was thinking jewelry and skipped over the camping gear. I think all Rusty's guns are accounted for."

Rusty handed over the keys. At least there would be no doors broken in.

When the officers went in something was still off. Something was missing. Where was Shadow? There should have been a chorus of barking when the cops went in. I wasn't worried about him. They all knew Shadow. He'd been the flower girl at my wedding. But where was he? It was very unusual for a sheltie to be quiet. And it was very unusual that he hadn't looked for me. Shadow was a sheepdog. Rusty and I were his flock. He was responsible for us, at least that's the way it seemed. So where was he?

"I figured out what's wrong in there," I told Schroeder.

"What?"

"No dog. He's a noisy dog. He should be barking at the guys. He should have rushed out the front door when they went in."

"What do you make of it?"

"I don't know. If he was outside he would have found me. If he was inside he'd be barking or looking for me. I don't see any sign of him."

"If Agnes got away up into the hills, do you think he'd follow her?"

"Not far. He knows his boundaries. He takes his responsibilities seriously."

We waited while the police made their way through the house room by room. There were no shots. No yells. I imagine it was a bit tense for the guys each time they entered a room but they only met silence. It was embarrassing and encouraging at the same time. I never liked to see the guys raid a house. The potential for being fired on was too high. They were all friends now, whether I had met them or not.

I remembered the days when a cop was simply a reason to hit the brakes, no matter how slow I was going. Now they cruised by my Jeep and waved. Occasionally I got pulled over just so they could ask about my latest search.

It didn't take them long to decide Agnes was not in the house, but I wasn't so sure. I knew they had been thorough. They had opened closets and looked under beds. Rusty knew all the places to look. Yet… nothing.

"Can I go in?" I asked Schroeder.

He nodded a go ahead. So did Rusty. Hmm, nothing felt off to Rusty.

"In the morning take a look at the area," he said. "Wake me if you find anything, anything at all."

"It's what I'm *not* finding that bugs me," I said.

He paused for a moment and headed for the house again. We went around the house calling Shadow's name. Usually just a bump or a door opening was enough to bring him running. Now? Nothing.

"You're right. This is weird. We have the car. We have the evidence that she was in there. All I can think of is that she slipped away while you were talking to me."

"And took Shadow with her? She wouldn't take Shadow. He'd slow her down. He'd attract attention. He's not worth much to her monetarily. He should be here."

It was puzzling but there was nothing we could do to change the facts. Agnes had gotten away and Shadow was missing.

Rusty called in a team to take fingerprints. We were up most of the night. We finally fell into bed a little before dawn, Hazel's dinner party nearly forgotten.

When the sun came up I wearily pulled myself out of bed and checked the grounds for Agnes's footprints. Hmm. There were none. I found a few close to the house, covered up by my scouting the night before. I expected to see a trail of tracks leading away into the junipers. This was bad news. How could she have gotten out the front door, down the cement driveway and past the police roadblock? I walked the road watching for footprints leaving it. If she had gotten away via the front yard she had to leave the road when she got close to the roadblock and then hide in the brush as she went around the barricade. It didn't make sense for her to do that. That still left a very long walk into town. It made more sense for her to go back to the party and blend in there. But I walked both sides of the road from one police barricade to the other and I didn't find any tracks that even remotely resembled Agnes's.

I crawled back into bed with a sigh and my head going a mile a minute. Where could she be? No tracks. No car. No Shadow. No Agnes. When Rusty didn't stir I got up again. I called Chase.

"I've got a puzzle. You left one day early. Got any ideas?"

I explained the situation.

"You circled the property?"

"Of course. I found my footprints, Shadow's old tracks. Agnes's tracks can only be found under the windows and I watched her put them there."

"So you know her tracks."

"Yeah, I know her tracks."

"None by the road?"

"Only cop prints."

"Now you've got me curious. I don't want to drive four hours back."

"I'm not asking you to."

"I know, but now I'm curious. I might have to just to satisfy my own curiosity. What's this woman wanted for?"

"She's a cat burglar. She steals jewelry."

"So what's she doing at your house? You don't wear jewelry."

So, I explained about the dinner party and the roadblocks and my house being a handy hiding place between the roadblocks.

"She knew it was my house because I was introduced at the party as Hazel's neighbor."

"Makes sense, but there's no tracks."

"Right."

I could feel the wheels in his head turning all the way from San Diego to Joshua Hills.

"And she's not in the house."

"Right."

"Damn. You're right."

"What?"

"It's a puzzle."

"No ideas?"

"Not from here."

"Okay, thanks anyway."

I went back to bed thinking the house was way too quiet. I should have already fed Shadow and run him through the agility course. Where was he?

Midmorning Rusty got up and went to work. We were both dragging. Something felt off to both of us but it wasn't just our missing dog. Things just didn't add up especially after I told him my findings tracking the area. He went to work to report the findings to Schroeder. I sorted laundry, just doing something that didn't require thought. I checked the drawers, wondering what needed washing the most. I noticed the drawers had been rifled through gently. It matched Agnes's MO. Everything was neatly put back in place except for one corner of the drawer where things had been turned over and not righted. What was in that corner? Oh shoot. The map. I dug down into the drawer looking for it. It was gone. What was it a map of? Why would Agnes want it?

"Rusty? We have a small problem."

"Small problem is relative when you say it. What is it?"

"When we were out at the building, putting things back in the boxes before we left, I forgot I had a map in my pocket."

"Okay, so far it still sounds like a small problem. Is there more?"

"When I got home I found it in my pocket and stuck it in a drawer until I could figure out what to do with it."

"Okay."

"Now it's gone. I think Agnes took it."

A long silence. It wasn't too tension filled. That was a good sign.

"What was it a map of?"

"I didn't get a chance to find out."

"Okay, we'll keep that in mind as we go. I'm not going to mention it unless we have to. It's just a piece of paper until we find out otherwise."

Whew.

I gathered up a load of colors and headed toward the washroom when I heard a yip. I stopped. That was Shadow. Where was he?

"Shadow? Come here, boy!" I called.

I listened. Nothing. I looked around the house, inside closets, inside cupboards… everywhere. I didn't do the laundry. I wanted to be able to hear. Later in the day I heard a scratching noise but I was in the kitchen and it was coming from the back of the house. Before I could figure out where it came from it stopped.

I started doing quiet jobs, dusting, dishwashing, bird feeder filling, so I could keep my ears tuned. I didn't turn on the TV or appliances that would cover up sounds. I was getting very bored and terribly curious. Finding quiet jobs wasn't easy to do in a house with only two people. We didn't do much to dirty it up. I was checking my email for the tenth time when Shadow appeared with a loud bark behind me. It didn't startle me. I was used to it. But at the same time it was incongruous. He'd been missing nearly a whole day. All the doors were closed and yet here he was. Did I have a teleporting dog? After checking on me he ran to his water dish, then looked at me expectantly. He was hungry and thirsty. I fed him like I always did but there was an eerie feeling to all this. After he ate he wanted to go out so I went outside with him and he quickly did his business.

I did another tour of the house examining each room for signs of a doggie exit. I found it in my bedroom. The closet door was open just far enough for a dog to have nosed through. That didn't make sense. I had checked that closet three times. If Shadow had been in a closet for even fifteen minutes he would have been barking and scratching to get out. Sheltie patience didn't last much longer than that. It seldom lasted five minutes. A whole day in a closet was an impossibility. So, where did he come from? It was time to do some down on the ground investigation.

I crawled around in the closet. It was a big closet as far as closets go. It was the walk-in variety but I could still see all the parts of it simply by sitting in the middle and glancing around. I looked at all the clothes hanging at doggie height. They were nearly all mine since Rusty could reach the higher bars easier and his work clothes needed to remain fur free. Shadow didn't usually go in the closets. He was a herding dog and felt trapped in small spaces so any clues in the closet were surely recent ones. There was no fur on the shirts and blouses but I did find some on the jeans and gym clothes. I parted the clothing on that rack and looked behind. All I saw was a closet wall. I felt the wall. It was odd. It was not sheetrock like the rest of the house was. I stood and examined the wall closer and found it was made in panels. At the top there was a track and at the bottom it looked like baseboards. It was made to look like a wall but it wasn't a wall at all. It could move. I looked for a button, like a garage door would have, but didn't find anything. I tried moving it and it slid quietly along its track revealing stairs going down into a dark, dry, subterranean vault. I took one step down the stairs, there was a funny noise in my head and I was out.

I woke up bruised, battered and handcuffed to the supports at the bottom of the stairs. Agnes sat on a couch in a small room. The walls were bare dirt. The floor was dirt but somebody had spread an area rug in the middle of the room to make it homier. It was like a cellar that had been converted to be more livable. The couch and rug helped. There was a radio and television, a small bookcase full of books. A bare light bulb hung from a beam in the dirt ceiling.

"I'm sorry about the fall," Agnes said. "I always worried about having to do that to Bernice. Gustaf said it wouldn't harm her but I always worried about it anyway. I'm glad I never had to use it."

"Use what?" I asked, shaken.

She pocketed a personal sized taser. That kind of explained the falling down the stairs part of this little adventure.

"What are you doing here? And where are we?" I asked.

"Congratulations. Bernice never guessed this room was here all the years she lived here. You are the first to find it on your own. I'd like to know how you figured it out."

"Dog fur," I answered. "What are you doing here?"

"Trying to stay out of sight until the police leave, collecting a few things I left here. Gus complicated things a little bit when he died. Bernice rarely left the house after that. This was my first chance to slip back in."

"What do you mean, 'slip back in?'"

"There aren't many people who remember the war. Having soldiers knock on the door. Fearing for their lives. Gus did. He dug this room when he made the house because he remembered the fear. He never had to use it but it was a comfort to him to have it here, just in case. He said it would withstand earthquakes. It was hidden from view. Nobody would find it, he boasted. Nobody, not even his wife. So when I needed a place to stay out of sight, he offered me refuge. Because he understood my fear, he said. I came here frequently. Bernice never knew. Never knew the room existed. Never knew of my presence here. I trust she won't find out."

"Not from me," I said. "Let her keep her memories. She adored Gus."

"I thought you were gone today," she said changing the subject. "The house was so quiet. I'm glad I was cautious. I really must be going. I hope you won't be down here too long. You can understand my need to tie you up, don't you? I hate to leave you like this but if I let you go I doubt I'll get home again. You have earned my deepest admiration. You are the one to come closest to catching me. I really don't want to go to jail."

Agnes pulled a long length of package sealing tape from a roll and put it over my mouth, wrapping it securely around my head. Yeah, right, you hate to leave me like this, I thought as I heard the sliding door close and latch. I wasn't sure if I heard the closet door close or not. I was alone. At least she left the light on. I imagined this room would be pretty dark without the lone light bulb.

As I lay there under the stairs I looked around as much as my bound hands would let me. The room fascinated me. I had my very own secret room! It might be useful for a trouble magnet like me. If I ever got out of there I'd have a refuge, a hiding place. If I'd had this room when Stern was after me I could have prevented a lot of trouble. I couldn't wait to show it to Rusty. The problem was getting out. Handcuffs are not easy things to get loose from and if Bernice had lived in this house for twenty years and never found this room what made me think Rusty would come down the stairs looking for me?

I tried prying my hands loose from the cuffs. It only gave me sorer wrists. I tried using the short chain on the cuffs to saw through the support, but I couldn't keep it up for long. I finally decided my best bet was noise. I'd heard Shadow from inside the house. I could make myself heard after Rusty got home.

I wondered what time it was. Rusty had gotten a late start to his day and I'd puttered quietly around the house for hours before Shadow had finally appeared. I was guessing it was mid-afternoon. There was no telling time without clocks, sun, or windows. Time seemed to be a secret in the secret room. I tried pulling the tape loose, but I couldn't find a good position to work in.

I finally decided to find a comfortable spot and wait. I was still sore from Gonzo's beatings and now I had a fall down the stairs to add to my problems. Shifting around caused sharp pains in my hip and knee. I finally just lay with my arms around the support and waited and waited, thinking, feeling embarrassed, listening. It seemed like forever before I heard a faint noise and then a faint bark. A greeting. Maybe Rusty was home. I thought of a signal to attract attention. I kicked the stair support, *bam, bam, bam*, wait, *bam, bam, bam*, wait. I repeated the signal over and over again and then I stopped to listen. Shadow was still barking. Was he barking at me? That wouldn't be unusual for him to bark at an odd sound. Was he barking at Rusty in greeting? I thought he would be done with that and on to other doggy pursuits. Maybe someone was at the door. He could bark forever if he thought someone was outside. I started up the signal again just in case it was someone who might get concerned enough to call Rusty. *Bam, bam, bam*, wait, *bam, bam, bam*, wait, over and over again.

I stopped to listen again.

"Cassidy?" Rusty called out from far away.

Bam, bam, bam, wait.

"Cass! Are you home?"

Bam, bam, bam, wait, *bam, bam, bam*, wait, *bam, bam, bam*, wait.

Shadow barking again. Could Rusty hear the signal through all the dirt and the closed closet? If I could hear him, he could surely hear me, I thought.

Bam, bam, bam, wait.

Maybe a general ruckus would draw more attention. I went back to sawing the support with the chain.

"Cassidy? Where are you?"

Saw, saw, saw.

"Stop!"

I stopped.

"Can you hear me?"

I sawed.

"Where are you? Don't answer. I'm in the bedroom. Am I close?"

I sawed.

"I'm going to list some places. Tell me when I get closer. The window. The bathroom. The dresser. The bed. The closet."

Saw, saw, saw. He opened the door.

"Cass, there's nothing here! Are you sure?"

Saw, saw, saw. I wished I could talk. I kicked the support some more hoping he could feel it in the closet.

"Babe, don't play games with me. This isn't funny anymore. Where are you? What did I do? Please come out."

I went back to the three hits. *Bam, bam, bam*, wait. He was a cop. He knew a distress call when he heard one.

"I'm standing in the closet and I tell you there's nothing here. There's nowhere else to look."

If only I could talk!

Bam, bam, bam, wait.

"Help me, then. Which way should I go? Left? Straight?"

Bam, bam, bam, wait.

He stepped forward, started shifting things around, tapping. The tapping was what I was hoping for. He'd be able to tell the wall was different. The tapping turned to knocking and the knocking turned to figuring. At last I heard the panels slide and the light from below drew his attention. He ducked through the two rods of clothes and onto the top stair.

"Cassidy?"

Bam, bam, bam, wait.

Hurried downward steps. A confused look around the room. Recognition as he spotted me under the stairs. He knelt down beside me then quickly stood.

"Hold on, I'll get a key and some scissors."

He ran up the stairs, found a handcuff key in his work clothes, pulled the scissors out of the junk drawer in the kitchen, and came downstairs again. He unlocked the cuffs and I rubbed my sore wrists as he slipped the scissors under the tape and cut it. I pulled the tape off my mouth.

"This is embarrassing," I said. He stood, hands on hips, a smirk on his face. It wasn't funny but I knew the story would be funny as it made the rounds of the station. He gave me a hand up but I couldn't stand yet. "Oh! Yikes!" I exclaimed as I tried to stand. "Agnes has a taser and she used it on me at the top of the stairs."

"You're kidding. How would Agnes know about this place?"

"You wouldn't believe me if I told you."

"Try me. I've seen a lot of weird things."

"Give me a hand."

We tried again and I limped over to the couch.

As he felt over my leg for swelling or broken bones I told him, "Would you believe Agnes and Mr. Morgan had a thing going?"

He looked at me skeptically. "You're kidding."

"Well, it may not have been an affair at his age. Agnes didn't go into that much detail. She only said that he made this room when he built the house because he remembered what it was like as a kid in World War II. He always wanted a place he could hide in, just in case. When Agnes was on the run one time he offered her refuge here. She became a regular. Not even Mrs. Morgan knew about this room."

"Where's Agnes now?"

"I don't know. She said she stopped here to pick up some things. When I followed her from the dinner she was stuck here."

"And Shadow followed her down here."

"Yeah, Shadow got to be a pain to her this afternoon and she let him out. I tracked him to the back of the closet and found the odd wall in the back. I stepped onto the landing and Agnes zapped me. Isn't this cool?"

"Yeah, so what do you think Agnes was looking for here?"

"She'd left some things behind. Then when Gus died she had trouble getting back in to retrieve them. When she left she was carrying a box."

"You mean all the time I've been working this case I've been sleeping right above the stolen jewelry?"

"It's possible. She didn't show me what was in the box."

"I don't want to go to work tomorrow."

"It's a weird coincidence but it makes a little bit of sense that the Morgans could tie into this considering their age. Wally was very taken with Agnes. Why wouldn't Gus?"

"So Agnes is gone again and knows we'll recognize her. She'll probably relocate now."

"I don't know. It depends on why she wanted that map. If the map contained some interesting information she might stick around and do some treasure hunting."

I limped up the stairs.

"You sure you don't need that x-rayed?"

"Give it a few days. All I did was fall on it."

"People die falling down a flight of stairs."

"Luckily, I wasn't one of them. It was worth the fall to find the room."

"I wonder what other secrets this house is hiding."

I hadn't thought of that. But how would I ever know what to look for? Anything odd, Cass, anything out of place. That's what you're good at, seeing things that are out of place.

Chapter 14

The doorbell rang the next day. It was Lou Strickland. All the stories floating around were conflicting. I'd been abducted and left to die. I'd been tasered and left to die. I'd been beat. I'd fought wild sand sharks. The stories were as wild as my life and he didn't know what to believe anymore so he came to find out.

"You're looking pretty good compared to what the stories say," he said.

"I'm glad this isn't the days of knights and bards. I don't think I could stand to hear ballads sung about my adventures. The stories are bad enough and I never actually hear them. Wild sand sharks?"

"Okay, maybe I was exaggerating."

"You? Or the person you heard it from?"

His eyes crinkled. He was in grandfather mode.

"I'm disappointed. I thought you really had taken on the sand sharks."

"I shot a wild rabbit and ate it raw. Is that rough enough for you?"

"If you had a gun why didn't you shoot Gonzo?"

"He threw it out into the desert for me and drove away. At least he did that much."

"Cassidy… I need to know."

His real reason for being there was to know if I could track, if I could handle a search.

"I don't know, Lou. The only way to know what I can take on is to try. You know I'll try. I've been beaten and spent three days walking across the desert with no water. I fell down a flight of stairs. Rusty is hovering over me like a mother hen and I'm going nuts. I've got a jewel thief on the loose and a mysterious map missing and I'm trying to put the two together and figure out what's going to happen next, but Rusty wants me to drop everything and it's just not in me to do that. If something comes up, call me. I'll try anything."

"I missed the part about falling down the stairs. That one hasn't made the rounds yet."

"Will you make sure it doesn't?"

A raised eyebrow.

"Look, you've had reason to need to find me, so I'll show you. But don't spread it around. It's no good if the wrong people know."

He leaned forward, interested. What would this kid come up with next? He seemed to be thinking.

"I discovered something about this house. Come here." I took him to the closet and shoved the clothes aside. "Look at this wall."

He looked carefully, noted the joints in the panels. He examined the edges, nodded his approval.

"Very ingenious."

"Believe it or not, my dog found it first. Pull to the side."

He placed his hand against the panels and they slid aside. He stared down into the dark below.

"Watch your step. They sure could have put the light switch at the top of the stairs but I guess if someone's looking for me I'd rather they enter the dark than surprise me with light." I went down into the secret room and flipped the switch. "Now you see why I don't want a lot of people to know about this? If anybody comes after me at home I've got an out."

"You can use an out."

"Definitely."

"I sure hope you never need it."

"I've had a few times when I could have used it. I'm guarding the knowledge of this room. So far only you, me, Rusty and Agnes know about it."

"Agnes?"

"It's another long story."

"That's what I'm here for."

"Then come to the kitchen. I'm going to fix lunch. You're welcome to stay."

As we were eating lunch silence finally settled in.

"So everything was true except the sand sharks?"

"Basically."

"And you can track?"

"Sure, I'll try. If I have to slow down, I just have to, but we haven't found a way, yet, to speed up a search. It happens the way it happens."

He nodded agreement.

"Oh, that reminds me. I did a search and the woman insisted I take something for my efforts. Let me find the check. I told her I'd donate it to the search and rescue team and she insisted on paying me anyway." I found the check Vivian had given to me. "I figure you can use whatever comes your way."

"What were you tracking that you got paid five hundred dollars?"

"A little dog. You didn't hear that one?"

"No."

"Golly, that was a fun one. I had to wrestle rattlesnakes and everything."

"Maybe that's where someone got the idea of sand sharks."

"Maybe."

"Cassidy, are you ever going to slow down? Someday reality is going to catch up with you. You can't live this charmed life forever. You're either going to have to back off from it or live through the consequences of it."

"It's not in me to slow down. Maybe someday it will be. But, right now, no, I wouldn't even consider it. I back off for Rusty's sake, but in the long term? No. I can't."

"How much do you think that body of yours can take? You're young. The way you're going you'll be old by the time you're forty. You can't expect to keep going the way you are now."

"Yes I can. But if it doesn't work out that way at least I know I put my all into it."

"All of how many years?"

"Tell you what. You give me work to do. Make sure I have my survival kit, don't freak out when my Jeep gets stuck in the middle of nowhere and I'll get into a lot less trouble."

"What's in your survival kit?"

"A hunting knife and a magnesium stick."

"That's it?"

"Yup."

"You have that and you promise to stick around a while?"

"Yup."

"Kid, what am I going to do with you?"

"Drop me anywhere with my knife and my magnesium stick and I'll make my way back. Hell, I did it with a 9mm and a pair of shoelaces. I'd have been better off with the knife and stick! I could have cut open the cactus easier and I could have actually cooked my food. I've spent many days in these mountains with nothing but those two things. The trick is to keep me busy and thinking without getting me interested in things that will bring on trouble…so use me. It's safer than leaving me idle."

He sighed, not understanding his little tracker at all. I was used to it. Rusty was the only one I could count on to understand me and even he had his limits.

Chapter 15

Thinking, that was what did it. If I just didn't think so much I'd live longer. I was sure of it. But I couldn't stop myself from thinking. And I was thinking about Agnes and that map. What had been on that map? I hadn't had time to look. Then it occurred to me that there were several other maps at the homestead. Maybe they were similar. Maybe if I knew what they said I'd get a feel for what had piqued Agnes's interest. Then I kicked myself. If I went out to that homestead Rusty would kill me. I'd be grounded for life. But what was the danger? I'd be less conspicuous alone than we had been with Chase. Once I got the snakes out I could get down in there, out of sight and no one would know the difference. All I needed was enough information to point me in the right direction. I remembered the person on the dirt bike. They had fled as soon as they were spotted, but why were they there? Why would they care if a few people were poking around the ruins of a house? I decided the operation had to be as low profile as possible. I couldn't go at night. Rusty would forbid it and I couldn't be sure about the snakes. Our visitor had showed up in the morning. So I decided afternoon would be the best time to go.

I returned to the station and quietly made my way to the K9 unit and borrowed their pole again. I sure would be glad when I didn't need this thing anymore. Wrestling rattlesnakes was not my idea of fun but I wasn't going to go down through the hole with them there and this time I did plan on going down into the hole. I didn't want anybody to see a person at the site if they rode by checking things out.

I ate lunch before I left. I packed a good flashlight and plenty of water. I wore desert camouflage and carried my camouflage rifle. I was set for my mission. The goal? To find out why Agnes had taken that map.

I left the rental car on the shoulder of the road and jogged across the desert to the old homestead. It reminded me of my time in Afghanistan but I didn't have to worry about land mines here. It didn't take me long to reach the house but then I had to get rid of the snakes. My rifle rested comfortably across my back as I reached in with the pole and swept it around, low to the ground. I only found one small snake and I dragged it well away from the area. I shined the flashlight around looking for more snakes. I waved the pole around again. Nothing. I did a quick tracking inspection of the area. Someone had been here, but they had only looked around, seemingly out of curiosity. I hoped that's all it was. They had stepped up onto the floor, but who wouldn't?

Any curious person would have walked around all over it. If they had been on the floor, had they removed the floorboards? There were only a handful of people who would know about the floorboards: the original owners, Rusty, Chase, me… and maybe the guy on the dirt bike.

I lay on top of the floor as I removed the boards. I shined the flashlight down in the hole knowing the snakes could be anywhere down there. When I was sure all the nooks and crannies that I could see were snake free, I slipped down through the hole in the floor, did a last flashlight inspection and pulled the pole, flashlight and rifle down in with me, then I pulled the boards back into place and settled in for a time of study. I turned on the flashlight and then opened the box the maps had been in. I pulled out a map. It was just a general map of southern California. I was amazed how few towns it showed. The roads were all different. The freeway didn't exist. The paved roads were few.

The commercially made maps just showed generalities. I needed specific information. I needed local information. I reached in for another stack of papers. The paper was brittle. I had to be very careful when I unfolded the papers that I didn't rip them apart. Folding them up was nearly as frustrating. At last I began finding smaller maps and a few with notes penned in, a dot with a name by it, an area traced out that I presume was property lines. Several of the penned-in dots had the same name next to them and the large areas also seemed to belong to the same family. Predominately I saw two names. A few minor properties had other names. I noticed one of the dots matched the location of the homestead but there was a dirt road that ran to it that was long gone. Wind and sand had taken possession of it. I was so engrossed in reading the maps that a movement against my leg made me jump out of my skin! I tensed instantly. The movement was constant. A soft, long stroke across my calf. A snake. I analyzed its movements estimating where its head would be. It was headed into the boxes. Damn. I didn't have room to move and I didn't want to shoot towards the boxes. Who knew what was in them? We'd found a pistol in them last time we looked. There could be eighty year old gunpowder back there. Did gunpowder work after eighty years? I didn't want to find out sandwiched between a thick wooden floor and the hard ground. Even I could smell the fear in that small area. So far the snake didn't feel threatened but if I moved around much that could change in an instant. I froze, glad I had plenty of stalking experience. I could stay still for a long time. As I sat there waiting for the snake to make up its mind I thought about my options. I didn't want to have to get out of that place quickly. Sitting cross-legged on the ground the floor was only inches above my head. To get out I needed to go around the boxes and I couldn't move that direction. I looked at the hole the snake had come through. Either way I had to pass over part of the snake to get there. Okay, Cass, just stay still. I felt a movement against my back. The snake checking out this warm blooded invader of his domain. Sweat trickled down my back and still I stayed frozen. The snake's head slipped down by my hip and I saw a small window of opportunity. I smoothly grabbed my rifle, pointed it at the snake's head inches away from the barrel and pulled the trigger. The snake's head vanished and its bloody, headless body thrashed around spraying blood everywhere. The snake didn't do much to stop the bullet, which continued on and blew away a large hole in the dirt bank enclosing the storage area. Dust and rocks flew. Blood flew. The smell of gunpowder was everywhere. I scrambled to the hole in the floor and shoved the boards up, coughing and fanning away the smoke.

Okay, enough. Maybe I'd found enough. I ducked down into the hole and grabbed the few maps that had some specific information on them and stuffed them into a cargo pocket of my combat pants. I grabbed my tools and worked my way out of the hole. What a mess! Blood everywhere. Time to head for home.

Halfway back to the car I realized a patrol car was parked behind my rental car. Shoot. Please let it be highway patrol. They might not know me. On the other hand, maybe I wanted to be recognized if I was walking up to them carrying a rifle, dressed in camouflage, and covered with blood. At least the guys who knew me would think it was halfway normal. I just didn't want this to get back to Rusty. Another car was cruising up and down the road. Shoot. No way was I getting out of this.

When I got closer I waved a friendly greeting. Recognition dawned on them. Smirks appeared where once they were all business. When I got closer their expressions changed from annoyed to curious. The other car circled around and parked behind the first patrol car. That was a good sign. If they were worried they would have blocked in the rental car.

"We had a report of shots fired," Ben Tomlin said.

"One. One shot. I know. I counted. It only takes one shot to blow away a rattlesnake at three inches," I said.

"You could have backed off just a little."

"Easier said than done," I countered.

"What's all this?" he asked fingering the bloody fabric of my pants.

"Rattlesnake blood. The snake kind of lost its head."

"What's the pole for?"

"Rattlesnake wrestling."

"Cassidy, do you do these things just to provide the station with endless story telling?" Jayce Thompson asked.

"No! You can't let this get back to Rusty. He'll kill me."

"I doubt if he believes us. He's kind of turned a deaf ear to the Continuing

Adventures of Cassidy Michaels. After the sand sharks…"

"It wasn't sand sharks. It was these same rattlesnakes. There was only one this time. Please don't tell him."

"What are you doing out here wrestling rattlesnakes?" Jayce asked.

"Well, first time, I was tracking a little dog. This time, I was looking for information on Agnes Cooper. I know. It seems like a stretch but it's less than you think."

I'd lost them somewhere. They heard about the little dog and they all knew about Agnes Cooper but the connection just didn't connect.

"I'll go tell the woman it was a hiker frightened by a rattlesnake. Cassidy, go home," Jayce said.

"Is that what I should write in the report?" Ben asked.

They all looked at me. Okay, I guess I really was frightened of it. That was a fair assessment that wouldn't get me in too much trouble.

"Sounds good to me," I said.

When I drove up to the house I knew I was in trouble. I opened the door silently and checked out the room before entering. I stalked to the wall separating the living room from the kitchen, dining room and den. I peeked around the corner. I stalked down the hall. I heard keystrokes coming from the office. That was good news. Maybe he'd be distracted and I could slip by before he noticed. I waited for the right time. He glanced down to read a file and I slipped past and into the bedroom. I quickly slipped out of the bloody camouflage shirt and pants, tossed them into the dirty clothes bin, and placed a towel on top so they wouldn't be visible. I put on jeans and a t-shirt, trying all the time to be silent. I went to the bathroom and checked for blood on other parts of me. There was a damp washcloth on the side of the sink so I used it to dab away the spots of blood on my hands and face. I brushed my hair. There, I was almost normal again. As close to normal as I could get without making noise, anyway.

I stepped across the hall and into the office and Rusty froze. Instantly froze. I saw him take in the room in the reflection of his computer screen. It wasn't pointed towards the door. He put his hand on his service revolver.

"Hey, it's okay, it's only me," I said. "Did you have a rough day? You seem overly alert or something."

"First tell me where you've been. Then tell me why you smell like a fireworks factory explosion."

"I've been exploring and I had to shoot a rattlesnake," I said.

"Cass… you don't get that full of gunpowder just shooting a rattlesnake."

"It was in close quarters."

"How close?"

"Very. Would you like tacos for dinner? That's quick."

He got up and followed me into the kitchen.

"I want you to sit down and tell me what you've been up to. If you had really gone exploring you would have told me where you went, what kinds of tracks you saw, and what the terrain was like. You're hiding something."

"Now, what would I be hiding?"

"Do you want me to list it all out? How about the *reason* you went? The place? Something that *happened*? Someone you ran into? Trouble you ran into? Umm, the fact that you weren't supposed to go *anywhere near that place*? Have I hit it yet?"

On the outside I was standing up to him, irritated that I couldn't do anything without it being stuck under a magnifying glass. Inwardly I was cringing, thinking he only cared, he only wanted to be able to trust me and I'd broken that trust. I was between a rock and a rattlesnake.

"Yeah," I said with a sigh. "You hit it."

Unfortunately irritated Cassidy was winning the battle right at the moment. I was waiting for the softer side to weaken the hard side. I didn't want to hide things from him but it seemed like, if I only did things he approved of, I'd do nothing at all. He was the one who got me thinking about Agnes in the first place and then he expected me to just drop it when my head was full of ideas and I was itching to get out. He was expecting too much if he thought I could just forget it. It was a puzzle, it had fallen apart and now I had to put it back together. I couldn't help it. If I left it broken it would take months or years to filter out and be just old, dead memories. I didn't want dead memories. A brain was for thinking and my brain was tuned. Once a puzzle was presented to it, it was a constant process until the puzzle was solved. Just like a search. Agnes was a search of sorts. The tracks were different but they were there. I just had to find them. They were in maps and patterns and social behaviors and cliques and… and I was making progress. But I wasn't making much progress on myself. So I stood there, guarding my emotions and reactions.

"Rusty, the map was the only thing Agnes took from us. I thought, if I went back to the homestead and looked at the other maps, I'd be able to see what had piqued her interest in it. So I went there. I was very careful. I went at a time of day when I'd be less noticed. I got rid of the snakes and crawled down under the floor and I covered the hole so it would look like no one was there. And I looked at maps. It was cramped and small under there and when a snake surprised me I shot it. It was a smoky, bloody, dirty mess down there for just a minute but all in all it was a successful trip. I found a map that might help me see what Agnes is up to. I'm sorry I went back, but I was careful and I did take precautions."

He leaned against the kitchen wall with a sigh of frustration.

"I asked you to stay away for your own protection. Did you read the journal?"

"No, I didn't even touch it. I was only interested in why Agnes wanted the information in the map."

"What if the people involved in that conflict don't want it brought back to life. If they find out there is someone who could reveal the things in that journal they would stop them. If they even thought you *might* know what's in that journal you'd be a target again. Babe, I don't want that. Any information you have can only make you more of a target. Did anybody see you?"

"No, nobody that matters. When I got to my car there were officers there investigating a shots fired report but I told them I'd just had to shoot a rattlesnake. They thought it all sounded a lot like typical Cassidy activity and went on their way."

"Okay."

"I wouldn't have gone back to the homestead if Agnes was caught. Only her interest in the map sent me there. My curiosity about it is satisfied and I won't be going back."

He seemed satisfied although I was really glad he didn't ask me what I'd learned. Disaster averted.

Chapter 16

Unfortunately, the thing that I learned from the map was where other similar places could be found. The family at the homestead was afraid of something. They had found places around the area to hide the things that really mattered to them and Agnes was on a hunt to find their jewelry. I was going to have to proceed very carefully. If one stash was watched the others could be too. They might have been long forgotten pockets of history, like the homestead. Or they might have been discovered and cleaned out long ago. Only finding them one by one would tell me. In my search I wasn't really looking for the stash itself. I was looking for Agnes. I wondered a bit what I would do if I found her but I'd have to worry about that when the time came. I set rules for myself. I would always go to a map location armed, with handcuffs and cell phone. If I found Agnes and I had a chance I would call Rusty. If not, there was the gun and cuffs option.

Something bugged me about the guy on the dirt bike, though. If he was interested in the things under the floor of the homestead, why didn't he get them out? And if he wasn't, why did he care at all who poked around the ruins of the house? So many questions and so few answers. It seemed like the more answers I got the more questions popped up. The more questions popped up the more my mind fiddled with it. It would be a never-ending cycle until Agnes was caught. I had senior citizen events to watch over, places to track and stake out, and one diligent husband trying to stay one step ahead of me.

I scanned the map on the computer and then I cropped off pieces of it so I had little pocket-sized maps with only enough information on them to take me to one place. If I only had one map on me at a time and I got caught I could only give them something they already knew. So, one little map in hand, I headed for the car and took Palm Drive all the way west until it nearly hit the foothills. After that a long-dead dirt road went off through a fenced off field. I parked the car.

The brush was thick in the field. I was sure I could disappear easily in there, if needed, so I crouched and slipped through the barbed wire and followed the barely discernable road up into the hills. The road ended and I got the map out. I'd seen no sign of tracks going in but I wanted to find out if this place had hidden secrets, too. If each family had hidden things before ill fate had befallen them Agnes might have an extensive jewelry hunt on her hands. Knowing what was hidden at each location would tell me if they held any interest for Agnes. So I searched. The map simply showed the two roads with a dot off to the side. There were some symbols on the map. One I took to be a building and another appeared to mark a natural landmark. There was a symbol next to the building. The hillside was covered with thick brush so I decided finding the building first might help me pinpoint things better.

Even the building was hidden by brush. Again, it was simply a foundation. This one didn't even have a chimney and what few pieces of the structure remained looked like burned wood. I walked the edges of the foundation, pulling brush away to see if there was space underneath. I couldn't see any way under it. The symbol near the building on the map turned out to be an old well. I tossed a rock down it and was rewarded with a splash. Hmm, the well seemed like a death trap for a youngster out exploring. It also seemed like a place I should remember if I was ever stranded in this area without water.

I stood on the foundation looking for the natural landmark on the map. What was it? A large tree? A rock? A ridge? Nothing jumped out at me so I headed in the direction of the landmark on the map. As I hiked, the hillside became steep. It was rough going and I began to question the symbols on the map. Maybe there was no significance to the dots but the foundation and the well told me otherwise. The building symbol had meant something and the well symbol had meant something. Now, what did a sideways Y stand for?

As I walked I naturally watched for tracks, but I didn't see any tracks here, not even old ones. It was too far off the beaten path. No one would think to follow a road that had been fenced off and dead for fifty years. I'd only been able to tell it was a road from the ruts. It was covered over with weeds and only a person used to noticing changes in the ground would see it at all.

I spent the whole day trudging through a small cleft in the hills looking for a landmark or a hiding place of some kind. I knew a hiding place could be small, a pile of rocks over an animal den, some valuables bound in fabric and stuffed in a hollow tree, a box buried. It could take a long time to find even one stash and there were six of them. I didn't even know if Agnes was following her map. She may have just noticed something very old and taken an interest in it just like I had. But even if I never saw Agnes this was interesting and keeping me out of trouble. I enjoyed the hunt. The puzzle of finding the place and seeking something hidden displaced the puzzle of finding Agnes. Agnes was Rusty's job. I had gotten interested in it because of our similar natures but Rusty would be glad I had something else to pursue, as long as he didn't know it involved a map from the homestead.

Animal tracks distracted me and I found myself nose to the ground up a game trail with a young doe just ahead. She stayed out of reach of me and climbed farther up into the hills. I shook my head to clear it. I wasn't out tracking, I reminded myself. I was searching for something. I turned around and made my way back to the foundation.

I stood at what I thought would have been the front door of the house. I looked at the countryside around me. If I were living here, the natural thing for me to do to go up in the hills would be to follow that little wash where the two hills met. It wasn't as steep and was easy walking. It led somewhere. It was the path of least resistance, especially before the land had gone wild, so that's the natural direction people would have walked. I looked at the map and it sort of matched. I'd have to follow it to be sure.

I didn't find anything that day. I looked in burnt out trees. I poked my head in animal dens. I walked for miles watching for anything that looked like a place a person would choose to hide something. I watched for anything man made. I came home empty handed but cheerful. I'd been out in the hills. I'd put miles beneath my feet. I had a goal and everything seemed right, if not productive. It was something I was enjoying and if something interesting happened along the way so much the better.

"You look cheerful today," Rusty said after work.

"I do? I had fun today. I went tracking. I saw a doe. She was on the move though so I didn't bother stalking her."

"Where'd you go?"

"Out on the west side of town, in the grassy foothills. There are lots of game trails through the grass."

He was satisfied with my answer and I thought, "Whew."

I decided to search one map area per day. Hopefully I'd run into Agnes's tracks and that would send me in another direction but until then the plan was to locate as many places on the map as I could in six days.

The next map took me to the west side of town again. It was out in the open in the middle of farmlands. Out here in the desert you don't see miles and miles of green fields like you might back east. Out here the farms are spread apart and separated by miles of desert. There will be a hundred acres of alfalfa or onions or carrots, surrounded by cactus, mesquite and Joshua trees. That's the way this farmland was. Dirt roads ran along side of the fields allowing me to get closer to the area on the map, but I was uneasy. The car would be discovered and my actions questioned. I decided it was too risky and backed out of that one. I went home and chose a different map.

This map took me way out west, almost to Gorman. I had to guess at the roads. The street signs had names now, unlike when the map was made. The map only showed lines. I'd brought up a modern mapping program on Rusty's computer and matched up the patterns to get an idea of where this place was, but it was only a guess. As I drove I saw fields of poppies and I thought I could play the dumb tourist if somebody asked me what I was doing out there. People from all over the country came out there to look at the poppy fields. Of course most of them didn't carry a 45 across their back. Hmm, maybe I should have gone for the 9mm. One road led to another and with each turn the roads got smaller and smaller. I really needed my Jeep. This rental car was designed for businessmen to drive from their hotel to meetings or from Joshua Hills to the airport. Dirt roads off in the boonies were foreign to it. It bumped and lurched and I worried about getting stuck. When the car had gone about as far as I thought it would go I got out and walked. Had I known about the poppies in this area I would have traded the rifle in for the pistol and brought a camera so I'd blend in with all the other people wandering around semi lost in the hills.

I got out the map again and tried to guess where I was on it. It wasn't a topo map and it wasn't necessarily to scale so it was all guess work. The road got rougher and rougher until I decided walking beside it was easier than walking on it. Poppies grew on the shoulders of the road, a bright orange path through the desert. When the road ended I looked for a building or a ruin but I didn't see one. There was farmland to the west and north, desert to the south and east. I decided the building would be more likely to be near the fields, a homestead abandoned after a bigger house was built. I searched the outskirts of the land, not wanting to venture onto private property. I compared the land around me to the map, then set boundaries that looked logical. The area that matched the building on the map was surrounded by barbed wire fences. Every quarter mile or so a sun-bleached sign hung. The signs facing south and west were faded beyond recognition but the ones facing north and east were still barely readable. They said, in red lettering: Danger! Keep out! I had to park on the south end of the field so I didn't read the signs until I'd already crossed the field. I ducked under the barbed wire fence and began my search.

I crisscrossed the land watching for any signs of a building or a hiding place. The terrain here was low rolling hills, with miles of dry grassland, brush, cactus and Joshua trees. It looked like it might have been good grazing land way back in the 1920's but one match and the whole place would go *poof.* It was dry as a tinderbox. The area seemed to have an unusual number of bones, bleached white by the sun and half covered by sand.

As I walked I kept noticing odd wires down in the brush. I stepped over them wondering where the rest of the fence was. Then I noticed that the wires were not lying loose on the ground. They were placed about ankle high.

When the thoughts about the wires niggled at my brain long enough, my trouble radar started going off. The next time I had to step over a wire I knelt down and looked more closely at it. Without touching it, I followed it to its starting point. I didn't have far to go. It was connected to a cyanide gun hidden down in the weeds. Yikes! The field was booby-trapped!

Cyanide guns were usually used to control nuisance predators around ranches. A piece of meat was attached to the top and when a coyote tried to take the meat the poison would explode into its mouth The powder would hit the saliva and a chemical reaction produced cyanide gas, eventually killing the animal.

Damn! I'd been stepping over these wires for hours! I was lucky I kept an eye on the ground. Then I thought about what might happen to Agnes if she were to try the same thing. I looked for the car. It was a half-mile away. Half a mile of booby-trapped field. I was torn. On one hand, if the thing hidden in this field was worth guarding with booby traps I wanted to see what it was. On the other hand, I could die doing it. It wasn't a death I looked forward to. I should carefully exit the field as soon as possible, and alert somebody. I did not want Agnes to stumble on this field the same way I had. I pulled out my cell phone.

"Hey, there, how are you?" Rusty said pleasantly.

"Fine, for now," I said uneasily. "I've got something here that needs investigating."

He didn't like the sound of that. "What is it?" he asked.

"It's a field. I'll give you directions but don't let the guys step off the road. It's booby trapped with cyanide guns. Do you know what a cyanide gun is?"

"Yeah," he said grimly.

"So far I've only seen one but I've been stepping over trip wires for hours. I'm going to head for the car and I'll check out the trip wires on the way."

"Cass, where are you?"

"I'll see you at the car. Don't let the guys leave the road."

"Cassidy! Don't move."

"I'll be careful, you know I will."

"Please, just wait. You have everything with you that you'd have at the car. There's no reason to risk it."

"I can show you what to look for."

He tried reasoning with me and I listened, then I gave him directions and, after we hung up, I picked my way carefully to the car. I found three more trip wires, also attached to cyanide guns. How much of an area had they covered? It was impossible to find them in all that brush. Only my natural habit of watching the ground for tracks had saved my skin. When I reached the car I retraced my steps to the last cyanide gun I'd found. One end of the trip wire was attached to the cyanide gun, the other to a stake in the ground. Someone had gone to a lot of trouble. There must have been a dozen of the things scattered in the field.

A single patrol car drove up the dirt road, lights flashing. Rusty leaped out as soon as the car stopped.

"We really need to get me another Jeep. This car is useless," I said.

"I told you to say put," he said.

"I've got one of the guns marked so you can see what's out there."

I started into the field and he jerked me back.

"Rusty, I've been out there for hours. Walking twenty feet down a path I've marked isn't going to trigger anything."

"For hours? *What were you doing out here?*"

"Looking for something. Look, here's one of the traps. It's attached to a stake on this end and a cyanide gun on the other. Usually these things are stuck down into the ground. Someone wanted to keep people out of this field. These guns are positioned specifically to target people. Someone is in big trouble."

"Yeah. You. Cass… this wire is invisible in amongst the weeds."

"You forget. I can see invisible things. I saw the wires; I just assumed they were part of a fence until I thought about it and looked closer. By the time I knew what they were I was a half mile that way," I said pointing. "That's where I was when I talked to you."

He ran his fingers through his hair and counted to twenty. He wasn't angry, not yet, but he wasn't sure how he should respond to this little adventure of mine.

About a half hour later a HAZMAT team arrived and pulled on protective suits making them look like tacky astronauts. Rusty talked to one of the men who approached me and asked to see the trap I'd marked.

"How many are there?"

"I have no clue. I'm guessing I stepped over a dozen or so trip wires but I was crisscrossing the area so I may have missed a lot."

"What area have you covered?"

"About half this fenced off area," I answered, pointing. "The eastern half."

"So we've got a square mile of cyanide guns to find?"

"I don't know about the land past the roads. Oh, and I found more of them towards the center of the area than I did on the sides."

They went into an alien looking huddle and Rusty jerked me out of there and took me back to town before I could try anything else. He took me to his office and slapped the report on the desk that I needed to fill out.

"Why *that* field?" He demanded.

"I reasoned it out that that field had what I was looking for."

"What made you think that?"

"A map. And I looked up the location on your computer."

"What did you expect to find there?"

"I didn't know. That's one reason I was having a hard time finding it."

"You went twenty miles out of town to look in some random field for some random object and you just happened to find the one field in the whole valley that is booby trapped?"

"Semi random, but yeah."

"Cassidy, do you know how close a call that was?"

"Yeah, that's why I called it in. I didn't want somebody else to stumble on it."

"And I suppose, if it had only been a danger to you, you would have just written it off as another adventure."

"I knew somebody might be coming there and I didn't want them to get hurt."

"And who might that be? What other person did you expect to target that particular field?"

"Agnes."

That baffled him for a bit but he chose to ignore it.

"Did you leave a note on the fridge? Would I have been able to find you if something *had* happened? Babe, cyanide is nothing to play around with!"

"I wasn't playing around with it. I stopped what I was doing and I called you as soon as I realized what was going on. And I did leave a note on the fridge but I ended up with a change of plans because the first place I tried looking seemed too dangerous."

"What in the world was more dangerous than cyanide guns?"

"People."

Chapter 17

Three more places to check out. I hoped they were easier than the first three. I didn't need any more booby traps. I'd run across booby traps in my tracking before. Fish hooks hanging in trees to cut people. A shotgun rigged to blast when a wire was tripped. Trip wires placed to release a warning noise to people watching for me. I was used to being careful about these things. Now that I knew the possibility was real in my searches I had to be extra vigilant. Vigilant for me, and for Agnes. I felt a need to protect her if she chose to pursue her own treasure hunt. She might be stealthy and clever but I didn't count on her having an eye for the invisible. With my trouble radar tuned I continued my search.

The next location seemed fairly safe. It was even in town. It was a house in an older part of town, and was still standing, although it was windowless and boarded up. A chain link fence kept out the easily dissuaded. I was not easily discouraged and the fence was loose so I parked to hide myself from view and quickly slid underneath.

This time there were tracks around the house. They were only partial tracks because of the thin grass. I examined the tracks closely. They could have been left by Agnes. It could also have been some older neighborhood kid bent on mischief.

The walls had graffiti sprayed on them. Kids probably found their way in there frequently. I did what I thought Agnes would do, slipping around the house to the back, feeling for loose boards over the windows. Most of the particleboard covering the windows was securely bolted down, but one window had three bolts removed. The fiberboard was held in place by one bolt. The other corner rested on a nail stuck in a hole in the siding. Remove the nail and the plywood swung down revealing a dark interior. I stuck my head into the opening and shined the flashlight inside. Yes! It wasn't positive proof but it seemed more likely to be Agnes than a kid now. Whoever had entered had not just climbed in. They had squatted in the window frame and very carefully placed their footprints where they would be the least noticeable. In my mind there were very few people who would think to do that. Agnes. Me. Chase. Elan? I doubted if Elan would think to do that unless he had scouting lessons with his grandfather and Chase. Neighborhood kids didn't even enter the picture in my head. It was Agnes. I was ninety percent sure. I hadn't expected to find her there, but it meant I needed to check out the rest of the sites and senior-proof them. I stalked from room to room doing my cop imitation. When I was sure the house was free of people I turned my attention to Agnes's tracks. They were not easy to see in the dark. I had to search out each one in the flashlight beam. Only the fact that this was the desert and the house had sat empty for many years allowed me to track her inside. The wood floors were covered with a fine powdery dust, especially thickest near the windows. I could tell that one room was used frequently by teenagers to hide out and smoke and do drugs. Cigarette butts and drug paraphernalia littered the floor. Burn spots dotted the wall near the group's meeting spot. It was a wonder they hadn't burned the place down. I'd have to tell Rusty about this house, too.

I didn't know which was more distressing to me, the risk to my life that was out in the field or this dark side of society that I mostly tried to pretend didn't exist. I could handle threats to me. I was used to those, but to see kids putting themselves at risk day after day saddened me. Then I wondered what the difference was between these kids doing drugs and me hiking through booby trapped fields, getting myself kidnapped and beaten. I decided the only difference, really, was that I hadn't done anything illegal. The basic premise was the same and it saddened me to put Rusty through that.

Cassidy, just go home, I told myself, you don't have to do this.

But I did. If Agnes had come here she would check out some of the other sites as well, especially if she had found anything here. I examined the inside of the house carefully, tracking Agnes as much as I could. It looked like she had followed the walls, probably feeling for inconsistencies that would indicate hiding places. Where she stopped, I stopped to see what had caught her attention. She had a sharp eye and a good feel for the invisible, I had to give her credit for that. Often when she stopped it took me some time to figure out what had caught her attention. I had to read the shallow tracks. Was she standing or squatting, reaching or looking at something? The tracks usually told me but often the house itself didn't. The walls were buckled from water leaking through the old roof. The floor was buckled from age. The boards creaked. The house groaned when the wind blew.

Pieces of wall had been torn away and Agnes had looked around in the nooks and crannies but she hadn't brushed away the spider webs to look deeper. A breaker box had been wallpapered over and then cut back out. The door hung open. I wondered if Agnes had opened it thinking it was a safe. I looked at the tracks to see if there was a quick backwards leaning to them but I couldn't tell. When I had followed Agnes around the house as much as I was able I started looking at other things. A panel covered a hole leading up into the attic. I found a metal bed rail that had been discarded and I used that to push up on the panel. It was hinged and the panel opened upwards. When it fell over with a bang another explosion rocked the house and I jerked the rail down, examining it. I was glad I didn't have a ladder! Someone didn't want people poking around up in the attic. If that was true, there was a reason for it.

The bed frame had a bracket on the side. I looked around and found the other half of the frame. I used the brackets like stilts and it gave me just enough height to reach into the hole and pull myself up. The gun up there was trip wired, so it wasn't going to go off again. I just had to be careful of any other wires up there. I braced myself in the opening long enough to look around. I declared the area right next to the hole to be safe and drew my feet up. I did it. I was in the attic.

Being careful to only step on ceiling joists, I sneaked around the attic, attuned to trouble. Boards had been laid over a section of the ceiling joists and several boxes had been stored up there. One box contained hand embroidered table runners, pillowcases and handkerchiefs. I imagined an antique dealer's eyes lighting up if presented with this box. Another box contained important papers. Once again there was a box of personal belongings and a small box… of fine jewelry. This was what Agnes was looking for. But she'd missed it. I pulled out the map and looked at it. There were three symbols on this location. Did one of them represent jewelry? I needed to go home and compare this piece of the map to the others, and figure out where Agnes was likely to look next. My curiosity satisfied, I started putting everything back when I heard a *boom, boom, boom…* "Open up! Police!"

Shoot! Not again. I stuck my head out the hole and yelled down, "I can't! It's boarded up! Try the window in back with a board that's swinging loose."

"Cassidy?" It was Kent Jacobsen. Double shoot.

"Yeah, Cassidy," I answered. "All's clear in here except for me."

I waited until they had both found the window and made their way into the living room.

"Up here," I told them.

They looked up through the hole in the ceiling.

"What are you doing here?" Jacobsen asked.

"Do you remember the shots fired report out in the desert?"

"Yeah."

"And the booby trapped field they called HAZMAT out to?"

"Yeah."

"I'm doing the same thing as I was then."

"Come down. Where's your ladder?"

"You're standing on it."

They looked around, saw the bed frame.

"This?"

"It worked. Can you scoot it aside so I don't land on it?"

He kicked the bed frame aside and I stood over the hole. I calculated my jump and skimmed through the hole, landing on bent knees. The floor gave way and all three of us landed in a dusty, dirty, spider-webbed heap in the crawl space under the house.

When the dust had settled and we all verified we were okay, I said, "You told me to come down."

"I think you better come with us," Jacobsen said.

On the way I heard the radio transmissions, getting Rusty's twenty, telling him to meet them at the station. Rats.

They led me to an interrogation room but it didn't worry me. I'd been there several times. I'd spill the beans. They'd shake their heads. I'd explain it all to Rusty. He'd give me the hands in pockets safety lecture. He'd take me back to my car. I'd go home and fix dinner.

"We had a report of shots fired," Jacobsen stated bluntly.

"One shot. Only one. I counted." I was getting tired of this and I imagined they were too. "They actually call in gun shots in that neighborhood? I thought they were used to it by now."

Sigh, "Okay, one shot," he said. "Explain it."

"It would be easier to explain back at the house," I said. "The attic was booby trapped. A gun was wired to the panel leading into the attic. I opened it with the bed frame pole and *bam!* I'm getting used to this now. After the rattlesnakes and the cyanide guns, I've become cautious. So one shot, aimed to take out anybody who ventured into the attic. Here's my sidearm, no shots fired. If you take a look at the attic you'll find one forty-five, aimed at the opening, one shot fired, no fingerprints."

"You triggered the shot and you went up there anyway?"

"I figured the gun wouldn't fire again. I watched for more triggers while I was up there. There appeared to be just the one."

"Did you find anything?"

"Yeah." I listed the contents of the boxes as I'd seen them.

"Why? Cassidy, we're used to your antics by now. We know you've got an agenda here. So… why are you doing this?"

"Agnes."

It took him a minute. "Huh? What does Agnes Cooper have to do with rattlesnakes, cyanide guns and booby trapped attics?"

"She's got a map. A map that shows where these places are. This is the first one of the spots marked on the map where I saw evidence that Agnes had been there. So I need to check out the other locations before she gets herself killed. In the process I was hoping I'd run into her, but so far that hasn't happened. I've got two more locations to check out."

"Why did she choose this house?"

"I don't know. She has a different map than me. Maybe her map has a key to the symbols on it. Mine doesn't."

"And how did you come to be in possession of said map?"

"Ummm, the rattlesnakes gave it to me? I'll put it back when I'm done. Actually I could put it back now, except Rusty won't let me. I have pieces scanned and printed out so I only carry one little section at a time. That way I can't give out any information except what the people already know."

"And who are the people?"

"I don't know. I only have two last names and I don't know who the good guys or bad guys were in the situation. It happened in the late 1920's so it's not like you can go after them."

The door opened and Rusty stepped in.

"Enough?" Jacobsen asked him.

"Enough," Rusty answered.

Jacobsen left and we were alone.

"I should have Jacobsen question you more often. You'll tell him more than you'll tell me."

"That's because Jacobsen won't ground me and make me feel guilty for holding back. I'm not worried about Jacobsen's feelings."

He put his arms around me. "I guess I can understand that. But I need more information than that. You said there were two more places left to check out?"

"Yeah."

"Where?"

"The map is at home. I only have one piece with me. See?" I handed him the little four by four inch square. "I need to get to these places before Agnes does. She wouldn't watch for a rifle in an attic. She wouldn't wonder about trip wires in a field."

"You're doing this to protect a jewel thief?"

"It didn't start out that way, but, yeah. And the house I was in *did* have jewelry in it. Agnes just didn't find it. But it gives me a hint to look at on the big map. The homesteads have symbols next to them. Since we know the contents of this house we can figure out where Agnes is most likely to look next."

"I should have known you were up to something."

I spread out the big map and compared symbols. The house in town had three symbols: I, $ and *. The homestead I first stumbled on had: $, I, ^. So comparing the two I had to guess I was information, papers, financial statements, accounting books. $ would be money, although I didn't see a box of money at the house, like I did at the homestead. Perhaps I needed to be a bit more thorough in my investigating. I had been focused on jewelry. The two symbols that varied were the * and ^. If I had to take a wild guess I'd say the ^ was the roof of a house and the homestead had contained household belongings: China, personal belongings, silverware, that kind of thing. So the * was the mysterious symbol that might mean jewelry. Maybe it reminded the owner of the facets of a diamond. I looked on the map for other * signs. There were two others. One was a place I hadn't checked out yet. The other was the homestead in the hills with the well that I had spent all day investigating.

"I'll go back to this one alone," I told Rusty. "I've already been out there. I searched all over the area and didn't run into any booby traps. Whatever is hidden there is just hidden very, very well. Seems like each family hid their valuables as well as they could. I guess how they chose to hide their possessions depended on their experience with the people they were hiding them from. One thing I don't understand is why these things are still there. You'd think someone in the past eighty years would have ventured up into that attic. I don't get it."

"Maybe they weren't put there eighty years ago."

"But then why put them *there*? Why not rent a storage unit or a safe deposit box? There are better ways to keep things around than hiding them in ruined houses."

"That, I don't know. I'm only speculating. We have two choices. The new site or the old one."

"The new one. Agnes went for the house in town first. The one I have already been to is the most remote. Agnes would probably visit the closer one first."

"Think we're too late?"

"Not if we hurry."

"You want to go out there today?"

"Why not?"

"Getting shot at and falling through a floor wasn't enough for one day?"

"I wasn't shot at. I was very careful not to get shot at. And I didn't exactly fall through the floor. I jumped."

"Did you have to take two guys down with you?"

"If they'd stepped back one more step they wouldn't have fallen through. Let me put on some desert gear if we're going out there. The tracks I saw at the house were recent, yesterday, maybe today. If we're going to catch Agnes or prevent her from walking into danger we have to get out there."

"Wear your vest," he reminded me.

"I don't know if I should. I've been shot at more in the vest than without it. I think it has a sign on it that says 'shoot me.'"

"Wear it."

I always put on my bulletproof vest with mixed emotions. It was a gift to me from a father whose son I found dead from hypothermia. It was a reminder of a failure. A tragic failure. Yet it had saved my life more than once. What an ironic twist. I couldn't save Carl Cranston but his father had saved me.

I dropped the rental car keys in Rusty's hand as we went out.

"What's this?"

"You're used to your Explorer. You don't remember how limited a car is. See how far it gets us. I bet we end up walking a mile or more."

"We don't have time to be walking a mile to this place."

"Sure we do. I've been doing it all week."

"Okay, I get the point. Let's take the Explorer."

I thought we'd end up taking it anyway because that's where all Rusty's gear was.

It bothered me that all the places I'd been to on the map were almost obliterated. There were plenty of houses around from the 1920's but not these houses. And they all belonged to one family. A big family to be sure but it seemed someone at one time must have had a vendetta. I hoped it didn't carry on for eighty years but the traps we were running into were not eighty years old. It was a little worrisome.

This site, as well, was mostly just an abandoned burned out house. Only one charred wall and the foundation remained. The foundation was cement. No place to hide things under there. We searched the edges of the foundation for a way underneath but found nothing. I searched the area for tracks.

"Now what do we do? We can't stake out this place hoping Agnes will walk up to it. She could see us from a mile away. I know I could do it if I was alone but I don't think we want to dig foxholes for a team of cops to lay out here in wait. If Agnes didn't show we'd never hear the end of it."

"Do you think Agnes knows what to look for? She may be looking for a structure like the house in town was."

"Well, so far that's the only one that has had some of the building remaining. Most of them are like this. But the map had symbols by this place. Where could they have hidden things here?"

"Maybe they burned with the house."

"I'm not counting on it. I'm going to do some poking around."

"Where? There's no place to look."

"There are *always* places to search. Maybe I'll only find rabbit tracks but there's always something."

I began walking. There was a little dip in the land that I couldn't see a reason for so I followed that. It was almost like a path and it bugged me. It wasn't a place where water had run off. Those kinds of little dips in the land were common on the desert but they were unmistakable for what they were. They looked like itty bitty pre-arroyos. This wasn't one of those. Another reason for small dips in the land were man made ridges, again, to channel water and prevent erosion in some unwanted place. This wasn't that either. The only other reason I could think of for that little dip to be there was a very well-worn path. A human game trail.

Rusty followed my actions knowing something was brewing but he couldn't imagine what. He probably thought I was wasting my time. As far as I was concerned the time spent exploring homesteads was more worthwhile than puttering around a clean house looking for things to do.

The path didn't go very far. I almost didn't see what it led to. At first I thought it was the hole where an outhouse had once stood. Then I thought it was something that had been buried and dug up. But then I noticed a roof of sorts. It almost looked like another foundation but as I examined the layout of it. I realized it was like a root cellar. The desert winds had blown in sand and it had filled in the doorway and covered over the roof. Rusty watched me as I walked around what looked like a dent in the ground. I walked around on the roof, noticing it gave underneath its load of sand. I kicked at the edges of it and heard sand filter down through the shake shingles.

"Go get the flashlight," I told Rusty.

Starting at one edge I pulled the sand away until I found the corner of the roof. I found the shingles loose and wobbly. They were cracked with age and a couple of them broke apart when I tried jiggling them. I pulled the shingles off until I uncovered enough of the roof to slip through. All the wood was rotten. Water had seeped through the shingles and settled on the planks beneath. After the planks had rotted, water had seeped into the cellar. Rusty handed me the flashlight and I shined it down in the hole. It was a damp and clammy place.

"If there was ever a gun positioned down there it's rusted together with age. Take a look."

Rusty shined the light down into the hole.

"How do you see these things? I'd have walked right over it thinking it was a sand dune."

"Walk on it. You'll see it feels like an old roof. I'm going in."

"Cass, you jump into these things too quickly. There's no use in going down there. You're not going to find Agnes down there and it could be another trap."

"If it is, it's a very old trap. Hand me the flashlight." He hesitated. "If there's something down there we need to know. Agnes's map might make this look attractive enough for her to do some searching here. If it's worth her while then we ought to know."

"How are you going to get out?"

"Well, hopefully, you'll give me a hand."

"If I wasn't here, you'd still go in."

"Yeah, but I'd have a surer way of getting out first."

Another visual check and I dropped into the hole. Rusty probably would have gone first if I'd given him the chance but the hole wasn't big enough and I was the curious one. I dropped into a squishy quagmire of stinky mud.

"Ugh! If there's something down here it better be good and it better be up off the ground!"

I followed the floor of the cellar to the back wall, my feet making a sucking sound whenever I pulled them out of the mud. The cellar wasn't large. I could barely stand up in it. Rusty would have to crouch over if he went in.

Rusty began walking around on the roof, seeing if it really did feel like an old roof. Sand filtered down on top of me.

"It's awful enough down here without you adding to it!" I called up.

In the back wall little mailbox-sized holes had been dug and I found rusty farming tools stashed in them. The farm was long gone. Desert had reclaimed it but still the tools remained. A wall of rocks hid something. I took the rocks down one by one.

"Cassidy? You okay?" Rusty called down.

"Yeah, just looking around. No jewelry yet."

I decided the one rock at a time method was too slow so I tried pulling the wall over. The rocks tumbled down into a heap and I shined the flashlight over them. I stepped over the pile and entered a small cave dug out of the back of the cellar. It was a small space, about the size of a card table. The rock wall had kept out the water so the floor was dry. I sat cross-legged inside. Dirt. And rock. Just a small cave dug out of the cellar.

Suddenly outside there was a splintering, crashing roar, and dust filled the little cave. I crawled to the opening and where the cellar had once been there was an immense pile of wood and sand.

"Cassidy!" Rusty called. He scrambled around on the pile pulling shingles and boards away. Looking for any way down through the mess. I couldn't see him, only hear him, and he was frantic.

All I could do was cough and wait for the dust to settle.

"Cassidy! Say something, please!"

"I'm okay!" I yelled between coughs. "I'm stuck, but I'm okay."

He heaved a sigh of relief. "I thought I'd killed you. Where are you?"

"I'm behind the back wall of a cellar. I'm sealed in but I don't think I'm in any danger."

"You were right, it's an old roof."

"You could have just trusted me, you know."

I shined the flashlight around the little cave. It was definitely man made. The walls were straight and the corners were neat. But that was it. At first. Since I had plenty of time to kill down there I started examining closer.

"I need tools to get you out. Are you sure you're okay?"

"Yeah. Go for it. I'm not hurt. Nobody's going to sneak up on me while you are gone. There's no booby trap. I'm fine."

Silence settled in when he left. I focused on the cave. If that proved to be a waste of time I'd see about getting out of there. I didn't know where I would put the dirt and lumber but I'd try. I shined the light along the wall. Still dirt and rocks. I thought the placement of the larger rocks was odd. I tried to think about other places I'd seen with exposed dirt. Arroyos. Arroyos sometimes had imbedded rocks in the sides, but not like this. I pried at a rock with my fingers. It didn't budge. I picked out a smaller rock and used it to scrape away the dirt around the edges of the bigger rock, then I tried prying the rock loose again. It fell to the ground in front of me with a heavy thud. Behind it, a hole had been dug in the wall, similar to the ones that the farm tools were in. I reached in automatically fearing scorpions or rattlesnakes but knowing sand sharks would be more likely. This hole had been blocked off for a long time.

What I felt puzzled me. I pulled out an odd object. Oh shit! Damn it, Cassidy! I couldn't drop it, it could go off. Since it was not triggering at the moment, I froze and examined the object. Okay, Cassidy, you can breathe again. Think, think. You're in a little cave with a live trap. You can't get away from it. Disarm it. I was afraid to move my hand. The trap was rusted so it was possible it was safe but I couldn't be sure. The device was a shotgun shell attached to a rattrap. Only the rust had kept me from losing my face. It was still dangerous. I realized I couldn't let the spring go without the arm hitting the head of the shell. Damn. I pointed the shell away from me and felt with my other hand in the hole. I pulled out…a small bar of gold. Not exactly what Agnes was hoping for but I bet she would be intrigued enough to look further. I put it back and put the trap in the hole so that if it went off it would fire into the back of the hole. Oh man, now that I looked at the walls there were several similar odd rocks. How many of them held traps? Did I dare open another one?

Rusty, why did you have to go away right when I need to be talked out of something? I counted the odd rocks. There were a lot of them. I looked at the placement of them. I picked one that I could easily stay out of the way of, if it went off. Then I braced myself to the side of it, scraped away the dirt around the edges and pried. The angle was awkward but I wasn't going to put myself in the line of fire. A couple more scrapings and more prying and the rock fell out. Instead of a thud, an explosion filled the small cave, making me jump!

The shot blasted the far wall of the cave and dust and rocks flew everywhere. So that's what the first one was supposed to do. I was glad I was prepared when one really went off! I coughed and fanned at the cloud of gunpowder that filled the little cave. I certainly didn't want my air contaminated any more than it already was.

Okay, Cass, the trap is sprung, it can't hurt you now. I reached into the hole, still staying well out of the way. I pulled out a small leather box. The leather was worn and the top layer was curled with age. I shook the box gently. It sounded promising. I opened the box, pointing it away from myself as I did. I was getting paranoid. I didn't even trust a little box. When nothing happened I looked inside.

Well, Agnes, here you go. Inside were two finely crafted rings and brooches. All the pieces were obviously handmade and each ring and brooch set was made to be worn together. How many other holes contained jewelry? There were several of them I didn't dare open because I couldn't get out of the way of them. Then I thought that there had to be a way to remove the contents without triggering a trap, otherwise, how would the real owners get them out? Since the trap was tripped and there was nothing in there to hurt me I reached into the back of the hole. I carefully felt around and realized the back of one hole had an opening to the next. I sat back. It was possible, if one started in the right spot, to deactivate the traps. Would it work backwards? What would happen if the shot went off and the rock was still over the opening? Would the rock take the hit or would I get beaned by a softball sized rock? Would it set off a chain reaction inside the little labyrinth behind the wall? I sat back and calmed my frazzled nerves. I didn't want to mess with a wall of booby traps but I wanted to satisfy my curiosity. So far I had found jewelry but not enough to really tempt Agnes. I wanted to know if there was more. And I was curious if I could outsmart this wall. It was a puzzle. As I sat there thinking about how I would go about solving the puzzle I heard a scraping sound outside.

"Cassidy? Are you okay?"

"Yeah," I yelled back. "I'm fine. I found something."

"What?"

"I found a little bar of gold and a little box with some jewelry in it."

"Help will be coming soon."

"No problem. I've got a puzzle to work on. If you hear weird sounds don't panic."

I didn't want to use the word explosion because he'd worry. An explosion is a weird sound, right? I was glad he wasn't here for the first weird sound. I hoped there wouldn't be more.

Okay, Cass, how can you see what's in the next hole without setting off a trap? I stuck my hand into the safe hole. Remembering that a shotgun blast could knock a good sized hole in a door, I decided getting beaned by a rock was a very real possibility. I felt the back of the next hole over. An object was lying in the back. I scooted the object in the back until it bumped gently against the object in the front. Okay, that hole wasn't safe. I removed the object that was in the back. It was another little box, which contained a pocket watch. I thought about the positioning of the trap. It would be pointed towards the opening of the hole. Nervously, and very gingerly, I turned the trap to face the back of the cave. Now if it went off it wouldn't shoot forwards, only to holes I'd already emptied. So far so good.

"Cassidy?"

Who was that?

"Yeah?"

"Just keeping tabs. You okay?" It was Antonio Rodriguez. Rusty had enlisted the help of the closest Fire Department.

"Yeah, so far so good."

"She's up to something," said Rusty to Antonio. "She's being too quiet."

More voices outside.

"So what are we doing?"

"Cassidy? What part of the cellar are you in?"

"If you were to enter at the door, just go straight back and then to the right."

"How far is it from the door to the back?"

"About five paces."

I heard digging overhead. I was almost disappointed that my time was limited.

Okay, the trap is turned to the back of the cave. All it can do is blast a hole in the side of the little niche and back the way I'd already come. I thought it was safe to try the rock. I scraped the sand away around the front of the rock and when it was loose I held it in place. I removed it slowly feeling for a trip line. Carefully, I scooted the trap to the back of the hole and into the hole behind, always keeping the shot pointed away from me and away from more traps. I stuck my hand into the hole and felt for the next.

It was a tense time knowing any moment a shotgun blast could rip through rock. I found several pieces of jewelry, enough to tempt Agnes. When the guys pulled away the last of the roof and peeked in at me they found me shoulder deep, feeling my way through the wall. I pulled my arm out.

"What are you doing in there?" Antonio asked.

"Only one of you at a time will fit in here. Let Rusty in first. He'll want to call in a team to deactivate all these things."

The guys exchanged glances.

"Don't touch that one," I said. "It's rusty but it's still very much alive. Here's the one I accidentally tripped."

I handed the trap to Rusty and he blanched.

"Where did you find this?" he asked.

"See these rocks? The bigger ones that don't seem to fit in? Behind each one is a hole with something stashed in it. In the front of the hole is one of these. Behind the trap is other stuff. Look, I found three boxes of jewelry, and one pocket watch. It's a death trap for Agnes. We have to disarm it all before she gets here."

"How did you get all this out if there's a trap in each hole?"

"See the last hole? That's the one that went off. After it was tripped I could reach from one hole to another. Each of these other holes has the trap scooted to face the back where it couldn't do any damage while I went on to the next one. Once I saw the system it wasn't hard to carefully work my way down the row."

He took a deep breath.

"You were trapped in a small cave with all these traps and you spent the time trying to figure out how to outsmart them? Cass, you could have killed yourself."

"Only by the first one and that one didn't fire."

He ran his fingers through his hair.

"And I was worried about the roof coming down on you! Out!"

"I will as soon as you move."

We crawled out of the little cave. I made sure to take the safe trap along to show the team what they were in for.

"I'm never letting you out of my sight again. I turn my back on you for a second and the next thing I know everything falls apart; you play deadly games in close quarters with explosives. Why? Cassidy, it was something that could wait. We could have called in a team and had it all disarmed. We have experts for this. What made you think you could just disarm a wall of traps and take the things out with you?"

"I had it figured out before I tried anything. I thought it through. You gave me plenty of time to do that. Look, I got through one whole row without getting hurt. I found out what we came here to find out. There's definitely enough jewelry in there to send Agnes on a treasure hunt. Look at these." He opened the little boxes. "And that's just one row's worth."

"Next time I'm going in first," he stated flatly.

"If you had gone in first you would have said there was nothing in there but a bunch of farming tools. You take in what you see and you don't get curious about oddities. We would have gone on to the next spot on the map without knowing anything about that little cave."

"Okay, next time I'll go in first and *then* you can look for oddities."

The firemen were putting their tools away.

"Antonio, Roger, thanks for coming out. I hope Rusty didn't make it sound like too much of an emergency."

"He was pretty calm this time. But we never know when it comes to you," Antonio said.

"Yeah," said Roger, "your circumstances have a way of turning in an instant, just like they could have today."

"Aw, guys I knew what I was doing or I wouldn't have chanced it. You think I want to set off booby traps in confined places?"

Antonio raised an eyebrow. He wasn't sure.

Rusty's team arrived and I showed them what they were up against and then turned them over to Rusty.

"Remember how we didn't want the contents of the homestead publicized? Well, having a bomb squad empty this cave isn't going to help that cause. You can count on word of this getting out. When you throw a rock at a pack of dogs the one that gets hit yelps. Let's hope no one yelps when this gets around. Be prepared for a call to Schroeder's office. He's going to need an explanation and he's not going to take my explanation alone. He'll stand up for you but you've got to show him we had reason to be out here."

Chapter 18

It was like a trip to the principal's office. I knew why I did the things I did. Getting other people to understand that was a whole other problem. Nobody appreciated Cassidy logic.

"Wait a minute," Schroeder said trying to get the past few weeks to make sense. "Agnes stole a map from you that you stole from a homestead and now you're following another map trying to catch Agnes on some wild goose chase because you think she is looking for the jewelry hidden at these locations? You've had the HAZMAT team out twice this week because of some wild goose chase that you don't even know will pan out?"

"First: the HAZMAT calls were legitimate even if Agnes never showed. I've proven there is a legitimate reason to check out each of the locations on this map. Second, I did find Agnes's tracks at one of the locations. We're lucky she didn't look as far as I did or we would have had a dead jewel thief."

"Oh, yes, the shots fired report. Cassidy, this department feels like a three ring circus with you on the hunt! I want you to stop. What have you done successfully?"

"In the hunt for Agnes or the weird map controversy?"

"Let's do the weird map controversy first since that's the reason you're here."

"There are six locations around the valley that someone doesn't want people to know about. Each of the locations I have visited has either had things hidden very well or protected by booby traps. I uncovered a field with cyanide guns, found an attic with a rifle set to go off if someone tried to go up there and a cellar full of booby trapped holes containing valuables. However, the first homestead I found by accident is the one that contained the information about all the others."

"You found it by accident?"

"Yeah, I was tracking a little dog for some lady and her dog disappeared under the floor. When I fished him out I found boxes of stuff hidden there."

"And why do all these finds matter?"

"Well, I thought we didn't want people stumbling into places where they could get themselves killed."

He put his head in his hands then rubbed his eyes wearily. "Okay, what about Agnes?"

It was a long talk. A very long talk. I thought I'd never get out of there. I thought he was going to deport me, make the Marines take me back and send me to Iraq, but he didn't. Maybe he thought Iraq had enough problems.

"What are you going to do next?" he asked.

"Well, there's one more location on the map that Agnes might hit. I guess I want to go back and make sure it's not booby-trapped. Now that I know what to look for maybe I can find it this time."

"You're going there looking for traps? What about Rusty?"

"He'll probably insist on going. Maybe I can slip out before dawn."

"You don't want him to go?"

"He's a cop, he's not a scout. He's careful of people but he doesn't have an eye for things like trip wires. He's got the analytical mind he needs for his job but it involves people and evidence. He doesn't profile a trail as he walks. He doesn't see odd things as odd. I'd rather go without him."

"Is there anyone you would go with?"

"Yeah, but I'm not going to call him for something this minor. All I want to do is go hike around near a homestead in the hills. I've been there once. It's nothing. But I want to be sure. I want to look at it with the new information and see what pops up. At any rate, I think we've Agnes proofed all the places she is likely to turn up except that one, so I want to be sure. After that I'll put the map away and forget about it. I could go back to the senior center tack. That as working."

"Just out of curiosity, who would you go with on these little scouting expeditions?"

"Chase."

"You're kidding. Most people only call Chase if they want an exterminator."

"He's not an exterminator. He's a nice guy, if you happen to be a little blonde tracker. And he thinks like me. He understands why I do what I do. He might think it's funny, but he makes the connections. I've tracked with him before. I trust him to see odd things. He sees things, invisible things, just like most good trackers."

"You think he'd find those booby traps?"

"Yeah, I think he would, once we filled him in on why we were looking for them."

I was finishing up dinner preparations that night when Rusty answered the phone in his office.

"What! No! …You've got to be kidding. There's too many things that can go wrong.… That doesn't mean there aren't any there. It only means she didn't know what she was looking for the first time.… Damn it, Schroeder, do you know what you're asking…"

He was not in a good mood when he came to dinner. I wasn't sure whether to push him to talk or not. I figured it would come out eventually. It didn't. He just got moodier. I didn't know whether to bring it up and suffer the wrath or let him stew. I thought I knew what Schroeder had asked. It was the only thing that would affect Rusty this way. Schroeder had told Rusty he couldn't go to the site tomorrow. I wondered what the plan was. *My idea* of the plan was what I'd been doing all along, just drive out to a site and see what I could see. But that didn't seem to match up with Schroeder's plan. He was supposed to be the one that went by the book. He would have to assign me a senior officer, if he sent me out, unless of course he wasn't sending me. But if he wasn't sending me I was on my own. That was fine with me, just unexpected. Now that he knew I was going and he couldn't stop me, I expected to be assigned a senior officer.

I always had my own personal backup although I hated to call on Rusty. I hated that tense, silent pause as he turned into a tight spring, both physically and emotionally. I knew he wouldn't get tied up in investigations tomorrow morning. He would want to be free if I needed him, which I didn't plan on doing. I knew he'd be doing piddly little detective chores that could be easily dropped. He'd study cases, not really thinking about them at all. He'd do anything to keep occupied. I figured I better call him when I got through so he'd know he could relax. I wondered why he expected me to go on with life as usual when he went on a raid. Yet he was on pins and needles as soon as things seemed out of his control with me.

The evening was tense and the tenseness grew as Rusty stewed about what could happen the next day. I felt like I was betraying him by going out alone. He could stop me. If he absolutely forbid me from going I would stay home. I didn't really expect to find much out there. Of all the locations it was the most remote, the most peaceful, the least likely to be booby trapped, seemingly devoid of secrets. But something told me that was precisely why I should go. If there was something out there the owners had been very careful and very clever and I wanted to see just how careful and clever they could be.

I didn't go at dawn. I didn't want Rusty to think I was sneaking out on him. I made breakfast, packed a day pack with snacks and water.

"Show me again where you will be," he said.

I handed him the map and then brought up his mapping program on his computer and zoomed in on the area so he could get a modern day view of it. I printed him a copy and traced the lines of the roads I knew I'd be taking and put a dot where the homestead was located.

"You'll be on foot?"

"Yeah, if I had my Jeep I could go farther but I don't."

"Would it help if you had the Explorer?"

"A little but I don't need to take your car. If you need to go in you need to be able to get there. The area between the car and the homestead is grassy. I can get down below grass level and disappear."

"Please don't disappear. I don't think I could take it again."

"I've got my cell phone. It's charged. The homestead is on this side of the hills so I should be able to get a signal. I've got food and water for the day. I'm armed. I'm alert. I'll be careful. Hopefully it'll be just as peaceful out there as it was last time."

As I drove away I felt the tension lift a little. It was just me now. I knew what I was doing, where I was going. I was just following my curiosity, like always. It just happened to be a little more complicated now. Booby traps, hidden jewels, abandoned buildings. I wondered again why the families had hidden their possessions and fled. Or had they fled? What did they think was going to happen that made them hide their things away and what kind of hatred did they have for their tormentors that they would set shot gun blasts to go off in their face and cyanide guns that caused a very painful and agonizing death? Even with the day bright before me something was off about it.

I made my way through the farmland and back into the neighboring foothills. I found the nearly invisible road and went to duck through the barbed wire fence but it had been cut and tire tracks led through the gap. The tread was from mud and snow tires. Wide tires. I wasn't chancing taking the car up there though. The road was too close to becoming an empty field for me to trust the car on it. I felt more comfortable on foot anyway. I could disappear on foot. When I noticed how recent the tire tracks were I decided maybe I ought to disappear from the very start. The driver was probably still around. The tracks went in but they didn't come out, at least not this way.

I walked down the tire track. That way the weeds I stepped on would look like the tires had crushed them. It wouldn't fool Chase but it would fool almost anybody else. When I neared the hills I cut into the trees. Where was that truck? I kept to cover as I circled the area. I found the tracks leading around the back of the homestead and up a cut in the hills. Around one hill, then another and I came across a second structure. The truck was parked near it but I didn't see any people. I took another scouting trip just out of sight of this new structure. It was a house but the front was made of rock and still remained intact. The whole front section of the house stood but fire had claimed the back rooms. I stood, watching the house as morning turned to afternoon. I was getting nowhere. Occasionally I saw a movement but nobody emerged. I wasn't going to explore the area if I could be confronted. Rusty had said there were other issues involved besides Agnes and a bunch of jewelry and I didn't want to get involved in it, whatever it was. So as long as the people were there I was unwilling to reveal my presence. This was the pits. If I went back to the original site they would see me when they left. If I stayed here I might have to stake out the house for a week. What were they doing down there? What could be so interesting in an abandoned house for this long? Then I had to laugh at myself. I'd probably spend this much time looking for the jewelry and booby traps, why not them?

Yeah, why not them?

I crept down to the house and made my way from window to window until I discovered where the people were. There was a man and a woman and they were baffled by something. The woman was fretful, worried about something. The man was more level headed but the woman was driving him to distraction. The man would try something and the woman would freak out and stop him. I smiled to myself. They were trying to disarm booby traps! If the traps were anything like the ones I'd run into I didn't blame the woman for worrying but she wasn't helping matters at all. I wondered what kind it was this time. I wondered how close to the window I should be.

Dang it, they could be at this all day. They could kill themselves. Was I a cop today, a tracker, or a curious hiker? Rusty would kill me if I confronted them. Come to think if it, *they* could kill me if I confronted them. And what exactly would I be confronting them about? Hell, it could be their house. Was there a procedure for this? Not until I knew they were up to no good. If I was convinced they didn't belong here I could call Rusty in. But nothing, so far, had told me they had done anything wrong.

Suddenly the man exploded, "Damn it Shay! Get out of here. If we're going to get this done you're going to have to go somewhere else."

"What? And let yourself get blown to smithereens?" Shay said.

"This was your idea. You wanted to come here before that meddling woman got here. Well here we are! Are you happy? Now let me work. Go find something else to do."

Shay walked off in a huff. I had to dive for cover because she went to the truck and paced. She opened the door and sat sideways in the passenger seat. There was a noise from the house and she leaped inside.

"Go!" ordered the man.

Shay went back outside so I shifted my position to keep the house between us. I slunk up into the trees and found a secure place to wait. I had a view of the house and the truck but couldn't really be sure what was going on inside. After a snack of trail mix and jerky I got tired of sitting around and changed positions. As I made my way from tree to tree I noticed a movement in the trees. I froze. Now I had to stay out of sight of three people! Shay and the man seemed to be no problem but who was this new addition? I decided to find out. I had to do a bit of triangulating to find hiding places but gradually I made my way around to a spot where I could watch the person on the hill and the people at the house. I found the movement again, barely a shadow flitting from place to place. What was it?

Shay saw it, too. She ran into the house.

"Dirk! Dirk, it's her! I told you she'd show up here!"

Dirk came out of the house. "Where?"

Shay pointed up the hillside. Damn.

Dirk went to the truck and pulled a rifle out from behind the seat. He took a couple of angry steps toward the hill.

There was a movement to the side. Oh hell, it was Agnes! Who had Shay seen?

I didn't think I'd done anything to make myself visible. I didn't want to move. I was almost sure I was still hidden but could I let them take Agnes?

Dirk warily scanned the hill looking for movement.

Agnes looked around for a way out but if she moved she'd be in real trouble. She and I were in the same boat.

Dirk advanced. The tension built as Dirk continued to scan the hillside, rifle at the ready.

I removed my rifle, which hung across my back. I wasn't ready to use it yet. I took my pistol from the holster and hid the holster with the rifle. Then I pocketed the pistol. In close quarters I was better with it, anyway.

Agnes was ready to bolt.

No, I thought, stay invisible! Don't move.

It was her or me. All week I had worked to protect her from just this kind of situation. Did Agnes even know I was there? She didn't act like it. She seemed to think Dirk had spotted her.

He pointed the rifle at the hill and fired.

Agnes shrunk back. That shot should have proved to her that Dirk didn't know where she was. If he did he would have aimed closer, even if it was just a warning shot. Dirk started toward the hill, ready to ferret us out and Agnes didn't know what to do. She was fine alone, given cover, a secure wall to sneak past or a doorway to duck into. This seemed to have her unnerved. She inched around the tree, keeping it between her and Dirk. This would work for a little while but a little farther and Shay would spot her.

A half second before Agnes gave herself away I decided I couldn't let her do it. I had to do something so I stepped forward. Dirk's eyes narrowed. He walked towards me rifle in hand. I was relieved to note he didn't know much about walking around with a rifle. He carried it at his side, pointing forward.

"Get down here," he said evenly. I walked with him down to the house. "Do you have any idea what a mess you've made of things? You've robbed us."

"I haven't taken anything."

"I don't believe you."

"It's her," Shay said. "I know it's her."

"How did you know about this place?" Dirk asked.

"I found it marked on a map. I was just curious what was here."

"Not good enough. Why have you been breaking into the stores?"

"They were on the map too. I was just curious why they were marked on the map, then when I saw all the trouble people went to to keep people out I got more curious. But I was just trying to solve a puzzle to satisfy my own curiosity. I have no desire to keep anything I've found."

"Now that I don't believe for a second."

"Just because *you want it* doesn't mean I have to. Let me go. You have nothing to lose by letting me go. For all I know this property is yours. You have every right to do as you please here. I'm not going to talk."

"No. I have a better idea. You know how these things work. I have a little job for you."

Gulp, I knew this was coming. I let them find me so they wouldn't force Agnes to do it.

"Do you know how dangerous this is? So far I've almost tripped a cyanide gun, been shot at by a rifle and nearly blasted away by a shotgun shell booby trap. Whoever these people were guarding their stuff against, they hated them. The traps were deadly."

"Then why risk it?"

"I'm a goody two shoes. Once I found out how dangerous they were I decided I had to protect other people from them. I couldn't just leave them for some innocent person to stumble across." Or some guilty person either, I thought, wondering where Agnes was.

"Then consider me innocent," Dirk said. Shay stifled a laughed. "Here, I have a little project for you. In the house."

He poked me with the end of the rifle but I wasn't particularly afraid of Dirk. He didn't know how to shoot. I was more afraid of the trap. The trap did know how to shoot, well, at least the ones I'd found so far. He led me into a back room, a library of sorts. One wall was covered with bookcases, no books. Dirk dug a yellowed piece of paper from his pocket. It said simply: you can't judge a book by its cover.

"It's what brought us to the bookcase. Either there's a book somewhere or it's just a reference to this place."

"It could be both. It could have been written when there *were* books here."

I began tapping around in the back of the bookcase, because it had worked for my closet. I did find hollow sounding spots but I couldn't find a way to open any panels. I tapped the shelves. I glanced at the edges of the shelves. I had an idea but did I really want to help these people? In one of the shelves an arrow was carved. It was above my eye level so I could only feel it.

"I need to see something," I said. I climbed the bookcase, beside the arrow. If it was going to do something it would probably be pointed forward. "Stand aside. There's no telling what we could run into."

The arrow seemed to be that, just a carved arrow. So what was it pointing to? I felt the edge of the shelf. Nothing. I turned around and looked to where the arrow might be pointing. It just pointed to the rock wall on the other side of the room. I started at the arrow and crossed the room. I felt the rocks looking for a loose one. This seemed familiar and I didn't like the looks of it. Okay, Cass, if there's a shot gun shell in one of these spots it's going to be at head height or chest height. A rock wiggled. I flattened myself against the wall. If my captors were smart they'd do the same.

Dirk yelled, "Stop! What are you doing?"

"Following the next clue. It's likely to be noisy so don't shoot me if I dive for cover."

"What is it?"

"How should I know? I'm just preparing for what I've seen so far."

Shay ran out of the house. "I can't watch!" she shrieked. She knew a little about these people too.

Keeping my hand as flat against the wall as I could, I worked the rock loose. A small explosion blew a hole in the bookcase wiping out the arrow. Wow, they had good aim!

Dirk lifted me off my feet and shoved me against the rock wall. My head hit with a *thunk*.

"Don't knock any more loose!" I yelled. "There could be more!"

"What are you trying to do, destroy the rest of the place?"

"What would you have me do? You told me to follow the clues! I'm following the clues! I'd be more than happy to let you do it but NO! You wanted me to. Now go see what's behind the trap."

He approached the wall with trepidation, then pointed the rifle at me.

"You do it," he said.

Shay was outside calling, "Dirk! Dirk are you okay?" He was trying to ignore her.

He really wasn't very smart. I reached in and took out the pistol. Dirk jumped back and cocked the rifle. I opened the chamber and checked for more bullets, turned the gun to show Dirk.

"They aren't going to waste ammo on a gun that is only going to fire once."

He relaxed. I closed the gun and dropped it in my pocket. He didn't think anything of it. This guy really needed a course in caution. This was getting interesting. I looked in the hole again and pulled out another piece of paper. It said, *In case of fire, all hands to the pump.*

Great. I handed the note to Dirk.

"Well? I only know of one pump around here. What about you?" I asked.

"The kitchen burned up with half the house," he answered.

"What about the well? If they anticipated the kitchen burning, they had to mean a different pump."

He pushed me towards the back of the house with the rifle. The possible uses for a pump in this case were numerous. They could have done anything. I wasn't touching it. I looked around for cover. It wasn't far away. I could probably escape from view given a few distracted seconds. How could I buy a second or two?

He pushed me to the back of what would have been the yard. There was the pump, traditional rusted red paint job, spout overhanging a cement horse trough shaped pool. I looked over the handle and pipe, the spout, the trough, trying to find anything that might hold a clue. One thing I did not want to do was move that handle. One pump and I could blow the whole house sky high. When the well didn't reveal anything I turned back to the pump.

"Try it," Dirk said.

"No," I answered.

"Do it," he said raising the rifle.

"Have you ever seen a pipe bomb?" I asked. "Put a pipe bomb in this contraption and you don't even have to rig a trigger for it. It triggers just with a pump of the handle. A good pipe bomb would take out the well, the house and your truck, not to mention you and me. If these booby traps have been sitting here since the house fire they are going to be real touchy. You try it."

He cocked the gun and put it to my head. Okay, maybe he couldn't miss at that range.

I jiggled the pipe to see if anything felt loose, like it had been taken apart and reassembled differently. A good well needed a good seal to draw the water up. A bomb did not. I tried turning the pump assembly. A good pump would be tight. This moved. Cautiously I kept turning. Turning it could be as dangerous as pulling the handle. When it was loose I tilted it so I could see down the pipe. Felt an icy wave of fear as it registered just what it was I was seeing. Had I raised the pump handle the mechanism inside the pipe would have pulled the pin out of a homemade incendiary device. Carefully I set the pump back down.

"We need wire cutters. Have you got some?"

Dirk didn't want to turn his back on me.

"Shay! We need some tools!" He yelled across the yard.

After a while Shay appeared with a toolbox, slowly lugging it with both hands. Dirk took it from her and looked around inside for wire cutters.

"What are you doing?" Shay asked.

"Disarming a pipe bomb," I said. When she looked alarmed I added, "It was his idea."

When I had clipped the wires that tied the pin to the pump handle I lifted the pump assembly out and set it on the ground. I looked down the pipe.

"Very ingenious, but where is the next clue?"

I wasn't going to poke around in the pipe so I gave the well another going over. I pried at cracks in the cement. I tapped, listening for differences. But the clue had specifically mentioned the pump. They wouldn't hide a piece of paper in a pipe. Why not though? It obviously wasn't going to pump water with a bomb assembled inside it. I looked inside the spout and pipe that I had taken loose. A small envelope was rolled up and clung to the edges of the pipe. Shoot, not again. I peeled the envelope free and handed it to Dirk. The envelope nearly fell apart as he opened it and pulled out another yellowed piece of paper.

"*One in the mine are worth two in the bush*," he read. "These are lousy clichés."

Gulp. A mine. I could just imagine trying to pick my way through a mine. Dirk poked me with the gun again.

"Walk," he ordered.

"Where? I don't know where any mine is! And we won't be able to see a thing if it's a tunnel."

"Walk, to the truck."

When we got to the truck he took a clipboard off the dash and flipped through the pages. The clipboard held maps, forms and notes, pages bent from use. I'd like to get my hands on that clipboard. Was it something he had for his job or had he been researching these homesteads? Which side of this family feud was he on?

Shay walked out of the house. Now that Dirk had things under control she was staying out of the way. That helped a little except I could never predict where she was.

"We have to go to the mine," he told her.

"You'll need a light," she said.

He felt around under the seats and pulled out a small flashlight. Oh hell. That was going to light up a two foot circle on the ground. We needed to watch for trip wires, guns hidden in nooks and crannies, dynamite. We were looking for a little yellow piece of paper. How did he expect to see a little yellow piece of paper with that thing?

Dirk prodded me in the direction of the first homestead. I had been hoping he didn't know enough about the area to know about a mine but apparently he did. I walked ahead of him purposely leaving a trail. If Rusty had to find me I wanted him to have some clues. We passed the first homestead and followed the curve of the hill away from the house. When we got to the mine entrance it was almost completely covered over with brush. I pulled it aside, snapping a couple of small branches. I taught Rusty enough tracking that he would notice recently broken foliage. The more activity I could create the better. We looked into the dark hole. Dirk jabbed me with the rifle.

"Go," he said.

"No way."

"Did you hear me?"

"Yeah. I'm not going in there. It's a death trap. I'd rather deal with you and the rifle than go in there."

"Okay, we can arrange that."

He pointed the rifle at me.

"I'm more dangerous with this little, empty pistol we found in the library than you are with that thing," I said pulling out my 9mm.

He thought it *was* the pistol from the library. He smirked.

"What are you going to do? Throw it at me?"

"No, it works better this way," I said firing a shot that tore through the side of his shirt and made him jump. "Now drop the rifle."

His eyes narrowed. He didn't like the way the tables had turned on him. He charged me and I jumped aside. He plowed into the brush beside the mine entrance, raised the rifle and fired. The bullet flew down the shaft.

"Don't fire that way! You're going to blow us to…" and a roar engulfed my words. I didn't even think about Dirk. I just ran for my life, picturing crates of dynamite exploding. There was no place to take shelter. No overhangs. No buildings. I dove behind a large tree. Rock and wood, sand and vegetation rained down on me. I made myself the smallest target possible. When the noise had settled I shook off the leaves and sand. I noticed a large rock a few feet away. I didn't think it had been there before.

"Dirk! Where are you?" I yelled. It seemed kind of strange to be looking for someone who had just tried to shoot me but I couldn't leave him trapped or injured somewhere. As I searched I pulled out my cell phone.

"Rusty? The big explosion you're going to hear about soon was out here. Send a crew with a dog. I've got one missing person."

"Cassidy? Are you okay?"

"Yeah, but I gotta find this guy. The whole hill blew and he could be buried. I hope he lost his rifle in all the commotion! I need to search."

"Wait! What do you mean the hill blew?"

"Um, blew up? Kaboom? As in a bullet went down a mineshaft and probably through eighty-year-old dynamite, which is no longer in stick form.

Look, I need to find this guy! I've got to go." I flipped the phone shut and thought quickly. Dirk had been standing right there. The ground had raised a few feet since then. Think, think, where did Dirk run? I put myself in Dirk's shoes. There was no use tracking him. His tracks were buried.

"Dirk! If you can hear me do something!"

Shay ran up to the mine as well as she could in heels.

"What did you do?" she cried.

"I didn't! Dirk fired down the mine shaft and it exploded."

We both started moving branches rocks, anything to get closer to where I thought Dirk should be. I was just guessing. It took me a while to figure out there was another searcher with us. I nearly jumped out of my skin. Chase? How the hell had he gotten here?

"Schroeder hinted at me that you might need help out here," he said.

"Well you could have helped a little earlier, like when you heard shots from the house or before I had to diffuse a pipe bomb!"

"You looked like you knew what you were doing."

"At gun point!"

"You've been there before. Why did you go through all that if you could have just shot the guy? You had your pistol on you the whole time."

Shay shot me a look like she didn't like what she was hearing.

"I don't like shooting people."

"Why did you come out in the first place? He couldn't see you."

"There was a woman. You probably mistook her tracks for mine. She moves like me, is about the same size. I need to track her down when all this is over. I let Dirk see me so he wouldn't have *her*."

"Why didn't you just pull your rifle and arrest the whole lot?"

"One, I was kind of outnumbered. Two, I'm not a cop today, no senior officer. Three, what would I do with them? My goal coming out here was to find the booby traps so Agnes wouldn't get herself killed. It kind of worked. As far as I know she is very much alive."

"Agnes?"

"A cat burglar we've been hunting for several weeks."

"You're not making sense."

"It's okay. Just help me find this guy. I really don't want him to die just because he tried to shoot me."

"You sound like there's an elite club out there of people who try to kill you."

"Wouldn't surprise me in the least," I said, pulling a branch from beneath a load of sand.

Shay was crying and calling Dirk's name over and over.

A black and white Bronco bumped onto the scene. Carla jumped out with a black lab on a leash.

"Do you have any clothes or something our missing person has held recently?" Carla asked.

"Shay, where's the truck?" I asked

"I know where it is," Carla said. She must have passed it on the way in. She and the dog jogged to the truck to give the dog a dose of Dirk's scent, then she released him and he tore up the hillside sniffing a mile a minute. We continued to search until the dog started digging at a pile of brush mixed with sand.

"Carla, I'm going to track down Agnes Cooper. She was here this morning. I know where her tracks start. If you can spare an officer I could use some help with the take down."

"What about Rusty?"

"Agnes is his case. He should be there. Send him after me."

I ran up the hill to retrieve my rifle and then quickly hit the trail. I was amazed how much Agnes's tracks resembled mine. Luckily, she didn't make a point to hide them. Her only goal had been to stay out of sight of the house. She had remained in the same place for a while after Dirk took me away. She stuck around and watched, moving from tree to tree. She knew the focus was off her so she felt free to move about. She had even hung around as I diffused the pump and followed when we went to the mine. The explosion had taken her by surprise and thrown her a good ten feet away. When the police started arriving she had backed off going up into the hills and then making a wide circle to the cars. Chase and Rusty caught up to me as I topped a hill, overlooking the cars below. The police had blocked off the two cars parked down there. One was my rental car. I hoped the other was Agnes's.

Rusty looked me up and down, then embraced me in a hug. "Cass, the things you get into! What am I going to do with you?"

"Agnes can't be far but, if she made it here, she knows she's without wheels."

"What's her state of mind?" Rusty asked.

"When she was hanging around the house she seemed relaxed and curious. As soon as the police turned up her tracks got more intense. I bet they change gears again now that she knows she's afoot."

"Does she know you're on her trail?" Chase asked.

"I don't think she knows I can track her. I think she is only running from the officers but she knows I might have sent them after her."

"Is she armed?" Chase asked.

"I don't know. I've never known her to shoot at people. She isn't a violent person, just a good cat burglar. When she had a chance to shoot me she just cuffed me to a stairway. She even apologized for knocking me down the stairs. I'm not worried about getting shot at."

"Can you find her?" Rusty asked.

"Yeah, no problem," I said hitting the trail again.

As I tracked Rusty and Chase talked. Rusty dragged as much of the story out of Chase as he could. At least Chase gave me the benefit of the doubt telling Rusty the precautions I had taken, explained the care I took before I took the pump apart. He told him how the explosion happened, that I refused to go in the mine.

"You should have seen the guy's face when he realized the seemingly empty gun was now fully loaded."

Chase tracked behind me. I knew he was tracking me as well as Agnes. He couldn't help it. I sure didn't mind him learning a thing or two about tracking me. Agnes's trail was interesting. She didn't hide her tracks but there were no scuffs. Her footprints were always in a perfect line. That was unusual. It made the tracking easier. I didn't have to hunt much side to side for the next track. Her trail went down the hill like she was heading for the road but then suddenly it veered back into the hills. I followed not even really needing to track as she waded through the dry grasses. The grasses bent in her direction of travel and I only verified Agnes's tracks as I went along.

About a quarter of a mile from the mine we found another house. It wasn't burned out but it was old and dilapidated, the siding was warped away from the frame and the paint was curled and eroded by the wind. At one time it had been a handsome house. Two story, it had a nice, big porch. I followed Agnes's tracks as she approached the house. Her steps didn't go to the front door. They circled around back and vanished. I examined the wall. In her climbing she had knocked off a lot of curled paint and the brittle wood had splintered under her weight. She had simply climbed the wall and entered the window on the second story, cat burglar style. I wished I had been able to watch her do it. I set my foot on a windowsill and pushed myself up. One hold led to another. The warped siding created many little bumps and bulges I could use.

"Cassidy, get down from there," Rusty whispered.

"This is how Agnes entered the house. Somebody's got to go in and we know this way is safe. She went this way to avoid traps so it seems logical to follow her. Don't go in the front door. I've seen too many guns rigged to fire through obvious openings. In fact, don't trust any door, no cupboards, no closets. Anything that opens could be rigged."

"But this house wasn't on your map," Rusty said.

"It might have been on Agnes's map, though. Nothing says we had the same map to follow."

As I neared the window I got out my pistol, just to follow procedure a little bit. I doubted I would shoot Agnes but she might not know that. There was no glass in the window but Agnes had opened it anyway, I presumed to avoid cuts from broken glass. I peered into the room. No furniture, just dust, cobwebs and threadbare curtains blowing in the breeze. The sun had bleached away all color and pattern and the weather had made the fabric brittle so only tattered remnants fluttered lazily at the window. I noticed little mouse trails in the dust on the floor and wondered what mice ate in an abandoned building. I wished I could follow them and learn their secrets.

Everything leaves a trail. Even ants, given enough time will wear trails in the dirt. Now, where was Agnes's trail?

I slid over the windowsill and dropped silently to the dusty floor below. I scanned the room from behind the gun. Chase dropped into the room behind me and grinned at the whole cop pretense.

"She hasn't left," he said quietly. "I checked around the house."

I nodded.

"Rusty'll catch her if she runs," he said.

"Don't open any doors," I told him. "If we set off any guns Rusty will come running and we don't want that."

I put an ear to the closet door. Nothing. I indicated the hallway with my eyes and Chase nodded. He took the lead knowing I'd hesitate to fire no matter what happened when we left the room. Chase flattened himself against the wall and then turned, following his .45 out the door. He took one step and fell through the floor to the living room below. In amongst all the crashing, splintering sounds I heard the zing of a bullet. I looked through the hole in the floor. Chase had tripped a booby trap on his way down, but since he wasn't standing when he tripped it the bullet went over him. Dust billowed around him and he coughed and fanned at the cloud.

"You okay?" I whispered down to him.

"I'm too old for this stuff," he gasped. He got up and went to the front door. "I think this door is safe now," he told Rusty.

I left the downstairs to the real cops and made my way, room to room, upstairs. I watched the dusty hardwood floors for tracks and there were plenty of those. Agnes was searching for something. Something very important to her. Important enough to take a few risks. What was it? And where was she?

I examined the doorway to the next bedroom for trip wires and triggers in the floor, then followed my sidearm in. One by one I found empty rooms. The guys met me on the stairs.

"Nothing," Chase said.

"She's here somewhere," I answered. "Time for a deeper look. If it's anything like the other house it's going to get noisy. When she hears shots she might make a run for it, so be prepared."

"What do you mean, shots?"

"I'll show you."

"Cassidy, no."

"All you have to do is anticipate the shot and stand aside. It could be a pistol, rifle or shotgun so you have be ready."

We went downstairs and began opening doors. We felt silly, all three of us flattened against the wall while I pulled open a door and nothing happened. It was a coat closet, no booby trap, no funny hidden walls, no loose floor boards, no secret carved clues in the woodwork, just an empty closet. The next door was the kitchen and the door in the kitchen held a pantry. No booby traps, only cobwebs.

"We've been through the downstairs rooms," Chase said.

"One more door to go but I can't imagine what it would be. A library? A den? This house wasn't built when houses had dens."

We approached the door wondering if our caution was misplaced but decided better safe than sorry and flattened ourselves against the hall wall as I silently turned the knob and pulled. Nothing happened but the door opened onto a stairway going down. A basement? Houses in this part of the country rarely had basements. Chase and Rusty stepped out onto the stairs testing them for sturdiness and promptly tumbled down the stairs. Agnes! I'd recognize that stun-gunning anywhere. I drew my pistol and approached the stairs cautiously.

"Agnes! Drop the taser! You can't hope to keep all three of us incapacitated long enough to get away."

I stepped to the doorway. There she stood, looking rather sad.

"Toss it up here. Toss it up here or I'll shoot it. You don't want to be holding it when I shoot it. I'm a good shot, but still, it's just not a good idea."

I aimed at the taser. She tossed it to the top of the stairs.

"Now, hands over your head."

My training was starting to kick in.

"Spread eagle against the wall."

I patted her down, making sure she was unarmed. Rusty would be proud. Usually I trusted people to not be armed. I got scolded every time I forgot to frisk somebody. I pulled the cuffs from Rusty's pocket and cuffed Agnes. She became agitated, almost frantic. She turned on me and, with one swift kick to the head, sent me flying across the room. So much for her interest in a self-defense class. I tested my teeth to make sure they were still there. She stepped over her hands so her hands were in front of her, then dashed to a large roll top desk. She pushed the top open and peered inside, opening drawers she searched intently. I stood and placed her at gunpoint again. She didn't seem to care. She was looking for something. Why? The police would just take it from her, but she was so intent in her search that I got curious, too. Opening one drawer after another she found all kinds of little tools. One drawer held a little bag of precious stones. A locked drawer frustrated her. What could be in the locked drawer if the owner had left priceless gems in a bag in a cubbyhole? She found a key and tried the drawer. When she pulled the key out of the drawer there was a loud *pop* behind the desk. It made both of us jump, then flames started licking up the wall behind the desk. Oh hell, this old house would go up in minutes. Agnes became even more frantic. She tried the key in the drawer again. It slid open stiffly and she drew out a leather case, also locked. She went back to the drawers. There were more locked ones and this frustrated her. She was more concerned about the desk than she was about the fire. There was something in there that she valued more.

"Agnes, we've got to get out! March! Up the stairs!"

Smoke began filling the room.

I turned to the guys. I'd never get them up a flight of stairs. Chase maybe. Rusty, there was no way.

Agnes took the case and headed hesitantly for the stairs. She didn't seem to be concerned about getting caught. She seemed more worried about leaving the contents of the basement.

"Rusty! Come on!" I said shaking him, gun still pointed in Agnes's general direction. I didn't really care if she got away. I could track her down again from here. There were more important things at hand. "Rusty, please! Chase, wake up!"

The wall behind the desk was blazing now. The only place for smoke to go was up the stairs.

"Rusty! Come on, we've got to get out of here! We don't have time for this! The house is burning up!" I shook him and shook him as smoke filled the room. I had to do something! Of all the times for Rusty to not have a radio, why did it have to be this time? Did I have time to run to the mine for help? I had to. I grabbed Chase under the armpits and locked my fingers across his chest. I pulled him up the stairs one impossible stair step at a time. He was more than the hundred sixty-five pounds I had practiced on in academy. At the time I thought, I better never have to do this in real life! Now here I was. Up, up the stairs, his heels catching on each stair. A sudden pull, a loosening of my fingers, an adjustment. I counted the seconds as I pulled some more. When we reached the top of the stairs things got a little easier I pulled Chase across the living room and out the open door and into the field. I dropped Chase in the field and sprinted back inside the house. I shook Rusty again.

"Rusty, please!" I begged. "Please wake up!"

I tried to pick him up, like I had Chase but he was just too big. I looked at the fire, now spreading beyond the desk area. Did I have time to make it to the mine? I had to, I just had to. I sprinted to the mine.

Schroeder's presence at the mine indicated the magnitude of the investigation. He had the highest rank so I went straight to him. I was supposed to stand, salute and wait to be addressed. I didn't have time for that.

"Schroeder! You've got to give me some help! Rusty needs help! He's in the basement and the house is on fire. I can't move him! I need two big guys. There's no time for the fire department. He was stun gunned and took a tumble and I don't know if he'll come to in a few minutes or if he took a knocking in the fall. A fire truck can't get in. It's got to be on foot. Please!"

Schroeder sent Big John Jankowski and two EMTs. They followed me back. I ran but made sure they could see me the whole time. They used that calm, firm pace that looked unnervingly slow but maintained a professional attitude in the face of chaos. When I saw the house again I nearly collapsed. It was billowing smoke. Rusty! Chase was sitting in the field looking puzzled. I raced past and into the house. Jankowski shouted for me to stop but I couldn't! I just couldn't! The smoke hit me and I had to back out. I took a breath of fresh air, held my breath and plunged into the smoky living room, then down the stairs. Oh Rusty! I found him still on the stairs.

The fire had made it up to the first floor and threatened to ignite the stairs. Where were the guys? I couldn't take the smoke much longer and that made me worry about Rusty. He'd been in the smoke all this time…

"Cassidy?"

I raced up the stairs.

"This… way," I said coughing.

"Out!"

"Not until… *cough, cough*… I show you where," I said turning back into the house.

With a growl of frustration Big John and an EMT followed me in. As soon as Rusty came into view John grabbed me by the arm and booted me up the stairs like a little kid. I tried to turn back but knew I'd just be in their way. As I walked out the front door the other EMT nabbed me. I shrugged away but he was used to that. He guided me to where Chase was sitting.

"It'll be okay. Just sit still. Cassidy, look at me," he said.

I looked at him but I didn't know him. It was weird not knowing an EMT. I was so used to Landon and Victor being there. I looked at the patch on his uniform. It was the same company as Landon's. The name embroidered on his uniform said Kipp Taft.

"I can't just sit here. I'll go nuts. How do you know me?"

"We all know you. Anybody who's worked with Landon knows you."

Chase knelt in front of me. "How'd I get out here?" he asked.

"Chase, I could move you. I couldn't budge Rusty. I had to get help. So I dragged you out and made a run for it. Hell, I need a punching bag. I need a tree. Anything to hit. I'm a mess. If anything happens to him I'll never live with myself. All this is my fault. If I'd just let Agnes go, if I didn't have to track her none of this would have happened."

"Where'd Agnes go?"

"I don't know. I could only do one thing at a time. She was cuffed when the fire started. I told her to get out. I figured I could always find her later."

Big John and the other EMT carried Rusty out. I started to get up but Chase and Kipp headed me off.

"Look, if I was going to keel over I'd have done it by now. I'm fine. Let me go."

"Help me find Agnes."

"Chase! I don't care about Agnes. I…"

"I know, but you need to stay away and you need to focus on something else. Let the guys work. When we hear the helicopter we'll head back. John, we're going after Agnes Cooper. She's only been missing about fifteen minutes. If we hurry we can catch up with her."

We could indeed. Agnes knew there was no use running and she'd been as shaken by the past events as I had. We found her sitting under a tree, the open leather case in her lap. She lovingly fingered the contents with her cuffed hands.

"I finally found it," she said with a hint of nostalgia in her voice. "I knew it existed but I didn't know where it was until your map gave me a clue. I had no hope of really finding it but I couldn't stop trying. The man who lived in that house made jewelry. He imported stones from all over the world and made wonderful, creative jewelry, each piece an original, no two alike. I own some of his creations. They were handed down through my family. The basement was his shop. He made the pieces here and sold them in the best jewelry stores up and down the state. He disappeared in 1926. Not many people know who made his jewelry. He only signed his pieces RK. When I found your map and saw all the dots with the name Kingsley on them, I knew I had to search and see if the legend was really true."

Leave it to Agnes to give me a history lesson on jewelry in the middle of her arrest. I felt sorry for her. I didn't want to send her to jail. I wanted to stop the thefts. I wanted to see Dottie get her rings back. But I didn't want to see Agnes behind bars. I sat beside her under the tree. She brought out a ring. It sparkled like new even after eighty years.

"Here's something you police won't understand at all," she said and lifted out a small pistol totally encased in precious stones. She was right, I didn't understand why anybody would dress up a gun like that. It was like making a shovel out of gold. The decorations only limited its uses. Some things were just made to be tools.

"Agnes, we've got to go. I hate to have to tell you this but, you are under arrest." Big John took over the arrest. He trundled her off to the mine and a squad car. Chase gave me a hand up and we walked back to the house. It wasn't far. My pace quickened and I gradually left Chase behind. As the house came into view I broke into a run.

A fire department helicopter buzzed in and took a tour of the situation. I hoped they jumped on the situation because it was a brushfire just waiting to happen.

I pulled up beside the EMTs still working, still waiting on an airlift. I knelt beside Rusty. I took his hand. I was relieved that his color was better. He felt okay. His leg was splinted. He was breathing although the noise of it was frightening.

"Cassidy," Chase said. "They aren't going to let you in the helicopter. I can tell you that right now."

"What! Why? I have to! I get lifts out of places with victims all the time. They let me go then."

"We'll get a destination from them as soon as they know. You'll be right behind the helicopter."

"But I want to be there."

"I know, kid, but they are going to have to do some things that you don't want to see."

"I don't care. I have to be there."

"You don't have to, if you can't."

We heard the clatter of the helicopter, but they couldn't land close to the house without spreading the fire into the dry grasses nearby. Chase knew what needed doing. He verified the hospital they were going to. It was in Joshua Hills. That was good news. It meant they were optimistic. It also meant doing all the piddly little details like getting cars home would be less hassle. I drove the rental car to the hospital. Chase arranged for an officer to drop the Explorer off at the hospital. I don't know what I would have done without Chase. He thought of everything. I would have stumbled along until I ran into a problem and then tried to figure it out. He left me free to think about Rusty. He rode with me, talking me through what I could expect. Just what everybody needs, an emergency consultant. He'd been through it all, seen all the hang-ups, seen how things might have gone a little smoother if only some little detail had been thought of, and he thought of them. He kept me sane, filling my mind with little things, not letting me dwell on the fear. Even when I was sitting with Rusty I could focus. Things didn't overwhelm me like they had in the past.

The EMT's got word to Landon. After Landon arrived I had a medical translator. Schroeder checked in daily. I was even able to call Kelly. He was shocked by the news.

"Kelly? I have some news," I said.

The line was eerily silent.

"It's bad news but it'll be okay. I thought you ought to know. Rusty was in a fire. He wasn't burned but he's got complications from smoke inhalation. He's on a respirator, but it's just to keep his airway open. They'll take it out when the swelling goes down."

A long silence, then, "I'll be right there."

He rushed in half an hour later prepared for a long wait in the emergency room but what he found was me and Chase sitting, talking in Rusty's room. He heaved a sigh of relief. Last time I'd been in this situation he'd found me barely able to function.

"Can you tell me about it?" Kelly asked.

A big lump formed in my throat. "No, Kelly, I can't. I can't think about it or I turn into an emotional mess. Maybe when I know he's fine and over a boxing match."

Chase got up and signaled for Kelly to follow. All I caught as they walked out the door was, "Don't push, she blames herself."

And boy did I. What could I have done differently? I could have dropped the case when Rusty asked me to. I could have been more careful. I could have kept Agnes from touching the desk and setting off the booby trap. I still wasn't convinced the booby trap had functioned properly. A fire obviously wouldn't stop someone from getting the things in the desk. I thought it had misfired and the fire was the result. But still, if I'd have just arrested Agnes and kept her in line the guys would have come around and taken over. I felt guilty for Rusty's accident and Chase's too for that matter. I even felt guilty for sending Agnes to jail. I needed something to feel good about. I looked at my big strong detective, his raspy breathing being monitored closely, his leg in a cast. The tube. I had to remind myself that the tube was a good thing. Or rather only having the tube was a good thing.

He stirred and I turned the chair around. I sat on the back of it, putting my feet on the seat so I could look down at Rusty.

"Take it slow," I said. "Don't push it. I know it feels weird."

His hand moved so I took hold of it. He seemed to tense a little.

"Can you hear me?" I asked.

Nothing.

Chase and Kelly walked in. Chase took the other chair. Kelly came up behind me and put a hand on my shoulder. I felt Rusty's hand try to move again.

"I can feel you there."

Every once in a while his hand would move and I'd perk up.

I asked Chase, "Have you talked to Elan? How are things going at the ranch?"

"I've heard more from Patrick. While you were missing he called every day. I got the impression he was hiding in the bushes when he talked to me," he said grinning. "He was mostly worried about you but I asked tracking questions to get his mind off his worries. He has hundreds of questions and Elan can't always answer them but they seem to have more fun just walking around doing chores together. He certainly keeps Elan thinking. I was counting on that. Patrick's questions teach Elan as much as they teach Patrick."

"Doesn't Elan consider him a pest?"

"Actually he is quite impressed with Patrick. He only asks intelligent questions and when he gets an answer he comes up with intelligent conclusions. Elan gets most of his work done while Patrick is in school. He likes the work, loves training the horses. He can't wait for Frank's Choice's first race. He's been working with the horse. He and Randy work well together. They have a lot in common as far as horses go. Something else you'd be interested in, he thinks Shasta misses you."

"I wonder what Randy thinks about that."

Rusty's hand moved again.

"Rusty? Are you there yet?"

His hand jerked a little harder.

"Don't try to talk. You can't talk yet."

This seemed to worry him. His movements became rougher and jerky.

"Shh, it's okay. You won't be like this for long. Relax, come on, relax." I stroked his arm. "We're doing good. We're right on track."

Kelly stepped in. "Rusty, it's okay. Cassidy's doing great. She's a trooper. Relax, you numbskull, you worry too much. If she needs anything we're all here. Chase is here. I'm here. Landon's in an out. Schroeder's on standby. Cassidy can't move without someone watching out for her."

He seemed to settle a little after that. I couldn't believe he was in any shape to be worrying about me.

That night was the worst. Kelly went home and Chase went to wherever Chase goes when he's in town. He said he needed to go over the case with Schroeder. I offered him the keys to our house but he declined. I sat with Rusty, worried that I would miss something if I fell asleep. I sat on the back of the chair watching him until I got drowsy and thought I was going to fall off the back of it. I got up and paced. I tried every trick in the book that I'd come up with on long guard duties. It didn't work. I'd just been through too much that day. Okay, I thought, half an hour. I'll nap for half an hour. I sat in the uncomfortable naugahyde chair, held Rusty's hand, and drifted off.

In my dreams I dropped Chase in the field and when I turned to the house again it was fully engulfed in flames. There was no time to run to the mine! I ran back in the house and the flames leaped at me. Panicky, I ran from room to room but I couldn't find Rusty. I couldn't see. The stairs to the basement were on fire! Suddenly alarm bells went off. Rusty's hand jerked violently. I woke up scared of the fire and then realized it was Rusty's breathing monitor going off. Nurses rushed in. They sent me out of the room. I was having trouble waking up, still halfway in the dream. I was scared for Rusty but as I settled down, I knew what had happened. My nightmare had worried Rusty. It upset him enough to interrupt his breathing. I knew he'd be okay. But I decided that I couldn't sleep with him.

"I'm sorry," I cried when they let me back in. "It was just a dream. It's okay. You can hear and you can feel. That's good. I'm sorry I upset you. Don't let my dreams get to you. I want to stay, but I can't if it upsets you."

By the time Chase arrived in the morning I was ready to drop but I was scared to. I didn't want to worry Rusty but the nightmares were not going to go away. When they came they usually stuck around until I found peace in the situation and I couldn't find that peace here, watching Rusty suffer for my actions. I would plunge right back into the fire as soon as I slept but I had to sleep or I wouldn't be in any shape to help Rusty. Chase could tell something was wrong.

"Go home," he ordered.

"It's a half hour drive. I don't want to be gone that long."

"I'll stay."

"I still don't want to be gone that long."

"Then let's get a cot. You can sleep here."

"I can't. I have nightmares about the fire and it upsets Rusty."

"Then try the car."

The Explorer was in the parking lot so I folded down the back seats and stretched out willing the nightmares to stay away. They didn't. I forced myself to stay there and try to sleep for an hour. First I had nightmares. The second time I dozed off I heard a knocking on the window. It was a cop. Jayce Thompson grinned at me.

"So you're the poor homeless person living in their car in the hospital parking lot. What's up Cassidy?"

"Apparently me," I answered. "Please let me sleep. Rusty's laid up in there and I haven't slept in forever."

"Okay. I think we need a code for you in our reporting. Shots fired? It was just a Cassidy call. Homeless people lurking in the hospital parking lot? A

Cassidy call. Mysterious explosions in the hills? It's just Cassidy. You know we could write off a lot of minor calls off to you and everybody would believe it."

"Good night, Thompson."

"I hope you can sleep. Tell Rusty I said 'hi.'"

"I will, he can hear now. Go up and say 'hi' yourself."

Thompson left to go say 'hi' to Rusty and I drifted back to sleep and into the fire. It was no use. Sleep was my enemy right now. I forced myself to lay still and just rest for an hour. Maybe rest would suffice while sleep was impossible.

I went back to Rusty's room and took up my watch.

"Any change?" I asked Chase.

"Talk to him. He can understand you. He needs to talk to you."

"Hey," I said to Rusty. "I'm back. You doing okay?" I took his hand in case he had a response. He began fighting the tube. "You can't talk. The tube will win every time. Just relax. You're doing great."

His hand moved. The jerky, worried movement.

"What is it? Don't worry about me. I'm getting along. Chase made me go take a nap. I didn't want to leave but I was afraid the nightmares would bother you."

More worried hand movements.

"Rusty, what's wrong? I can't guess what's on your mind. Do you want to know what happened? It was a fire. You're here because you were in the smoke too long… I can't tell you the whole story. I just can't. Just get better and then maybe, maybe I can… We got Agnes. While we were waiting for the helicopter we tracked her down and Big John hauled her in."

That was the most detail I could handle at the time. He fought the tube some more and I tried to calm him. I knew he was frustrated with his circumstances. He was used to being in charge and in control and everything was out of his control right now.

"Rusty, calm down. The tube is there because your throat is swollen from the smoke. The more you irritate it the longer the tube stays in. Just relax. Nothing's going to happen while you're here. We've just got to get through this and we'll do it faster if you stay calmer."

I knew reasoning with him was almost useless. But at least it kept me talking and he could hear my voice.

Chase and Kelly switched off, passing on an update.

"Kelly, you have a life, too. Go home. You can't spend your afternoons here. You have work to do. You have a wife. She misses you. She doesn't want you hanging out here with me."

"When I'm convinced that you're taking care of things on your own I'll go home. You haven't convinced me yet. When was the last time you ate a meal?"

"Dang, why'd you have to pick that? Yesterday."

"I'm going downstairs to get something. What do you want?"

"Anything that will keep a while and I can pick at," I said burrowing in my pack and handing him my wallet. "Get something for you, too."

Kelly left and I sat with Rusty again. "I swear, these guys are worse than living at home on the ranch." He felt around for my hand and found my knee. His actions seemed more coordinated now. "Rusty? Can you open your eyes? I want to see your eyes. I miss you so much. Can you open your eyes, just for a second?"

I didn't get to see his eyes then, but later in the day he seemed to reach a milestone. His eyes opened and he looked around. His hand movements were controlled. Now he just needed his voice back, but at least I could read his expression.

"There you are. I've waited a long time to see those eyes. Next we need to let your throat heal. You'll be rid of that old tube soon."

His eyes held a question but I was afraid to know what it was. Still, I had to try.

"What is it? I told you what happened. I told you we got Agnes. You know I'm being watched over day and night and can't even sneeze without the guys handing me a tissue. What else is there? Schroeder will explain the work aspects. I've told you all I know about your condition. If you want the scientific terms for it all Landon can help with that. He's due in here in a few hours."

The question didn't go away.

"Rusty. You want to know why I can't tell you what happened, don't you?"

His expression softened. Shoot. Just thinking about it enough to form an answer brought tears to my eyes.

"I can't. To do that I have to admit something and I can't even think it again. I can't. Please don't ask me that. Just get better. It's the only way I can cope. If I have to go back I'll…I just can't. I'm sorry."

I toughened up inside, sat a little straighter and pasted a look of confident optimism on my face. It didn't fool Rusty. It seemed to make him sadder.

A doctor and two nurses walked in.

"Miss, could you step out of the room for about fifteen minutes?" the doctor said.

"He's my husband. Whatever you need to do, you can do with me here."

The doctor looked at me weird. I know, I know, I thought, what's a kid like me doing married to a hunk like him? I was used to it.

"We're just going to do a quick exam. If everything checks out I'll still ask you to leave while we take the tube out," the doctor said. Then he turned to Rusty, listened to his lungs.

I worried. To me Rusty's breathing still sounded awful. I hoped they would take the tube out so Rusty could talk again.

"Take a deep breath," the doctor told him. "So far so good." Then he nodded to the nurse.

"Mrs. Michaels?" the nurse said guiding me to the door.

Kelly came, too. The nurse didn't stop at the door though. She guided me down the hall to a waiting room.

"Kelly, what am I going to do? He's going to want to know what happened and I can't say it. I just can't. I know he won't blame me, and he needs to know but I can't say it. It sticks in my throat and I turn into a basket case. Look at me! I can't even talk about talking about it. Just talking about it this much makes me want to go to the station and take on the punching bag."

"Sit down," he said.

I sat and brought my feet up into the chair and put my head on my knees. That told him more than anything I could say verbally. He knelt down and pulled my feet down.

"Look at me," he said. "I've only heard this from Chase, so let me see if I've got this right. You tracked Agnes to a house and you searched the house for her. You found her in the basement. There was a fire and you were able to get Chase out but you couldn't move Rusty. So you ran for help from the officers at the mine."

I nodded. "Chase doesn't remember part of it. They went into the basement first and Agnes stun gunned them. They were out while I cuffed Agnes but then there was something she had to see before we hauled her off to jail. I couldn't take her in myself. I needed a senior officer and I wasn't going to leave the guys…I was an idiot. I let her look and when she did she triggered a booby trap. It started a fire. I had one able bodied but cuffed cat burglar, an unconscious Rusty and Chase and a fire to deal with. I told Agnes to get out. I figured I could always track her down later. I…I knew I couldn't move Rusty. Even Chase was a rough haul. Up all those stairs…When I chose to pull Chase out it took precious minutes. The house was old and dry and burned easily. The basement was filling up with smoke…the only way for the smoke to get out was up the stairs. Now Rusty's paying for it." Up went the feet, out came the tears. "I left Chase in the field and ran to the mine. I brought back help but Rusty's the one paying for my inability. Why did I do it? How *could* I? Damn it, now I can't even go back in there without upsetting him." I cried, just sitting there in my usual hiding position, curled into a little ball.

"Cassidy, come on, no hiding. Come on. You can cry, as long as you do it here." He held out his arms. "Would it help if I told Rusty?"

I shook my head no.

"Why?"

"I have to face it eventually. He can't know I blame myself. It'll just make him feel worse."

"*You* can't blame yourself. Nobody would expect you to be able to move Rusty."

"But I could have dropped the search for Agnes when Rusty asked me to. I could have run for help before I pulled Chase out."

"Then Chase and Rusty would both be in the same boat. Chase is amazed you *could* have pulled him out. And he knows it cost you. He understands why you feel like you do even if he doesn't know how the fire started. He knows it was bad and he knows you had to make a choice."

"A choice that hurt Rusty."

"You think Rusty wouldn't have chosen to make that sacrifice for Chase? If Rusty could have told you to get Chase out he would have."

"But I left him there, unconscious, unable to do anything but breathe smoke. I'll never forgive myself. But it'll be better as soon as Rusty's all right."

"And he will be. Just wait and see. He'll be out of here soon and then what will you do?"

"I don't know. Rusty wanted to go someplace. He needs to be able to relax and get out and play and build some good memories. He needs to see everything be all right for a while. I'll need to stick close to home."

"Mrs. Michaels?" the nurse said poking her head into the waiting room. "You can go back now."

I looked at Kelly. Kelly gave me a hug before leading the way back to Rusty's room. I felt like I was going to face a firing squad.

"Rusty's going to want to know the facts."

"And?"

"He should know them. Just keep it general. If there's any way, keep my feelings out of it."

"Why?"

"Because he's got enough problems right now. We'll deal with my feelings later, when he's got the facts all straight in his head."

I was saved from the telling for a little while. Rusty was tube free but he was also very sore. He lay there exhausted. I sat quietly with him and stroked his arm so he'd know I was there. He opened his eyes.

"There you are," he whispered hoarsely.

"You don't need to talk if it hurts. I know those tubes are no fun."

He lay quietly for a while but his curiosity got the better of him.

"I don't remember a fire," he said.

"I know. Agnes got you with the taser when you entered the basement."

"Must have been some stun gun. How did I break a leg?"

"Agnes stunned you at the top of the basement stairs."

"And you got Agnes?"

"Yeah, we got Agnes. Chase and Big John helped me."

"Good job, babe."

I just shook my head.

"What?"

"Nothing."

"Hon," he was down to a whisper. "You can't fool me."

"You were unconscious. You were gray. We were lucky you were breathing on your own. The EMTs only had their orange boxes. We had to wait for a helicopter to get oxygen. I had to leave you to go after Agnes. I knew I had to stay out of their way but I just wanted to let Agnes go. It was too much. I had to leave you twice not knowing what would happen, not knowing if you'd survive my decisions." I had to stop. "We got Agnes but there was no victory in it. Then after all that they wouldn't let me in the helicopter."

He felt around for a hand, always needing to feel things be okay.

"Are you okay?" he asked.

"Most of the time. I have my moments."

"Why the nightmares?"

"You know I have nightmares."

"I know. It's the only way I can tell when you've been truly affected by something. You only have nightmares when you're hurt deeply."

Dodging the issue I told him, "I relive the fire, except it's bigger. I'm scared and I can't find you. That's not the way it was in real life. In real life I knew where you were. I led the guys right to you. In the dream I can't find you and the house is in flames and falling around me. But it's not the fire I'm scared of. I'm afraid I won't find you in time."

He fell silent, thinking, resting his voice.

"You went in that burning house?"

"I had to. Big John yelled for me to stop but I couldn't. I had to know."

He struggled with that. I hated what I was doing. Only half telling things to keep my emotions in check.

Rusty continued to improve. He went through physical therapy sessions to increase his endurance and get his wind back. His voice was still raspy when they finally released him. When we got home I dragged him to the old brown couch and fell into his arms. This time I needed my minutes. I was still battling. Still having nightmares. Still kicking myself. I was glad he took it as worry.

Schroeder came over. At first he'd visited at the hospital to get progress reports. Now he needed to know the details. He tossed a file folder on the table.

"This is what happened from Agnes's point of view. Now I need it from your point of view."

I read through the report. Agnes had been very detail oriented. She'd drawn the right conclusions and everything. She knew I stepped forward to save her skin. She guessed right at what Dirk had made me do. She sure saved me a lot of explaining. The report fell apart when she stun gunned the guys. She wasn't going to admit to assaulting a police officer. I gave Schroeder the real story including why Agnes had been looking for that particular place and what she had found. She admitted tripping the booby trap. She had left the house intending to run away but she knew she would never get far in handcuffs and without her car, so she had simply given up and spent the time proving to herself that she really had found Ronald Kingsley's jewelry making shop. It was worth it to her just to have found it. It confirmed something in her. It was the fulfillment of a dream.

"Will any of the women get their jewelry back?" I asked Schroeder.

"A few. We'll contact the owners. They will have to come forward and identify it. Those with proof of ownership will have it easy. Those who insured their jewelry will have identified it somehow."

Dottie. I'd never know if Dottie got her rings back. But I'd know I did all I could to make that come about.

Chapter 19

Rusty's mom was elated when she saw us standing at her door. There were big hugs all around until she noticed Rusty's crutches.

"What happened to you?" Bev asked.

We'd come to San Diego for some peace, to splash in the pool and walk the beach. But I couldn't put the fire behind me. Every reminder of it sent my emotions spiraling. I tried not to let it show.

"From what I hear I got beat by a little old lady," Rusty joked. His voice was almost back to normal but it still faded if he talked a lot. Another reminder.

"How long can you stay?" She asked.

Rusty looked at me. He wasn't sure who we were here for this time. He wasn't sure what it would take.

"Mom, I don't know," he confessed. "We came to…"

"Regroup, I know," Bev answered. "I'll call Sandy. Maybe she will come for dinner tonight. And you're not sleeping in the attic. You're not climbing all those stairs with crutches."

"We like the attic, crutches or no crutches. We like to sleep out on the balcony," he said.

Cody came home from work beaming, "Hey! Little Sis! You're still in one piece!" Then he saw Rusty. Every time Rusty joked about his leg I sank deeper. By the time Bill and Sandy had joined the group I was having a hard time staying pleasant. We barbecued around the pool and then Chase walked in. Cody got up and got Chase a plate and a beer just like he always did.

"Aren't you going to ask Rusty what happened to him?" Cody asked Chase.

"Nope. What have you been telling them?" he asked Rusty.

"That a little old lady beat me," Rusty answered.

Chase shrugged. "Yup, she got me, too," Chase said.

"Wait a minute," Cody said. "You were there and Rusty was there? In Joshua Hills? This has Cassidy written all over it."

Everybody looked to me and I was stuck. How could I tell Rusty's family what happened when I still couldn't even admit it to myself? I couldn't even talk about it to Rusty!

"Yeah, I was there, too," I managed to say.

"There were three of you, against one little old lady, and Rusty came out of it with a broken leg?"

"One little old lady in the dark with a stun gun," I added.

"That still…"

"At the top of a flight of stairs," I added. "Rusty took the worst of it because he was the first one in." And that was as far I could go. I pretended to go to the kitchen for a refill and quietly disappeared. I put on some shorts over my swimsuit and went for a walk. After a while I went for a run and when I was all run out I went for another walk. When I feel good I can run five miles. I maintain that, since I have to do a lot of backpacking, and it was required for academy, I just figured it was good to maintain an easy five miles. When I feel rotten I can go seven because I push myself. I kick my ass. I use the run to give myself a good cussing out, physically. So by the time I stopped running I was beat and I was probably seven miles from the Michaels' house. And I still didn't know the city very well, so I was lost. Well, not really lost. I could find my way back. It was just going to take some figuring to do it. I knew to head uphill and I knew to watch for streets named after explorers. It was late at night when I finally dragged myself into the house. Rusty stood as I came in the door and started to hobble over.

"No, don't walk on your leg," I told him. I walked over and gave him a big, worn out hug.

"You can't run from this forever," Chase said.

"Who said?" I asked.

"It's going to beat you unless you do something about it."

"How much did you tell them?"

"Just enough so they think you're a hero," Chase said.

"Oh Chase, you didn't. Please say you didn't."

That night the nightmares were particularly fierce. I woke with a start thankful I hadn't woken Rusty. I paced the attic on silent feet. It didn't help. I put on my swimsuit and dropped the rope ladder that went from the balcony to the ground. I climbed down and slipped into the pool. I swam laps under water so it wouldn't be noisy but I had to stop because I couldn't swim under water and cry at the same time. No matter what I did I felt worse. Not only did I dream about the fire now, I dreamed about the hospital. All the hopelessness I had felt was magnified. And when I dwelled on them I felt the same hopelessness woven with guilt and I was miserable. I swam and swam trying to out swim my emotions. Running hadn't worked. It looked like swimming wouldn't work either.

There was a scrape of a chair on flagstone and I froze, surprised I had heard it in my haste amongst the water noises. It's a little hard to freeze in seven feet of water. I made my way to the side and hung on, ears tuned for the smallest sound.

"Rusty's right, you are hard to sneak up on," Bill said. Rusty's dad.

"Thanks," I said trying desperately to reel in my emotions.

"What are you doing out here all by yourself?"

"I woke up and couldn't sleep. I needed to work something off and I knew Rusty wouldn't want me to go running."

"Is what Chase said, true?"

"From Chase's point of view? Probably."

"Then why the conflict?"

"Chase doesn't know the whole story. He's missing about ten minutes. But it's ten minutes I'd give anything to go back and fix."

"Ten minutes?"

"If anybody knows how much can happen in ten minutes it's you. Our luck made up for my stupidity."

"Chase says you saved their lives."

"Bill, please," I cried. "I can't talk about it. I just can't." I pulled myself out of the pool and headed for the ladder but Bill beat me to it.

"You can't say what?"

I was shaking with sadness and rage at myself and anger at him for pushing.

"Please, let me go. If you were almost anybody else you'd have a fist fight on your hands right now. You've pushed too far. I'm in fight or flight and if you don't back off I'm… I'm…I don't know what I'll do."

"Chase is right, you can't run from this."

"Chase is usually right. As long as Rusty's okay the memories will fade. Rusty said they would, once, after a different bout of trouble. These will too."

"How long? Can you wait that long?"

"I have to. I just have to."

"You don't have to, give it to me."

"I can't! You'd hate me. If you knew…"

"Nothing could make me hate you," he said releasing the ladder. I climbed up and looked at Rusty still sleeping. It wasn't like him to sleep through things. Usually, a slight noise was enough to put him on guard. Voices woke him easily. I had thought just my being in the pool would wake him up. I thought it meant he was still recovering from the smoke and that made me sadder. I paced the attic until I gave up, and curled up in a beanbag chair I found deep in the recesses of the attic. I moved a game controller out of the way and cried myself to sleep.

"Cassidy? Hon? What you doing here? Are you okay?"

I opened my eyes and took in my surroundings. I could see why he wondered. I was deep under the eves of the roof wedged in between the TV and a bookcase full of game cartridges and paperbacks. A half played game of backgammon lay on the floor by my head.

"Yeah, I'm fine. I just had a rough night and I didn't want to wake you."

"What if I want you to wake me?"

"You had plenty of chances. You must have needed the sleep."

He noticed the swimsuit, the hair that dried scrunched up in the beanbag chair.

"Hon, I need my girl back. Can you find her for me?"

"I'm trying. Let's go see if she's at the beach today."

"I don't think we're going to find her by going different places."

"It can't hurt to try. Maybe some good memories will replace the bad ones."

The sun was warm and sparkled on the water as I felt a swell coming behind me.

"Don't try to stand up," Cody said as he comfortably treaded water beside the surfboard. "Just ride the wave in for now. Later you can kneel on the board. But don't try to stand from the very beginning. It's all in the balance."

I looked to Rusty watching from the beach. He couldn't swim with his cast on but he enjoyed the sand and sun. Even at the beach he watched for trouble. I'd found it here before but today trouble wasn't looking for me.

I felt the wave lift me up and felt a rush of wind as the board slid through the water. Chase skimmed down the face of the wave beside me. He was a seasoned surfer, taking it up before I was born. Cody was teaching me, gradually. The wave crested and the surf engulfed the surfboard, knocking me flat. I disappeared board and all while the water pounded around me, tossing the board around and driving me to the sandy ocean floor. I was tethered to the board, so all I had to do was not panic and eventually I'd be near the surface again. When the turbulence ended and I popped to the surface I saw Rusty, on his feet, waiting. I climbed back up on the surfboard and paddled out again.

"One of these days I need to learn how to steer," I told Cody. I turned the board over to him. I knew he wanted to surf a lot more than he wanted to watch me fall off the board.

When I swam to shore I saw that Bill and Bev had joined the group. They had a picnic lunch. I was afraid to face Bill after the night before but he didn't hold it against me.

"We have fried chicken or roast beef sandwiches," Bill said.

"Sam at the taco stand promised to tell me all about Rusty's crazy childhood at the beach but Rusty always finds a way to prevent that from happening."

"You can't believe Sam anyway," Bill said. "He's seen so many kids come through here. He gets them all mixed up."

"You think so?" I asked. "Let's see."

I ran over to the taco stand, partly because Rusty couldn't catch up to me in time, partly because I wanted some space. Sam looked at me for a second before he made the connection. He was pretty sharp. He'd only met me once or twice before.

"We have a bet going," I told him. "I need a story about Rusty to prove a point."

"Rusty? Michaels?"

"Yeah."

His grin broadened.

"Okay! When Rusty was about fourteen he came out here with Tony and we had a battle of the stands, Rusty and I against Tony and Herschel the hotdog man. I cooked tacos as fast as I could and Herschel cooked hotdogs as fast as he could and the boys ate as fast as they could. The boys set up a table between the two stands and they had to finish their hotdog or taco before they could run back for another one. Rusty ate twelve tacos, but Tony only ate nine hotdogs. Then there was a conflict because the tacos fell apart and we weren't sure if Rusty really ate a dozen tacos or if he fed the seagulls the tacos. Rusty argued that if he fed the seagulls all those tacos then he'd still be eating. Before they could settle the bet both boys turned green. When they tried to dig up the money to pay for the tacos and hotdogs they came up a couple of bucks short. Rusty walked around in a hotdog costume to make it up to us. He brought in a lot more customers so we all called it even."

"Thanks Sam," I said and bought a plate of nachos and cheese.

"Well?" asked Rusty when I got back.

I grinned, "Did you or did you not challenge Tony to a taco/hotdog eating contest when you were fourteen?"

He grinned back. "I was so sick. Tony was worse. That's why I ended up walking around in the hotdog suit."

"Oh, Rusty, you didn't," Bev said.

"Sam said Rusty ate twelve tacos and Tony ate nine hotdogs."

"That's all?" Bev said. "I thought you boys were going to eat us out of house and home."

"That was after a three scoop sundae and churros from the boardwalk," Rusty admitted.

"You didn't do anything like that when you were a kid, did you?" asked Bev.

"I did a lot of dumb things in my time but they rarely involved food. Rusty's heard the stories."

"Most of Cass's food stories are about weird things she's had to eat to survive: gopher snake, vole, raw rabbit, cactus. It amazes me the ways she discovers how to survive on nothing. Cassidy lives by her wits."

Yeah, I thought, and one of these days, if I'm not careful, I'm going to die by my wits.

"I think I need half a roast beef sandwich to go with these nachos," I said.

We sat and ate and visited, glad the night before hadn't damaged our relationship. After we ate I stretched out on a towel to rest.

"Are you tired?" Rusty asked.

"Yeah, I hardly got any sleep last night."

"Same nightmares as usual?"

"Sort of, hospital dreams get mixed in, too, but only the scary part."

"What can we do?" he asked.

"Wake me up if I start tossing and turning."

"That's not what I meant."

"Okay, sit where you'll cast a shadow on me."

"That's not what I meant either."

"I know."

I dozed off, thankful for even a little bit of peaceful sleep. Even ten minutes would help. At first I slept well, I have no idea how long it was but I found myself at the one place I couldn't stand seeing. The staircase. Rusty? Or Chase. I had to choose. The fear felt like a lightning bolt made of ice that stabbed straight through me. I could move Chase. I couldn't move Rusty. The choice. The decision would affect the rest of my life. If anything happened to Rusty I'd never forgive myself. But Chase had a chance. I had to give it to him. I had to. And in the dream when I chose Chase my world fell apart. The fire flared up consuming everything. I woke up crying. When I found the present again I was embarrassed.

"I told you to wake me," I said through angry tears.

"Cassidy," Bill said. "He was going to but I asked him not to. I wanted to see how deep this hurt goes."

"Well, you still don't know," I said bitterly and I got up to leave but Bill followed.

"Dad, stop," Rusty called, but Bill followed anyway.

"The crux of the matter lies in why you think I would hate you for what happened. Whatever that is, you're dumping more hate onto yourself than I could ever conjure up for you."

I broke into a jog.

"Cassidy," he said jogging beside me. "Tell me what it is. Stop and tell me in one sentence what's eating you alive."

I broke into a run. He stuck to me like glue. I headed for the water and he tackled me. I went face first into the sand and an old lady ran up and started beating on him with a beach umbrella.

"You leave that poor girl alone!" she yelled.

He ignored her.

"Don't go in the ocean feeling like this. It's dangerous… Cassidy, tell me. Just one sentence."

The lady turned beet red and walked off down the beach.

"I can't! I can't even admit it to myself…"

"Yes, you can, or it wouldn't affect you this way. What's doing this to you?"

The ocean's roar was nothing compared to the battle in my head. I had to run, or hit something, or cry, so I cried. Face first in the sand with people walking all around us, I cried, "I chose Chase. How could I do that? I chose Chase." Bill just sat there, Rusty's worried look on his face. "How could I leave him in that old dry house? It was burning! But Chase had a chance. I could give Chase a chance. So I chose Chase."

"You went for help…" Bill said.

"With the basement filling with smoke. A quarter mile. Help was a quarter mile away, on foot, and the basement was filling with smoke. And I didn't know what kind of help there was. I knew I could get two cops to help get him out. But that's all I could count on."

"If Rusty hadn't made it, what would you have done?"

"I would hike into the hills and never come out. I'd walk until I couldn't walk anymore and when I was rested I'd walk some more. No food, no water. And I wouldn't come back."

"Chase would have found you."

"No he wouldn't. Ask Chase. If I knew he'd come after me, even he wouldn't be able to find me. But we made it. It was touch and go for a little while and it was scary for a long while, but we made it."

"Are you sure? Because Rusty's not. He'll never be whole until he sees you be whole."

"I know. Bill, even when Rusty was semiconscious, he was worried about me. I tried to answer his questions about what happened. I thought he was worried about the case, what had happened, all the facts, but no matter what I told him, nothing would console him, until Kelly told him I was all right, that the guys were there for me. Chase and Kelly and Landon and Schroeder. When Kelly told him I was all right and I had backup he calmed down."

"So the real heart of the matter was you hate the fact that you chose Chase over Rusty."

"And he suffered for it. I hurt him. That's what hurts. My stupidity hurt

Rusty."

"If you could go back and change those ten minutes, what would you change? Would you leave Chase? I don't think so."

"I'd hold my suspect at gun point and not let her move. I let her curiosity get to me. What she was doing seemed harmless and I was curious, too. She tripped a booby trap and it started the house on fire. If I could go back I'd keep Agnes spread eagled, at gun point, until the guys woke up and took over."

"So you learned something from all this. I'm sorry you had to pay the price for it that you did. Would you choose Chase again?"

I sighed, "Yeah, I'd choose Chase again and it would be just as hard and painful as it was this time. Every time I felt Chase's heel catch on a stair I counted the seconds it was costing Rusty. But I'd do it again. Because Chase *did* have a chance. I had to give it to him."

"So when are you going to quit punishing yourself?"

"I don't know. What do you think?"

"I think there's healing in forgiveness. I think you can start right now. Choose to forgive yourself and even if you don't feel forgiven you'll have taken a step. Even if you have to do it every day, choose to forgive. You'll find those days coming less often and then one day you'll know you don't need to do it anymore. When that day comes you'll be whole again. Will you do it?"

"I… I don't know if I can."

"I'm not asking you to do it all at once. I'm only asking you to take the first step for your own good."

"I don't want any good for me. I don't deserve it. I need a good thrashing. I'd feel better if I just had a good thrashing."

That saddened him and that's how I knew I had his forgiveness. If he could forgive me, maybe Rusty could, too.

"You've thrashed yourself enough. It's not helping. It hurts those around you to see you go through this. Forgive yourself. Stop this cycle you've put yourself in. You've faced it. You've put it in words. You can see it. Now put it behind you."

He stood and gave me a hand up.

"You're forgiven. You wanted my forgiveness. You've got it. I couldn't hold onto any ill feelings while I watched you dream. Your hurt runs deep and it's only there because you love my son. You love him so much it hurts. I can't fault you for that. Now you need to forgive yourself."

We headed back. He kept looking behind us. I didn't realize how far I'd run before Bill stopped me. He looked behind us again.

"What are you doing?" I asked.

"Seeing if you put it behind you yet."

"You can't see that."

"I'll be able to see when you've done it. It'll free you and you'll be more like my favorite daughter-in-law again."

"I'm your only daughter-in-law."

"I'll know when it happens," he said confidently.

Rusty stood and crutched his way over when he saw us coming. Bill joined Bev on the beach blanket so Rusty and I could talk.

"Why is it always the dads you gotta watch out for?" Rusty joked, knowing my dad had his own quirks.

"It's okay, he's a wise man. And he cares an awful lot. Any guy who will tackle his daughter-in-law and endure a beach umbrella beating just to talk has got to care, right?"

"He didn't…" Rusty said heading back for the blanket.

"Rusty, don't. I know why he did it. It's okay. He meant well."

"I should have waked you, no matter what Dad said. Where does that much sadness and fear come from? I can't imagine one person capable of handling that much sadness."

"If I could I wouldn't have nightmares. Your dad says I won't find peace until I've forgiven myself. But I can't."

"Why? You didn't do anything wrong. What can you possibly have to forgive yourself for?"

Don't run, I told myself. You can't run from Rusty. You have to face it so just toughen up and get through it.

He saw the walls go up and he stopped.

"This is a brown couch issue, isn't it?"

"Yeah," I admitted. "But there's no brown couch."

"I can take you home. We can use the attic."

"No, it's just time. I don't have the strength to hide it anymore."

We walked in silence for a while as I gathered my thoughts. I finally thought I had found a way to explain what was in my heart. When we found a quiet place we sat down.

"One time Landon and I were on our way to the compound to get our cars after a search. There was a traffic accident and we got out to tend to the victims. Landon treated a mom and a couple of kids and I went and talked to the guy in the other car. He freaked out and fled the scene and I tracked him to a little bar and grill. He turned out to be one of the men you were looking for. I went in to ID the guy from the accident scene and you and a team of cops converged on the place not knowing I was in there. Do you remember that?"

"Yeah. I remember. Alfonso."

"You were fixing to send the bomb squad robot to stun grenade the place. You called me to say you were going to be late for dinner and you found out that I was in the bar and grill. You said, if you'd gone ahead with the plan and launched things into the restaurant to bring Alfonso out and then found out I was in there you'd have been a basket case."

"And I would have."

"I did worse. I did worse to you and it wasn't just uncomfortable things like pepper spray. And the only reason for it was carelessness. If I'd just followed procedure the fire wouldn't have happened. But I slipped and it cost you. It could have killed you. Every decision I made cost you. When I let Agnes look in the desk, it cost you. And when I chose to pull Chase out of the house it cost you more. I relive every second of that time a hundred times a day. Because I hurt you. I ask myself a hundred times a day, how could I choose Chase? I'm a basket case, because I hurt you."

He was quiet for a long time.

"You can't continue like this," he said. "I don't have any easy answers for you, but you can't continue like this. You're going to beat yourself to a pulp and I can't watch you do that. Decide you're moving forward. When it slows you down just tell yourself, that's in the past and you're moving forward. Then do it. Don't let it drag you back."

"You really want me to do that?"

"I think it will help. I want my girl back. I want to see you fly free again. I love to see you go after life. It's beautiful when you really enjoy life, whether you're on the trail or at the beach or stalking deer. When you're really living you're the most beautiful thing in the world."

"So, you can forgive me? For what I did to you?"

"I hundred times over, if that's what it takes."

I was forgiven. Rusty still loved me. I didn't quite understand it but I could accept it.

"Okay," I said. "I'll try."

"You'll try what?"

"I'll try to forgive myself and I'll try to move forward without running. I won't let it drag me back. I don't know if I can do it, but I'll try."

"That's my girl. That's more like it. What do you want to do to move forward?"

"First? I'm going to learn how to surf, or at least how to spot a wave and steer. Maybe I'll even learn how to stand up."

"You really want to learn how to surf?"

"I want to learn anything that will get me outside. I'd rather be doing something at the beach. The more active I can be the less I will think about things that get me in trouble. That's why I tell Strict to put me to work, why I went to ATV training. Will you teach me rock climbing?"

"After the cast comes off."

"Okay, first though, surfing. Let's go see if Cody is tired of it. Maybe he'll let me have a turn."

Cody had just flopped down on the towel ready to call it a day.

"Go on. Chase is out there. He'll help you," Cody said. I wrestled the surfboard under my arm and jogged slowly down to the water. I paddled out to wait my turn. I tried to leave the good waves for the experienced surfers who could appreciate a good ride. My only goal was to learn how to read the waves. I could do that by watching. It was what I was good at, careful observation, pattern recognition, watching the surfers' feet on the board, translating it to board movements. Tracking on the water. Chase paddled up and sat on his board.

"Chase, I'm not running anymore."

"What are you doing?"

"Actually I'm tracking the surfers. I'm learning surfing tracker style."

Little laugh lines. "If anybody can do it, you can. So, if you're tracking have you noticed the difference between a regular foot and a goofy foot?"

"A what? A goofy foot? Give me some time to observe. I've only been doing this a few hours."

Chase always knew the right questions to ask to get me thinking. A goofy foot? I began watching people's feet. Most people put their left foot forward. I imagined myself if I ever learned to stand on a surfboard. How would I stand on one? Well, after falling off a hundred times. When I knew what I was doing, how would I stand on a surfboard? I decided it would be left foot forward. If most people led with their left foot, then the people who put their right foot forward must be goofy footed. While I was figuring all that out I was watching feet, and the board's reactions to the foot movements.

A wave swelled underneath me and I could tell this one had my name on it. I stayed out the way of the experienced surfers so I wouldn't infringe on their territory, but this wave had strayed into my territory. I lay on the board trying to feel just that right time when I could catch the wave.

"Paddle! Paddle!" yelled Chase. "Okay, wait, wait…now!"

As I skimmed down the wave I looked behind me. No fire, so far so good.

A couple of waves later Cody paddled out.

"Where'd you get the surfboard?" I asked, because I was using his.

"This one's yours," he said. "The color was Rusty's choice. He said it had to be visible from the air."

Leave it to Rusty, anything to help me move forward. I bet we took a lot of trips to the beach, too. Cody and I traded boards. I let him take the next wave, watched the timing, the movements. When it was my turn I found the crest, almost missed on the timing, I had to hurry. Up, up it went then…then down! It went down and the board slipped forward. Everything felt right. My heart leaped. Now, to stand. Getting from a prone position to a standing position on a moving board was impossible, just a little off and I was tossed off the side, the wave lost to me. Again and again, it was a matter of balance. Once I got the side-to-side motion under control I had to work on forward backward position. Time after time I was too far forward and the board plunged into the water, dumping me over the front. When I was exhausted I rode the board back to the beach and flopped down on the blanket. Rusty grinned glad to see me doing something besides thinking.

"So," Chase said as he walked up with a drippy hotdog, "Did you figure it out?"

"Yeah."

"Yeah. Not I think so. No questions?"

"No, I figured it out. A regular foot is someone who surfs with their left foot forward and a goofy foot is someone who surfs with their right foot forward. I told you I was tracking out there."

That night I thought I would be too tired to have nightmares but I was wrong. Rusty woke me gently and held me until the fear subsided.

"You okay?" he asked.

"Yeah, it's just…"

"Nope, no looking back," he said. "Only forward."

Sigh, "Okay, so how am I supposed to do that with only an attic and my thoughts?"

He winked at me, then got up and tossed the ladder over the balcony. We snuck down the ladder. Descending a rope ladder in a cast is not easy.

"If they'd given me a choice, I would have told them to give you a cast you could swim in, but they didn't ask."

"It's okay, I can watch."

"Guess my bathing suit being in the downstairs bathroom doesn't mean anything."

"Not in the middle of the night."

He sat on the side of the pool, one leg in the water, broken leg on the side of the pool. I slipped out of my tank top and panties and dove into the pool, then paddled up to Rusty. I tickled his leg with my fingers and he splashed me with his foot. He pulled out his foot and turned around, dangling his hands into the pool. I swam into his touch and gave him a kiss. The porch light switched on and Bill stuck his head out the back door.

"Dad!" Rusty said.

“Sorry,” he said grinning. “What are you doing up in the middle of the night?”

“We’re not looking back,” I answered from the shelter of the poolside.

“That’s better,” he answered and went inside.

Chapter 20

One piece of the puzzle refused to die. Why hide valuables and then booby trap the hiding spots? It didn't make sense. I wrote it off as a hate crime for a while, but that didn't stop my thoughts from straying back to the mysterious traps I had encountered. They were meant to kill, that was obvious. But why kill somebody? Surely not to protect their belongings. Finding a body near a booby trap would only lead to an investigation and the investigation would lead to confiscated evidence. And why booby trap something, making it risky to ever retrieve it? I didn't understand it at all. The mine especially grated on me. I never did see what was in that mine. Maybe the explosion had nothing to do with the traps. The first homestead I found had gunpowder stored under the floorboards. Dirk's single shot could have been chocked up to bad luck.

"Did you read that journal we found?" I finally asked Rusty.

"Only a small portion of it. It isn't easy to read. It was written with a fountain pen and the cursive is bad."

"Whatever happened to it?"

"I'm not telling. If you have asked this many questions about it you're curious enough to read it and the information in it is best left in the past."

Rats. I thought it might contain a clue.

I even visited Agnes. But she was scared to talk about it. She thought anything she said would be used against her. I guess I really can't blame her. I did read her her rights.

Finally, out of boredom and desperation to close the case in my own mind I went back to the homestead that started it all.

I drove to the nearest parking spot and followed my old route to the homestead as early in the morning as possible. Snake wrangling was getting old. This time I only found one large rattlesnake but it made me leery about entering the crawl space again. I wore old clothes that I wouldn't mind throwing away afterwards just in case the crawl space was as awful as the last time I saw it.

The crawl space looked like something out of a horror movie. Dried snake blood still covered a large area. The skin and entrails had dried and hardened. I noted the clean spot in the middle where I had been sitting when I had to shoot the snake. Luckily, I was not squeamish. A little dried snake blood was not much of a turn off.

I lowered myself through the hole, sat cross legged on the ground, and looked around before turning on the flashlight, and pulling the boards over the hole. I shined the flashlight across the boxes wondering where to start.

I opened the box that I found the map in. I thought I might have missed something important. The first time I was in a hurry and just looking for anything to get me started, so I could assume there was something more in the box. I remembered to pass over the commercially made maps. I watched for the little hand drawn ones. There were several more detailed maps of the individual properties. But they didn't show me anything I hadn't already seen in person, that is until I worked my way further down the stack. I found a small map of a single property. The layout of the property didn't match any of the others I had seen. It had a hill nearby and I recognized the name of the hill. I thought about the lay of the land in that area. I had tracked there in the past. Like many desert areas animal tracks showed up easily in the desert sand there. A small community had grown up at the foot of the hill. I just wasn't sure where this property fit into the layout with the other ones out there.

I hesitated to go there. People who lived outside of town frequently did so because they wanted elbow room and they didn't appreciate strangers nosing around where they didn't belong. The police frequently had trespassing calls out there.

Oh, what the heck, I thought, the worst that would happen was I'd get caught, the police would be called, I'd tell the officers I was out tracking, they would believe me and tell me to go home, so I'd do it.

I drove to the hill. That was the easy part. After I stopped the car and took a look around, though, I didn't see any structures that fit the map. I knew the house on the map could have been reduced to a single foundation and that the foundation would not be visible until I was very close to it, so I began walking around in the desert between the houses and the hill. Rabbit and lizard tracks abounded. The rabbit tracks especially. The lizard tracks exhibited the typical herky-jerky tail swipe and claw mark configuration. I noticed the lizards were mostly very small ones. A typical lizard track had a four inch tail drag and the claw marks were a little over a finger's width apart.

In the distance I noticed a light green house. Under the eaves the green was darker telling me the house was painted long ago and the light green had faded in the intense sun. Like many houses in the area there was no fence. A shed stood in what would have been the corner of the back yard. It, too, was faded and weathered. The door hung slightly crooked. There was a vent on the roof to provide air circulation inside. A failed garden was taped off beside the shed. Nothing worthwhile would grow here. There were only a few withered plants inside the plowed area. The rest had been pulled and discarded. I didn't see any recent tracks inside the garden area.

I avoided the house and walked a wide circle around it. A dog barked and the curtains at the sliding glass back door jerked around as the dog jumped against the curtain. I steered away from the house in case the owners let the dog out.

The next house was tan and could have been yellow in the past. This house had a rough wire fence. The dogs that ran the fence line could have easily jumped out, but they didn't. They didn't have to. They were shepherd mixes and appeared to be very capable of keeping strangers away from the house.

I was guessing the gray house used to be blue. There was no fence and no barking. A set of antlers was mounted at the peak of the garage, which was separate from the house. A green car sat in front of the garage. It was an old car. In a former life it was known as The Thing. I had only seen a few in my lifetime and I had asked Old Frank, our ranch foreman, what they were when I was a teenager. Old Frank knew everything, but when he said it was The Thing I had to look it up. Sure enough, there was a car called The Thing. I didn't blame the car manufacturers one bit for opting for The Thing as a car name. That's just what they looked like.

The house was quiet. The car looked content just sitting there. The curtains didn't move. The breeze even seemed to cease. Usually there is a constant breeze, if not a howling wind, in the desert. I tried to remember if I had felt a breeze at the other houses but I hadn't paid attention. I was even tempted to back track and see if the wind had just vanished or if the glowering gray house just had that effect on people. I stood waiting for a breeze but it remained still.

As I passed the gray house the land sloped downward. At the bottom of the hill a small arroyo ran through the desert. It was only a few feet wide and a motorcycle track ran up the arroyo, obviously this was a dirt bike path to some place more interesting to visit. I followed the arroyo a little bit until it turned. Then I noticed something made of rock behind the hill. I cut across the base of the hill and discovered a house made of rock. The roof was long gone and the windows had been bashed in years ago. The door had graffiti scrawled on it, though it didn't seem to be any of the gang symbols I remembered from training. He door creaked when I moved it. On the backside somebody had painted a picture of Waldo. I ran into pictures of Waldo every once in a while on bridges, fences, trees and now doors and I smiled every time. Good old Waldo.

After my previous experience with rocks and the things they could hide, I was wary. I knew not to stand directly in front of anything that I tested. Whether it was pistols, or rifles, or rat traps, the traps only had a small area where a person was in real danger. However that area was the most natural one for anybody looking for something. It was rather awkward testing all the rocks without standing in front of them. I kept my eyes open for any hints, like the arrow in the bookcase. I stomped around on the foundation listening for wobbly spots that might indicate a loose brick or empty space underneath. *Stomp, stomp, stomp, cachick.* Shit. That *cachick* was not a wobbly brick. It was a gun cocking.

"Figured you'd show up eventually," a gravelly voice said. "Didn't expect someone like you till I saw the news. Thought it would be someone older."

"Come out where I can see you," I said.

"*HAR har har*," he laughed bitterly and then broke into a hoarse cough. "Most people ask me to turn away. Damn son a bitches. Only perfect people are allowed in public these days."

"Nobody's perfect," I said trying to engage him in conversation. Dang, what did they say in that crisis negotiation class I took? Schroeder suggested I attend it since trouble seems to occur everywhere I go. "What's your name?"

"Aint no concern of yours," he said.

"Okay, well, then why am I being held at gunpoint?" I asked.

"Because," he said as he stepped into the house. He wore a bandana over his face like a bank robber but I could tell he wasn't going to rob a bank. He squinted at me and the bandana shifted with the slight movement. "It's payback time."

He was slightly on the tallish side, and fat from lack of exercise. He needed a haircut and shave. His clothes were old. He didn't care anymore what he looked like.

"I haven't done anything to you," I pointed out.

"You have." He spat on the ground and I wondered how he knew the exact angle to miss the point of the bandana. "You been to nearly all the other settlements. I saw you on the news. You're sharp. Gotta give you that. Which means I gotta be extree careful."

"I'm not going to hurt you. I was just tracking in the area and noticed the ruins. Ruins of houses are interesting, but if this is your property…"

"Shut up! You are not here just for the heck of it. You caint get me to believe that for one stinkin' second. You might have made yourself scarce and avoided the cameras but they did show the 'young woman' who found the other stores."

He was growing angrier. It was when his temper flared that I noticed the bandana fit his face wrong. It hung just above his cheekbones and interfered with his vision. Then I realized why it hung so oddly. The man had no nose!

"So," I said. "How do you fit into this mystery? I am only here wondering why the stores were booby trapped. It didn't make sense to me to set up a trap that would only draw more attention to the belongings being hidden."

"I don't care about them damned Kingsleys," he growled. "Nor about them Packards. I don't want no part of their treasures and belongings and stuff. But they's coming back. Some day. And when they do they're payin'."

"For what?" I asked.

"For this," he spat as he pulled down the bandana. I was glad I had figured out the reason he wore it. I was surprised by the extent of the injuries but maybe being in the Marines and police reserves had hardened me a bit. I wasn't repulsed by his face. I cringed inwardly imagining the pain and heartache the man had endured, but I managed to stay focused on the situation and not the disfigurement.

"Who did that to you?" I asked as compassionately as I could.

"Rufus Packard. Nine seventeen p.m. on July eighteenth nineteen hundred and sixty-two. On a rare cloudy day. Right in the face."

The fact that he remembered the date and time after so many years was bad news. This man was bitter and his anger had been kindling for fifty years.

"You're too young," I said.

"Taint. He done it to a kid! Dropped outa school! Never held a job!" *Bammm!* I jumped to the side. "Folks are scared of me!" *Bam!*

"I'm not related to Rufus Packard," I said. "You've got no reason to hate me."

"You're undoing all my hard work. Sooner or later I was going to catch me a Packard."

He stepped forward, an old fashioned western style revolver pointed directly at my chest. It reminded me of old cap guns, but this was no cap gun. He'd proved that already. I wondered if he found it at one of the homesteads.

"I'll leave," I said. "I don't have to find any more of the stores."

"Liar! If you were going to stop you wouldn't be here now! You'll bring in the po-lice to undo all my work. If I let you go I bet you bring them back here."

He took another step closer.

"What's your name?" I tried again. One thing we did learn in training was to look for ways to identify with the other person. People respond better if they hear their name.

"Quit school because they called me Pinocchio. Kids ran away from me," he spat. "Those days plastic surgery was brand new. Nobody had it done, cept movie stars and rich folks."

"Look, I know it wasn't easy, but you can't blame Ru…" *Bam!*

Okay, maybe he could. He only had three shots left. Maybe I could get him to waste his bullets.

"Since you seem determined to kill me anyway, how many other houses like this are there?" I asked.

He pointed the gun at me and lurched forward.

"I'm guessing two," I said. "You'd save one more of these sites in case I found this one."

He stopped as if he should have thought of that, then scowled. "This is the only one I can keep close tabs on. Now how would you like your nose? Inside your head?"

"You really think you can hit my nose?" I asked. "Shooting me isn't going to fix your problem. You've *let* Rufus…" *Bam!* "Ruin your life. Your lack of friends, schooling and job were a result of *your* decisions, nothing…" *Bam!* "more."

He was down to one bullet and that bullet had my name on it. So far his shots were simply to scare me but it didn't work. The fewer bullets there were in his gun the safer I was.

"No one person can ruin your life, except you," I said expecting him to fire the last shot.

"Says who, you pretty little wench?" He said as he got in my face. My usual move for this situation wouldn't work on this guy. I was known for my right hook, but he didn't have a nose to break. I decided it was going to hurt but maybe it would rattle his brain a little, so I brought my right fist up into his jaw as hard as I could. He roared some intelligible sound and raised his hands. He grabbed me around the neck. I twisted and ducked to the right.

I had a rifle across my back but apparently he hadn't seen it. I hate shooting people. The only thing I hate worse than shooting people is when they shoot at people I know. I had killed men in self defense but it was the hardest thing I've ever done. My training said to shoot him. My heart cried, "No!" My analytical mind said that my rifle could be used in a multitude of ways, but then it argued that it could also be used against me. I was putting way too much thought into surviving. I had survival instincts that superseded in times of trouble. Instinct was the way to go. When I twisted away from him I put some distance between us and I let Dangerous Tracker Woman take charge. She whipped the rifle around and cocked it in one motion.

"You're underestimating me," I said. "Drop the gun and kick it this direction."

He stood there numb from shock at the way the tables had turned.

"Drop the gun and kick it this way," I said again with a little more force. "Now!"

"That thing ain't legal," he said as he gawked at my rifle.

"Drop it!"

"How'd a little thing like you get a gun like that?"

"I'm going to tell you one more time to drop your gun. If you don't do it I'll make you drop it. Where would you like it? In the hand? Maybe you'd like an ear pierced? Now. Drop it."

He was scared. When he got scared his mouth started up.

"Is that an automatic?"

"Drop it on the count of three," I said as I took aim. "One… two… three." Please drop it, please… I aimed the rifle at the gun and pulled the trigger. The pistol spun out of his hand and he jerked in surprise.

"Semi," I said, "and even my permits have permits. Now spread eagle on the floor."

He amazed me when he actually did what I told him to. I frisked him taking away his wallet, a pen, and a handful of spare bullets. There was still one bullet left in the pistol.

"You planted all those booby traps hoping to kill yourself a Packard?" I asked.

"Took me months. The waiting was the hardest part. Them Packards… I know they'll be back one day."

I took that as a confession so I got out my cell phone. I disguised my voice.

"Joshua Hills Police Department how may I help you?"

"I'm hearing gun shots near my house! Lots of gun shots! Can you send an officer out here? I usually hear them far away but these sound like their in my back yard!"

"Yes ma'am and do you have an address?"

I guessed at the number based on the layout of the town. I knew the nearest street because I had driven it to look for places to track. They sent an officer after I added, "And please hurry! I'm scared and alone!"

I flipped the wallet open and checked my prisoner's ID. Calvin Kingsley. One of the land wars survivors. I stood over Calvin with my rifle aimed and ready.

"Why'd you change your voice?" Calvin asked.

"Because they know my voice," I said.

"Ha, how would they know your voice?"

"I… uh… I'm married to one of their detectives and I'm a reserve deputy. Now I want you to get up slowly. Keep your hands where I can see them and walk toward the street. We're going to wait nice and findable for my backup to arrive. Up. Hands up."

Maybe I learned a thing or two from my encounter with Agnes.

He got up slowly and stood with his hands over his head. "To the street," I said. "Don't run. I can take you down with one shot. Your pistol has fired five so you've proven to be a threat."

He began walking, glancing back forlornly at his pistol.

"Don't worry, the police know what to do with that," I said.

As we walked between the houses, the dogs charged the fence again. Calvin steered toward the gray house. The breeze was still and the air felt leaden.

"Away from the house," I instructed. The farther we were from the house the less likely he was to bolt. "Farther."

The dogs lunged and barked. When we were as close to the dogs as we were going to get Calvin lunged.

"Dino! Rocky! Git her! Git her!"

"Hold it right there!" I yelled at Calvin. The black and tan dog jumped over the fence.

"Git her! Bite her!" he yelled at the dog. It stood beside Calvin growling. Its ears were back but its tail thrashed back and forth rhythmically. Calvin began backing away.

"Stop where you are! Keep your hands up!"

When the second dog saw the first dog getting in on some action it, too, jumped the fence. Calvin stood there waiting for the dogs to take action and distract me. The dogs stood bristling before me, barking and wagging. I kept Calvin at gun point.

"They must think I have a snack," I said. "Keep walking."

"But…"

He turned and the dogs began running circles around us barking up a storm.

"It isn't very nice," I said to Calvin. "Sacrificing your neighbor's dogs just to get away from the police. I've killed a dog with nothing but a hunting knife, but these dogs don't deserve to die. They're just acting."

The dogs frightened me but I had to put up a brave front if I was going to get Calvin to cooperate. I hoped that didn't include shooting his neighbor's dogs. It wasn't too long ago that I was attacked by fighting dogs, so Dino and Rocky unnerved me a bit. I wanted to run, but I knew I couldn't. To run would invite a chase and Calvin would get away.

Calvin turned and walked toward the street. He knew his time was severely limited. Off in the distance we could hear sirens, but the officers still had to find us. Calvin looked desperate. The dogs still barked, though only in warning. Suddenly Calvin turned around and charged straight at me. I should have shot him. I should have. But I didn't. He grabbed the gun and tried to wrestle it loose from my grip. I hung on for dear life.

"Cal… it's no use! They're almost here!" I yelled.

With a wild yell he pulled up on the weapon lifting me off my feet. I gripped the rifle, swung my feet forward and let my weight pull the gun down. I slid between Calvin's legs pulling him into a spectacular flip. He landed on his back with an *oooff!* I twisted the gun loose and stood over

Calvin a total mess, hair flying, covered with dust, dogs barking.

The first black and white pulled to a stop and the officers jumped out. There I stood, Calvin at gun point, the dogs barking at the action.

"We had a report of shots fired," Big John Jankowski said.

"Six. Five for him. One for me. Just one. I counted."

"How was your day today?" Rusty asked when he found me in the kitchen after work.

"Oh, so so," I said. "Why?"

He leaned against the wall and watched me work.

"There's a story going around the station."

"Oh?"

"Something about you capturing a felon."

"Oh, that must have been Calvin Kinglsey," I said.

"Hon…"

"I told you my day was so so. It didn't rate even a so so until Big John showed up. But it turned out okay."

"His gun looks like a prop from an old west movie."

"Thanks."

"So it's true?"

"Uh, yeah. Sorry."

He smirked. I thought I was going to get a sound scolding but he smirked. "Cook enough for three. Chase was curious enough to make the drive. He wants to track it."

Cassidy Michaels, Dangerous Tracker Woman, and dinner cook. I guess I could live with that.

PART 2

HUNTING TROUBLE

Chapter 21

"Don't move."

I froze. When you get in trouble as much as I do, a phrase like *don't move* could mean a lot of things. When the guy who says it to you is used to you getting into trouble, and he's a detective, you tend to listen to him. Add to it the fact that I attract felons and I didn't know what was coming.

Rusty looked cautiously around me and darted back.

This was strange. Usually if he wanted to observe someone inconspicuously he moved as little as possible. He watched with his eyes, acting as normal as possible. He glanced over my other shoulder.

Usually I was the one who spotted suspicious characters. It got to the point where I was afraid to go to a restaurant. I'd been approached by drug dealers, con men, and murderers, so I never knew what to expect.

Rusty took a drink of his beer and set it down still watching over my shoulder, then quickly switched to the other shoulder. Something happened behind me and he relaxed for a bit.

The waitress arrived with our food. Rusty took a plate of ribs and mashed potatoes, set it down and smiled broadly over my left shoulder. His expression changed to one of disappointment. The waitress set down my pasta.

"Does everything look okay?" she asked. "Can I get you anything else?"

"Everything looks great," I answered. "Rusty?"

"Yeah, everything's fine," he answered, distracted. He hadn't even looked at his food.

"Okay," the waitress said. "Let me know if you need anything else."

As the waitress left Rusty's eyebrows shot up and he shot a surprised look over my shoulder. The disappointed look came back. Then the surprised look. This was very odd.

A sticky hand appeared over my shoulder. It grasped a soggy animal cracker. A squeal and the hand moved quickly hitting me in the eye with mushy cookie. I jumped. Rusty laughed at the baby, a big hearty laugh that filled the restaurant. I wiped cookie mush off my face and scooted over.

Rusty was flirting with a baby! Why hadn't I thought of that before? He wasn't watching felons. He was playing as inconspicuously as he could. That big old softy! I looked over my shoulder and big brown eyes looked back, curly black hair encircling a cute half-toothless smile. The little girl scrunched down in her seat and Rusty looked disappointed. She popped up and Rusty looked surprised. I smiled. Rusty looked embarrassed.

"You never flirt with me like that," I said.

"You don't play peek-a-boo," he countered.

I watched in quiet amusement as Rusty played games over the booth with the little girl behind me. It progressed from peek-a-boo to hide and seek. The little girl was a notorious flirt and Rusty flirted back. She offered the cookie to Rusty. He shook his head no.

"That's baby's cookie. This is Rusty's cookie," he said, holding up a half eaten rib.

The little girl turned around, selected a different item of food and offered it to Rusty.

"That's Mommy's French fry," he said.

Mommy turned around, got a glimpse of Rusty, turned scarlet and made the little girl sit down. Rusty looked disappointed and not for the baby's sake.

Things got very quiet at our table. He knew not to mention kids and I knew not to mention kids but the subject hung in the air between us. It wasn't a point of conflict, just disagreement. I wasn't ready to settle down and be a mom and he loved kids. He teased me saying that I was enough like a kid for him, but I knew. He wanted a family. And I wanted time without being tied to the house. But how much time was enough? How much time did we have left? And what about searches? I was the area tracker for search and rescue. I needed to be able to take off at a moment's notice. How could I do that with kids? And what was more important, staying home with the kid or finding someone in trouble? I didn't have any answers so I didn't want to bring up the questions.

The little girl peeked over the booth and Rusty smiled back. She batted her eyelashes at him and he gave her a one finger wave. The peek-a-boo game resumed. I heard giggles behind me. Rusty's eyes were laughing. He was having fun. It was good to see him having fun even if it brought questions to mind that I'd rather not deal with.

Rusty would make a great dad. He loved to play and interact. He would be an effective disciplinarian. I would not. I tended to see the kid's point of view and justify what they did. I did it with my nephew, Patrick. I'd do it with my own kids, too.

The family in the next booth finished their meal and packed up all the paraphernalia associated with small children. In addition to the little girl they had a very young baby. They packed up toys, rattles, bottles, little plastic cups, a blanket, car seat, and a diaper bag bigger than my backpack. My backpack could hold a week's worth of camping supplies. They looked like modern day nomads except they only carried baby supplies.

The little girl climbed down from the booth and toddled over to our table. She batted her eyelashes at Rusty and waved bye-bye. Rusty waved bye-bye back. The mom blushed again as she retrieved the little girl. The dad gathered up the car seat and diaper bag in one hand, the baby in the other and walked out. The mom followed leading the little girl, patiently helping her walk.

Rusty sighed and got back to the business of eating ribs.

At the same time that I battled with myself over the subject of kids, I thought I was missing out, and that feeling is what I thought Rusty felt as long as I put it off. It felt a bit empty. As long as I had a trail to follow, a job to do, and people counting on me I could put away the empty feeling. There was a world out there just waiting for me to get out in it.

Rusty smiled. He knew what was in my head. It was all the things we never said to each other.

"What would we do when Strict calls? You can't just drop your job and put it on hold for a few days. Especially the first year. A lot of searches happen in a year. What would we do? I wouldn't impose on our parents even if they were in town. I could be trapped at home for eighteen years!"

"Babe, you're exaggerating."

"Okay, so just think in terms of the first year, can you imagine me sitting at home for a year when Strict needs me? I can't leave someone out there if I could find them. A search is no place for a kid. Even if I went out on my own, without SAR, a search is no place for a kid. It's a strenuous, nerve wracking time. A kid doesn't need to be exposed to that kind of intense urgency. They shouldn't. Sure, I want to take my kid tracking but not during searches."

Rusty just let me talk wanting to see what was in my heart. He didn't have any answers.

"These things just have a way of working out," he finally said.

"No magically wonderful babysitters are going to float down out of the sky and tell me to go on the search. There is no fairy godmother for search and rescue."

"We prioritize."

"So what's more important, the kid or the search?"

"Hon, I don't know. All I know is there are plenty of families involved in law enforcement. My mom and dad did it. If you had any other job we'd have the same problem."

"No, if I had a regular, paying job we would just do day care. But it's not that kind of job. It's a drop everything and run for the hills job. I think of Stella and Marcel. Stella was an eleven year old girl with epilepsy. By the time I found here she was covered with scratches and bruises from having seizures out in the woods. We made camp and after dark I did a circuit of camp with a flashlight. She saw the lights and came running. She was scared. She didn't know if she'd ever get home. I sat up with her all night while she had seizures. When I think of the time she was out there, every minute counted. It's things like that that push me. Marcel lay under a dead tree. It took a hike in, carefully following track to track to find him. No plane would have found him. No amount of tromping through the woods would have worked. He had to be airlifted out. I never heard if he made it. Rusty… every time I go out it could be like that. I can't turn my back on them. I can't. I can find them, so I have to."

"Strict has other resources."

"Yeah, the erase-all-the-tracks method. That's what happens in field searches. The searchers erase all the information I need to do it the easy way."

"People were found before you came along. They will be found if you have to stay home with a baby."

"In time?"

Sigh, "I don't know."

The first problem was a big one. Kids would keep me from searches. But the issue had personal effects, too. Was I depriving Rusty, selfishly, from something I knew he wanted? When I got right down to it I had to say yes. And then I felt guilty for putting others before Rusty. I felt guilty for making myself less available to Strict and I felt guilty for not giving Rusty something he truly desired. So no matter what I did, I was the one in the wrong. Then my selfish side would kick in and say, "Hey wait a minute, you have a life too, you know. Do you want to spend the rest of it being a mom?" and I had to say, "No," and then I felt guilty for that too.

Chapter 22

Things had been rather quiet since my last bout of trouble. I stayed close to home while Rusty recovered from a broken leg. I'd managed to leave behind the nightmares and I was moving forward. It was hard to do at home. Left in an empty house with nothing but a few chores to do, my thoughts would catch up to me. It was a constant battle to put the trouble behind me and go forward when there was nowhere to go. Each night I had dinner on the table and we ate together, just the two of us. The hills were calling but I stayed home anyway. Rusty could see that it couldn't last much longer. I was going to go nuts.

"I need my Jeep back," I said one night at dinner.

"Do you want to go look? It can't hurt to look at cars at night. There's no sales people to bug you."

"I want my old Jeep back. Not the new one. The one I had when you and I first met. That Jeep and I were friends. We knew each other. We thought alike. It takes a long time to break in a Jeep. The new ones aren't friendly like my old Jeep was."

"Cass, you're talking like your car had feelings. It was just a machine, a tool to get you from one place to another. Do you want to look for a used one?"

"No, it's just not the same letting someone else break in your Jeep for you. Why can't Jeeps be like Levi's? Wear 'em, wash 'em, go horseback riding in them and they fit. Maybe it's the metal in the Jeeps. Metal would be harder to break in than cloth."

He smiled and shook his head. Sometimes Cassidy logic eluded him.

"I still think we should get you a sexy sports car."

"No way, I'd get stuck my first trip into the boonies."

"How about a motorcycle to go with it? You could take the bike out into the hills. It would be small enough that you could wrestle it loose if you got stuck and you'd still have a car to drive to town in."

"Can we find an insurance company that will take me?"

"Cass…"

"I'm not kidding, three cars in the past few years. I wouldn't insure any of my cars!"

My first Jeep was car bombed by Tyrone Trent to make a point to the police. My BMW was rolled when Trent decided the Jeep wasn't a big enough point to the police. He'd followed me and forced me off the road in a wild car chase through the desert. The new Jeep was tossed in the California Aqueduct to make Rusty think I was dead. He didn't believe the ploy for a second. But nevertheless, I'd gone through three cars in a very short span of time. Maybe a motorcycle would be the way to go. I'd had a license since I was a teenager.

"I'll go look tomorrow. I can ride into town with you and by the time I walk to a dealership it'll be open."

"You're not walking. Take the Explorer. I can use another car."

And so I found myself a dirt bike. A street legal dirt bike. One I could wrestle over just about anything. I took it out in the hills and put on the speed. Yes! I could fly out into the hills with this. I could wind up the arroyos and find tracks where even the Jeep couldn't go. I was free again!

After putting the bike through every test I had handy, I stopped at the top of a hill out in the desert to check the time on my cell phone. Yikes! I better get back to town. Rusty would be getting off work soon.

I was riding to the station, feeling slowed down by the stop and go of city traffic, when I saw an ambulance ahead. Its lights were not on, so I pulled up beside it. Landon was driving it, so I stayed with it until he got curious. Then at the next light I took off my helmet. His expression was plain, oh, no, not a bike. He opened his window.

"Pull over," he yelled, "next driveway!"

"Okay," I replied.

When the light turned green I sped off, found out the next driveway was where the ambulance company was based and turned in. Landon got out of the ambulance and stood there hands on hips while I took off my helmet.

"Well, at least you got a helmet, too. Are you insane? The Jeep wasn't enough trouble? You're going to kill yourself with that thing."

"I was careful. I bought one I could handle. If it gets stuck I can just wrestle it loose. It flies over the hills and it handles the arroyos well. I was just heading to the station to meet Rusty for dinner. He was the one who suggested a motorcycle. He thought it would be more maneuverable in the hills. What do you think?"

"I think it's going to be a week or less before we're scouring the desert looking for you."

"That's why I got bright green. I thought it would stand out."

"Great, glad to hear you're thinking ahead."

"You can't fool me. You want to try it out. You want to do all the things you don't want me to do. Admit it."

"That's different. I'm not a trouble magnet."

"So, you admit it?"

He grinned.

"Ha, I told you," I said. "I'm off to the station."

"When do I get to try it?"

"After Rusty. He hasn't seen it yet."

I parked the bike at the station and went in to Rusty's office. I peeked in the little window and knocked like I always did.

"You found one," he said smiling.

"How did you know?"

"Helmet hair. We see a lot of helmet hair in this profession."

"Rats."

"So what did you get?"

"You know me. I got a workhorse, street legal, dirt bike, two-fifty so it's light and maneuverable. I tried moving a four hundred around. It was too heavy to be practical for me. I wanted to get a four hundred so it would be better for both of us but I couldn't talk myself into it."

"You've got your wheels again. You just can't go grocery shopping on it. So what are you going to do about that?"

"I don't know, what would Skipper drive?"

I look a lot like a Skipper doll. Some Halloweens I even dress up like Skipper to hand out treats. Since I have more of a military background I kind of think of myself as Skipper meets GI Joe. I'm petit, blonde, with a knack for being dead on with a gun. I prefer not to use one though. Being a trouble magnet, I walk a very fine line when it comes to loaded weapons. I worry that I'll need one and I worry about what I might have to do if I carry one. I own a handy little 9mm. I have to for my work. When I get a call I need to be prepared to look and act like a cop. That's another area I have trouble with. Technically, I'm a tracker but the police have an odd assortment of jobs that trackers can get called on for.

"Skipper would ride around in Barbie's bright pink convertible," Rusty said. "But I can't see you doing that."

"Me neither."

"Before the car, though, we're getting you a leather jacket. One tumble on the bike and you'd be full of gravel."

"I feel silly. Green bike, white and green biker jacket. All I want to do is ride around in the hills. I'm not going to be racing or motocrossing or doing anything dangerous. I'm just looking for tracks."

"Oh yeah? How fast did you get it up to when you were 'just testing it out' in the hills? You said it flies over the hills. That means you were going fast enough to need a leather jacket. And wear your helmet, too."

Sigh, yes Daddy, I thought.

Benny Trujillo stopped at our table, noted the helmet on the table and me in the biker jacket.

"Are you nuts?" he said to Rusty. "She's going to kill herself with that thing!"

"I will not," I replied. "I've ridden motorcycles before. I only wrecked one once!"

Both guys looked at me.

"A long time ago…I was just a kid."

"You're just a kid now," Benny said.

"I was even more of a kid. I was fourteen. I told you about that," I said to Rusty. "It was right after Barton Fartston stuffed me in my locker. My dad was mad because I wrecked the bike and somehow between the two incidents I broke a leg and my dad was mad because we'd never know if Barton broke it or the accident broke it."

"Ah, yes, right before the barrel racing competition. I remember now."

Benny huffed, "And you don't think she's hell on wheels. If she was like that at fourteen, you better hang on Rusty! You're in for the ride of your life."

To make matters worse, Landon walked in. He swaggered over.

"I knew I could find you here," he said. "Gotten a ticket yet?"

"Of course not," I said. "I've only had the bike for six hours. Besides, the cops stick to pavement."

Now all three guys were wondering. I thought I better shut up.

I decided I better get dinner on track. "Benny, I'll have the Enchiladas Diablo."

"Are you sure? You know that one's spicy."

"I'm feeling adventurous tonight."

"Is that bike bringing out the Mexican in you? Because you're asking for spicy, like *Mexican* spicy."

"That's okay, I like spicy sometimes."

"Okay, one Enchiladas Diablo and one pitcher of water. Rusty?"

Rusty ordered a combination, a nice, safe mild combination, probably just in case I couldn't eat the enchiladas. Landon joined us and ordered carne asada.

Benny Trujillo and his brother owned Trujillo's Bar and Grill. Most of the cops and rescue workers frequented the place, knowing they could find a friend there in the evenings. With Benny Trujillo and Landon knowing about the bike, it didn't take long for word to get around the station and speculation abounded. Pretty soon there was a pool going on betting on what kind of trouble I'd get into next. Rusty wasn't betting. He preferred to let them think he trusted me with the bike.

For a few weeks I kept the station waiting, the pool increasing in value a little each day. I took the bike out almost every day for a few hours. I tracked coyotes in the desert. I found little used mountain roads that took me into the backcountry of the forest. I took the bike out to the hills where kids rode on weekends. While they were in school I skimmed over the jumps, racing over their paths. I was ecstatic. One day I sped through the foothills following Sunset Drive to Lost Hills Road. I pulled up to my house and Landon was standing in my driveway looking very serious.

"You need a cell phone inside that helmet. How soon can you be ready?"

"What's going on?" I asked as I pulled off my helmet.

"Strict has been calling. I told him I'd stop by and pick you up. That was an hour ago."

"I'll be ready in ten minutes."

"Does that mean I can ride the bike for ten minutes?"

"Sure," I said, opening the garage door. "Just leave it here when you get back."

I rushed into the house, grabbing the phone as I went by.

"Rusty?" I said as I heard the phone being picked up in his office.

"What is it?" he asked already worried.

"Nothing, I've just got a search. I don't have any details yet. Landon was waiting for me when I got home. I guess Lou has been trying to call so I am kind of rushed. Can you get the details from Strict?"

"Yeah, I'll call after dark like usual, and get the update."

"I'm sorry the notice is so short. I'll be back as soon as I can. I'll have to take the big pack, since I don't have any idea how long it is."

"Take care of my girl out there."

"I will."

"How much water do you have?" Landon asked when I came outside with my pack.

"Three days worth, like always."

"Three desert days?"

"Oh hell, this is a desert track?"

"A car broke down out in the back country. The driver tried to hike out."

"Don't they usually do an air search first in cases like this?"

"Been there, done that."

"Oh, where can they be if they aren't visible from the air? You can see beetle bugs from a low flying helicopter out in the desert. There's nothing to hide them."

"That's what we are hoping you can tell us."

"Okay, let me fill up the camel pack and I'll be ready."

I took the pack into the house and filled the built in water reservoir. This was going to add another couple of pounds to my pack but it couldn't be helped.

"Okay, pack, hat, hiking boots, water and more water. I think I'm ready."

I closed the garage door and we were off.

"How long has our ten sixty-five been missing?"

"Just long enough to do an air search. It hasn't been a day but we wanted to get a jump on it because of the water situation."

"Good idea, I've been in their shoes. It's no fun walking the desert with no water."

Base camp was over a mile away from my starting point. An officer drove us to the car where I was able to get an idea of what I was in for. I got a good look at the tracks, the stride, and the kind of person I was working with. It was a young woman. She had done a lot of walking around her car. She popped the hood open and looked around inside. The tracks at the front of the car showed a lot of weight on the front part of the foot. She'd done a lot of looking around under there. Probably didn't understand a lick of it. She'd left the hood up as a sign of distress. She opened up the backdoor and poked around inside, pulled something out and headed down the road.

We got back in the car and drove a mile or so back down the road and the officer let us out where the tracks left the road. I looked off into the distance to see what had drawn the woman's attention enough to cause her to leave the safety of the road. There were buildings off in the distance. I thought if they were visible they were reachable. The air search would have covered the whole area between the car and any nearby buildings. I was sure the search had been extended to those buildings and any buildings close by. So, where was our ten sixty-five? It was up to me to find out.

"Does this woman have a name?" I asked Landon as I followed the tracks.

"The car is registered to a man. Our ten sixty-five is a woman, so no, not so far."

"You should be doing the tracking," I told Landon. "This is easy. You should get some practice in."

"The tracking is your job."

"I may not always be around. It can never hurt to have another skill."

"Oh yeah? If I can track Strict will send me out without you. I wouldn't want that to happen."

"You don't have to tell him you can track."

"If I'm tracking I can't watch you."

"I ought to smack you one."

"In my dreams."

The tracks led on through the desert. This girl was not used to hiking. Her tracks were not sure. They tended to falter a lot. The first half mile off road she did well, but then she began stopping briefly and awkwardly. Her footprints looked like she was shifting a heavy object around trying to find a way to carry it comfortably. Who would try to carry a heavy object on a cross country desert hike? It was insane. She needed to conserve her energy. The heat and the lack of water would exhaust her resources quickly even without carrying unnecessary burdens. What could be worth the risk of dehydration just to carry it out?

I stopped at one of her, now frequent, stopping places and examined the tracks carefully.

"What's up?" Landon asked.

"Something's going on here. Something we should know about."

Normal, heavy tracks leading in. Pressure points shifting out and back with the right foot, forward and out with the left foot. Feet spread slightly, then moving to normal standing position. A couple of steps and another quick shifting and she was off again. This went on for over a mile before I figured out what was happening. I stopped to examine a resting spot. It wasn't in the shade when I got to it but it would have been earlier. Even while resting she carried this thing, whatever it was. Next to the print where she sat was an odd dent in the ground. I got out my magnifying glass. It was smooth and rounded and small. Only about a half inch long. My trouble radar was nagging at me. It was the edge of a shoe, but not the woman's shoe. It was too small.

"Landon, we now have two ten sixty-fives."

"What?"

"I've been wondering what this woman was carrying across the desert. It's a child. This little dent in the sand right here is from the back of a child's shoe."

"How old?"

"Young enough to be carried for two and a half miles. Maybe the kid was sleeping when the car broke down. We'll just have to watch for little kid tracks."

The mom began taking breaks frequently. She stopped every couple hundred feet or so. She was not used to walking long distances. She had a heavy burden, no water. When her steps began wandering I worried. Then she began stumbling frequently. If she went down she tended to stay down for a moment, gathering her strength. At last she set the child down. And he crawled through the dust a little ways before she gathered him up. When the mom saw the baby crawling away she scrambled after him but her strength didn't last long. About a hundred yards later, after her unsteady footsteps became more and more erratic, I found the print of a woman's body in the sand and the *brush, brush* motions of a crawling baby. He crawled over to a mesquite tree and pulled himself up, then toddled around. He went back and checked on mom and then toddled off to investigate his surroundings.

I sat for a moment, gathering my feelings. One year old, loose in the Mojave Desert. As long as he didn't run into a snake I thought he'd be okay. He'd be hungry and thirsty but not as bad off as his mother. He was still rested.

"The mom is more likely to need medical attention. I'll follow the baby. You stay on the mom's trail. Don't move on unless you know it's the right way. She's been pretty easy to track. She's going to need you when we find her. The baby might be fine. It shouldn't take me long to find him. He couldn't have gone far."

Babies are easy to track. They don't think about their tracks, they scuff a lot. They're slow. This baby toddled around looking at the various desert plants. Every once in a while he turned back to keep track of his mother. Gradually his interests brought him farther and farther from his mother's side. I found several branches that had been mangled in his investigations. I hoped he hadn't eaten any of the plants he handled. And I hoped he didn't investigate any cactus.

I heard him long before I found him. Loneliness and a tumble had frustrated him. He sat in the middle of the desert crying his little lungs out. I continued to follow his tracks until I was certain where he was. When I approached he wasn't sure he wanted to play with a stranger. He stood unsteadily and got ready to run. I jogged up and scooped him up before he could decide whether I was friend or foe. No matter what conclusion he came to, I had to get him back to his mom. Unfortunately, not being a mom, I didn't even think of what my actions might do. I pulled him up and set him on my hip with a big *squiiiiish*. Oh, yuck, arg! His diaper was full! And I had zero diaper changing supplies, not to mention, I'd never done it before. All I knew was it was necessary for everybody's well-being that the baby's diaper was changed as needed. Okay, well, so far we weren't in too bad of shape. I thought Landon would have some disinfectant wipes in his first aid kit. Maybe we could figure something out.

"Where's your mama?" I asked the squalling, squirming bundle in my arms. I followed my tracks back to my starting point and took off after Landon. He hadn't gotten far. He was making very slow progress from track to track.

"I'll trade you," I said walking up with the baby awkwardly trying to squirm loose, dirty diaper smells wafting skyward.

"Cassidy, just act like you mean business. Act like you know what you're doing and kids assume you do."

"But I *don't* know what I'm doing. I've never even babysat. Jesse did all that. I helped with the foaling. I know what to do with a baby horse but I've never dealt with a baby human."

He took the baby from me.

"Hey, buddy! Come to Landon. What have you been up to? Did you see the desert? Where's your mom?"

He turned his nose up at the diaper.

"Yuck, you've got a mess in there. Let's clean you up."

He set the little boy down and fished around in his backpack. Disinfectant wipes and a protective waterproof pad were the best we could come up with so he folded it this way and that until he had a diaper sort of arrangement. He deftly changed the baby's diaper.

"Someday you *will* learn how to do this. There's nothing hard about it. Just act like a mom and go through the motions like you mean business and they usually calm down. They just need to know someone is in charge. Especially these little ones. Then when they get to be about three the uniform is the big attraction. They will listen to anybody in a uniform. They think the job is cool. So you make them your special buddy, keep a calm firm attitude."

"But I don't have a calm, firm attitude."

"You do when it comes to tracking."

"Tracking doesn't involve people. It's people I have a hard time with."

Landon rolled up the dirty diaper into a nice compact package and used the Velcro tabs to fasten it closed.

"Pack it in pack it out," he said handing me the package.

Okay, I could live with that. At least he didn't make me change the diaper. I put the diaper in my trash bag, wound it up tight, and stuck it in my pack, then I focused on the trail. The mom had lain on the desert floor long enough for junior to get out of sight. When she came to the mom had been frantic. She didn't know to look for tracks so she just walked around frantically calling to her little boy. There was nowhere to look. When we stood where she had stood the desert was open. No place for a baby to hide. She walked around and around afraid to leave the area but knowing she had to. Which direction? She couldn't even begin to guess. One was as good as another to find a lost baby. She started circling but she lost her bearings and the circles wandered farther and farther from the starting point and farther and farther from safety. Landon carried the baby as I followed the trail. The little boy carried one of Landon's extra water bottles just like he would a baby bottle. His dark eyes watched everything around him. He'd had his first haircut and looked too grown up behind the baby face.

"Can you say *mama*?" Landon asked him. "Say *MAMA!* real loud. Maybe she will hear you."

He kept up a constant chatter asking the baby questions he knew he'd never get an answer to, just to keep him busy. He fished out his keys and let the baby play with them. Into his mouth they went. Landon seemed unconcerned.

The mom's circling became more and more erratic. She stopped often. She stumbled often. I could feel her fear. In the middle of the desert, lost baby, no water, flagging energy. What could she do? She had to find her child. The desert was too big. If she left she'd never be able to find the same area again.

I began to see a disturbing trend. When the mom fell she didn't get up and keep going; she was becoming distraught. She would lie on the ground and strike the ground with her fists. She curled into a fetal position. The trail was leaching into my brain. It happened a lot to me. I'd profile as I went and read things into it that were remarkably vivid. I began to feel the feelings I imagined the person I was tracking was experiencing. I was feeling desperate even though I knew it didn't do any good.

"Cassidy, you need to stop. You're putting too much into this. We'll find her today. All the tracks are fresh. I think junior here needs a snack. Did you bring any cookies?"

I sighed and stopped. I took off my pack and rummaged around until I found the cookies.

"You can't just give him one though. They have nuts. You asked for nuts so now you get to pick them out before you give them to the kid. I can't stop. I need to keep going. I know what it feels like to be in the middle of nowhere with no water. I wasn't sure I'd make it and I knew what I was doing. This woman doesn't and she knows it. We need to find her."

The radio crackled. I expected it to be Strict asking Landon for a status update. Instead it was a different voice. He asked to talk to me on the telephone. I wasn't sure if I could get a good signal but I gave him my number.

"Cassidy?" he asked.

"Yeah, what's up?" I asked.

"It's Antonio." Antonio Rodriguez. He worked for the fire department.

"What's up?" I asked again, wondering what the fire department had to say about this little search.

"It's my wife, Cass, can you find her?"

Antonio's wife and little boy?

"Yeah, I'll find her. The tracking is easy. It's only time and a lack of water that is the problem."

"Where are you?"

I checked the GPS and read off the coordinates.

"What's she doing clear out there?"

"She's looking for something. She keeps circling. She thinks she is circling the area she last saw what she is looking for but her circles are off so she's basically doing this huge corkscrew trail deeper into the desert, thinking she is making wider circles around one point."

"What could she be looking for?"

"Don't worry, we're onto it. By the way, what's your little boy's name?"

"Ricardo, but we call him Ricky, why?"

"He's doing great. He's here with us. Don't worry, we'll find Eva. I just need to stay on her trail. I'll find her today. I need to track but you know how to reach me. Try not to worry."

I ended the call and pocketed my phone.

"The baby's name is Ricky. We need to finish this. Landon, it's Antonio's wife. No more profiling. I'm just going to follow this trail. Today. We're not leaving her out here tonight. When we find her we're flying out. She's in no shape to hike out. The only reason she's still on her feet is because she's searching for Ricky."

"Hey Ricky!" Landon said cheerfully. "Where's Ricky? Where is he?" Landon turned his face away and quickly looked back. "There he is!" Ricky hit him in the eye with the water bottle.

Okay, Cass, make this one fast track. You've only got four hours of daylight. Hit this trail and hit it hard.

"Look out Ricky! It's Dangerous Tracker Woman! She's gonna find your mom. Stay out of the way!"

I didn't know how much of this baby talk I could stand, so I hit the trail. Hard. Eyes to the ground, I kept to the trail. The spiral turned into more of a scalloped pattern because when Eva's tracks crossed I took the more recent path. It was quicker than following her actual trail.

If Landon needed help he knew where to find me. He lagged behind, juggling Ricky, occasionally letting him walk, then picking him up when the pace was too slow. Ricky got cranky and bored. The keys were not enough entertainment for him. We couldn't stop to entertain the kid so we pressed on, cranky baby and all. I was hoping Eva would hear him and come running. She didn't and that had me worried.

I tracked harder. We hit a patch of hard pack. Nearly sandstone, it had been swept clean by the desert winds. This told me just how desperate Eva's situation was. I could even track her here. If she'd just been walking her steps would have been invisible but she wasn't walking. She was in a mad rush, scrambling. It spoke volumes about her mental state. I stuffed my thoughts away and only looked at the tracks.

A short time later I was watching the ground when I heard a cough. It wasn't a simple, something-doesn't-feel-right cough. It went on and on. I glanced back at Landon. He was fine. But he had heard it too. I looked around and Eva stood in the distance, hands braced on her knees, coughing like crazy, still scanning the desert for Ricky. I jogged over to her.

"My baby!" she managed to say between coughs.

"It's okay, we found him. Landon's bringing him. It's okay." I took off my pack and found a water bottle. I opened it and handed it to her but she staggered off to meet Landon.

"Oh, my baby! Mi hijo, mi hijo." She sank to the ground crying, cradling her little boy. Just rocking back and forth crying. I had to turn away. I got choked up. Landon gave me a hug, giving Eva and Ricky a few minutes before he had to return to business.

"Ten sixty-five found," he told Strict.

"Ten forty-five?"

"Ten twenty-three." Stand by.

"Ten four."

Five seconds later my cell phone rang.

"Antonio, she'll be fine. We just can't get near her. She's too busy hugging Ricky. She's fine. She'll need fluids, but she's fine."

"I'll never complain about rescuing you again. You're an angel. Cassidy… thanks."

"Thank you, Antonio. We'll meet you in town. Bring a diaper bag if you can."

Landon gave Strict our coordinates and asked for a lift out. When he finished he turned to Eva. She still didn't want to turn loose of Ricky.

"Come on Ricky," I said, prying the boy loose. "We have to let Landon work. Let's go for a walk." Then to Landon, "Where are those cookies?"

"We've got time, cook up the macaroni and cheese you're always cursed with. Why do you buy that stuff if you don't like it? Kids cannot live by cookies alone."

"What if *I* want a cookie?"

"Then they're in the bag beside my pack."

I fired up my stove and heated water but I didn't let it boil. When it was just starting to steam I turned it off and poured some into the pouch of macaroni and cheese. I sealed the top and let it cook. Ricky tried to grab hold of anything I was touching. I had to keep him close, yet not let him touch anything that might burn him. I handed him little bits of cookie. I ate the bits with nuts and he ate the bits without nuts. I thought that to be a mom you'd have to grow an extra arm or two. Then I had to cut up all the noodles. Cutting up noodles in the bottom of a foil pouch with a short handled plastic spoon was more challenging than tracking down Eva. Yep, I thought, just give me a plot of ground and some tracks. That I can do. Trying to play octopus with a hot stove and a baby? Cutting up slippery noodles in a slippery bag just so the baby could eat? No thanks.

We got our lift into town. Ricky checked out fine. Antonio showed up, diaper bag in hand, and did a quick change. Then he went to see how Eva was doing. I ended up with a cranky baby in a busy hospital. As darkness settled in Rusty called Strict and got an update, finding out we were at the hospital. I was never so relieved to see him as when he walked through those double doors. He saw me pacing the halls with a cranky kid in tow, tired and dusty from the trail, full backpack and gear. He came to my rescue. He took the pack back out to the truck. I'd rather he took the kid. I didn't know what to do with a kid in a hospital! No toys, no kid type food, no experience. All I could manage was to keep him out of harm's way. After that I was lost. Rusty came back shortly and took Ricky off my hands. My arm was numb from carrying him around. I thought he weighed a ton but when Rusty picked him up he suddenly got little again. I sat in the lobby with a sigh of relief.

"I'll be back in a few minutes," he said and disappeared.

The few minutes stretched out and I wondered if we were spending the night there but at last Rusty reappeared.

"Are you ready to head for home?" he asked.

"Uh, yeah. How's Eva?"

"She'll be fine. There's just a lot that they need to attend to so I told Antonio we'd take care of Ricky until things settled down."

"You did what!" I said.

"I told him we'd babysit. Just until Eva's released."

"Rusty! I don't know the first thing about taking care of a baby! I don't even know how to *talk* to a baby! I haven't changed diapers! I've never even babysat and now you want me to keep a one year old for days? What do I do with him?"

"Practice," he said matter of factly. "There's nothing much you can do wrong at this age. I got his car seat, diaper bag, a little bit of food. He'll be fine. I'll help."

"You bet you will. You'll be lucky to get to work tomorrow."

"Babe, you are worrying over nothing. I bet Eva is released tomorrow. It'll be great."

Yeah, great for who? I thought.

Chapter 23

The first problem we had was sleeping arrangements. We couldn't have a one year old loose in our house but Ricky wasn't inclined to lie down and just go to sleep. He was in a new place. He wanted to see things. I thought I should count my lucky stars that he was comfortable enough in my house to want to investigate. Had he been frightened of us we could have had even more of a struggle. As it was he seemed to accept us as something close to normal.

The couch? The guestroom? He couldn't sleep there. He could climb down and toddle off without us knowing. We decided one night wouldn't spoil him so he slept in our bed between us. The only problem was he wasn't ready to sleep.

The second thing I noticed is that a diaper bag holds about a dozen diapers. Since a baby might need changing anywhere from every ten minutes to every few hours I wondered how long our supply would last. We were a long drive from the nearest grocery store. I kept my fingers crossed on the diaper situation.

"Come on, Ricky, lie down," I said, patting the bed next to me.

He gave me a mischievous grin and popped his head down, then popped right back up.

"Time to sleep, lie down," I said again.

No way was he going to lie down. I lay there tired and exasperated.

Rusty got up and took Ricky with him. He carried him around. Ricky put his arms around Rusty's neck and rested his head on his shoulder. No fair. That's what I wanted to do. Rusty walked and talked quietly to the baby on his shoulder jiggling him gently, rocking back and forth. When Ricky brought his head up Rusty gently hugged him close putting his head back down, rocking, gently rocking.

"I know this is a weird place," Rusty said to him softly. "Mama will be back soon. All we have to do is wait. In the morning you can play with the doggy. We'll go for a ride in the car…." He rambled on and on. He even made me sleepy. And gradually Ricky got drowsy, too, until his big brown eyes were droopy and he drifted off to sleep. Rusty rocked him all the way to the bed and all the way down and lay the sleeping child gently down and slipped in behind him.

We lucked out that first night. Ricky slept until first light, then he started tossing and turning and fussing. He'd been shy and withdrawn the day before but he woke up a whole different person. First he was cranky. I figured out it was because he needed changing. Oh boy, here we go. I laid him down next to his diaper bag and he sat back up. I decided there was no reason he had to lie down until I took inventory. Diapers, baby wipes, baby powder, baby lotion, rash cream, a bottle…

"Baba!" Ricky said enthusiastically.

"After we change you," I told him.

Formula…formula? Ricky was a year old. What happened to good old milk? Three jars of junior baby food, a package of teething biscuits, a cloth diaper, three bibs, a set of plastic keys and a stuffed bear with a rattle inside. I laid Ricky back down, took off the dirty diaper and turned to get another diaper out of the bag. A second later and he went off like a Roman fountain, right into my lap. He was lucky I didn't freak out easily. I grabbed anything in sight and tossed it over him, which didn't help much. It just made two wet spots in the carpeting instead of one. We moved to a different spot.

"Practice, *humph*," I said. "Is this a conspiracy? If Rusty thinks this is going to make me want to be a mom he better think again!"

"Baba!" said Ricky.

"Yeah, I'll baba you. You just wait. Diapers first, then the puddles, then the baba."

I wiped him all over with baby wipes. I thought I remembered that being a necessary part of the procedure, from what I'd observed in women's restrooms. I opened up a diaper. Which way was the front? They looked identical. If they looked identical then it didn't matter, right? He raised up his legs, used to the whole procedure. I slipped the diaper under him and brought the tapes around. Hmm, this didn't look right. I tried to untape them and try again but I thought I'd end up tearing the fabric so I decided it didn't matter that much. Backwards diapers were not the end of the world.

Okay, the puddles. I took Ricky to the bedroom and plopped him on the bed next to Rusty.

"I have a mess to clean up. He's all yours for a few minutes."

I got paper towels and soaked up as much as I could. How could someone so small hold so much liquid? I sprayed the area with pet stain remover, rubbed it in and made a note to vacuum later. Pets and kids were about the same, I figured. Ricky came in and grabbed the paper towels and ran through living room, the roll thumping and bumping behind him, leaving a trail of paper towels behind him. I raced after him. Shadow thought it was a game so he ran after Ricky, nipping at his heals, herding the little sheep just like a good sheepdog was supposed to do.

"No, Shadow! Sit! Stay!" He didn't sit. He was too excited about playing. I grabbed Ricky and took him back to the bed.

"Now I have paper towels to clean up. Keep him here for just a few minutes."

"Huh?" said Rusty.

No use rolling them back up. I accordion folded about two hundred paper towels and put them on the counter.

"Baba!" said Ricky.

"Okay," I said, "baba time."

I got the bottle out of the diaper bag. It was a plastic tube with a nipple on top. How was a plastic tube supposed to hold formula? I assumed I was supposed to use the formula or it wouldn't have been packed. I emptied the diaper bag looking for something that would work with a plastic tube to hold liquids. In the bottom of the bag I found a small box with rolled up plastic in it. I pulled one out. Bottle size plastic sheet. Hmm.

"Baba!" said Ricky.

"I know, I know, I'm trying. I'm new to this. Give me a break."

I looked at the plastic sheet. It was two layers. Ahh, okay, I think I get it now. I took the formula, plastic sheet and Ricky to the kitchen, pried the empty bottle from his tight little hands.

"Babaaaaaaa!" he wailed.

I ignored him hoping he'd wake up Rusty.

Let's see, the plastic sleeve goes in the tube. I unscrewed the plastic ring, then thought the nipple probably needed washing if it had lain in a diaper bag for days on end. Then I thought it had already been in Ricky's mouth half a dozen times that morning. What was the use? I inserted the plastic sleeve in the plastic tube and bent it over the top. Walla, a bottle. I read the instructions on the can of formula, put in the right amounts of powder and water, shook it up, then microwaved the whole thing and learned real quickly that formula inside a plastic bag heats very fast and builds up pressure. The bottle went off like a Megablaster squirt gun inside the microwave. I yanked the door open. Now the bottle was too hot for a baby. I took the lid off and added some cold water but there wasn't enough space to add enough to cool it down. I left the bottle on the counter to cool and cleaned up the microwave. All the time Ricky was dancing around wailing, "Babaaaa, I wan baba!"

A sentence! He spoke a sentence! I picked him up and gave him a big hug.

"Good boy!" I said as if I was praising Shadow for a job well done.

"Baba!" he continued to cry. So much for praise.

I checked the bottle, still too hot. I put it in the refrigerator. We took a quick walk outside while I fed Shadow. Ricky only managed to eat one kibble before I stopped him.

"We won't tell Mommy about that," I advised him.

"Goggy," said Ricky.

While he was watching the doggy he forgot about the bottle so I had Shadow jump over the hurdles. Ricky was thrilled.

"Goggy! Goggy!" he giggled.

When we got back to the kitchen the bottle was cold. I handed it to Ricky anyway. I thought I'd prefer it cold and he wasn't young enough to need it body temperature. He took a sip, looked at it weird and then started carrying the bottle around the house by the nipple. I thought I better keep the carpet cleaning supplies handy. Does pet stain remover work on formula?

I turned to the refrigerator to see what I had to cook for Rusty's breakfast. When I turned back around Ricky was finger painting formula designs on the coffee table. Oh great. I got a damp dishcloth and cleaned up the mess. How many messes could we have in one morning? I picked Ricky up and took him over to the old brown couch and held him while he drank his bottle. Rusty walk in on the idyllic scene. He sat on the freshly scrubbed coffee table and laughed at me.

"See, I told you it would be great. You're taking all this easier than I thought you would," he said.

"Ha, you miss the past half hour of constant frustration and catch two seconds of peace and everything is perfect."

"It can't be that bad. He's hasn't been awake an hour."

"You'd be amazed how many messes we can create and clean up in an hour."

"Do you want me to take him for a while?"

"No, we're okay. Go shower. Then you can watch him while I shower." Mine was going to be a long shower, I decided, I'd make sure of it.

Two minutes after Rusty left the bottle was empty and Ricky was ready to play. Only problem was there was nothing to play with. One set of plastic keys and one teddy bear rattle held his attention for about two seconds.

I heard Rusty's shower start. Shoot. I called Hazel.

"Hazel, help!" I said. "I'm babysitting a one year old and I don't have any toys. What do I do?"

"Give him a bath. Babies will play in water until they turn into little pink prunes. Just don't turn your back on him. If you have any plastic cups throw those in the tub and you'll be set for half an hour or so. After that turn a bunch of pots and pans over on the floor, give him a wooden spoon and put in your earplugs. Do you have any kids' books? Maybe you can read to him."

We tried the bath. Ricky loved playing in the water, especially seeing how much of it he could get on me, the floor and the towels I stacked too close to the tub. I found a couple of measuring cups that were plastic, a few freezer containers and he poured water from one to another. He floated the empty ones on top of the water, then dumped water in them with a smaller container until they sank.

"Hey, you're doing baby math," I told him. "How many cups does it take to fill a bowl?"

He splashed and water sprayed up into my face. I wiped the water out of my eyes and sat beside the tub and splashed water around with my fingers. I was glad I wasn't dressed for the day.

"Water," I said. "Can you say *water*?"

He splashed again. "Awa," he said. Okay, I guess that was close.

"He's saying *water* in Spanish," Rusty said behind me.

"Agua!" I said. "I should have thought of that. I do know that much Spanish. Are you a bilingual baby? You know goggy and awa and baba."

"Looks like you can skip the shower," Rusty said.

"No way, I'm taking one and I'm taking my time. And you're going to watch this kid and see how much work it is."

I started to pull Ricky out of the tub but he thrashed around yelling, "Awa, awa." He still wanted to play. I put him back in the tub.

"Go on, we'll be fine," Rusty said.

I took a long hot shower. I took my time, enjoying the quiet. I shampooed and conditioned my hair. I shaved my legs. I soaped up with bar soap, then shower gel. Let's see what else could I do in here? After I rinsed and dried off, I dried my hair and curled it and put on makeup. I was determined; Rusty *was* going to put in his share of the work. Let him figure out how to keep a toddler occupied for hours on end. Ricky couldn't *live* in the bath. Sooner or later Rusty would have to take him out and then what would they do? I chose clothes that wouldn't be hurt by a little baby food. Good old jeans and t-shirts. When I came out Ricky was toddling around the living room couch and Rusty was crawling around the other side. Every once in a while Rusty would pop up and call out, "peek-a-boo!" Yup, he definitely had Peek-a-boo perfected. Ricky beat on the seat of the couch and laughed.

"A boo!" he said enthusiastically.

Was anything hard for Rusty?

Ricky snuck around the end of the couch. "A boo!" he said.

"Oh! You scared me!" Rusty said, then acted like a growly monster and chased Ricky around the couch until Ricky tackled him from behind. They tumbled on the floor, the baby giggling.

I went to the kitchen to start breakfast but Rusty stopped me.

"Don't fix anything for me. There's a couple of things I need to do in town and then I'll check on Eva. Do you need me to pick up anything while I'm gone?"

"Ask Eva and Antonio what Ricky can eat. Does he eat normal people food?"

"Of course he does," Rusty answered.

"So far all he's wanted is a bottle."

"Baba!" said Ricky.

"Try scrambled eggs. That usually goes over well. Just make sure the pieces are small. I bet he eats most everything as long as it's cut up and isn't too spicy."

"I don't know, he's Mexican. He might even do spicy."

"Don't make this hard. You think yourself into a box and then you can't get out of it. Just go with the flow."

"When I did that I cleaned pee out of the carpet and formula off the coffee table. He's really good at flowing."

Rusty gave me a reassuring hug. "Don't make this hard. If you spend the day playing and don't get a thing done, that's okay."

Playing. I'd love to spend the day playing, but we waved bye-bye to Rusty and watched him drive away, then Ricky started filling his diaper. Rusty! Come back!

Ugh! Why did messy diapers have to be so… so… messy? I untaped the diaper and looked inside. I don't get grossed out easily. I've hunted and field dressed deer. I've eaten raw meat in order to survive. The thing here was that I had a zillion nooks and crannies of a squirmy kid who wanted to get up and play. How to clean all this… this… yuck out of all those nooks and crannies, all I could do was start and I went through about a hundred baby wipes. The stack of soiled baby wipes was bigger than the mess of a diaper. This time I got the diaper on frontward. When I finally let Ricky up he gave me a disgusted look and I returned it. He got shy and hid behind a chair.

"Ricky, come on. Want to play Ringo Star?"

I went to the kitchen and arranged a drum set of pots and pans and sat Ricky behind them. I handed him a spoon. He just looked at me like, now what? I took his little hand and brought the spoon down on a pot. It gave a satisfying bang and Ricky jumped, startled, and burst into tears.

"It's okay! Ricky, look," I said beating out a rhythm on the pots and pans. Ricky cried louder, so I picked him up and walked the house. Ten minutes later I was still pacing the house, Ricky howling. Okay, time to try something else. I checked his diaper. I couldn't cook without putting Ricky down and I hated to put him down when he was crying. How could I get food into the kid without putting him down? I set him on the dining room table since I didn't have a high chair. I got out a box of cereal and put a handful of Cornflakes in front of him.

"Are you hungry?" I asked. "Ricky, look, cereal, you like cereal?" He perked up a little when he saw the flakes before him. While he picked up each flake individually, I cooked a scrambled egg. So far so good. I cut up the egg small and put the egg pieces in front of him, too. He ate all the cereal and left the egg. He started rubbing his eyes. He ground Cornflakes into his face. I picked up some egg and offered it to him. He turned away. Okay, no egg. I got a fresh dishcloth and dampened it and wiped off his face. This started him fussing again. Sigh. I checked his diaper. Since he wasn't really hungry. This fussiness must be because he was tired. Now all I had to do is figure out how to get him to sleep. I walked him and jiggled him and rocked him and he squirmed and fought it. My arms were getting leaden and my steps were slowing and I was going for the next level of resolve.

Half an hour later Ricky was still squirming and fussing. Maybe he wasn't tired. Maybe he was bored. I knew he should be, so we went for a walk. He chased Shadow calling out, "Goggy! Goggy…" as we went along. Shadow did not want to be caught so I chased Ricky and Shadow through the junipers. Suddenly Ricky changed course, still yelling out *goggy* and then I saw what kind of a goggy he found. It was a skunk! I'd never even seen a skunk around here. No skunk tracks, nothing. Leave it to us to find the only skunk in southern California. I ran forward and scooped Ricky up as he continued reaching for the goggy. Whew! That was close. I carried Ricky as I backtracked the skunk. I hadn't seen skunk tracks very often. I'd only seen a few on Santa Cruz Island. I followed the trail and it wandered around and led up into the forest. I set Ricky down and he began picking up rocks and pine needles. I thought it was great, exploring the woods kid style. He popped a rock into his mouth.

"No! No rocks," I scolded fishing around in his mouth for the offending object. He bit down on my fingers. Ouch! "Ricky, give me the rock." More fishing around. I found and extracted it with a sigh of relief and picked him up again but he'd had a dose of freedom and wanted to explore. Unfortunately, every opportunity for exploring involved touching and hopefully tasting too. Just looking was not an option. I pulled rocks and weeds, pinecones and sticks out of his greedy little grasp.

Rocks were gocks. Pinecones were cocones. Sticks were ticks.

We were half a mile from home when Ricky filled his diaper again. We didn't have the diaper bag so we hightailed it for the house. Ricky still wanted to explore so he didn't want to be carried. I put him on my shoulders, stinky diaper and all and made a game out of touching tree branches.

"Get the tree! Get the tree, Ricky!" *whack!* "Good job!"

Dirty diaper smells wafted around my face all the way home. I was thinking the skunk was lucky smelling the way it did. Dampness started leaking through onto my neck. I tried not to think about it as I hiked along. When we left the trees he wanted to take a whack at the junipers so I zigzagged my way from bush to tree. He leaned way out to whack a branch…squish…waft…ugh!

"Ricky, this has got to stop."

I began jogging gently and he grabbed hold of my hair laughing and bouncing along. We hurried in the back door and over to the diaper bag. A hundred baby wipes later we were back to square one.

Next I had to figure out how to make lunch with a baby loose in my house. I hadn't had time to baby proof anything. I sat Ricky on my dining room table and cut up a banana in tiny pieces. Then I cut up a slice of lunchmeat in tiny pieces. While he was trying to pick up slick banana and pieces of meat I made myself a sandwich. Every minute or so I turned around. It only took him one minute to mash banana into his hair and another minute to nearly fall off the table. I rushed over and put him in the middle of the table again. How moms got anything done, I'd never know. I only half made my sandwich. It had meat and cheese slapped between two slices of bread. I couldn't bring myself to turn my back on Ricky long enough to hunt for more ingredients. He ate a few banana bits and a few meat bits and started looking at my sandwich longingly. I cut off a corner and handed it to him and he took it apart. He squished the bread until it looked like Silly Putty, then looked at my sandwich again.

"Want a bite?" I asked.

"B-bite!" he said.

I held up the sandwich and he took a bite and dragged all the meat out of it. He grabbed the meat and kept going. Was this a trick? I ate my bread and cheese sandwich half-heartedly. Then I found out how hard it is to get dried banana off the dining room table. After that I found out how hard it is to get dried banana out of baby hair. Note to self: highchair- necessary. Ricky cringed and whined as I tried to comb the banana out of his hair.

"I'm sorry, baby. You put it there. Now, it's got to come out," I said.

He squirmed and whined and rubbed his eyes.

"Mama," he whined.

"Mama will be here soon. She's getting better. She'll be back soon." I wasn't sure who I was reassuring, him or me, but I hoped it was true.

"I wan mama, mi mama," he pouted and rubbed his eyes. "Baba."

"Okay, kiddo, a baba we can do."

I decided banana hair was second place to the comfort of a small boy. This time I was a little smarter. I filled a pan with hot tap water, prepared the bottle and then stuck it in the hot water to warm. When the bottle was warm I handed it to Ricky. He took it and went to the front door.

"Mama?"

"Not yet kiddo, Mama will be here soon. Nap time."

“Me wan dada.”

“Yeah and me want mi Rusty, too. Please go to sleep. You need a nap.”

I took him to the bedroom and laid him down but he got up as soon as I turned my back. I refused to get angry with him. He wasn’t being disobedient. He was just out of sorts and I couldn’t blame him for that one bit. I was out of sorts, too, though, and that didn’t help matters at all. He dragged his feet and rubbed his eyes and whined. I picked him up and carried him around. The house got too confining so I walked out back. Big mistake. He decided the corral and gazebo were perfect toddler-size monkey bars. The activity perked him up and he was raring to go again. He climbed all over the lower corral bars swinging like a little monkey. When would I learn? Go with the flow, Cass. He was headed for sleepytown. Why did I have to exit at playland?

“Ricky? Want your baba?” I asked hopefully. The baba was forgotten. The baba was history. Sigh. I watched Ricky swing like a monkey as I called my sister.

“Hello?” she said absentmindedly.

“Hi Jesse, It’s Cass.”

“Cassidy! What happened? *Are you okay*?”

“Yeah, of course, well, it depends on what you mean by okay. I’m frustrated and tired and I need some advice.”

“Golly, what kind of trouble could you get into that you’d want *my* advice? I don’t know anything about getting kidnapped or lost in the woods.”

“It’s the kid nap part I’m having trouble with. How do you get a kid to go down for a nap?”

“You’re kidding. Right?”

“No, I’m babysitting a one year old and every time I think he’s getting tired he just wants to play some more. But I don’t have anything for him to play with so he is wearing me down.”

“Don’t worry about it. When he gets you all worn down he will get bored and nap with you.”

“That doesn’t help much. I don’t want to nap. I have things to do.”

“Make him a warm bottle and snuggle with him. He’ll conk out.”

“I did the warm bottle and then he saw the corral so he’s climbing all over it and I can’t get him back in bottle mode.”

“I can’t believe you took on a one year old. I thought you didn’t like kids.”

“I love kids! I really do. I prefer them to be old enough to reason with. Ricky isn’t old enough to reason with.”

“Well, just forget about what you need to get done. He won’t be around for long. You’ve only got to keep him occupied for a few hours, right?”

“I don’t know. His mom is in the hospital. She might get discharged today but it could be a few days. He spent the night here and I've had him all day."

"Oh, I'm so glad to see you're finally getting used to the idea of having kids! I can't wait for you to finally change your mind."

"Well, this isn't changing it very fast. No Ricky! No rocks! Rocks aren't food. Hold on." I fished the rock out of Ricky's mouth and received another bite. "I think Rusty was hoping I'd get used to the idea, too, but leaving me with a one year old for a day isn't doing the trick."

Ricky stopped his climbing for a minute. His face turned red as he strained.

"Oh great, he's filling his diaper again. I hope I have enough baby wipes left."

"How many do you have?"

"About a third of a package but it takes about that many to change him."

"Cassidy! You need some lessons. It should only take a few. I wish I could show you. You always do everything the hard way. Use the clean part of the diaper to wipe off most of it. Then use the baby wipes. While you have him inside for his diaper change give him his bottle again and I bet he settles right down for you. He'll feel better after being changed and you can try snuggling with him again. Warm snuggles work well for naptime. I can't wait to tell Mom you've been babysitting. She will be so shocked. I bet she calls you this evening."

Oh great.

"Okay, I'll see what I can do. I guess I better go so I can change this kid. Talk to you later."

She hung up and probably called my mom first thing. I took another rock away from Ricky and then took him in the house.

"No! Play!" he said pulling away and heading for the corral again.

"Nope, time for a diaper change," I said, as I dragged him kicking into the house. He swung the bottle around by the nipple and the rubber slipped through the top of the ring. The contents went flying coating Ricky and me with a nice even coating of, now cold, formula. It's just a small mess, I told myself. It's a simple clean up job, just change clothes, change Ricky, change Ricky's clothes, mop the floor, make a new bottle, warm it, strangle the kid and he'll go to sleep. Easy, right?

I had to admit, Jesse's instructions made diaper changes a lot easier. I only used six wipes. I might survive until Rusty arrived. Ricky didn't have another set of clothes so he ran around in his diaper until I could wash his clothes. I changed my clothes, made another bottle and took Ricky to the bed. I lay down with him and pulled him close. He struggled to get up.

"No, no, lay down. Nap time," I told him.

He asked for his mama, his dada, the goggy. He wanted to play. Anything but nap.

"I told you she was an angel," Antonio said.

When I opened my eyes Antonio and Rusty were standing over me. Ricky was sleeping peacefully in my arms, finally! Leave it to Rusty to arrive the one time when peace reigned.

"Angel? Huh! If you wake this kid up it's no angel you'll be dealing with! How's Eva doing?" I disentangled myself from Ricky praying I didn't wake him up. He startled a time or two but drifted off again quickly.

"She'll be fine. She keeps asking about Ricky so I told her I'd come check on him. Do you need anything?"

"Yeah, everything! A bed he can't climb out of, toys, clothes, diapers, baby wipes. He keeps asking for you and Eva but he seems patient enough when I tell him you're not coming yet."

"Sounds like everything is going great," Antonio said.

Yeah, great, I thought, if you call *great* one little mishap after another.

"I'll run home and get the things you need. I should be able to bring back everything except the crib."

When Antonio had left Rusty turned to me.

"How is it really going?" he asked.

"You're not leaving this house until tomorrow," I said.

"Babe, it can't be that bad."

"I haven't had two minutes to think except to figure out how to either clean up messes or how to entertain Ricky. I'm going nuts here."

"You don't have to entertain him the whole time. Just make sure he doesn't hurt himself."

"Okay, tell you what, I'll go wake him up and you can see how easy it is to let him entertain himself. He has no problem entertaining himself. He eats rocks and sticks and grass. He finger paints with formula on the coffee table. He unrolls paper towels. There are lots of things he can do here."

"I think you need a little break. Why don't you take a ride on the bike?"

Chapter 24

Yes! I was free, for as long as my conscience would allow me to be. I turned the bike down Lost Hills Road heading for some dirt bike tracks nearby. I wasn't interested in tracking I needed to burn off excess frustration and energy. I needed to free my mind. Concentrating on speed and maneuvering over the jumps and through the washes took my mind away from the tensions of small messes and paying constant attention to a small child. One trail led to another trail. I wrestled the bike, purposely pushing myself. I wanted to find out what I was capable of close to home before I tried to see how far this bike would go. A few other people were out on the trails. I didn't know anybody so I kept to myself.

I examined the arroyo ahead. It was thin and deep. The sand was loose. Would the bike handle sand this deep? When I'd rode dirt bikes as a teen we didn't have deep sand and jumps. There were just rolling hills dotted by oak trees near my parents' ranch. The main dangers were unexpected low-hanging branches of the large, ancient trees. Desert biking was different and, I decided, a lot more fun. I looked at it like a motorized obstacle course instead of a ride in the hills.

I picked out the challenging spots of the arroyo, deciding ahead of time how I would handle them. I hit the gas, the front wheel lifting off the ground. I wanted to attack the sand with some speed. In my Jeep a slow, constant crawl through sand worked best. The motorcycle was a lot different. I got a run at the sand planning to skim over the top and let the momentum carry me through. I hit the soft, dry section of the wash and the sand flew out behind me. A dust cloud rose over the arroyo.

A curve came up. It was less sandy but it was too sharp for me to take fast. Maybe later, after some experience. I slowed, gauging the turn. How fast could I take it? There was a sharp noise and the front wheel of the bike slid out from under me. The rest of the bike twisted around grinding my leg into the dirt. My first reaction was, oh shit, not again.

After the crash my instincts sent me diving for the shelter of the arroyo wall. I didn't even think about my leg. Something in my brain knew that sound. Knew it was not a normal dirt biking sound. And when my thinking got that far I remembered in an instant what it was. I'd heard it thousands of times. Thousands of rounds fired in practice. It was the sound of a rifle shot.

As I sheltered in the bend in the arroyo I analyzed what had happened, the angle the wheel twisted, the way the bike fell. The shot had to come from my left from fairly close by. Damn. I was unarmed. I didn't have my pack. No water. No wheels. I was glad I stuck close to home but it was still a few miles and I didn't know what my present situation was. Was I dealing with some crazy person who had a grudge against dirt bikers? Or was this targeted specifically at me? Being a trouble magnet, I had to assume the person could still be after me. Where was he? Where was the person who shot my new bike? This was aggravating.

Forget the bike, Cass, there's more important things going on right now, like finding the danger. I flattened myself against the arroyo wall, listening. I heard the crunch of footsteps on dry ground. Tiny rocks turning underfoot. A figure loomed above me. Dirk. I hadn't seen him for a while, not since the mine exploded. He must be royally ticked.

It was his fault that the mine had exploded but he could easily blame me for his misfortune. After the dust had settled and I got some experts on scene to find him I had gone looking for a burglary suspect that I knew was in the area. I never knew what became of Dirk. Now I did. I was relieved to know he had made it, but I was a little worried about his state of mind. Did he really blame me for what happened? He was still a lousy shot. Well, he was a lousy shot if he was trying to shoot *me*. If he was really shooting at the bike tire he'd improved remarkably over the past few months.

"It's payback time," he said. There was a glint in his eyes that I didn't like. His words didn't scare me as much as his look. It was feral, like he'd slipped over the edge. His body seemed bent peculiarly. What had the explosion done to him? Buried him alive, I remembered.

I determined right at the start that he was not taking me. And he wasn't shooting me either, although I didn't yet know how I was going to stop him.

"Payback for what?" I asked.

"For all the pain, all the humility. You cost me. You and your meddling. You cost me everything and now it's going to cost you. What are you willing to pay? Your health? Your family? How about your little boy?"

"The boy's not mine. I'm just babysitting."

"Yeah, right. How about your husband?"

"If you've got something against me. Take it out on me. Leave the others out of this." I had to really think to not give Dirk any information. I tended to use names when I talked about people, and I tended to talk too much. I had to keep a careful rein on my words.

"The way to make you squirm…is to make you worry. Make you stew. Like I stewed under a ton of mud. Suffocating. Thinking I'd never get out alive."

"I looked for you. I called in the team who found you. I didn't have to do that. If I hadn't called them you'd be dead and only Shay would have known where you were. Shay couldn't get the help for you that I could."

"Damn it!" he yelled and fired haphazardly. He was on the edge. He was slipping. "Shay left me. When the going got tough, she split. She left me for dead and never looked back!" Another shot into the bank next to my head. Dirt and rocks peppered me. "You fucked up my life!" He took two faltering steps towards the edge of the arroyo. "You fucked up my job!" *Bam!* "You fucked up my health!" *Bam!* "You ruined me!" *Bam!*

All the time the bullets were flying I stayed small. I let him rant. He couldn't shoot as emotional as he was. He was just blowing off steam and though I got my share of near misses and flying rocks I finally heard the click of an empty chamber and ran hell bent for better cover. At first he just stood there, not believing I was just turning my back on him, then that angered him, too. He got on his dirt bike and charged after me. He ran me down, the hit sending me careening into the dirt bank. He sped past, a yellow blur. I climbed up out of the arroyo where I had more room to maneuver and took off running until I found a group of Joshua trees. I put a tree between him and me and stood statue still except for my heavy breathing.

Okay, Cass, you have breathing room. Think. Put yourself in stealth mode and head for home.

Cover was sparse. Hiding my footprints was tough but came naturally to me. Slowly I made my way across the desert, only moving forward when I knew Dirk was not watching. Away in the distance I could hear the buzz of his dirt bike as he rode back and forth looking for me. Then faintly, "Damn you Cassidy Michaels! This isn't the end. You'll be hearing from me again! You'll pay! You'll pay like I had to!"

Why do people always blame me?

I ran home when I was sure Dirk had given up. I ran almost blindly, just trying to get there. When I came to Lost Hills Road I stumbled out onto it, heard a screech of brakes and dove for the other side. I couldn't believe how rattled Dirk had made me. I was ashamed of it, so ashamed I didn't bother looking at the driver of the car. I scrambled up and kept running.

The house lights were on by the time I got home. It looked so peaceful I didn't want to interrupt the tranquility of it. A car pulled up. Antonio. He got out and rushed over to me.

"Cassidy! Are you okay? What are you doing out here?" He looked me up and down, saw the scratches from the flying gravel, the blood stained leg of my jeans, the haggard expression. "What the hell happened to you?"

I couldn't talk. Everything was a jumble. I was still in flight mode.

"Come on," I finally managed to say and headed for the house. I entered the house and let Antonio in, then locked the door behind us. I went to the back door and locked it too. I checked all the windows, the door to the garage.

"Cassidy, slow down, kid," Antonio said.

Rusty came in holding Ricky. He looked so content just having a little one in his arms. It started the old conflict in me and along with the new one they ganged up on me.

"I didn't hear the bike," Rusty said.

"Hang on," Antonio interrupted. "Something happened. Cassidy, what were you running from?"

This drew a startled look from Rusty.

Looking at Rusty he said, "I nearly ran her over when she ran out of the desert. No bike. She was on foot running for her life. What was it?"

I still couldn't bring myself to talk. I hated this. Bringing trouble down onto Rusty like this. I could deal with it on my own. But I couldn't take the hurt it caused Rusty. The scratches, the bloodied leg. I could deal with that. Dirk I'd deal with as things came up but every encounter, every scratch, every bruise, hurt Rusty, too, and all the fear and running turned into sadness.

"Where are your first aid supplies?" Antonio asked.

"Bathroom medicine cabinet," Rusty replied. He set Ricky down and he toddled off down the hall looking for his dada.

Rusty started with questions he knew I could deal with.

"Where's the bike?"

"In the desert."

"Did you crash it?"

"No."

"Did it break down?"

"No," I gulped. "The tire was shot out."

He paused.

"Chance shot?"

"No."

Antonio returned with a bunch of minor first aid supplies.

"Cassidy, this isn't going to do it," he said. "Will you go to town?"

"No, it's just scratches."

"The leg is not just scratches."

"I ran a couple of miles on it. It'll be fine."

"If you ran a couple of miles on it you probably made it worse."

Ricky was happy with his dad there. He ran around talking baby talk. Shadow made the rounds between me and Ricky. Ricky squealed with delight and toddled off after Shadow calling, "Goggy! Come goggy! Me wan goggy!"

"What do you mean it wasn't a chance shot?"

"It just wasn't."

"How can you know?"

"I talked to the guy."

A quick pause. "You know who it was?"

"Yeah. I know who it was enough to pull his record."

"Who was it?"

"Dirk."

"Who's Dirk?"

And then I remembered. Rusty didn't know who Dirk was. Schroeder knew. Chase knew. But Rusty didn't. Aw hell.

"Do you remember when I called to tell you about the mine explosion? Dirk caused it. He fired at me and the shot went down the tunnel and set off some old dynamite. The hill blew. Dirk got buried in the explosion. I searched for him until Carla arrived with a dog and backup. I didn't know what happened to Dirk after the mine explosion. You'll have to ask Schroeder that. But I do know it was Dirk. I recognized him and talked to him. I know it was him, beyond a shadow of a doubt."

"How dangerous is he?"

Very.

"He wants revenge."

"How dangerous is he?"

"I'm going to change out of these clothes before they become permanently attached to me."

"Cass, how dangerous is he?"

"He's a lousy shot."

"Cassidy…"

He's like Teague Stern with a motive, I thought, fighting the fear again. Teague Stern was cruel. He'd nearly killed me.

"Very," I finally said. "Be careful. Find out from Schroeder what he looks like so you won't be surprised by him. Stay armed. If I need to take care of Ricky tomorrow I should do it someplace else. Dirk knows where to find me here."

"Don't worry about Ricky," Antonio said. "You've got enough to deal with. You're right about the jeans though. You better go change or you'll take your skin off, too."

The jeans were worthless by the time I cut them up enough to get them off. I had to leave little threads embedded in the scabs. My knee was ground raw from being pinned under the twisting bike. My elbow was next. I should have worn the leather jacket but I was in a hurry. I needed space and I'd needed it fast. Antonio doctored the scrapes as much as he could. He picked out little rocks and brushed away the sand that would fall off. He cleaned and disinfected and tried to bandage it but I stopped him.

"The bandages will just stick. It'll be okay."

Ricky stood watching. He touched a scrape. "Owie," he said. He reached up to be held so I pulled him into my lap. "Kiss better," Ricky said and planted a slobbery wet baby kiss on my arm.

Antonio continued to work on my knee. He didn't find any broken bones but he wasn't satisfied with the way things looked either. He felt around. Bent the knee. Felt some more. Pulled out a small rock.

"This is going to give you fits unless you see a doctor and get better care for it. If you let it dry out straight it will break open when you bend and if you let it dry out bent it will crack when you straighten it. The area's too big for this home first aid kit business. Look, I keep finding more rocks. You need to go where they know how to locate them. You don't want to heal up with rocks imbedded in your knee." He knew me. He knew I wouldn't go to town. He knew I wouldn't see a doctor.

"I've had worse. It'll be fine," I assured him.

We had a short stare down.

"You're more stubborn than you are smart, you know that."

"Yeah, I know that."

"Have you ever had your IQ tested?" he snapped.

"Sort of."

"How do you 'sort of' have your IQ tested?"

"When I was in boot camp a group of us decided we had to be either really smart or really stupid to get ourselves into the Marines. So Denisha Williams downloaded an IQ test off the Internet and we all took it. It was awful. It took me an hour of looking cross-eyed at the screen, trying to figure out which shape was different, do mathematical problems, figure out word puzzles. Unfortunately a lot of it was pattern recognition and that's what I'm good at so I came out looking like a genius. I was glad it wasn't an official test."

"What did you score?"

"I'm not telling."

"Why?"

"Because being smart isn't a good thing sometimes."

"If there was a Mensa group for *stubborn* people you'd qualify."

"Yeah, I guess."

"So what did you score?"

"Thanks for tending my knee. What are you going to do with Ricky?"

"What are you going to do about your new stalker buddy?"

"I'm going to be armed. I'm going to go track down my bike. And then I'm going to go talk to Schroeder and find out what happened."

"I'll take Ricky with me. Maybe they will let me take him in to see his mom."

Rusty appeared in the doorway again. He looked grim.

As Antonio placed Ricky in his car seat and prepared to take him home, Rusty gave a sigh of resignation.

"I'm sorry, Rusty. You would have kept him as long as you could. And I would have watched him in town if Antonio needed me to. But Dirk threatened him, thinking he was mine. I wouldn't keep Ricky here. He'd be in more danger than me."

Ricky waved at us, palm out, fist opening and closing. A baby wave. I sighed, too. Okay, I admitted, I'd rather have a hundred baby messes a day than the mess I was in now. At least a baby only loved you more at the end of the day.

I knew Rusty was feeling stressed when he led me to the old brown couch. He pulled me into his lap and pulled me close. How could I do this to him? I'd warned him before we married, I was a trouble magnet and there was nothing I could do about it. And he assured me I wasn't trouble to him. But we'd seen trouble and then we'd seen more trouble and in rare times we'd seen wonderful peace. Peace we could luxuriate in. But it never lasted.

We sat that way for a long time. Usually our couch time either strayed into touching or talking. Rusty was too worked up to go the touching route.

"Dirk is FTA."

"So he's on the run and he's not going to be tracked down at home in his easy chair."

"I'll find him."

"No! You can't do that."

"I can."

"He won't hesitate to shoot you. He wants to hurt me. He threatened you and he threatened Ricky. I told him, if he had something against me, to take it out on me, but I don't know if he will. I'm sure not going to count on it."

"Babe…" There was a long emotional pause. "Don't take this guy on. Please. If he comes after you consider it a life or death matter. Shoot him. Before he can get a hand on you."

"I saved his life and now you want me to shoot him?"

"Schroeder thinks the guy's unbalanced. He wasn't sure he could stand up in court. He's twisted somehow. If he gets his hands on you…you don't know the things he can do in the state of mind he's in."

"I know enough."

"So you will defend yourself?"

I was a Marine. They taught us well how to kill a man. I'd been through sniper school. They could teach me how to kill. Efficiently. I could shoot Dirk and kill him with one shot, on the run. I had the know-how, the skill. You can teach a person to kill, but you can't make them pull the trigger. And I always had trouble with that last little detail because I'm an optimist. I know there are other ways, nonlethal ways, to get away. They might be painful but it was usually a physical pain. I could deal with the physical pain easier than the mental pain of taking a life. I'd killed before. I still had nightmares about it. It was when instinct took over. When it was the only option. Even when it was the only option it hurt. It hurt for years. It would never go away. I didn't know if I could do it again.

"I'll defend myself," I assured Rusty. But I won't kill him, I thought.

"And I'll find him. Before you have to."

"Schroeder won't give you the case."

"Schroeder won't know. This is personal."

We were at an impasse. I couldn't stop Rusty from looking and he couldn't make me shoot Dirk.

The next morning I donned jeans feeling the material scrape against the scabs with every movement. The initial pain was over. Antonio was right. When I straightened my leg first thing in the morning a long crack formed in the scab and started the wound to bleeding again. I winced, cleaned up the blood, then went about my routine. I showered paying particular attention to the wound on the side of my knee. I dressed in jeans, bullet proof vest, camping shirt, hiking boots and 9mm.

"Where are you going?" Rusty asked.

"I'm going to retrieve my bike. I'll have to track myself back because I don't remember exactly where it is. I'm ashamed to admit the tracking will be easy. There was only about a half mile where I worried about my tracks."

"You're not going alone."

"You need to get to work."

"I'll make you a deal. Take me with you and I'll take the bike to town and get a new tire for it."

"You'd do that anyway."

"Don't take me with you and I'll toss you over my shoulder right here and now and take you to town with me. How are you going to get it out?"

"I was going to push it. I bought a 250 so I could handle it. Now I get to find out if I made a good choice."

Unfortunately, I was right, the tracking was easy. I was glad Rusty couldn't read the desperation in my tracks. Chase would have had a hard time with this trail. Not because of the difficulty but because he knew me too well. He'd know exactly what was in my head. I was tempted to erase the trail as I went just to erase the feelings it brought to mind.

The motorcycle lay where I had left it. Rusty climbed the arroyo and scoped out Dirk's perspective. I saw him analyzing the scene as he imagined it.

"He stood right here and he still missed?" he asked.

"I told you. He's a lousy shot. He was a lousy shot at the mine and he's still a lousy shot. Let's hope if he really wants to kill me he'll try to shoot me."

The joke was lost on Rusty. He took out a camera and began photographing the scene. He took a picture of the tire where the bullet entered cleanly and where the bullet left a gaping, ragged hole. He handed me rubber gloves.

I walked over to the bike but the ground caught my attention.

"Rusty, wait. Don't go closer."

I circled the bike, reading the ground. Dirk had approached the bike, knelt down. I looked closer at the motorcycle. Nothing seemed unusual to me but something didn't quite feel right. Last I remembered Dirk he was patrolling the desert looking for me. Why would he return to the bike?

"Dirk was here. At the bike. But I don't know why. Why would he care about the motorcycle?"

"Was it running when you left it?"

"Yeah, I didn't have time to shut it off."

"But it's off now."

"Why would Dirk care enough to turn off my motorcycle?"

I let Rusty finish taking pictures, then I turned the bike over. I took the barrel of my pistol and used it to push the ends back into the hole to make the tire roll better. Rusty cringed. This wasn't a use for a firearm that he approved of. I pushed the bike down the arroyo towards home.

"Cass, wait," Rusty said, hurrying after me. He lifted the motorcycle and put it up on the hard pack where it would roll easier. "Help me find the slugs."

Mentally I put myself where I was when Dirk had shot at me, let the flashback loose, heard them hit around me and the search was on. Eventually, we found three.

It was a long, slow, quiet walk back. I pushed the bike, my knee nagging at me with every step. Rusty knew I had to feel like I did my share but after a while he couldn't take it anymore.

"Cass, stop, please, let me help."

"It's my bike and my bout of trouble. I'll do it."

"I'm telling you to stop. Babe, you don't have to do it all on your own."

I sighed with resignation. I was used to getting through trouble bouts. In a way it helped me deal with them. While I had my bike and I was pushing it home I was pushing Dirk into the background. If I stopped my thoughts would have free reign and I didn't know where they would take me. But I knew Rusty needed to help so I handed over the bike to him. I had struggled the whole way, but he pushed it easily. It irked me. I knew he was a lot bigger than me so the bike would naturally be easier for him to push, but it still irked me.

When we got home he loaded the motorcycle into the back of his Explorer and got ready for work. I stewed. I'd be stuck at home. Alone. No wheels. Nothing much to do. Just me and my thoughts. I'd go nuts.

"Can I go to town with you?" I asked when he was ready.

"Sure, what are you going to do there all day?"

"I don't know. If you don't need the Explorer I'll go to the gym, practice at the firing range, talk to Schroeder."

"I don't recommend talking to Schroeder. I already did. You won't like what he has to say about this Dirk character."

"Maybe I'll go chase down a purse snatcher at the mall." Seems like every time I go to the mall something happens there. Banks get robbed. Purse snatchers suddenly get itchy fingers.

"Are you afraid to stay home?"

"Me? Scared? No, not exactly. I just don't want to be left alone with my thoughts. I need something to occupy my mind. But I'm not really scared. If anything I'd be more afraid of having to hurt Dirk than scared for my safety. I could take the bike in to be fixed."

"Not until it's been looked over at the station. When they release it I'll take it to be fixed. Keep your cell phone on. If I need the truck I'll give you a call."

"Okay," I said with a hug and a kiss.

In town I wandered around town doing random errands. I didn't get into town as much as I used to. I went when the cupboards were bare or when I got a search call, but in general it just seemed too far away to go for no reason. I got my hair trimmed. I went to the post office. I ate lunch. I was at the pet store buying a thirty-pound bag of dog food when my cell phone rang.

"Cass, are you okay?" Rusty said.

"Yeah, I'm fine. Hold on." I dumped the bag of food at my feet so I wouldn't have to talk under a thirty-pound load.

"What was that?" he asked.

"Dog food. What's up?"

"Are you sure you're not being followed?"

"Pretty sure, why?" I looked around for any suspicious characters. No one ducked for cover when I did my quick scan. I didn't see Dirk.

"Can you come to the station?"

"Sure. Why?"

"I just need you to come to the station."

I found Rusty in the one spot I didn't want to find him. At the punching bag. Usually I was the one who took out my frustrations on the punching bag. Anywhere else I'd know things were in control and he was just doing his job. Not here. He'd learned something and it wasn't good. When I walked in all the other guys quietly disappeared.

"I'm sorry, babe, I'm losing it. I just had to see you. I keep playing this what-if scenario in my head and…I just couldn't take it anymore."

"That's okay. I don't mind coming. What happened?"

"I know why the bike was turned off when we found it. It wasn't because Dirk wanted to conserve your gas."

After a bone crushing hug he led me to another part of the station. A part I had never seen before.

"Don't touch it," he admonished needlessly as we approached the motorcycle. "What do you see?"

It took some searching. My bike looked sad, like it was in the hospital or something, even though I couldn't see anything wrong with it other than the blown out tire. It had to be something subtle. Something Dirk had done. Something dangerous. Very cleverly hidden. Rusty pointed it out to me, a single wire leading from the starter of the bike to a tiny hole in the gas tank. A hole just big enough to snuggly fit one wire. One twist of the key and…

"I keep picturing you picking up the bike from the Kawasaki place, hopping on happily, turning the key, pushing the button… and it could have so easily happened that way. I could have gone to work thinking it was a normal day. Not knowing in a half second it would be over. Not knowing until word came back to the station, through Schroeder…And I just needed to see you." He ran his hands through his hair and it fell back down just like it always did. He took me by the hand and we went to the Explorer. I got in and he drove… and drove. I waited patiently. I knew when he had worked through what was in his head he'd go back to the station.

He didn't go back to the station. He drove forever. He got on the freeway that led to the L.A. basin, then got off and drove around in the mountains, wandered down into Santa Clarita. Eventually he pulled into a parking lot all the way down in Ventura. He was nearly out of gas but he wasn't out of worry so we walked. The beach seemed to call to Rusty just like the mountains called to me. I dragged him down to the water. He was in his suit and I was in jeans so we weren't exactly dressed for the beach. I rolled up my jeans and waded. I knew what he needed. When he felt like this, he needed to see me be happy and healthy. I had to let him think it could stay that way. I waded. I ran down the water's edge. I let the tracks distract me.

"Tell me about it," he said.

"You hate when I read the sand at the beach."

"Read it to me."

"Okay, these footprints were made by a man, smaller than you, thin. He was carrying stuff. Maybe he was going to fish in the surf. See? The handle of the poll hit here. He's got a long gangly gait. I kind of picture Ichabod Crane on a fishing trip."

"Find another one."

We shifted positions on the beach.

"Here's a young woman she's out for a jog. No, she's meeting someone. See? Here's another set of tracks. The other set is a guy. They walk down the beach bumping hips together. They know each other. They are comfortable together."

A group of teens appeared ahead. Rock music blared from a boom box. Some of them were playing volleyball. A couple of kids were boogie boarding. The tracks joined the group.

"Which ones are they?" he asked.

"They're all about the same size. I'd have to watch them for a while. The guy has a longer stride than the girl so maybe the guy is the one in blue Hawaiian print trunks. Then the girl is probably the one he is most familiar with. The girl in the red bikini top and cutoffs has her eye on him. Maybe it's them."

"I wish I'd known you when you were that age."

"No you don't," I answered. "I was too hard. I needed breaking. I wouldn't have been the one playing volleyball or boogie boarding. I'd have to pick the hardest thing to do. I'd swim around the pier. I'd run the beach. I wouldn't have sat around listening to music and chatting. That was Jesse. I was off pushing myself."

"Why?"

"I was expected to live up to Steve's example."

Steve worked for my dad. He was perhaps my best friend while I was growing up but he wasn't an easy man. He was rough, tough and hard to bluff and believe me I tried to bluff him many times. He had a heart for kids. He watched over me on the ranch, taught me to ride, and got me out of trouble more times than I could count. But he was an awfully hard man for me to emulate. He could tame a horse. He downed a buck with one shot every hunting season until my dad let me try. He could rope and tie a calf in ten seconds and I always took at least twice that time. And he could flank the big calves while I had to leg over the little ones. So I pushed and hardened myself so one day I would be ready for Steve's job. I was expected to take over the ranch someday. I had to be tough. I got too tough for my own good.

"Your dad didn't know what a treasure he had."

"He didn't want kids. He wanted me to grow up, so he wouldn't have to raise me."

"Is that why you don't want kids?"

"No! Rusty no! And it's not that I don't want kids."

"I'm sorry I pushed Ricky onto you."

"I'm not." And it was true, looking back. I was glad I had that short time with Ricky.

Rusty looked at me hopefully.

I stopped walking and turned to face him so he'd know I was serious. "It was frustrating. I still don't think I could do that full time. Ricky showed me I'm still too hard to be a mom. But I'm getting closer. Have patience. I'm trying. I'm really trying…okay?"

Little laugh lines appeared around his eyes. I'd given him hope. I pulled him back towards the pier.

"Where are we going?"

"We're too dressed up to have fun. Let's go get some beachwear. The salt water will be good for my knee."

He allowed himself to be pulled along, his mood lightening a little as we went. When we were outfitted in swimsuits we headed for the water again.

"I wish I'd brought my surfboard, but I didn't know we'd end up here."

"Are you still determined to learn how to surf?"

"I'm not *determined*. I just think it never hurts to have options wherever I go. It can't hurt to know how to surf and it might turn out to be fun."

"I think you're mistaken. Look at you, you're just like a kid. Babe, you're not as hard as you think. You're tougher than most but there's a heart in there, a joy that hard people don't have. Believe me, I see a lot of hard people. You're not one of them."

"The joy wasn't there until I met *you*. Remember when I was supposed to meet you in town? You wanted me to meet Lou and I got stuck up in the mountains. You drove up to retrieved me. Since it was too late to make the appointment with Lou you asked me to dinner. You asked me to wear a dress. You didn't know how much you were asking when you did that. I gave you a good scolding as I struggled with the dress, with the idea of getting all made up, and I felt so awkward."

The little laugh lines appeared again.

"I'm sorry…"

"I'm not. I needed it. You always know what I need even when I don't. I need you to push me in directions I'd never think to go on my own. I don't *think* you stuck with me to change me, but you have. I'm not the same person you met when you were looking for Silva, and I'm glad. I don't want to be that person anymore. And I want to keep changing. I want to be happy as a mom. Right now that wouldn't happen. But maybe someday it will."

"How did you have fun as a teenager?"

"Fun? I guess the closest to fun I had was the tension of competition when I was barrel racing. It was the concentration of stalking a deer, seeing how close I could get. But fun? Deep down fun? It wasn't really part of me. I felt at peace when I was out tracking, or riding. But fun? I wouldn't call it fun."

"When we were on our honeymoon you said the survival part was fun."

"Because I was with you. Come on. I'm with you now, so I can have fun." I stepped into the ocean. It was cold but I kept wading until the water was waist deep and the swells reached up to my shoulders. I loved the ocean as much as Rusty did. It was freeing. The mountains were good and solid but the water and ocean breezes lifted my spirits. The mountains took concentration. The ocean freed my mind. I could forget things at the ocean.

It was a rare lull. Play time. A time when we just enjoyed each other. We laughed a lot, swam a lot, walked the beach until we found an ice cream stand. We ate ice cream for dinner not caring if it was bad for us or not. I had fudge brownie and Rusty had black cherry.

"I needed this," said Rusty. "I don't want to go back. I want to rent a boat and go sailing off to explore the Channel Islands and visit Catalina. I want to take you far away and live every day like this afternoon."

We were sitting on a low wall overlooking the ocean. The sun was setting over the ocean setting the sky afire. We were still barefoot, in nothing but swimsuits. He straddled the wall and I sat in front of him leaning against his chest, feet stretched out before me. He kept dripping ice cream on me. A big glob of chocolate dripped off my cone.

"Mmm, fudge brownie with cherries on top. Can I lick it off?" he asked.

"Not until we get home."

"Can I drip in some interesting places?"

"Not until we get home."

"Oops," he said as a drop fell down the front of my swimsuit.

I hopped off the wall and climbed back on facing him. I wrapped my arms around his neck, and drew him down into a kiss.

"Oops," he said again with a mischievous look. He wiped the drip off my chest with his finger and licked it off.

"Maybe we should head for home. You can drip whatever you want on me there."

We went to the truck and I started pulling on my jeans over my swimsuit.

"Do you have to?" he asked.

"Depends on where we're stopping."

"Just for gas. You can wait in the truck."

I threw the jeans back in the truck and settled into the front seat. He pulled his work shirt on, left the top three buttons undone and rolled the sleeves up.

The house was dark when we got home. Shadow thought he'd been forgotten. I quickly fed him and let him out. Necessities out of the way, Rusty scooped me up.

"You've been driving me crazy all afternoon."

"So you like this swim suit?"

"You is what I like. Now where are those drips?"

"They are exactly where you wanted them to be."

"I wish."

He found the drips plus a whole lot more. How did I live without this man so long? How could I stand it alone when he was out there? I didn't know but I was so grateful he'd knocked on my door that day. And I was so thankful he'd stuck with me. And for just a little while I was able to forget Dirk was out there, and Rusty could feel me be alive beneath him.

A few hours later I woke to a dim house and sleepy husband. It couldn't get better than this afternoon. Oh god, it was good. When the minutes counted we tended to treasure them, make them rich and valuable to us. I turned to Rusty and snuggled close stretching the minutes. It brought back flashbacks of what life was like without him. The sorrow. The loneliness that drove me running for the mountains. The days of hunger doing survival trips into the mountains. The hunger battling it out with the sorrow of losing my first husband. Why did I put myself through all that when Rusty was out there? Because life was hard. I answered myself. *You* were hard. It was all you knew. So it's what you did. I couldn't believe it myself and I'd lived through it. Days of living off the land. I learned volumes. I could now survive in almost any environment. But it was so hard. I was lucky to have lived through it. I was never far from the Jeep but hunger haunted me and sorrow kept me running. Rusty rescued me from all that without really knowing it. Stop it, Cass, you're going to start crying and then Rusty's going to worry about you and…and it was too late. Rusty was too quiet beside me. He was awake, feeling the wheels turning in my brain. I snuggled closer.

"Thank you for today," I said.

"What's wrong?"

"Nothing. I was just contrasting the present to the past. Thank you… for my present. It's so much richer than my past. I don't know how I survived it, but I can take joy in today. As long as you are here."

He pulled me close and I was at peace again. He was very still which meant he was checking his emotions. I felt treasured like that. Him holding me close. Guarding me. I slipped into a quiet, contented sleep, safe. For now I was safe. No sorrow. No fear. Just blissful peace and rest. We slept like that for a long time.

Chapter 25

Morning arrived right on schedule. Rusty returned to work. He had a lot to do after taking half a day off. I thought he'd work late. I locked all the doors and prepared for a boring day indoors. I was determined, Rusty was going to have a worry free day at work and arrive home to a perfect house and a happy wife. I started at the front door and examined each room for what needed cleaning. In the living room I looked for a way to rearrange the furniture. The room was never used. It was stiff and uncomfortable, so I was looking for a way to loosen it up. I scooted the furniture around and no matter what I did it still felt stuffy. Maybe that's because it had the old brown couch for competition. The old brown couch was just the opposite. It was comfortable, in a lumpy sort of way. It was familiar. It was home. I looked at the living room couch. It didn't feel stuffy just looking at it. Maybe it was the room itself? I couldn't pinpoint it. It was like the pictures Mark Mireau had taken of Dangerous Tracker Woman. We couldn't tell why I changed from one set of pictures to the other but something was different. There was something different about this room that couldn't be seen, only felt. I tried to remember how the furniture was arranged when we bought the house from its previous owner. The placement seemed odd. I pulled and tugged my furniture into the same configuration. I sat on the stuffy couch trying to figure out why they liked it that way. I couldn't spend all day on the living room. I decided the furniture was fine. The room was just stuffy, that's all there was to it. I'd always prefer the den. I could live with that. I vacuumed the floor and dusted the furniture and pictures. I moved to the windowsills and doorframes. The molding around the front door was odd. It was different from the rest of the house. It was wider. And it felt loose. I knew this house held secrets. I'd already found a secret room in the back of my closet. So when the molding felt loose I began working at it. It was stubborn until I found just the right motion and when I did the molding swung away like a little door, revealing a long thin compartment behind. Inside hung an ancient rifle. I went to the garage and found the box of rubber gloves. Rusty always had a pair of rubber gloves handy when he went to work. As I pulled the gloves on I thought I'd seen too many investigations. There was no reason to use rubber gloves on this rifle. It wasn't involved in any crime. I pulled the gloves on out of habit, or maybe because of my training.

I knew who the rifle had belonged to, a man named Gustaf Morgan. We had bought the house from his widow, Bernice. Gustaf must have been an interesting character. With the gloves on I took down the old rifle. I checked the magazine. It was still loaded, though the magazine wasn't full. Gustaf wasn't taking any chances. So much for a boring day at home. I was curious what other secrets this house held. It turned from a cleaning day into a hunt.

I moved from the living room to the dining room. Not much to do there. One table, six chairs. I vacuumed the floor and went on to the den. There was no help for the old brown couch. It took over the room and it was as old as dirt, but I wouldn't part with it until it became one with the earth. It was our comfort zone. It was L shaped, so if we sat in one section of it we faced the TV, and if we sat in another section of it we faced the fireplace. I dusted and vacuumed, then I went over the room with a fine toothed comb. Any odd moldings around windows? By the back door? It seemed to me that if Gustaf was worried about people who came to the door he'd be equally concerned about people who came to the back door. I searched the entire room, but nothing seemed unusual. I was beginning to see Gustaf in a new light though. He was a thinker. What was in that mind of his?

The guestroom held another surprise. The shelf separating the clothes bar from the top of the closet wasn't just a shelf. It was a box and inside I found documents. I wasn't nosey enough that day to read them, but it was interesting. Gustaf was getting more and more eccentric the more I knew about him.

Other shelves that appeared to be wide in a decorative sort of way were actually hidden compartments. I found one other hiding place. It was one I expected to find. In fact I was disappointed that it was so simple and I hadn't seen it earlier. I knew the window seat in my bedroom opened for storage. I kept blankets in there, but after all the other things I had found that day I thought further investigation was called for. I removed all the blankets and examined the inside. It appeared to be a wooden box, neatly lined with cedar. What I found was that each of those cedar panels came out and behind them was a neat compartment. It was a little disappointing that of all three panels all I found inside was one key, but what was the key to? After the house was clean I started dinner. Rusty came home to a big pot of spaghetti.

"How was your day?" he asked hesitantly.

"After dinner I have something to show you."

"You didn't answer my question."

"It was…interesting."

"Interesting? You stayed home and cleaned house and it was interesting?"

"Yeah, I'll show you why after dinner." We sat down to eat dinner. "What do you know about Gustaf Morgan?" I asked as I scooped out a serving of noodles.

"I know as much as you do. He built the house, he liked to sit in the bay window and watch the wildlife. He owned Morgan horses," he answered adding a scoop of sauce.

"He's an interesting character. That's all you know?" I said dishing up noodles and sauce for me, too.

"That's all Mrs. Morgan told us. Why?" He shook Parmesan cheese all over his sauce, then stirred it all up. He cut it up with his fork. He was a cutter. I was a twirler.

"I think I found more questions than answers."

"Okay…it's a door," Rusty observed.

"What's different about it?" I asked. "If I can find it dusting, you can find it on your own. He opened and examined the front door. He knocked around on it. It was good solid wood. He ran his hands over the molding."

"Cassidy, it's a door. It's completely normal."

"That's what Gus would like you to think. The molding is way too wide."

"Why? What's wrong with wide molding? It's decorative."

"Then why didn't he continue it throughout the house? Look."

I swung the molding open revealing the rifle behind it. Rusty stepped back, a sheepish grin on his face. He, too, put the gloves on before taking the rifle down.

"It's loaded," I warned him.

He looked the weapon over with an analytical mind. I watched him make mental notes about it. He hefted it. Felt the balance. He read the labels on it. Checked the magazine. Looked down the barrel.

"Nice piece, but not enough to keep you occupied for a day. What else did you find?"

"I wonder why Gustaf would feel like he needs a rifle at his front door. I know he was a bit paranoid just to have dug the secret room but he seems to have planned ahead for some type of trouble to come. The other things are just odd. I don't know that there is anything of interest in them. One contains documents and the other only held a key."

I showed him the two other hiding places I found and he just shook his head.

"I never in a million years would have thought to take apart the window seat or look inside a closet shelf. So it was too thick for a closet shelf. It was attractive and functional."

"Now I'm curious what the key unlocks. I didn't find any hidden locks."

"Have you checked out the barn?"

"No, but that's an idea."

"Any sign of Dirk?"
"No, it's been quiet all day."
"Maybe we should put *your rifle* in that compartment by the front door."

Chapter 26

During tough times I hope for searches to come up. It gives me something to focus on besides my trouble and since I am normally accompanied by armed men it is safer to be out on a search than it is to be anywhere else. Rusty hated for me to be gone overnight but conceded it served a multitude of purposes. I was working, getting my outdoors fix in, and staying out of trouble. So when Lou Strickland called the next day I was ready to roll.

"This should be a fairly straightforward search. Your ten sixty-five is parked on a mountain side. He's in good health, good spirits, just lost. He radioed his buddies back at camp and they spent yesterday trying to find him and gave up. They convinced him to find someplace and wait. Hopefully he's got water but he's at least not expending a lot of energy or using up resources. I expect a hike in and a hike out, nice and simple."

I nodded. My eyes already strayed to the ground. I tried to focus on Lou.

"Where can I get a sample of the tracks?"

"We had a hiker report he saw Lenny on the trail about two miles down. That's your starting point. I put it about… right… here," he said bending over a map. I looked the map over for landmarks. There wasn't much to identify the place. I'd have to watch the trail.

Again I just nodded assent. I got the picture. I was ready to go.

"Cassidy? Are you okay? You're not acting like yourself."

"Sorry, yeah, I'm fine. I don't feel great but there's nothing wrong. The trail's still the best place for me."

"Why are you going armed? You usually only go armed on apprehensions."

"I've got reason to feel a little apprehensive. So far it's just been one confrontation and some threats. But they are threats I have to take seriously. The guy shot my motorcycle out from under me and then when I ditched it to get away he rigged it to blow when I started it up."

"Nice guy. Does he have a motive?"

"Yeah, I apparently ruined his life."

"I see."

"It's complicated. Schroeder can fill you in of you need details. I need to hit the trail."

Sometimes searches don't turn out like I plan. I always have a firm goal in mind when I start out, a realistic picture of the situation, and what I can expect the outcome to be. *Usually*, I am pretty accurate. If I think I can find a person in a day I usually do. And I have an idea when I start out whether I am in for a grueling, brain-numbing rocky search or a quick hike through the forest search. This search was different. For one thing I didn't feel well starting out. It was just a vague, something's not quite right feeling. Landon and I hiked the two miles to our starting point. When the tracks were clear I stopped and studied them so I'd recognize them off trail. Lenny's buddies had messed up his trail in their searching, but I managed to get an idea of Lenny's stride. I noted his tread. Wear spots didn't show up well on the trail. It was too gravely.

By the time we followed Lenny's tracks off the trail I felt rotten. I was wondering if I was getting a fever or coming down with a cold. It wasn't following the usual symptoms of a cold, though. Usually I get a sore throat and then it spreads to other inconvenient areas. This just felt like a vague unwell feeling, so I kept going. Our missing person was dealing with more than a cold coming on. He'd been out in the open over a day but reports said he hadn't gone far.

After an hour of tracking I decided Lenny Patelli would be an easy find. He moved through the forest like a bulldozer despite his small stature, or maybe because of it. Sign of his passing came in tracks, broken branches, kicked rocks. He gave me plenty of clues. I even began to wonder why he didn't just track himself back. It would have been an easy job.

"You're being unusually quiet," Landon observed.

"I feel rotten. I prefer to keep my rottenness to myself. If you can think of something cheerful to talk about, I'd be glad to talk."

"Cookies. Did you bring cookies?"

"I always try to bring cookies. I've become a cookie slave. When Strict calls, first I check to see if I have cookies. Then I tell him when I can be there."

"You're kidding."

"Yeah, I'm kidding. But I do try and have cookies ready, even if they have been sitting in the freezer for a few weeks. You'll have to wait for them to thaw."

Lenny's tracks did a ninety degree turn and I looked around for what might have drawn his attention. It wasn't a spontaneous decision. He'd stood there considering his options and then turned to the right and set off again at a sprightly pace. He was enjoying his hike, enjoying being out in the woods. I hoped he wasn't going to try to climb the mountain because I was not up to a mountain climbing expedition. The reports did indicate Lenny was at a higher elevation than when he started out. He'd given his buddies a rough idea of what his surroundings were like and he was definitely higher up than we were now.

The feverish feeling grew and then the kind of feeling all women hate when they are in the woods. I excused myself and told Landon to keep to the trail and I'd catch up to him in a few minutes. I went off away from the trail to take care of necessities thinking something was off with this. This was the wrong time. And I thought maybe I needed a new prescription for my birth control pills if these weren't working right.

I had decided things definitely were not right when I began "chasing butterflies" every fifteen to twenty minutes. The feverish feeling turned to a weak feeling and the weak feeling turned into a shaky feeling and still I kept to the trail, stopping frequently.

"Cassidy, are you okay?" Landon asked after my tenth side trip.

We were closing in on Lenny Patelli so I admitted, "I don't think so, when I get out of here I'm going to town. I need to see a doctor."

A half mile later my stomach clenched in pain. I paused on the trail waiting for the pain to subside but it didn't. I pressed onward.

"Landon, when we find Patelli, call a helicopter, whether he needs one or not. There's no way I'm hiking out."

He sat me down.

"Cassidy, you're white as a sheet. Tell me what's going on."

"I don't know, it's… it's female related. I thought I was coming down with something but now I'm bleeding like crazy, my stomach hurts, even my shoulder hurts. Why would my shoulder hurt? We have to find Lenny. Come on, we're getting close."

How close a call that was, I didn't know. Landon reluctantly let me continue. We found Lenny Patelli waiting like he said he would, but we found ourselves in a race against time. Landon called a helicopter knowing I wouldn't ask for one unless something was very wrong. I could hear the conversation between Landon and Strict.

"Ten sixty-five found, ten forty-five A," Landon started out.

"Ten four, good work," Strict answered.

"Strict, we need a pick up."

Dead silence.

"Ten-nine?"

"We need a pick up. Cassidy is sick. She's been making trail stops all day."

"How sick?"

"She asked for the pick up, that's how sick."

"Right."

I sat next to a tree and the pain grew until I couldn't sit anymore. I curled into a fetal position on the ground and just waited. I knew it could be hours.

Lenny walked over and asked, "Hey, are you okay?"

"You ever ride in a helicopter?" I managed to say.

"No, why?" he answered.

"You may get your chance."

Landon came back. "Oh, god, Cassidy, what have you done to yourself?" Then into the radio, "Put a stat on that helicopter."

Landon began talking to me like a patient. "Cassidy, I need more information. Talk to me. You said this is female related. When was your last period?"

"I don't know. I'm on the pill. It had to be at the end of the card."

"The card of pills?"

"Yeah."

"Do you *know* that?"

"I think so. I don't keep track. I just trust them. I don't think about whether or not I had my period. If I don't, I count myself lucky. It's no fun. You couldn't understand."

He smiled at me but his expression was grim.

"Could you be pregnant?"

"No, I told you…"

"It doesn't mean a thing."

He'd been taking my pulse and he opened his pack to get out other equipment. The blood pressure cuff first. He took it twice. My fingers were cold in spite of the heat of the day, but I felt feverish too. The pain wasn't easing up, if anything it was getting worse, the bleeding was getting worse, too.

"No, Cass, stay with me here. I need you to think. Where does it hurt?"

"Lower abdomen, right side," I managed to mumble.

But I couldn't think. I was past thinking. I remember worried eyes. Being rolled onto my back. Palpations where I said it hurt. More worried eyes. He went to his pack. Everything blurred together. I fought the haze descending on me knowing Landon would feel better as long as I was lucid. I could hear the clatter of the helicopter and I looked up into the big red, white and blue underbelly of an air ambulance. Strict took my request seriously. By the time the basket was lowered I was delirious and I don't remember being lifted into the bay of the helicopter.

All I know from Landon's description later was that it was a race against my body. I was bleeding fearfully fast. Nobody really knew why. They had found the nearest emergency room that could take a critical case and away we flew, the sound of the blades a distant rhythm that rattled around inside my brain.

Lenny found himself on an unplanned trip to L.A.

The fastest examination in the history of ER ensued and I was whisked off to surgery.

Strict had called Rusty while I was still on the mountain and Landon called in a destination from the air. Rusty found Landon frantically pacing the halls.

"What happened?" Rusty demanded.

Landon told him he didn't know, and explained what I'd told him.

"You're the EMT," Rusty demanded. "You must have some idea."

"I do, but I don't know if I'm right. I'm hoping I'm not. The doctor will explain it all when they find out more."

Rusty turned on him. "I need to know what she's fighting in there. I have to. Even if it's not right. Even if it turns out to be all wrong, it gives me something to latch on to."

Since Landon had something to latch on to he could understand.

"I think she's having a miscarriage."

Rusty stopped, still as could be, then he found a waiting room and sat down, head in hands.

"If you'd told me she fell, or got shot, or her ten sixty-five turned on you two and beat her to a pulp, I wouldn't have been surprised. I can expect things like that. You could tell me she'd been snake bitten, or attacked by a mountain lion and I could believe that. I never in a million years would have guessed she went out on a call in that condition."

"I don't think she knew, or had thought of it. She just felt out of sorts when we started out. No need for concern. I didn't know how serious it was until she asked for a pick up. We knew our ten sixty-five was in good shape to walk out. We thought we'd locate him and follow our trail back. But Cass, went downhill frighteningly fast. I called in to report our missing person found, in good shape and asked Strict for the pick up. When I turned around Cassidy was on the ground."

When they asked for more information from the hospital staff they got the standard, pat answer, "She's in good hands. They're doing what they can. We'll tell you as soon as we know more."

The nothingness of unconsciousness morphed to a sort of delirium of dreams. I felt like I was floating between nothingness and reality, but reality wasn't a hospital room, it was woods, some woods I'd only seen once in my life, the green woods of Minnesota, and a river teaming with fish. A bear walked up to the river and I wanted to go down and hide in the brush and watch it. This floating business was for the birds.

I couldn't control where my mind took me. It took me away to places I'd seen, experiences I'd had, but I couldn't stop. I reached for reality. I felt something there but my mind wouldn't let me stay with it. A car wreck. A fire… Rusty, please, Rusty, wake up. Rusty and Chase and the fire. Make it stop. Please make it stop… Making cookies with Patrick. I could remember they had too much vanilla, but I couldn't remember my name. Voices, hushed voices in the dreams, and odd sounds that didn't fit with the scenes. I could identify the voices of Rusty and my mom in a fuzzy sort of way. Others I didn't know.

At last the drifting stopped and I felt heavy, so heavy that I couldn't move. Everything was an enormous effort. I tried to open my eyes. It was too much. I tried moving my hand. I knew I was successful when a hand squeezed mine. I hadn't even realized it was there. I grasped back and felt the squeeze again, then heard a shift in position next to me, some pressure on the bed.

"Cassidy?" Rusty said quietly.

I squeezed.

"Can you hear me?"

Another squeeze. A calming.

I tried again to open my eyes.

Softly beside me, "Relax, hon, it's okay. Relax and it'll come easier."

I tried again. I got them open but they wouldn't stay open. I caught a glimpse of Rusty before they fell closed again. I felt like I was fighting a battle, just to open my eyes. I tried to say something but realized I couldn't.

He took my hand in his. "Can you squeeze?" he asked.

I tried, not knowing how successful I was. It was a weak squeeze at best.

"Can you understand me?"

I squeezed.

"Do you remember what happened?"

Another squeeze.

"Do you know what caused this?"

How to say no? I tried two squeezes.

"Okay…if you knew you'd have questions. I just wanted to be able to give you the answers, but it can wait."

Sometimes when I woke up Rusty was right there ready to encourage me. Other times he had to pull himself out of the depths of despair to talk to me. I didn't understand it. It made me wonder what had happened while I'd been out, but it wasn't me that was causing his grief. I continued to improve slowly, painfully slowly.

Landon was there when I woke up again. When he saw my eyes open he scooted closer.

"Cassidy?"

I tried to talk but the respirator wouldn't let me.

"She'll answer your questions if you hold her hand. One squeeze for yes, two for no," Rusty told him.

Landon hesitated to take my hand, but he seemed to need to talk somehow.

"Can you hear me?" he asked.

One squeeze. He relaxed a little, thinking.

"Do you remember what happened?"

One squeeze.

"You scared me, kid. Just to see you come this far is hard to believe. You're a fighter. You know that? I don't know how you made it through. I thought I'd lost you. I wouldn't have given you a chance and now look at you."

I weakly pulled my hand loose and, in rough sign language, finger spelled C-O-O-K-I-E-S-I-N-P-A-C. It was a tremendous effort and nearly sent me over the edge into sleep again. He looked puzzled at first but I knew he understood. He had taught me the letters on a long search one time. He went to the closet and found my pack and got out the Ziploc bag of cookies. The worry seemed to fade as he saw the humor in my situation. I finger spelled I-O-U and then slipped over the edge hoping he'd share with Rusty.

I woke to find my mother sitting with me.

"Hi there, I sent Rusty for a walk. He needed some fresh air. I have to push him out the door to get him to go. He spends way too much time in this chair. You okay?"

A weak squeeze.

"Everybody back home is rooting for you. Just rest. You need quiet rest first."

I tried to talk, but gave up in frustration.

"Patrick sent this for you." She held up a coloring book of wildlife. She showed me several pages that he had colored. "He called it a reminder book, so you'd be reminded of who was thinking of you at the ranch. He made everyone color a page. Look, even Dad colored a page for you. When you feel better you can read what everybody wrote to you."

A nurse entered the room pulling on a surgical mask.

"You'll have to leave the room for just a minute," he said. "I'll call you back in when I'm finished."

Mom obediently left and went to update Rusty. The nurse turned to me and I saw those eyes. I panicked. It was Dirk! It was Dirk and I couldn't move! He stared down at me enjoying my plight.

“What are you doing here?” he asked. “Trying to deprive me of my fun? I watched the house for days. Took me a while to find you.” He was pacing around looking things over. I couldn’t answer him. I couldn’t get away. I was helpless. “Let’s see. How can I make you squirm? Let’s see how you do without this ugly tube. See if you feel like I did under all that dirt, pushing sand away, trying to make a small pocket of air.”

I turned my head away from him but I was too weak to fight it. Out came the tube with a searing pain. In my panic I was breathing okay. To me it felt like flight mode. Quick ragged breaths. If I could have run I would have but I couldn’t even sit. When the tube was removed all the sensors on the machine went crazy. It started a piercing beep. Dirk looked alarmed, knowing real nurses would be heading this way quickly. “You’ll die little girl. One of these days, with me watching…” he said, then he dashed out the door. A real nurse came in, took in the situation and looked at me with a disapproving glare, like I’d taken the tube out myself. I couldn’t have even if I’d wanted to. She called in other nurses and the room filled with people. I was still in flight mode. I turned away from her efforts.

“No, stop!” I frantically rasped. “Need to talk. Let me talk! It wasn’t a nurse. It was a man. Get Rusty. Please, get Rusty!”

A nurse stood guard over me while another nurse went away. I was fading and I couldn’t do that. I had to talk to Rusty…had to… I fought it, tossing and turning, anything to keep feeling until Rusty burst through the doorway.

“Cass! Babe, shhh…it’s okay…be still. I’m here.”

“Rus…”I gasped. “Dirk was here. Took out the tube. He thought I couldn’t breathe without it. Alarm scared him off.”

I was gasping for air but I was breathing. Rusty flipped open his cell phone and called the police.

“What was he wearing?”

“Hospital scrubs, mask too.”

“Babe, I have to go look. I’ll be back as soon as I can.”

“No tube,” I gasped at the nurses. “Please…give me a chance without it.”

I lay there concentrating on breathing. The nurse called the doctor. I faded out, still fighting the nurse.

I woke with a start, expecting to see Dirk. The tube was still gone.

“Rus…” I whispered.

“Shh,” he said. “Take it slow. You’ve been through a lot.”

“I love you.”

He smiled and tears sprung to his eyes.

“You don’t know how long I’ve waited for those words.”

“How long?”

"Too long. Don't worry about it."

"So weak."

"I know. You've got every right to be. You've got a long, hard job ahead of you, but I know you can do it."

"Dirk?"

"They're still looking for him. This is a big place. They can't stop every nurse they see and there are a lot of male nurses here. I won't leave again, babe, I'll be right here. Don't worry. He won't get near you again."

I could feel the cruel fingers of sleep dragging me down. I fought it but sleep won.

Later…

"Rusty?" I said weakly.

Landon appeared.

"Hey," he said. "You can talk again."

"For a short time," I whispered. My voice would come and go as my strength came and went. He had to listen closely and concentrate on listening.

"Thanks for the cookies."

"Did you share?"

"Yeah, Rusty got some, too. You shocked both of us when you used the sign language. We didn't know you could think enough to do that. Rusty was grinning like a fool for hours."

"Does he understand the letters?"

"I showed them to him. Just like most people, he'd learned them as a kid and forgotten half of them."

"Why would I have trouble thinking?"

"You still don't know what you've been through, do you?"

"No, I can't stay awake long enough…to find out. Appendicitis? Appendicitis wouldn't do this to me."

"No. It's not my place to tell you. You need to talk to Rusty. He's having a rough time of it. He's had too many quiet hours to think. He needs to talk to you."

"Where is he?"

"I told him I'd stay. He's here. He's just taking a nap."

We fell silent, me from weakness, he because he was uncomfortable with the topic.

"Landon, can you read me a book?"

"A book? What book?"

"Little coloring book, from my family."

He looked around, found the reminder book on the table and opened it up.

"The first page shows a wolf cub." He showed me the picture, definitely colored by Wyatt. "Dear Aunt Cassidy, get better quick. From Wyatt."

"Wyatt's five and he doesn't know me very well," I explained.

"Here's one of a bobcat, done by Steve," he said holding up the picture. Coloring wasn't Steve's forte. "Kiddo, how do you get yourself into these things? Take care of yourself. We're all rooting for you. If you're well enough to read this book your recovery's certain. I know what a fighter you can be. Don't let us down. Steve."

"What does Patrick say?" I asked.

Landon leafed through the book until he found Patrick's page. It was a picture of deer, carefully colored and shaded. His expression changed and he said, "Cassidy, I can't read Patrick's page until you talk to Rusty."

"Why?"

"You'll understand when you get to read it."

The next day I woke and found I could move easier. This was a good thing because I was sick of the bed. I felt trapped in it. Being able to shift around a little helped although it also told me that I had stitches. I couldn't move enough to see them but I knew they were there. I also noted I had no clothes on. I looked around. Monitors were everywhere, IVs; there was barely room in the little alcove for the bed and a chair. Rusty noticed the movements.

"I'm here," he said dragging himself out of the chair. He was looking haggard and worn. He needed to shave. The sandy brown stubble reminded me of our time in Minnesota. It gave him an attractive outdoorsy look. He tenderly pulled the sheet up where it had shifted from my movements.

"Rusty…what's wrong?"

"Nothing, babe, it's okay."

"No, something's bothering you, whatever it is I want it, too."

"I'll talk when you're ready."

"I'm ready."

"Hon, you only stay awake a short time. I don't want to burden you with…"

"Burden? You… Rusty… you can't burden me. Wondering what's wrong is what burdens me."

He sat on the side of the bed and looked me in the eye. He looked sad but his eyes looked hopeful. "Babe, there was something I loved very deeply and it was taken from me before I knew it existed. I just keep thinking of what might have been and wishing I had a glimpse of it before it was lost to me."

I was puzzled. I still didn't understand. I couldn't even think of the right questions to ask.

"What? What was it?" I managed to say.

He couldn't answer for a few moments. "Our son, babe, we lost our son and I didn't even know until he was gone. I feel silly mourning someone I never even knew existed but I can't help it. I keep remembering all the things we did with Patrick, thinking it could have been like that. But it won't ever be. I should be thankful that you're going to be okay. And I am, more than words can say, but I'll always miss the son I never had."

Our son. The words hit me like a freight train. I couldn't process them. I could feel myself falling.

"Rusty… I'm so sorry… I didn't know."

"Shh, it's not your fault. It would have happened anyway. It just could have happened under more controlled circumstances."

It took days before I'd reasoned out his words. The doctor spelled it out in medical terms. Ectopic pregnancy. I'd lost one fallopian tube. The tube had ruptured. The surgery was messy. I was lucky, I was told. A person having a rupture under the conditions I was in should have died. An hour more on the mountain and I wouldn't have had a chance. If Strict had simply called a helicopter for a pick up, I wouldn't have made it. Only lucky timing and Strict and Landon's quick thinking got me through.

Landon brought the reminder book when he visited again and let me read the messages that revealed what had happened to me.

Patrick said, "Dear Aunt Cassidy, I wish I didn't ask you for a baby cousin. I don't need a baby cousin if it hurts you. Please get well. I miss you. Love Patrick."

And from Jesse, "Hi Sis, sending you a dose of love long distance. I'm so sorry you lost this baby. Don't worry, you'll have another chance. I can't wait. Take care of yourself. Love, Jesse."

Everybody colored a page. I sadly noted there was no page from Old Frank. After I was moved to a normal room I asked for crayons and colored a page in Old Frank's honor.

A deep sadness settled into me. A piece of me was missing, but I wasn't sure what it was. I just missed something, something I couldn't get back. How can you miss something you never knew? I thought maybe I was just depressed because the recovery seemed so long, but that wasn't it. It was nameless.

"Did you have a name for him?" I asked Rusty one day when I was almost ready to leave the hospital.

"Not really. Do you remember the little boy you were stuck in the mine with?"

"Trevor, yeah."

"When we rescued Trevor I thought if I ever had a son it would be like the feeling I got when you and Trevor came out of the mine. Out of the darkness, into the light, into life again. So the name Trevor was there in the back of my mind, except… except this time Trevor didn't make it."

Rusty mourned Trevor for a long time and I felt guilty for it. I knew he wouldn't want me to. He and I were coping in our own ways. My challenge was coping physically. I hadn't exactly made things easy on myself, pushing myself on the trail. I'd lost a lot of blood and put myself at terrible risk. The recovery was very slow. Rusty stayed sad. He tried to turn the sadness into caring for me. He made me rest and brought me things he thought I'd like. He made me eat when I didn't feel like it. My weight had plummeted alarmingly. Every time he turned around he was caring for me, but he wasn't finding peace for himself.

I asked myself the inevitable questions. Did I want a baby? No. Did I want that baby? If it were possible. If I'd have known, I'd have done anything I could to save that baby, but I didn't know, and by the time I did it was too late. I was told a pregnancy like that could never have gone full term. I knew there had been no hope for him from the very beginning so there was nothing I could have done, but I still felt guilty for Rusty's loss. I wondered what Rusty's little boy would have looked like. I wondered what Rusty's reaction would have been when I told him. I imagined Rusty playing with his very own little boy. And all the things I imagined were pleasant, things I would miss now. Was it worth it? Days on end of dirty diapers, constant attention to one little baby so I could make that come true? I didn't know.

When I went back to my doctor in Joshua Hills Rusty insisted on going along. The doctor assured me there was no reason I couldn't get pregnant again, that many women get pregnant with only one fallopian tube. He then gave me a different prescription for my birth control pills and advised me to stay home and rest for several weeks.

"Is there any reason I can't do search and rescue calls if I'm pregnant?" I asked the doctor.

"If you think you might be pregnant, or even if you just miss a period, come see me. We'll do a pregnancy test and, when it's appropriate, we'll run an ultrasound to make sure everything's fine. If everything appears normal, there's no reason why you can't go on calls the first two trimesters. The closer to your due date you get, the more you have to wonder if you want your baby born on the side of a mountain somewhere. You'll have to make choices. As far as I'm concerned, you can do anything you feel capable of, once we get you checked out."

Rusty laughed at the idea. "If it's a boy we can name him Cliff and if it's a girl we can name her Brook."

"Rusty," I reminded him, "I'm still taking the pills."

"I know, but if you ever stop, would you tell me?"

Chapter 27

When Rusty went to work I was bored stiff. I had chores I could do but I had no interest in doing them. My energy level was unpredictable. I never knew when I started a job if I'd be able to finish it. I paced the house wishing I could do more, then I'd start a job only to have to quit in the middle of it. Rusty came home to cold mop buckets in the kitchen, half sorted laundry, half the dishes washed. He always sighed and tracked me down. Usually he found me asleep on the old, brown couch, sometimes in the bay window watching the birds or the deer. I was lonely. I needed to get out. I felt useless, and I still felt incomplete somehow.

"You don't have to do all these jobs you start," Rusty told me over Chinese takeout. "The world will not end if you don't mop the kitchen floor."

"I don't do it to clean the floor. I do it to see if I can. And then I can't and I feel worse."

"Just say *no*. When you're tempted to work, just say *no*."

"I'm bored to tears."

"That maybe we can fix."

Rusty's way of fixing my boredom was to send friends to visit. Every day someone new was at my door. First it was Kelly. When Kelly came I opened the door wide.

"Hey there, Trouble! Long time no see!" he said.

"I've been out of commission," I complained.

"What in the world could put *you* out of commission?" he asked knowing I bounced back from everything life threw at me.

"Will you walk with me?" I almost cried. "I haven't been out of the house for weeks. I can't walk far but it would help if I just got out."

"Sure," Kelly said.

"Don't answer so quick," I said pocketing my 9mm. I went to the bedroom and came out with Rusty's rifle. I handed it to Kelly. He looked at the rifle, then at me. "Do you still want to go?" I asked.

"Yeah, but I want the story as we go."

So I started talking as we walked up into the junipers, but I didn't get very far. Pretty soon I was winded from walking.

"I have to get stronger," I gasped. "I need to be ready for anything and right now I can't even walk a half mile. I want to track. I want to hike into the mountains. I want to sit under a tree and let squirrels take nuts out of my hand. The mountains are calling to me and I don't have the strength to go."

"What did this to you?" Kelly asked.

"I went on a search with Landon…" The words caught in my throat but I tried to keep going. "I didn't know I was pregnant. The thought never even entered my mind." I paused, unsure how to explain it to a man. "I started having problems on the trail and I pushed myself until I found my missing person. I shouldn't have done that. I should have stopped and told Landon what was going on. He would have done something sooner but I didn't know. I had no idea how serious it was. I just knew I had a person to find and I was in pain. I can deal with pain. I can deal with things on the trail. So I dealt with that, until I collapsed." I couldn't walk anymore. I sat down on the ground for a rest. "Do you know what a tubal pregnancy is?"

He nodded.

"That's what it was. It ruptured on the trail. And I pushed myself until I'd nearly bled to death. But, Kelly, I don't think that's why it's been so hard. I can't figure it out. Something's gone. Something I can't get back. And it's gone for Rusty, too. He's had a hard time dealing with this. He mourns for his little boy. It's all my fault and there's nothing I can do to make it right. And that's what makes it rough. He tries to keep things upbeat, but he is so sad. I know seeing me well again would help him but I can't. I can't do anything. I try and I try and everything beats me."

Usually a joker, Kelly was taken aback; he didn't have a joke for this.

"Rusty didn't tell me all this. He just said you could use a visit. All that doesn't explain the rifle, though. Why are we armed?"

"Because I've got a lunatic stalker after me. He blames me because he survived a bout of trouble and everything's gone wrong since then. And it has. He isn't the same person as he was before the explosion. He is bent and acts like he is in pain. He lost his wife and his job. The explosion was his fault but he blames me for his present circumstances. When the explosion happened he was buried under a mound of dirt. He wants revenge and the only way he is going to get it is to see me squirm. Since he was buried and couldn't breathe he seems fixated on making me feel the same way. When I was in the hospital he disguised himself as a nurse, snuck in and removed the respirator tube from me. He wanted to watch me fight for breath, but when he took the tube out the machine started beeping, and the nurses came running. That was the second time he tried to kill me. So that's why we're armed and that's why I don't go out alone. I don't think I could take him on like this."

"Is there anything I can do?"

"Yeah, give me a hand up."

He got up and held out his hand. I was ashamed I had to use it. When I stood up I had to wait a bit before walking again. I looked at the hills. The hills would have to wait another day. When we turned around I realized we hadn't even gotten out of sight of the house. On the way back some coyote tracks caught my eye and I slipped into tracking mode until I got winded again. I stopped and looked around and Kelly just grinned at me.

"Now that was good to see," he said. "You didn't even know you did that, did you?"

"No, I thought I was going home."

"You walked farther tracking than you did hiking. Are you going to follow the dog?"

"It's a coyote, and no, I'd never catch him. They can see me coming from a mile away. I've tried before."

"How do you know it's a coyote?"

"Placement, size, the relative size of the toes, the way it travels. Coyotes trot everywhere. A dog walks, trots, wanders, stops. Dogs get distracted easily. Coyotes are more focused. Come on, I need to sit again. Gee, I hate this. Thanks for coming with me. I was going stir crazy in the house."

"I'm glad I came."

"Can I get you something?" I asked when we got back.

"No, but you can sit while I find something."

"It's a deal. Iced tea."

I fell asleep as he made his way around the kitchen. He waited patiently while I napped. He was sitting in a chair close by reading a book when I woke up. My iced tea was in front of me, on a coaster. The ice had melted.

"I didn't want to just disappear on you," he explained.

"I'm sorry. You could have woken me up."

"You needed the rest."

Next was Strict. He knew all the background. He was more concerned about when I would be able to track.

"I don't know, Lou, right now it feels like forever. Come walk with me. It helps to get out."

So once again I headed out into the hills. When I got winded he stopped me.

"Cassidy, you're pushing too hard."

"I have to. Look… we haven't even gone a quarter of a mile."

"Still, you're pushing too hard."

"How am I going to build back up if I can't push myself?"

"Slowly, kid. You're the only one pushing. We're all just sitting back hoping you don't go too far."

Strict wasn't helping. I went home more frustrated than I was before.

When Rusty came home I asked to go to town. I wanted a jab at the punching bag. I knew I'd only last about two minutes but I was going nuts.

"Cassidy, stop, babe. Please. What's eating at you?"

The bag swung back hitting me full in the face. Down I went.

"You distracted me," I said struggling to get up. "Damn it, there's got be *something* I can do. I can't walk. I can't do housework. I can't do anything."

"Just wait until tomorrow. I've got a surprise for you tomorrow. Today you can go out to dinner with me."

"Do I look as bad as I feel?"

"You're beautiful."

"Yeah, right."

It was good to be out in the busyness of a restaurant but even that was wearing to me. I tried to be happy and upbeat but I fell asleep on the way home and woke up in bed with the sun shining through the windows.

Rusty was right about tomorrow's surprise. My sister, Jesse, was the last person I expected at my door. Jesse took one look at me and wilted.

"Cass, I never thought I'd see you like this. I know Mom said it was bad but it's been weeks!"

"I know."

"I shouldn't have brought the kids."

"You brought the kids? That's great! Where are they?"

I looked outside and both boys had their faces plastered against the truck window. Wyatt was impatiently anxious and Patrick was hanging back. He seemed to know, this wasn't going to be a tracking visit. He looked older than his seven years, like he was trying to be strong through the worry. I was his Aunt Cassidy. Nothing could get Aunt Cassidy down. I walked out to the truck and opened the door.

"If you see bad guys in the backyard call the police from *inside* the house," I admonished Patrick. He looked sheepish but I was serious. "Thank you for the reminder book. You remembered Rusty's reminder books, didn't you?"

"If it works for Uncle Rusty I thought it would work for you, too," Patrick said.

"It helped a lot. I still have it. I'll keep it always."

"You're sure this is okay?" Jesse asked.

"I haven't been cooking. If you can live with whatever Rusty brings home it's the best thing that could have happened."

She unloaded the truck putting toys in the den, suitcases in the guestroom.

"Do the deer still come every day?" Patrick asked.

"Not every day, but frequently. I haven't seen the mountain lion again so it should be safe."

"Do the Stellars jays still come to your house?"

"If we put out peanuts. I haven't fed them for a few weeks. How long are you staying?"

"I don't know, it depends on how long you can stand us," Jesse said. "I told Rusty we could stay four days but if it's too much for you we'll go home earlier."

"No! You can't do that. Rusty really needs time with the boys."

And boy, did he. He knew what was waiting for him at home. He got off from work early. Rushing into the house, he hugged those boys until they squirmed to get loose. I was a little worried that having the boys here would make Rusty miss Trevor even more, but he dove into it with more joy than I'd seen in weeks.

"Wyatt, have you ever ridden in a police car?" Rusty asked over pizza.

He remembered Patrick's list of preferred kid food and brought home pizzas. Pepperoni for the boys. Hawaiian for me. And all meat for him. Jesse had a little of each.

"Do I hafta go to jail?" Wyatt asked.

"Uncle Rusty wouldn't let them put you in jail," Patrick assured him. "Even when we almost got arrested he didn't let them put us in jail." Then he figured out that he'd said too much and zipped his lips.

Rusty had planned the four days well. Friday morning he took the boys with him to work. I doubt he got anything done. He probably took the whole day off. They got to ride in a police car and he gave them a choice of the toy cars in his desk drawer. Wyatt brought home one of Rusty's reminder books to color in.

"So that's where you got that idea," Jesse told Patrick.

Pat showed his mom Rusty's reminder book. "Uncle Rusty has kids in his office and sometimes they need something to do, so he lets them color these books so he can remember each kid. Some of the kids don't have moms or dads, and some of them have had bad things happen to them. He looks at these books when he gets discouraged and then he goes out to catch bad guys again so kids don't have to hurt like that."

I got a lump in my throat hearing it summed up like that. Why did Patrick always do that to me, reading into a simple coloring book what was in Rusty's head?

While the boys were with Rusty, Jesse took me shopping. It was what Jesse did best. She had instructions from mom to buy what we needed. We didn't need anything so she stretched the instructions to include anything I liked. That was mom. She loved spending money on her girls. I had to be careful when I shopped with her. I gave myself a limit even though she never placed one on me.

My phone rang while we were shopping. “Make sure Jesse and the boys brought swimsuits,” Rusty said. Swimsuits?

“Okay. Do we have plans?”

“Yeah, we’re going to the beach tomorrow. Patrick can track and swimming will be good for you. Wyatt can build sand castles and Jesse can watch the guys.”

“Rusty!”

“Well, am I right?”

“Okay, yeah, you’re right.”

We shopped for swimsuits. I didn’t buy one because I had too many. Too often Rusty and I found ourselves at the beach on an unplanned trip and bought a new one. Jesse just liked shopping, so she shopped for a new swimsuit.

“This makes me look like a watermelon,” she complained.

“Maybe something without green vertical stripes would be better,” I conceded.

“Here try this on,” she said.

“I’m not buying it,” I told her. “I’ve got enough.”

“It can’t hurt to try it on.”

When I tried it on she sniffed at me, “It’s no fair. You take anything off the rack and put it on and you look like a model for it. I look and look and end up thinking of myself as a watermelon.”

“Try red Hawaiian flowers instead of green stripes.”

“Now I look like a spoiled tomato.”

“Are you hungry? You keep comparing yourself to food.”

“No, food is just what makes me not like swimsuits.”

“Not spoiled tomatoes. If you brought one, why look for another?”

“Because mine makes me look like a Thanksgiving turkey.”

I laughed. “Okay, here’s my method. Stay in the dressing room and I’ll bring you one of each. Make three piles: a *yes*, a *maybe*, and a *no* pile. When I come with more swimsuits hand me the *no* pile and we’ll just go through the whole bunch.”

“That’s your shopping method?”

“Usually, well for things I’m not used to buying. Jeans and tops I can just buy a five or seven but dresses and swimsuits and stuff like that I use this method.”

Jesse tried on every swimsuit in the store in her size and her *yes* pile was very small. She tried on the two she thought she liked best and I chose the one I thought James would like and she chose the other one because she thought it was more like what a mom would wear to the beach.

"Who cares what a mom would wear? Just because you're a mom doesn't mean you suddenly quit being a sex goddess."

"Cassidy! Maybe you could wear a sexy swimsuit. You've got the body for it. I could never..."

"You like them both. So would you rather look like a mom at the beach or like a woman having a great time at the beach?"

"Cassidy, I swear. Mom would never approve of this."

"When do you go to the beach with Mom?"

She held up the two swimsuits she looked at one with a grumpy expression and went *hmm*. She looked at the other one with raised eyebrows and went *HMM*. I laughed. It felt good to laugh.

I had to stop after each store. Even walking a store wore me out. I sat down outside a department store while Jesse made the rounds of the perfume counter. I watched the people like I always did, watching them make invisible footprints, watching for the odd man out. Anybody acting strangely. Invisible tracking.

No shoplifters in my corridor today. No purse-snatchers. Only, oh hell. I looked away, thought for a minute, nervously. I shouldn't be by myself. There's safety in numbers, especially when I felt like this. I pretended not to notice Dirk standing behind a pillar watching me. I wandered into the store, found Jesse, and then asked the woman at the counter to call security. I watched the pillar out of the corner of my eye. When a uniform approached I explained there was a man wanted for attempted murder, last seen behind the pillar.

"He's tall and bent. Wearing jeans, a long sleeve shirt. Blue. He's got dark brown hair, dark brown eyes, light brown leather deck shoes. Wear point on the tip of his left shoe and the inside of both heels. He's carrying a bag and may be armed."

They looked at me weird when I described the bottoms of his shoes.

"I'm a tracker. I know how the guy walks. I know where those wear spots are."

"Yeah, right," they said to themselves as they wandered toward the pillar. When Dirk wasn't there anymore they made their way down the mall watching for a man like I had described.

"Shoot," I said. "I thought I'd gotten lucky." Then to Jesse, "We'd better go."

"Why? We're just getting started!"

"No we're not. We need to leave this place and when we leave you'll follow my instructions to the letter."

"Why?"

"Because we might be followed and if we're followed I want you to know what to do. If we're not followed, we can go to another store. I want to get molds for building sandcastles. Do you surf?"

"Ha! Me surf? I barely ride a horse anymore. Do you?"

"I'm learning. I don't actually surf yet. I mostly stay out of the way of the real surfers and try to read the waves right. It takes practice. Cody is teaching me when we go to San Diego, but I try his patience."

"You are the luckiest girl in the state," she sighed. "Being married to Rusty and having Cody for a brother-in-law. I can't wait to go to the beach. I've never seen Rusty in swim trunks before!"

"Jesse!"

"What? You don't like me watching your husband? Everybody else at the beach is watching him."

"I guess I'm just surprised you admit it. Okay, I'm going to watch our tail and, if I tell you what to do, follow my instructions."

"You've been around cops too much."

"No, I've been followed too much."

In a way I was hoping we *would* be followed so I could get a car description and license plate number. When no tail showed I sighed and told Jesse she could drive to another store. I thought today was going relatively smoothly considering it was me and I was going shopping. The two usually spelled trouble and I was in no shape for trouble.

We managed to find a big plastic pail of sand toys. I added a beach ball and two plastic swim rings to the cart.

"How good can the boys swim?" I asked.

"They've never seen enough water to learn."

"They can't swim?"

"Where would they learn?"

"Jesse, you know how to swim. Where did you learn to swim?"

"We had lessons at a swimming pool in town. Remember?"

"Oh yeah. So the boys don't know how to swim yet? Should we get them life preservers instead of swim rings?"

"Patrick wouldn't be caught dead in one. He'll want to learn how to swim without one. Wyatt would love one."

There they were again, Patrick taking after me, Wyatt taking after Jesse. I put the swim rings back and bought two life preservers. Even if we only used one I needed to treat the boys equally. I got Patrick one with sharks on it so it would look cool and I got one for Wyatt with beach balls and sun graphics because he was more of a kid. Even though I expected Pat to refuse to use his I hoped he would. The ocean was no place to learn how to swim.

After stocking up on beach toys I was beat. I needed to go home and nap. Jesse planned a dinner and called Rusty.

"The boys asked for hamburgers," he said.

"They always ask for hamburgers. They can't live on fast food."

"Four days won't kill them."

"No, but it'll spoil them."

"Not if it's just their Uncle Rusty doing it. They aren't going to expect you to suddenly turn into a junk food junkie. Make a salad if you want vegetables."

"I swear, that man is impossible," Jesse said hanging up.

"Give him a break. It's the first time I've seen him smile in a month," I called from the bedroom.

"It is?" Jesse asked as she sat down on the side of the bed. "He's taking this miscarriage harder than you."

"He's always wanted kids. He lost a kid. He didn't get a chance to meet him but he knows what it could have been like. He's mourned ever since he found out what happened. And he knew long before I did. He spent days sitting in my room thinking about it with no one to talk to. To me the hard part is just getting well. I know that seems kind of backwards. Usually it's the mom who knows, who goes through the feelings. He needs this time with the boys. I think he wanted me to see what it was like having kids in the house again and he's trying to make it fun for me. He knows me too good. It's going to work, just wait and see."

"What would you have named him?"

"I hadn't really thought about it. We call him Trevor after a little boy I rescued from a mine cave in but that's not what we would have named him."

"Would you stick to the tradition?"

"Not for Dad. If there was an old west name that worked, we'd go with it, but if not we wouldn't feel obligated to stick to his 'tradition'. Knowing me our boy would probably be named Otto because he was born in the car."

"You've got to be kidding. Otto? Would you really name a little baby Otto?"

"It was a joke. Now let me rest or I'll be in no shape to enjoy dinner. What is it?"

"Hamburgers."

"Oh, goodie."

Rusty arrived home with Wyatt on his shoulders.

"Duck!" he said as he approached the front door.

"What?"

"Duck," Rusty repeated. Wyatt still wouldn't fit under the door jam.

"Duck, duck, goose!" Patrick said. He swatted Rusty on the rear and ran under his legs and through the front door. Rusty ducked, too, and with both of them ducking they fit through the doorway.

"We got hamburgers and French fries and onion rings. Onion rings are vegetables and ketchup is tomatoes and pickles are cucumbers and there's lettuce and tomatoes on the hamburgers, too," Patrick announced.

"And mustard is a weed, so it's a vegetable, too," added Wyatt.

"And I suppose soda is a vegetable, too?" Jesse added.

"No, it's almost all sugar but that gives people energy," Patrick said.

"Oh, I see," Jesse said disapprovingly. I hoped Jesse seeing Rusty in swim trunks would make up for his food choices.

"I got to ride shotgun in a police car," Wyatt told his mom. "I didn't get a shotgun, though."

"Well, that's good. You're not old enough for a shotgun."

Patrick added, "I got to see Mr. Schroeder and Officer Thompson and Officer Jankowski. Mr. Schroeder tells good stories. You didn't tell me you had a motorcycle! We picked it up. It's cool! Can I ride it?"

"You picked up the bike? From the station or from the shop?"

"The shop, they fixed the tire, gas tank and starter. They wanted to know how you messed it up that much after only 200 miles. They thought I had a hell of a teenager. They were even more puzzled when I said it was my wife's."

I explained to Patrick, "You can't ride it unless we get you a helmet and you have to let an adult drive."

"Aww, rats."

"When you're old enough to have a license we'll teach you how to ride one," Jesse said.

"You will? My mom knows how to ride a motorcycle? My mom? My scrapbooking mom?"

"What's so odd about that?" Jesse said. "I learned when I was a kid."

"How come you never ride one?" Patrick asked. "If I could ride one I would ride it every day. I could get to the deer flats in five minutes."

"And scare all the deer away in two seconds," I reminded him. "It's still better to ride horses or walk there if you want to stalk deer."

The next day we packed up towels and beach toys, life preservers, and the surfboard.

"Wow! Aunt Cassidy! Are you a surfer like Uncle Cody?" Patrick asked.

"Not quite. I haven't learned how to stand up on it yet. It's kind of tricky."

"You will do it! You're good at everything."

"Thanks Patrick, but I don't get to practice very much."

We all piled into the Explorer and Rusty pulled out onto Lost Hills Road. Before we even got to the freeway Wyatt asked, "Are we there yet?"

"No!" said Patrick exasperated. "It's four hours."

"We're not going to that beach. We're going to a closer one," I told Patrick. "It's only two hours away."

"We're not going to Cody's beach?"

I laughed. Mission Beach *was* just about Cody's beach. Everyone there knew him, locals and tourists alike. But we weren't going to Mission Beach.

"No, it's too far for a one day trip."

"We could stay two days! Then Mom and Wyatt could visit Bill and Bev and Cody and Chase."

"We can't be gone two days. Uncle Rusty has to work."

"Aww, rats."

Fifteen minutes later Wyatt asked, "Are we there yet?"

Rusty smiled, glad for the kid chatter. "When we park, we'll be there," he said.

"When will we park?"

"When we get there."

"When will we get there?"

"When we park."

"But…"

"Wyatt! Let's play a game," suggested Jesse. "Let's play car Bingo. That's something even Wyatt can play. The first person to spot a dump truck, yell bingo!"

"I can't see the other cars," complained Wyatt.

"You can see them good enough to spot a dump truck," Jesse told him.

We drove and drove and never did see a dump truck. I could have sworn there was always a dump truck on I-14, and for sure on the 405. We pulled into the parking lot and parked. We all jumped out and Wyatt yelled, "Bingo!"

Sure enough, a dump truck was parked in the parking lot.

"Good job, Wyatt!" gushed Jesse. "You won the game!"

"What did I win?" Wyatt asked.

"The game!" Jesse answered.

"But what do I get?"

"You get to be Bingo champion for the day."

Patrick looked like all these games were for little kids. He was ready to get down to business.

Rusty grinned from ear to ear as he led his little troop down to the beach. He carried my surfboard under one arm and an ice chest full of drinks with the other. We all gathered up the beach toys and towels and followed him. Rusty staked out a spot and then ran back and took the basket of sand toys from me.

Jesse slathered sunscreen on the boys. Patrick fought it, because sunscreen was for sissies. Wyatt put up with it grudgingly. He was ready to play in the sand. Jesse settled down on a beach blanket to watch Rusty. I wanted to swim but I tracked with Patrick first just to humor him.

"Tell me what kind of person made the tracks. Following them is easy in this sand, so go a step further. Is it a man or a woman? Big or small?"

He tracked along happily describing the people to me. He was incredibly accurate, though I think he was only basing his guesses on the size of the tracks.

"And this man has been hurt. One of his feet drags when he walks. It's hard for him to walk in this deep sand. I bet he heads for harder ground." Patrick was right. The man found firmer ground and stopped there for a while.

"What do you think he is doing?" I asked.

"He is just watching people and resting. Then he goes back up the beach the way he came."

We followed the man's tracks and he went past our picnic spot and stopped again. We never did spot the man but Patrick did well profiling him. We went back to the beach blanket and I sat to rest. Just walking up and down the beach had taxed me.

"Pat, how would you hide your tracks in all this sand?" I asked.

"Can't. They show up too easily."

"You can't hide them completely but you can keep them from being identified as yours. There are ways, so think about it for a little while."

When I was rested again I headed for the water, surfboard under my arm. I was always amazed how the long, bulky things were so easy to carry. Once they were balanced they just kind of hung there. Rusty trotted after me. He took the board from me and stayed with me while I paddled out to a waiting spot.

"You sure you're okay out here?" he asked.

"Yeah, it doesn't take a lot of energy to sit here and wait for a wave."

"Don't try standing yet. Just work on timing and use your tether. You need to keep your board close. It's a good resting place if you run out of energy."

"I know. I won't be out long. Go play with the boys. And don't tell Patrick about the fish and sharks. He'll either be scared to get in the water with them or want to learn scuba diving before he can even swim."

Little laugh lines appeared as he tread water beside me.

"Be careful," he said before giving me a light kiss and swimming away. It was a slow day at the beach as far as surfing went. It didn't help that I picked an out of the way place to practice. Surfers tended to be territorial and I didn't want to invade their space. In San Diego I got more practice because I had Cody watching out for me. He was my ticket to the good waves. Here, I was on my own. I had a long rest on the board before I finally caught a wave headed the right direction. I paddled into position. I could hear Cody's voice in my head, coaching me. Line it up, find the crest, when the timing is right… right… GO! GO! Go for it! Yeah! I rode the wave in, jubilant, then turned around and paddled out to deeper water again. I was winded by the time I reached my waiting spot. I stretched out on the board, catching my breath.

There were a lot of swimmers out that day. People bobbed around in the water. Kids were snorkeling and boogie boarding closer to shore. Parents guided toddlers along the surf line, lifting them out of the water when the wave was too deep. Rusty waded around with Patrick. A wave swept over him and Pat braced for the cold, jumping and letting the wave carry him towards shore. Rusty stood over him ready to help when Patrick went too far.

Another wave came my direction and I went through the motions again, knowing I had to do it many more times to get the feel. The rush riding the wave down was amazing and tiring at the same time. I couldn't do this many more times before I'd have to go rest. The wave broke over me and, like usual, I got dumped off my board. Holding my breath I waited for things to calm down, then popped to the surface. Winded, I held onto the board and rested. I was drifting in close to shore so I paddled out again. Each time I paddled I had to rest longer. I couldn't even climb onto the board when I reached deep water again. I had to just hang on and wait for more energy. While I was waiting I looked to shore. Rusty was watching me, concerned I hadn't climbed onto my board. I tried again and he went back to playing with Patrick. Deeper and deeper they went until Pat finally accepted a piggyback ride.

I pushed against the board trying to get it under me and balanced when suddenly something grabbed me and dragged me down from below. I gasped for breath before the water closed around my head. I thrashed around, trying to escape. Hands pushed my head down, down. Hands! It was a person! This calmed me in a way. It gave me options. First I tried for the eyes and my hands met a mask. I pulled at the mask and my assailant struggled back. I tried for the groin but in the water I couldn't get a good thrust going. My strength was draining. My side ached from the unexpected movement. I had to do something fast! I grabbed the tether for my surfboard and pulled, pulled until the board was right overhead, then I yanked hard pulling the end of the board down into my captor's face. *Bam! Bam! Bam! BAM!* Right into his face. My lungs burned! I had to breathe but I forced myself to wait. I pulled again on the tether, hard, driving the board between us. It wouldn't go far. It was designed to float and this time when it rose the tip ripped the mask off my attacker. I big bubble of air burst to the surface. He let go of me groping for the mask, trying to get things back in control. I pushed away and frantically swam toward the beach. When my head broke the surface I coughed and sputtered and swam, the surfboard scooting along behind me. I swam until my fingers scraped mud and then I staggered through the surf to safety. Ground. Nice firm ground. And air. I sat heavily in the hot sand watching for my attacker, exhausted.

I looked for Rusty. He was standing in the surf, Patrick on his back, watching the water. He waded to shore and sent Patrick to stay with Jesse. He was worried. I stood shakily and gathered up the surfboard, found the balance point and started walking. Rusty was just about to swim out to my waiting spot when he spotted me walking down the beach. He jogged towards me. He took the surfboard from me and was going to jog with it back over to Jesse when he realized it was still attached to my ankle.

"What happened?"

"Just let me sit down."

"Cass, what happened?"

"Dirk's still mad at me."

When I finally got to the blanket I told Patrick, "If you see the man who drags his foot, tell Uncle Rusty quick." Then to Rusty I said, "I can't believe it. Patrick and I tracked Dirk and I didn't even notice. I'm slipping. I should have known it was him. I should have noticed a tail."

"Want to see how I hid my tracks?" Patrick asked.

"In a minute. Let me rest first."

"What happened?" Rusty wasn't going to be content until he got the whole story.

"He waited until I was tired. I was trying to seat my board but I was having trouble climbing up. He yanked me under water and held me under."

"How do you know it was him?"

"I guess I don't, but it fits his MO. He wants to see me suffocate. He said so and he tried it once before in the hospital."

"What's a MO?" Patrick asked.

"A method of operation. It's the way a bad guy chooses to act."

"Is that a police code?"

"No, it's just an acronym."

"How did you get away?" Jesse asked. I was glad it was her. I could abbreviate my explanation to her.

"Surfboards make good battering rams. I hope I didn't break it."

"That's my sister for you, always using what comes to hand. If you hadn't had the surfboard you'd have grabbed a fish and beat him with that," Jesse said. Patrick laughed at the mental picture.

Wyatt said, "A fish? Where would she get a fish?"

"In the water?" Jesse said.

"There's fish in the water?" Wyatt asked, alarmed.

"Of course there's fish in the water. Fish live in the water. But they don't like people. They swim away if you get close."

"How big are they?" Wyatt asked.

Jesse was catching on slowly. "Oh, they are only little," she said.

Wyatt wasn't to be conned though. "Where do the big fish live? Where do whales live?"

"They live waaaay out there in the deep, deep water, not up here where people swim."

"Where do sharks live?"

The questions went on and on and I was glad to let them. I didn't want to think about Dirk and drowning. I wanted Rusty to forget it and have a fun day. I made sure there was an adult with the boys at all times and I rested. After a while I noticed security patrols frequented the area and wondered if Rusty had called in the incident.

"Want to see how I hid my tracks?" Patrick asked again.

"Of course I do," I answered. "Show me."

"I'll show you the first one and then you gotta track me," he said.

"Okay."

He led me to a single track and pointed it out. It was definitely Patrick's track. I looked for the next one. He was clever, that kid was. I had to give him credit. His next track he'd used another person's footprint. He knew his small tracks would show up inside a big print so he only put pressure on the outside edge of his foot and matched the line of his footprint to the one already in the sand. The next footprint was too far away for him to reach so he had to use another footprint that was pointed in a different direction. Patiently and very carefully he had zigzagged his way over a multitude of other people's tracks. At one point he took three careful steps down a length of seaweed washed up onto the shore.

"Pat! You did a great job! That was really good thinking. I bet Uncle Rusty couldn't track you."

He looked disappointed. "But you could," he said.

He needed a boost. "Only because you'd told me you'd hid them. If I was just looking for a trail of Patrick tracks I never would have seen them."

"Really?"

"Really."

"Could I have tricked Chase?"

"I don't know. Chase is used to me hiding my tracks. He probably expects you to, too."

"I'll have to practice at home and see if I can trick Elan!" he said excitedly. Mission accomplished. Patrick was now thinking about what his own feet told people.

Rusty was on alert now. He was watching people, suspicious. It saddened me. I wanted him to have fun. He planned this day to play with the kids. So… I determined I'd have fun with the kids. I had tracked with Patrick, so next it was Wyatt's turn.

"Wyatt, do you want to swim?"

"No, I don't want to go with the fishes."

"The fishes stay away. I went in the deep water and I didn't see any fishes. I tell you what, we'll just put our toes in and if you see any fishes just tell me and I'll lift you out of the water."

"Why does the water turn white when it gets to the sand?"

"Because it's busy. Have you ever put water in a jar and shaken it up real hard? It looks white while all the particles are mixing up and there is lots of air in it. Then when the water settles down the white goes away. The ocean is the same."

He shied away from the water when we got close. It took some time just to get his toes wet and even then it happened accidentally.

"Do you see any fishes out there?" I asked.

"No, they're hiding."

"Do you see any place for them to hide?"

"No."

"That's because the hiding places are in deeper water. It is nice and open and sandy here so the fish are a long ways away."

Wyatt tried my patience but I was glad to have some time to actually talk with this, normally silent, nephew of mine.

"I'll pick you up and you look in the water. If you see any fishes, let me know."

He reached up to be held so I picked him up and waded out about knee deep. Every few minutes I'd ask him if he saw fishes. I held him over the water so he could get a good look. When I waded deeper he clutched me tighter. He worried when his feet dangled in the water but no little fishes nibbled on his toes.

"See the people swimming? They aren't scared of fishes."

I spent half the afternoon easing Wyatt into the water. I didn't think we made much progress in the water department but I'd made progress with Wyatt. He knew me better by the end of the day. He talked more than I had ever heard him talk in his life.

Watching me with Wyatt calmed Rusty's frazzled nerves. By the time Wyatt and I waded out of the water and made our way up to the beach blanket Rusty was laid back, soaking up the sun.

"Still got your toes?" Rusty asked as I walked up.

"Yup, the fishes didn't even touch us."

"How do you put things behind you so fast? Most people wouldn't have gone near the water after being pulled under like that."

"I'd even go out and try a couple more waves. In fact, I think I should. If Dirk is somewhere watching I'd like to show him he can't scare me."

"It would just make him double his efforts. Don't tempt him."

"Uncle Rusty? The man at that booth might know about that bad man," Patrick said.

"What man at what booth?" Rusty asked.

"That one," Pat said pointing.

"Why would the man there know anything?"

"I went back and I followed the tracks of the man who dragged his foot when he walked. His tracks go up to that booth and then they go around it. It's cement around it but people have tracked in enough dirt you can still see he drags his foot. He took something from over there and went away to the parking lot or something. I couldn't follow him because Mom would get mad and there's not enough sand in the parking lot. But maybe that man knows something."

"Aunt Cassidy? Do you have a piece of cardboard and some string?" Wyatt asked.

"I'm sure we can come up with a piece of cardboard. I don't know where you're going to find string on the beach. What do you need it for?"

"My sand castle needs a drawbridge."

There you go again, I thought. The two boys were like night and day. One off tracking a violent criminal, the other making elaborate sandcastles, carving windows and doors, and digging a moat. Two completely different personalities, just like Jesse and I had been growing up.

Rusty climbed the slight rise to the booth. I looked for a piece of cardboard and a string. It seemed strange that the request of a five year old boy seemed as important as an attempted murder charge. Nevertheless, I looked and I found a piece of cardboard that we cut to size and I lent Wyatt a shoe lace to complete his project. He looked his castle over.

"Aunt Cassidy? Can I go over to that hamburger stand?"

"Wyatt!" Jesse scolded. "You don't ask Cassidy for things like that. If you want a sandwich you'll have to wait and eat lunch with the rest of us."

Wyatt hung his head. "But I don't want a hamburger. I only want to go over there and look for something."

"I'll go with him," I offered.

Wyatt happily scampered over to the stand and began looking around on the ground. He picked up one thing and carried it around. He found two more, compared them, then saw another under the wheel of the cart. He worked it loose and compared the four. He chose the best three and found a trashcan to throw his discard in.

"What are you looking for Wyatt?"

"I saw people walking away from that stand with little flags stuck in their hamburgers and they were just throwing them away. I wanted flags for my castle. See? I have three towers and now I can add flags to it."

"That was very observant for you to notice that. They'll look great on your castle."

"Oh look," he said. "Somebody lost it, but it's broke. It'll work better than string." He bent down and picked up a broken necklace chain. It was cheap and useless, except as a chain for a drawbridge on a sandcastle. He ran back and added the finishing touches.

"Mom! Look! I finished it!" Wyatt announced.

"Wyatt! That's a wonderful sandcastle and look how you dressed it up! You're so creative."

Wyatt beamed as Jesse took a picture of his creation. Then she took one of him sitting next to it. Just like his mom, I thought. My mom had countless pictures of Jesse holding up some completed project or modeling a new dress. Her pictures of me were snuck while I was in the barn, doing chores, working with the horses. I was never looking at the camera. I was always focused on a task.

Patrick looked smug as Rusty came back. "Good call, buddy. The guy didn't even know his scuba gear was missing but he remembered talking to a guy that matched Dirk's description." That was all the praise Patrick needed. He'd been right and now he knew it. He was happy.

The day was wearing on me. It was a good one though. I'd been more active than I had been in weeks. I fell asleep curled up on the beach blanket and I woke up with an umbrella over me and Wyatt asleep beside me. Rusty and Jesse were talking quietly.

"…she's not against the idea. She's just not ready to settle down."

"If she doesn't settle down one of these trouble bouts is going to kill her." Jesse said. "She tries to make light of it so I won't worry. But this was too close. She could have drowned out there and we wouldn't have known a thing until somebody found an empty surfboard. Do you think it's good for her to learn how to surf?"

"It can't hurt. At least the landing's soft. I can't stop her from trying. Besides, have you seen the look in her eyes when she tackles something new? There's real joy there. I can't take away anything that brings her joy. And she'll learn. As soon as she recovers from the surgery she'll be back out there pushing herself to stand on the board."

"Why can't she find a nice, *normal* hobby?"

"She did. You have to be around law enforcement to see it. We see a lot of reserve officers who are basically hobby cops. They go out when they want to see some action. Cassidy isn't like that. She goes when they call. She goes no matter what it costs her. That's why she ended up in CCU. She didn't know she was going through a serious medical condition. A person was lost. No questions asked. She had to find them. She won't turn down a call and that is what makes the idea of parenthood hard for her. She'd be torn between two worlds."

I was still feeling lazy and I was wondering what else I was going to learn about myself so I lay still.

"How can a woman not know she is pregnant? How far along was she?" Jesse asked.

"Ten weeks."

"She should at least have had morning sickness. If she gets pregnant and never has morning sickness I am going to be so jealous!"

"No you won't. She's gone through that and more. Count your lucky stars you've never seen what she's been through. Just watching it… even when I can't see it, like today. It was so close and we didn't know a thing was going on. What would I do? All I'd have left is minutes, treasured minutes."

"Minutes?"

"Cassidy didn't want to marry me. She said it wouldn't be fair to bring trouble on me like she'd been through. I didn't know what to say. I was dying inside. I wanted anything she'd give me. Minutes. Even just minutes. So the good times we call our treasured minutes… and they're adding up. She's given me so many treasured minutes. Like the joy in her eyes when she tries to surf. If I can see that again I'll be a happy man."

"Just wait until she finally does get pregnant. You catch the look in her eyes when they plop that wet, wriggly, pink, wrinkled, little baby on her chest and you'll know. She'll be ready."

"I hope so."

"And hey, there's no hurry. You haven't been married long."

"I'm an old man at the station. There's so many guys there in their twenties who already have kids. I'm really going to get teased if it ever really happens. They're going to call me grandpa."

"Grandpas are old. You're not old," put in Patrick.

"Thank you, Patrick. I don't really care when it happens. I just wish I could know if it will. I can live with the idea of not having kids, but if that's the way it's going to be I'd like to get into that mindset. Instead, every time the subject of kids comes up Cass feels pressured and things get awkward."

"Did you know she called me while she was babysitting that one year old?" Jesse laughed. "She'd gone through two thirds of a package of baby wipes to change two diapers. She didn't know what to do with the kid. He was fighting sleep and she had no experience. I could sympathize but there wasn't much I could do long distance."

"She really never even baby sat as a teenager?"

"No. She didn't need to. Dad kept her working the horses. She had a gift for it. Some of our winners are due to Cassidy's work. To dad Cassidy was a son and she took to it. It was like she was the brother and I was the sister."

"You know, I could be really mad at your dad if I let myself. Not that I expect Cass to be a baby expert. But to force her into the role of a boy just because she didn't fit the plan was unfair to her. She'd have learned all the ranch work on her own just because she's a worker, likes to be outdoors, and likes horses. But to make her live up to Steve's example when she was just a kid. It was unfair."

"You know what Cass does when life throws her a curve ball? She catches it and figures out how to make use of that ball and when she throws it back whoever threw it better watch out. Dad got what he had coming to him. Cass rejected the ranch life. She joined the Marines just like a parent should be proud of their sons doing and she made her own life."

"And her life is still curving. She's still fighting to be herself. She just seems to hope the curve doesn't end in total normality. I don't think it will. But I don't know what to expect either."

Was that what I was doing? I didn't feel like it, although much of my life did feel like a rebellion of sorts. Rusty crawled over to me.

"Cass? Hon, it's getting late. We need to pack up."

"One more time," I said.

"One more what?"

"One more wave."

"We'll be all wet for the ride home. We need to stop and eat dinner."

I didn't want to go. I'd been outdoors and more active than I had been in weeks. I wasn't totally bored and exhausted. I wanted to take advantage of it. "Okay," he finally said. "If I can go with you. I don't trust Dirk."

As I paddled out I was thinking through this ride. My mistake so far in standing on the board was standing too far forward. The tip of the board would dig into the water and toss me off. So… this time I needed to come to a stand farther back on the board. What would happen if I stood too far back? The tip would rise. And what happened when the tip rose? I didn't know but I was about to find out. All the other surfers had gone home so I didn't have to wait long for a wave. The first one I got wasn't a particularly big one but I got into position.

Wait, wait, feel the swell. Keep with it. I felt for the time, just the right time, where was it? There… there! The board started down the wave. I pushed up, brought my feet under me. Back, not forward, the board felt unsteady. I found a balance spot thinking it would dump me over the side but it didn't. Shakily I rose to a crouched position, hands out for balance. The board shook under my feet. Balance wasn't quite sure but… I did it! I did it! Once.

All I did was ride the wave down but I was jubilant. Rusty swam after me and clasped me in a hug when he caught up to me. His eyes were laughing as he scolded me, "I told you not to try standing until you were healed up." We hung on the board just grinning at each other. "I knew this day would come. I was waiting for it. I hoped I'd be there when you did it." And when he said it I knew why he wanted kids. So many shared firsts. So many treasured minutes. I'd give anything to see Rusty like this. "Come on, let's go find a restaurant that doesn't care what we look like and celebrate."

"But I can't quit now! I'll lose it!"

"You won't lose it. You learned something from it. You'll get dumped in the ocean again no matter how good you get but you won't lose it. Not you. You'll remember the foot placement."

I hoped he was right. I decided it was more important to emerge from the sea victorious.

When we got back to the beach Wyatt was jumping up and down in his excitement.

"Aunt Cassidy is a real surfer now! Can I try? Can I try?"

"First you have to learn how to swim. Then you have to learn how to swim with the fishes. When you can swim with the fishes you can learn how to surf."

"Oh goodie! Can I swim with the fishes? Now?"

"Swimming takes practice. You'll have to spend time learning. You can't learn it all in one day."

"Can I swim with the fishes just a little bit?"

I wasn't going to make him sit in a stuffy restaurant when he wanted to swim with the fishes. Rusty sighed and went to the hamburger stand. I put the life preserver on Wyatt and led him to the water. I held him and waded out until I was waist deep and the surf wouldn't wash over Wyatt as he tried to swim.

"Do you see any fishes?" I asked.

"No, they're hiding in the deep water."

"Right. Now I'm going to put you in the water. The vest will make it so you float. Ready?"

I set him down and his eyes got big. He wriggled around feeling the water around him. I stepped a few steps away. "Point your body toward me and kick with your feet," I instructed. "Have you seen scuba divers on TV? Point your toes like flippers and kick."

He reached for me and kicked his feet. He barely moved but he made progress. When he'd kicked his way all two feet toward me I pulled him up.

"Good job! This time I want you to kick with your feet and push the water towards your feet with your hands. There's two ways to do that. Can I set you down while I show you?"

And so we spent another half hour with Wyatt learning how to swim with the fishes. I always knew, if kids had a good reason to learn, they could learn anything. All they needed was a good reason, so when a good reason came up you had to be ready to take advantage of it. Wyatt emerged from his little swimming lesson ready for more.

"I swam with the fishes!" He told his mom as he ran up the beach, "They stayed away because they were scared of us."

He stood on my surfboard acting like a surfer. Patrick tracked the beach close by. We all dried out and brushed off and headed for the nearest restaurant.

"Mom, can I have a corndog?" Patrick asked.

"There's all these good things on the menu and you want a corndog? There's shrimp and scallops and fish and even shark and you want a corndog?"

"There's shark? We could eat a shark?" Wyatt asked excitedly.

"You can have whatever you want," Rusty said.

"I want a shark!" Wyatt exclaimed.

"That's an adult meal. You can't eat that much," Jesse said.

"But Uncle Rusty…"

"He can have shark if he wants shark. Have you told him what calamari is yet?" Rusty said.

"Don't you dare," Jesse said.

When the orders were taken Patrick ordered a corndog and Wyatt ordered shark. I ordered Manhattan clam chowder because I'd been to this place before and I knew the Manhattan clam chowder was an educational experience for the boys. Rusty ordered an appetizer knowing he'd end up eating most of Wyatt's shark.

When the food arrived I laughed because Wyatt jumped down from his chair and hid behind his mom. Smack dab in the middle of my bowl was a large, whole crab.

"Wyatt, come here. It's dead. Patrick, come look."

"What is it?" Wyatt asked.

"It's just a crab," Patrick answered annoyed with his brother's caution.

"Pat, next time we go to the beach we'll have to watch for crabs and track them. They walk sideways. See their feet? I bet the tracks are interesting, little sideways scratch marks. Do you want the claw?" I said lifting the claw hand of the crab. Wyatt shivered and Patrick said, “Cool! Can I have it?”

“Don’t tease your brother with it,” I admonished him as I broke it off.

He stood there making the claw open and close. Wyatt snuck around and peeked over his brother’s shoulder.

“Where do crabs live?” Wyatt asked.

“In the water with the fishes, but some of them come on land. Sometimes we see them on the beach.”

“I swam with crabs?”

“Yeah, but they stay away from people, too.”

I pulled the meat out of the crab’s leg and handed some to Wyatt.

“Ewe! That’s crab muscles!”

“Yeah, eat it.”

“Eat it? I’m not eating crab muscles!”

I laughed at him knowing he was gung ho about eating shark muscles, he just didn’t know it. I ate my crab muscles and enjoyed it. Wyatt watched me cautiously as I cracked open the crab and added the meat to my chowder.

“Shark is weird,” Wyatt announced. “It’s not like fish and it’s not like animals.”

“Do you like it?” Jesse asked.

“I guess. I’m mostly eating it to freak out Dad. He’s going to think it’s gross to eat a shark.”

I thought I better call James and warn him to act appropriately grossed out.

“Aunt Cassidy? What kind of tracks would a seal make?” Patrick asked.

“Well, you know they don’t have paws so the tracks are going to look very different from the animals you are used to. Imagine them when they move. They push with their flippers and they push with their back ends. So the tracks would look like a drag mark with flipper pushes next to it.”

“Cassidy, how do you stand all the questions? He drives me nuts with his questions.”

“He asks good questions. It tells me he is thinking. I’d be more worried if he *didn’t* ask questions.”

“When they pull with their flippers they push with their tails,” Pat said after giving it more thought.

“You’re right, so what do you think a tail push looks like?”

“I’m full,” announced Wyatt.

Jesse looked annoyed but Rusty jumped in, “Did you eat some veggies?”

“I ate some.”

“Good job, are you sure you’re full?”

“Yeah, I’m stuffed.”

“Can I try it? I’ve never tried shark before.”

Wyatt handed over his plate and sat watching me eat crab muscles and soup, while Rusty finished off the shark.

The trip home was very quiet. After a few questions from Patrick the boys got tired and fell asleep and the darkness settled in. Rusty carried Wyatt into the house and put him to bed on the couch in the den. He went back for Patrick but Pat had been conditioned. One touch and he was awake and alert.

"Elan has a saying, 'your ears can sleep while your eyes are awake. While your eyes are asleep your ears stand guard,'" he told us. "He makes me tell time with my eyes closed. I have to guess where the sun is. Or if it's night I have to figure it out by the amount of light. He says each stage of the night or day have different feelings to them."

Jesse thought it was very odd but it made sense to me. Awake or not Patrick was ready for bed. He found his bed in the den and plopped down tiredly.

"I don't know about you but to me today was glorious!" I said, stretching. The incision pulled and the muscles complained but all in all I felt much better than I had the day before.

"You almost died and it was a glorious day?" Jesse said.

"Two very bad minutes don't ruin a glorious day. It was still wonderful. I love the beach. I could rest when I needed to and play when I wanted to. I haven't felt that well in weeks."

The bed shook and I jerked awake. Was it a dream? I was tired of being alert all the time. When it was just wariness I didn't mind so much but this wariness was different. I was tired of trouble. The bed shook again and I realized it was Rusty. Oh, Rusty. He only had nightmares when he was really worried. Sometimes nightmares stemmed from things he imagined could happen to me and sometimes it was an old hurt. Sometimes my trouble brought the old nightmare back but he hadn't had that one in a long time.

I wasn't sure it was safe to wake him. I knelt on the bed ready to jump out of the way. There was only a few seconds in there between sleep and reality where I had to be careful but I'd learned the hard way that those few seconds came rather quickly. This wasn't one of those times. I shook him gently and he was awake in an instant, eyes wide, breathing quick. He just looked at me and knew. The fear faded and relief came over him. We're okay, his look said. We're okay and at home and she's here and she's whole. Everything's okay. I lay back down beside him.

"I don't know what it feels like to not be able to breathe," he said quietly. "It's only what I imagine it to be like. I know it's happening but I don't know where or how to get there in time. I feel what I imagine you are going through and I have to find you…"

"You found me. I'm right here."

"For how long?"

"Forever, I'm here forever."

I awoke suddenly again but this time it was for a different reason. Someone was in the room. This person wasn't stealthy, although they were trying to be quiet. When they climbed up onto the window seat I knew it was Patrick.

"Pat, it's too early for the deer. Go back to bed."

"Can I try to stalk them if they come?"

"Of course, but they won't come until it's light out."

"Can I eat cold pizza for breakfast so I'll be ready when they come?"

"What would your mom fix for breakfast?"

"Scrambled eggs and fruit and toast."

"Then let's see if we can come up with scrambled eggs, fruit and toast."

"Aww, rats."

"You've been getting your way for dinner. Do it Mom's way for breakfast. I'll fix it for you. Close the door on the way out and I'll be right there."

Rusty grinned at me as I rolled out of bed and went to put some clothes on.

"Go back to sleep. It's too early to get up," I said to Rusty.

"Then why are you?"

"I've got a nephew ready to stalk deer. Can't turn down a deer stalking nephew. You buy them hamburgers and pizza. I get up at insane hours and stalk deer."

"Don't wear yourself out."

I wondered what the plan was today and what I might need energy for.

In the kitchen we found eggs and bread. The only fruit we had was an old cantaloupe. I hadn't done much grocery shopping since coming home.

"Well, how about if I mix up some orange juice?"

"Can I have milk?"

I smelled the milk.

"Only if you are very brave."

"Orange juice is fine."

He scarfed down his scrambled eggs and toast and gulped down his orange juice then ran off and dressed in khaki pants, a camouflage t-shirt, and moccasins. Oh dear, I thought, it's contagious. He went out to the backyard and went through his little ritual of silently inviting the deer to visit. I would never understand it but I wouldn't stop him from identifying with animals in any way he felt comfortable. I liked to sit under trees and feed squirrels from my hand. He liked to talk to the deer. What was the difference, when you came right down to it?

When the deer silently stepped out onto the grass in the side yard Patrick was raring to go.

"Hold on, has your mom ever seen you stalk deer?"

"I don't think so. The deer flats are a long ways from the house."

"Let's give her a chance."

The best place to watch the deer was from my bedroom, so I went to wake Rusty, but he was already awake watching for the deer. He hadn't watched me stalk deer in over a month. It was one of his favorite things to do.

"Mind if Jesse joins you?" I asked. "She's never seen Patrick stalk deer."

"Okay, I'll get dressed."

I went to the guestroom.

"Jesse?"

"Hmm?"

"If you want to watch Patrick stalk deer head for the bay window. Rusty's already there. He'll show you where to look."

She gave me a "you've got to be kidding" look.

"Come on sis, you'll be glad you did. He's good at it. I bet he's better since he's been working with Elan."

Jesse cracked an eye. I hoped she didn't look too closely into a mirror before going to the window.

"Aunt Cassidy! Come on!" Patrick urged quietly.

"We want the deer to come all the way into the yard, anyway. We have a minute."

He walked to the den, peeked out the window and came back. Jesse got up reluctantly and ran a brush through her hair. Patrick ran to the back door.

At one time the deer had been used to my outdoor activities. They would come to the fringes of the yard even if I was outside working. Now they were more cautious. They hadn't seen me in a while and they certainly didn't remember this other little human. I thought it made a good test of our stalking abilities.

"Open the door as quietly as you can," I instructed.

We slid outside and I silently closed the door before Shadow could dash out. Patrick knew what to do. He was in stalking mode from the very first. He no longer looked to me for guidance. He watched the deer and took his cues from them. I followed and went into my own stalk behind him, letting him choose the way. He walked out to the end of the patio and knelt down, thanking the deer for visiting, then he rose and took two crouched steps towards them. Their heads shot up and they watched him. He seemed unconcerned. He knew they'd watch him. He was a stranger after all. It looked more like he was approaching a frightened child than a herd of deer. He didn't intimidate. He advanced when they would accept advances and he stopped when they showed fear. This was a different way of stalking than I had done. To me distraction was my main tool. When the deer ate I moved. When they sensed me and stopped I froze. We advanced step by very cautious step. I watched Pat place each foot carefully and silently. He kept his eye on the deer, not on the ground. The more he closed in the lower he crouched. I became so absorbed watching Patrick that I forgot about the deer and finally I decided to let him go on alone. I was just starting to lower myself to a nice non-threatening wait when a shot echoed off the barn. Instinct took over and, instead of lying to wait I dashed forward tackling Patrick, shielding him from harm. At the same time something hit me in the head. I tumbled forward, taking Patrick down with me. I vaguely felt him squirming around beneath me as stars danced around in my head. I could hear Jesse's frantic yelling from the bay window and the sliding door as Rusty ran out, gun drawn.

"Aunt Cassidy! You're squishing me!" Patrick said squirming.

"Pat, lay still!" Rusty shushed him.

When the stars settled down I rolled off of Patrick, holding him down.

"Shh, stay down. The bad guy might be out there," I told him quietly. "See the door? I want you to move the same time I do. Stay low."

I pushed Patrick into the house ahead of me. Jesse was freaking out, dancing around the den screaming, "Cassidy! You're shot! You're shot!"

"I'm not shot. If I was shot I wouldn't be in here. I'd still be out there. I'll track it all later and see what happened."

I picked up the phone and dialed 911 and reported shots fired, the address, told them it was Rusty Michael's house so they wouldn't need the address, then found my rifle. I thought I should wash up a little bit but I didn't want to leave Rusty out there alone. The blood trickled down my left temple and dripped off my jaw onto my shoulder.

"Cassidy! Get in the house!" Rusty said sternly as I slipped behind the large shrub next to the patio.

"We need to head him off before he reaches his car. Let's try around front. His car is bound to be on the road."

"No! Get in the house!"

"I will, as soon as your backup gets here. You need my eyes."

I scanned the trees looking for any movement that might be our shooter. I wasn't convinced yet that it was Dirk. This didn't feel like something he would do, even though he'd taken shots at me before. He seemed to have decided I needed a nice slow death, not something quick like a shot to the head. I wondered if maybe some sudden bout of depression had sent him over the edge. Clinical psychosis could be unpredictable and sudden.

Rusty joined me behind the shrub.

"Is Pat okay?"

"Yeah, just squished, and disappointed that he couldn't stalk the deer."

I caught a movement, pointed it out to Rusty. He nodded. I moved to the next shrub making my way around the house, pausing in each hiding place to make sure I was still invisible. We continued around the house carefully keeping the last known movement in view. There was a sudden rumble from behind the trees.

"He came on his dirt bike," I told Rusty. Rusty dashed to the garage.

"No don't!" I called after him.

Damn, I had to remember not to leave the keys in it at home.

The yellow dirt bike shot out of the trees and down to the road and Rusty took off after him on my motorcycle. Okay, now I was convinced, it was Dirk.

Dirk had the advantage of a bigger bike and less weight. I pulled out my cell phone and called the station, asking for a phone connection with the responding officers. Big John called me back.

"What's going on Cassidy?"

"Watch for a yellow dirt bike. The green one is Rusty. They headed towards town but I don't know that they will stay on the pavement. They're both armed but Rusty can't shoot his rifle from the dirt bike. I don't know if he has his sidearm."

I heard Big John relay something over the radio.

"Where are you?" John asked.

"At home."

"Is everybody okay?"

"Yeah," I said as a drip landed with a wet splat on my shoulder.

"I'm pulling onto your street. There's two other cars responding."

"No! Go help Rusty."

"Too late, I'm here."

Big John pulled up, took one look at me and picked up his radio.

"Don't you dare!" I told him. "You didn't give me a chance to get cleaned up."

"Dang, Cassidy, if you weren't up walking around I'd swear you took a shot right through your skull! What happened to you?"

"I haven't figured it out yet. Things happened too fast."

Big John towered over me. "I'm calling number thirty-one." Number thirty-one was the nearest rescue squad.

"You are not." I said, "I'm only allowed one call per week per station."

"That's a joke. They just say that because of all the stories."

"I'll fight you for the radio." This was a joke because Big John was easily twice my size, but he took me seriously.

"Damn it, Cassidy, have you seen yourself?"

"No, but I know I'm a mess. I know I'm bleeding. If you'll put down the radio I'll go quietly to my room and clean up. Now go help Rusty. He might need it."

"I'm not leaving you until I know for sure you're okay. I can hand you over to an EMT or you can prove to me you're not shot."

"Okay, what can I do?"

"Tell me what happened."

"I can't do that until I've tracked the site."

"Okay, then track the site."

I sighed with exasperation then led him around the house and read aloud what I saw back there.

"My nephew and I were stalking deer. Patrick was stalking ahead of me and doing a pretty good job of it so I was going to set this one out and let him proceed on his own."

"Patrick? Seven year old Patrick was stalking deer?"

"Yeah, he takes after me in that department. Anyway, I heard a shot so I tackled him. Something hit me in the head as I came down. You can see where we landed. So if I was coming down this way, the thing that hit my head had to come from that way." I took a few steps, eyes to the ground. About six feet from where my head would have been was the deep impression left by a leaping deer. "Here's your proof. The shot scared the deer and one of them ran straight at us and caught me in the head as it bounded away. If Dirk was in those trees where we saw him it all adds up." I turned around and looked for the spot where the deer had come down. It was there plain as day, four deep hoof prints and the marks from its dewclaws as it bounded away again.

"You're trying to tell me that hole in your head is from being kicked by a deer?"

"Yeah."

"And you're not shot."

"I'm not shot."

"I don't believe you."

"John! Even Patrick will tell you what happened. If I took Pat up in the trees he could even give you the name of the man from looking at his footprints! If Patrick can do it why won't you believe me?"

"Patrick tracks?"

I stood as tall as my five foot four inches would let me. It's not a good idea to stand up to a cop but these guys sort of knew me. "Go help Rusty," I said.

"My orders are to secure the house. Rusty has the help he needs. Air support has been called in. They're on top of it. Can you ID the footprints?"

"Easily, even Patrick can ID those footprints."

"You're not kidding are you?"

"No, take him up into the trees. He'll profile the tracks for you. He'll tell you it's the same man we tracked at the beach, that he drags his foot due to some injury. If you ask the man's name he'll tell you it's Dirk."

"He doesn't live around here, does he?"

"No, he lives up north."

"Whew, I don't think we could take another little Cassidy loose down here."

"John, just secure the house so you can go do real police work."

"This is getting interesting. You're telling me you have a seven year old nephew who tracks and profiles criminals and stalks deer."

"Yeah, but you know Patrick. Rusty had him at the station two days ago. He said he saw you there."

"Hey, Patrick!" Big John said brightly as we entered the house. "I need a tracker and Cassidy says you can ID the guy."

"Me?" Pat said uncertainly.

"He doesn't believe you can track good enough to ID the guy."

"You mean you want me to tell you who did it? How should I know who did it?"

"Trust me," I said. "You'll know. Go show Officer Jankowski how good a tracker you are. The bad guy's long gone. Uncle Rusty is following him on the motorcycle. You know not to step on the tracks as you go. Go read the trail to Big John. I'm going to try and wash some of this blood off."

"You're not going to help me?"

"If I go help you Big John won't believe you did it all by yourself. You can do it. I know you can do it or I wouldn't send you out there."

He reluctantly led Big John out into the hills. He hadn't even really seen where Dirk had stood but I knew the dirt and I knew the tracks. They would be easy to spot. The drag mark was unmistakable.

The blood was stubborn. I'd ruined my shirt. When I looked in the mirror I didn't blame Big John for thinking I was shot. It did look like a small, round dark hole in my head, but once I'd washed it as well as I could, it looked a lot better.

Big John came in shaking his head in dismay. He sat down at the dining room table and began writing out his findings while it was fresh in his mind.

"Well, was Patrick helpful to you?" I asked.

"Umm, yeah. It was spooky. I swear, it was like watching a miniature you.

He showed me where the guy camped, where he stood to watch you, where he stood to take his shot. And it all added up. I couldn't believe I was actually listening to a little kid."

"Where he camped?"

"He told me he'd seen those footprints at the beach yesterday, that the guy had tried to drown you when you were out surfing. I didn't know you could surf!"

"I can't. I was practicing. I've only managed to stand up on the board once. Is the camp still there?"

"Yeah. You didn't know?"

"No. I wondered why he was up so early. He doesn't seem like the type to be an early riser. I'm surprised the deer showed up with a camp nearby."

"Aunt Cassidy?" Patrick interrupted. "Would you go show Mom you're still alive. She's laying in bed blubbering about you getting shot."

I went to the guestroom and there was Jesse, curled up in a little ball on her side crying away. What's worse, she was crying into the phone. She better not be talking to Mom, I thought. She was. Oh man. This day was just getting started and already it was getting flushed down the toilet. Rusty off after a gun-toting psycho. A cop in my dining room. A sister and a mom who thought I was dying. What would Wyatt come up with this morning?

I sat on the side of the bed.

"Jesse, give me the phone." No response. "Jesse, I'm not shot! Don't scare Mom like that. Now give me the phone!"

While I was trying to get the phone from Jesse, to calm down my mom, Wyatt walked in sleepily.

"I'm hungry. Can I make smiley face pancakes?"

Yeah, I thought, that's what we all needed, smiley face pancakes. Let's all sit down and put sticky syrup all over smiley face pancakes and maybe today will magically turn around.

"Just a minute, Wyatt."

I walked around the bed, plucked the phone from Jesse's hand and talked to my mom.

"Mom, I'm fine. Jesse just saw me all covered in blood and panicked."

"How did you get covered in blood?" She shrieked. Mom was not ordinarily a shrieker. Jesse must have gotten her worked up.

"Mom! Has everyone gone nutso on me today? I'm fine. I'm not even bloody anymore. Jesse was upset over nothing."

"Nothing?" Jesse shrieked with good reason. Jesse was a shrieker.

"Yeah, nothing. Would everybody please just settle down? Look at the boys. They aren't upset. Patrick isn't even upset and he was there!"

"You had Patrick with you and you got shot?" Mom asked.

"We were stalking deer and I didn't get shot."

"Are you sure?" Mom asked. "Everybody seems so sure."

"I think I'd know if I got shot. Mom, go have a cup of coffee with Martha. You'll feel better. I'll call you back when things have settled down. Right now I have a cop in my dining room. A sister who thinks I've been shot. A nephew wanting to make smiley face pancakes and a husband off on an apprehension. And it's not even seven thirty! Life shouldn't get this complicated so early in the morning. I need to sort this all out."

"Okay, dear, I'll let you go."

"Thanks, love you."

"I love you, too," she said as she hung up. One down.

"Jesse, you need something to do. Help Wyatt make smiley face pancakes."

"Smiley face pancakes?"

"It was his idea."

"Okay, that sounds like fun. Are you sure you're not shot?" she sniffed.

"I'm sure. A deer kicked me in the head. I found the tracks."

"Leave it to you to get kicked by a deer and make everybody think you'd gotten shot."

Jesse wandered out to the kitchen in her pajamas and dashed back to her room with another shriek.

"You didn't tell me there was an officer in your dining room!"

"There's an officer in my dining room," I told her, but she just glared at me. "And he doesn't care what you wear to cook pancakes as long as you offer him some."

Patrick got tired of all the hoopla. He went to the back yard and filled the bird feeder and staked out a spot in the bay window. I wanted to kiss him. The one cool head in the midst of chaos.

Jesse put on her best jeans and a flattering top, brushed her hair and styled it a little, redid her makeup and came out ready to play little Suzy Homemaker for Big John. Wyatt added ingredients to the bowl according to her instructions. When Rusty came home dusty and windblown he walked into a very odd house. Wyatt stood over the stove saying, "Can I put a bunny face on mine? I like to eat the ears first."

"Of course you can make a bunny pancake," Jesse said. "Excuse me, Officer? Would you like some pancakes?"

"Yeah," said Wyatt. "We can make happy face, kitty cats, bunnies, doggies. I even figured out how to make a raccoon pancake but the mask is a little bit tricky."

"What kind of doggies?" Big John asked.

"I don't know, like bunnies except the ears go down instead of up. Oh and snowmans. We can do snowman shaped pancakes, too."

"How about round?" Big John asked.

"Aw, he doesn't appreciate pancake artists," Jesse said.

"Okay, since you want a challenge, try to make a giraffe shaped pancake," Big John said, just to make them be quiet. It didn't work.

"Ooo, a giraffe?" Jesse and Wyatt went into a huddle. "Cassidy? Do you have a baster or a pastry bag?" Jesse asked.

"Top drawer next to the stove," I called out as I hugged Rusty. He was disappointed. The chase had not gone well. He sat down heavily next to Big John.

"Uncle Rusty, what kind of pancakes do you want?"

"Surprise me," Rusty answered.

Jesse got out the baster and filled it with batter. There were elaborate hand motions over the griddle.

"Oh yeah," said Wyatt. "I think we did it. How are we going to flip it?" Then after a short wait, "Don't break it! Don't break it!" Another huddle. They slid the giraffe pancake onto a platter and added spots of peanut butter. Wyatt ran to get the camera and took a lopsided picture of his creation before handing it over to Big John. Rusty grinned. I was glad to see he wasn't too depressed. A giraffe pancake could still cheer him up. Big John just poured on the syrup and dug in. Wyatt watched his creation get devoured in thirty seconds. "Would you like another one?" Wyatt asked.

"Wyatt, let's just make a whole stack and people can eat what they want."

Yes, I thought, brilliant idea.

"I want to make a bunny. I'm starving."

"Okay, make a bunny. Then you can eat."

"Welcome to the three ring circus," I told Rusty.

"It's better than the rest of my morning," Rusty said. "Dirk gave me a run but he was just able to go faster. He's still giving them a run but there wasn't much I could do."

"It's okay, I was worried what might happen if you caught him anyway. You weren't armed right. You didn't have a way to get backup. What would you have done if you caught him?"

"*After all he's done to you?*"

He didn't have to answer. Rusty probably would not have had a choice. Against one man, Dirk would have defended himself, and Rusty would have shot back. Rusty, John and I knew what would have happened. We kept quiet.

"Is your house always this crazy?" Big John asked.

"No. Only rarely. Isn't it great?" Rusty answered.

"Um, yeah, great. Cassidy, I know Patrick walked me through all the tracking but, you know, this would sound more valid if it came from you than from a seven year old kid," John said.

"Okay. Well, tell them I said it then."

"You at least need to know what he said so if you need to testify it'll stand up in court."

"Don't worry. I plan on tracking it just out of curiosity. I'm sure whatever Patrick told you was right. He wouldn't have said anything unless he was sure. There's really a camp out there that Dirk stayed at?"

"More than one night by the looks of it."

"I'll go track it. I need to know what he's been up to. This camp is all news to me."

Rusty listened with interest. This was news to him, too. A platter of pancakes appeared and Rusty took two cats and a bunny. He pulled off the ears and ate them separately. I took what I thought must have been a dog and put jelly on it. Jesse made good pancakes. I wondered if she used the milk in the fridge.

Patrick walked in and Jesse gave him a surprised look.

"Pat, do you want a pancake?" she asked.

"The usual?" Patrick asked.

Jesse looked into the bowl.

"I'll try."

In a few minutes she produced Patrick's pancakes, three small pancakes shaped like paw prints.

"Sorry, I only had enough batter for three."

"It's okay, I already ate. Aunt Cassidy made eggs and toast."

Big John looked at Patrick's plate. "What kind of tracks are those supposed to be?"

"Cats. If they have claws they are dog tracks. If they are big they are lion tracks. These are small so they call them cat tracks. They aren't quite right, but I don't care since I'm just going to eat them."

"Well," said Rusty getting up from the table. "Are you ready for some action?" he asked Big John.

Big John looked over the stack of pancakes. He'd only eaten a giraffe.

"Let's go see how things stand," Rusty told him. "I want this guy brought in *today*."

I followed him out to Big John's squad car. So much for today's plans. As always I told him to be careful and he said he would, but there was a hardness to his look. He brushed my bangs away from the cut on my head. All the things Dirk had tried to do to me were driving him. As they pulled away I knew he meant business.

Dirk had a long day ahead of him.

It was time to see what Dirk had been up to for the past few days. How could I have missed all these tracks? My tracks with Kelly and Strict had gone another direction, but still. I was slacking if there was a camp fifty feet from my property line and I didn't know about it. I had to get better. Dirk was going to catch me and there wouldn't be anything I could do. I had to do something to build myself back up. I had to be ready for a fight.

I located the camp and where he kept the bike parked. I found the place he had stood to shoot from. I stood in almost the same spot, looked down into my yard, and imagined the scene below from Dirk's vantage point.

He had to really hate me, I thought. It drove him. It kept him awake when he would normally be asleep. He'd been awake and ready when I came out of the house at six a.m. Something was eating at him and I didn't like what it was.

I went into the house and found a clock. Nine o'clock and I had two small boys and a sister who didn't know what to do at my house. I caught Patrick heading for the backyard.

"Pat? Where are you going?" I asked.

He seemed melancholy. "I need to tell the deer I'm sorry. They probably think I tricked them. I invited them to come and then they got shot at. I hope they aren't scared to come back."

"They'll be back. And they won't hold it against you," I told him.

He was outside for a long time. I guess apologies take longer than invitations.

"Cassidy, let's go get the boys a helmet. They'd love to ride the bike," Jesse said.

"That sounds dangerous," I answered.

"Why? We'll take it easy. The boys know to hang on."

"It sounds dangerous because I want to buy Rusty a bike, too."

"Oh, yeah, that kind of dangerous…You wouldn't choose Rusty's bike for him anyway. A guy wouldn't let a girl pick out his motorcycle for him. I think there's a rule about that somewhere."

"Yeah, I think so, too. But what if Kelly knew exactly what Rusty would like?"

"No, I think it's a rule, guys have to pick out their own motorcycles. Guy's tastes in motorcycles are usually very particular. Even a guy who wouldn't be caught dead on one knows which one he'd want if the dream machine were to suddenly appear before him."

I nodded in agreement. "Okay, let's go get the boys a helmet and drool over the bikes."

"Oh, cool!" exclaimed Patrick when we walked into the motorcycle dealership.

"We're only here for a helmet," I told him.

"Why didn't you get this one?" he asked pointing out a huge cruising bike. It was gold, with lots of chrome.

"That bike isn't practical for me. I have to be able to lift it by myself. If I'm out in the hills and lose the bike I have to be able to right it to get it home."

"How can you lift a motorcycle if you lose it?" Wyatt asked.

"If you lose it on a bike it means you tip over."

"Oh."

"Why didn't you get this one then? It's cool too."

"I'm not racing. I'm just trying to go out in the hills without getting stuck. Kids, I shopped very carefully before selecting my two-fifty street legal dirt bike. I'm not interested in a racing bike or a cruising bike or a motocross bike. We're here for a helmet so you can ride my wimpy little two-fifty, unless it's not cool enough for you anymore."

"Here's what Rusty needs to go with your bike," Jesse said.

Oh yeah, I thought, practical, big, black. It had Rusty written all over it. I wished it had Rusty's approval. I was just kidding when I said we'd drool over the bikes, but here I was. Okay, helmets, just look at the helmets. Patrick and Wyatt tried on all the kid sized helmets until we'd narrowed it down to a red one or a black one.

"I like the red one," Wyatt said.

"I like the black one," Patrick countered.

"We only need one and it doesn't matter what color it is," Jesse said.

"Black blends in with shadows," Pat said.

"Red is cool," Wyatt said.

"Sorry, Pat, but I'm going to get the red one. Now that you mention blending in we want you kids to be visible in case something does happen."

"Oh, oh it's steep!" said Wyatt nervously as I drove down the hill.

"Lean when I lean," I said heading for a corner.

He leaned but I felt his grip tighten whenever we went around a curve or came over a hill.

"Go faster!" yelled Patrick.

I sped up a little and he laughed behind me. A hill was coming up.

"Go faster!" he said again.

"I'm not going to go fast enough to leave the ground. That's dangerous with a passenger."

"Aw, I want to fly."

"Not today."

"Will you do it while I watch?"

"Okay."

I let him off the bike and turned the bike around, drove up the road and turned around again. I hit the gas, unsure just how fast I needed to go for this particular hill. The front wheel left the ground, and the ground dropped away beneath me. Pat jumped up and down next to the road as I zipped by.

"I can't wait until I'm big enough to do that!" he said.

When we got back to Jesse's ranch truck I got off and gave her a turn.

"Who wants to go? Wyatt it's your turn," she said.

"Are you going to go fast?"

"We'll take it easy."

Jesse and Wyatt took off slowly.

"Aren't you scared the bad man will come after you again?" Patrick asked.

"Not today. He's kind of busy staying away from the police today. If they have the helicopter on his tail he's going to have a rough time shaking them."

"Will Uncle Rusty catch him?"

"I don't know, Pat. I hope not."

"Why? Don't you want them to stop that guy after what he did to you?"

"I do want him to get caught. I'm hoping he will see all the police coming and give up. I worry about Uncle Rusty catching him. If Dirk sees one man coming after him he will be more likely to shoot or fight. I don't want anybody hurt even though I do want him to be caught."

"Does Uncle Rusty hate Dirk?"

"I don't know. I hope not. I don't. I doubt there is anybody I could really, truly hate."

"How come you don't want Uncle Rusty to hate Dirk? Dirk did mean things to you."

"Hate doesn't solve anything. It hurts the person doing the hating more than the person the hate is directed to. Just look at Dirk. He hates me and it only makes him worse. His hate is going to land him in jail and it could kill him if he isn't careful."

"How could hate kill a person?"

"He gets so mad he makes rash decisions. If he makes rash decisions with the police after him he could get shot down."

"Mom sure is taking a long time to make the circle."

"You have to go slower with Wyatt. He doesn't like to go fast. How long has it been since your mom has ridden a motorcycle?"

"I didn't even know she could."

"I hope she remembers how it's done. The shifting is a little different than a car."

Late in the afternoon Rusty came bumping down the road. I'd left a note on the fridge telling him where we'd be and what we were doing.

Jesse took more turns on the bike than I did. I had to rest between runs and after a while it was a fight to stay awake while Jesse was out riding.

Rusty stepped out of the Explorer arms open wide.

"I'm sorry babe. I wasted a day and Dirk ended up losing us in L.A. traffic."

We sat in the bed of the ranch truck waiting for Jesse to get back with Wyatt. Patrick was casting around the truck for tracks. I didn't have the energy for another run.

"There's a motorcycle at the dealership that has your name written on it," I told him. "I was so tempted to buy it so we could go riding together."

"Why didn't you?"

"Because there's a rule. Guys have to choose their own motorcycles. Besides, most husbands wouldn't want ten thousand dollar surprises to turn up in the garage suddenly. Whether or not you get one is your decision. But I do wish we could go riding together."

"You do?"

"Of course I do. Anything I do I'd rather do with you."

"You would?"

"Rusty, you're acting like I only married you so I'd have a roof over my head! I married you because I love you twenty-four seven. When you're gone I miss you and when you're here I want to be with you."

He looked at me as if he was trying to figure out if I really meant it.

"Where's Pat?" he said.

I glanced around.

"He was looking for tracks."

"He probably found some."

"Oh shoot, I don't have the energy for this."

Rusty stood up in the bed of the truck and looked around, then hopped down. I grew a little concerned when he held out his hand for me to jump down, too. It meant he hadn't seen Patrick and that was odd because we could see for miles out on that flat desert. Rusty and I began a large circle around the truck watching for little boy footprints leading away.

"Over here, Cass," Rusty called from the opposite side of the truck. I jogged over, getting a stitch in my side. Patrick's footsteps milled around, just wandering. I followed them seeing myself at seven. Bored, just looking for some kind of trail to decipher. A trail was a puzzle and a puzzle was not to be ignored by an active mind. When he found a trail he had squatted down studying for a bit, with good reason, he'd only seen a similar trail once before and it had been old. This trail held promise. I only hoped he wasn't trying to find the maker of the tracks.

"Rusty, keep your eyes open. He's tracking a snake. I don't know if he will stay back. He's very curious about how animals move so he's likely to get closer than he should."

I followed the tracks swiftly until I noticed a change. I stopped and studied to make sure I was reading it right. Patrick wasn't just walking anymore. He had slowed down and he was walking sideways, bent over. His weight was more on the front of his feet, now. He stood still watching, then walked two or three steps sideways. I calculated the distance from the snake's track to Patrick's footprints. It was only about five feet. I pictured him following the snake, watching its movements, watching the way each push of the snake's body left a little ridge of sand behind.

"Give me a boost up. He can't be far," I said to Rusty.

He made a step with his hands and raised me until I had to use his shoulder to steady myself. I looked around. I could see Jesse making her way back towards the truck on the dirt bike. I was glad about that. She'd been out for a long time and I was beginning to think something had happened to her. I scanned every direction and at last I saw a small movement slightly off from the direction the tracks led.

"Okay, drop me, we're close." Rusty lowered me down so the jump down wouldn't jar me. The tracks led over a small rise and on the other side we found Patrick, just as I imagined him, stooped over, studying the movements of a large rattlesnake.

"Patrick! Get back!" Rusty scolded. "Do you know what that is?"

"Yeah, it's a rattlesnake. Isn't it cool?" Patrick answered bending over, watching intently.

The snake continued on its way. It didn't seem concerned about being followed by a little human.

"It is cool, but also very dangerous," I answered.

"Wait'll I tell Elan! He'll think it was cool too. I saw a snake track when I was with Chase but we didn't know what kind it was. I need to figure out what kind this one is."

"Memorize the pattern on its back and the shape of its head and you can look it up when we get home. But we've got to go. Your mom is back at the truck again."

"Do we have to? I never got to track a real live snake before."

"I know, Pat, but rattlesnakes can be deadly. You're lucky this one doesn't mind you being close. I'm surprised he isn't rattling at you."

"I want to hear him rattle! I never heard a rattlesnake before."

"Nope, you're not going to hear it today either. When they rattle they are saying, 'back off or I'm going to bite you!' and believe me, you don't want a rattlesnake to bite you. Now leave him alone and let's go home."

He left the rattlesnake behind reluctantly.

"What do rattlesnakes eat?" Patrick asked as we walked along.

"Small animals."

"How to they catch them? Mice are fast and snakes are slow."

"You're lucky you only saw that snake while he was moving slow. They can move fast when they need to. They can go down in burrows and find mice and baby rabbits down there."

"They can't eat baby rabbits! Baby rabbits are… cute."

"Sorry kiddo, that's just a fact of life."

I did okay while I had the distraction of the search but walking back was rough. I was winded and had to stop frequently. The day was taking its toll on me. I climbed back into the bed of the truck where I could sit down and catch my breath.

"You need to slow down," Rusty said.

"I *was* slowed down until Patrick went missing."

"How many times did you go out on the bike?"

"Just twice. Jesse went more."

"Yeah!" Patrick said. "And she flew! Mom won't go fast. It's boring when Mom drives."

Rusty gave me a disapproving look.

"He asked me to go faster," I said defensively. "We had a great time."

"I wish I could have joined you. I'd have accomplished more riding all over the hills than I did chasing Dirk. But at least I knew he was far away from you. I was glad the rest of your day was relatively safe."

"Uncle Rusty, are you going to take a turn? Can I ride with you?" Patrick asked.

"Okay, one quick one and then we need to get dinner."

"Will you go fast?"

"I don't know. I've never been over this road."

As he took off with Patrick holding onto his belt loops Pat asked, "Will you fly?"

They weren't gone long and Patrick got off the bike grinning broadly. I guess Rusty went fast enough.

"What do you want to do on your last day here?" Rusty asked.

Patrick's eyes got big, "You mean we get to choose?"

"Well, within reason. It's up to your mom."

"I want to go to San Diego!" Pat said irrefutably.

"That's at least an overnight trip. You're supposed to go home to the ranch tomorrow."

"So? We can go home from San Diego," Pat had this all worked out.

"We can't just drop in on Rusty's parents!" I said. "Five people is a lot to deal with."

"They said to come back whenever I could," Pat argued.

It was true, Rusty's parents would love having the boys. The boys could practice swimming in the pool. I just hated to surprise Bill and Bev like this. I looked at Rusty. Rusty looked at me. We both looked at Jesse.

"What do you think, Jess? Do you want to go visit Rusty's parents?"

"Wow, this is certainly a surprise. You don't want to go to the beach again? Or an amusement park? Or the zoo?"

"No, Bill and Bev don't have any grandkids. They have this cool attic full of books and toys and they have a pool and a pool table. And Cody will teach me how to ride a skateboard and Aunt Cassidy can go surfing. Cody's teaching her how."

I think the prospect of seeing Cody in swim trunks swayed her. Now we all looked to Rusty.

In a way a trip to San Diego was just what I needed. I thought I'd last about half an hour walking an amusement park or a zoo.

"Oh! Patrick! Look how much you've grown!" Bev squealed as she rushed out the front door. "And Wyatt! It's good to meet you. How old are you?"

"I'm five," Wyatt said from behind Jesse's legs.

"Can I show Wyatt the attic?" Patrick asked.

"Most certainly. I got all the toys out and put some of the books away," she said with a wink. Last time we had visited Patrick got his hands on a paperback that wasn't exactly rated G.

As the boys ran upstairs Bev turned to Jesse. "And you must be Cassidy's sister. I'm Bev. Make yourself at home. Maybe Cassidy can show you around."

We found the boys in the attic. Wyatt was playing with Rusty's old toy cars and Patrick was heading for the stairs down. He had a thick book in his hands.

"Look, Aunt Cassidy! It was a western diamondback rattler! See? The pattern on his back is exactly the same as the one in the book. And it says they live in the desert and they are out in the daytime and they are one of the most dangerous rattlesnakes. Cool! Will Chase be here for dinner?"

"Chase has an open invitation and reads minds so he probably will."

"What was a diamondback rattler?" Jesse asked.

"I tracked a rattlesnake! While you were out riding the motorcycle I tracked a snake, just like this! Isn't it cool!"

Jesse turned to me. "You let him track a rattlesnake? Are you nuts!"

What could I do? If I admitted Patrick got away from me I'd be in trouble for not watching him. So I just said, "We were careful. He didn't get close to it."

"Next thing I know you're going to teach him how to cook and eat gopher snake!"

Patrick jumped on that one, "Oh yeah, can we? Will you show me how to catch a snake? A harmless one?"

"No!" said Jesse. "I was being sarcastic."

"But I might have to know how to catch a snake. What if I'm lost in the mountains and all I can find to eat is a snake? I might have to know these things."

"Pat, when you were following the rattlesnake it went pretty slow, right?"

"Yeah."

"Well, if you know a snake is harmless and you have to catch it, just don't scare it. Sneak up on it like you are stalking and when you catch it be gentle. Some snakes don't even mind being caught if you are gentle. If they get scared they can be real fast, so if you scare it be prepared for a fight. You have to know it's harmless first, though. A poisonous snake could kill you."

"I'm going to read this book. I'll find all the harmless ones."

"It just amazes me what a reader that boy is," Bev said behind us.

Patrick was a reader even before Jesse knew it. She puffed up proudly when Bev praised her son.

Not to be outdone in the wildlife department Wyatt chirped, "I swam with fishes!"

"Oh! You did? You must be a good swimmer."

"I'm going to be a surfer like Aunt Cassidy! I'm not scared of fishes."

"An admirable goal," said Bev. "Oh, it's so good to have little ones in the house again! I can't wait…"

"Mom, can I talk to you?" Rusty interrupted.

"Of course," Bev answered following him down the stairs.

I followed. I wanted to find out how Rusty felt about the subject of grandkids.

"Mom, please… I know it's tempting to talk about the possibility of grandkids… but now isn't a good time. You almost had a grandkid. We didn't even know Cassidy was pregnant before she lost the baby. So, can you just enjoy the boys? I invited them down because I needed some activity. Some kid activity. It's going to be hard to send them home tomorrow."

"How long ago was it?" Bev asked.

"She's been home about a month."

"What are you doing forcing her to deal with company on top of what she's been through?"

"Jesse knows not to expect big meals and a spotless house. I've been bringing meals from town when I come home from work. Jesse cooks, too. It's been a good distraction. We all went to the beach this week and Cassidy got to surf. She stood on the surfboard for the very first time. That's what made Wyatt decide he wanted to be a surfer. It helped him overcome his fear of the fish and Cassidy taught him the basics of how to swim. She can do almost anything for short periods of time."

"Maybe I should cancel the volleyball tonight."

"That's not necessary. Just let Cass sit when she needs to. Don't push and she'll be fine."

Jesse was in for a treat. Rusty and Cody both battling it out in the pool over the volleyball net.

I joined Jesse and the boys in the attic.

"You can make beds on these mattresses," I showed her the pile of comforters. "I love sleeping up here on the balcony but I don't recommend doing that with the boys here. The bathroom is halfway down the hall on the left. Rusty and I will be in the next room down. The bedroom on the right is Cody's and should probably have a warning sign on the door. Bev won't be upset if you find things for yourself in the kitchen. Remember, the backyard is all pool so the boys need an adult out there with them. Come here," I said leading Jesse downstairs. I took her to the guestroom where Bev had hung pictures of the kids growing up. "Here's pictures of Rusty when he was little."

There was one of Rusty graduating from kindergarten and one with a school picture for every year from kindergarten through high school.

"Doesn't it make you wonder what your baby might have looked like?" Jesse asked.

"Yeah, someday maybe I'll find out."

"Look at this expression," I said pointing to a picture of Rusty being tackled by another kid in Junior High football.

Jesse looked and looked just like I did when I spent any time at all in this room.

"Ohmygod," Jesse exclaimed. "Here's what he looked like when he graduated from academy."

He looked so young. He had to have been twenty-two. He couldn't start academy until he was twenty-one. I wondered how much of his aging was my fault. Rusty was still handsome. Women of any age would find him attractive because he was almost ageless, but seeing the contrast between graduation and today was disconcerting. When I turned around Bev was standing in the doorway.

"I like to look, too," she said. "It's all good times."

"Rusty looks so young at graduation," I said.

"They always do. If you look closely some of those guys are forty but you wouldn't guess it. They are so set, so ready to go out and be real cops. You see the same guys after a few drug busts and a few major car accidents and they look different. Reality leaves tracks on men. Women, too. Women more on the inside than the outside."

Maybe that's why I had changed so much. Maybe reality was leaving tracks inside me.

"You've seen a lot, are the changes for the better?" I asked.

"It depends on how a person chooses to use them. Some become bitter and hard. When they do they look bitter and hard. Some develop a sense of humor to deal with the harshness of the job. You see it in little laugh lines around the eyes and a gentler attitude."

I didn't know what to say. How had I changed Rusty? That's what I wanted to know.

"Cassidy, I see the question. Are you worried about the answer?"

Yes, I'm terrified, I thought. What if I'm slowly killing him? What if I really am making him into an old man before his time?

"What do you see when you look into his eyes? Have you ever seen anything there besides love?"

Yeah, I've seen lots and lots of worry. I've seen worry about my safety. Worry about my health. Worry about what I might choose to do in spite of what was safe. Worry about what other people might do to me. I've seen sadness and now even mourning. And I've seen joy, pure, simple joy, passion and longing. And love.

"Do you want to know what I see?" Bev asked. "I've never seen Rusty happier than when he's with you. There's a contentment that wasn't there before. He enjoys you. When you move he watches you. When you talk he listens to you, even if you're not talking to him, even if you're in the next room. When you're away he misses you and when you're near he reaches for you. He's attuned to you. That doesn't happen without love."

I decided I'd have to find the answer myself. I knew Rusty loved me. The question was whether his love for me was good for him or not.

We all gathered in the living room to visit and Patrick immersed himself in the field guide. Wyatt had found art supplies and was drawing something. The conversation turned to Tony and Sandy and Cody.

"I hate to think of him in twenty years, still riding around town on that old skateboard, still hopping from one job to another at Mission Beach. He's got his degree now. He could be doing something useful. But what is he doing? Renting kayaks to tourists, and having his picture taken with every girl who walks by. He'll never make a living renting kayaks," Bev said about Cody.

"Maybe he sees what Tony does and knows it's not the life for him. He sees his degree as a ticket to office monotony."

"Then why did he major in business?"

"Because it's the subject his mind could understand. The fact that his heart and his mind don't run along the same lines kind of got lost in the doing of it. Now he needs to find a way to get them to match up."

Patrick, always the logical thinker suggested, "If he is good at business and skateboarding, he should open a skateboarding school, or a surfing school. I know he's a good teacher, too. He taught me to ride a bike and roller blade."

Cody was a puzzle, a very handsome, likeable puzzle. The one puzzle I didn't have to figure out. That was his job. He came home with his usual boisterous racket, skateboard strapped to his back, carrying his bicycle up the stairs and into his room. When he was at home it always stood at the end of his bed. There were high fives all around for the boys. When he hugged me he stepped back. I knew I'd lost weight but I hadn't thought much about it.

"I thought I told you to stay out of trouble," he said.

"It's good to see you, too," I answered.

It was one thing Rusty and I hadn't planned on when we brought Patrick to visit Rusty's family- the endless explanations. Bev had heard it; there was still Cody, Bill and Chase to go. I doubted Sandy would notice. She would talk shopping with Jesse.

The house gradually filled up as people came home. Rusty's appearance was reason for a party at his parent's house. The guys grouped around the barbecue grill and Jesse and Sandy visited under an umbrella beside the pool. Bev came and went from grill to table to kitchen. Wyatt wanted to swim with the fishes again.

"But there aren't any fishes in the swimming pool," I told him.

"It's okay, I can swim without fishes."

We went to the shallow end and I helped him float and learn to tread water. Then we tried again to make some progress with forward motion. Patrick watched from the side of the pool. He was taking notes. He was studying swimming the same way I had studied surfing, watching the techniques so he could try them later.

Later Patrick slipped into the pool and tentatively felt for the depth of water where he could practice but still touch bottom. It took him a long time to make his way the short way across the shallow end but each time he tried it he got farther faster. I was still working with Wyatt trying to find the stroke that would carry him three feet in some sort of efficient manner. He would understand the motion when I did it but when he tried to do it by himself he just wriggled around in the water, not making much headway. Still, he was getting comfortable in the water. He wasn't afraid to try.

After the barbecue the adults took over the pool. Patrick and Wyatt were designated goalies.

"There aren't goalies in volleyball," Patrick said.

"Okay, then you get to be the ball boys. When the ball leaves the pool it is up to you to get it back in play."

"I want to play volleyball," Patrick said.

"Pat, you'll get tromped on, trust me, they tromp on me," I said.

And boy did they. I had to sit it out. The guys got too competitive for me.

There was a movement next to me and Chase sat in the chair beside me.

"How's business in Joshua Hills?" he asked.

"Slow, I hope."

"You still tracking for Strict?"

"I haven't been called out in a month."

"That's unusual. So, when you did go out, did you find your man?"

"Yeah, it was an easy search."

"But…"

"But, what? It was an easy search."

"Usually when you tell me about a search you tell me how long it took, how far you hiked, what the conditions were."

"Okay, the guy had only gotten a few miles off the trail. He got turned around, called his friends to help him out of his spot. They couldn't locate him so they called Strict. This guy was a simple tracking call. Patrick could have done it. Elan could have done it. You could have done it with your eyes closed. He just busted through the undergrowth. I hardly had to watch for tracks. He was a good boy and found a place to wait. We found him. It's that simple."

"I know they've had calls down there."

"You've called Strict. You check up on me, just like you check up on Patrick at the ranch."

Chase looked odd, halfway amused, halfway concerned. He knew more than he was letting on. He gave me a 'just a second' look, reached behind him and yelled, "Gotcha!"

Patrick jumped about three feet up in the air and came down with an, "Aww, rats."

"Strict wouldn't tell me why you were off his call list. He said it was personal."

"He probably didn't want to have to explain it all. I had a few problems on the trail."

Patrick accidentally came to my rescue. "Chase, I tracked a western diamondback rattler!"

"How do you know? Did you ask him his name?"

"No, I remembered what he looked like and looked him up in a book."

"So, what does a rattlesnake track look like?"

"It looks like a wide line in the sand when the snake is going straight. When it turns or it is looking around it looks like a hose laid there, except the patterns are more scattered than a hose would be. It was cool! I never saw a rattlesnake before!"

I got up and fixed Chase a plate, pulled a beer out of the refrigerator and set it down in front of him. He and Patrick were talking tracking. I quietly went to the guestroom and closed the door. Why did Chase's questions bother me so? It wasn't because I didn't want to explain it all to a guy. It had a deeper reason than that. After lying there a while I thought it was because, when I admitted I had the miscarriage, I felt that empty feeling again.

After a while there was a knock on the door.

"Who is it?" I asked.

"Sandy," the voice said.

I cracked the door. I didn't want to be rude to Rusty's sister.

"You okay?" she said.

"Chase wants to know why I'm off Strict's call list."

"He knows. He was feeling you out, seeing how hard you were taking this."

"I don't even know myself. Sometimes I am fine with it and at odd times it hits me and I can't even talk about it. I didn't want to be pregnant. So you'd think I'd be glad to be free of that. But I can't be."

One of these days I wanted to go to my in-law's house without a problem. Before when we'd gone there it was to put trouble behind us. Sometimes it worked. Sometimes we found more trouble in San Diego than we'd left behind us in Joshua Hills. Someday I was going to return and we were just going to be happy together. I was determined.

It was rough saying goodbye to the boys. Rusty had playtime with them in San Diego. He enjoyed watching me work with the boys in the pool. He played tag with them and watched as they rode Cody's bike up and down the street. He hugged me tight when they switched the luggage from the Explorer to the ranch truck and drove away. The boys looked sadly out the window of the truck as they headed back to their ranch life. The gloom descended on Rusty again and we went into our quiet house.

A week passed with the only activity happening around the house being my boisterous sheltie demanding to be let in and out. We attempted the agility course, but I still couldn't run it. I walked him through it.

I walked up to the camp Dirk had left behind. I doubted he was stupid enough to use it but I had to check. The camp was cold but there were signs of Dirk's passing around the house. A chill went up my spine. The tracks weren't fresh but they were put there after the chase.

I got worried enough about my recovery to go back to my doctor. Would I ever be back to my old self? I asked. He said it had only been six weeks, that even a normal surgery should take eight weeks to recover from. A rupture like I had, the shock I'd been in from blood loss took a toll on many different parts of my body. I was told to have patience.

Chapter 28

There was a knock on my door. I looked out the peephole. It was Strict. I opened the door reluctantly.

"Tom's got a case," he said not beating around the bush. "A car abandoned on the side of the road. It's been linked to a man who disappeared over a week ago. Chase won't take this case. He'd say there was no use. He'd say there's a dead body out there. The family wants a search. I can send a bunch of guys out to tromp through the bushes or I can send you."

"I can't," I said, the words sticking in my throat.

"What's the problem?"

"I can't walk far enough. I can't carry a pack. It would set me back even further than I am now."

"Can you profile to me for a little while, point me in a direction?"

"This has been okayed by Tom? Usually the guys don't like me to get involved in their cases."

"You'll probably be going out with Tom and Landon. I want Landon to go because he knows what to watch for as far as you're concerned. And the obvious reason that you might actually find the guy. When Landon says to stop, I want you to stop."

"Does Tom know what he's asking?"

"Yeah, he knows, he's looking for clues, any information you can give him as you track will help even if you don't go far."

"Does Rusty know I'm doing this?"

"Are you?"

"I won't go behind his back. Call him. Tell him the score. Then you're on your own. But I'm warning you, he's going to fight it."

"I've seen it before and I'll see it again."

I went to change clothes and the arguments floated down the hall.

"Even if it's only a quarter mile, we need what information we can get….You know Wilson will stop her….She'll be back before dinner…This isn't a search. It's just information gathering. She sees things we miss…. It's *all* going to be slow going. I want her to take her time, get everything she can out of the trail…We need *something*. A direction. An attitude. Clues. Anything."

I wasn't sure what to wear. This was police business but if I had to track in my uniform I'd last about ten minutes. I opted for lightweight camping clothes. The more time I could spend on the trail the more information I could pull out of it.

When Strict pulled up to the car we could see a crowd of people had gathered. Cops, family. A young woman stood beyond the police tape crying. A wife? A sister? An older couple stood resolutely beside her keeping a stiff upper lip in spite of their fear. The man approached Landon as we got out and looked over the car.

“Please, find our son,” they pleaded.

“We’ll do our best,” Landon replied. People usually addressed Landon instead of me. He fit their image. I didn’t care. I preferred to work in the background. I wasn’t in uniform, so they probably wondered why I was there.

Victor and Rosco arrived. The EMTs who would work with Tom, should the need arise.

I walked around the car reading the ground. The driver had left the car in some haste. The tracks were pressed deep. They had emotion behind them. What that emotion was I couldn’t yet say. I looked around for other tracks. There were none. There was only one man in the car. He had left the car on his own and headed into the woods, heels biting deep, hurry in every move. Hmm, maybe not hurry. Maybe anger, maybe grief. Whatever it was it affected him deeply. I looked closely at the inside of the car, doing my best not to touch anything. Had he brought anything with him? It was hard to say. Tom would know that. He had already gone over the car once.

Landon was not at all sure this was a good idea. He didn’t want a repeat of my last call. He knew I was having a rough time bouncing back.

Tom was all business. He needed facts and he needed them as soon as possible.

“Tom, I can track the driver of this car but we don’t know that he’s your missing person.”

“It’s okay, just tell me what you see.”

So I told him what I knew so far and we went into the woods. The trail continued at a quick pace. The man was venting. He kicked rocks, pinecones. When branches hung within reach he tore them down. He was like the Tasmanian Devil thrashing his way through the forest.

I had to take it slow. Fortunately tracking is usually a slow pursuit and reading and profiling was even slower.

It was a hard trail, not so much following it but reading it. It beat on me emotionally as well as physically. The trail seeped into my head. There was a desperation in the tracks. A fleeing. I wanted to flee, too. I didn’t want to reach the end of this trail.

“The trail is a few days old,” I told Tom as I went along. “The man we’re looking for is over six feet tall. Rather heavy. And he’s an emotional basket case.”

"Can you see any sign of an injury?"

"I'll watch for it, now that I know to."

He nodded.

"What kind of injury?" I asked. "That would help."

"It could be anything. There was a domestic dispute. In his hurry he fell down half a flight of stairs. Could have hit his head. Could have bashed his hand into the railing. Could have broken a leg. We don't know."

"Well, his leg appears to be fine. He's not favoring his foot or his leg. He's just bulldozing the forest down and doing a lot of venting. Look, another branch torn loose. And it's not just a few leaves picked off as he goes by. He grabs the whole branch and rips as much off as he can. If the branch doesn't come loose he spends a few seconds ripping and tearing. He's probably tearing up his hands but he doesn't seem to care. I've been in his shoes. He's trying to waste himself."

"Waste himself?"

"He's wearing himself down. Battering himself into submission. Trying to get his body as beaten as his emotions. Hopefully his emotions gave out before his body did. If the emotions win we're looking at a long trail. The emotions will drive the body a long way."

"And you know this…because…"

"I told you, I've been in his shoes. In these mountains. I usually ran out of emotions in about three days. Three days of starving myself by living off the land. I don't think this guy's going to go looking for game trails or whittle himself a snare. He's not going to watch for a spring. He's…he's wasting himself."

I was winded and flagging. Landon watched carefully. My little troupe was patient, especially Victor. Victor knew I was pushing myself. He'd seen me on enough searches to know I was running on empty.

When I began stumbling often Landon sat me down. He shoved a water bottle into my hand.

"Rest," he said, then went and conferred with Victor.

"It can't hurt, if she'll let you. Remember, it's still a walk back."

"Yeah, I know."

He came at me with the blood pressure cuff. I didn't have the energy to protest and that told him something, too. He didn't look pleased with the reading, but he put the cuff away.

"Well?" said Victor.

"It's high, for her. Not dangerously high."

"How much more do you think we can do?" Tom asked.

I felt like they were talking about an old car that was losing parts as it went down the road.

"I'm more worried about the hike back. She's already gone farther than I thought she could."

"I can always get her a lift out," Tom said.

"Not Cass, you don't know her if you think she'll accept a ride out. I've only seen her get a ride out when the whole team went, or she was on her deathbed."

If we thought the trail was bad before, it turned downright nasty. We began finding things on the trail. Credit cards with a bullet hole through them. His driver's license, with a bullet hole through the picture. The picture would have been helpful to me. I looked at it through the evidence bag. Six foot two, two hundred and sixty pounds. I was right, a big guy. Heavy.

Next we found photographs, again with holes blown through them. In group photographs it was obvious certain people were blown out of the picture. Tom found it fascinating. I found it grim. I thought about Dirk wanting to get me out of his picture.

The walking began wearing on me again, the emotions of the tracks leached into my brain until I was on edge, nervous, and exhausted. My heart hammered in my chest. When I stumbled across the body I was too dazed at first to know. I thought we'd found another discarded thing on the trail, but after I stumbled over it, I saw it was him. And he was very still. And there was a gun in his hand. And part of his head was missing. And I couldn't take it anymore. I stumbled off into the forest and sank to my knees.

He was dead. I knew he'd be dead. Something in the trail had spelled death to me. Something in the intensity of the tracks. The desperation of the man's flight. It seemed too sudden, too final. But it didn't change the facts.

Usually I blamed myself if a search turned out for the worst. I didn't blame myself this time. He'd died long before I hit the trail. He'd been dead within hours of leaving his car. But the trail, the body, the finality of it all was too much. I needed to shut it out. The emotions in my head, the ache in my heart, and the physical exhaustion were overwhelming. I needed to get home, but my feet wouldn't work.

"Cassidy, look at me," it was Landon. He knelt down and looked me in the eye. His expression calmed.

"Go help the guys. I'll be okay."

"I'm going to set up a tent. I want you to rest."

"No. I'll be okay."

"I want you to rest, *in a tent*. So I can find you. If I let you go you'll vanish on us. You'll find a spot and blend into the undergrowth. We need you findable and rested."

I didn't fight it. I knew the investigation would take hours and I had to rest before trying the hike back. When I got to the cars I still wouldn't have a ride home. I'd come with Strict.

The tent was slowly raised nearby and I crawled into it. I was out within minutes. I wasn't picky about sleeping conditions. I'd slept in these mountains plenty of times without gear so a tent was a luxury. And Landon was right, if I wasn't assigned a spot, I'd have found an out of the way place, a peaceful place where nobody would think to look or walk and it would have been an irritating nuisance to find me. Police don't get along well with irritating nuisances. It's not in the book.

People came to ask me questions but it was like swimming through quicksand to try and answer them. They gave up and left.

"Are you sure she's okay in there?" Tom asked Landon. "She's not unconscious?"

"She's just beat. Why?"

"It's not like her to ignore a person's presence. She's always way too aware for my liking, yet she didn't stir when I talked to her."

Landon crawled into the tent. He took my pulse, brushed the hair out of my eyes.

"Cassidy?" He ran a finger down my cheek. "Kid, are you okay? Come on, answer me, just enough so I know you're there."

"How long?" I asked.

"I'll take you back whenever you're ready. Tom has some questions. I don't know if they need to be answered here or he can talk to you on the phone later. It's going to be a while before they all head back."

"Not yet."

"Okay."

I drifted off again into a deep sleep. I could hear activity and voices but none of them penetrated until I heard the doorbell plain as day. I looked through the peephole and Dirk stood on the other side of the door. He'd come for me. My heart did a quick tap dance and my breath quickened. I determined right then that he wasn't going to get the advantage. I was going to fight this guy with every ounce of my strength. If I lost, I was going down fighting. I didn't answer the door. I ran to the bedroom and searched for my rifle. We always kept it in the same place but it wasn't there. I looked for the 9mm. I frantically searched the house for anything to defend myself with but they were all gone. Through the windows I could see Dirk walking around the house, his foot catching on little bumps, his steps awkward. He looked for me like a cat stalking prey. There was a shattering sound and I knew he could get into the house. I couldn't let him corner me. The back of the house was a dead end. I sprinted for the front door but when I tried to get out I couldn't. The knob wouldn't turn. Dirk was coming and he wanted to see me die. He wanted me to suffocate. He wanted to watch as I fought for my last breath. I stood at the front door as he stepped towards me. That dragging foot and the quick step that followed echoed in my brain. His feral eyes seemed to look right through me. I felt hands on my shoulders and I pushed to get past him. I twisted and he wrapped an arm around me. It slipped up around my neck and he squeezed, dragging me through the house. I kicked and squirmed. I reached for his feet trying to trip him up. He slung me onto the bed and stood over me. He gripped a pillow and slowly lowered it towards my face. My breath was coming in quick gasps as I opened my eyes. I kicked out at the face and lunged forward, my fist connecting with a crunch. I didn't know if the sound was my knuckles or his nose but my fingers complained almost as loudly as my attacker. He tumbled backwards, a puzzled expression on his face. It was Landon. It was just Landon. I crumbled. I wanted Rusty so badly. He made bad things go away. Dirk couldn't do anything if Rusty was there. In spite of having half a dozen cops within calling distance, I felt vulnerable. Oh Rusty, I'm losing it, I thought.

I stumbled out of the tent and into the woods. Landon stumbled after me.

"Cassidy, stop!" he called, but I kept going. I knew the cars were this way but I really didn't have a head on my shoulders yet. All I knew was I wanted to be home. I wanted the world to go away. I didn't want teams of cops investigating the dead bodies I found. I didn't want killers stalking me. I didn't want nightmares causing me to attack good friends who were only trying to help. I lurched through the forest heedless to the things that stood in my way. Landon kept after me until he caught me by the arm. I turned on him, and when my arm came back to strike him again, I realized what I was doing and stopped with a wretched sob. "Hush, it's okay," Landon said wrapping his arms around me. "Who was it this time?"

"Dirk, he's still after me."

"No he's not. It was just a dream."

"I know, it wasn't realistic, but he's still out there. Sooner or later I'm going to have to face him."

"It was just a dream."

"He hates me. He wants to see me die."

"Hush, it was just a dream."

"Ask Rusty, it's not just a dream. I need to go home. I'm losing it, Landon. I'm too weak to take on Dirk. I need to go home. I'll go with or without you but I need to go."

"Give me fifteen minutes. I need my pack and my tent. I need to tell Tom we're leaving."

"No, I don't want to talk to Tom."

"Cassidy, what's wrong with you? I've never seen you like this. You're not all here. You're almost panicked."

"I'm beat. I'm just beat. Physically, mentally, emotionally. And I've got too many things to deal with. I can't deal with a killer. I can't even deal with my recovery and I feel so weak. I hate it. I hate it all. And my first reaction is to run but I can't even do that. I don't have the strength."

The walk back was more like a flight. I tried to just hike but an urgency drove me until I was almost jogging. I couldn't keep up that pace for long. Landon kept up but he didn't understand it at all. When my strength gave out I'd sit under a tree waiting until I could go on. Landon took off his pack and tried to get me to eat, to drink, but I was too agitated. I don't know how the weakness and exhaustion drove me, but it did. The worse I felt the more I needed the comfort of home. After my third rest stop I couldn't even walk. I stood up to walk and my legs wouldn't support me.

"What do I have to do, hogtie you? Cass, stop. You can't go on like this. You keep this up and you're not going to make it out. If you pass out on me, I'm calling a lift."

He knew I'd take his threat seriously. If there was one thing I didn't want it was a lift. It would probably mean a trip to the hospital. He finally got me to eat a granola bar and that made me thirsty so I took a drink. It still took a couple of tries before I could go on. By the time we reached the cars I was staggering through the trees. Landon opened the Search and Rescue car so I could sit. The people who had gathered at the car had moved to the base camp to get word via radio. Landon put his pack in the back seat and sat in the driver's seat, undecided.

"Landon, I want to go home. If I can just go home I'll lock all the doors and sleep for a week."

He started the car but he argued with himself all the way home. When the Explorer wasn't in the driveway he followed me into the house and made sure everything was okay.

"Are you sure you'll be all right?" he asked.

"Yeah, I'll lock the doors and I'll rest. Rusty will be home after work."

He left grudgingly.

The old brown couch beckoned. I collapsed into its lumpy brown comfort. As exhausted as I was, I thought sleep would come quickly, but instead the exhaustion fed the thoughts niggling at the back of my brain. I could still feel the emotion of the trail. Still see the bullet holes through little bits and pieces of a nameless man's life. Still see the body as I tripped over it. Still feel the mind numbing exhaustion that caused me to be so inattentive that I didn't see his lifeless form until I was on top of it.

Through all the things that had happened to me, I was still glad to be alive. Even when I was hanging by a thread, when my life was in the balance I wanted it to tip just a bit more towards life, towards continued existence. When I was beaten and left to die I fought it, fought for life. And when I was so filled with sorrow that all I knew to do for it was to run, eventually life won. The man's body haunted me. The sorrow and the finality of it made my heart ache.

My body ached from the hiking, pushing myself too far. My mind ached from watching the trail, seeing the hurt, the violence in the man I tracked. My heart ached with sorrow and fear. As I lay there as useless as could be, every noise made me jump and listen closely, analyzing it for possible danger. But what could I do about it if Dirk showed up? I was barely able to walk after all I'd done that day. I longed for Rusty. I needed him to put the pieces back together. That thought made me pause. And why did I need that? I thought. Why was I all of a sudden so dependent on Rusty? I used to do anything in my power to prevent him from seeing me like this, weak and emotional. I'd flee to the mountains and deal with it on my own and now I just lay here yearning for him, reaching out over the miles to town, trying to send him a silent prodding to come home. Please come home. I need your arms around me. I need to know today will get better. I need to smell your old brown sports coat. And then the tears came.

He came in quietly knowing I could be sleeping. At that point I didn't know what I was. I was in a limbo of sorts, too spent to stand, too drained to react. He sat down on the floor in front of the couch and watched me cry quietly. I opened my eyes and he was there. I reached out to him and he rubbed my back.

"Rusty… come here. Please, come here," I cried. "I need you so bad."

His eyes narrowed. "I'm going to clobber Wilson, next time I see him."

"No, don't, I already did," I said, my voice still shaky.

He sat on the couch and drew me down into his arms. Finally, I knew I'd make it through the day.

"He was supposed to keep this from happening."

"Just hold me. Please. Make today go away."

"Okay, babe, it's okay."

"No more violent tracks. No more bullets holes. No more pushing for the next few steps. No more stumbling blindly over dead bodies. No more worrying about Dirk today. No more nightmares."

"No more, it's all over."

"I need some strength. Can I soak up some of your strength?"

"Take all you want."

"I want to be well again. I'm so tired."

"I know babe. You will be well again."

"How long?" I cried as I sank deeper and deeper into despair.

"Patience," he said quietly as he pulled me closer.

"I need to soak up some patience, too, then."

Gradually I settled into an uneasy rest.

"We need some dinner," Rusty said. "Let me go fix something, even if it's just breakfast or sandwiches. I know you don't want to go to town."

He got up and started poking around the kitchen. The phone rang and Rusty got it so I wouldn't get up.

"Hello?" he said. Then he went to the window and began looking out to the hills around the house. "No, you're not getting two seconds," he said angrily. He moved from window to window, even after he hung up the phone. It had to be Dirk. That was the only thing I could think of that would send Rusty to the windows like that. A couple more phone calls and Rusty went back to the kitchen. He didn't mention the phone call, not wanting to upset me, but I knew. And I knew, at least tonight, I didn't need to worry.

Chapter 29

I was tracking for Tom again, this time with full knowledge of what the outcome would be. I could see the body, crumpled on the ground, with a bullet hole through one side of the head and the other side blasted wide open. Glock 45. Pistol. One shot to the head. This time I didn't stumble over the body. I knew it was coming. I expected it. I dreaded it.

"Cassidy, babe, wake up. Come on, back to me." Rusty shook me gently. "Cass… no more nightmares. Remember? We're here. Just the two of us. Come here, I've got you." The words flowed and I gradually relaxed, snuggling deeper. Hiding from my memories. Turning to the one good thing I had. My Rusty.

Morning dawned and I didn't stir. Rusty's alarm went off and he shut it off, saw I was still there and went back to sleep. Half an hour later I shook him gently. "You're going to be late for work."

"I'm not going to work. I already called Schroeder."

"I thought you called Schroeder about the call from Dirk."

He paused a second, a little surprised I had made the connection. "He wanted to talk to you but I wouldn't let him. He asked where you were yesterday but I didn't give him an answer. He said he'd be watching. He said he'd find his chance. He said he had a plan. So I'm not going to work. I'm on stake out. I'm staking out your place."

The talk brought Shadow to our bedside. I groaned and got up to feed him and let him out. Rusty followed me. When I went outside he came out, sidearm ready, he scanned the hills. I did my minimal morning responsibility and went back to bed. Shadow was disappointed but the morning routine had been fulfilled so he ate his food, then found a place to wait for something more interesting to happen. Rusty wasn't disappointed. He didn't mind going back to bed at all.

"This is a cushy job," he said. "I could get used to this. Beautiful woman, comfortable bed."

"Mmm, how close do you need to stake me out to make sure I'm safe?"

"As close as possible."

"Is this an inside operation?"

"Hmm, could be. I better check."

He burrowed under the covers and planted kisses up my legs, across my stomach, up my body. Yesterday was fading quickly from my mind as I anticipated what was coming. Rusty's magic fingers. I could have shot Dirk myself when there was a crash outside and Shadow lunged at the bay window barking furiously. Rusty and I grabbed our nearest weapons and lunged for the window, too. Rusty whipped the shutters aside. Dirk ducked into the trees as Rusty and I stood there in our birthday suits. Dirk turned around and Rusty stepped in front of me, raised his gun and fired through the window. Dirk continued his flight. Was he walking differently? I couldn't tell because Rusty pulled me away from the window and ran to pull on some pants and shoes.

"Rusty! No! He's armed!" I yelled but he took off after Dirk, anyway. I pulled on jeans, and a t-shirt. Rusty needed backup! I wasn't going to let him chase down an armed man without help. Lousy shot or not, Dirk might just get off a lucky shot. By the time I got out to the yard Rusty was out of sight so I ran to the camp. As I passed the barn an arm came out of nowhere and brought me up short. Jayce was lucky I didn't blast his head off! I turned, began leveling my gun and saw uniform. He grabbed my hand and forced it away until he knew I wasn't going to shoot.

"What are you doing here? And why didn't you see Dirk when he snuck up on the house?"

"We were told to patrol the area. We were driving by and we heard shots. When I pulled up Rusty told me to stop you, so I'm stopping you."

"Go help Rusty!"

"Not until I know you'll stay home, inside, with the doors locked."

I figured Jayce was a bigger help to Rusty so I went to the house in frustration. At least he would shoot. I still had my doubts of whether I would or not. I knew I'd only fire if I thought it was in defense of another. I wouldn't fire simply to stop Dirk.

I went to the house and locked the doors so Jayce would leave and help Rusty. Inside I was fighting it. But I really wasn't capable of helping much. Just running to the barn had tired me. All I could say was I was a better shot than most of them but what good was it if I wouldn't shoot? When I thought about it I'd most likely complicate things for them. I paced the house. When I grew weak and shaky I slapped some deli meat between two slices of bread. I stood in the kitchen eating my makeshift breakfast. Shadow sat obediently at my feet waiting for tidbits. Every once in a while he glanced down the hall. I thought he expected Rusty to come out and I dearly wished Rusty would. Food was more important to Shadow. I tossed him a bit of bread and he caught it and sat again. He knew carrying on and begging only got him a cold shoulder. As long as he minded his manners he had a good chance of getting something. Another glance down the hall a quick check on the sandwich. A click of a gun. I froze, sandwich midway to my mouth. Shadow ran to the hall, barked twice in greeting and ran back to the sandwich. Some watchdog.

"Nice of your husband to leave a nice big window open for me," Dirk said.

I'd remembered the window when Jayce sent me home but I didn't remind him of it because I wanted him to join the chase. I didn't worry about it because I thought Dirk would be on the run. Great, I thought, I am in no shape to take Dirk on. I even wondered if I had enough energy to take Rusty on and he only wanted a little playtime.

"You've got lousy timing," I told Dirk.

"It was more entertaining than what I had planned. Gave me some ideas. I hadn't thought of watching you die nude."

I took a bite of my sandwich. I had to stall for time.

"I meant you have bad timing because the police could be back any time."

"I'm not worried. They aren't following me. They just think they are. I just need a few minutes."

"If you think it's only going to take a few minutes to kill me you better think again. I can be a royal pain in the ass."

"I was hoping you would be, because I don't want you to go down easy."

"It's a deal. I won't."

"We need to be going."

"No. Rule number one for being a royal pain in the ass is to not cooperate with your captor."

"Walk," he said. "Or I'll shoot."

"Please, do," I said. "So far you've only managed to waste bullets when you've shot at me. Oh, and you blew up a mine."

That made him mad. "Let me tell you about the mine. That mine held more money than I've seen in a lifetime. The money, had the family survived, should have been mine. My family was driven away, murdered, some brutally. The family was almost cleaned out by land grabbing politicians. My mother fled to another part of the country but she always told me, while I was growing up, that there was a fortune, a family fortune buried somewhere in the foothills outside Joshua Hills, California. I spent years researching family history. I came out here to restore the family name, to find the family roots, to discover the family fortune. Instead I found ruins and cryptic notes and a meddling kid. It was a pleasant surprise when I found out you weren't a kid. I'd have had trouble killing a kid. Come to find out you're a cop. That was some surprise."

"I'm not a cop," I said, though technically I might be, if I had a senior officer, if I had a job to do, then maybe. But I was a lousy one, one they couldn't count on. So, although I had the uniform and the sporadic authority, neither I, nor they, considered me a cop. "I'm a tracker."

"You? Ha, that's a good one. That's even harder to believe than you being a cop."

"I was tracking a woman when you met me. She was looking for Ronald Kingsley's jewelry making shop. She found it. You found me."

"Well, at least one of us came out ahead. Kingsley's shop was worth a bundle. He was my great uncle."

"She didn't get to keep it. She was arrested."

"You mean it's still there?"

"Not exactly. Last I saw the house it was engulfed in flames."

"You're just full of good news," he said sarcastically. "We need to take a little ride."

"You're not getting me past the door without a fight."

I slid down the counter gradually aiming for the knife drawer. As I did I was mentally scanning the house. Where had I left my cell phone? Where was my gun? I was cornered in the kitchen, but if I had a chance where should I go? Dirk closed in. I wasn't going to make it to the knife drawer. I feinted a lunge towards it and when he dashed in to stop me I shoved him into the cupboards. His head hit with a heavy thud. I dashed past while he was figuring things out and tipped over a dining room chair as I ran by. He swore as he ran after me. I grabbed Rusty's cell phone off the nightstand as I stumbled toward the broken window. I was deciding quickly that I couldn't outrun Dirk. Just this little tussle had me winded and aching. I pocketed the phone. I didn't want Dirk to know I had it. He grabbed my arm and hauled me back. I swung around and grabbed his gun hand. He brought it down and I pushed it away. If it was a battle of strength he was going to win. He forced me to the floor. I kicked and punched ineffectually. My strength was fading fast. The search had taken a toll on my stamina. Dirk's hands closed around my throat.

"I hadn't planned to do this here but you aren't... giving me... much... choice!" he growled. "I *will* see you die."

In my thrashing around I felt something with my fingers. It was nice and solid, metal. The gun! It was the gun! I reached, desperate to get that handle in my grasp. Each time I felt it, it slipped just a few inches farther away. I needed that gun! It was down to a life and death fight now and he wasn't getting me this easy. I squirmed in the direction of the pistol, stars dancing where Dirk's face should have been.

"Poor little girl, she's turning blue. You better get some air little one," he sneered with mock sincerity.

Okay, I thought, finally grasping the gun in my hand, one breath for you, then one for me. I brought my hand up. I hated the only angle I could get, but I was fixing to black out. I didn't know what this angle would do and time was growing short. I pointed the gun at his side and a wretched sobbed squeezed past Dirk's fingers as I pulled the trigger.

Dirk's eyes got big, not believing what had happened to him. He got to his knees but his lungs were filling quickly with blood. I struggled loose as Dirk knelt nearby feeling the wound in his side. I staggered to my feet. I didn't know what to do. I was in so much shock all I could do was call for help. I dialed 911 and croaked out that I needed an ambulance and the police. I gave them the address.

"Are you in immediate danger?" the woman asked.

"Just get them here fast," I said.

"Please stay on the line. What is the condition of the injured party?"

"He's dying!" I cried. "But I need to hang up. I need to call the police."

"That isn't necessary. Please stay on the…"

I hung up. I had Rusty's phone so I flipped through the numbers until I came up with Schroeder. I didn't wait for his questions to start.

"Schroeder, Rusty's with Thompson and Jacobsen. Call them off and send them here."

"Cassidy, I can't just call them whenever I want."

"Then get ahold of the person who does! I've got a guy dying in my bedroom and I need help!"

"What?"

"You heard me. I've got to go. I can't stand this…Schroeder please…"

The stupid thing was Dirk wasn't quite dead. Even as he was dying he found the strength to give it one last try. With a strangled gurgle he staggered toward me and launched himself at me. He pinned me to the wall leering at me, hands groping for my face, grasping my neck. I kicked him in the groin and he started to double over but his grip was too strong and he was leaning into me. He dragged me down with him, spasms wracking his body. Mentally I recoiled. I couldn't take in the violence. My brain shut it out. All I could do was lay there quietly sobbing.

"Cassidy?" I could hear through the phone. Schroeder was still there.

A rescue squad arrived first, followed by the ambulance. Landon recognized the address over the radio and took the call. He banged on the door.

"Cassidy!" he called out.

I could hear the noises out front but they barely penetrated my numb mind. I knew if I didn't go answer the door, they'd kick it in, but I couldn't force myself to move. More voices. They didn't want to enter a potentially dangerous situation but Landon's voice argued over the others. There was quiet and then he was climbing in the broken window. He ran to the front door and unlocked it then ran back to me.

"Cassidy? Girl, come on. Talk to me."

"I killed him," I sobbed. "I had to. Landon, I think I killed him."

"Don't think about it. Help me here. What are the injuries?"

"I shot him. Through the side. He was choking me. I had to. I swear I had to. He would have killed me."

"Don't think about it," he repeated. His partner got the information he needed though. "What about you?"

"I don't care about me," was all I could cry. The struggle was still going on in my head the blows, the shot echoed on and on. Landon checked me over. He felt for broken bones. He palpitated for internal injuries. When Rusty walked in Landon quickly took him aside. Rusty almost slugged him.

"Michaels, wait half a second. Cass is okay. But I don't know what to do. She needs you but it's going to take patience. Maybe I should take her in. She can't take this. She had to shoot the guy. She's got bloody handprints around her neck, around her arm. But I can't find anything physically wrong with her. She's just in shock." He got out of the way and Rusty pushed past. I still lay on the floor, just sobbing. I'd turned on my side and covered my head with my arms, trying to block out everything I could.

"Babe? It's Rusty. Come on. Come here. It's okay."

No response, just quiet sobbing.

"I know you had to. Cassidy, you wouldn't have shot him unless you had to. Try and think of something else."

No response. I thought I'd cry for the rest of my life. People came and went. Tom tried to get a statement out of me. All he could do was gather evidence. Finally, Rusty was able to gather me up and sit with me on the floor, just holding me. Schroeder arrived, looked around the room and hung up the cell phone.

"Let's try this from a different angle," Rusty said. "Who was the guy on the yellow bike?"

No response, at first, then a sobbed, "I don't know."

At least it was words.

"Did Dirk know who he was?"

"I think so."

"How'd Dirk get in? The door was locked."

"The broken window."

"The kid on the bike was just a diversion?"

"Yeah."

"What did he do to you, babe? What made you do it?"

That put me over the edge again. "He was going to take me away. I wouldn't let him. He lost his temper. He was choking me. Rusty… I had to. It was my only chance. Make it go away. Make it stop. It's all I can see."

"Shh, open your eyes. Come on, open your eyes. You'll see it's just me."

I opened my eyes and I did see it was just Rusty. Rusty sitting near an immense pool of blood. Blood splattered on the walls and furniture. A bloody handprint smeared down the wall. I hid my eyes again.

"Oh, babe, I'm sorry. We won't stay here tonight. We'll find someplace else."

But we didn't. After the police cleared out Rusty helped me shower. He helped me into flannel pants and a tank top and we lay down in the guestroom. For several days I was barely there. I was still weak from the surgery and the search, then the fight. The mental strain pushed me over the edge until I almost didn't care if I got better. Rusty told me when to eat and when to sleep. If he didn't I would have simply existed in a world of violence and blood. Nights were the worst. Nightmares haunted me. I was scared to go to sleep because my thoughts ran uncontrolled. At least when I was awake I could slow them down.

"It's like she's stuck in time," Rusty was telling Kelly. "She lives the attack."

"Like after Stern."

"Yeah."

"She'll come around. Give her time."

"How much time? Sometimes I think the more time she has the deeper she sinks."

They were talking like I wasn't there, and in a way I wasn't. I wasn't there enough to argue. Hell, I couldn't argue because it was all true.

"She lost a baby, tracked a suicide case, and was almost strangled. All that hit physically as well as psychologically. Each of those has serious complications. It's going to take time."

It wasn't the attack that haunted me, though. It was the shot.

PART 3

THE LONG RIDE HOME

Chapter 30

I never would have guessed Rusty's solution to my problem. All I can say is I thought he was nuts.

A man rang my doorbell one evening. I was afraid to open the door. Seems like whenever I open the door disaster enters my life. Rusty went to the door and opened it without looking out the peephole. He must have been expecting someone. I wished he'd told me so I could have been dressed for company. There stood a middle aged cowboy. He wore very worn and faded blue jeans over dusty boots, a white western shirt with the sleeves rolled up to his elbows and a bent up straw cowboy hat. He took off his hat when he saw a lady was present. He had serious hat hair. The band was pressed into his slightly overgrown hair. His blue eyes were sharp, reflecting a kind heart and a quick mind.

"Cassidy, this is Farley McGyver. Farley, this is my wife, Cassidy."

I shook Farley's hand and he said, "Good to meet you." His voice was quiet and kind making me think he knew more about me than I did about him.

I was wary. This had the smell of one of Rusty's surprises. I had to be nice but I wasn't sure I was happy about whatever he had up his sleeve.

"Farley has a project for you. If you will take it on, I think it'll be good for you. He has a three-year-old horse that needs to get used to people. I told him you had experience with horses, that you were particularly good at gentling unruly horses in training."

I looked at him dumbfounded. He wanted me to *train a horse*? When I couldn't even walk around the block?

"What are your plans for this horse?" I asked Farley. My voice sounded like it was coming from far away, but it was important to keep the ultimate goal in mind when training a horse, so I persevered despite my reluctance.

"He was given to my school. I have horses that handicapped kids ride. It helps them develop balance and self-esteem. Their coordination improves dramatically when they learn to ride and care for a horse. I have kids in and out of the stables all day. I can use all the horses I can get but I can only have horses at the ranch that I can trust with the kids. If I get one I can't let the kids ride, I foster it out. All I need is someone to work with him. It doesn't matter how long it takes as long as it's done right."

"So you just need him to respond to basic riding commands and be gentle with kids?"

"If that's possible. If you have really good luck with him I've got some kids getting advanced enough to try jumping. It wouldn't be high jumps, just enough so the kids have to develop some better riding skills."

"Is he saddle broke?"

"He was at one point. The former owners didn't have time to devote to him so he needs a refresher course."

"Is he sound?"

"Yes, and he's a beautiful horse. The kids love pintos because they are flashy. The kids will learn anything to be able to graduate to this horse."

"And we're not on a time table?"

"None at all."

"Because I've got some handicaps of my own right now."

Farley looked concerned.

"Do you think this horse is too much for you?"

"No horse is too much for me. Put him in the corral."

He raised an eyebrow at that but Rusty just grinned. Okay, he had me. I wanted to see this horse. While the men brought the horse around back I changed into jeans, a camouflage t-shirt and boots. I brushed my hair. I was amazed how much I had let myself go in my depression. When I went out back, already tired from just getting dressed, there was, indeed, a beautiful pinto horse in the corral. He was ready to be out of the trailer and he had energy to boot. He pranced around the corral tossing his head. I walked to the corral and ducked through the fence. Rusty almost stopped me.

"What's his name?" I asked.

"The kids wanted to name him Apache because they think he looks like an Indian pony. Then one kid pointed out that he's a patchy horse so the name stuck."

"Where's the rope?" I asked.

He handed one over. I formed a loop and walked toward Apache. I lassoed him easily, much to the surprise of both men. I followed the rope closer. I looked over the horse from head to toe. He stamped his hoof at me and I gave him a stern "ah ah" so he'd know he was overstepping his bounds. I lifted his hoof and he jerked his leg away. I tried again. I wanted to make sure he was properly outfitted and I wanted to see if he was used to being handled.

"Where's his tack?"

"You're not going to try and ride him today, are you?"

"He's that rusty?"

"That's your call."

I led Apache around the corral. He was spunky. I wasn't sure if he was ready for a rider or not but I wanted to find out while Farley was still here.

"Let's give it a try."

I didn't get to ride Apache that day. He startled whenever the saddle touched his back. He was going to take some work. He was used to a halter but fought the bit. Farley put two saddles, a bridle, about a week's worth of hay and a couple of grooming brushes in the barn. I had me a horse. Temporarily.

"You sure you're okay with this?" Farley asked.

"No," I admitted. "But it's worth a try. We'll be working each other."

When Farley was safely down the road I faced Rusty, hands on hips. "What makes you think I'll take in any mean spirited horse that someone else doesn't want to work with?"

Rusty just grinned broadly. "It's working already," he said. "It's good to see you mad."

"What?"

"Babe, you've been so depressed I didn't even know if you knew how to feel any more. It's a good sign that you're mad."

"I'm not mad yet. Why do you pull these things on me without talking to me first?"

"You know why."

"I do?"

"You know you can't say no to a horse. But if I talked to you ahead of time you wouldn't have felt up to it. Give you a horse and a challenge and I knew you'd be up to it. Farley always has a horse he needs worked. He chose Apache specifically for you. You can't go on a call anyway, so why not work on you and Apache for a few weeks?"

"*You* are a sneak!" I said.

"Thank you," he replied smugly.

He was also a genius. At first I could only work with Apache feeding and socializing him. Just feeding Apache tired me. While I rested and he ate I ran my hands over him. While he was still calm I picked up each hoof. After a few days I began working on his hooves with a pick. I didn't do any riding for several days and, when I did, I only rode late in the afternoon when I knew Rusty would be home soon. Riding didn't take much energy but it took plenty of concentration. Concentration on the horse took my mind off of the attack. I dragged into the house each evening, but I dragged in after working, not lying around having flashbacks all day.

When I finally did climb into the saddle Apache gave me a run for my money. Before I even sat in the saddle he tried to knock me off by squashing me against the fence. When I jumped into the saddle and moved my leg out of the way of the fence he began dancing around, trying to shake me. He didn't really buck but he was clearly irritated at having a passenger. I just sat the saddle rubbing Apache's neck and talking to him, telling him what a good boy he was, making friends from my perch on his back.

"Babe, you're amazing," Rusty said. "Do you know how far you've come in the past week? You haven't had nightmares for a couple of nights."

"I'm doing better during the day, too," I admitted. I could feel it, but I no longer lived the violence of the attack. The gunshot would be with me for years, but I'd managed to leave some of the violence behind.

Apache was slower to come around. He'd tolerate me in the saddle but he spent most of the time trying to get me off. He was young and feisty and didn't want to be restrained. He wanted to be in control. I couldn't let him. So my determination got a work out. It was a gradual process, half peer pressure, making friends, learning trust. The other half was the opposite, establishing authority. The two worked together in an odd way and each day it had to be attacked from a different angle.

Every morning I fed Apache and groomed him, checked his hooves, legs, ears, and teeth, not because I was worried about him but because he needed to be used to handling. I fed him little bits of carrot with the admonition to "be gentle." When I fed him whole carrots he nearly tore my hand off grabbing at the treat. Smaller pieces he had to feel around for and there was more time to talk to him and praise him when he was gentle.

We worked on all the basic commands in the saddle and some that I deemed necessary for his job. I taught Apache to stay put when his rider left him. I'd ride for a while and get off and he was supposed to stay until I told him otherwise. It was important that, if his rider fell off, he stand by patiently. So at first I stayed close and upright. But he needed to know that, no matter what his rider did, he still had to stay, so I lay on the ground, like a fallen rider waiting for him to break his stay so I could correct him.

One day, as I lay on the ground, Rusty came home and looked out the back door. I heard the back door open and hurried footsteps. I waited to see if Apache would stay. As Rusty climbed over the corral fence Apache shied away and I corrected him.

"Ah ah! Stay!" I told him. I put him back in place.

"Oh god, Cassidy, you scared me half to death. I thought you'd been thrown."

"We're just training. He's learning to stay."

"You could have told me that *before* I had a heart attack."

"I love you, too," I said with a kiss.

Apache's first trail ride showed me some areas we needed to work on. I put on the western saddle, glad I could finally lift it easily. I pointed Apache down Lost Hills Road and we set out at a leisurely pace. He startled when a car eased by on the road but I held him to a walk, praising him as the car disappeared down the road. I took note, we needed to practice working in the midst of distractions. Rusty could help with that. We continued down the road and then up a little dirt road that I knew went deeper into the hills. When the road opened out I sent Apache into a nice easy canter. He enjoyed stretching his legs and I enjoyed the free feeling of just being a girl on a horse on a ride in the hills. It reminded me of summers as a kid near my parent's ranch.

The desert and junipers gradually turned to pine trees. Apache was used to wide open spaces but as long as I was there he seemed to accept his surroundings. I heard a motorcycle coming down the road and braced for Apache's reaction. Unfortunately it was some damn fool person who enjoyed a good show. When he saw a horse on the road he gunned his engine. The loud buzz of the engine made Apache go crazy. The motorcycle roared by and Apache reared. As the bike roared past he bucked. I was hoping he'd give the motorcycle a good kick, but he took off running as fast as he could down the road as I cursed the motorcycle rider a mile a minute. If the circumstances were different I would have enjoyed the run but the road twisted and turned and I was afraid he'd barrel into a surprise as he dashed around the turns. There was a ranger truck ahead and a man stood by the side of the road with a chainsaw.

No! I thought as the man pulled the cord and the machine started up with a sharp buzz. Apache startled in another direction. He barreled off the road through a patch of thick undergrowth. He tripped in his hurry and we both rolled down the embankment, horse and rider a tangle of arms, legs and tack.

"Don't move," a voice told me gently. It was the ranger with the chainsaw.

"Where's my horse?" I asked.

"Don't worry about the horse. Just stay still. Paramedics will be here soon."

"Paramedics? No! Send them back."

"No way, look at you! Nothing's pointing the right direction."

"Well, it will be in a minute. Send them back. I'm only allowed one call per station per week. I don't want to use up my one call on a tumble off a horse."

The ranger just gawked at me, not believing I was still in one piece.

I started sorting out limbs. "How long was I out?"

"Fifteen minutes. What do I have to do pin you down?"

"The paramedics will tell you that doesn't work. They'll see it's me and get out their little clipboard. I'll sign their little form that says I refuse treatment and they will go home shaking their heads just like they do ninety-nine percent of the time. It's that little one percent they worry about, so they come. Of course, they are also coming because they don't know it's *me* yet. You just watch. When they see it's me their whole attitude will change."

"Who *are* you?"

"Trouble. How long have you worked up here?"

The ranger would have laughed at that if he hadn't been so worried. A little blonde woman, named Trouble, yeah, right.

"Five years," he said.

"I'm surprised we haven't met yet. You work with Kelly Green?"

"Occasionally."

"Ask Kelly Green who Trouble is. If you tell him about this, he won't be the least bit surprised."

The red rescue squad truck pulled to a stop on the road above us. By then I had all my limbs going the right direction and I was picking sticks and leaves out of my hair. The guys jumped out and got their trusty medical boxes off the truck.

"Hold it," Antonio said. "It's just Cassidy."

He put the box back and walked forward, hands on hips, an irritated look on his face.

"Don't blame me! I didn't call you. He did," I said pointing to the ranger. "Did you see a brown and white pinto on your way in?"

"We weren't exactly looking for a horse."

"Was Rusty's Explorer at the house when you passed?"

"We passed him coming up Sunset Road."

"Shoot."

"You need a ride?"

"No, I need to find my horse. Can you stop by the house and tell Rusty not to worry, that I'll be home as soon as I find Apache?"

"I guess," answered Antonio. "I still owe you one for finding Eva."

"No you don't. But if Rusty's worried he might just call you out to look for me, so it might be worth your while to stop."

"How are you going to find your horse?" the ranger asked.

The paramedics and I all looked at each other wondering which one of them would answer first.

"If there's one thing this kid can do it's find a horse."

"Yeah, catching up with him today might be the tough part," I added, "and I'm not going to catch him standing around talking. Where's your handy little form?"

"You're really going to let her off that easily?" The ranger asked. "She was unconscious when I got to her. I would have sworn every bone in her body was broken."

"What happened?" Antonio asked withholding judgment a few minutes more.

"I took a tumble with a horse."

"A tumble? That was *not* a tumble," the ranger insisted. "The horse rolled over the top of her! I didn't expect her to survive."

"Sounds like a normal Cassidy call to me," said Antonio, then he ordered me to sit. I sat with a sigh. He got out his box, gave me the quick check: pulse, blood pressure, light shined in the eyes, felt for broken bones.

Antonio got out his clipboard and put the proper form on top. I signed wondering how thick the folder for these forms was and how many of the forms in it had my signature on them.

"Thanks guys," I said to the paramedics.

"Take care, Cassidy."

"And thanks…"

"Tate."

"Thanks Tate, you talk to Kelly and you'll find out more about me than you ever wanted to know."

I walked down the embankment and looked at the crushed branches and trampled ground.

"Are you sure you're okay?" Tate asked.

"Yeah, just getting my bearings. I'm a tracker. I'm trying to see how banged up the horse is. I'll be on my way shortly."

I found Apache's trail and followed it easily. A horse is about the easiest animal to track. They are big and heavy and their shoes leave distinctive prints. They trample brush. I heard the chainsaw start up again behind me. Antonio drove away with a wave, back to my house and the station. It was hard to assess Apache's injuries. The brush was thick and hid the intricacies of the tracks. He was on his feet and moving. That was good news.

The main problem was I was not up to walking very far. Since the miscarriage I had one mishap after another. I had been housebound for weeks before Apache came along and since then I had only walked enough to train him. Walking from house to corral to barn did not take much effort. I walked slowly, conserving energy, knowing I might need some left over when I located the horse. If he didn't want to be caught I might have a chase on my hands. Maybe I should have had the guys send Rusty out here looking for me.

It was getting late and I had no food or water along. I knew if I had to head for home, I'd make it eventually. The problem was the eventually part. I thought about how far it was. I was guessing three or four miles. Normally that was a morning's hike. Now it was anybody's guess how long it could take. I sighed and admitted I'd bitten off more than I could chew. I decided it was more important to be findable. I could come back in the morning and locate Apache with better resources, so I headed for the road. By the time I got there I had to rest. I alternated walking and resting as I made my way homeward. The sun set and still I kept up the pattern until bright headlights appeared in front of me and the Explorer pulled up.

"Hey beautiful! Headed my way?" Rusty said.

I climbed into the Explorer and he took me home. He tried to keep things upbeat but the fact remained. I was beat and I had a horse loose in the woods.

"Maybe he'll come back on his own. You always said that horses have barn radar."

"I don't know if he considers our house his home. He might remember the way. He might want to come back here but he hasn't been here long. I still need to go back out and find him."

"I think I can help," Rusty said.

"How?"

"You think this hasn't happened to Farley's troublemakers before? I bet if we need a horse to get us out there to find Apache he'll bring us a horse that'll do the job. He'll probably be amazed Apache was ready for a trail ride."

"He obviously wasn't."

In the morning Farley brought two horses, saddled, bridled and ready to go.

"Are you okay?" he asked me. "Rusty told me what happened."

"Yeah, I scared a ranger half to death, but I'm okay. Apache needs to learn to work with loud noises around him. I didn't know that when I set out. Cars, motorcycles, chainsaws. He panicked at any loud noise. Are these riding horses we're on, or roping horses?"

"Riding horses. I don't have much use for a roping horse with kids doing beginner exercises in a ring."

"Okay, I'm used to working with roping horses. I just wanted to know what to expect."

The difference could mean catching Apache or losing him again. A roping horse has an entirely different reaction to a chase than a riding horse. A roping horse knows the cues, and senses when to stop and help set the rope. A riding horse only obeys commands related to riding. What it boiled down to was that I couldn't count on my horse to help once the rope was set.

I led Farley to the last place I'd seen Apache's hoof prints and we started down the trail again. When the tracks were clear I rode, when they weren't I walked. Farley was puzzled. Guess I hadn't made it exactly clear *how* I was going to find Apache.

After the tumble down the hill Apache had rolled to his feet and bolted downhill. He had run until he figured out the forest was not a racetrack.

Undergrowth impeded his movements so he slowed down. He walked in an agitated gait, still stressed by the events of the day. After he settled down he began doing what any horse will do if left to his own devices. He grazed. He walked. He grazed some more. As I read the tracks to Farley he stopped me.

"Wait a minute. How do you know what he did? Did you see him? Rusty said the ranger found you unconscious."

"I'm reading his tracks. I grew up with horses. I know what their feet do in every possible situation. I have no problem reading the tracks. I had an accident and I haven't built up my strength enough to walk this far. Otherwise I would have just stayed out here last night and stayed on his trail."

"You're not making sense. You grew up with horses so you know what their feet do?"

"And I'm a professional tracker. I work with the search and rescue unit in Joshua Hills, at least I did until this accident."

"Hell, I've been just looking out into the trees hoping we spot him and you say you're on his trail?"

"Yeah."

Apache headed in the general direction of home but when he got to Lost Hills Road he continued on into the junipers. He liked the wide open spaces and used it for a short run. Usually a horse on its own does very little running. Seeing Apache running for the fun of it showed me he was too young and too spirited to be forced into a life of trotting around a corral with a little kid on his back. He was destined for bigger things, at least until age caught up to him.

When we found him it was obvious he was going to give us a chase. I tried the easy approach first. I rode towards him talking quietly, loop ready to drop over his head, but every time I got near he gave me a mischievous look and pranced away.

"Are you ready for a run?" I asked Farley.

"I'm not *that* good with a rope."

"Okay, you block him in on one side and I'll give it a try."

We closed in on Apache and he tossed his head daring us to try it. When we got close he ran out of reach. I looked at Farley. Farley looked at me. He nodded. I put the heels to my horse and it bolted forward. Apache thought it was a game. He snorted and took off running. I was glad to see his legs didn't pain him. I expected some injuries from the tumble he took.

Feeling a good solid horse beneath me felt wonderful. He reached out with his hooves. He pounded across the desert after the fleeing paint. I opened up the loop ready for a toss but I never got close enough. Apache was just too fast, too game. My horse was older, smaller and sturdier. He was a workhorse but he wasn't used to rounding up spirited youngsters. Three times we tried to lasso Apache and he outran us every time. Farley and I regrouped.

"Think we should call it a day?" he asked.

"No. I've got one more trick up my sleeve. It's going to take time and patience but it won't wear the horses out. I need you to distract him. Let him think you're trying to catch him but don't chase him."

"What are you going to do?"

"Stalk him."

"You've got to be kidding. Here?"

"Just distract him."

I slung the lasso over my shoulder and got off my horse. I walked off to a nearby juniper and gave Farley the go ahead signal. He rode toward Apache. I snuck from tree to tree to bush until I had an angle I could work with. Apache watched Farley carefully, trying to figure out this new game. I snuck up on him slowly. Every once in a while he'd look around for me and I froze. I stayed calm, like I was just standing around in the desert for no reason. He didn't consider me a threat. The man on the horse though, he might still be, so he watched Farley. Farley's eyes crinkled in merriment as he saw me get ever closer to Apache's flank. By the time I was close I began rethinking my plan. If I lassoed him he might try to drag me off through the desert. What if I just got in the saddle?

While Apache was watching Farley I motioned him closer. Farley shot me a questioning look and I nodded. He started toward Apache, who startled a few quick steps closer to me. I timed my leap carefully. Foot in the stirrup, a quick pull and I was in the saddle. Apache was irritated. He bucked around and Farley watched and worried as I rode it out.

"Stop it you knucklehead," I said to the horse. "Just remember, I've got the carrots."

Carrots? He knew that word.

I rode up beside Farley. "Guess he still needs some work," I told him, then I detailed how far we'd come and what I had learned we needed to work on. We gathered up the other horse who had stood by obediently. We talked as we rode. He asked about the accident and my experience at the ranch. As we neared the road I listened carefully for cars, motorcycles, anything motorized. We crossed the road to my house and put the horses in the corral.

"Come out to the school," Farley said. "I can use all the volunteers I can get. It would keep you on your feet walking beside the horses as the kids ride. You can teach them the commands, and be there in case of trouble. I need people with your experience. Just try it once for a few hours, see if it's something you could enjoy. I know just seeing a kid who one day was a listless wheelchair case suddenly perk up at the site of a horse keeps me going. Even if they never ride they seem to come alive when they see the horses. Kids who struggle with leg braces can ride with ease. It gives them freedom from their handicap. Give them a half hour lesson on a horse and they feel they can do something. It carries on to other parts of their lives. They try to walk, they use their hands. They care for the horses, too. You should see it."

"Give me a ride home and I'll look at your school," I said.

The horses had a full day, so there wasn't any further training for me to do that day. Apache was safely ensconced in his corral again, so I rode to the school with Farley in the school pickup.

"You'll find this place a little different than most of the horse places you're used to," Farley said. "I'll tell you about each case as I can. Don't ask about the kid's handicaps in front of them. We try to get them to forget their handicaps. To their face they are any normal person. A kid might be thirty but inside they are still kids. Take Terrel, for instance. Terrel is thirty-two but he plays video games. He can play video games with his eyes shut and win but he can't spell his name. He'll tell you his name is Terl. But he's a great kid. He rides Brownie. That's another thing. The horses have weird names because the kids name them. You can guess why Brownie has his name. We also have Lassie, Socks, Yoshi, Giant and Indy. Indy is our other pinto. Yoshi got his name because he has a big nose. He reminded Terrel of the little dinosaur on the video games. Giant is big. He's a draft horse. All the names have reasons behind them but the meanings aren't always clear to outsiders."

The variety of horses on Farleys ranch was as wide as the variety of kids who came and went all day. Six-year-old Sarah rode Indy. She came in a wheelchair accessible van but she walked to Indy's stable one lurching step at a time. There were hand rails all around the stable for the kids who needed a steady support. A volunteer helped her saddle and bridle the little horse and helped her into the saddle. I watched as the volunteer guided the horse out to a large corral. Sarah's eyes shown as she rode quietly around the corral. The volunteer stood before the horse.

"Now Sarah, do you remember how to turn the horse? Show me how to turn right."

The little girl reined left but had the motion down correctly.

"That's left, but that's good!" the volunteer praised. "So how do you turn left?"

And so it went. It was all easy stuff. Things I had known all my life.

"Cassidy? This is Bailee," Farley said. "Bailee has been coming here for two years. Haven't you Bailee?"

The girl just looked at Farley with big blue eyes. She stood tall for her nine years but her hands curved inward and her fingers were stiff.

"Bailee is a super rider, aren't you Bailee? This is Cassidy. I want you to show Cassidy your horse."

I followed the young girl to the stable where she stopped in front of Socks's stall.

"Mine harse," Bailee said with difficulty.

"He's a beautiful horse," I told her. In reality Socks was an old horse and looked old in every way. His black coat was graying but his white socks still stood out boldly. He was a kindly horse, though, nuzzling Bailee and standing quietly as she groomed him. Bailee grasped the brush with difficulty. It hurt me to watch her although she enjoyed every minute of the time she spent brushing the horse. I grabbed a brush and went to work on the other side. When Socks was brushed to her satisfaction she led me to the tack room. I could see that each piece of tack had a laminated list clipped to it with the kid's names on it. There were saddles of all shapes and sizes and bridles with different configurations. Bailee needed a bridle with the reins tied. That way she could rest it over her withered hands without losing a rein. Some of the saddles had straps designed to keep the kids in place. Some had extra handholds. Bailee had a normal saddle and she *was* a super rider. She showed me a wall where clipboards were kept. In big, bold letters her name shined on the top of a clipboard in purple glitter paint. It was obvious Bailee had written the name herself. The letters were scrawled but legible and it was decorated with pink flowers with neon green squiggles for stems. I took down Bailee's clipboard and read: Three circuits. Walk. Trot. Canter. Pole weave. Gate.

Farley looked over my shoulder.

"A circuit is a figure eight in the corral. We do figure eights so the kids get more practice reining. Let's go. Ready Bailee?"

Farley led me through a class with Bailee. As she rode out of earshot he told me her story. "She was a normal kid until a car accident. She had head injuries. There was some paralysis from strokes and therapy helped her work through most of it. Her hands are bent from lack of use. She can read and write but she barely speaks. She's quit trying to talk except the few words she knows well. One day she had a birthday party at her house. She was excited because she had received a horse figurine for her birthday. She kept trying to tell me she got a sma harse. I just smiled and told her that was great, not knowing what she meant by sma harse. If she does say something, listen. It's very important that what she says counts. Many of these kids get fixated on something. With Bailee it's horse books. She can be a normal kid in a horse book. She can be a normal kid here, living a horse book."

When Bailee finished a figure eight at a walk Farley called out, "Now a trot!" Her eyes lit up with each advancement through the sequence. She found the gate to be a challenge. The trick was to open a gate from the saddle, ride through it and then close it. It was new to her. Her hands didn't help but Farley knew she could accomplish the task. He didn't raise his voice in any way but he insisted the gate had to be closed and latched properly or else the horses would get away. She understood but she wrestled with the gate and when she finally got it he clapped and grinned broadly and when she dismounted he hugged her cheerfully.

Every Tuesday and Thursday I showed up at Farley's school. I tried to get there around the same time Bailee showed up. I always arrived at the school with mixed emotions. It was hard for me to face the kids. Their challenges seemed too big. How could they take it? But put them on a horse and they could do anything. It was heartwarming and humbling. Each day brought a little more lifting and a little more walking and the work with Apache was challenging. After his great escape he reverted a little and we had to go back to corral work again.

Then one day I realized I wasn't tiring as quickly and I could work around the house again and I didn't get winded like I used to. Only problem was now I didn't have time for all those household chores I'd tried so hard to do. I was too busy. I had to find a way to start backpacking again. That was my last hurdle before I'd be ready to track again. So I began wearing my pack to the school. Bailee looked at me weird. We got along great now even though it was in a quiet way. We enjoyed each other's company. She patted my backpack and gave me a questioning look.

"What?" I asked good naturedly, trying to get her to form words.

She thought for a moment. "What you do?" she asked.

Words!

How to explain the pack though?

"I need to carry a pack for my job. I got hurt. I couldn't carry it. I'm getting better so I try to wear the pack to get used to it."

"You yike me," she stammered.

"Of course I like you," I answered.

She got frustrated. "You yike me, try gate. Use to it." Her struggle with the words touched me. Yes, I was just like her. She used to be able to open a gate. Now she was relearning, getting used to it. We were all in this life together.

"You're doing great on the gate. You and Socks are learning together. That's even harder than learning by yourself and you're doing great!"

I went through that whole lesson with a big lump in my throat, watching Bailee struggle. I hardly noticed my pack on my back.

For some reason Farley never questioned the pack.

When I had been wearing the pack to the school for about a week I had a surprise visit. I was carrying my pack to my new Jeep when Strict drove up.

"How did you know?" he asked.

"I don't know anything. I'm going to the riding school. Bailee's lesson starts in half an hour."

That got a strange look.

"What's with the pack?"

"The usual. I've been wearing it at the school and around the house doing chores so I can get used to the weight. Why?"

"So, are you used to the weight? I came to see how you were doing. Figured you'd be bored stiff, sitting at home. I have a job for you if you are up to it. Rusty thinks you might be."

I couldn't believe I was torn between a search and a kid at the school. Bailee would be disappointed if I didn't show up. She was finally talking to somebody. How could I not go? I thought through the contents of my search pack. It was ready. Was I?

"I have to talk to somebody first. You talked to Rusty?"

"Yeah."

"Do you want to go with me? Or should I meet you up there?"

"How long will it take?"

"An hour tops."

We tossed the pack into his Suburban and I gave him directions to the school. When we got there I found Farley.

"I need to go on a search, I'll be gone for a few days. Can somebody take over with Bailee until I get back?"

"I will. She's not going to be happy though."

"I know. I'll talk to her." Strict followed me to Socks's stable. "Hi Bailee!" I said brightly.

She smiled her usual lopsided grin.

"Remember I told you I had to carry a pack for my job? Well, I need to go. My job is to look for lost people and there's a person who needs to be found. Farley will do your lesson with you and I'll be back soon."

Her lower lip trembled. She searched for words. Oh shoot, I didn't think it would be *this* hard.

"How yong?" she asked.

"Maybe one day, maybe a few. But if I don't find them they might get hurt."

"Yike me," she said, thoughtful.

"I don't want them to get hurt. I'll be back as soon as I can. You'll do good at your riding. Show Farley how far you've come. Show him you can do the gate easily now."

She nodded that she would. I turned to go.

"Chas!" It was the closest she could come to my name and it was the first time she had tried it.

"Yeah?"

"Me yike you."

"I like you, too. I'll be back soon," I said with a hug.

I never in my life thought a kid could affect me like that. I walked to the Suburban teary eyed.

"Cassidy!" Farley said as he ran up. "She talked! Does she talk like that to you?"

"She's coming along," I answered.

"You're an angel," he said.

"I'll be back, just as soon as I find my man."

"What are you doing here?" Strict asked indicating the school grounds.

"I'm working and walking and getting used to my pack…and I guess I'm helping a little girl learn to talk again. I've come as far as she has lately. If it weren't for the horses and the kids I'd still be at home half mopping my kitchen and giving up in disgust."

"Do you think you can backpack?"

"All I can say is, I'll try and I won't give up. I assume I'm going out with Landon again?"

"Yeah, until we know for sure, I want you and Wilson paired up as much as possible."

"He cares too much. I worry about him."

"He cares too much to let you hurt yourself. We both know you will if left to your own devices. So you're stuck with him for a while."

"Who am I looking for?"

"Did you have to ask that?"

"I always want to know who I'm looking for."

"All I can say is ignore the TV cameras. You're looking for Sherri Champlain."

"You've got to be kidding. How'd *she* get lost? Don't at least half a dozen paparazzi know where she is?"

"That's what got her lost, trying to get away from the crowds."

"How long has she been missing?"

"Overnight, not long by our standards. Her agent called, said she was supposed to be on the set at six-thirty this morning. He tracked her down to a campground and her friends said she took off in disgust because the photographers wouldn't leave her alone. She didn't want to be photographed camping. Said she needed a bath and at least an hour in front of the mirror, then she'd be ready for the camera. The cameras never stopped so she took off straight into the mountains."

I groaned, "What a first search to call me out on! TV cameras, mountain climbing, probably rocky terrain, half the world waiting on me. Why me?"

"Because you're good at it."

Base camp was a movie set. Where there was usually a trailer, a lean-to and a picnic table, there was all that plus three television crews, three fire trucks, two police cars, and half of Landon's coworkers. Light towers stood ready to blast forth as soon as the sun set. A helicopter circled overhead. Damn, this wasn't a search. This was a parade! Strict and I got out of the Suburban and he marched up arms crossed. Half a dozen volunteers met him on his way to the table.

"If I didn't call you about this search previously, go sit down," he called out over the crowd.

They all started milling around dejectedly. I sure wished one of them was a tracker. If there was ever a case I'd hand over to someone else this was it. I shunned publicity. The cameras, the tense waiting were going to grate on me. I wasn't sure I was capable of physically enduring the search and now I had the whole world watching me struggle through it.

Landon and I remained standing and Kent Jacobsen and Jayce Thompson stepped forward. I groaned again. I knew why they had been picked. They were used to working with me. They had the patience and experience. But they also expected things to get weird on any case I was involved in.

Strict nodded approval and then looked to me. "Crowd control," he said simply. As usual they were all outfitted with radios. I preferred to hike unencumbered. I also like to leave the gadgets to people who appreciated them. The guys liked the radio. Any of the trappings of search and rescue they took on willingly while I just made sure I had my food, water, and stove handy. "Follow Landon," he told me.

Landon led me around the back of base camp where a simple campsite was located. Nobody was in it. I assumed whoever camped there was part of the crowd at base camp.

"Here's her shoes," Landon said pointing to a picnic table. On it was six pairs of shoes.

"Who brings six pairs of shoes on a camping trip?" I asked.

"Sherri Champlain," he answered.

I looked over the soles. They were all nearly new. No wear marks on any of them.

"Do we know what kind shoes she took off in?"

"Hiking boots."

"Brand new, too?"

He looked at the pile of shoes. "Probably."

"Do we have any sample tracks?"

"Umm, yeah, we have a whole gaggle of tracks, unfortunately I think all Sherri's friends also have identical brand new hiking boots. Take a look at the camp."

Damn, he was right, tracks everywhere, same size, nearly the same tread.

"Okay," I said with a sigh. "Do we at least have a direction?"

"The cameras came from that way. So…"

"Isn't there a friend somewhere around here that we can get some directions from?"

"We'll have to wade into the crowd to find them."

"No thanks, I'll find it."

As I slipped into the forest to begin my half circle of the camp I could hear Strict answering reporter's questions.

"Our time table depends strictly on the terrain involved. I don't expect a find until tomorrow. Sherri has a day's head start on us. Only she knew where she was heading. All we have to go on is the clues she left behind. We've got the best crew there is. They will give this search their all and then some."

It took three ever-widening passes before the tracks thinned enough to pick out Sherri's tracks. The attitude in them was different from her friends. Her friends' tracks milled around wandering in zigzag lines. Hers led in a straight line away from camp and headed into a thickly forested, but rugged, canyon. She stopped frequently to look behind her. Unfortunately the canyon she chose was rocky, desolate and held no promise of water unless it rained. If it rained it would turn into a flash flood zone. Trees had been washed down the canyon from previous storms, but fortunately this wasn't the rainy season. There were plenty of rocks and fallen trees to complicate the movements of the photographers following her. Unfortunately, that meant there were plenty of rocks and trees to complicate our movements, too. The helicopter followed our every move. The only advantage to that was that maybe Sherri would hear it and try to signal it.

"Well, Michaels won't have to call in for his nightly update. He can just turn on the TV and watch you," Jacobsen said.

"Thanks, Kent," I said, but I was glad he reminded me. If at all possible, I needed to keep a positive attitude. I didn't want Rusty to see me struggling on the trail.

Struggle I did, though. It only took about a half mile for my pack to weigh a ton. Each step up the canyon became a challenge. I kept my head down, eyes on the trail. I made sure, if I ever looked at the helicopter it was with a cheerful attitude. I kept my troubles to myself.

"Couldn't they have sent a dog on this search?" I thought aloud.

"They brought a dog in. It smelled the tent and found every girl who had slept in it except Sherri. It smelled like perfume and the whole group smelled like a perfume counter."

"Don't they know perfume just attracts bugs?"

"Maybe they do now."

Sherri was sorry she wore brand new hiking boots. Her steps began changing as she hiked. Maybe she was getting tired, maybe the new boots were irritating her feet. She pressed on. I doubted she could have lost the photographers this quickly. We certainly hadn't. We came to a rock wall and Sherri's footprints led to the base. When I didn't see any sign of her following the base, I started up.

"Let me go first," I told the guys. "I need to look for sign."

Sign was in short supply on that rock wall. About halfway up I wondered what this looked like on TV. Hell, why did the press have to be so darned persistent? I reached for the next handhold, felt a ledge and heard a fierce rattle. I jerked my hand back and nearly toppled right off the rock. I held on with my left hand as small rocks rained down on the guys below.

"Cassidy!" Landon called.

I struggled to find handholds while I pictured the rattlesnake investigating my one handed hold on the rock. I imagined viewers all over the country holding their breath.

"Are you okay?" Jacobsen asked.

I located a pair of footholds and stood, pressed against the rock while I steadied my nerves.

"Did you see where my hand was?" I asked.

"No, we were talking," Landon admitted.

"Well, don't go there. There's a rattlesnake on the ledge."

I climbed horizontally across the rock before I started up again. When I looked at the ledge where the rattlesnake lay I saw Sherri's bootprint, halfway covered by the snake.

"The snake is right there," I called down, pointing.

When I got to the top I cast around for more tracks but things were still very rocky. I found the edge of the rocks and studied the ground, back and forth, back and forth until I found sign of Sherri's passing. I took note of her track, went back and waved the guys up.

"Look out for the rattlesnake," I warned them.

They all wisely shied away from the very handy looking ledge.

"You are the only woman I have met who would stay on a rock with a rattlesnake right next to her," Jayce said.

“I’ve had a little experience with rattlesnakes,” I reminded him.

After the climb up the rock Sherri seemed to have lost her pesky photographers because her trail turned from an angry escape to a pleasant hike. She must have been hot, tired, and thirsty but she continued on. I couldn’t. Once I’d determined that Sherri was okay and her trail was clear I had to stop. I took off my pack and sat down under a tree to rest.

“Sorry, guys. I have to,” I said. My breathing had turned to huffing and puffing and the day was starting to feel unusually warm, even for southern California. We had topped out. That was good news. It was a rough climb and had taxed any reserves of energy that I had. I couldn’t expect to stay on the trail as I had in the past. My recovery was just starting to look positive. At home I was nearly back to my normal self, much to Rusty’s relief. Every time he came home and I was doing something active he stopped and watched and when I came to a stopping point he reached out to me. His hands strayed more now that he knew I felt like a woman again. His hugs were wonderful. But a search was not normal household chores. It was carrying thirty-five pounds on my back on a hot, dry trail. It was climbing mountains with that thirty-five pounds on my back. And it was just plain work. Hard work, after what I had been through.

“You’re doing a lot better than I feared,” Landon said when he caught up. “I didn’t want Strict to send you out but he said this was too high profile to just go beating the bushes over. Strict wasn’t sure if you’d be ready either. That’s why he went after you himself. What did you do to convince him?”

“Well, I was loading my pack in the Jeep when he arrived. He thought I knew about the call already but I was just getting ready for work.”

“You’re working now? What are you doing?”

“It’s not what you think. I’ve been teaching kids how to ride horses. And I’ve been training a rowdy horse. I’m trying to get him in shape for beginner riders but I don’t think he’s going to make it. He’ll need an experienced rider for the next five years. You don’t want to hear what he did to me last week.”

“Oh yeah? You know I’ve got to hear it now.”

It was just part of a search, hearing the latest Cassidy Michaels adventure. I noticed the guys stayed right behind me as I told the story.

“And so I went out to this school, met the kids, met the horses. I work with this kid named Bailee. Farley says she is nearly uncommunicative but I must have done something right. She speaks a few words now if she feels strongly she needs to get a message across. I hope she managed the gate okay today. I can’t wait to see what Farley wants her to learn next. You should see her when she’s allowed to just ride. She turns into a whole different kid.”

I was just rambling now and the guys had probably lost interest, but the talk made the miles go easier.

"When I get home I need to ride the motorcycle around Apache's corral and get him used to noises. I haven't ridden the motorcycle since the attack so he's never seen it. Maybe I can get him used to noise that way."

I paused, studying the ground. Sherri was not an easy person to track. She moved quickly and lightly through the woods. She didn't seem like the type to take off on long cross-country treks or climb rough rocks. She must have been really mad. I thought she would stay fairly close to camp, so I thought we would find her fairly easily. Her pace slowed down considerably once she was beyond the reach of the cameras. It was time for her to rest, find something entertaining to do, head for home, anything.

Every half hour or so I had to sit and wait for my body to catch up. The pack dragged me down. Landon worried when I stopped. He knew how driven I usually was on a search but I couldn't push myself that hard without giving out on the guys completely.

The tracks led on into shady little pockets of the mountains. I was glad Sherri was sticking to the shade because I needed every spot of shade I could find. As the day wore on the shade became darker and darker until I had to admit I could no longer see the tracks. I wearily called a halt. I took off my pack, leaned it up against a tree and sat. And sat. The guys pitched their tents and started their stoves and still I sat. Landon sat down next to me.

"You okay?"

"Yeah."

"Need some help?"

"No, just a dose of energy."

"I'll add some water to mine and you won't have to get your stove out."

"Thanks."

"Did you bring cookies?"

"Oh, Landon, Strict took me straight to the school and then we came straight out here. I never went back in the house. I just took off. I didn't even call Rusty because Strict had already talked to him."

"That's okay."

"No it's not. First I almost died on you, then I socked you in the jaw. It's a wonder you will go anywhere with me anymore. The least I can do is remember to bring cookies."

"I'm just glad you were around to sock me in the jaw."

"I'll give you some cookies when we get back to town."

Jacobsen and Thompson looked disappointed.

"And I'll send a batch to the station, too. I usually carry them along on searches but Strict surprised me."

When Landon's water started boiling I dug out a backpacker meal and pulled the tab to open it up. Landon poured water in my pouch, then his, and we sat there holding our dinners, shaking them occasionally to feel how done they were.

"So you teach riding at a school?" he said, just for something to talk about.

"A couple of days a week. And I train that knucklehead horse. But I have to admit, it got me on the right track. Getting Apache to act like a gentleman has taken my mind off my health and wrestling that big horse has given me a gradual workout. I walk around the school, helping the kids. I can't dwell on my problems when I see theirs. Kids who will never graduate from high school. Kids who will never walk normally. Kids, like Bailee, who barely talk, who can only live a normal life through their imaginations. I thought I'd seen my last search. There were so many weeks of hardly being able to walk. I thought I was all done in."

"Two months ago I thought the same thing," Landon said. "When they wheeled you into surgery, I didn't expect to see you again. I've seen some desperate situations. I've had heart attack victims in my ambulance. At least with a heart attack there's a plan. You run through your options and hope it works. With you I didn't even have a procedure, only a guess. If I didn't have my training to fall back on I'd have been a basket case. I was running through percentages in my head. How much blood could one person lose before there was no turning back? This percentage meant one thing, that percentage meant another. I didn't want to think what it could mean for you. You were way into the danger zone before we got over the mountains." He paused to collect his emotions. He was uncomfortable with the guys seeing him keyed up over it, but he also seemed to need to talk. Jacobsen and Thompson knew Landon. Landon was a permanent fixture at the station when he wasn't working his day job. And he was available twenty-four seven for Strict, so the guys knew him from there too. The officers frequently had to call Landon to accident scenes. So he was well known throughout the police and fire departments.

"How's Rusty taking all this?"

"He's had a rough time of it. First he mourned for his little boy. Then we had some opportunities to have kids around and he perked up. Then we both kind of settled into a blue funk while he missed the kids and I missed being able to accomplish anything. I used to think when you are down there's nowhere else to go but up. But I'm beginning to learn things can always get worse. So I've been trying to look up. Like when I surf and I get pushed to the ocean bottom. I know eventually I'll rise to the surface. It might be a long hard tumble before it happens but I look up and eventually I make it. This has been one long tumble in the surf, but I can breathe again. I'll be okay. And Rusty will, too."

I was hungrier than I thought. I quickly finished off the whole backpacker meal and searched around for dessert. I was glad I felt like eating. For two months I'd barely eaten enough to keep going. My weight hung around a hundred five. It was time for a change. It was time to workout again. It was time to build a new me.

I packed up my trash and pulled out my tent. Landon helped me set it up. I wouldn't have used it if it weren't for the guys. For some reason they had trouble letting me sleep out in the open when they all had tents. If I had my choice I'd just roll out my sleeping bag when it was time to turn in, but I knew from experience that if I did that I'd quickly be offered one of their tents. Chase was the only cop I knew who respected me enough to leave me to my own devices. No, I corrected myself, that wasn't it. I blamed it on an over developed sense of chivalry, while Chase accepted the fact that I didn't give a hoot about chivalry. I just wanted to be left alone to be as eccentric as he was. Whatever it was, I knew I had to set up a tent, so I did it, wishing the guys would happen to think they were also forcing me to carry an extra five pounds all day when I didn't need to.

It was a rough night. I was afraid I'd have nightmares and wake up the guys, so I tried to hold myself to a light doze. All night long I lay there wondering how long I had lain there, wondering how much longer until first light. I always got up at first light, as soon as it was bright enough to see. I'd eat a quick breakfast and hit the trail while it was cool and I could make good time. I lay there wondering about the time until suddenly I realized there were voices outside my tent.

"Do you think she's okay? Usually she's the one rattling our tents," Jayce said.

"At least she's resting," Landon answered. "I'm glad she's over the nightmares. I expected another sock to the jaw."

Thompson laughed. "You'd go in there just to get it, too. You've got to put her behind you."

"I know, I've tried. I even dated someone for a while."

"Oh yeah? Who?" Jacobsen said.

"After Cass's wedding I kept in touch with Michael's sister, Sandy, but it didn't work out. She's too much of a city girl and she said I was arrogant and conceited."

I laughed silently. Yep, that about summed it up. It's exactly what my first impression of Landon and Sandy had been. Sandy would always be a city girl, but Landon was only arrogant and conceited until you worked your way past that and got a glimpse of his heart.

I rustled around so they would know I was awake.

"It's not easy finding someone who understands the profession. At first the uniform's a draw, but after being stood up a time or two because of emergency calls most girls give me the cold shoulder. That, and the fact that after seeing as much as I've seen, they all seem shallow. When I get off the job, I don't care what brand shoes a girl is wearing. I just want everything important to be on an even keel. I thought maybe Sandy would understand that. She was raised in a family with cops. But it wasn't like that. Rusty's sister and Cassidy's sister are so similar; you'd think they came from the same family. So right now there is nobody."

I brushed my hair real quick hoping my bangs weren't sticking straight up. One thing about camping is I never had a mirror. The guys had never run away in fright but I often wondered what I looked like first thing in the morning. At home it depended on what happened *before* I fell asleep. If I woke up to a crazy hair day I could usually blame Rusty.

I climbed out of the tent and quickly collapsed it by pulling the two pegs and pulling the poles out of the pockets. I pulled the poles out of their sleeves and set them aside. Landon folded them up for me while I rolled up the tent, pushing all the air out from the rear to the open front door of the tent. I looked around. The guys had eaten breakfast and gathered up their belongings so I pulled out my trail mix and shouldered my pack.

"You should make trail mix cookies," Landon observed.

"Then I could get sick of trail mix and cookies at the same time," I countered. "Besides, the trail mix has to melt and then freeze back together. It wouldn't do that if it was in cookie form."

"Learning all the intricacies of trail life is important," Thompson observed sarcastically.

"Ha, I bet you send your steak back if it isn't medium rare," I said. He couldn't argue with that. "So I like my trail mix melted. You like your steak medium rare. What's the difference? Tell you what, I'll make trail mix cookies and send them to the station. I bet chocolate chip wins."

"With nuts," added Landon.

It was good to have meaningless conversations on the trail. That was what trails were for. Seemed like a lot of meaningless trail conversations involved food. We'd had the macaroni and cheese debate more times than I could count. Why did I bring macaroni and cheese pouches if I didn't like them? The answer was, they magically jumped into my basket at the store. I just grabbed one of each kind and macaroni and cheese was always on the rack, probably because nobody else wanted it either. So I'd come home and ask myself why I bought macaroni and cheese and stick it in my pack and then not eat it unless I was desperate. I had purposely prepared it for myself once, when it was the last thing in my pack, and once for Patrick, because it was kid food.

Then there was the great hot chocolate/instant coffee debate. Was there more caffeine in hot chocolate or coffee? And who could stand instant coffee? The debates went on and on, mile after mile, unless there was a story they hadn't heard or hadn't shared.

"What's happened on the job lately that is interesting?" I asked as I tracked.

"There was a morning not long ago…we were patrolling this neighborhood when we heard shots. We pulled over and Jacobsen sees this guy running off. He gives chase so I go see what else is happening. I'm looking the house over when this woman comes running out in her pajamas. I stopped her from walking into something she shouldn't and she nearly shot my head off."

"Very funny, and I wasn't quite in my pajamas," I said.

"What about that guy who tried to hold up the Fifth Street Market?" Jacobsen said.

Thompson continued the story, "Get a load of this, the guy goes in, gun in hand, right? He sticks up the place but he doesn't have room in his pockets for the money so he lays down his gun, gets out his wallet and the cashier picks it up. The cashier points the gun at the guy and we walk in and slap the cuffs on him."

"With my luck I'd be behind him in line and he'd turn out to be the guy Rusty was looking for," I said.

Sherri's trail was turning towards the mountains again. Despite the late start we were making good time. I followed the tracks in amongst the trees and into a small cleft in the rocks. Oh no, rocks. Please, don't go there. But before I could buckle down and get too discouraged I heard an "Eep!" and a noise of something moving in the bushes. I held out an arm to stop the guys and peered into the brush.

"Wait here," I told them. I removed my pack and pushed the branches aside. There sat Sherri disheveled and dirty. Her leg was obviously broken but that was the least of her worries.

"Oh!" she cried. "Go away! Don't look at me!"

"Sherri, we all know who you are. You've been stuck up here for two days. Nobody expects you to be gorgeous. Believe me, these guys have seen women in every state you can imagine." Then I rethought that statement and blushed. "I didn't mean that the way it sounded."

"Don't let them see me!" she hissed.

"I have to. They're the ones who know what to do. I'm just the tracker."

"I think we found our ten sixty-five," Jacobsen observed.

The officers stood back smirking. Landon was on the radio reporting our find. Codes fired back and forth but Landon didn't have any more answers until he could get a look at his patient. Every time a guy stepped forward

Sherri retreated farther into the brush, cussing up a storm at the pain in her leg.

"Okay, everybody hold it," I said. "Just stay put. Give me fifteen minutes."

I crawled under the brush pulling my pack along. I opened it up and dug out my hairbrush, a bottle of water and a clean sock.

"Here," I said handing her the brush. "You know you're just giving the reporters time to close in. They were quiet until the radio tipped them off. Give that helicopter five minutes to get over the mountains and you're in the news again."

She was an expert with a hairbrush. Five minutes later her hair was brushed and teased into a glorious halo of blonde. I poured some water into the sock and handed it to her. She looked at it with distaste.

"It's clean," I assured her.

She dabbed at her face being careful not to rub.

"Do you have any moisturizer?"

"Ha, you're lucky I have a hairbrush and a wet sock."

"No eye shadow? Liner? Lipstick?"

"Do I look like I use that stuff on the trail?"

"Can I have more water?"

"Yeah, you can even drink it. Are you hungry?"

"Starving."

I handed her the trail mix.

"You're torturing me!" she shrieked. "It's covered with chocolate! It'll make me break out."

I dug into my pack again and came up with a granola bar. She read the calorie count before opening it.

"Tell me about your injuries. What happened?"

"It's my leg," she wailed. "I'm going to be out of work for months. Arnie is going to kill me."

"Arnie?"

"My agent. I'm in the middle of a huge production and I don't have two months to spend on crutches! I'm supposed to save the world! I'm supposed to make out with Prescott Hughes in the Bahamas! I have to wear a sexy black dress in a nightclub scene! Casts are not sexy!"

"You look great!" I said with as much confidence as I could. "Let Landon take a look at your leg."

"Landon, aye? Sounds like a cool guy. Is he single?"

"Yeah, he's a cool guy and he's single."

"You're sure I look okay?"

"You look terrific. When the news helicopters show up just smile real big and all your fans will throw a party in your honor." Hoo boy, did I believe any of what I was saying? Maybe a little. Mostly I was just trying to get home sooner.

She fluffed her hair a little and checked her nails. They had sunsets with palm trees painted on each one.

A pink and purple helicopter made a few passes and Sherri scooted back in the brush. When it had us located it hovered overhead a minute. A bay door opened and a shiny black head poked over the opening. The helicopter was so close I could see the shiny black head had tons of eye makeup on. He wore an expensive suit and a silk tie that blew around in the wind. Not a hair on the man's head moved. It was the guys' turn to shrink back. They didn't like this pushy helicopter pilot. They assumed it was sent out by some fashion magazine to take pictures but when the shiny black head disappeared we barely heard from above, "BOMBS AWAY!" and a package came down with a bubble wrapped thud and bounce. The contents rattled in a familiar way and Jacobsen ran to pick it up.

"Ooo, bubble wrap!" he said and popped three bubbles.

Sherri gave the helicopter a toothpaste commercial smile and called up excitedly, "Oh! Thank you, Arnie!"

There was no way they could hear her above the clatter of the helicopter blades. She waved hysterically as the helicopter bobbed, seemingly in answer, and then flew away.

Jacobsen opened the package and inside was a Day-Glo pink makeup case and a box. He passed the contents through the brush to me and I passed it along to Sherri. Behind me I could hear the *pop, pop, pop* of the bubble wrap. Thompson got out his pocketknife and asked for a piece so Jacobsen reluctantly cut it in half. As Sherri meticulously applied moisturizer, then foundation, powder, blush, eye liner, mascara, eye shadow and lotioned her arms and nicely shaved, unbroken leg the two officers gave us a bubble wrap demonstration and debate. Thompson rolled the bubble wrap and twisted it popping at least fifty bubbles with each twist.

"That's cheating," Jacobsen said. "A true bubble wrap connoisseur will only pop one bubble at a time."

"I never claimed to be a connoisseur. I say kill and destroy. I have power over the helpless bubbles. They are all doomed."

Jacobsen: *Pop, pop, pop...*

Thompson: *sizzzzzzle, pop, pop, unwrap, retwist, sizzle, pop...*

Then Jacobsen: *pop, pop, pop...*

It was the Bubble Wrap Wars. Who would win? Slow and steady? Or kill and destroy?

"Okay," Sherry sniffed. "I think I can do this now."

I crawled out and handed the situation over to Landon.

"We're going to need a lift out," I told the officers. They called in to Strict on the radio, reporting the patient's condition and asking for a helicopter.

Landon was having fun. He oozed smooth compliments. He was good at that. He was a flirt and Sherri enjoyed being flirted with.

"How did you manage to fall off a cliff without breaking a nail?" Landon asked.

"I can't break a nail. I'm going to be in a hand lotion commercial tomorrow."

"Let me see," Landon said.

Sherri held out her hands.

"Wow, not a scratch!"

A helicopter clattered overhead. I looked up at it. News. I was waiting for a yellow and green one. I stood out in the open ready to flag it down but with all the news helicopters around I probably didn't need to do anything.

"Clear plastic? How tacky!" Sherri said about the inflatable splint.

"It's clear for a reason. They can take x-rays through it. Don't worry; you'll make it into a fashion statement. Everyone will want one."

Two more helicopters joined the first one.

"Oh!" Sherri wailed. "Don't let them see me!"

"Calm down," Landon advised her. "You know how they can zoom in. Just smile up at them. Show them how much fun a broken leg can be. Your fans will be relieved you were found and glad to see your spunk."

"Do you think so?"

"I know so. Just wait until you read your mail over the next few weeks. Maybe you can get a custom cast at the hospital. Start thinking about what color you want. Maybe you can get one to match your nails. Have your friends sign it, then sell it on eBay. You'll make an extra couple grand just from auctioning off that old cast."

So went Landon's examination. Landon stayed under the brush with Sherri, keeping her spirits up, giving her a pep talk so she would cooperate when it came time for transport. Finally the green and yellow helicopter appeared overhead, and a basket was lowered from above. Two EMTs jumped out of the basket, unclipped it and set off to find their patient. We pointed the way.

"Cassidy? You coming?" Landon asked.

I thought about the load, the TV cameras, the peaceful hike back. Sherri would probably insist on being taken to L.A. and I had no desire to find my way home from there. In spite of the long hike back I waved them off. I stayed behind until the helicopter lifted up and headed south, then I put on my pack and headed for base camp. Jacobsen and Thompson filed in behind me.

The news helicopters wavered a little bit so I waved up at them as I hiked into the forest.

The hike back was much easier than the track in. It was nice easy hiking until we got to the canyon. After the rough night I still had to rest about every half hour. I told the guys to go on ahead and I'd catch up but I knew it was useless. Landon wasn't there and somebody had to make sure I didn't fall head first off the rock or hike myself to death, so they pretended to rest when I rested.

"You know you don't have to hike behind me. I'm not tracking. You're not going to mess up the trail. Besides if I walk behind you I'll learn your tracks. If you run into trouble on the job you might want me to be able to recognize your tracks."

"You'd recognize our tracks on sight?"

"If you'd just give me a chance."

"You mean you could pick out our tracks in a group of mixed tracks?"

"If… you'd just give me the chance. Once your patterns are logged into my brain I remember things like that fairly easily."

"Whose tracks can you recognize?"

"Well, Rusty, of course. Chase, Big John, all the hands on my parent's ranch except Elan, the new one. Patrick, Kelly Green. There are several dead people I'd recognize if they suddenly came back to life: Dirk, Old Frank, Tyrone Trent, Mario Peccati, Carl Cranston. That's depressing. I don't want to think about that. Can we change the subject?"

"But you're saying if we changed shoes, you'd still be able to pick us out of a crowd?"

"It depends on a lot of things. If I knew you were missing and I knew your mannerisms and I knew to watch for you I think I could. If I was walking across the field at the fairgrounds and saw your tracks I wouldn't suddenly say, 'Jayce and Kent came through here!' Rusty and Chase are the only ones that stand out that clearly to me. There have to be a few clues first."

"Dang!" said Jacobsen but nobody suddenly wanted to walk ahead of me. It was ingrained in them. The tracker goes first. Or maybe they were worried about going too fast and leaving me behind.

Jacobsen was still popping bubble wrap one bubble at a time, while Thompson was searching a limp sheet of plastic for that one elusive bubble. He handed it to me. I ran the plastic through my hands and said, "There's still one more," even though I didn't feel any. He examined the sheet as he walked. "One problem with the kill and destroy method is they might not all be completely dead. They might just be squished and limp and laying there helpless. But they aren't quite dead yet."

Pop, pop, pop, went Thompson's bubble wrap.

The canyon went steadily downhill until we got to the rock wall. I was tired. I looked down the face of the rock and the thought of climbing over the edge with my pack on was daunting. Up was no problem. I was used to the balance issues on the way up. I took off my pack and rummaged around in it. Sometimes I had a light climbing rope but I didn't this time. Shoot.

"Cassidy, what are you doing?" Jacobsen asked.

"I was hoping to climb down without my pack on. I was looking for a rope."

"You're in luck. We don't want you to climb down with your pack on either," Jacobsen said.

"You're allowed to ask for help," Thompson added.

"I don't need help. I can improvise. I'm good at improvising. A rope would just be easier."

Both guys gave me an impatient look.

"Do you have any problem with the climb without the pack?"

"No."

"Then climb down. We'll take care of your pack."

I looked over the edge.

"Rattlesnake's gone. Or at least in a different spot," I reported.

I backed over the edge finding footholds, feeling my way down until I could find handholds on the rock. I inspected the ledge and found it snake free. When I reached the bottom Thompson started down. Jacobsen handed down my pack and Thompson passed it to me.

Base camp was in transition as we dragged our way in. The search had been over for a long time but a group of reporters was still hoping for an interview. Strict was still in residence. He had to be as long as civilians were hanging around. He was relieved to see us so he could kick everybody out.

"Well, guys, they're all yours," I said, but Thompson grabbed the back of my pack before I could get away.

"Oh, no, you don't. You're the tracker. You know the answers. We were just crowd control."

"Then control this crowd!" I said walking away but he still had hold of my pack.

"Cassidy… it was your search. Just stay and answer a few questions."

"I don't know what to say. Sherri doesn't want them to know everything!"

"Then fudge a little."

Then it was too late. We were trapped.

"Good job finding Sherri Champlain," a reporter said to Jacobsen and Thompson. "What condition was she in when you located her?"

"We didn't find her. Cassidy did," Jacobsen said. Aw gee thanks guys, I thought shrinking back, but they pushed me in front of them and closed the gap so I couldn't escape.

"She looked remarkably well considering she was out in the open for two days." Thanks to a last minute fashion rescue by a greasy agent and a searcher with a hairbrush.

"Was she injured?" the reporter fired at me.

"That is privileged information. You'll have to ask her or her agent that question."

"Did she talk to you when you found her?"

"Yes."

"What did she have to say about her ordeal?"

"She was more concerned about getting back to work."

"And when do you think that will happen?" another reporter asked.

"Just as soon as possible," I said, dodging the question. "Get me out of here or the cookie deal is off." I mumbled to the guys behind me. They just smiled at the cameras.

"Where is Sherri now?"

"I presume somewhere in L.A. Since I didn't go, I don't know where they went."

"How did you find her so quickly?"

"I followed her tracks."

"What happened on the cliff that made you fall?"

"I didn't fall, and it wasn't a cliff. It was a twelve foot rock and a rattlesnake just gave me a warning to stay off his ledge."

"Are rattlesnakes common in these mountains?"

"I've seen a few."

"Do you think Sherri ran into a rattlesnake?"

"I doubt it."

"How long does it usually take to find a person in Sherri's situation?"

"That depends on many things. Sherri was relatively easy to find. I've had searches take hours and searches that took four days. It depends on how long the person has been lost, how far they traveled and the terrain they chose. Some soils are easy to track in and some are nearly impossible. We have a wide variety of soil types in these mountains. I've tracked most of them."

"You look familiar. Have we interviewed you before?"

"I have been involved in a few news stories over the past few years. The mine collapse, the follow up wedding story. Those were me. I was also the officer missing from a stakeout a little while back."

"And the mysterious shopper at the mall who took down the bank robber. I saw that on TV," interjected Jayce Thompson.

"I really should be going," I said pushing my way between Thompson and Jacobsen.

"But will Sherri be all right?" half the reporters asked at once.

"She'll be fine," I shot back.

The house was quiet until I walked in the front door. Shadow met me with his usual enthusiasm. It was hard to tell if he missed me. I got the same greeting whether I walked to the barn and back or I was gone for a week.

Life went on and so Rusty was at work, catching the news off and on throughout the day. He'd know very soon that Sherri was found. If he didn't catch it on the news, Jacobsen and Thompson would arrive at the station soon.

I grabbed a carrot from the fridge and headed out back to see how my charge was getting along without me. I broke the carrot into pieces as I went. As I expected, Apache had been fed and watered in my absence but he hadn't been brushed or ridden. I slid the carrot pieces into my pocket but I couldn't fool Apache. When I came close to him he nudged my pocket. I took out one piece and climbed into the corral.

"Gentle," I said as I held out the carrot on my palm. He took the carrot and I went to the barn and got out a brush and started to work. I needed to relax, but to a girl who grew up around horses, grooming horses was a relaxing activity. Apache must have missed me a little. He stood still while I talked and brushed. He paid attention, ears swiveling as I moved around, brush in constant motion. After a light brushing he looked better and I put the brush away and got out the lead line. I walked him out to the grass and let him graze a little. He was a perfect gentleman. I thought he was hiding an ace up his sleeve so I remained cautious. He didn't try anything that day so I put him back in the corral and went into the house determined to work with him after my trip to the school the next day. Then I remembered the work I was going to do on the motorcycle. I went to the garage. I started the bike with the door closed and when it was settled down to a nice quiet idle I opened the door and slowly eased the bike out and around to the back yard. At first I just left it idling next to the house where Apache could hear it. I walked to the corral. He was prancing in circles, ears pricked, senses alert. I entered the corral and talked to Apache, petting him, reassuring him the noise was okay. When he had settled a little I walked back to the bike and pushed it closer. He did a little playful bucking when the bike came in sight so I went and talked to him again. The bike rumbled gently, the horse paced and tossed his head and pawed the earth. So far so good, I thought and moved the bike closer. As long as the bike was just sitting there Apache settled. As soon as it moved he got fearful and antsy. I shut it off and put it in the barn before I went too far and panicked him.

Rusty wasn't sure what to expect when he got home. He knew I could be worn out from hiking, so he was relieved to find me up and about. I was looking over my chocolate chip cookie recipe wondering if trail mix cookies would be really good or really tough. I was imagining what dried fruit would do in the oven if you baked it into a cookie.

"It's good to have my girl home again," he said wrapping me in a hug. "Thank you for having patience with the TV reporters. I know how hard you tried to avoid them."

"So, what's your theory on bubble wrap? We had a big bubble wrap debate on the trail."

He grinned. "The guys were still popping bubble wrap when they got to the station. My theory is it doesn't do much good if you pop it so I leave it alone."

"You don't pop bubble wrap?"

"No."

"I've known you all this time and I just assumed you would at least pop a few of them. Even I have to pop a few of them. It's not normal to not pop bubble wrap."

"I never claimed to be normal," he said.

"Do you push the buttons on those irritating animated holiday animals in stores?"

"No."

"Rusty! You mean you never got curious about what a Valentine's Day kung fu hamster might do? You never wondered what a mechanical ukulele playing stuffed gorilla might do?"

He grinned, amused at my curiosity. "No, but I have to admit I watch over your shoulder when you do it."

"Okay, that's more like it."

"Knowing you, the hamster would have a black belt, but so far they've proved harmless."

It was so good having meaningless conversations again. For the longest time Rusty came home to a silent house while I slept, recovering from some chore that proved to be too much for me.

"Let me get out into the desert before you start it up," I told Rusty. "Then ride around as close as Apache will let you. If he seems upset, back off. He just has to get used to the noise and activity. He'll never be fit for kids until he's accepted surprise noises as normal."

"Are you sure this is wise?"

"As long as we're out in the open we'll be fine. If he runs all I have to do is stay in the saddle. If that happens just put the bike away. We'll know he isn't ready for this exercise. I'll be back as soon as he tires out."

And so I spent an hour slowly riding Apache out in the desert while Rusty quietly rode big circles around the horse. Apache bucked and startled and Rusty fretted, thinking he'd do something just a little too suddenly and I'd be thrown. I waved him closer. Things were more under control than they appeared to be. I was familiar with Apache's natural reaction to noise. He was just fearful and nervous. Nervousness was to be expected in a horse his age and it usually resulted in movement. Herd animals run from prey, so they run from frightening things. Round and around we went until I was tired of the monotony of it. I called Rusty on the cell phone.

"I'm going to run him. Try making a pass and see what he does."

"Okay."

I hung up and gave Apache a spirited kick to get him going. This youngster didn't need much prompting. He'd rather run than do anything else, so I pointed him down the road and he took off and found a comfortable pace. Rusty passed us on the bike off at a distance then turned around and made a pass closer to us. Apache's nostrils flared. His ears pricked forward and he stared down the motorcycle. The buzzing grew nearer. Apache held his own. The motorcycle kept on. This was a game of cowboy chicken and I was willing to bet Apache would chicken out first. I held on with my knees as he pounded forward. Ready for a sudden lunge to the side. Instead Apache stopped in midstride nearly throwing me over his head. My legs tightened automatically gripping the horse as I followed his erratic movements. He whirled around and took a flying kick at the motorcycle as it went by. I hung on hoping Rusty wasn't watching me. I'd ridden many a green broke horse and Apache's bucking didn't bother me. I just moved with the horse. The motorcycle sped off and Apache turned and watched it go, stamping his foot angrily. My cell phone rang.

"I say we call it a day," Rusty said.

Farley followed at a distance as I met Bailee the next day. She brightened immediately when she saw me coming and she had plenty to say, well, for her anyway. She was excited.

"Chas!" she hugged me happily. She pointed to herself with her clenched hand and said, "Saw you. Me did."

"You saw me?"

She nodded.

"Don't tell me, on TV?"

"Yes! You… I see."

She held up a tabloid newspaper with Sherri's picture on the front and a long article inside. She held up a pen and the newspaper.

"What? You want my autograph?"

She beamed. Oh, what the hell. It was useless, except to make a little girl happy. So I signed it: To Bailee, a super rider at McGyver's riding school. From Cassidy Michaels who tracked and found Sherri Champlain in the woods of California. Then I decorated it with hearts and stars and handed it back to Bailee. She read it and her smile brightened the whole stable.

"Are you ready to ride?" I asked.

She went to Socks' stable and hugged the old horse.

"Mine harse," she said.

"Can you say Socks? Horses like to hear their names. Can you say Socks' name?"

She thought for a moment and I thought she was going to withdraw but she hesitantly said softly, like she was experimenting by herself in her room, "Mine… Shocks… mine Shocks."

"That's great!" I praised her. "You can say Socks' name! When he does what he is supposed to, praise him. He will like to hear your voice and he will respond better.

"Shocks…" she said over and over, practicing.

As we brushed out Socks' coat I made sure to use short phrases as I went. When I found tangles in his mane and he didn't flinch I said, "Good boy! Good Socks!"

Bailee looked like she was taking notes. As she rode she said, "Goo… Good Shocks. Good harse."

"What's wrong, babe?" Rusty asked that evening.

"Nothing," I answered truthfully. Nothing was wrong. The problem was it was so right I didn't know how to deal with it. Bailee's brain was working, forming new words where they didn't exist before. All she needed was a reason. Was there anything love couldn't do?

"Cassidy?"

I looked at him pushing down the emotions bubbling just below the surface. Love caused all manner of strange things to happen. It made a little girl want to speak again. It made a detective hunt down a renegade horse to draw his wife out the depths of despair. It drew people to do things they never thought possible, teaching in a place where joy and cruel reality fought hand to hand. It was the story of my life, trouble and peace fighting it out. But I loved this life. And my love was growing. I could feel it expanding and swelling.

"Cassidy?"

Maybe there was space in my heart for my own child. To see my own child learn and grow. To see Rusty's sparkle in their eyes. To see their curiosity about the world expand and grow…

"Hon…"

If he only knew what was in my head he wouldn't interrupt, I thought. Maybe, some day, I'd have that chance, to see my own child figure out how to say words, to walk, to soak up life. That's what I wanted for my child…to soak up life, like a little sponge.

"It's all right," I told Rusty, "and it's getting better. You'll see. Would you come to the school with me?"

"You? You want me to come to the school with you? That's your project."

"It's not a project. Do you remember when I asked you to come to the hideout with me but you didn't know why?"

"Yes, I remember that weekend as if it were yesterday."

"Was it worth it? You weren't sure you wanted to walk four miles for something you didn't know was there. Was it worth the hike?"

"It was priceless. It was the first ray of hope I had for us."

"Would you come to the school with me?"

"Of course, when you put it that way. I would do anything for you. I didn't know it meant that much to you."

"It didn't at first. But something has been happening that I want you to see."

On the way to the school I told Rusty all about Bailee. He had never actually been to the school before but the station had a program for teenagers wanting to work their way into law enforcement and Farley supported that. Rusty met Farley on one of his frequent visits to see how the kids were doing. He sponsored a riding day for the Junior Officers so they could have a day as mounted police.

"How old is this kid?"

"Nine, and she really does very well. Even a normal nine year old wishes she could ride like Bailee. When I started here she only said two words, 'mine horse.' She has come up with several others since I started working there."

I took Rusty to Socks' stable and we waited for Bailee. The more I looked at the old horse I wondered how many rides he had in him. But Bailee didn't see him that way. Socks was a friend and no matter how old he got and how big Bailee got they would be friends forever. Having seen the demise of many an old horse I only prayed Socks had one more ride in him than Bailee.

After sharing the newspaper with me Bailee felt like she could share other parts of her life. She ran to the stable with an odd lopsided gate that didn't slow her down at all. I pointed her out to Rusty so he could see the state she was in even before she got there. In her hands she clutched a book.

"Hi, Bailee!" I said with a big smile. It always paid off to be bright and cheerful. It was contagious and put off total frustration just a little bit longer.

"Chas!" She held out the book.

"What have you got here?"

"Mine."

"What is it?"

"Mine…" a few seconds of thought, "book."

"It looks like a great book! I read books like that when I was a kid, too."

"Look!" She showed me the cover. On it was a girl running the barrels on a black horse with white socks. "Dis… dis me! I do! I do dis."

Oh man! I was all for it but I wasn't the boss. Farley was the boss. Farley knew the right steps. I couldn't go over Farley's head. But this was important. This is what Bailee wanted. If a kid wanted something there was no stopping them, except unbelieving adults. Unbelieving adults had a horrible way of squashing kids' dreams.

"You want to do barrel racing?" I asked.

"Yes!" she said emphatically.

I looked at Rusty. Rusty looked at me. I took Bailee's clipboard down. She was supposed to ride English today. That was a big step for a kid in itself. It meant she was getting better at balance, not needing the support of the big, wide, western saddle. But Bailee had the barrel-racing bug.

"Bailee, I have to ask Farley before we can do barrel racing. I brought a surprise for you, too. This is Rusty. He's my husband. He wants to see you ride. He's heard you're a super rider. Show him how to get Socks ready for your lesson and I'll talk to Farley."

As always she gave the horse a hug, saying, "mine harse." She worked a brush over her withered hand and got to work.

I handed Rusty another brush and said, "I'll be right back."

"Show me what to do," Rusty said to Bailee.

"Farley, we have a slight problem," I said.

"What's that?"

"It might be nothing. And it might be you."

He cocked his head like Shadow did when I asked him if there was a squirrel in the back yard.

"Maybe you should tell me about this problem."

"Bailee wants to try barrel racing."

"How do you know that? She can't even say *barrel racing*."

I held out the book. "No but she can say, 'this me.'"

"Oh really!"

"Yeah, Farley, she doesn't have to try it at a gallop. As long as she is working towards it. It'll be good for her coordination. She knows how to steer a horse. That's all barrel racing is is steering a horse around barrels. Why can't she do that slow until she's ready to do it faster?"

"I'll think about it."

"Think fast."

"What?"

I stood up to Farley and gave him *the look*. "Little girls' dreams don't last forever. She will do anything to be like this kid. So let her be like this kid."

"That kid is fictional."

"Bailee isn't. Bailee's a real kid with a real dream. Scratch the English saddle. Give me three barrels."

"She's ready to ride English."

"She thinks she's ready to try barrel racing. She is! At least slow."

"What if Socks isn't ready for barrel racing?"

"He can at least take them slow. That's part of riding, knowing what you can expect out of your horse."

Farley and I had a short stare down.

"You can't slash her dream," I told him. "Come talk to her. She wants this bad enough to talk. Come see for yourself."

"I'll be there in a minute."

Yes! That was better than him coming with me anyway.

"Bailee, Farley wants to talk to you about your riding. You need to convince him you can do it! He knows you're a super rider. Show him you have what it takes to do barrel racing."

"Me?"

"Yes, you. I know you can do it. You convinced me. But you need to talk to Farley. He sets up your lessons. He'll be here soon." I handed her the book. "Tell me about the story. What in there got you interested in barrel racing?"

It was like making a shy kid get up in front of a group and give a speech. She was terrified.

"Dis harse," she said tapping the cover of the book, "he… sick… dirl…" she drew a blank. "Dad… say harse… no good."

"What's the girl's name?"

"Sam… Sam say harse… good harse… care of harse."

Farley walked in dumbfounded. Bailee was talking. Making conversation. Describing a book.

"Did the horse get better?"

"Yes! He… fast. Sam have…" another pause while she thought very hard "big dream… her harse… be rodeo harse."

It was the standard girl meets horse story, but she didn't know that. After what Farley saw he didn't take a whole lot of convincing.

"Bailee, show Farley what you want to do."

She looked at Farley like she'd just been sent to the principal's office. Then her eyes brimmed with tears. Farley took an emotional step back. If he said no it would be like taking candy from a baby. He'd feel like a heel.

"Mizzur Mac…" That alone took Farley McGyver by surprise. "Shocks good harse… me want… ride like dis." She held out the book to Farley.

"You do?"

"Yes!" Yes can be the most beautiful word when it comes from somebody who has heard a thousand no's.

"This is going to take work, you know that."

"Yes!"

"You don't mind starting out slow?"

"No!"

"You'll listen to Cassidy?"

"Chas! Yeah!"

"Cassidy? Have you ever done barrel racing before?"

"Yeah, it's been several years but I can teach it, no problem."

Bailee's eyes lit up. She was going to learn barrel racing!

"Mizzur Mac! Dang you!" I laughed at her excitement and hoped Farley knew she was saying thank you. "Dang you, Chas!"

"You're welcome, Bailee. I like barrel racing, too. Is Socks ready to go?"

I'm afraid Bailee was a little disappointed in her first barrel racing lesson.

"You know how to turn left and right but there are patterns involved in barrel racing. You have to know the sequence by heart and you have to make the turns as tight as you can without knocking the barrels over. We'll work on the turns first. Socks has to listen to you slowly before you can expect him to obey quickly. He's used to figure eights but he has never done the cloverleaf pattern before. So this is going to be new to him."

Farley and Rusty set up the three barrels and I walked Bailee and Socks through one run.

"Remember the pattern, because if you go on the wrong side of the barrel it messes up the whole run. You need to circle each barrel in a clockwise direction."

As she came to the first barrel I walked quickly beside Socks' head calling out directions.

"Clockwise, tight, very tight turn, around, around some more. Okay aim for the next barrel. Okay do it again. Tight, as tight as you can without touching the barrel…" Next she needed to do it without me walking along side coaching. That was more frustrating. I called out the orders but Socks wasn't listening very well. I thought it might help if Socks had some experience barrel racing. I doubt the little horse had ever been used in competition. When I could see the frustration level mounting I pulled Bailee off the cloverleaf.

"Just canter him around the outside. You both need a break."

As she rode I talked to Farley.

"If she's going to get anywhere at this she needs a horse who has done it before."

"Indy might work better. He's younger. He enjoys surprises so, even though he's never done barrel racing, he'd take to it better."

"Maybe that would work."

But Bailee would hear none of it.

"No! Shocks… good harse! Me… Shocks… do both… we learn. Shocks my fren."

"Can I ride Socks?" I asked Bailee.

"You? Ride Shocks?"

"Yeah."

"Shocks mine harse."

I smiled because I knew four other kids rode Socks as well, but to Bailee Socks was her horse.

"Maybe he needs a teacher, too. He has never done the pattern. Maybe if I run him through the pattern a few times he will listen to you better."

"Shocks, me learn…both. We do…" She was thinking the word together but it just wouldn't come out.

"You want to learn together." I summed it up. "Okay, that's fair. It's harder but I know you can do it because you're a super rider! Let's try it one more time. I'm going to jog beside Socks. Maybe we can do it at a trot. Ready?"

Off we went. I prodded the lazy old horse around the turns calling out, "tight, tight turns, rein him tighter, there you go!" By the end of the run I was exhausted but Rusty was leaning against the corral fence grinning ear to ear. He hadn't seen me work in a long time and to see me standing up for a little kid and helping her realize a dream made him feel as good as it did me.

As she put Socks back in his stable her face was a study in contrasts. On one hand she got to try barrel racing. On the other hand she was not even close to being good at it.

"Every lesson it will get easier, you'll see. It's never easy when you are both learning something new at the same time. I thought you did good for a first time! Remember the first time you tried the weave poles? It was hard.

But now it is easy. The barrels will be the same way. Pretty soon you'll be flying around those barrels and we'll have to time you with a stopwatch."

She gave me a big hug, "Dang you, Chas."

"Tell your mom what you did today. Moms love to hear what their kids did, especially if they did such a good job."

"Mom… don talk… me. Mom talk… Mizzur Mac."

"Well, you talk to her, anyway. She needs to hear your voice. The more you talk the easier it'll get."

I encouraged her but her words bothered me. Mom don't talk to me.

"Me talk you. You talk me."

"You can always talk to me," I assured her.

Again Rusty was puzzled.

"Cassidy? What's wrong?"

"Is it always this heartbreaking and wonderful working with kids? Seems like every day Bailee makes me cry with joy and weep in sorrow."

"No, not always. In my job you see the dark side of kids too often. I think a family loses the highs and lows in the business of everyday life. It's not like that all the time."

On Thursday I showed up at the school with a book about equestrian events. Farley glared at me.

"You can't show that to Bailee," he said.

"Why not?"

"She'll want to do all of them."

"So?"

"So she can't do all of that here. It's impossible."

"Why stop her?"

"She isn't capable of…"

"She's capable of anything she's allowed to do. She's just as capable as me. She could enter gymkhanas if she progressed far enough."

"That's a big if."

"What do you see, Farley? Do see Bailee's capabilities or her limitations? So she has trouble talking. So her hands are crooked. She can do anything she puts her mind to. Or is that what you're afraid of?"

He glared at me.

"I choose to see her capabilities. I'll teach her whatever she wants to learn, because I had the chance to learn whatever I wanted. I might have had to teach myself, but I did it all. If we don't have the equipment, I'll figure something out. If she isn't ready I'll tell her how we need to work towards her goal. But I will not tell her flat out no. Kids learn what they want to learn. If

Bailee wants to learn something there is no stopping her. Giving her information isn't dangerous."

"What will you do when her dreams are bigger than reality?"

"Then we try and stretch reality. But we try. That's it. We try. She won't fault me if I fail as long as I try. Six months from now we'll see who knows more. Your star pupil or Bailee."

"What in tarnation did Michaels get me into?" he said, forgetting completely that he invited me to the school himself.

That day I took Bailee through the cloverleaf over and over. She wanted to be timed but Socks always managed to balk at one turn or another unless I was jogging along beside him. Socks needed more training than Bailee did. After her lesson I gave her the book. We opened it up to the pages on barrel racing and she exclaimed over the action shots of women competing in rodeos.

"I do dis…" she said over and over wishing she had more words.

I turned to the page with the cloverleaf diagram. I traced the path with my finger.

"Take a crayon and trace the path over and over so the pattern is in your head. If you can get it to be automatic it'll be easier to remember in the saddle."

She flipped back to the action shots.

"I do dis…"

"What do you want to do Bailee? Tell me? Your head knows the words. You know it's called barrel racing. You know they do barrel racing at gymkhanas and rodeos. You know more about it than most kids because you read."

"Me want… Chas, words… be gone."

"I know how you feel. I'm in no hurry. If a word gets stuck just try. We'll find it."

"Me want…" I thought she gave up in frustration but then she said, "Me… have little brover. He… he…" she got frustrated and held up two fingers.

"He's two?"

"He talk… better'n me."

"That's great!" I said and she glared at me. She didn't consider it a good thing. "What? You don't think he should be praised when he says a new word? He is going at his own pace. He didn't have a car crash to set him back. You did. It takes courage to do what you are doing. You earn every word. Every word you say I celebrate. I love to hear you talk. You should celebrate your brother's words too. It will make you both feel better. And when he knows enough words he will celebrate your words, too."

"You like… my talk?"

"Of course I do! Tell me, when you read do you pronounce the words in your head when you read?"

"Me… yes."

"So you know what all these words sound like in your head?"

"Yes?"

"So when you read, try to say them out loud. You know what they sound like…"

"Say words?"

"Yeah, like this," I said pointing to the chapter title. "Tell me what these three words say."

"Woe mans row dee o eve ents," she read.

"That's great!" I exclaimed loudly. "That's exactly what it says. See? You can talk! All you need to do is focus on it and think how it sounds." I found another title. "So, tell me what event you want to learn. The words are right here." I pointed out the words.

"Barl rais ing."

"There you see? Barrel Racing! You can talk. You can do anything you set your mind to. All you have to do is want it bad enough. You want to talk? Try reading words out loud. Eventually your brain will get used to them and you won't have to struggle to find them."

And so it went. Half of Bailee's lesson was in the saddle and half of it was in friendship. That's really all she needed, a big sister to celebrate her words, and to give her high fives when Socks made it all the way through a turn without balking.

"Good harse! Good Shocks!" she said enthusiastically.

When she progressed enough to be timed, I sent her to Farley to ask for a stopwatch. She ran off and I trailed behind wanting to see Farley's reaction.

"Mizzur Mac?" Farley turned, knowing it was Bailee and knowing he had a game of twenty questions ahead of him to find out what Bailee needed. "Chas say she time me… if you… got watch. You got watch?"

After Farley picked up his jaw off the floor he said, "You mean a stopwatch?"

"Yeah."

"I've never had need of a stopwatch. Let me check the office."

Bailee followed him to the office and waited while he searched the drawers.

"How are your lessons going?" Farley asked not expecting an answer but needing to fill the quiet.

"Good! Shocks go throo patterns good. Slow… but good. Now we must speed."

"Bailee, you're talking so much better! Tell me what Cassidy did. How did she help you talk?"

"Cass iddy? She Cass iddy? Me say Chas. She like Chas."

"So what did Chas do to help you talk?"

"Me read book. Many many words. Me talk words in book. We read book… barl racing. So I learn rules, patterns. Me like pictures. Me say words in book. Chas like hear me talk. I read. I talk. Now, more words I can talk."

Farley nearly forgot the stopwatch, just listening to this silent girl giving him a complex explanation of exactly what she'd been doing for the past month or so. He searched a couple more places before giving up.

"I'm sorry Bailee, I don't seem to have a stopwatch."

Sigh, "Okay," she said. "Me look my house. Maybe next time."

She caught me eavesdropping, but thought nothing of it. "Mizzur Mac no have watch."

"Okay, I'll buy one and then we'll have one to use whenever we want."

"Your name… not Chas?"

"Chas sounds just fine to me."

"What you real name?"

"Cassidy, but really, Chas is fine with me. It's your special name for me. You're the only one who gets to call me Chas."

She looked thoughtful and I was curious what she would decide. "Shocks ready to go! We do barl racing!"

In the meantime, Apache was his ornery self. I rode him every afternoon. I rode the motorcycle around the outskirts of the property getting him used to noise and motors and moving machines. I probably scared off every deer for miles around and they quit coming to my house in the afternoons, but I knew the motorcycle conditioning was temporary and the deer would come back.

"You see?" Rusty told me. "You don't go looking for trouble and it won't go looking for you. How long has it been since you've run into trouble?"

"It's quiet," I admitted. "Too quiet."

"It's not too quiet. You've kept busy. You're making progress at the school. You're making progress on Apache. You're back to work at home. Everything is right on track. This is what things should be like."

"Almost," I answered.

"What do you mean, almost?"

"Something's still missing."

I tried to figure out what it was. Did I miss the mountains? Could be, but it didn't feel like the itchy feet I used to get. Was it the empty feeling I felt after the miscarriage? Could be, but it wasn't a physical ache any more. Did I miss the small victories I felt with Bailee that I wanted for my own child? Could be, but I didn't have time for a baby. Whatever it was it was vague and sneaky. It lingered outside, feeling its way in occasionally and then backing out silently. It was like a peeping tom. I could see its tracks under the windows and when I wasn't busy doing something I'd feel something out there…watching.

Chapter 31

I thought I must be nuts but logic told me it was time for another trip to the ranch. It wasn't the going that made it crazy. After all, my family lived there. It was just a friendly visit. But it wasn't quite just a friendly visit. For one thing I had an ornery horse who needed socializing, and noise conditioning. Apache would get plenty of that at the ranch. Cars and trucks coming and going. People around all the time. Dogs wandering the property.

Another reason I wanted to go to the ranch was because I knew Bailee would think she had stepped right into a storybook. Yes, I was determined Bailee would get to go. She could play with Patrick and Wyatt. Patrick would talk her ear off and Bailee would get plenty of chances to communicate. She could ride almost any horse she wanted to with supervision. There were real cowboys and real ranch business and a big boisterous group of people to interact with. I just knew this was the right thing to do. So I had Rusty watch for a small block of time that he could take off and, when it neared, I asked Farley for Bailee's phone number.

"Um, yeah, hello?" Bailee's mom said in a distracted manner.

"Mrs. Roland? This is Cassidy Michaels…"

"I don't want none." Now I knew where Bailee's bad grammar might be coming from.

"Mrs. Roland, I'm Bailee's riding teacher at Farley McGyver's school. I was calling to see if you would consider allowing Bailee to go on a little trip with me."

"Bailee? You want to take Bailee on a trip? You know that girl can't even talk?"

"I know she *can* talk and I know she can ride. The place I would like to take her to is the quarter horse ranch where I grew up. She would be supervised every minute and she would get to ride new horses. There are other kids there who would play with her. I think she would really enjoy it."

"Huh. Never known that girl to enjoy something. She's always so quiet. Spends most of her time with her nose in a book. What makes you think she wants to go to a ranch?"

"Mrs. Roland, it's just like the places she reads about in her books. She'll love it."

"Well, you're welcome to take her. How long will she be gone?"

"Four days. If it's easier she can just come home with me after her Thursday lesson. She can spend the night at my house and we can take off early the next morning."

"Hallelujah, I'm gonna take Brandon to my parent's house and go live at the day spa!"

I hung up, discouraged even though I had Mrs. Roland's permission to take Bailee along.

"I suppose it's illegal to shoot lousy parents," I said.

"I suppose you're right but believe me, I've been tempted over the years. Did she let Bailee go?"

"Yeah, unfortunately she was a little too eager to let her go. She's letting Bailee travel to another town with someone she doesn't even know! She didn't ask what Bailee needed. She wasn't worried about Bailee missing school. Can't we just accidentally adopt her while we've got her?"

"I'm afraid things like that are easier said than done."

"I know."

"You really wish you could do that?"

"Well, I know why she lives in a fantasy world of books now. I wish her mom could see Bailee as a real person with real emotions and real dreams. She doesn't see it though and Bailee won't open up to her so her mom never sees what a bright kid she is."

"I've heard all this before, with Patrick. Now look at him. Patrick is doing great."

Next was my dad. Usually I called Mom about these things but I needed a few things like a corral, permission to bring another horse, and the use of some equipment. Like usual Martha answered the phone with, "Gordon's Quarter Horses, this is Martha speaking."

"Hi Martha, it's …"

"Cassidy!… Is everything okay?"

"Yeah, everything's fine. I was thinking of coming up there for a short visit. Before you turn me over to Dad I wanted to tell you there will be three of us for four days. Is that all right?"

"Three of you? Who are you bringing along?"

"A little girl I've been teaching. She loves horses and wants to learn how to do barrel racing. She loves horse books so I thought she might like to live a horse book for a long weekend."

"That sounds wonderful. Your mother will love having a little girl in the house again."

"Wait, Mom can't buy anything for this girl. Bailee can't come home with a bunch of new clothes and toys. No way. You've got to stop Mom. Bailee can't be doted on. She just needs to be welcomed and made to feel like she belongs there, that's all. I mean it, Martha. Can you talk to Mom?"

"But, why? You know how your mom loves to dote on kids. It doesn't matter to her that this girl is a student of yours."

"Bailee just wants a dose of ranch life. If she gets inundated with gifts it's going to make it awfully hard to face reality when she gets back. She'll have all these things reminding her of what life *could* be like. And when it doesn't match up with the life she is stuck in it'll rebound on her."

"A few trinkets is not going to spoil a girl who is used to nothing."

"Okay, just make mom wait until we get there before she does anything. Please? Can I talk to Dad? I have another guest but I need to talk to Dad about him."

"Him?"

"It's a horse."

And so ensued a long discussion on horse training and it was all stuff I knew from just being around the ranch for years but he finally relented. Relenting was Dad's way of saying yes.

"And Dad, please don't be too particular about how Bailee addresses you. I'll tell her what to call you but if it doesn't sound like Mister Gordon to you, just accept it. The guy who runs the school is Farley McGyver and Bailee calls him Mizzur Mac. She isn't being disrespectful or making fun of him. That's as much of his name as she could say for the longest time. She calls me Chas, although she can say Cassidy now. When I met her the closest she could come was Chas and it stuck."

"She's your student. She should call you Missus Michaels."

"It's not that kind of a school and I prefer Chas."

Tuesday when Bailee came for her lesson I should have thought about my words before I said anything. At first she was disappointed.

"Bailee, I have to go on a trip."

"How long?"

"Four days."

She could count. She knew four days meant I'd be gone Thursday. Her face fell.

"Bailee, wait, I wanted to know if you would go with me. I'm going to a place you might like to see. Would you like to visit a ranch? A real ranch?"

"Me? Go *with* you?"

"Yeah! My parents live on a ranch. They raise quarter horses. There are horses of all ages. You can meet my horse. His name is Shasta."

"What color Shasta?"

"He's gray. You'll know him. He's the only gray horse at the ranch."

"My mom never say yes."

"I already talked to your mom. You can go if you want."

She gasped, "My mom say yes?"

Way too quickly, I remembered.

"Yes, when you come for your lesson on Thursday bring four days worth of clothes. You'll need jeans, clothes like you wear here for your lessons."

The whole lesson was filled with questions.

"You mom, dad live ranch?"

"Yes, I grew up there. That's how I know about barrel racing and riding."

"I ride, too?"

"Of course!"

"What horse I ride?"

"You can ride Shasta."

She pulled up, stopping Socks.

"But Shasta your horse."

"I'll share my horse with you." I share him with the whole ranch, I thought, but she didn't see it that way.

"I sorry Chas. I selfish. You ride Shocks."

"Thank you, Bailee, but you're training him just fine. He's doing better on the barrels. He's learning just like you."

"I do barl racing with Shasta?"

"Sure."

"He fast?"

"There are many faster horses. But he'll give you a good run."

"Who fastest?"

"The fastest horse? You can't ride him. His name is Frank's Choice. He's still in training but he's the fastest horse."

"You ride him?"

"Yes, I've ridden him."

And so it went all through the lesson. I walked the whole lesson beside Socks's head because if I was in the middle of the corral Bailee would still yell questions across the yard. All the yelling brought Farley who was amazed at Bailee's progress both in the saddle and in the conversation. So I followed Socks around and helped him through the tight turns.

"You have brovers? Sisters?"

"I have one sister. You'll meet her."

"Mizzur Russy going?"

"Yes."

"There kids at ranch?"

"Yeah, they are younger than you. Patrick is seven and Wyatt is five. Patrick is very outspoken. He will probably ask why you talk differently. What will you tell him?"

"I say, because I'm me. He tease me?"

"No, he's just curious."

"He ride harse?"

"He has a little pinto horse, named Snoopy."

"There cow boys there?"

"They don't wear cowboy hats but they are modern day cowboys. They only wear hats when they get dressed up or they go to rodeos and races where hats are expected."

For once she was ready to go home after her lesson. She wanted to go pack.

I spent Wednesday packing because I knew there would be no use trying to pack with Bailee asking a hundred questions on Thursday. Shadow knew something was up. He paced the house and eyed the suitcases warily.

Bailee was waiting for me when I got to the school on Thursday. I noticed Mrs. Roland didn't stick around to meet me and I wondered if she even told Bailee to have fun at the ranch. Did she even say goodbye before she drove away, leaving a nine year old girl and suitcase at the front of the barn?

Bailee's questions started even before I got to the stable.

"You have harse like Shocks there?"

"No, the only black horse they have is a huge pure black horse. His name is Satan. Don't go near him. He's a beautiful devil of a horse. Nobody can ride him. If he charges the gate to his stall, don't worry, it's reinforced steel."

"I take pictures?"

"Sure."

When she was riding she pushed Socks for more speed but the old horse only managed a slow lope. I think she was trying to prepare for the trip, hoping she would be able to run the barrels. I wasn't sure she *should* run the barrels even if the horses would, and I knew my dad's horses would. That bothered me a little, knowing all the horses there were used to speed and experienced riders. Would Bailee be content going at her own speed when the horses were ready and willing to do more? Did Bailee have the balance she needed in a truly high-speed hairpin turn? I'd have to play it by ear.

"Chas, you ride Shocks. See if he go faster for you."

"Are you sure?"

"Yes, I wan know. I no push him if he won't go faster. If he go faster I know to try."

"I've never ridden him before. I better ride him around the outside before I try the barrels."

If there was one place Socks would run it was in the long straightaways.

Now I was in a pickle. If I got Socks to gallop, Bailee would want to gallop too, yet I wasn't sure Socks had much more galloping left in him. The trick, I decided, was to get just enough out of the horse to keep Bailee trying, then sit her down and have a heart to heart talk. That was going to be rough. Socks was her horse. To her he was almost immortal. He'd always been there for her so he always would be. But a nine year old girl has a lot more years left than an eighteen year old horse.

I climbed into the saddle. The stirrups were too high but I'd make do. I'd use them the same height Socks was used to feeling his cues from Bailee. I gave Socks a kick and started him around the corral. The little horse was responsive to me. I attributed that to my no nonsense attitude. He quickly moved from a walk to a trot. As I rode him I analyzed my motions and the resulting movements of the horse. Horseback tracking, if you will. Every action has a corresponding effect. In this case it wasn't tracks on the ground I was concerned about but the response of the horse. As long as my actions were a demand for obedience Socks proved to be a wonderful horse. As soon as I backed off and asked permission first he began thinking maybe he could say no. How could I translate this into something Bailee would understand?

Socks had a nice easy lope. I bet he was a breeze to ride back in his working days. I urged him to a gallop. His ears swiveled. A question. What? He was saying, this is a school for handicapped kids. You can't ride like this! And when I tightened my knees and gave him a firm kick and I hardened my attitude I was saying, oh yes I can! And he said, oh, okay and eased into a slow gallop. I galloped him along the fence line and thundered up to the fence where Bailee was jumping for joy. Her Socks *was* a good horse. He just proved it. When I tried him at the barrels he went into a lope easy enough but he slowed down at each barrel. I was getting a feel for what this horse needed but Bailee wasn't going to like what we needed to do. Making him run the barrels fast was like asking him to run into a brick wall. He backed off and took the cautious route. Basically, he wasn't going to bash into that wall. So we needed to back up and convince Socks he had what it took to maneuver around the wall. When I had completed the cloverleaf with little more success than Bailee I rode over to where she stood and dismounted.

"Bailee, tell me, what is the rule for being in a library."

She looked at me wondering what libraries had to do with barrel racing. "No running, no talking. Must talk, then quiet."

"And what happens of you talk and be rowdy in the library?"

"Teacher punish you. Send you away."

"What happens if you run in the halls at school?"

"Teacher yell, send you office."

"Well, I think Socks is obeying the rules. This is a school. Most of the kids can't ride well enough to gallop so he thinks the rule is No Galloping. When you ask him to run you are asking him to break the rules. He doesn't understand that the rules are different for barrel racing. And you can't just tell him he can run. He doesn't understand English. So, how do you tell a horse to run when he thinks he can't?"

"I don know."

"When you are at school who is allowed to run in the halls?"

"Nobody."

"The principal could if he wanted to. Nobody would yell at the principal if he ran in the halls. They would just think he was in a hurry and he was the boss. You don't tell the boss what to do. So… you need to be the principal, to Socks. You need to prove to him that you're the boss. You make up the rules."

"Me?"

"Yes, you. The rider is the boss, not the horse. You are the principal, the one to be obeyed without question."

"Me?"

"Yes. Now how do you go about acting like the boss to a horse? What if a boss went to work and all he did was hope his workers did their job? Do you think much work would get done?"

"No, people lazy. They see boss no care, they no care, too."

"But what if the boss comes in and says, 'All right everybody! Here's what we're going to do! In the next two minutes we're going to run these barrels as fast as we can! Now go to it! Go! Go! One, two all right one more, faster!' Do you think those workers would run the barrels?"

"Yes, if they know job and boss say run, they run."

"Socks is the same way. You have to tell him to run with your voice, your signals, and your attitude. When you kick him to say go faster put some muscle behind it. Act like a big boss!"

"He think I mean. I no want him hate me."

"He won't hate you. He needs a friend *and* a boss. Horses like clear directions. The clearer you are the more likely he will be to respond. We're running out of time. Try one more run. Think like a big boss! See what happens."

She climbed over the fence mumbling, "Me big boss, me big boss." She went around to Socks' head, looked him in the eye and said, "Come on Socks! We do it. Fast."

The little horse looked at her, seemingly saying, yeah right.

Bailee got into the saddle and urged Socks forward.

"Don't go straight into the barrels. Take him on a lap first. Talk to him with your body. Tell him who's boss. You're the boss and you say run!"

Socks moved from a walk to a trot to a lope and Bailee urged him to give her just a bit more. Socks said, this kid sure is kick happy all of a sudden. Then the last straightaway came up and Bailee's posture changed. She squinted over Socks' head. She leaned forward. She kicked Socks as firmly as

I thought she could and Socks went, "huh? What?" And Bailee's attitude said, "run in the halls! I'm the boss. I say run in the halls!" And Socks said, "Yes Ma'am!" His head came down and his reach extended just a little bit and he moved into a gallop. He pounded down the fence line.

"One lap!" I yelled. "Just one!"

She turned the horse and took another lap, black hair flying, smile as wide as the clear blue skies and behind me I heard, "Cassidy! Are you nuts?"

Farley.

"Yeah, I'm nuts," I answered. "Talk to me later. For now I've got a kid so jazzed she's going to be impossible to live with. We only have time for one barrel run. One barrel run won't hurt."

"Cassidy, I don't know whether to hug you or boot you off this ranch for good. Bailee can't ride like that."

"She *is* riding like that."

"You have no control over the ride. One stumble and she'd be toast."

"One stumble and any of us are toast. You forget, I've been toasted more than once. She's proving she can do it. Look at her. She's leaning with the horse. She's showed him who's boss. She's *doing* it!"

Bailee came back around and pulled Socks up to a stop. She was grinning ear to ear. "Mizzur Mac! Shocks do it! Shocks good harse!"

Before Farley could say anything I said, "Okay, Bailee, while Socks is still in go mode take him through the barrels just once. Be prepared for the sudden turns. Rein him tight. He's going to slow down for the turns but I have a plan for that later."

"Time it!"

"Okay." I got out the new stopwatch. "Ready? One, two, three… Go!"

It took her a full forty-one seconds to do the cloverleaf but it was a lot better than she'd ever done before. I hoped she didn't know that a truly good run was less than fifteen seconds.

High fives with Bailee consisted of two semi-closed fists knocking together but they contained all the enthusiasm of the real thing. She gave Socks a big hug before leading him to the stable. I recorded her new time and followed.

In the barn she was chattering away to her horse.

"Shocks, you do so good! Next time I bring carrot. I go to a ranch! Chas take me. I wish you could go. I wish you come home with me. You my fren. Every day I wish I ride…"

I smiled broadly at Farley, daring him to try and smother the enthusiasm in the barn, then followed Bailey in.

"Bailee, you did great today! Are you ready to go to my house?"

"Me care of Shocks."

"Yeah, I know, we'll get Socks situated first. You've never seen my house. I have a horse at my house, too. He's in training. So far he isn't rideable. He needs a lot of work. That's why he's going to the ranch with us. He needs to be around other horses and more people and he needs to get used to noises. I'll be working with Apache off and on while we're gone. You'll like him, though; he's a pretty horse. I have a dog, too. His name is Shadow. He likes kids."

Socks needed more grooming than usual because he wasn't used to running. I checked his mouth to make sure Bailee hadn't gotten too rough with the bit. It was easy for horses to develop irritated spots from the tack. Even the fluffy saddle blankets could cause chafing. They get tossed around a tack room and pick up little sticks or rocks or nails. So checking the tack on a regular basis was a good idea. Keeping an eye on the horse at all times usually tipped me off before tack became a problem.

Bailey was sitting on the edge of her seat as we drove to my house.

"Where your house? Other town?"

"No, it's in the same town, just in the foothills. It's a good place to keep horses. There's lots of space to ride. I can ride straight from my house into the desert."

When we got to the house we walked around back and I introduced her to Apache.

"He big hars."

"Yeah, don't go in the corral. He isn't very friendly either."

"Where you dog?"

"He's in the house. I can hear him barking. He's a noisy dog."

We went around to the driveway again and got Bailee's suitcase out of the Jeep, then entered the house through the front door. When we stepped into the house Shadow was there to greet us.

"Shadow, sit!" I said.

Shadow sat.

"This is Bailee. Can you shake hands? Shake hands with Bailee!"

Shadow offered a paw. Bailee shook it.

"He always listen you?"

"No, but he's pretty good. He knows lots of commands. He'll sit, lay down, stand up, jump, go up and down obstacles, run through tunnels. Did you see all the obstacles in the back yard? That's Shadow's playground."

"Dogs gots play ground? I no have play ground. Only play school. Me hate school. Kids mean. Me like Mizzur Mac school."

"I'm all packed up for the trip but I need to make cookies. Do you know how to make cookies?"

"You *make* cookies? You no buy cookies?"

"I buy cookies at the store but these are special cookies. They're for some friends. I'll make them and take them to the station and freeze a few. You can help. You can even have some of the cookie dough. It's a rule, you have to snitch some cookie dough or the cookies don't rise."

She helped me measure and mix up the cookie dough and we talked about school, and mean kids, and boys, and horse books. We made a couple dozen cookies without nuts and then I added nuts to the rest of the dough.

"Why you put nuts now?"

"The cookies without nuts are for Rusty. The rest are for Landon and the other officers. They prefer nuts. Do you like nuts?"

"Me like chocolate. What officers?"

"At the station. We'll deliver the cookies to the station and then we'll go out to eat with Rusty. And then tomorrow morning we'll go to the ranch."

"Mizzur Russy at station?"

"Yeah, he works there."

"Me no go station."

"Why? All the police are friends. They like kids. You can meet my friends. They'll thank you for the cookies."

"Me no go station. Mom say police come door, no answer. She say go my room, close door, read book, be quiet."

My mind was going a mile a minute but all I said was, "You don't have to worry about going to the station. The police are your friends."

At the station it took some prying to get her out of the Jeep and then she was like my shadow, joined at the hip.

"Cookie delivery!" I said cheerily as I deposited a bowl of cookies on the front counter. "I had a helper this time. This is Bailee. She made the cookies."

"How did you know I'd been on double shift?" The woman at the counter said. "I'm starving, but I don't get a break for another half hour. Maybe I'll survive now. Mavis! Cassidy brought cookies!"

Mavis came in from another office. "How come you only bring cookies when I start a new diet?"

"Because you start a new diet every day," the first woman said. "They're good, too. Got nuts."

I went through the door to the back of the station and Bailee almost made a break for it but decided invisibility was her best friend at this point. An officer walked down the hall toward us and she shrunk behind me. A kid version of stealth mode.

"Hey, Cass, can I have one?" he said.

"Sure, Bailee made them," I said holding out the bowl.

"Bailee, you did a great job. You even remembered the nuts."

"See, Bailee, you don't have to be scared of the police, as long as you remember the nuts."

I went on and left a bowl on the counter where the guys checked in evidence. There was another desk at the back door. Bailee had started to relax a little until she saw all the police cars lined up out back. They looked official. They looked like they meant business. They meant a knock on the door. I still had three more deliveries left. These were smaller bags. One went to Tom. I led Bailee down the hall and we knocked on Tom's door. He opened the door and Bailee jumped back with a quiet, "eep!"

"Cookie delivery," I told him.

"Hey Cassidy! You ready for a fight?"

Bailee gripped me from behind crouching out of Tom's sight.

"Not today. Bailee, this is silly, come out. Come here, this is Tom. He's a detective. Come out and say hi. He isn't going to fight you. He only fights me. When a case gets me frustrated I come box with Tom. He's nice, even in boxing gloves."

I squirmed around trying to get Bailee to let go but she wouldn't. Tom gave me the hush sign and knelt down. He peeked around my legs and met Bailee face to face. He flashed her a big, friendly grin and held out his hand. "Hi, I'm Tom."

"Me Bailee," she said timidly.

"Did you make these cookies?" Tom asked.

"Me hep Chas."

"Well, thank you. I know you were a good helper. Did she let you lick the bowl?"

"Yeah."

"Bailee is learning barrel racing," I said hoping to draw her out.

"Nawww, a kid like you learning *barrel racing*? That's a big kid sport."

"Me big kid," she said standing a little taller. "Chas, you fight Tom? You police, too?"

Tom busted out laughing. That about summed it up.

"Sort of, I'm a reserve deputy. That means I'm only a policeman when they let me, which means almost never. Remember I told you my job is to find people? Sometimes when I find people I work with the police."

"She *is* good at finding people," Tom admitted.

"Well, I have another delivery to make. We're off to Schroeder's office."

I wondered what Bailee would do when confronted with Schroeder's stern form, dressed in his always crisp police uniform, buzz cut. Even I went *eep!* sometimes when I saw Schroeder and I knew he was a friend. I knocked on his door, glanced in his window and went *eep!* He came to the door and I grinned at him nervously.

"Would you do me a favor?" I asked quietly.

"What's that?"

"Go sit behind your desk… and smile a little"

"Is there a reason I need to be sitting down? What are you going to tell me? Do I want to hear this?"

"It's not that. You just need to look a little less intimidating."

He gave me an "oh, come on" look.

"Please?"

He went and sat behind his desk but he was having trouble with the smile.

"Thanks," I said entering his office. I pulled Bailee in with me. She looked at the closing door like a prisoner condemned for life.

"Bailee, this is Mister Schroeder. He's the big boss of the station."

Schroeder's smile came a bit quicker now.

"We're making cookie deliveries before our trip to the ranch."

"You'll be gone until Tuesday?"

"Monday night."

"No trouble for a long weekend, eh?"

"Thanks to Bailee I haven't given you trouble for months."

"What do you mean, thanks to Bailee?" He looked closer at Bailee and she shrunk behind me again.

"Don't do that. She's scared enough of you already."

"How are you keeping Cassidy out of trouble? I want to know how to do that," Schroeder asked.

"I no know."

"I've been teaching riding at Farley McGyver's riding school. Bailee is my student," I said. "She's learning barrel racing."

"Farley teaches barrel racing?" Schroeder asked.

"No, I do. Farley would rather I didn't."

"Ah, so you're making trouble for McGyver instead."

"Sort of. There's a little controversy over that. Bailee is doing great. Farley sees her doing great and worries. Kind of like what I do to you, on a small scale."

"Gotta get them started early?"

"Very funny."

He opened the bag of cookies. "Cassidy makes the best cookies," he said.

"I didn't make them, Bailee did."

Schroeder leaned forward and Bailee hid again.

"You know what that means?" Schroeder asked.

"What?" Bailee asked.

"It means I need to share something with you." Schroeder dug around in his desk drawer and came up with a little coloring book about the police force. Bailee had to come out of hiding to accept it, but she didn't look very happy. She looked at the pictures. An officer listening to a lost child. An officer riding a horse, smiling like an idiot.

"Police ride horse?"

"Sometimes. We have a few mounted police."

An officer directing traffic. I never saw so many smiling officers as I did in that book. A loud *knock, knock* made Bailee jump like she'd been shot. Rusty opened the door and stuck his head in.

"Hey beautiful, I knew you were here when I saw all the cookies. Bailee, are you ready for some dinner?"

"Yes!" If it means getting out of this station in one piece, I imagined her thinking.

"Schroeder, I'll be back Tuesday."

"All right, have a good trip."

"Will do."

"Don't get into too much trouble," he admonished me.

"It's almost impossible where we're going. I spent eighteen years figuring out all of the trouble I could so they're wise to me now."

"Eighteen years? Is that how long it takes?"

"No, that's just how long they had me for."

Bailee had never been to a restaurant before. She wasn't sure what to do so she kept quiet and read the menu wondering at all the pictures of food.

"Do you know what you want?" I asked her.

"No, I no know what it is."

"Well, what do you like to eat?"

"Cake, never eat cake. Only school party get cake."

"Well, you can't eat cake for dinner but you can have some for dessert. Do you like beef? Chicken? Pasta? What do you eat for dinner at home?"

"Me eat stew and biscuits. Sometime chili an bread."

"What do you like to eat at school?"

"They have pizza? School pizza look good. I never buy lunch."

We looked on the menu. This wasn't exactly a pizza place but we found little kid sized pizzas on the children's menu.

"What do you eat for lunch at school?"

"Always bring one sanwich, one carrot, sometime juice. Bring carrot if one left from cook dinner. Maybe, special day there piece canny. One piece. I save canny, for walk home."

Rusty was reading his menu but I could tell he was listening carefully. "Your mom's going to have a heyday," he said.

I was thinking the same thing. I was having a heyday just buying her a kiddy pizza and a piece of cake.

As Rusty ate his megamushroom and Swiss burger he watched Bailee. You'd think she'd been given a precious gift. She ate the pizza slowly, taking the smallest bites that still had pizza flavor to them. I finished my chicken fajitas and still Bailee carefully shaved off pieces of her pizza. When she got to a slice of pepperoni she cut it in quarters and made sure a piece was on each of the next four bites. I doubted she was this meticulous with stew and biscuits.

"Would you like dessert?" I asked trying to hurry her up a little bit.

"Cake too?"

"Sure."

"Chocolate?"

"I don't know, let's see what they have on the menu."

I plucked the menu from the end of the table and turned to the desserts. Their cake looked rich. It was called Triple Truffle Treasure. I thought Bailee would make herself sick.

"Are you sure you can eat all that?" I asked.

"Yes!"

"Okay, we'll take one Triple Truffle Treasure."

"And three spoons?" the waitress asked.

"No, just one."

"Good luck!" she said shaking her head and walking away.

When the waitress put the cake in front of Bailee her eyes popped out of her head.

"That's what they all say," the waitress said. "Are you sure you don't want more spoons?"

"No, but maybe a small box," I answered.

Just like the pizza, Bailee carefully ate one layer of cake at a time. There were seven layers and she made it through about three of them. The waitress packaged up two thirds of a pizza and two thirds of a Triple Truffle Treasure. Did that make it a Double Truffle Treasure? She put the two boxes in a bag with some napkins and a fork and we headed for home.

Halfway there we heard from the back seat, "This more than my birthday ever!"

Another slice of pizza disappeared and a smidgen more cake got eaten. When we got home I showed her the guestroom and where the bathroom was.

"This big bed?" she asked.

"Will you be okay in here?"

"I be okay. Is just big big bed."

She climbed up onto it and bounced gently, smiling a little. She stretched out and pulled the pillow over like she had never felt such comfort. What was it about this kid that made me feel torn all the time? To think she only got cake at school birthday parties, and she only got pizza when a friend took her out to dinner. Normal kid things. To think she thought an ordinary bed was a luxury. I didn't mind her being used to stew and biscuits. A kid ate what was served. A kid grew up however their parents lived. Maybe I was spoiled. In fact, I knew I was. I was spoiled rotten, but it seemed other kids could at least be spoiled a little. A little spoiling was good for them.

"We need to get up early in the morning so get a good night's sleep. If you need something in the night you know where things are in the kitchen and the bathroom is just across the hall."

"Me n Shadow do… tricks?"

"You mean the obstacles? You want to take him through the agility course?"

Her eyes brightened.

"Yes!"

"You're going to need some help. He thinks I'm the boss so I don't know if he will listen to you."

We went out back, Shadow dashing out the door before us. Bailee lunged for him.

"It's okay, he won't run away," I said. "Shadow, work time, come!"

He dashed over and sat at my feet.

"Shadow, heel!" I commanded walking toward the first obstacle. I chose the tunnel because I knew Shadow loved the tunnel and it was one of the easier ones for Bailee to try. "Shadow, sit!" He sat and then I addressed Bailee. "Okay, watch me. Say 'Shadow, go through' and make a tunneling motion with your arm. Go through! Just like that."

Bailee stood beside the tunnel, "Shadow, go through!" she commanded.

Shadow cocked his head at me. "Well, mom?" he seemed to say. "The kid says go through. Should I go through?"

"Go on," I said.

He dashed through the tunnel and came back around. Bailee laughed at him.

"Shadow! Go through!" she said.

I gave him the okay and he ran through again. This time though he was ready for the next obstacle so he waited for us to follow to the next one.

"Maybe it would help if I showed you how it's normally done. Let me run him through the course and then you can try it. Listen to the commands because those are the words he knows. Shadow! Heel!"

I jogged to the first obstacle, the A frame.

"Shadow! Up! Go up! Okay, come down!"

Next the dog walk because it was similar to the A frame.

"Go up! Come, Shadow, up! Good boy! All right, down."

The tunnel.

"Go through!"

The hurdle.

"Jump!"

The broad jump.

"Jump again!"

The seesaw.

"Shadow, go up, over, come on! Good boy. Easy, easy. Okay, down"

Shadow didn't like the seesaw because it moved. The collapsed tunnel.

"Go through! Go! Go! Good boy!"

The weave poles.

"Weave! Shadow weave! Good boy!"

The tire jump.

"Jump, boy! Good dog!"

The crossover.

"Shadow up! Up! Good boy, slow, wait." Shadow waited on top of the crossover. He was waiting for a cue on which way to come down. I didn't know the official commands for agility so we used *to me*, *away*, *forward* and *back*.

"To me!" I said and he ran down the board that ended at my feet. "Heel!" I said walking back to Bailee. "See, that's how we do it, at a jog. When he competes he will be timed and the fastest dog to do the whole course wins."

"He good! You teach all that?"

"Yeah, we had a couple of very boring years and we worked on agility." The years after Jack died, I remembered sadly. Not too sadly, though, the memory was fading and my life now was much fuller than it ever had been then. "You don't have to do them in that order but you have to keep going, so don't stand there deciding what to do or he just might take off without you and that's a bad thing, too. He has to be corrected for that."

Bailee didn't have much luck with the agility course. When Shadow balked I went over and gave the right signals.

"Try just the jumps and tunnels. Those are his favorites."

And so Bailee played with Shadow until it got too dark to see and then we all turned in.

"Did you bring something to do on the drive? It's a four hour drive."

"I bring books. But I want see everything. I watch."

"Well, keep a book handy. It's not a very interesting drive."

"Everything interesting," she said and I thought maybe that was one of the things I liked about this kid. "Walk to school. Every day is same but every day different. Man walk little dog. Woman walk big dog. Cats in yards. Birds. Me like walk school. Me watch."

And sure enough, I learned a lot about the drive I'd made so many times.

"What grow those trees?" They were oranges.

"Look Chas! Bird houses under bridge." Sure enough, they were cliff swallows.

"So many cows!"… "Them have horses, look one like Shocks!"… It went on and on. In spite of breakfast she brought along the pizza and cake and it slowly disappeared on the drive. She was on the edge of her seat when we turned down the white fence leading to the ranch house. There were going to be plenty of nose and fingerprints on the windows.

Shadow recognized the turn onto the road and came to attention, too.

Patrick came tearing out of Jesse's house and jumped on his bicycle. He dumped the bike at the porch steps and waited for us to get out of the Explorer.

"Pat, go fetch Randy. I need some help with an obnoxious horse."

Apache didn't like the trailer one bit. I was surprised there wasn't a hole kicked in the side of it. There were thumpings and bumpings inside.

Patrick jumped on his bike and pedaled away. Pretty soon Randy came jogging up from the barn with a lead rope. Between the two of us we managed to get Apache out of the trailer and calmed. Randy stood there holding the lead with a firm hand, Apache skittering along beside him. Bailee climbed down from the back seat, took one look at the handsome cowboy and fell in love. Randy was everything the books talked about, minus the hat.

"Chas," Bailee said tugging on my shirt and staring off after Randy, "How old Ranny?"

Oh gee. "He's twenty-five. There's lots of people you need to meet. This is Patrick. He's my nephew. Patrick, this is Bailee."

Patrick extended his hand tentatively. "It's nice to meet you," he said because it was expected of him. He didn't look like he was very pleased, though. Bailee, shook it, also tentatively. Who wanted to shake hands with a seven year old kid when there was a real cowboy around?

"Where'd you get that wild pinto?" Randy asked.

"He belongs to the school where I teach riding. I'm supposed to make him fit for young kids to ride. Right now he needs socializing and noise conditioning. I'll work with him here in the busyness of the ranch and see if that helps."

"Oh yeah!" Zack said clumping up onto the porch, "We got us a new ice pack bet going. That horse'll have you on the ground before you know it."

"I ride him at home. He *is* saddle broke. He just has… issues."

My mom hurried out the front door making the screen slam and Bailee jump.

"Cassidy! You're home! Rusty! It's so good to see you again!" she said amid a flurry of hugs. Bailee just watched her, inching a little behind me. Martha followed, always next in line for hugs. She eyed the child beside me. I gave Martha a hug and then Martha went on to hug Bailee too.

"Are you ready for some real ranch cookin'?" Martha asked.

"I think so," Bailee answered. I wondered if she was picturing pots of stew and chili like in the kids' westerns she read. If there was one thing Martha knew how to do it was cook.

"Bailee, this is my mom, Mrs. Gordon."

"Call me Betty, dear."

"And this is Martha, she helps my mom with the house and cooking."

"More like I run the place," Martha said.

"Randy and Zack work with the horses. Zack looks for opportunities to make bets on how much trouble I'll get into. Zack, it's no fair startling the horse just to win five bucks. I do need some noise distractions but not for the purpose of winning a bet. We need to ease him into it."

"Show Bailee to her room," Mom said.

We walked into the big ranch living room with the fireplace burning brightly, the big overstuffed couch and easy chairs beckoning. Beyond she could see the huge dining room, table stretching from one end of the room to nearly the kitchen, chairs for a dozen people, and beyond that windows provided a view of the old oak trees and yellowed hills behind the ranch. The living room was probably the same size as Bailee's house.

"This is the house I grew up in," I told her. "I'll give you a room close to mine. You'll even have your very own bathroom. My sister and I didn't even get to fight over bathrooms because every bedroom has its own bathroom. It's almost like a hotel."

Martha and Mom should turn it into a dude ranch. I went from room to room looking to see if Martha had fixed one up especially for Bailee. I hit the bullseye in the room across from mine. Most of the rooms were decorated the same in rust, deep green, and blue gray but Martha almost always added floral arrangements to the dressers and added little personal touches when she was expecting a guest. In this case she lined up horse models on the windowsills, put a saddle on a quilt rack in the corner, and put pretty little bottles of strawberry cream shampoo, conditioner, lotion, anything a little girl could want in the bathroom. There were even hair styling gadgets in the drawers.

"Hey, Bailee, Martha went all out for you, look," I said opening the drawers. Curling irons, mousse, hot air rollers, little samples of makeup and nail polish were lined up in the drawers.

"Me no know how to use that stuff. Mom get mad I use hers."

"Well, this is here for you. You can use it if you want to. You can play with the horses on the windowsill, too. Oh, and if you want a real show, take that lasso off the saddle and ask Patrick how to use it. He's learned a bunch of rope tricks."

"Pat rick?"

"Yeah, my nephew."

"Little Pat rick."

"Yeah."

"Not Ranny?"

"Randy can show you how to rope a horse. Patrick can show you how to twirl a rope over your head, jump into and out of a moving rope and twirl it at your side. He's pretty good. Besides, Randy is too old for you."

"An Pat rick too young."

"Give him a chance. Patrick will surprise you. He can ride and rope and tell a good campfire story. He can track animals and people. You can find him hanging out with Elan. You can recognize Elan because he has long straight black hair and he doesn't wear boots."

"Why he no wear boots?"

"He likes to feel the ground beneath his feet, just like me. I'll wear boots when I train Apache but when I'm not working I wear moccasins."

"Indian shoes?"

"Yeah, but Elan wears them because he *is* an Indian."

Rusty clattered in with our rolling suitcases and Bailee's little bag.

"Do you want to see my room? It's been cleared out but it's the same decorations I chose when I was a teenager."

We walked across the hall and entered my cowgirl room. The bedspread had western silhouettes all over a buckskin background: bucking horses, cactus, barbed wire, and sheriff stars. The curtains matched with contrasting toppers. A border of grazing horses circled the ceiling and the walls were painted a very light tan. A picture of Shasta and I adorned one wall. It wasn't there when I was a kid. My mom had added that after I left home. The windows overlooked paddocks of grazing quarter horses. When I was sick my mom would have Steve put Shasta in the paddock under my window so I could watch him. It wasn't comforting, though. It made me itch to get out again and often I did, sneaking out at night I'd ride Shasta around the paddock bareback. My mother never questioned why my pajamas were full of horse hair and she never told me I'd just get sicker going out at night in nothing but my PJs. Somehow my mom just knew, there was only so much she could do.

"Chas, we see your horse?"

"Sure, we need to stop by my dad's office on the way. Remember, he's not as stern as he looks. You must call him Mister Gordon and you must be respectful. If you do that he's a big old softie."

"Why? He look mean?"

"No, he doesn't really look mean. He looks nice. Do you remember Mr. Schroeder? He looks stern and he acts stern, well, Dad doesn't need to look stern. Don't worry, just be polite."

"What you mean, be polite?"

"Call him Mr. Gordon, remember to say *yes, sir* and *no, sir*. You know, all those things they taught you in finishing school."

"What finish school? I'm fourth grade."

"I was just kidding. Finishing school is where you go to learn all those extra manners that normal people don't know exist."

I'm afraid my attitude about my dad didn't help much. I approached the office door hesitantly. I knocked gently and peeked in the open door, just like I had since I was about four years old. He looked up from his books.

"Come in, Cassidy," he said just like he might if I'd been living at home all this time. "What can I do for you?"

"Nothing, just reporting in and introducing you to a friend. This is Bailee," I said turning around, but Bailee was still outside the door. I gave her an impatient look, sympathizing a little. "Come on, Bailee, say *hi* to Dad and then I'll show you the horses. You want to ride Shasta? Then come say *hi*."

Bailee came around the doorway and stood there like she was facing a firing squad. Dad stood up behind his desk, dwarfing it. Bailee stood her ground.

"Bailee? I'm Mr. Gordon. I'm Cassidy's dad. It's good to meet you."

"Yessir," squeaked Bailee.

"Do you like horses?"

"Yessir."

"Do you have experience on a horse?"

"Yessir." The squeaks were getting fainter and fainter and I was afraid she was going to make a run for it.

"Tell me about the riding you do."

"Yessir, Chas, teach me barl racing. I ride Shocks. He black horse. Got white shocks. He good harse."

"I'm sure he is. So, you're learning barrel racing? A young thing like you?"

"Yessir."

"She's doing great at it, too," I put in to give Bailee a little boost.

"And you want to see my horses."

"Yessir!"

"You go on to the yard and wait for Cassidy. She'll be along in a minute."

"Yessir."

He waited until she was out of earshot and then said, "What happened to her?"

"A car wreck."

"How long ago?"

"Two years."

"Two years and she's still like that?"

"Yes sir. She doesn't have a lot of support. I think when the doctors said they'd done what they could her parents used up the therapy that was on her insurance and called it quits. She's come a long ways in the speech department. If she cares enough to talk she figures out enough words to get by."

"What about her hands?"

"I don't talk about her hands. She guides a horse. She can hold things. She writes crudely."

"She got a head on her shoulders?"

"Yes sir, a good one. She's a year behind in school but she reads at a higher level than most kids in her grade."

He stared at his feet for half a minute.

"She a Randy?"

"In a way. I know she has a mother and a brother. I know she has a home. But, yeah, in a way."

Randy was taken in by the ranch because he was homeless. Dad wasn't asking if Bailee was homeless, well, in a way he was. What he was really asking was if she was a child in need. I knew to answer his questions and not question back. He'd reach his own conclusions about Bailee and it didn't surprise me in the least when he appeared at the barn and stood quietly off to the side. Like I told Bailey, once Big Wayne Gordon got a dose of respect he was a big old softie.

"These harse bigger! Much much bigger."

"You're used to Socks. Socks is a small horse. Think you could ride a horse this big?"

"Yes! I ride any horse! I ride Shasta."

"Which horse do you like the best?"

"I like Shasta, cause know you choose best. But honest? Me like this one," she said pointing out Buck.

"He's a good horse, too. What is it about him that catches your eye?"

"Him… I lose word. Not strong, sort of… but… he look like he smart, he know his job… an me like his color. His color like cowboy ride to hide. Many harse his color in old west book."

"You've got a good eye. Would you like to ride Buck?"

"Can I?"

"Yeah, I wouldn't bring you here and then keep you from riding."

I saddled Buck and Shasta. Bailee wanted to do it but she couldn't reach to lift the saddle and bridle and we didn't have the special platforms that aided her at the school. I climbed into Buck's saddle, found a good length and tied the reins so Bailee could hold them easily. Once she was in the saddle I adjusted the stirrups for her. When we were both saddled up I led the way to the track. I wanted to find out what she was capable of.

We walked half a lap letting her get used to being on a bigger horse. When we moved on to a trot and she rode easily, knowing to use her knees to gentle the bouncing.

"Be ready when we move on to a canter. These horses are used to taking off like a shot. When they are asked to speed up it is usually to catch something already moving or to put some miles behind them in a hurry. They aren't like Socks where you have to ask multiple times. These horses are ready to go. Are you ready?"

She waited until she'd settled in her mind exactly what she needed to be ready for and then she nodded, concentrating on the horse. I watched her give Buck a kick and he jumped to attention. Bailee was startled at first, then eased herself back down into the saddle smiling broadly at the feel of a real horse beneath her. I stayed by her side.

"This big big horse!" she laughed.

Buck's canter was as fast as Socks' halfhearted run of the previous day. We did one lap at a lope. She was used to these three gaits, she just wasn't used to horses of this caliber. Farley's horses were all donated. Their problems had been worked out but some of them, like Socks, were donated because they needed an easy retirement. They loved the kids and the kids loved them. The burdens of each day were easy. The weight on aching joints was light. Farley balked at the barrel racing because he had to. He had to put safety first. It was his duty even if his heart saw a free spirit who needed to soar. He had a school to run, a school with a reputation. He had an image to maintain and that image was not one of galloping barrel racers. It was of handicapped kids learning and growing. It was slow paced. Smiling kids on smiling horses doing nice, safe things. Bailee, I feared, was fixing to outgrow the school. And when that happened what would become of Socks? Bailee was content there until I came along. Maybe she'd have been better off with a nice firm *no* when she asked about barrel racing.

Bailee became almost invisible at the dinner table. The ranch hands were talking work a mile a minute. Mom and Jesse were talking shopping a mile a minute. Patrick was looking at Bailee jealously. Wyatt wanted his mashed potatoes with butter not gravy. The mountains of food were intimidating to Bailee, too.

"Excuse me y'all but we have a guest at our table tonight," Dad announced. "Please welcome Bailee Roland. She came with Cassidy and Rusty to do some riding. Bailee, I think you've met most everybody except Steve, Elan and James."

They all gave Bailee a nod of acknowledgment. She looked back as she slunk down in her chair.

As the bowls and platters were passed I placed a little bit of everything on Bailee's plate.

"You don't have to eat it all," I told her. "Save room for dessert."

She brightened at the prospects of something sweet.

"Chas," she whispered. "This your big family?"

I looked around the table. "Yeah, this is my big family." The real one was smaller but I accepted the hands as family, too. They had eaten meals with us longer than I could remember. They watched over Jesse and I as much as our Mom and Dad did, maybe more. Elan was a newcomer to the family but seemed to have settled in. He and Steve had just gotten back from an errand so I hadn't had a chance to see how he worked out in the normal scheme of things.

"So, Trouble, what kind of trouble have you gotten into since your last visit?" Steve asked.

I tried to think of what had happened to me that I wanted Bailee to know. So I told the story about looking for Sherri Champlain.

"Something's still eating at you." Rusty pointed out as we lay in our room that night.

"I think I did the wrong thing letting Bailee try barrel racing. Now we're stuck in a Catch 22. She's got a horse who can't possibly be a barrel racer. Farley can't support Bailee's dream because it endangers his school's reputation. Bailee is getting a dose of real horses and she's not going to be content doing little exercises at Farley's school but she won't abandon Socks because they have bonded. I don't know what to do. I can't undo any of it."

"Take Shasta home with you. She can do barrel racing on Shasta, and visit Socks at the school, just like always. You'd have your horse home with you."

"No, Shasta stays with the ranch. This is his home."

"Your dad's been looking at Apache. I don't know what's stewing in that noggin of his but it might work to your advantage. Feel him out. I think he sees a young, fit horse and he sees some of his work horses getting up in years."

"You're kidding. He can't just claim Apache. Apache is Farley's horse."

"He could offer to buy Apache. You admitted you didn't think Apache was destined for Farley's school anyway. Maybe you can bring a barrel racer to Farley's school and get Apache off your hands at the same time. Watch and see what happens."

Just what I needed when I was trying to sleep, more ideas to stew on. I went to the window and looked out over the paddocks.

"I hope it's easier with our own kids," I said.

"It will be. Part of the problem is that Bailee is not your child. If she was, you could teach her anything you want. It's all these other factors that complicate it."

"Well, that's a relief anyway. I really believe in encouraging kids in the direction of their passion."

"What about husbands? You're sure encouraging *my* passions standing there in the window like that."

"Especially husbands. Husbands should follow their passions, too."

"It helps if husbands and wives share the same passions," he said as a kiss closed over my mouth.

I got up with the sun knowing as soon as Bailee was up I'd have little time to work with Apache. I took a quick shower and went down to the paddock, caught the stubborn animal and tied him to the fence while I saddled him and bridled him. I rode him around the large paddock before venturing out to tour the rest of the ranch. I wanted him to see it come alive, to hear the tractor start up that brought hay to the horses in the pastures, be near the shouts of men and the noise of tools and the clanging of the triangle that called the cowboys to breakfast. With each sound Apache jumped and I held him to a controlled walk. I didn't coddle him and tell him everything was okay. If I reacted to the things he feared he would know it was dangerous. I had to treat the sounds as everyday occurrences and something to accept no matter how it made him feel. I couldn't change the way noises affected Apache but I could change his reaction to them. And eventually, maybe they would become a more normal part of his life.

I caught my dad watching. He did indeed have his eye on the flashy pinto.

"You think he'll ever be fit?" Dad asked as I rode by. Apache heard a door slam and skittered away from it. I brought him back to a walk and made a u-turn to come back around to Dad.

"I give him 5 years to be ready to settle down enough for those kids. But I hate to do it to him. He'll make a good horse for an experienced rider with just a little conditioning, but to get him to slow down enough for Farley's school? I'll have to take all the fight out of him and I'm fixing to tell Farley I won't do that."

Dad just scratched his head, but I could tell he agreed with me.

Zack hurried by but Dad stopped him. "Zack, are you heading up to the house to look for me?"

"No sir, I'm heading up to the house for a stack of pancakes."

"The bell hasn't rung yet."

"Hey, Zack," I said. "If you'll ride the dirt bike around the track for me, then you'll have a quick way up to the house when the bell does ring. Apache needs to get used to being around machinery."

I rode Apache to the racetrack and put him into a nice steady lope. The more energy he used up running the less he'd have left to fight with. I kept him at it until Zack appeared with the dirt bike.

"Take it easy at first," I told Zack. "No loud engine gunning when you're close to him. Just ride around and gauge your actions based on how he reacts to you. My job is to maintain control of the horse."

Zack put-putted around the track and I rode Apache pretending everything was rosy and bright, wrestling Apache back in line whenever the dirt bike got too close and it startled him. Round and around we went until Martha rang the triangle on the back porch. Zack stopped and looked to me for permission to go.

"Go on, you earned your pancakes this morning," I told him.

Zack hit the gas and took off for the house in a cloud of dust and Apache went ballistic. As I fought to stay in the saddle and ride out Apache's panic attack I thought I should have known Zack had the attention span of a flea. I pointed Apache down the track and gave him the go ahead to run off his anxiety. Once he had a direction things could be controlled easier.

"That damn kid, will he ever get a head on his shoulders?" Dad said as I rode past.

"Looks like you got your hands full with that one," Steve said of Apache.

"What do you think?" Dad asked Steve.

"If Cass has trouble with him you really want him around here?"

"You don't want to deal with him?"

"It's not that. You know we've had worse cases than a noise spooked horse."

"He's a young un."

"Take some training. Bet he's not broke for roping."

"He's half way there," I put in. "He knows to stand still when his rider is gone. He needs to be taught what to do after a calf is roped, but you've done that before. It's just the noise problem I'm working through. Well, that and the fact that he's just too much horse for what Farley wants to do."

"Do you think this Farley character would be keen to a trade?" Dad asked.

"What kind of a trade?"

"You put Bailee up on the horses, see which ones she takes to."

"I plan to but I don't know what Farley will think about a trade. Apache was given to him to use at the school. He might feel funny trading him off if he was a gift."

"See what Bailee thinks, then we'll talk again."

Everybody was finishing up breakfast when I finally got back up to the house. After the riding that morning I needed to groom my horse before turning him loose again. Ranch rule. I automatically just did it, but it put me late for breakfast. I felt bad making Bailee fend for herself in the big house. Martha was sitting next to Bailee at the big dining room table. Most of the hands had come, eaten, and gone on to do other ranch chores.

"So, what would you like for dinner tonight?" Martha asked Bailee.

"Pizza?"

"Pizza? Really?" Martha asked. "I don't think we've ever had pizza for dinner. Maybe for lunch if I have all the ingredients. What about dessert?"

"Cake?"

"What kind?"

"Choc lat."

"If you make pizza, be sure and invite the boys. They love pizza. That's one of the first things they ask for at my house," I said.

"Chas! Today we barl race?" Bailee asked, glad for a familiar face.

"Are you sure you're ready? Yesterday you were only cantering. When a horse is trained in barrel racing they take it at a gallop. Are you sure you're ready for the speed and the quick turns?"

"Yes!"

Somehow I knew she'd say that. I would have at her age whether I was ready or not. I was always ready to try. I also found out the hard way that I wasn't ready to try everything that I thought I was. I wasn't sure I wanted Bailee to learn the same way I had.

"Are you ready to try a different horse? I think Mack would be a good choice for barrel racing."

"What color Mack?"

"He's bay. He's a good horse. He's smaller than Buck but he's smart. He has a good feel for the barrels."

I ate a scoop of scrambled eggs as I talked because Bailee was raring to go.

When we got down to the corral the barrels weren't set up yet so I had to retrieve them from behind the barn. They were big, bulky oil drums, painted red, white and blue. They had always been awkward for me to move, so as a kid I had developed my own way of transporting them. I pulled them over on their side and one by one I hopped on top of them and walked backwards rolling the barrel forwards. Bailee laughed at me when she saw me walking on top of the barrel.

"Chas! What you do?"

"I'm just putting the barrels in the corral."

"But why you do that?"

"It's funner and I can't carry them. Go open the gate."

She ran and opened the gate and ran back.

"Me try?"

"Sure," I said hopping off.

She climbed up awkwardly, but the barrel shifted under her, dumping her off.

"Try again," I said.

She climbed up and I held up a hand for her to balance. She stood shakily. I waited for the shaking to stop then told her, "Walk backwards, slowly."

One step and the barrel moved too quickly and she had to jump down again.

"It takes some practice," I admitted. I hopped back up and began moving the barrel again. By the third barrel I had lost patience walking them and just shoved it ahead of me. We went to the barn and I introduced her to Mack.

"Mack's a good horse. Old Frank favored him, and Old Frank had an eye for what makes a horse tick."

"Who Old Frank?"

"He used to work at the ranch. He was like a grandfather to me. He passed away earlier this year."

"Why he die?"

"He was just old. But if Old Frank saw something in Mack you can be sure he's got what it takes to do the job."

We saddled up Mack. I adjusted the bridle to fit and we were in business. Bailee rode Mack to the corral. She seemed a lot more comfortable with Mack than she had with Buck. I thought it was because Mack was closer to the same size as Socks.

"Be ready," I told Bailee. "Always be ready for anything when you are in the saddle. Horses are unpredictable. Try taking the barrels slow first. Do you remember the pattern?"

"Go far side barrel, tight turn."

"Good! Do you want me to go through it or do you want to take it on your own?"

She grinned at me and put her heals to her horse with such a firm determination that Mack leaped forward and Bailee did a backflip right off his back end and landed in the dirt with a thud.

"I swear, she looked just like you when she did that," Dad said, shaking his head.

"Bailee! Are you okay?" I said running to her aid.

She was scratched and bleeding, dusty and still in shock from the fall but she just said, "Him fast harse!"

"I told you slow and I told you to be ready for anything," I reminded her.

Mack stopped then came back and nuzzled Bailee's shoulder.

"Him yike me," she observed.

"Come on, let's get you up to the house and get these scrapes washed out."

"No, me want try it."

"We will, as soon as we make sure you're okay," I said thinking I sounded an awful lot like Landon and Antonio, and Bailee was sounding a lot like me.

On the way back to the house we saw Elan and Patrick, noses to the ground, puzzling something out.

"What them do?" Bailee asked.

"They are tracking. It's an interest they both share so they track together and teach each other the intricacies."

"What tracking?"

"Tracking is following tracks, maybe they see dog tracks or fox or coyote tracks. Maybe they are learning to tell one person's tracks from another."

Patrick looked up and saw me with Bailee and looked disappointed. I thought I better do something with him later.

Bailee sat through my ministrations grudgingly. She had torn a hole in the knee of her jeans but it looked like they were about due to rip anyway. I also noticed they were about two inches short.

"What happened?" Mom asked.

"Mack fast horse!" Bailee said, proud of her little adventure.

"So I see. Are you okay?"

"Yes, me fine, only Chas think I need all dis."

"We can't send you home with your clothes all torn up. We'll go to town and get you some new ones," Mom said.

She was just looking for any excuse to go shopping for Bailee but maybe if Mom took Bailee to town I could spend some time with Patrick and Rusty.

Zack walked in, looked around and said, "Rats!"

My guess was that he was checking on the icepack bet.

Back at the corral I showed Bailee just what she could really expect out of these horses.

“Just watch one run. You’ll see you have to expect the horse to move erratically. You have to lean with the horse, be ready when he speeds up and slows down. Grip with your knees and stay firmly in the saddle.”

I climbed up on Mack, rode him to position and got a nod from Bailee before I set my heels to the horse. Mack leapt into an instant gallop and I turned him toward the first barrel. I reined him in a tight circle around the barrel. One, two, three barrels and a run for the start, a quick pull up and we stopped in a cloud of dust.

“Yes! Yes! Mack fast horse! Me try now?”

Again I asked, “Are you sure you’re ready?”

“Yes!”

I was beginning to see what I put my parents through. I climbed down and helped her climb up.

“Be ready. Lean into the leap. It’s going to be fast. Don’t push for speed, just take it easy.” Yeah, right, I thought. Bailee had as much restraint as a snowball going downhill. “Ready? Wait until you are really ready. Remember what happened last time and plan for it.”

“Come on Mack, you fast horse! We do dis!”

She crouched over the saddle, counted to three and brought her heels down. Mack leapt to the command and ran straight ahead.

“Turn him! Turn him to the first barrel!” I called out.

She reined right and Mack headed for the first barrel. I didn’t stress a tight turn at this speed. She needed to feel the turn and lean with the horse. The turns could be refined later. Now it was just important to get a feel for the ride and learn what to expect.

“All right! Go to the next one!”

Three barrels and she headed for the start again. Mack thundered toward me and I jumped out of the way.

“Chas! Me did it! Me did it!”

“You sure did!”

“Mack! We did it!” She said hugging the horse’s big neck. Mack tossed his head in agreement.

After two more sloppy, but successful, runs I declared a rest time for Mack. He didn’t really need it but Bailee would run him into the ground if I let her and I knew I had to parcel out my time. Mom would be thrilled to take Bailee to town and then I could spend time with Rusty or Patrick.

I admonished my mother, “Don’t go overboard! Bailee isn’t used to having a lot. She doesn’t need fancy things to be happy. Think basic. She’ll probably need help with buttons. Try to have patience and don’t correct her English. A couple of months ago she barely spoke so she’s doing wonderful now.”

Mom and Bailee were gone for hours. As soon as they pulled out of the driveway I found Patrick. I walked down to his house and heard voices from the tree house.

Patrick: "I know I need to share. I just get to see you guys a couple times a year and then she brings this *girl* along. I just want things to be like always, that's all."

Rusty: "Me, too, Pat, but Bailee helped Aunt Cassidy be strong again and Cassidy wants to help Bailee, too. She hasn't forgotten you. You have to understand where Bailee comes from to understand why it was important for her to be here. I don't expect you to understand it, but you've got to accept it."

Pat: "She gets to see Aunt Cassidy twice a week! I only get to see her twice a year!"

Rusty: "But it's not Aunt Cassidy that Bailee needs here, it's a chance to be like you for just one weekend."

Pat: "Like me?"

Rusty: "You live a life Bailee can only dream about. It doesn't seem like anything special to you but some kids would do anything to live like you do. Bailee's one of them. Instead of getting mad at her, try and show her what it's really like. Show her Snoopy. Tell her how you work with him. She needs to learn how to get along with horses. If you show her she will know it's something a kid can do."

I climbed the ladder and peeked into the tree house.

"Come on down," I said. "Grandma took Bailee shopping."

Pat and Rusty grinned at each other. Finally!

"Poor Bailee! Does she know what she's in for?" Pat said.

"Girls take to it better than boys," I told him.

They didn't really want to do anything. They just wanted time so I climbed up into the tree house with them. After a while Wyatt climbed up, too.

"Aunt Cassidy, will you teach me how to swim?" Wyatt asked.

"We don't have enough water here at the ranch."

"Will you draw me a picture to color?"

"Huh! You have come to the wrong person. I don't have an artistic bone in my body."

"Yes you do. You made the picture on your wedding cards."

"Only because I didn't have any choice."

"How can you not have a choice?" Pat asked. "They were your cards."

"I just made one as an experiment. I didn't plan on actually sending those out. But then the news people saw the card in Uncle Rusty's truck when they were trying to dig me out of the mine and they found out we were getting married. So they blew up the whole wedding story and used the card in their broadcast. Since everybody thought that was the wedding announcement I had to stick with it, so I had copies made."

"Well, you still did it. You can draw."

"Thanks, Wyatt."

"Well? Will you?"

So we all climbed down from the tree house and spent the next hour drawing silly pictures. First he asked for a lion, then a horse. Then Patrick got into the whole idea of drawing for his own purposes and asked me to draw different animal tracks.

"You know, you boys can try riding the cloverleaf when I am working with Bailee. You will just have to take turns. Bailee would like it if you joined us."

"She talks funny. She doesn't like me."

"She talks funny because she is learning to talk again. When she was seven she was in a car crash. She's just like you except she has to work a little harder to communicate. The more she is around kids who talk normally and talk *to her* the more normal her speech will become. And it's not that she doesn't like you but that she is scared that you'll feel exactly like you do. She would like it if you rode with us. We can get out a stop watch and have a competition."

"But I've never done barrel racing," Patrick said.

"But you've got more experience on a horse. You know how to get Snoopy to do what you want."

And so I ended up with a kiddy competition. Wyatt was too intimidated by the roughness of the sport but Patrick took to it. After Bailee tried riding Mack she also rode Chet and Shasta but something brought her back to Mack's stall again and again. There was just something in the horse that she liked and Mack liked her, too. Patrick rode Snoopy, the little pinto horse that James had bought for the boys to learn on.

Bailee was proud of the new clothes she brought back from her shopping trip with Mom. She now had real western jeans, boots, western cut blouses and a white cowboy hat. She strutted around in her new clothes and rode straighter in the saddle. She even showed her new outfits to Mack who just wanted to know if the pockets contained any treats for him.

Dad watched the goings on with interest. He seemed pleased with Bailee's choice of mounts.

Mom followed Bailee's actions with interest, too. She noticed the change in the girl when she had new clothes and she followed Bailee around in the background taking pictures. I think she was planning some project. Her and Jesse were always coming up with crafty things to do together.

Bailee put her all into the barrel racing, except when the horses needed a rest. Then she prowled the barns and corrals looking for Randy.

Apache continued to be his ornery self. I spent several hours on the track with Rusty riding the motorcycle around. I rode Apache around the ranch while cars were coming and going. I always got the same reaction out of him. He pulled away, forgetting the job at hand. If the engine was loud he bucked gently. If the noise came too close he struck out with hooves. When things were quiet he cooperated fine. He loved to run and he even ran the barrels a couple of times without mishap. We had a showdown of the pintos and Apache won easily because Snoopy and Patrick were both smaller. The little horse just didn't have the get up and go that Apache had.

"Cassidy, I'd like to talk to you about that horse," Dad finally said. I met him in his office. "What are McGyver's plans for Apache?"

"Well, eventually he'd like the kids at the school to be able to ride him."

"And these kids…"

"Are handicapped. Bailee's a good rider but there are a few more advanced. Farley said he had a couple of kids ready to try jumping if he had a horse trained to it. Most of the kids simply ride in figure eights around a corral. But they do it proudly."

Dad thought for a minute.

"Apache will never take to a life like that."

I repeated my 5 year prediction.

Dad nodded. "But he'd take to the work here."

"You'd have to talk to Farley about that."

"You got a phone number?"

I wasn't sure I liked Dad's manipulative ways but I also could see that trading Apache for Mack had a lot of advantages. Apache would have a home where he'd be used. Mack would head for a more settled life and after twelve years he was ready. Bailee would have a horse she could learn barrel racing on.

"Dad, what if Farley won't let Bailee learn barrel racing at the school?"

"I aim to find out. And what if he won't? I could trade him for Chet and you could have Mack. Bailee could work on her barrel racing with you on the side. Or I could trade him to McGyver if Bailee can work on barrel racing at the school."

"What about Socks? Bailee won't turn her back on her old friend."

"Hun, I can't do everything. What do you want?"

What *did* I want? I didn't know. I didn't want a horse at my house permanently. I didn't want a student showing up at my house every few days like clockwork. I liked Bailee. I was convinced we were linked for some time to come, but it was through the school.

"So, you've decided you'd give up Mack and Chet if you can have Apache? You're going to be short a work horse."

"If I need another I can bring up a colt I've got in training. Apache's got spunk. He's a looker. People will notice him when they come see the quarter horses."

"You can't breed him. He isn't a quarter horse. I don't think he's registered as any particular breed."

"That's okay."

"What're you going to do if you have people here looking at the horses and Apache decides to go berserk because somebody started up a car when he wasn't expecting it?"

"Randy and Elan will work with him."

"I need to think about this before you call Farley. I need to figure out a way to talk to Bailee, too."

"You'll find her in Mack's stall."

Dad was right. Bailee was in Mack's stall. She'd brushed him to a shine and she was laying on his back braiding the last of his mane. He looked silly. I had to be very careful how I talked to Bailee. I didn't want to commit to anything but I needed to find out how we were going to make this work. It was tempting to just take Apache home and forget about it but....

"Bailee? Do you miss Socks?"

"Sometimes, me used to long weekend no ride."

"What would you say if I told you Socks will never be a barrel racer? He's an old horse. He shouldn't be ridden that hard. The ride you got out of him Thursday is about the best you can expect."

"No, him good horse."

"He's a wonderful horse, and he loves you. But he isn't capable of what you want him to do. If you push him it will eventually hurt him. It'll make his knees hurt. That's why Farley has him at the school. He's too old for hard work so he does easy work with kids. Kids don't weigh much. They're a light load to bear. They ride slow and easy. You know other kids ride Socks, too. They ride like you used to, in figure eights, slowly doing weave poles. That's the work Socks should be doing for his age."

"No, Socks, good horse." It was all she could let herself believe and I didn't blame her.

"You've ridden Mack. What do you think of him? Do you think he could beat Socks?"

"Yes, Mack always beat Socks."

"Even with lots of practice?"

She thought about that. Yeah, even with lots of practice she seemed to decide but she wouldn't voice it.

"If you had a choice, to ride Socks or to ride Mack, which would you choose?"

"Chas! You no ask that! Me no choose! Me have no choose!" Her words got more jumbled the more upset she became.

"What if you did have a choice? Would you choose to ride Socks gently or would you choose to ride Mack around the barrels, maybe even learn to jump?"

"I…I…I no choose. Me can't. Me love both."

I gave Bailee a tearful hug. "Okay, I'm not asking you to choose. I've got my answer."

"Farley I need an honest answer," I said without preamble. "If you had a horse capable of doing barrel racing, would you let Bailee try it? I've got her up here at my parent's ranch. She's run the barrels. She can do it. If I could find a way to bring a horse down there for her to ride, would you let her do it?"

"Cassidy, you don't know what you're asking."

"Yes I do, you don't want Bailee to do barrel racing because it isn't part of the image you want for your school. So what's more important, your image? Or Bailee?"

"Cass…"

"This horse can jump. He's ready for your better riders. He's trained in everything you can think of. So, are you willing to forego your image to let some kids advance in their riding?"

"Cassidy…"

"I'm coming home tomorrow. My dad's going to offer you a trade. He has two horses that are ready for riding. The only problem I can think of with either of them is one of them is fussy about his back hooves. Other than that, they can deal with kids, they can do the exercises, they'll do jumping. They'll do English or Western. One is twelve and the other is thirteen."

"He wants to trade these two horses for Apache?"

"Yeah, he won't do it unless it benefits Bailee."

"What?"

"You heard me."

"Letting Bailee do barrel racing is what this deal hinges on?"

"Not really, but pretend it does." Suddenly I had an idea. "Would it help if I emailed you some pictures?"

"Yeah."

"Will do."

"Mom! I need to see those pictures you've been taking."

"What are you doing? Those were going to be a surprise for Bailee."

"They still can be. I just need a few to send to Farley McGyver."

I popped out the little memory card and slid it into the slot on my dad's computer.

"How did you take a hundred and sixty pictures of one kid in one weekend?" I asked my mom. "I just need two or three that show Bailee doing barrel racing on Mack and Chet."

"Bring up the thumbnails," Mom suggested.

"What are you doing?" Rusty asked as he walked into the office.

"Strategizing," I answered.

"Uh oh, I don't like the sound of it."

"Help me find a couple of pictures that will sway Farley to Bailee's side."

"Try this one," Mom said and I double clicked to increase the size.

"Nope that's Shasta."

"What about this one?"

"As long as we're going off these tiny pictures we're going to be guessing. We might as well just look at them all big."

We flipped through the pictures writing down numbers left and right. Mom was noting the pictures she wanted to scrapbook for Bailee. Rusty was writing down numbers he thought would sway Farley, plus a few he wanted for himself. I wrote down file numbers of pictures that I thought would impress Farley. Turned out we were all looking for different things.

"This one shows Chet's form."

"This one shows Bailee coming around the barrel. I like how the dust is flying. There's real action in that picture."

"Here's one that shows Mack pretty good."

"I like this one, it looks so peaceful."

"She's not even riding in that picture."

"I know but it shows the bond between her and Mack. You can see she just wants to be there with him."

"Rusty, you're a guy. What is Farley thinking? Which would sway you?"

"First of all these pictures are for his information. Send him one of each horse that is strictly information. He will see the horses are sound, they are obeying their commands, they pay attention. Don't send the picture that shows the dust flying. It's not the image he wants for his school. Send the pictures that emphasize the control of the horse. This one is good. It makes it look like Bailee has control of the horse even though Mack's galloping in the picture. See what I mean? He doesn't mind speed he just doesn't want his school to become a rodeo. So emphasize control. Then once you have his attention and he's thinking this might be a good deal whop him one upside the head with the one of Bailee and Mack in the barn, where he can see into her eyes."

I looked at Mom. Mom looked at me.

"Sounds like a plan," I said.

"I'm still putting the barrel racing pictures in the scrapbook," said Mom. "She'll feel like she was a real barrel racer."

"I feel like a traitor to men everywhere telling you to send that picture," Rusty said. "It's mean to do that to a guy."

"I won't tell him you suggested it."

An hour after I hit the send button I got a call from Farley on my cell phone.

"Cassidy, that was a mean, cruel thing to do to a guy," he said.

Ha, ha, it worked! I thought. "So, what do you think of the horses?" I asked.

"You've ridden these horses?"

"Many times."

"How's Apache coming?"

"I can ride him. He still spooks when he hears loud noises. I still give him five years to be settled down enough for your school. He's too young to lead a quiet life. He needs a few years of rough and tumble training. He's a man's horse. These guys on the ranch will continue his training. It's what they do every waking hour. They train horses for racing and working. They can take whatever Apache can dish out."

"You say your Dad will be calling?"

"Yeah."

"Okay, I'll be ready for him."

"What are you going to say?"

"I don't know."

I had to be content with that so I went and found Bailee. She was in the barn talking to Mack.

"I no know what to do, Mack. Tomorrow I have go home. I no want to." She stroked his blaze. "You good horse. You good for Ranny. Ranny say you good horse. He say you work har… I no wan go home. No wan go school. Kids be mean. You no mean."

I wondered if this was the same conversation as the one in the picture I sent to Farley. Mack nuzzled Bailee's pocket.

"I go get more," she said and went to the barn office. She opened a little refrigerator and took out a carrot. I didn't even know there was a refrigerator in there but Bailee did. She returned to Mack's stall, "You have all carrots you want while I here," she told him.

I started putting an English saddle on Shasta.

"Chas, what you do?"

"I want to show you something. Farley wanted you to start learning to ride English. I want to show you where that might lead."

"Me no want ride fancy English."

"It's not fancy, it's just more practical to use an English saddle for some activities."

I walked Shasta out to the corral where I had set up some low jumps. Shasta had always enjoyed jumping. I even entered him in competition as a teenager but when I went off to boot camp our jumping days just about ended. I knew how Bailee felt leaving Mack behind because I had felt the same way turning my back on Shasta seven years ago. Had it really been that long?

"You don't want to do this in a western saddle. The saddle is heavy. There is too much leather flapping around. It would be like trying to run track and jump hurdles wearing a carpenter's belt. You want things sleek, light and easy to move in."

I set Shasta up for the first low jump. He thought I was getting soft in my old age but I didn't want to show Bailee more than Farley would let her do at the school, so the highest jump was only about three feet. I made a point of stopping and setting up for each jump even though I knew Shasta could manage the whole course in one smooth run. I wanted Bailee to take this seriously. When we moved on to jumps where Shasta's feet had to actually leave the ground she began getting interested.

"You say Mizzur Mack let me do this?"

"Yeah, but you skipped learning to ride English. You'll have to go back and start from scratch on the English riding before you can start jumping."

"Me try now?"

"Sure, no jumping yet. The saddle feels different. You need to get used to the balance of it. You'll need to work your way back up through the gaits. And even if you think you learned it here you will have to do it again for Farley."

I figured if Bailee was going to push the rules she might be encouraged to push them in a direction that Farley would accept.

She didn't like the English saddle at first. Most kids used to riding western felt unsettled on an English saddle. It felt high and the side to side movement was different. There was no horn on the saddle, although Bailee had been wisely taught not to use one. She was taught to ride sitting straight, hands on the reins or one hand on her thigh. So her balance was good.

"Chas," she said from her high, slightly shaky perch, "jump in this saddle not safe."

"Yes, it is. I just showed you. I just did it. Once you get used to riding English you will see. It just takes practice."

And so we practiced and Bailee never did feel really secure in the saddle but she was working at something horsy and new and it held her interest.

"Me wish Mack jump," she said.

"Mack knows how to do these jumps. He's been taught almost everything there is to know."

"Mack do this?"

"Yeah!"

"Chas, me no want go home. Me stay here. Work ranch."

"You know you can't do that."

"Why? Ranny do it."

"Randy didn't have a choice. He didn't have parents. He needed a place to live."

"That how works? No mom, no dad."

"Bailee, you have a family. They love you. They want you home. You can't stay here. If we kept you here it would be kidnapping. It's illegal."

"But, I be sad. Leave Mack, leave dis your family."

"You just have to remember, you got to visit my life for a little while but your life is different."

"Why? Why be different?"

"Because, it's what you were born to. When you grow up you can choose more what life you want to live, but as a kid you have to live the life of your family. I had to when I was a kid. When I got grown up I chose a different life, one that took me to Joshua Hills. That's where I got to meet you. I was lucky, because I got to meet you. I'm glad I got to do that."

"You no miss you family, you ranch, you horse?"

"Yeah, a little, but I like my life in Joshua Hills, too. I like teaching at the school. I like my job. I like my family there too."

"Who your family Joshua Hills?"

"My family? The search and rescue team, the officers, the firemen, my friends, we're like one big family. Rusty has a job there. It's just home to me."

Bailee rode and rode, her mind wandering, just enjoying being in the saddle. I didn't push for more than just her being comfortable in the saddle. The more saddle time she got the more natural it would be when she had to concentrate on lessons.

"Okay, Bailee, we need to put Shasta back in his stall and wash up for dinner. Martha will be ringing the bell soon."

"She always make big big supper?"

"Yeah, even when we're not here."

"She always make choc lat cake?"

"No, she made it because she knows you like it. She usually makes a pie or a cobbler."

Bailee was moody at dinner. She knew it was her last dinner at the ranch. She looked around at all the faces, now familiar to her.

"Mister Godon?"

"Yes, Bailee?"

"How old workers dis you ranch?"

"Well, Bailee, they are all over twenty and right now we have all the trainers and jockeys we need."

"Have to be twenty?"

"No, eighteen with experience training horses."

"How you learn train horses?"

"That's a problem. Most city kids don't have a chance to learn how to train a horse. Good trainers are hard to find."

"Me learn. I fine way."

She went around the table.

"Mister Steve, how you learn train horses?"

"My dad worked a ranch in Montana. We lived in a little house kind of like James and Jesse do, so I had access to the ranch. I tagged along when he was working. He didn't do much training, but I learned how horses think, and when problems came up I started thinking how I'd solve them. I guess I just had the right mind for the job. I could think like a horse."

"James? How you do it?"

I was amazed Bailee was talking at all and here she was monopolizing the table.

"I don't do much training. I do more of the hands on work of the ranch. I'm more of a hand. Me and Zack. Steve, Elan and Randy do most of the training. They decide what needs to be done and then we all do it together."

I thought that was interesting. I knew James had worked here since Jesse and I were in high school. That's how Jesse and James had met. But I'd always assumed he trained the horses, too.

"Elan? How you learn train horses?"

"My family raised horses. I grew up around them. Basically I was the same as Steve except I grew up in Arizona. I went to school on the reservation and helped with the horses after school."

"Elan's dad and his grandpa and his great grandpa were trackers!" Patrick said.

"Yes," added Elan. "But tracking doesn't put food on the table like it did in the old days. So now we pass down tracking as a tradition. A skill. And the family raises horses."

The talk continued on the various ways to live a ranch life but what it mostly boiled down to was that it was in the blood. Horse people were mostly born that way, which was discouraging to Bailee. She was not born to it and there was very little she could do about it.

"Mister Godon? How I ever learn train horse with hands don't work?"

"Your hands do work. You eat, you write, you grip the reins," Dad answered patiently. He wasn't used to counseling young girls at the dinner table.

"They never be strong." She thought for a few seconds, wanting to make a point but not having the words to do it. "Got to be strong to train horse. Strong people follow their hands, their strong mind. Takes two things. I have strong mind but can't follow my hands. My hands. My hands want more. Want to be strong as my mind."

Bailee did have a strong mind. It took a lot of strength to say as much as she did that night. I wished Farley could be there to see just how strong Bailee was becoming. She was no longer the timid child I had met my first day at the school. She was a girl with a purpose. She had confidence. If she would take the time to form sentences correctly she would be a kid others looked up to, instead of made fun of.

Each day at the ranch Bailee came up with a different cowgirl outfit that Mom had bought her. She insisted on wearing the white cowboy hat even though she didn't need it. Her boots were already getting scuffed from constant work around the horses. She didn't worry about the scuffs. She seemed to consider them to be experience marks. Real cowboys had worn boots. She wouldn't be a real cowgirl until her boots showed it. So she worked hard in those boots. As I walked around the ranch I saw more of Bailee's tracks than anyone else's. She didn't sit still for a minute. Even when I was off doing things with Rusty and Patrick and visiting with my mom and Jesse, Bailee had been with the horses.

Apache continued to be trainable, but he spooked easily. I was beginning to see a little progress in the normal noise of everyday life. He didn't mind moving cars as long as they were quiet. Farley was going to have a long wait for this horse, though. Noise conditioning was something you couldn't push. Push too hard and it backfired.

I was catching a few peaceful minutes with Rusty when Patrick ran up. He stood waiting to be acknowledged.

"Grandpa wants to see you," he said.

"Okay, Pat, thanks for coming to get me," I answered. It looked like Patrick had taken over my messenger boy job.

Oh boy, here we go, I thought. What had Farley decided?

I stepped into the doorway of Dad's office with Bailee's hopes in the balance.

"You sent for me?" I said and my dad looked up from his work.

"It's time I called McGyver. Are you sure this is what you want?"

"It's not what I want that counts. I want what's best for Bailee and the horses and the ranch. I'm not going to pine away if Apache stays here. I know you'll work with him and he'll be happier here. If I end up taking him home I'll continue working with him on my own."

"And what about Bailee?"

"I don't know what's best for Bailee. She's going to heartbroken to leave. She'll be a little less heartbroken if Mack comes with us. But bringing Mack back forces her to make a choice she doesn't want to make."

"That girl's got gumption. Most kids would be scared to ask me about the ranch. She'll be a real handful pretty soon. Soon as she sees she has a chance at life she's gonna take off after it and nothings gonna stop her. Them hands of hers. They can be straightened. She's still young. The advances they have made. Her hands can be fixed. Her speech has improved just in the days she's been here."

"Her hands won't be fixed. Her parents don't have the money to do it. They did what they could after the crash. That's it. It's done."

He pursed his lips, stared at his hands.

"Would Bailee like them fixed?"

"I don't know, Dad. To be honest, even though her hands are a source of ridicule from the other kids and she hates it, standing up to it is part of what makes her Bailee."

"But is she Bailee who can take anything? Or is she Bailee who would do anything to make it stop? It takes strength to take the ridicule but it also takes strength to take a risk on a new life. It has to be hard trying to do things with hands like that. What would she do with normal hands?"

"I don't know. I hope she'd grab hold of life and haul for all it's worth."

"That's your spirit talking. What do you think she would really do?"

"I don't know, Dad. If it were possible, I'd be there to point her the way. I'd hand her the rope."

"This reminds me of when you told me about Randy. Got the same tight pit in my stomach. Thinkin' of a kid with their future on the line. I gotta tip it to the right. It's a hangin' there and if I just tip it. Maybe it'll sway to the right and the kid can make a go of it. You, you never stood still long enough to feel a tip. Never could catch you long enough to point you. You'd head for the dangdest things and all I could do was warn all the hands to look out."

I was beginning to see what Mom could see in him. Why did it take twenty-seven years for me to see it? And how was it that Rusty could see it all along?

"Sending Mack to the school won't make Bailee normal. It'll just give her more options."

"Cassidy, what is it I got too much of around here?"

Pride was what came to mind first but I was beginning to doubt that now.

"Money," he answered. "I got enough. Enough to tip that scale. Do you think Bailee's parents would get the treatment done, if someone would pay for it?"

"I don't know. I've barely seen her mom. I don't know if she has a dad."

He sighed. "I got connections. Maybe I'll find a way so's they don't even know."

This conversation was getting odder and odder. Next thing I knew he was on his computer. I was wondering if the conversation was at an end. Then he asked, "Where's them pictures your mother took?"

"They're in mypictures/betty/baileescrapbook."

"Leave it to your mother to give me what I need."

He clicked through the pictures until he found one that clearly showed Bailee's bent hands. He inserted the picture into a short email to a friend.

"Don, think you can do something about this?" was all the message said.

"Who's Don?"

"A surgeon in L.A. He bought a horse a few years ago. He bets on the races. He has a home near town. He gets around. Occasionally flies kids to hospitals across the country for treatments they need and can't get up here. He's got a heart for kids."

I wasn't sure what to think. I thought it was meddling in affairs that were not his own. But if it worked…

"Dad, I only brought Bailee here for a weekend of barrel racing. I didn't plan on it being a life changing experience."

"Now, there you go. You never know what's going to turn into a life changing experience. Tell me what you were thinking when you went to the grocery store two years ago."

Most people wouldn't know what he was talking about but he was referring to the time I went grocery shopping and got carjacked. Rusty was the detective in search of the man who carjacked me. If it wasn't for that trip to the grocery store I wouldn't have met Rusty.

"I get your point," I told Dad. "What do you want me to do? Should I talk to Farley first?"

"No, you run along. Watch around you. And be ready to hand over that rope you were talking about."

Chapter 32

It was hard to pretend everything was normal. I didn't have any real information, just possibilities, so I couldn't tell Bailee anything, yet the possibilities were all jumping around like popcorn in my head. What if I couldn't see the rope when it appeared? Bailee couldn't go through this without some backup. I only expected minimal support from her mom. Her mom had lost faith. She'd run out of possibilities and now was not the time to let that happen.

Fortunately, Bailee was still in horse mode. Rusty was enjoying the peace and quiet of the ranch. He could frequently be found in the hammock on the back porch. He talked ranch talk with Steve and Randy. He walked up to Jesse's house and played with the boys. He watched me and Bailee ride. We all enjoyed a relatively trouble free weekend. Only Zack was disappointed and I wondered if anybody actually bet on my side, that I wouldn't need an icepack.

The clock stood still as I waited for news from my dad.

"Chas? Me ride Mack one more time in morning?" Bailee asked.

"Of course, we don't have to leave until after lunch. You'll have some riding time. Make sure you are all packed up before you go to breakfast and the rest of your time can be spent riding."

She was happy with the answer, though not with the circumstances. I wished I could tell her we'd be bringing Mack back with us but I didn't know. My dad and Farley were both unpredictable. If Farley was predictable he would have given me his answer over the phone. I suspected he didn't want to take my word on the condition of the horses if he could talk to a real quarter horse breeder.

Everything seemed to be in slow motion. Rusty and I sat in a tense wait sitting close on the couch in the living room. Despite the warm weather there was a fire in the fireplace. Bailee appeared at the hallway. She stood watching us, just sitting quietly. Rusty tightened his arm around my shoulders and I snuggled closer. Bailee turned away.

"Did you want to talk to us?" I asked.

"No. I just go barn an… an I go now."

"And what? You can talk to me. You're not interrupting anything. We're just waiting for my Dad."

"I no want talk. I just never saw… me mom, me dad, they never close. I glad see you close. I go barn now." And she ran off.

"Well, at least now I know she *has* a dad," I said and I snuggled closer because that melancholy feeling Bailee left me with was back. I tried to remember if I'd ever seen my mom and dad snuggling on the couch and I couldn't bring a time to mind, but I'd never questioned their love for each other. Then I remembered last Christmas when Rusty and I made love under the Christmas tree. I'd asked him what he'd do if our kids caught us at it, and he said he'd tell them, "Daddy loves Mommy, get used to it." I knew he was just kidding but the memory warmed me back up anyway.

"I feel the wheels turning," he said softly.

"I'll tell you later," I answered.

We didn't get an answer from Dad that night. I knew there was still time but it would be nice to be able to ease Bailee's mind. When night came I went to the barn and dragged Bailee back to the house.

"But I only see Mack little time!" she complained.

"I know, but you need to sleep, too. You can see him in the morning," I said feeling like a traitor. How many times had I slept in the barn simply to be with the horses? Many times, but that was different. It was my barn, and my family. Bailee's mom would not like it if I let her sleep in the barn, so I couldn't leave her out there.

"Now will you tell me what was on your mind?" Rusty said after I got Bailee safely settled in her room. It was late. I'd given her as much time with Mack as I could. She told me again that she didn't want to go home and I told her again that I understood but she just had to. The whole time I was wishing I could tell her that Mack was coming too, but I couldn't. I wouldn't lie to her and so I left her sadly trying to sleep, waiting for the dreaded day to come.

"Are you ready for bed?" I asked.

"Yeah, I guess it's about time. Now what were you thinking about."

"Bailee reminded me of last Christmas," I said as I unbuttoned his shirt.

"With Patrick?" he asked.

"Ummm, yeah, well the part without Patrick. Remember? We fell asleep after making love under the Christmas tree and I woke up worried that he'd seen us?"

We were both topless now. He ran his hands over me gently waking up all my nerves until I shivered pleasantly.

"And what am I supposed to be remembering about that night?"

"I asked you what you would do if our kids caught us making love under the Christmas tree."

He smiled at the memory. "So what would *you* do if they caught us at it?" he asked.

"I don't know. I like your answer even if it was a bit impractical."

"Daddy loves Mommy, get used to it," he said with a deep kiss.

"Mmm, Mommy loves Daddy, too."

"It's been so peaceful. I wish it would last," he said. "I've got my girl back. We haven't had trouble in weeks. You've got something to work at that's rewarding to you. We're all set. You can help Strict. You can teach Bailee. Maybe between the two and an occasional camping trip we can keep trouble away."

"And what would we do with so much peace and quiet?"

"I bet I could figure out something," he said, hands straying farther.

"If I stay out of trouble do I get to see what it is?" I asked.

"How about a demonstration, would you like that?"

"I think I'd like to participate more."

He was perfectly willing to let me participate, in fact after just a few minutes he didn't have any choice. Once Rusty expresses an interest nothing much holds me back. I never know what the effects are going to be from time to time but I always know it's going to be quite a ride. If I've had a bout of trouble he can me so tender and caring it makes me ache for more action just so I don't have to watch the worry in his movements. When we are both turned on it can be an all out brawl. Sometimes it is flirtatious, teasing fun. This time it was somewhere in the middle, like a roller coaster ride through daisies. It was soft and fast and filled with good feelings and wild rushes.

"So, that's what we're going to do with all that peace and quiet we're looking forward to?" I asked.

"Every chance we get."

"And we're still going to have enough energy left to work?"

"Of course. The more you do it the more exercise you get, so the better your stamina is."

"Oh, so this is an exercise program now, is it?"

"Babe, you know that's not it."

"Maybe I need to work on certain muscle groups? We could start a new fad. Muscle building sex positions. Of course selling the video might be a little risky considering your job."

He laughed. "And what muscle group should we start with?"

"Abs, everybody wants to flatten those abs. If we can find a position that works we can make millions."

We kind of lost track of the research aspect of it as the night went on. It started out a playful experimentation and quickly turned into a fit of laughter as one position after another turned out to be either impossible to maintain or too weird to be acceptable. I have to say, I slept like a rock when we finally gave out and I woke to a morning I needed plenty of energy for.

I knew the day would be rough, particularly for Bailee. There was no sense in asking my dad anything until later in the morning so I went to Apache's paddock and checked on him. His ears perked up when I came to the fence and he pranced around expecting to be fed. I didn't feed him. It was easier for the hands to just make the rounds with the tractor. One reason I put him in a paddock was he'd be forced to deal with the tractor each morning.

I went to the barn to check on the horses and saddle Shasta for one last ride before I went home. I thought Bailee would be appearing soon, eager to get a start on her last real try at barrel racing but what I saw in the barn stopped me in my tracks.

Mack was gone.

I looked around for a hand. No one was around. There was a barrel on its side with hay stuffed under the sides to keep it from rolling. Bailee's tracks were all around the barrel, her boots landing heavily as she made her way up and down the barrel trying to saddle and bridle Mack. It was hard to believe she'd managed it on her own. How had she gotten the girth tight enough? Just the fact that she'd done it upped my respect for her.

I searched the barn for anybody who might have seen her. I cornered each hand but they had just been tending to their duties. Shoot, how long had she been gone? She could have been out all night. If no one had seen her take off she probably left in the night. How far could she have gotten? On horseback? Many miles. I couldn't track her on foot and expect to catch up. I quickly went to the Explorer and took out Rusty's daypack. I dumped it and gathered up the things I could use. I filled all the water bottles. I was on my way to my room to tell Rusty what I was up to when Dad came out of his bedroom.

"Dad, I need to know what Farley said. It could be important."

"We talked for a long time," Dad said, "Mostly about you. McGyver didn't worry so much about the horses being fit. He trusted you to judge them fair and after talking to me he trusted me to do right by him. But…"

"Dad, I'm kind of in a hurry. Bailee ran away and I need to go find her. It would help me bring her back if I knew what you and Farley decided."

"Mack and Chet are going to the school. I sent him some more pictures, some that showed the horses taking the jumps."

"Will he let Bailee do barrel racing?"

"That I don't know. We got to talking."

"I really need to go find Bailee, Dad. We can talk later. She took off with Mack and there's no telling how far she got last night."

As I entered the bedroom to tell Rusty what was going on he was out of bed in an instant. Cop reflexes. He relaxed when he saw it was just me but he also felt the tension in the air.

"Bailee ran off with Mack," I told him as I pulled off my boots. I pulled on moccasins. Tracking shoes. "I'll have to take Shasta out to find her. If she was putting miles in I've got a search ahead of me."

"She should know better than this. She knows she can't stay."

"Emotional girls can justify just about anything in their own mind if they try hard enough."

"I'll go with you."

"No, this is going to take some girl talk. It's going to mean a heart to heart talk and you would just make it harder. If I'm not back by midafternoon you'll have to call Farley and Bailee's mom."

"Cass, don't go out there alone."

"I'll be fine. I'll be back as soon as I can."

"This isn't as simple as locating a person and turning them over to Landon. Bailee's not going to want to go home and you can't do anything to change that. How are you going to get her back?"

"If I can talk to her, I can get her back. She can't run forever. She's got to eat and she's got a horse to feed. She didn't think of that when she took off. She's got more problems than just not wanting to go home. She'll have to come back or run her horse into the ground and she won't do that. If there's one thing I can count on, she'll take care of the horse. She might accidentally go too far but she won't hurt Mack."

Rusty pulled on pants and a t-shirt and followed me downstairs. I went to the kitchen and put several apples and a few carrots in the pack. There wasn't much in the way of backpack friendly foods at the ranch. They didn't have a search and rescue pack ready at all times like I did at home. Patrick was in the kitchen getting breakfast. Whether he ate at home or at the ranch depended on what he planned on doing with Elan that day. It was a short walk from one to the other so it didn't really matter where he was as long as he was somewhere findable. He watched all the goings on with a puzzled look.

"Cass, take Randy or Steve," Rusty was saying as he followed me around the kitchen.

"If I was going to take somebody, I'd take you. But this is a kid who just doesn't see reality the way she should. She just needs a girl-to-girl talk. She'll come around. Bringing a guy with me will just slow down the process."

"At least bring your cell phone," he reminded me.

"I've got it."

He followed me down to the barn and helped me saddle up Shasta.

"I'll be back as soon as I can. You know how these things go. If the tracking is good I'll be back soon. If I have to stop and read sign it's going to be a while. Horses are easy to track on foot but I need to ride to keep up with her. It's a matter of balancing speed and readability."

"Hon, be careful."

"There's nothing back there that'll hurt me."

"I know, but I have to say it anyway."

I gave him a kiss before climbing into the saddle. He stood in front of the barn looking lost as I rode away. The backpack thumped against my back as Shasta cantered off. When I got to the back gate of the ranch proper I was amused to see that Bailey had unlatched the gate and closed it behind her without dismounting. She had mastered the gate and the horses wouldn't get away. I did the same and picked up her trail on the other side.

Mack wasn't hard to track but I couldn't ride as fast as Bailee had and still see the tracks. One look at her fast pace and I was afraid I'd be on the trail for days. Even if Bailee got hungry or scared or just headed back because she reasoned things out, I had to finish the trail and right now the trail was heading at a good steady lope straight into the hills. I tried tracking at a lope. I couldn't do it. The ground went by too fast. I could manage a trot as long as the trail stayed rough and the ground stayed soft. I kept Shasta to the trot, using my legs to ease the bouncing and push me forward where I could watch Bailee's trail over Shasta's shoulder.

As I rode along I had plenty of time to think but my mind only found the same little circle of thoughts. Bailee didn't want to go home. She didn't want to leave Mack, or Randy. Surely she knew Randy was a lost cause. There was no way a twenty-five year old man was going to be interested in a nine year old girl. She didn't want to leave the ranch, where everything was right, at least in her mind. She didn't want to go home to a mother who wouldn't even talk to her, and a brother who could talk better than her. I could use Socks to lure her back. She knew staying up here was turning her back on Socks. Now that Mack was coming with us that might nudge her homeward.

I didn't like the look of the sky. Dark clouds were gathering. So far they were in the distance but more were coming. Rain on a search was bad news. It would dampen the spirits of even the most determined runaway, a kid who was tired, hungry and trail worn. The only positive aspect of rain was that it brought water. If Bailey had no water maybe she would try to gather it for drinking. I imagined the trail fading before my eyes and prayed the rain would stay away.

The tracks continued uphill and down. The sun was well up in the sky when I began getting hungry. I knew Bailee must be wearing out, having been up all night. Would she stop to rest? Or was distance a driving factor? Did she bring anything along to eat? Did she even think of bringing water? At least she was riding. She wasn't using up the resources she would be if she were hiking, but Mack was. Horses need water, too.

I was relieved when Bailee stopped to rest her horse. She didn't dismount but she slowed him down and let him wander. He tried to wander back to the ranch and his stable full of hay but she pointed him into the hills.

I kept Shasta to a trot while Bailee walked her horse. At least we could gain a little. The trail got a little confusing and I dismounted as I puzzled it out. What was going on here? Mack was stopped. I could tell that easily enough from the tracks. I led Shasta away from the site so I could walk around and study it out. As I did I heard the creak of saddle leather and I looked up and around. In the near distance was Patrick on his little pinto horse, Snoopy. Snoopy got his name because his spots matched the spots on Charlie Brown's famous beagle.

"Patrick! What are you doing here?" I asked annoyed.

"Tracking!" he said confidently.

"Who are you tracking?"

"Shasta and Mack. I just want to help."

"Then go home."

"You're tracking Bailee."

"So I am and I need to be able to work without worrying about you."

"You don't need to worry about me."

"Good, then go back to the ranch."

"I can't. I don't know where it is."

"Good try but it won't work. If you can track good enough to find me you can track good enough to track your way back."

"Rats, I think I can help, if you will let me."

"Yeah, how?"

"I can think like a kid. Bailee's a kid."

"Did you bring any food or water? Aren't you hungry?"

"I have jerky and pemmican."

"Pemmican? What are you doing with pemmican? How do you even know what it is?"

"Elan and I made it. He teaches me all kinds of stuff. We made it out of venison, cranberries and cherries. He says it isn't authentic with the cherries but I like it better. You want to try it?"

"I think we better save it for when we really need it. All I have is apples, carrots and water."

"Does that mean I can stay?"

"Call your mom and tell her where you are."

I handed him my cell phone and he took it reluctantly. He had been missing for hours. Elan would be able to tell that Patrick had followed me, so maybe they wouldn't worry, but Jesse and James should still know where he was. I puzzled out the area while he spoke to his dad. I sighed with relief that he'd reached James instead of Jesse. Jesse would have a fit and James would find out the situation, find out Pat was okay and tell him to be good.

Bailee had dismounted, which I assumed meant a pit stop. She kept hold of the reins as she went about her business. Guess she didn't know the horses were trained to stay quietly by their rider. While she was on foot she continued on her way walking and leading Mack. Shasta followed as I tracked Bailee. I was so focused on tracking that it wasn't until I heard Shasta behind me that I thought to mount up, but then I noticed a stumble in Bailee's tracks and that drew my attention again. Maybe I should stay on foot.

"Aunt Cassidy? Why did Bailee run away?"

"She doesn't want to go home."

"Why wouldn't a kid want to go home?"

"Have you seen the books she reads?"

"Yeah, a little. They're girl books."

"Yeah, but they are horse books. Lots of girls go through a horse crazy stage, so horse books are really popular for girls. Bailee reads the horse books and when she got to come to the ranch it was the life she always dreamed of, just like a book, so she doesn't want to leave it."

"I don't see what's so great about it. It's chores and more chores and when those are done it's school and after school it's more chores, then homework."

"What you see as work, Bailee sees as play. She'd love to have your chores, well, at least for a week or two. The problem is Bailee's mom thinks she isn't capable of doing chores."

"Why?"

"She doesn't talk to Bailee. I bet she doesn't even know that Bailee *can* talk. She thinks Bailee can only read horse books. She thinks Bailee is useless."

"But that's not true. She might be a pest but she's got more going for her than that."

Spoken like a true boy.

"Bailee can do anything she sets her mind to, well, besides knitting. I bet she'd have trouble knitting. But who needs to know how to knit these days? She could be anything she wants to be."

"And she wants to be a horse trainer so she can work for Grandpa," Pat added.

"Yeah."

"You know how likely that is?"

"Not very. But nothing's stopping her from being a horse trainer somewhere else."

"Her hands."

To me Bailee's hands were just part of Bailee. I didn't think of them as a handicap.

"Let me concentrate on the trail," I said. "Or we'll never find her."

Bailee's feet were really dragging, but if she was tired, why didn't she ride? I examined Mack's hoof prints but they seemed normal. She wasn't walking because of Mack.

"Aunt Cassidy?"

"Let me read. I'm trying to figure out why Bailee isn't riding. Why would she walk if she could ride?"

"Because she can't see in the dark," Patrick said.

"Wouldn't she trust Mack to see the way?"

"Not if he stumbled in the dark. She might think she was smaller and closer to the ground so she could lead the way. She might be walking to protect Mack's legs."

I began watching the tracks and they stayed in the clear, avoiding branches that would have been hard to spot in the dark. Patrick just might be right.

"If she's a new rider a stumble might have scared her," Pat continued.

"She's not a new rider but she has only ridden in a corral," I told him.

I wondered what stage the moon was at. Was it light enough to see? I was a little bit busy last night. I wasn't exactly thinking about how much light there was outside. If Bailee did a lot of walking at night we may have a better start than I thought.

"I told her twernt no use runnin'," Pat said and I swore it was Old Frank's voice when he said it.

"Pat? Are you sure you're seven?" I asked, but he just looked at me weird.

"Yeah."

"I know. You just aren't sounding seven."

"That's what Steve says, too."

"So Bailee talked to you about this?"

"Not exactly. She was talking to Mack. She said she wouldn't go away. She'd find a way to stay. I told her you'd make her go back 'cause she had to be with her family. That you wouldn't let her quit school, that school was important even if you hate it. She got mad at me, but I don't care. It don't matter to me if she's mad at me. I thought it was more important to get her to listen than win a popularity contest with some kid I might never see again. So I gave her what for. I told her there was no hiding from you. You would find her no matter where she was and you'd make her go back. She doesn't know you can find anybody no matter what they do."

"Oh, Pat, she probably thought you were just arguing with her. I hope she doesn't think you're mad at her, too. And, it's not exactly true. The only reason I can find her is she took off into the hills. If she headed for town I'd have to turn it over to Uncle Rusty."

Bailee walked for a long time. When I was convinced I wasn't going to learn much from her trail, I rode again, simply following the trail. The sky grew gray but I pressed on.

"This is cool," Patrick said. "I never got to watch you track before. I mean we tracked animals together, but then you were teaching me. I never seen you doing it jus' to be doin' it."

"So, do I really change into Dangerous Tracker Woman?" I asked.

"What?"

"My partner says I morph from Cute Cassidy into Dangerous Tracker Woman when I get serious about tracking."

"That's silly. There's no such thing as Dangerous Tracker Woman. You aren't dangerous."

"I hope not," I said remembering all too vividly the shot that killed Dirk. Guess I'm only dangerous when cornered. I shuddered quietly to myself and kept going. Now my mind was going a mile a minute. Part of it was tracking. Part of it was worried about bringing Bailee back. And part of it was trying frantically to stuff away flashbacks of that one shot that would haunt me for the rest of my life.

I had other one shots that haunted me, too. I had to do something to stay out of trouble. Trouble didn't just mean trouble for me. Unfortunately all too often others were hurt. I had lots of training and plenty of backup. When trouble hit I had a defense. That was usually bad news for anybody bringing trouble my way. Yup, somehow I needed to figure out how to keep trouble away. I didn't know how many more bouts of trouble I could endure and I didn't know how many bouts of trouble Rusty could stand to watch me go through. Maybe it would be best to settle down. Maybe I should find a nice quiet hobby. Yeah, right. I didn't think I had it in me to sit quietly at home. But something had to give. And I had a feeling I had to be the one to do it.

But first I had to find Bailee. I could identify with the kid. How many times had I run away, not as a kid, but from life in general? And what was she doing but trying to run from life. Just as I had found out, she couldn't run from reality even if it stunk. Flight was only a temporary reprieve. Reality had a way of stalking even the most elusive person. The only ray of hope I offered was that reality eventually could change. I was proof of that.

Mack's tracks were easier to follow than Bailee's and I knew unless there was a big scuffle the two were inseparable, so I followed the horse. Shasta kept to a trot. Eventually Bailee struggled into the saddle again and rode. She had been out on her own for hours. I was willing to bet she was getting a little dose of reality. She had a horse to take care of. She had very little food or water. There was no place to go to find hay or water. She was lost, or at least she didn't know how she was going to get along out here. Her rosy picture of staying with Mack wasn't quite working out the way she hoped.

"Aunt Cassidy, I'm hungry," Patrick said.

"Then eat something. You knew when you came along we were short on rations. Just keep that in mind as you go."

"What about you? Aren't you hungry?"

"Yeah, but I've got more important things on my mind than my stomach. I'm used to tracking through the hunger. I think about how my missing person must be feeling and then hunger doesn't seem like such a big deal anymore. I wonder if Bailee is hungry."

The tracks went on and every once in a while Mack would attempt to turn back and go home but Bailee pointed him away from the ranch. I had to give him credit. The horse knew where he belonged but he was obedient anyway. I knew if push came to shove the horse would win. Would Mack push?

Patrick slowly chewed on a piece of venison jerky to stave off the hunger and make this food last. Jerky was good for that. You could chew on jerky for a long time without eating much.

As the minutes went by I fell into the tracking. Sometimes the trail pulled me in until I forgot what I was doing. My surroundings narrowed and my focus was only on the ground. I'd been tracking like this in my own little world without realizing it when Patrick said, "Aunt Cassidy? How far are we going? I'm getting all wet."

I looked up into a fine mist. I was all wet, too, and now that I noticed it I was also very chilly.

"Until we find Bailee," I told him, eyes straying back to the trail. "A little rain won't stop me. In fact it usually speeds me up. Rain wipes out tracks so we need to keep going."

Back to the trail I went pushing Shasta just a little bit harder. Now I was noticing faint raindrops hitting the tracks, each drop a little track eraser. I hoped Bailee was taking shelter somewhere. I hoped this was convincing her she didn't want to be by herself out on her own. Out on her own was not a rosy kids' story. The main character didn't have to live happily ever after with her horse by her side, a blanket of roses over his back or a shining trophy on the shelf in her room. Reality meant feeding yourself and your horse, finding water, getting soaked in the rain, getting lost in the hills with no one to find you because your trail got erased by a storm. Reality meant hiding in the brush, shivering as the rain made its way through and slipped down the leaves into the one dry spot you had left.

"Aunt Cassidy? Don't you think she's gone back already?"

"It doesn't matter. Unless we hear from the ranch we stay on the trail. Turning back is not an option. If the rain erases the trail completely we call in reinforcements but we don't quit. When you chose to follow me you took on the whole mission, rain, hunger and all. You have to remember that. When you chose to stay you chose to be part of the team and the team is going to bring Bailee back to the ranch. So your purpose is to do anything you can to help, even if it's something you don't like. You're at a good stage to learn what that means. I had to learn it the hard way."

"What do you mean, you learned it the hard way?"

"Well, the teamwork involved in running a ranch and training horses is mild. You have an unruly horse. You work on his problems. That's easy. You see that happening on the ranch all the time. When I joined the Marines I joined a team of sorts. When you enter the service you perform their mission, whatever that is. They sent me to boot camp. I thought I was going to die just *training* for the hard stuff! But there was no backing out. I was part of the team for four years. Four years is a long time to take on a mission whether you agree with it or not. They sent me to Afghanistan. It was hard. Every day was hard. Even the easy days were hard. Some days were hard because of the work. Some days were hard because of the suffering we saw. The violence was all around us. I slept in a tent or a foxhole for six months straight. I can say I ate every day. Can't say it was good every day. Some days I think I ate more sand than real food. The sand was awful. It got in everything. We longed for rain just to make the sand stay still for a day or two but then the camp would turn to little rivers of mud, flowing downhill however it could, sometimes right under our tents. It was a long six months. I was beginning to think all the color had gone out of the world because everything was sand color. The landscape, the buildings, our trucks and Jeeps, even our clothes. After a while even the people's faces became sand colored. First we burned, then we tanned, then we gave up on caring what color we were and walked around with a fine coating of dust. Oh, man, I never want to go back there. So you see, a little rain and a little hunger when Bailee's still out there is a little thing to me. Once you do it a time or two you'll get more used to the concept, this rain and this trail will feel more like an inconvenience. You'll know the mission is more important than a lack of comfort."

Water was running down my hair and dripping into my eyes. Patrick was faring little better. I stuck to the trail. The horses hung their heads but they kept on. I watched as the tracks slowly filled with water. When I wasn't sure what was tracks and what was puddles we had to stop and wait out the rain. I pulled the horses under the biggest, thickest tree I could and tied them to it, then Patrick and I sheltered nearby.

"Come here, kiddo," I told him. "Sit facing me and we'll be warmer." I pulled him into my lap and we sat together to share some warmth. "I hope Bailee stopped, too," I said.

"Some missions stink," Patrick said with a shiver.

I laughed. "You're right, some missions stink but I don't count this as one of them. This is just wet. A stinky mission is much worse. It's when you are tracking for the police and your missing person tries to kill your team. Now that stinks."

"Did that happen to you?"

"Once."

"You're right, that stinks. I'll stick to rain. I don't know what I'd do if that happened to me."

When late afternoon rolled around my cell phone gave a weak ring from the depths of my pack. I dug it out as quick as I could but it quit ringing before I could find it. I looked at the missed call. It was from Rusty. I called back so he wouldn't worry.

"Hi," I said. "Just letting you know we're okay. I just didn't get to my phone in time."

"Is it raining where you are?"

"Yeah, we had to give up tracking. We're holed up waiting for a break."

"Cass, come home, we'll figure something out."

"No, you know, even with the rain, this is the best clues we have telling us where she is. She doesn't know these hills. She can't track her way back. Someone's got to find her."

"A nine year old kid isn't going to brave a storm. She's going to take shelter."

"Another reason I should stay out here. If she stops I can catch up quicker."

"Babe, you have no gear. You can't stay out overnight."

"I can and I will, if I have to."

"She'll turn up."

"Rusty, I'm going to find her. Part of the reason she's out here is her parents make her feel like she's not worth the effort to look for her. Somebody's got to show her that she's worthwhile. I'll do anything I can to find her."

"Think of Patrick."

"I am. Patrick knows he signed on for the whole mission. He's doing fine."

"He's only seven."

"I know how old he is and I know he can make a logical decision. He made it. He had a chance to go back. As long as he could track his way back I'd let him go but that option is out now. He knows what he's in for. He's in it until the tracks are gone or we find Bailee."

Pat added, "Tell him some missions just stink."

"I heard that," Rusty said snickering.

"If anybody knows about stinky missions it's Uncle Rusty," I said.

"Don't hurt my girl out there," Rusty admonished.

"I won't."

"I love you."

"I love you, too."

"Aw, mush," said Patrick as I hung up.

"Just wait. Someday you'll feel mushy about somebody and you won't think it's mushy. You'll want them to know how much they're loved."

"Is tracking through a rain storm mushy?"

"What do you mean?"

"You told Uncle Rusty you wanted Bailee to see she was worth the search. Is that mushy, too?"

"Yeah, Pat, it's mushy too, just a different kind. Bailee needs to see someone cares enough about her to stay out in the rain and look for her."

"Guess I can see that. I think the rain is easing up. Think there will be anything left of the tracks?"

"I hope so."

Fortunately the ground was very thirsty. The rain got soaked up and there was very little standing water. If I'd have been tracking a person it would have been a lost cause but I was tracking a horse and the sharp print of Mack's hooves still stood out, rounder than they were before, but still visible.

"Walk for a while," I told Patrick. "Watch the tracks. Take note of how eroded they are after a good rain. It's important, in the long run, that you know what tracks look like after different lengths of time have gone by, after different types of weather. Rain, wind, snow, they all make tracks look different. Things fall onto the tracks hiding them. You have to learn all about the effects of time and weather to be a good tracker. You rarely have to look for someone who just disappeared hours ago. Usually they've been missing at least a night."

"But people don't get lost up here."

"You'd be surprised. One of these trips Uncle Rusty will take you to the police station and you can talk to the officers here. They see more action than you hear about. Besides, the police don't just need trackers to find lost people. Sometimes I get called out just to tell them what happened at a crime scene."

"Like I did with Big John? I mean, Officer Jankowski."

"Yeah and you can call him Big John when you're talking to me."

It was kind of nice having someone to talk to on the trail. I thought Patrick was learning something from it. I know I would have when I was his age. Plus, we were getting back some of the time I'd given to Bailee. It seemed the more Patrick learned about tracking the more he wanted to pick my brain for facts, stories, anything interesting, much the same way I did with

Old Frank as I was growing up. What goes around comes around, I thought.

Mack was giving Bailee a hard time again. He didn't like the rain. He knew he had a nice, warm, dry barn waiting for him at home, with hay and friends and occasional carrots. Bailee dismounted and led Mack on foot up away from the mud. I realized these tracks were left after the rain stopped.

"Pat! Look. These tracks are recent. How can you tell?"

He bent over the tracks a short time. "They aren't worn down by the rain. The mud is stuck to Bailee's boots. So it was after the rain started, probably after the rain stopped. We're getting close!"

The going was not easy for Bailee. She slipped as she led Mack to higher, dryer ground. When she mounted up again chunks of mud fell off her boots as she rode.

"Look, Pat, see the way the top of the mud clumps is lighter? That's because it's had time to dry out. The more of the clump that is dry, the longer it's been sitting there so you can gauge the age of the tracks by things around them. These have barely started to dry out so we have to be really close."

The trail was plain as could be. We trotted the horses down the trail of tracks again.

We didn't need to track Bailee very much farther. Her tracks turned and in the distance there was a house with a barn and outbuildings. In front of the barn there were three police cars. A rescue squad and ambulance stood by, just in case. A group of people crouched behind the cars. A woman and an officer stood beside the house talking. The woman was waving her hands around clearly upset over something. I put my heels to my horse.

As I got closer I could see that officers were flattened against the sides of the barn, high-powered rifles at the ready.

"This is such a peaceful community," the woman said loudly. "I can't believe this is happening! He scared me out of my slippers, he did, sneaking around the property like that! I'm just so glad you got here in time! He won't get away now, no siree!"

"Hold your fire!" I yelled as I came riding onto the scene.

The officers turned. Six rifles aimed at me, then when they saw who approached they lowered their weapons, still wary. This call was getting stranger and stranger for them. Somehow, it didn't seem odd to me. One thing I forgot, to these officers I wasn't little Cassidy Michaels, Rusty's wife. I was just some weird girl riding into a crime scene with a kid in tow. They didn't know if I was friend or foe, or some insane person with suicidal tendencies.

One officer stepped forward gun at the ready.

"Put your hands over your head!" he barked.

Oh, come on, I thought, but I put my hands over my head. I looked to Pat.

"Pat, put your hands up like they say. It'll be alright."

Pat put his hands up nervously.

"Now, dismount!"

I pulled my feet out of the stirrups and swung one leg over the saddle and slipped down, hands still over my head. They looked at me like I'd just performed a great riding stunt. Patrick used his hands to dismount. The officer patted me down quickly and guided me to the house where the civilians were kept.

"Look, you can't go in there guns drawn, expecting to drag out a prowler. You've cornered yourself a nine year old girl. You've probably scared her half to death. Let me go in. I'll bring her out, no problem."

The officers all looked to the woman and she vehemently shook her head.

"I saw! I saw a man sneak in there!"

"You might have seen someone sneak in there but it was no man. I've been looking for a girl. She left my father's ranch on that horse. She's not going to hurt anything…"

"Oh, no you don't!" cried the woman. "Girl or not, they are not to be sneaking around my house and my yards! I want them removed and I want them to be taken in. People these days have no respect for other people! No respect at all! Maybe a trip down to the station and a day in the clink will teach 'em a thing or two."

I thought about Bailee in the barn. Frightened of police officers, knowing they were armed, watching them act precisely in the manner she feared them. I ached for her.

"Captain," I said, "your men don't need to be armed. Bailee isn't armed. She can't even hold a gun. Her hands are bent. She's only a kid. Let me talk to her."

He nodded at his men and they rushed the barn entrance.

"No!" I cried. "Don't shoot!"

There were yells of "Freeze! Don't move! Put your hands over your head!" All the typical police hype. Then one officer walked out of the barn.

"Brandt? You gotta see this."

I followed the captain into the barn. There sat Patrick next to Bailee on top of a pile of hay.

"You didn't do anything wrong so they can't arrest you. Just be tough. Do what they say and it'll all work out. Don't be scared. They just *look* scary. Most of them have kids, too. They don't want to shoot a kid." On and on he went talking to Bailee, keeping her from doing something that would get her in trouble. Being the calm in the midst of chaos. Bailee sat there white as a sheet, hands over her head. Eyes like saucers.

"They won't hurt you long as you don't move. Just listen to them and do 'xactly as they say," Patrick said.

"How you know dese things?" Bailee asked.

"I watch too much TV, I guess, plus Uncle Rusty takes me to the station. I know the policemen. They like kids. They tell me stories."

Bailee caught sight of me behind the group of officers. Brandt was half stern superior, half concerned dad. He had a trespasser on his hands and an angry woman who wanted justice. And he saw a scared little girl who just needed to be returned to her family. Bailee looked more afraid of me than she did of the officers surrounding her. Cops or no cops she had something to make right so she began climbing down the stack of hay bales.

"Bailee, no!" whispered Patrick.

"Chas… me sorry."

She looked like a half drowned rat. Hair in half dried ringlets. Damp clothes still clinging to her scrawny frame. Mud caked boots. She stood before the group of policemen, hands still over her head. She gave them a pitiful look and slowly lowered her hands. She bowed her head readying herself for whatever came at her. They all just stood there rooted in one spot. They knew what to do with a violent criminal. They weren't sure what to do with a contrite heart.

"Chas… me stupid, stupid girl. Me ruin everything. Mizzur Godon mad wit' me. You mad wit' me. I can't keep… my promise to Mack. Me go jail. Mom be mad wit' me."

"You're not going to jail," I told her. "You didn't do anything that wrong."

"Me a thief. I am. I had to. Mack hungry, thirsty. He tired."

I looked around. "Call off your men, Captain," I asked him.

He jerked his head toward the door and they all hung their heads as they filed out. Brandt stayed behind.

"Chas, I no steal for me, on'y for Mack. I worried for him."

"You should have just brought him home then. You knew I'd find you. I told you my job is to find people."

"How? How you find me? I no un'er stand. I no tell you nothin'. How you know?"

I pointed to the ground. "See the tracks people leave when they walk? I followed your tracks. That's how I find people when they are lost. I mostly track people but horses are even easier to track. I think we better call Rusty and let him know everything's okay."

I got out my cell phone and speed dialed Rusty. I thought his legal mind would be useful in Bailee's situation.

"Cassidy, you okay?"

"Yeah," I said, "Ten sixty-five found, ten forty-five A…" I hadn't even realized I'd slipped into radio talk until Captain Brandt took a step back and rethought this situation. In my usual choppy mixture of ten-codes, occasional penal codes and plain old English I relayed the situation to Rusty. Half an hour later he pulled up in the Explorer looking every inch the man in charge.

I knew despite the length of a search I usually was only a few miles from civilization but it was still a little aggravating that I spent all that time searching only to have Rusty drive there in thirty minutes. While Rusty dealt with Brandt and Mrs. Farthington I dealt with Bailee. She stood next to Mack, petting him sadly.

"They send me away and I never come back," she said quietly for Mack's ears only. "I bad girl they never want back. They send me away."

"Bailee, sit down. We need to talk. First of all, we're not sending you away. You and I and Rusty have to go home but nobody's sending you away."

"I no go home," she sniffed. "I promise Mack."

"Horses don't understand about promises. They take whatever comes to them and they work at whatever a person tells them to do. Mack has a job to do."

"I work hard. Mizzur Godon no be sorry he let me stay. On'y now he no take me back."

"Dad knows you need to go home. Your mom is expecting you tonight. I bet she misses you."

"Mom no miss me. Mom glad I gone."

"Bailee, don't say that. Your mom will be glad to see you again."

"Mom glad I gone. Mizzur Godon glad I gone."

"Nobody wants you to be gone," I told her. "I would be really sad if you went away. I'd be really sad if you didn't come home with me. Farley would miss you. Mack and Socks would miss you."

"Oh," she cried. "Mine horse. Chas, what I do?"

I put an arm around her shoulders.

"Come home with me. Things will be better than you think."

"I no leave Mack."

"Mack's coming with us. He's going to go work at Farley's school. You'll be able to see him just like you see Socks. He'll be right there at the school. He's getting a new job to do. Mack and Chet both. My dad needed a young spunky horse for ranch work and Farley needs settled horses that are well trained. They arranged a trade, so Mack is coming home with us."

She didn't jump for joy at the idea. She pondered it a while.

"Mack leave your ranch?"

"Yeah, but Farley will be good to him. He'll do well at the school. He's worked hard at the ranch. It's time for him to try something new. If you go home you can help make the transition easier for him. You're the one who can really put him to the test. You can show Farley what a good horse he is, Chet too. Will you do that?"

She had a purpose. She could do something worthwhile. She looked like she was pulling herself together, readying herself for a tough haul.

"Today's Monday. Your lesson at the school is supposed to be tomorrow. We won't be able to get home tonight unless we hurry. As soon as Captain Brandt lets us go we need to head for home."

"Lady be mad at me."

"You can't really blame her. But you can show her that you're sorry. I'm sure Rusty offered to make things right. The price of a flake of hay and a bucket of water can't be too steep."

"I pay her back. Me got money. Me got…" she took a small wad of bills out of her pocket. They were all damp one dollar bills. "Seven dollars." She got up quickly and dashed to the house.

"Bailee, wait!" I called out "Let Rusty finish first. He knows how these things work." But she took off.

She went to the front door of the house and rang the doorbell. Captain Brandt answered the door expecting it to be one of his officers. All eyes turned to Bailee. She squared her shoulders. She stepped onto the plush carpeting and made her way through Mrs. Farthington's designer living room. I cringed at the trail of mud.

"It's the principal of the thing," Mrs. Farthington was telling Rusty.

Only I could see the exasperation in his eyes. He maintained a patient exterior.

"A child should not be allowed to take whatever they want whenever they want. A child who grows up like that will turn into a little felon. You of all people know what happens when children are allowed…" then she saw Bailee standing before her looking decidedly unfelonish.

"Ma'am, I sorry me steal from you. I done wrong. I pay back you. Dis my money. If it not 'nough, I sorry." She handed Mrs. Farthington the seven damp one dollar bills. Mrs. Farthington looked like they were burning a hole through her conscience. She didn't need Bailee's money and she was losing her battle and her demand for justice. Bailee gazed up at her with hound doggy eyes waiting for her verdict. If Bailee had done this to my mother, my mom would have cried. Mom was a sucker for hound doggy eyes.

"You'll not steal again?" Mrs. Farthington said, arms crossed.

"No, I on'y steal for mine horse. I hungry. No eat today…but I no steal for me…on'y mine horse…on'y 'cause he need it. I no steal again."

Mrs. Farthington was a hard-edged old gal. She wasn't giving in without a fight.

"See this mess you made? There's a vacuum in that closet."

Bailee went back to the porch, took off her boots and tiptoed to the closet.

She removed the vacuum cleaner and awkwardly began unwrapping the cord. It wasn't an easy feat for a kid with hands like Bailee's. We all stood around watching until Patrick stepped forward and took over. He unwound the cord and found a plug for it and Bailee obediently vacuumed Mrs. Farthington's floor. She wasn't happy about the job but she seemed to realize it was the easiest way out of her predicament. It took less than a minute to perform the task but each second that ticked by only made Bailee look less and less like a renegade child and more and more like someone you just wanted to take under your wing and love. All she needed was a little warmth, a lot of caring, a smidgen of encouragement and she would blossom and grow. I wanted to be around to see that happen.

When the floor was clean Patrick wound up the cord again and Bailee put the machine away. Everything she did brought focus to her hands and I thought about the email my dad had sent. One sentence sent across the labyrinth of technology to land in the hands of the right person could change a life. Where was that message now?

Rusty and Brandt exchanged a few words and Mrs. Farthington swept her front porch furiously as Patrick, Bailee and I tended the horses. We still had a long day ahead of us. It was a long ride back but before Rusty and Brandt were finished talking the big ranch truck pulled up to the Farthington house with a horse trailer behind. Randy and Zack hopped out. The men loaded Shasta, Snoopy and Mack up. Bailee looked longingly at Mack as he disappeared into the trailer. Mack was out of her hands, she knew. Her only hope was I had told her the truth.

"Cassidy? Patrick? Anyone riding with us?"

Bailee's eyes lit up at the prospect of riding back in the ranch truck with Randy, but Rusty brought her up short.

"Bailee, I need to talk to you," he said.

She looked to me for help so I followed her over. Rusty squatted down so he'd be at her level.

"Captain Brandt is going to let you go but I am accepting responsibility for your actions until I turn you over to your parents. Do you know what that means?"

Her big blue eyes passed worriedly from one man to the other.

"It means if *you* do anything wrong, *I* get in trouble for it."

"I no do nothing wrong."

"No running away, no stealing, you owe Mr. Gordon an apology for taking his horse."

Yikes, I was glad I didn't have to do that. I think I'd rather go to jail. Hound doggy eyes might work on Mom but I had my doubts about Dad.

When we got to the ranch I had to give Bailee credit. She took stock of her situation before taking on my dad. She made sure Mack was in his stall, fed and watered.

"Ranny? Mack okay?"

Randy turned to her, arms folded, looking like a pissed off cowboy. Bailee took a step back.

"He's fine, but you lucked out taking him out in a storm, making Cassidy go after you. You could have gotten you both killed out there."

Bailee looked like this was a small dose of what she was going to have to deal with in the office of Big Wayne Gordon. Would she have the answers?

As Bailee talked to my dad Rusty loaded the Explorer. I thought Bailee needed my help more than Rusty did so I followed her to the office. I stayed in the background, mostly observing, only there for backup should she need it.

She looked like a little waif standing in the office door. She waited for Dad to finish what he was doing before timidly saying, "'Scuse me, Mr. Godon, sir."

Dad stood and I flinched. Did he have to do that? He was intimidating enough just sitting. He walked to the doorway and towered over Bailee.

"You think you can take my horse and make off with him in the night and not face repercussions?"

"No sir, me know there be… I know me in trouble. I hope there would."

Dad froze. Bailee had taken him by surprise. He'd been walking back into his office, Bailee following. He turned and looked down at the girl again then he reached down and just picked her up. He was gentle. He walked over to his desk and set her on it, then took a chair facing her. He slouched down, crossed one leg over the other, and folded his hands in his lap. This was very strange to me. I was used to the supreme authority posture. I stood in the doorway.

"What do you mean, you hoped there would be? Do you know what that could involve?"

"I not know when I do it. I know now. You send me jail. Maybe you could. I not know this risk. I think you get mad, make me work. You think work pun… punish me. But I want work. I take Mack so you punish me."

"If work won't punish you, what will?"

"Dad," I interrupted. "It's not your place to punish Bailee. You got your horse back. He's unharmed."

"Stay out of this," Dad boomed at me.

"What punish me? Nothing. You make me work, I be happy. You do nothing, I be sad. You send me away I be sad. I bad girl. I deserve punish. I be sad you no punish me."

Dad looked uncomfortable.

"Cassidy? Go pack or something."

I stiffened. He wanted to talk to Bailee alone. But what would he do? I remembered the father from my childhood. Bailee wasn't ready to face that man. I was grown up and I still had trouble with it. He shot me *the look* and I knew there was no arguing with him. Still…

"Cassidy, have you ever known me to be unkind or unfair?"

I stuck my hands in my pockets and slouched out. He got up and closed the door. Gulp!

I found Rusty waiting on the porch; truck fully loaded except for a change of clothes for me and Bailee. I'd forgotten all about my clothes.

"What's going on?" he asked.

"Dad's talking to Bailee."

"Who's going to win?"

Big Wayne Gordon versus the little drowned thief.

"I don't know. I hope both of them."

He put an arm around me and squeezed, "That's my girl," he said a little amused.

Bailee came out a short while later. She wasn't happy. She was very serious. I took her to change clothes and get ready for the trip home. She kept her serious attitude until she began talking.

"Chas, you so lucky," she said, still serious. I thought she was going to say that I got to grow up on a ranch. I had my own horse. But she said, "You have daddy cares 'nough to be tough."

Gulp again. What had he done this time?

"What do you mean?"

"He find punish for me."

She pulled off the shirt unconcerned about modesty. It was just us girls.

"What did he do?"

"He no do nothin'."

"Then how did he punish you?"

"He… I have use Mom's words… he read me riot act." Then she grinned a little. "He say I no can do bad to get what I want." I counted the words in that sentence. I was amazed. "He say he no punish to do bad. He say on'y one thing punish me for good. But he say he can't make me do it. He say me have to want, really want do good." She gave me a look with those hound doggy eyes she was so good at. "Chas, I no want do bad. He say for punish I have to go school, everyday, get good grades. He ask me I get good grades. I say, no, but I hate school. He ask why and I say kids mean, make fun me. He say I go school, get good grades I be horse trainer. I follow his punish and maybe I be horse trainer. On'y school come first. School most important."

"He's a wise man," I told her. "He's right, you know."

She brightened, "He no send me away. I know we go home. He say I come back when school out, if I want. He check my grades. He say I do good school, I learn horses, I be horse trainer."

"That's not a promise, you know, horse training is a talent that has to be reinforced. It's not an easy life."

"I know. He say kids tease me less more I like them. He say I learn talk like other kids they no tease me. He say to talk like I read in books. I say I try. He say I doing good but he know I can do better. I never hear that. You lucky you dad believe kids always do better."

I pulled a fresh shirt over her head and she changed jeans. We rinsed off her boots and scrubbed them on the bootbrush out front. She wouldn't wear her old tennis shoes home. She had to show off her boots to her mom. She found her hat, too. I brushed out her hair.

Her eyes shown when she saw Randy loading Mack and Chet into the trailer.

"I ride here?" she asked, indicating the horse trailer.

"Nope, it's unsafe and illegal," Rusty answered. "We'll stop and eat and you can check on him."

We walked down to say goodbye to all the other horses then there were hugs all around. Patrick presented her with a lasso.

"If you're going to be a horse trainer you gotta be able to catch 'em," he said. "Aunt Cassidy can show you how it's done."

"I learn it, I learn everything," she said climbing into the Explorer.

We pulled up to Bailee's house late that night. She left Mack behind in the trailer reluctantly.

"You'll be able to see him tomorrow at your riding lesson," I told her.

"Mizzur Mac's school not be same after your ranch."

"Maybe not but Socks will still be Socks and Mack will be glad to see you again."

"Socks really old for horse?"

"He's too old to be ridden roughly. He likes quiet rides now. Imagine having to run with sore knees. You can do it but it hurts. He'll do it for you but it would be kinder to let him slow down."

"Mack old for horse, too?"

"Mack's good to go for several more years. He'll give you a good ride."

She tried the front door but it was locked so she rang the bell. A man came to the door. He was scruffy, dressed in holey jeans, an undershirt and grimy socks. His hair had grown down over his collar.

"You're late," he said simply.

"Me have long day," she said without even thinking about it.

"*What* did you say?" the man exclaimed in disbelief.

Bailee thought about my father's words and corrected herself slowly, "I had a long day," she annunciated carefully.

"Whoa, wait a minute," he grabbed Bailee by the shoulders and turned her around. "What did you do with my kid?" he asked me.

"She's had some practice in the speech department," I explained. "She likes to talk horses."

"Come in," he said, still looking at Bailee.

I motioned for Rusty to come in.

"We can't stay long. We have horses in the trailer that need to be unloaded."

"Okay. Was Bailee any trouble for you?"

I wasn't sure what Rusty had told them about Bailee's little escape.

"Bailee did great," I fudged. "She rode all the work horses and did a little barrel racing and went on a ride into the hills. She got along well with the ranch hands and my family. She probably ate more chocolate cake than was good for her but I think all in all she had a good time. Bailee, tell your dad what you liked about the ranch."

I so much wanted her parents to know Bailee could talk.

Bailee thought about it. She said, "Me ride horses every day. Ever' body friendly. What I like most… is people take care me. No matter what. They take care people."

I thought she'd say she got to do barrel racing. I never thought about what Bailee really needed, a firm, loving hand.

"I'm glad you had a good time," I said. "Will you be at your lesson tomorrow?"

Bailee looked at her dad.

"Yeah, she'll be there."

"If you have time we can use extra time tomorrow. We have two horses to ride."

"You wan' see new horse? Mizzur Mac get two new horses. Mack and Chet. Mack my fren. You wan' see?"

"Just for a minute. Brandon's asleep."

We went out to the trailer and Mr. Roland pet Mack and Chet through the window. He at least seemed a little friendlier than Mrs. Roland.

"They look like great horses," Mr. Roland said. "It looks like we have some talking to do. Bailee, what do you say to Mr. and Mrs. Michaels?"

Bailee came back and gave us both hugs. "Thank you, Chas, thank you Mizzur Russy."

"You're welcome, Bailee. Get a good night's rest. We have riding to do tomorrow."

My house seemed extra quiet. We unloaded the horses and put them in the corral. I'd have to get up early and take them to Farley's school in the morning. After the events of the day I was exhausted and wired at the same time. We lay in bed that night gently snuggling, quietly talking.

"It was so good to see you working with Bailee. You really care for that kid. She's worked her way into your heart, hasn't she?"

"Any kid would. I see what they could become and I just want to bring that out in them."

"I wish the trip hadn't rebounded on Bailee."

"It's my own fault…The whole time I was looking for her I just hoped it didn't break her. I was so afraid she wouldn't go home. I was afraid… I was afraid for her future. She's talking now. She's got a goal. She's safely home. We lucked out."

"We didn't luck out. You cared enough to give Bailee a dose of what she needed. You have a heart for kids. I so wish you could see it. Patrick, Wyatt, Bailee. Any kid you get to spend any time with comes out ahead for it."

"You really want kids, don't you?"

"Babe, we don't have to get into this again."

"Show me," I said.

"Show you what?"

"Show me how babies are made."

Little laugh lines appeared around his eyes. His mouth closed over mine and he showed me. For the next hour we laughed through a lesson neither one of us really needed but he got the idea. I was making my way over to his side. I was willing. I was his. I was alive and happy beneath him. His happiness was secure. At least for now.

Chapter 33

Bailee went on to learn barrel racing, although we never decided to go on to competition. We stretched Farley's patience for a while and then went on to English riding. Bailee spent a half hour on Socks, riding him just to warm up, and to have one on one time. She was confident in the saddle now. She spoke without hesitation. Her grammar was improving. She took my father's words to heart and paid attention to how sentences were constructed and, although she still lost words, she was able to come up with enough of them to communicate comfortably. After her half hour with Socks she put him in his stall and worked a half hour with Mack. She now brought two carrots to class and I wondered if her lunches were suffering for it. About a month after we returned home Bailee came to her lesson in a different frame of mind. She usually got right to work grooming her horse, waiting for help with the saddle and bridle and she rode with a purposeful goal in mind. Not so this time.

"Is everything okay at home?" I asked.

"I'm going to be gone for a while," she said.

"Really? Where are you going?"

"I'll still be here but I won't be able to ride for a couple of months. I can't stand it, Chas, I'll die of boredom and loneliness. I'm going to miss the horses so much! And I don't even know if I want to do this. I've gotten so used to just being me. I'm afraid I'll be different if they fix my hands. I'll be in bandages and some kid at school will have to help me write. This sucks!"

Oh, man, I thought, Dad did it! After all that, he actually went through with it!

"But Bailee, just think of all the things you will be able to do without a struggle when it's all over. It's going to take some work but you're used to that. You'll have to go to physical therapy and they'll teach you how to use your new hands."

"But I'll be just like any other kid. If I talk right and my hands get fixed there's no reason Farley has to let me come here. I won't fit in."

"Hey, Farley does this to see kids succeed in life. You have a place here no matter what happens. Who knows, you could become a volunteer and help teach the little kids. Once you've gotten the riding experience you need you can help others along. You'd be great at that because you know how tough it is. Stick with Farley's school. He will always welcome you here."

"But I'll be gone two months."

"It's okay, it'll feel like a long time but you'll make it and you'll be better off for it. Just think how it'll help you become a horse trainer. You'll be able to handle the ropes."

She was still moody. It was a big step she was taking and it felt like a big risk.

"Does it hurt to have an operation?"

"Not while it's happening. It will be painful for a while but you will learn to work through the pain."

"Have you ever had an operation?"

"Unfortunately, yes."

"Was it hard?"

"Bailee… you helped me get over it. I thought I'd never get well again but you and Apache helped me. Your operation won't be as bad. And I'll be there for you, just like you were here for me."

It was a long haul. As Rusty and I waited for Bailee to come through the surgery I paced the halls, I sat quietly in a little plastic chair, Rusty's arm around me. We made small talk but it was a tense six hours. How could it take six hours?

"What if she goes through all this and it doesn't work?" I asked.

"You can't play the what if game, Babe, I've done it too many times. It doesn't work. You've just got to have faith in Bailee just like I always have faith in you."

"But she's just a kid."

"I think the same thing when you're the one. I'm sorry, Cass, I know you're not a kid but you've got so much life in you. I can't help it."

"What if we have kids and I'm still a trouble magnet. I don't think I could stand being a trouble magnet mom, too."

"You'll just have to choose your trouble more carefully. Be the trouble making mom for the soccer coach."

"Rusty, you know I don't choose my trouble. Trouble just stalks me."

"Look at Patrick and Bailee. Have they ever gotten into any trouble because of you?"

"You know they have. Bailee wouldn't have run away except for my meddling and Patrick got into lots of messes when he visited us. He got stuck in a tree, he called the police on Mark, he could have gotten shot…"

Bailee's parents were around. They juggled Brandon and took turns making snack food runs. When Bailee came out of surgery her dad was with her. Her mom was distant.

"She's asking for you," Don Roland said. It was the pits, just being a visitor. All I could do was take ten minutes here and ten minutes there.

"Hey, Bailee," I said quietly at her bedside.

"Chas, this weird," she said. I noticed she'd slipped back to little kid talk again but thought she'd find her vocabulary again once her mind was clear.

"I know. It'll feel weird for a while. Just be glad it does. When the weirdness fades you'll start noticing your hands more. Then you'll wish things were weird again. It'll be okay. Just do what the doctors say."

"Tell you dad I did better in school. Maybe this operation help, too. Teacher say I get bad grade in math because she no understand my scribbles. Maybe scribble less after I get better."

It was a good sign that she was able to think and talk about school even in her fuzzy state.

"You just think about getting better. You can catch up on school later."

Later arrived and I visited Bailee at her house, helping her with homework. She did indeed have a lot to catch up on but she seemed to understand it. Her bedroom consisted of a twin bed in a metal frame and a small dresser in a plain white room in a small apartment. Brandon toddled in every once in a while. Bailee now talked better than Brandon did. He was a chatterbox and I wished Rusty could babysit him so Bailee and I could work in peace. She didn't get all the right answers and that led us to some one on one tutoring, but there was no reason for her to get bad grades. She struggled with juggling facts, but I did, too. I never cared what year the Napoleonic Wars were or who was president in 1812, so we both struggled a bit, but at least we had a sense of humor about it.

Occasionally the Rolands would let Bailee come to my house and Rusty would come home to find us bent over a school book, reading horse books out loud, or putting Shadow through the obstacle course. He knew dinner might be a little late but chocked it up to kid time.

My card of pills ran out and I debated. Bailee called me to say her physical therapist gave her permission to ride again and that made the debate easier. Time with Bailee or one of the boys always swayed me towards Rusty's side. Strict called me out on a search and the debate turned into an all out argument. In the end, I never did fill the prescription. I went on the call. It was a rough search. Three days with a heavy pack. Rocky ground. Wild animals in camp. But that is another story.

www.ingramcontent.com/pod-product-compliance
Lightning Source LLC
Chambersburg PA
CBHW020627020726
47494CB00001B/77

* 9 7 8 1 7 7 1 4 3 2 4 9 8 *